KING PENGUIN

SOLARIS
THE CHAIN OF CHANCE
A PERFECT VACUUM

Stanislaw Lem was born in 1921 in Lemberg. During the German occupation of Poland he was forced to work as a mechanic and also took part in the Resistance. From 1939–41 he studied medicine at Lemberg and from 1945–8 at Cracow. He practised as an intern before studying philosophy and science and worked as a research assistant on a psychology project. He is interested in cybernetics and in the philosophy and history of science.

He has written over twenty books, both fiction and non-fiction, which have been translated into twenty-one languages, as well as some lyrical verse, television plays and essays on assorted topics. He wrote his first science-fiction novel, *The Man from Mars*, during the war. His other works include *Cyberiad*, a study of Krysztof Meyer's Polish opera, *The Star Diaries* and *The Invincible*. *Solaris* was the first of his books to be published in England. In 1973 he was awarded the Nebula Award for his literary achievement.

Stanislaw Lem has lectured at the University of Cracow and broadcast on Polish television. He is married with a son and lives on the outskirts of Cracow.

STANISLAW LEM

SOLARIS

THE CHAIN OF CHANCE

A PERFECT VACUUM

A KING PENGUIN
PUBLISHED BY PENGUIN BOOKS

Penguin Books Ltd, Harmondsworth, Middlesex, England
Penguin Books, 625 Madison Avenue, New York, New York 10022, U.S.A.
Penguin Books Australia Ltd, Ringwood, Victoria, Australia
Penguin Books Canada Ltd, 2801 John Street, Markham, Ontario, Canada L3R 1B4
Penguin Books (N.Z.) Ltd, 182–190 Wairau Road, Auckland 10, New Zealand

First published in one volume in Penguin Books 1981

Made and printed in Great Britain by
Richard Clay (The Chaucer Press) Ltd,
Bungay, Suffolk
Set in Monophoto Ehrhardt

CONTENTS

Solaris

CONTENTS

I

THE ARRIVAL

At 19.00 hours, ship's time, I made my way to the launching bay. The men around the shaft stood aside to let me pass, and I climbed down into the capsule.

Inside the narrow cockpit, there was scarcely room to move. I attached the hose to the valve on my spacesuit and it inflated rapidly. From then on, I was incapable of making the smallest movement. There I stood, or rather hung suspended, enveloped in my pneumatic suit and yoked to the metal hull.

I looked up; through the transparent canopy I could see a smooth, polished wall and, far above, Moddard's head leaning over the top of the shaft. He vanished, and suddenly I was plunged in darkness: the heavy protective cone had been lowered into place. Eight times I heard the hum of the electric motors which turned the screws, followed by the hiss of the shock-absorbers. As my eyes grew accustomed to the dark, I could see the luminous circle of the solitary dial.

A voice echoed in my headphones:

'Ready, Kelvin?'

'Ready, Moddard,' I answered.

'Don't worry about a thing. The Station will pick you up in flight. Have a good trip!'

There was a grinding noise and the capsule swayed. My muscles tensed in spite of myself, but there was no further noise or movement.

'When is lift-off?' As I asked, I noticed a rustling outside, like a shower of fine sand.

'You're on your way, Kelvin. Good luck!' Moddard's voice sounded as close as before.

A wide slit opened at eye-level, and I could see the stars. The *Prometheus* was orbiting in the region of Alpha in Aquarius and I tried in vain to orient myself; a glittering dust filled my porthole. I could not recognize a single constellation; in this region of the galaxy the sky was unfamiliar to me. I waited for the moment when I would pass near the first distinct star, but I was unable to isolate any one of them. Their brightness was fading; they receded, merging into a vague, purplish glimmer, the sole indication of the distance I had already travelled. My body rigid, sealed in its pneumatic envelope, I was knifing through space with the impression of standing still in the void, my only distraction the steadily mounting heat.

Suddenly, there was a shrill, grating sound, like a steel blade being drawn across a sheet of wet glass. This was it, the descent. If I had not seen the figures racing across the dial, I would not have noticed the change in direction. The stars having vanished long since, my gaze was swallowed up on the pale reddish glow of infinity. I could hear my heart thudding heavily. I could feel the coolness from the air-conditioning on my neck, although my face seemed to be on fire. I regretted not having caught a glimpse of the *Prometheus*, but the ship must have been out of sight by the time the automatic controls had raised the shutter of my porthole.

The capsule was shaken by a sudden jolt, then another. The whole vehicle began to vibrate. Filtered through the insulating layers of the outer skins, penetrating my pneumatic cocoon, the vibration reached me, and ran through my entire body. The image of the dial shivered and multiplied, and its phosphorescence spread out in all directions. I felt no fear. I had not undertaken this long voyage only to overshoot my target!

I called into the microphone:

'Station Solaris! Station Solaris! Station Solaris! I think I am leaving the flight-path, correct my course! Station Solaris, this is the *Prometheus* capsule. Over.'

I had missed the precious moment when the planet first came into view. Now it was spread out before my eyes; flat, and already immense. Nevertheless, from the appearance of its surface, I judged that I was still at a great height above it, since I had passed that imperceptible frontier after which we measure the distance that separates us from a celestial body in terms of altitude. I was falling. Now I had the sensation of falling, even with my eyes closed. (I quickly reopened them: I did not want to miss anything there was to be seen.)

I waited a moment in silence before trying once more to make contact. No response. Successive bursts of static came through the headphones, against a background of deep, low-pitched murmuring, which seemed to me the very voice of the planet itself. A veil of mist covered the orange-coloured sky, obscuring the porthole. Instinctively, I hunched myself up as much as my inflated suit would allow, but almost at once I realized that I was passing through cloud. Then, as though sucked upwards, the cloud-mass lifted; I was gliding, half in light, half in shadow, the capsule revolving upon its own vertical axis. At last, through the porthole, the gigantic ball of the sun appeared, looming up on the left and disappearing to the right.

A distant voice reached me through the murmuring and crackling. 'Station Solaris calling! Station Solaris calling! The capsule will land at zero-hour. I repeat, the capsule will land at zero-hour. Stand by for count-down. Two hundred and fifty, two hundred and forty-nine, two hundred and forty-eight . . .'

The words were punctuated by sharp screeching sounds; automatic equipment was intoning the phrases of the reception-drill. This was surprising, to say the least. As a rule, men on space stations were eager to greet a newcomer, especially if he was arriving direct from Earth. I did not have long to ponder this, for the sun's orbit, which had so far encircled me, shifted unexpectedly, and the incandescent disc appeared now to the right, now to the left, seeming to dance on the planet's horizon. I was swinging like a giant pendulum while the planet, its surface wrinkled with purplish-blue and black furrows, rose up in front of me like a wall. As my head began to spin, I caught sight of a tiny pattern of green and white dots; it was the station's positioning-marker. Something detached itself with a snap from the cone of the capsule; with a fierce jerk, the long parachute collar released its hoops, and the noise which followed reminded me irresistibly of Earth: for the first time after so many months, the moaning of the wind.

Everything went quickly after this. So far, I had known that I must be falling; now I could see it for myself. The green and white checkerboard grew rapidly larger and I could see that it was painted on an elongated silvery body, shaped like a whale, its flanks bristling with radar antennae. This metal colossus, which was pierced with several rows of shadowy apertures, was not resting on the planet itself but suspended above it, casting upon the inky surface beneath an ellipsoidal shadow of even deeper blackness. I could make out the slate-coloured ripples of the ocean, stirring with a faint motion. Suddenly, the clouds rose to a great height, rimmed with a blinding crimson glare; the lurid sky became grey, distant and flat; everything was blotted out; I was falling in a spin.

A sharp jolt, and the capsule righted itself. Through the porthole, I could see the ocean once more, the waves like crests of glittering quicksilver. The hoops of the parachute, their cords snapped, flapped furiously over the waves, carried on the wind. The capsule gently descended, swaying with a peculiar slow-motion rhythm imposed on it by the artificial magnetic field; there was just time to glimpse the launching-pads and the parabolic reflectors of two radio-telescopes on top of their pierced-steel towers.

With the clang of steel rebounding against steel, the capsule came to a stop. A hatch opened, and with a long, harsh sigh, the metal shell which imprisoned me reached the end of its voyage.

I heard the mechanical voice from the control centre:

'Station Solaris. Zero and zero. The capsule has landed. Out.'

Feeling a vague pressure on my chest and a disagreeable heaviness in the pit of my stomach, I seized the control levers with both hands and cut the contacts. A green indicator lit up: ARRIVAL. The capsule opened, and the pneumatic padding shoved me gently from behind, so that, in order to keep my balance, I had to take a step forward.

With a muffled sigh of resignation, the spacesuit expelled its air. I was free.

I found myself inside a vast, silver funnel, as high as a cathedral nave. A cluster of coloured pipes ran down the sloping walls and disappeared into rounded orifices. I turned round. The ventilation shafts were roaring, sucking in the poisonous gases from the planet's atmosphere which had infiltrated when my capsule had landed inside the Station. Empty, resembling a burst cocoon, the cigar-shaped capsule stood upright, enfolded by a calyx mounted on a steel base. The outer casing, scorched during flight, had turned a dirty brown.

I went down a small stairway. The metal floor below had been coated with a heavy-duty plastic. In places, the wheels of trolleys carrying rockets had worn through this plastic covering to expose the bare steel beneath.

The throbbing of the ventilators ceased abruptly and there was total silence. I looked around me, a little uncertain, waiting for someone to appear; but there was no sign of life. Only a neon arrow glowed, pointing towards a moving walkway which was silently unreeling. I allowed myself to be carried forward.

The ceiling of the hall descended in a fine parabolic arc until it reached the entrance to a gallery, in whose recesses gas cylinders, gauges, parachutes, crates and a quantity of other objects were scattered about in untidy heaps.

The moving walkway set me down at the far end of the gallery, on the threshold of a dome. Here there was an even greater disorder. A pool of oily liquid spread out from beneath a pile of oil-drums; a nauseating smell hung in the air; footprints, in a series of glutinous smears, went off in all directions. The oil-drums were covered with a tangle of tickertape, torn paper and other waste.

Another green arrow directed me to the central door. Behind this stretched a narrow corridor, hardly wide enough for two men to walk side by side, lit by slabs of glass let into the ceiling. Then another door, painted in green and white squares, which was ajar; I went in.

The cabin had concave walls and a big panoramic window, which a glowing mist had tinged with purple. Outside the murky waves slid silently past. Open cupboards lined the walls, filled with instruments, books, dirty glasses, vacuum flasks – all covered with dust. Five or six small trolleys and some collapsible chairs cluttered up the stained floor. One chair alone was inflated, its back raised. In this armchair there was a little thin man, his face burnt by the sun, the skin on his nose and cheeks coming away in large flakes. I recognized him as Snow, a cybernetics expert and Gibarian's deputy. In his time he had published articles of great originality in the Solarist Annual. It so happened that I had never had the opportunity of meeting him. He was wearing a mesh shirt which allowed the grey hairs of his sunken chest to poke through here and there, and canvas trousers with a great many pockets, mechanic's trousers, which had once been white but now were stained at the knees and covered with holes from chemical burns. He was holding one of those pear-shaped plastic flasks which are used in spaceships not equipped with internal gravitational systems. Snow's eyes widened in amazement as he looked up and saw me. The flask dropped from his fingers and bounced several times, spilling a few drops of transparent liquid. Blood drained from his face. I was too astonished to speak, and this dumbshow continued for so long that Snow's terror gradually communicated itself to me. I took a step forward. He cringed in his chair.

'Snow?'

He quivered as though I had struck him. Gazing at me in indescribable horror, he gasped out:

'I don't know you . . .' His voice croaked. 'I don't know you . . . What do you want?'

The spilt liquid was quickly evaporating; I caught a whiff of alcohol. Had he been drinking? Was he drunk? What was he so terrified of? I stood in the middle of the room; my legs were trembling; my ears roared, as though they were stuffed with cotton wool. I had the impression that the ground was giving way beneath my feet. Beyond the curved window, the ocean rose and fell with regularity. Snow's bloodshot eyes never left me. His terror seemed to have abated, but his expression of invincible disgust remained.

'What's the matter? Are you ill?' I whispered.

'You seem worried,' he said, his voice hollow. 'You actually seem worried . . . So it's like that now, is it? But why concern yourself about me? I don't know you.'

'Where's Gibarian?' I asked.

He gave a gasp and his glassy eyes lit up for an instant.

'Gi . . . Giba . . . No! No!'

His whole frame shook with stifled, hysterical laughter; then he seemed to calm down a little.

'So it's Gibarian you've come for, is it? Poor old Gibarian. What do you want with him?'

His words, or rather his tone of voice, expressed hatred and defiance; it was as though I had suddenly ceased to represent a threat to him.

Bewildered, I mumbled:

'What . . . Where is he?'

'Don't you know?'

Obviously he was drunk and raving. My anger rose. I should have controlled myself and left the room, but I had lost patience. I shouted:

'That's enough! How could I know where he is since I've only just arrived? Snow! What's going on here?'

His jaw dropped. Once again he caught his breath and his eyes gleamed with a different light. He seized the arms of his chair with both hands and stood up with difficulty. His knees were trembling.

'What? You've just arrived . . . Where have you come from?' he asked, almost sober.

'From Earth!' I retorted angrily. 'Maybe you've heard of it? Not that anyone would ever guess it.'

'From Earth? Good God! Then you must be Kelvin.'

'Of course. Why are you looking at me like that? What's so startling about me?'

He blinked rapidly.

'Nothing,' he said, wiping his forehead, 'nothing. Forgive me, Kelvin, it's nothing, I assure you. I was simply surprised, I didn't expect to see you.'

'What do you mean, you didn't expect to see me? You were notified months ago, and Moddard radioed only today from the *Prometheus*.'

'Yes; yes, indeed. Only, you see, we're a bit disorganized at the moment.'

'So I see,' I answered dryly.

Snow walked around me, inspecting my atmosphere suit, which was standard issue with the usual harness of wires and cables attached to the chest. He coughed, and rubbed his bony nose:

'Perhaps you would like a bath? It would do you good. It's the blue door, on the other side.'

'Thanks – I know the Station lay-out.'

'You must be hungry.'

'No. Where's Gibarian?'

Without answering, he went over to the window. From behind he looked considerably older. His close-cropped hair was grey, and deep wrinkles creased his sunburnt neck.

The wave-crests glinted through the window, the colossal rollers rising and falling in slow-motion. Watching the ocean like this one had the illusion – it was surely an illusion – that the Station was moving imperceptibly, as though teetering on an invisible base; then it would seem to recover its equilibrium, only to lean the opposite way with the same lazy movement. Thick foam, the colour of blood, gathered in the troughs of the waves. For a fraction of a second, my throat tightened and I thought longingly of the *Prometheus* and its strict discipline; the memory of an existence which suddenly seemed a happy one, now gone for ever.

Snow turned round, nervously rubbing his hands together.

'Listen,' he said abruptly, 'except for me there's no one around for the moment. You'll have to make do with my company for today. Call me Ratface; don't argue. You know me by my photograph, just imagine we're old friends. Everyone calls me Ratface, there's nothing I can do about it.'

Obstinately, I repeated my question:

'Where is Gibarian?'

He blinked again.

'I'm sorry to have received you like that. It's . . . it's not exactly my fault. I had completely forgotten . . . A lot has been happening here, you see . . .'

'It's all right. But what about Gibarian? Isn't he on the Station? Is he on an observation flight?'

Snow was gazing at a tangled mass of cables.

'No, he hasn't left the Station. And he won't be flying. The fact is . . .'

My ears were still blocked, and I was finding it more and more difficult to hear.

'What? What do you mean? Where is he then?'

'I should think you might guess,' he answered in a changed voice, looking me coldly in the eyes. I shivered. He was drunk, but he knew what he was saying.

'There's been an accident?'

He nodded vigorously, watching my reactions closely.

'When?'

'This morning, at dawn.'

By now, my sensations were less violent; this succinct exchange of questions and answers had calmed me. I was beginning to understand Snow's strange behaviour.

'What kind of accident?'

'Why not go to your cabin and take off your spacesuit? Come back in, say, an hour's time.'

I hesitated.

'All right,' I said finally.

As I made to leave, he called me back.

'Wait!' He had an uneasy look, as if he wanted to add something but was finding it difficult to bring out the words. After a pause, he said:

'There used to be three of us here. Now, with you, there are three of us again. Do you know Sartorius?'

'In the same way as I knew you – only from his photographs.'

'He's up there, in the laboratory, and I doubt if he'll come down before dark, but . . . In any case, you'll recognize him. If you should see anyone else – someone who isn't me or Sartorius, you understand, then . . .'

'Then what?'

I must be dreaming. All this could only be a dream! The inky waves, their crimson gleams under the low-hanging sun, and this little man who had gone back to his armchair, sitting there as before, hanging his head and staring at the heap of cables.

'In that case, do nothing.'

'Who could I see?' I flared up. 'A ghost?'

'You think I'm mad, of course. No, no, I'm not mad. I can't say anything more for the moment. Perhaps . . . who knows? . . . Nothing will happen. But don't forget I warned you.'

'Don't be so mysterious. What's all this about?'

'Keep a hold on yourself. Be prepared to meet . . . anything. It sounds impossible I know, but try. It's the only advice I can give you. I can't think of anything better.'

'But what could I possibly meet?' I shouted.

Seeing him sitting there, looking sideways at me, his sunburnt face drooping with fatigue, I found it difficult to contain myself. I wanted to grab him by the shoulders and shake him.

Painfully, dragging the words out one by one, he answered:

'I don't know. In a way, it depends on you.'

'Hallucinations, you mean?'

'No . . . it's real enough. Don't attack. Whatever you do, remember that!'

'What are you getting at?' I could hardly recognize the sound of my own voice.

'We're not on Earth, you know.'

'A Polytherian form?' I shouted. 'There's nothing human about them!'

I was about to rush at him, to drag him out of the trance, prompted, apparently, by his crazy theories, when he murmured:

'That's why they're so dangerous. Remember what I've told you, and be on your guard!'

'What happened to Gibarian?'

He did not answer.

'What is Sartorius doing?'

'Come back in an hour.'

I turned and went out. As I closed the door behind me, I took a last look at him. Tiny, shrunken, his head in his hands and his elbows resting on his stained knees, he sat there, motionless. It was only then that I noticed the dried bloodstains on the backs of his hands.

2

THE SOLARISTS

In the empty corridor I stood for a moment in front of the closed door. I noticed a strip of plaster carelessly stuck on one of the panels. Pencilled on it was the word 'Man!' At the sight of this faintly scribbled word, I had a sudden longing to return to Snow for company; but I thought better of it.

His crazy warnings still ringing in my ears, I started off down the narrow, tubular passage which was filled with the moaning of the wind, my shoulders bowed under the weight of the spacesuit. On tiptoe, half-consciously fleeing from some invisible watcher, I found two doors on my left and two more on my right. I read the occupants' names: Dr Gibarian, Dr Snow, Dr Sartorius. On the fourth, there was no nameplate. I hesitated, then pressed the handle down gently and slowly opened the door. As I did so, I had a premonition, amounting almost to a certainty, that there was someone inside. I went in.

There was no one. Another wide panoramic window, almost as large as the one in the cabin where I had found Snow, overhung the ocean, which, sunlit on this side, shone with an oleaginous gleam, as though the waves secreted a reddish oil. A crimson glow pervaded the whole room, whose lay-out suggested a ship's cabin. On one side, flanked by book-filled shelves, a retractable bed stood against the wall. On the other, between the numerous lockers, hung nickel frames enclosing a series of aerial photographs stuck end to end with adhesive tape, and racks full of test-tubes and retorts plugged with cotton-wool. Two tiers of white enamel boxes took up the space beneath the window. I lifted some of the lids; the boxes were crammed with all kinds of instruments, intertwined with plastic tubing. The corners of the room were occupied by a refrigerator, a tap and a demisting device. For lack of space on the big table by the window, a microscope stood on the floor. Turning round, I saw a tall locker beside the entrance door.

It was half-open, filled with atmosphere suits, laboratory smocks, insulated aprons, underclothing, boots for planetary exploration, and aluminium cylinders: portable oxygen gear. Two sets of this equipment, complete with masks, hung down from one of the knobs of the vertical bed. Everywhere there was the same chaos, a general disorder which someone had made a hasty attempt to disguise. I sniffed the air. I could detect a faint smell of chemical reagents and traces of something more acrid – chlorine? Instinctively I searched the ceiling for the grilles over the air-vents: strips of paper attached to the bars were fluttering gently; the air was circulating normally. In order to make a relatively free space around the bed, between the bookshelves and the locker, I cleared two chairs of their litter of books, instruments and tools, which I piled haphazardly on the other side of the room.

I pulled out a bracket to hang up my spacesuit, took hold of the zip-fastener, then let go again. Deterred by the confused idea that I was depriving myself of a shield, I could not bring myself to remove it. Once more I looked round the room. I checked that the door was shut tight and that it had no lock, and after a brief hesitation I dragged some of the heaviest boxes to the doorway. Having built this temporary barricade, I freed myself from my clanking armour in three quick movements. A narrow looking-glass, built into the locker door, reflected part of the room, and out of the corner of my eye I caught sight of something moving. I jumped, but it was only my own reflection. Underneath the spacesuit, my overalls were drenched with sweat. I took them off and pulled back a sliding door, revealing the bright-tiled walls of a small bathroom. A long, flat box lay in the hollow at the base of the shower; I carried it into the room. As I put it down, the springlid flew up and disclosed a number of compartments filled with strange objects: mis-shapen forms in a dark metal, grotesque replicas of the instruments in the racks. Not one of the tools was usable; they were blunted, distorted, melted, as though they had been in a furnace. Strangest of all, even the porcelain handles, virtually incombustible, were twisted out of shape. Even at maximum temperature, no laboratory furnace could have melted them; only, perhaps, an atomic pile. I took a Geiger counter from the pocket on my spacesuit, but when I held it over the debris, it remained dumb.

By now I was wearing nothing but my underwear. I tore it off, flung it across the room and dashed under the shower. The shock of the water did me good. Turning beneath the scalding, needle-sharp jets, I scrubbed myself vigorously, splashing the walls, expelling, eradicating from my skin the thick scum of morbid apprehensions which had pervaded me since my arrival.

I rummaged in the locker and found a work-suit which could also be worn under an atmosphere suit. As I pocketed my few belongings, I felt something hard tucked between the pages of my notebook: it was a key, the key to my apartment, down there on Earth. Absently, I turned it over in my fingers. Finally I put it down on the table. It occurred to me suddenly that I might need a weapon. An all-purpose pocket-knife was hardly sufficient for my needs, but I had nothing else, and I was not going to start searching for a gamma pistol or something else of the kind.

I sat down on a tubular stool in the middle of the clear space, glad to be alone, and seeing with satisfaction that I had over half an hour to myself. (By nature, I have always been scrupulous about keeping engagements, whether important or trivial.) The hands of the clock, its face divided into twenty-four hours, pointed to seven o'clock. The sun was setting. 07.00 hours here was 20.00 hours on board the *Prometheus*. On Moddard's screens, Solaris would be nothing but an indistinct dust-cloud, mingled with the stars. But what did the *Prometheus* matter to me now? I closed my eyes. I could hear no sound except the moaning of the ventilation pipes and a faint trickling of water from the bathroom.

If I had understood correctly, it was only a short time since Gibarian had died. What had they done with his body? Had they buried it? No, that was impossible on this planet. I puzzled over the question for a long time, concentrating on the fate of the corpse; then, realizing the absurdity of my thoughts, I began to pace up and down. My toe knocked against a canvas bag half-buried under a pile of books; I bent down and picked it up. It contained a small bottle made of coloured glass, so light that it might have been blown out of paper. I held it up to the window in the purplish glow of the sombre twilight, now over-hung by a sooty fog. What was I doing, allowing myself to be distracted by irrelevancies, by the first trifle which came to hand?

I gave a start: the lights had gone on, activated by a photo-electric relay; the sun had set. What would happen next? I was so tense that the sensation of an empty space behind me became unbearable. In an attempt to pull myself together, I took a chair over to the bookshelves and chose a book familiar to me: the second volume of the early monograph by Hughes and Eugel, *Historia Solaris*. I rested the thick, solidly bound volume on my knees and began leafing through the pages.

The discovery of Solaris dated from about a hundred years before I was born.

The planet orbits two suns: a red sun and a blue sun. For forty-five years after its discovery, no spacecraft had visited Solaris. At that time, the Gamow–Shapley theory – that life was impossible on planets which are satellites of two solar bodies – was firmly believed. The orbit is constantly being modified by variations in the gravitational pull in the course of its revolutions around the two suns.

Due to these fluctuations in gravity, the orbit is either flattened or distended and the elements of life, if they appear, are inevitably destroyed, either by intense heat or an extreme drop in temperature. These changes take place at intervals estimated in millions of years – very short intervals, that is, according to the laws of astronomy and biology (evolution takes hundreds of millions of years if not a billion).

According to the earliest calculations, in 500,000 years' time Solaris would be drawn one half of an astronomic unit nearer to its red sun, and a million years after that would be engulfed by the incandescent star.

A few decades later, however, observations seemed to suggest that the planet's orbit was in no way subject to the expected variations: it was stable, as stable as the orbit of the planets in our own solar system.

The observations and calculations were reworked with great precision; they simply confirmed the original conclusions: Solaris's orbit was unstable.

A modest item among the hundreds of planets discovered annually – to which official statistics devoted only a few lines defining the characteristics of their orbits – Solaris eventually began to attract special attention and attain a high rank.

Four years after this promotion, overflying the planet with the *Laakon* and two auxiliary craft, the Ottenskjöld expedition undertook a study of Solaris. This expedition being in the nature of a preliminary, not to say improvised reconnaissance, the scientists were not equipped for a landing. Ottenskjöld placed a quantity of automatic observation satellites into equatorial and polar orbit, their principal function being to measure the gravitational pull. In addition, a study was made of the planet's surface, which is covered by an ocean dotted with innumerable flat, low-lying islands whose combined area is less than that of Europe, although the diameter of Solaris is a fifth greater than Earth's. These expanses of barren, rocky territory, irregularly distributed, are largely concentrated in the southern hemisphere. At the same time the composition of the atmosphere – devoid of oxygen – was analysed, and precise measurements made of the planet's density, from which its albedo and other astronomical characteristics were determined. As was foreseeable, no trace of life was discovered, either on the islands or in the ocean.

During the following ten years, Solaris became the centre of attraction for all observatories concerned with the study of this region of space, for the planet had in the meantime shown the astonishing faculty of maintaining an orbit which ought, without any shadow of doubt, to have been unstable. The problem almost developed into a scandal: since the results of the observations could only be inaccurate, attempts were made (in the interests of science) to denounce and discredit various scientists or else the computers they used.

Lack of funds delayed the departure of a proper Solaris expedition for three years. Finally Shannahan assembled his team and obtained three C-tonnage vessels from the Institute, the largest starships of the period. A year and a half before the arrival of the expedition, which left from the region of Alpha in Aquarius, a second exploration fleet, acting in the name of the Institute, placed an automatic satellite – Luna 247 – into orbit around Solaris. This satellite, after three successive reconstructions at roughly ten-year intervals, is still functioning today. The data it supplied confirmed beyond doubt the findings of the Ottenskjöld expedition concerning the active character of the ocean's movements.

One of Shannahan's ships remained in orbit, while the two others, after some preliminary attempts, landed in the southern hemisphere, in a rocky area about 600 miles square. The work of the expedition lasted eighteen months and was carried out under favourable conditions, apart from an unfortunate accident brought about by the malfunction of some apparatus. In the meantime, the scientists had split into two opposing camps; the bone of contention was the ocean. On the basis of the analyses, it had been accepted that the ocean was an organic formation (at that time, no one had yet dared to call it living). But, while the biologists considered it as a primitive formation – a sort of gigantic entity, a fluid cell, unique and monstrous (which they called 'pre-biological'), surrounding the globe with a colloidal envelope several miles thick in places – the astronomers and physicists asserted that it must be an organic structure, extraordinarily evolved. According to them, the ocean possibly exceeded terrestrial organic structures in complexity, since it was capable of exerting an active influence on the planet's orbital path. Certainly, no other factor could be found that might explain the behaviour of Solaris; moreover, the planeto-physicists had established a relationship between certain processes of the plasmic ocean and the local measurements of gravitational pull, which altered according to the 'matter transformations' of the ocean.

Consequently it was the physicists, rather than the biologists, who put forward the paradoxical formulation of a 'plasmic mechanism', implying by this a structure, possibly without life as we conceive it, but capable of performing functional activities – on an astronomic scale, it should be emphasized.

It was during this quarrel, whose reverberations soon reached the ears of the most eminent authorities, that the Gamow-Shapley doctrine, unchallenged for eighty years, was shaken for the first time.

There were some who continued to support the Gamow-Shapley contentions, to the effect that the ocean had nothing to do with life, that it was neither 'parabiological' nor 'prebiological' but a geological formation – of extreme rarity, it is true – with the unique ability to stabilize the orbit of Solaris, despite the variations in the forces of attraction. Le Chatelier's law was enlisted in support of this argument.

To challenge this conservative attitude, new hypotheses were

advanced – of which Civito-Vitta's was one of the most elaborate – proclaiming that the ocean was the product of a dialectical
development: on the basis of its earliest pre-oceanic form, a solution
of slow-reacting chemical elements, and by the force of circumstances
(the threat to its existence from the changes of orbit), it had reached
in a single bound the stage of 'homeostatic ocean', without passing
through all the stages of terrestrial evolution, by-passing the un-
icellular and multicellular phases, the vegetable and the animal, the
development of a nervous and cerebral system. In other words, unlike
terrestrial organisms, it had not taken hundreds of millions of years to
adapt itself to its environment – culminating in the first repre-
sentatives of a species endowed with reason – but dominated its environment immediately.

This was an original point of view. Nevertheless, the means whereby
this colloidal envelope was able to stabilize the planet's orbit remained
unknown. For almost a century, devices had existed capable of creating
artificial magnetic and gravitational fields; they were called gravitors.
But no one could even guess how this formless glue could produce an
effect which the gravitors achieved by the use of complicated nuclear
reactions and enormously high temperatures. The newspapers of the
day, exciting the curiosity of the layman and the anger of the scientist,
were full of the most improbable embroideries on the theme of the
'Solaris Mystery', one reporter going so far as to suggest that the
ocean was, no less, a distant relation to our electric eels!

Just when a measure of success had been achieved in unravelling
this problem, it turned out, as often happened subsequently in the
field of Solarist studies, that the explanation replaced one enigma by
another, perhaps even more baffling.

Observations showed, at least, that the ocean did not react according
to the same principles as our gravitors (which, in any case, would have
been impossible), but succeeded in controlling the orbital periodicity
directly. One result, among others, was the discovery of discrepancies
in the measurement of time along one and the same meridian on
Solaris. Thus the ocean was not only in a sense 'aware' of the Einstein–
Boëvia theory; it was also capable of exploiting the implications of the
latter (which was more than we could say of ourselves).

With the publication of this hypothesis, the scientific world was torn by one of the most violent controversies of the century. Revered and universally accepted theories foundered; the specialist literature was swamped by outrageous and heretical treatises; 'sentient ocean' or 'gravity-controlling colloid' – the debate became a burning issue.

All this happened several years before I was born. When I was a student – new data having accumulated in the meantime – it was already generally agreed that there was life on Solaris, even if it was limited to a single inhabitant.

The second volume of Hughes and Eugel, which I was still leafing through mechanically, began with a systematization that was as ingenious as it was amusing. The table of classification comprised three definitions: Type: Polythera; Class: Syncytialia; Category: Metamorph.

It might have been thought that we knew of an infinite number of examples of the species, whereas in reality there was only the one – weighing, it is true, some seven hundred billion tons.

Multicoloured illustrations, picturesque graphs, analytical summaries and spectral diagrams flickered through my fingers, explaining the type and rhythm of the fundamental transformations as well as the chemical reactions. Rapidly, infallibly, the thick tome led the reader on to the solid ground of mathematical certitude. One might have assumed that we knew everything there was to be known about this representative of the category Metamorph, which lay some hundreds of metres below the metal hull of the Station, obscured at the moment by the shadows of the four-hour night.

In fact, by no means everybody was yet convinced that the ocean was actually a living 'creature', and still less, it goes without saying, a rational one. I put the heavy volume back on the shelf and took up the one next to it, which was in two parts. The first part was devoted to a resumé of the countless attempts to establish contact with the ocean. I could well remember how, when I was a student, these attempts were the subject of endless anecdotes, jokes and witticisms. Compared with the proliferation of speculative ideas which were triggered off by this problem, medieval scholasticism seemed a model of scientific enlightenment. The second part, nearly 1,500 pages long, was devoted exclusively to the bibliography of the subject. There would not have been enough room for the books themselves in the cabin in which I was sitting.

The first attempts at contact were by means of specially designed electronic apparatus. The ocean itself took an active part in these operations by remodelling the instruments. All this, however, remained somewhat obscure. What exactly did the ocean's 'participation' consist of? It modified certain elements in the submerged instruments, as a result of which the normal discharge frequency was completely disrupted and the recording instruments registered a profusion of signals – fragmentary indications of some outlandish activity, which in fact defeated all attempts at analysis. Did these data point to a momentary condition of stimulation, or to regular impulses correlated with the gigantic structures which the ocean was in the process of creating elsewhere, at the antipodes of the region under investigation? Had the electronic apparatus recorded the cryptic manifestation of the ocean's ancient secrets? Had it revealed its innermost workings to us? Who could tell? No two reactions to the stimuli were the same. Sometimes the instruments almost exploded under the violence of the impulses, sometimes there was total silence; it was impossible to obtain a repetition of any previously observed phenomenon. Constantly, it seemed, the experts were on the brink of deciphering the ever-growing mass of information. Was it not, after all, with this object in mind that computers had been built of virtually limitless capacity, such as no previous problem had ever demanded?

And indeed, some results *were* obtained. The ocean as a source of electric and magnetic impulses and of gravitation expressed itself in a more or less mathematical language. Also, by calling on the most abstruse branches of statistical analysis, it was possible to classify certain frequencies in the discharges of current. Structural homologues were discovered, not unlike those already observed by physicists in that sector of science which deals with the reciprocal interaction of energy and matter, elements and compounds, the finite and the infinite. This correspondence convinced the scientists that they were confronted with a monstrous entity endowed with reason, a protoplasmic ocean-brain enveloping the entire planet and idling its time away in extravagant theoretical cognitation about the nature of the universe. Our instruments had intercepted minute random fragments of a prodigious and everlasting monologue unfolding in the depths of this colossal brain, which was inevitably beyond our understanding.

So much for the mathematicians. These hypotheses, according to some people, underestimated the resources of the human mind; they bowed to the unknown, proclaiming the ancient doctrine, arrogantly resurrected, of *ignoramus et ignorabimus*. Others regarded the mathematicians' hypotheses as sterile and dangerous nonsense, contributing towards the creation of a modern mythology based on the notion of this giant brain – whether plasmic or electronic was immaterial – as the ultimate objective of existence, the very synthesis of life.

Yet others . . . but the would-be experts were legion and each had his own theory. A comparison of the 'contact' school of thought with other branches of Solarist studies, in which specialization had rapidly developed, especially during the last quarter of a century, made it clear that a Solarist-cybernetician had difficulty in making himself understood to a Solarist-symmetriadologist. Veubeke, director of the Institute when I was studying there, had asked jokingly one day: 'How do you expect to communicate with the ocean, when you can't even understand one another?' The jest contained more than a grain of truth.

The decision to categorize the ocean as a metamorph was not an arbitrary one. Its undulating surface was capable of generating extremely diverse formations which resembled nothing ever seen on Earth, and the function of these sudden eruptions of plasmic 'creativity', whether adaptive, explorative or what, remained an enigma.

Lifting the heavy volume with both hands, I replaced it on the shelf, and thought to myself that our scholarship, all the information accumulated in the libraries, amounted to a useless jumble of words, a sludge of statements and suppositions, and that we had not progressed an inch in the seventy-eight years since researches had begun. The situation seemed much worse now than in the time of the pioneers, since the assiduous efforts of so many years had not resulted in a single indisputable conclusion.

The sum total of known facts was strictly negative. The ocean did not use machines, even though in certain circumstances it seemed capable of creating them. During the first two years of exploratory work, it had reproduced elements of some of the submerged instruments. Thereafter, it simply ignored the experiments we went on pursuing, as though it had lost all interest in our instruments and our activities – as though, indeed, it was no longer interested in *us*. It did not possess a nervous system (to go on with the inventory of 'negative knowledge') or cells, and its structure was not proteiform. It did not always react even to the most powerful stimuli (it ignored completely, for example, the catastrophic accident which occurred during the second Giese expedition: an auxiliary rocket, falling from a height of 300,000 metres, crashed on the planet's surface and the radioactive explosion of its nuclear reserves destroyed the plasma within a radius of 2,500 metres).

Gradually, in scientific circles, the 'Solaris Affair' came to be regarded as a lost cause, notably among the administrators of the Institute, where voices had recently been raised suggesting that financial support should be withdrawn and research suspended. No one, until then, had dared to suggest the final liquidation of the Station; such a decision would have smacked too obviously of defeat. But in the course of semi-official discussions a number of scientists recommended an 'honourable' withdrawal from Solaris.

Many people in the world of science, however, especially among the young, had unconsciously come to regard the 'affair' as a touchstone of individual values. All things considered, they claimed, it was not simply a question of penetrating Solarist civilization, it was essentially a test of ourselves, of the limitations of human knowledge. For some time, there was a widely held notion (zealously fostered by the daily press) to the effect that the 'thinking ocean' of Solaris was a gigantic brain, prodigiously well-developed and several million years in advance of our own civilization, a sort of 'cosmic yogi', a sage, a symbol of omniscience, which had long ago understood the vanity of all action and for this reason had retreated into an unbreakable silence. The notion was incorrect, for the living ocean was active. Not, it is true, according to human ideas – it did not build cities or bridges, nor did it manufacture flying machines. It did not try to reduce distances, nor was it concerned with the conquest of Space (the ultimate criterion, some people thought, of man's superiority). But it was engaged in a never-ending process of transformation, an 'ontological autometamorphosis'. (There were any amount of scientific neologisms in accounts of Solarist activities.) Moreover, any scientist who devotes himself to the study of Solariana has the indelible impression that he can discern fragments of an intelligent structure, perhaps endowed with genius, haphazardly mingled with outlandish phenomena, apparently the product of an unhinged mind. Thus was born the concept of the 'autistic ocean' as opposed to the 'ocean-yogi'.

These hypotheses resurrected one of the most ancient of philosophical problems: the relation between matter and mind, and between mind and consciousness. Du Haart was the first to have the audacity to maintain that the ocean possessed a consciousness. The problem, which the methodologists hastened to dub metaphysical, provoked all kinds of arguments and discussions. Was it possible for thought to exist without consciousness? Could one, in any case, apply the word thought to the processes observed in the ocean? Is a mountain only a huge stone? Is a planet an enormous mountain? Whatever the terminology, the new scale of size introduced new norms and new phenomena.

The question appeared as a contemporary version of the problem of squaring the circle. Every independent thinker endeavoured to register his personal contribution to the hoard of Solarist studies. New theories proliferated: the ocean was evidence of a state of degeneration, of regression, following a phase of 'intellectual repletion'; it was a deviant neoplasm, the product of the bodies of former inhabitants of the planet, whom it had devoured, swallowed up, dissolving and blending the residue into this unchanging, self-propagating form, supracellular in structure.

By the white light of the fluorescent tubes – a pale imitation of terrestrial daylight – I cleared the table of its clutter of apparatus and books. Arms outstretched and my hands gripping the chromium edging, I unrolled a map of Solaris on the plastic surface and studied it at length. The living ocean had its peaks and its canyons. Its islands, which were covered with a decomposing mineral deposit, were certainly related to the nature of the ocean bed. But did it control the eruption and subsidence of the rocky formations buried in its depths? No one knew. Gazing at the big flat projection of the two hemispheres, coloured in various tones of blue and purple, I experienced once again that thrill of wonder which had so often gripped me, and which I had felt as a schoolboy on learning of the existence of Solaris for the first time.

Lost in contemplation of this bewildering map, my mind in a daze, I temporarily forgot the mystery surrounding Gibarian's death and the uncertainty of my own future.

The different sections of the ocean were named after the scientists who had explored them. I was examining Thexall's swell, which surrounded the equatorial archipelagos, when I had a sudden sensation of being watched.

I was still leaning over the map, but I no longer saw it; my limbs were in the grip of a sort of paralysis. The crates and a small locker still barricaded the door, which was in front of me. It's only a robot, I told myself – yet I had not discovered any in the room and none could have entered without my knowledge. My back and my neck seemed to be on fire; the sensation of this relentless, fixed stare was becoming unbearable. With my head shrinking between my hunched shoulders, I leant harder and harder against the table, until it began slowly to slide away. The movement released me; I spun round.

The room was empty. There was nothing in front of me except the wide convex window and, beyond it, the night. But the same sensation persisted. The night stared me in the face, amorphous, blind, infinite, without frontiers. Not a single star relieved the darkness behind the glass. I pulled the thick curtains. I had been in the Station less than an hour, yet already I was showing signs of morbidity. Was it the effect of Gibarian's death? In so far as I knew him, I had imagined that nothing could shake his nerve: now, I was no longer so sure.

I stood in the middle of the room, beside the table. My breathing became more regular, I felt the sweat chill on my forehead. What was it I had been thinking about a moment ago? Ah, yes, robots! It was surprising that I had not come across one anywhere on the Station. What could have become of them all? The only one with which I had been in contact – at a distance – belonged to the vehicle reception services. But what about the others?

I looked at my watch. It was time to rejoin Snow.

I left the room. The dome was feebly lit by luminous filaments running the length of the ceiling. I went up to Gibarian's door and stood there, motionless. There was total silence. I gripped the handle. I had in fact no intention of going in, but the handle went down and the door opened, disclosing a chink of darkness. The lights went on. In one quick movement, I entered and silently closed the door behind me. Then I turned round.

My shoulders brushed against the door panels. The room was larger than mine. A curtain decorated with little pink and blue flowers (not regulation Station equipment, but no doubt brought from Earth with his personal belongings) covered three-quarters of the panoramic window. Around the walls were bookshelves and cupboards, painted pale green with silvery highlights. Both shelves and cupboards had been emptied of their contents, which were piled into heaps, among the furniture. At my feet, blocking the way, were two overturned trolleys buried beneath a heap of periodicals spilling out of bulging brief cases which had burst open. Books with their pages splayed out fanwise were stained with coloured liquids which had spilt from broken retorts and bottles with corroded stoppers, receptacles made of such thick glass that a single fall, even from a considerable height, could not have shattered them in such a way. Beneath the window lay an overturned desk, an anglepoise lamp crumpled underneath it; two legs of an upturned stool were stuck in the half-open drawers. A flood of papers of every conceivable size swamped the floor. My interest quickened as I recognized Gibarian's handwriting. As I stooped to gather together the loose sheets, I noticed that my hand was casting a double shadow.

I straightened up. The pink curtain glowed brightly, traversed by a streak of incandescent, steely-blue light which was gradually widening. I pulled the curtain aside. An unbearable glare extended along the horizon, chasing before it an army of spectral shadows, which rose up from among the waves and dispersed in the direction of the Station. It was the dawn. After an hour of darkness the planet's second sun – the blue sun – was rising in the sky.

The automatic switch cut off the lights as I returned to the heap of papers. The first thing I came across was a detailed description of an experiment, evidently decided upon three weeks before. Gibarian had planned to expose the plasma to an intensive bombardment of X-rays. I gathered from the context that the paper was addressed to Sartorius, whose job it was to organize operations. What I was holding in my hand was a copy of the plan.

The whiteness of the paper hurt my eyes. This new day was different from the previous one. In the warm glow of the red sun, mists overhung a black ocean with blood-red reflections, and waves, clouds and sky were almost constantly veiled in a crimson haze. Now, the blue sun pierced the flower-printed curtain with a crystalline light. My suntanned hands looked grey. The room had changed; all the red-reflecting objects had lost their lustre and had turned a greyish-brown, whereas those which were white, green and yellow had acquired a vivid brilliance and seemed to give off their own light. Screwing up my eyes, I risked another glance through a chink in the curtain: an expanse of molten metal trembled and shimmered under a white-hot sky. I shut my eyes and drew back. On the shelf above the wash-basin (which had recently been badly chipped) I found a pair of dark glasses, so big that when I put them on they covered half my face. The curtain appeared to glow with a sodium light. I went on reading, picking up the sheets of paper and arranging them on the only usable table. There were gaps in the text, and I searched in vain for the missing pages.

I came across a report of experiments already carried out, and learned that, for four days running, Gibarian and Sartorius had submitted the ocean to radiation at a point 1,400 miles from the present position of the Station. The use of X-rays was banned by a UN convention, because of their harmful effects, and I was certain that no one had sent a request to Earth for authorization to proceed with such experiments.

Looking up, I caught sight of my face in the mirror of a half-open locker door: masked by the dark glasses, it was deathly pale. The room, too, glinting with blue and white reflections, looked equally bizarre; but soon there came a prolonged screech of metal as the air-tight outer shutters slid across the window. There was an instant of darkness, and then the lights came on; they seemed to me to be curiously dim. It grew hotter and hotter. The regular drone of the air-conditioning was now a high-pitched whine: the Station's refrigeration plant was running at full capacity. Nevertheless, the overpowering heat grew more and more intense.

I heard footsteps. Someone was walking through the dome. In two silent strides, I reached the door. The footsteps slowed down; whoever it was was behind it. The handle moved. Automatically, without thinking, I gripped it. The pressure did not increase, but nor did it relax. Neither of us, on either side of the door, said a word. We remained there, motionless, each of us holding the handle. Suddenly it straightened up again, freeing itself from my grasp. The muffled footsteps receded. With my ear glued to the panel, I went on listening. I heard nothing more.

3

THE VISITORS

I hastily pocketed Gibarian's notes and went over to the locker. Work-suits and clothes had been pushed to one side as though someone had hidden himself at the back. On the floor I saw the corner of an envelope sticking out from a heap of papers and picked it up. It was addressed to me. Dry-mouthed with apprehension, I tore it open; I had to force myself to unfold the note inside.

In his even handwriting, small but perfectly legible, Gibarian had written two lines:

Supplement Dir. Solar. Vol 1.: Vot. Separat.

Messenger ds aff. F.; Ravintzer: The Little Apocrypha.

That was all, not another word. Did these two lines contain some vital piece of information? When had he written them? I told myself that the first thing to do was to consult the library index. I knew the supplement to the first volume of the annual of Solarist studies; or rather, without having read it, I knew of its existence – but was it not a document of purely historical interest? As for Ravintzer and *The Little Apocrypha*, I had never heard of them.

What next?

I was already a quarter of an hour late for my meeting with Snow. With my back to the door, I looked the room over carefully once more. Only then did I notice the bed standing up against the wall, half concealed by a large map of Solaris. Something was hanging down behind the map; it was a pocket tape-recorder, and I noted that nine tenths of the tape had been used. I took the machine out of its case (which I hung back where I had found it) and slipped it into my pocket.

Before leaving, I listened intently with my eyes closed. There was no sound from outside. I opened the door on to a yawning gulf of darkness – until it occurred to me to remove my dark glasses. The dome was feebly lit by the glowing filaments in the ceiling.

A number of corridors spread out in a star-shaped pattern between the four doors of the sleeping quarters and the narrow passage leading to the radio-cabin. Suddenly, looming up in the opening which led to the communal bathroom, a tall silhouette appeared, barely distinguishable in the surrounding gloom. I stood stock still, frozen to the spot. A giant Negress was coming silently towards me with a smooth, rolling gait. I caught a gleam from the whites of her eyes and heard the soft slapping of her bare feet. She was wearing nothing but a yellow skirt of plaited straw; her enormous breasts swung freely and her black arms were as thick as thighs. Less than a yard separated us as she passed me, but she did not give me so much as a glance. She went on her way, her grass skirt swinging rhythmically, resembling one of those steatopygous statues in anthropological museums. She opened Gibarian's door and on the threshold her silhouette stood out distinctly against the bright light from inside the room. Then she closed the door behind her and I was alone.

Terror-stricken, I stared blankly round the big, empty hall. What had happened? What had I seen? Suddenly, my mind reeled as I recalled Snow's warnings. Who was this monstrous Aphrodite? I took a step, a single pace, in the direction of Gibarian's room, but I knew perfectly well that I would not go in.

I do not know how long I remained leaning against the cool metal wall, hearing nothing except the distant, monotonous whine of the air-conditioners. Eventually I pulled myself together and made my way to the radio-cabin. As I pressed down the door handle, I heard a harsh voice:

'Who's there?'

'It's me, Kelvin.'

Snow was seated at a table between a pile of aluminium crates and the transmitter, eating meat concentrate straight out of a tin. Did he then never leave the place? Dazedly, I watched him chewing until I realized that I, too, was famished. I went to a cupboard, selected the least dusty plate I could find, and sat down opposite Snow. We ate in silence.

Snow got up, uncorked a vacuum flask and filled two tumblers with clear, hot soup. Then he put the flask down on the floor; there was no room on the table.

'Have you seen Sartorius?' he asked.

'No. Where is he?'

'Upstairs.'

Upstairs: that meant the laboratory. We finished our meal without exchanging another word, Snow dutifully scraping the bottom of his tin. The outer shutter was in place over the window and reflections from the four ceiling lights gleamed on the laminated surface of the transmitter. Snow had put on a loose black sweater, frayed at the wrists. The taut skin over his cheekbones was marbled with tiny blood-vessels.

'What's the matter?' he asked.

'Nothing, why?'

'You're pouring with sweat.'

I wiped my forehead. It was true, I was dripping wet; it must have been reaction, after my unexpected encounter. Snow gave me a questioning glance. Should I tell him? If only he had taken me into his confidence . . . What incomprehensible game was being played here, and who was whose enemy?

'It's hot. I should have expected your air-conditioning to work better than this!'

'It adjusts itself automatically every hour.' He looked at me closely. 'Are you sure it's only the heat?'

I did not answer. He tossed the utensils and the empty tins into the sink, returned to his armchair and went on with his interrogation.

'What are your plans?'

'That depends on you,' I answered coolly. 'I suppose you have a research programme? A new stimulus, X-rays, that sort of thing . . .'

He frowned.

'X-rays? Who's been talking to you about that?'

'I don't remember. Someone dropped a hint – on the *Prometheus* perhaps. Why, have you begun?'

'I don't know the details, it was an idea of Gibarian's. He and Sartorius set it up together. I wonder how you could have heard of it.'

I shrugged my shoulders.

'Funny that you shouldn't know the details. You ought to, since you're the one who . . .'

I left the sentence unfinished; Snow said nothing.

The whining of the air-conditioners had stopped. The temperature stayed at a bearable level, but a high-pitched drone persisted, like the buzzing of a dying insect.

Snow got up from his chair and leaned over the console of the transmitter. He began to press knobs at random, and to no effect, since he had left the activating switch off. He went on fidgeting with them for a moment, then he remarked:

'There are certain formalities to be dealt with concerning . . .'

'Yes?' I prompted, to his back.

He turned round and gave me a hostile look. Involuntarily, I had annoyed him; but ignorant of the role he was playing, I could only wait and see. His Adam's apple rose and fell inside the collar of his sweater:

'You've been into Gibarian's room,' he blurted out accusingly.

I looked at him calmly.

'You *have* been in there, haven't you?'

'If you say so . . .'

'Was there anyone there?'

So he had seen her, or, at least, knew of her existence!

'No, no one. Who could there have been?'

'Why didn't you let me in, then?'

'Because I was afraid. I thought of your warnings and when the handle moved, I automatically hung on to it. Why didn't you say it was you? I would have let you in.'

'I thought it was Sartorius,' he answered, in a faltering voice.

'And suppose it had been?'

Once again, he parried my question with one of his own.

'What do you think happened in there?'

I hesitated.

'You're the one who should know. Where is he?'

'Gibarian? In the cold store. We took him there straight away this morning, after we'd found him in the locker.'

'The locker? Was he dead?'

'His heart was still beating, but he had stopped breathing.'

'Did you try resuscitation?'

'No.'

'Why not?'

'I didn't have the chance,' he mumbled. 'By the time I'd moved him, he was dead.'

Snow picked up a sheet of paper from the fitted desk in the corner and held it out to me.

'I have drafted a post-mortem report. I'm not sorry you've seen the room, as a matter of fact. Cause of death – pernostal injection, lethal dose. It's all here . . .'

I ran my eyes over the paper, and murmured:

'Suicide? For what reason?'

'Nervous troubles, depression, call it what you like. You know more about that sort of thing than I do.'

I was still seated; Snow was standing over me.

Looking him in the eye, I said:

'I only know what I've seen for myself.'

'What are you trying to say?' he asked calmly.

'He injected himself with pernostal and hid in the locker, right? In that case, it's not a question of nervous troubles or a fit of depression, but of a very serious paranoid condition.' Speaking more and more deliberately and continuing to look him in the eyes, I added: 'What is certain is that he thought he saw something.'

Snow began fiddling with the transmitter again.

After a moment's silence, I went on.

'Your signature's here. What about Sartorius's?'

'As I told you, he's in the laboratory. He never shows his face. I suppose he's . . .'

'What?'

'Locked himself in.'

'Locked himself in? I see . . . you mean he's barricaded himself in?'

'Possibly.'

'Snow, there's someone on the Station. Someone apart from us.'

He had stopped playing with the knobs and was leaning sideways, staring at me.

'You've seen it!'

'You warned me. Against what? Against whom? An hallucination?'

'What did you see?'

'Shall we say . . . a human being?'

He remained silent. Turning his back as though to hide his face

from me, he tapped the metal plating with his finger-tips. I looked at
his hands; there was no longer any trace of blood between the fingers.
I had a brief moment of dizziness.

In scarcely more than a whisper, as though I were imparting a
secret and afraid of being overheard, I said:

'It's not a mirage, is it? It's a real person, someone you can touch,
someone you can ... draw blood from. And what's more, someone
you've seen only today.'

'How do you know?'

He had not moved; his face was still obstinately turned to the wall
and I was addressing his back.

'It was before I arrived, just before I arrived, wasn't it?'

His whole body contracted, and I could see his panic-stricken expression.

'What about you?' he said in a strangled voice, 'who are you?'

I thought he was about to attack me. It was not at all the reaction I
had expected. The situation was becoming grotesque. Obviously, he
did not believe that I was who I claimed to be. But what could this
mean? He was becoming more and more terrified of me. Was he
delirious? Could he have been affected by unfiltered gases from the
planet's atmosphere? Anything seemed possible. And then again, I too
had seen this ... creature, so what about me?

'Who is she?' I asked.

These words reassured him. For a moment, he looked at me search-
ingly, as though he was still doubtful of me; then he collapsed into his
chair and put his head in his hands. Even before he opened his mouth,
I knew that he had still not made up his mind to give me a direct
answer.

'I'm worn out,' he said weakly.

'Who is she?' I insisted.

'If you don't know ...'

'Go on, know what?'

'Nothing.'

'Listen, Snow! We are isolated, completely cut off. Let's put our
cards on the table. Things are confused enough as it is. You've got to
tell me what you know!'

'What about you?' he retorted, suspiciously.

'All right, I'll tell you and then you tell me. Don't worry, I shan't think you're mad.'

'Mad! Good God!' He tried to smile. 'But you haven't understood a thing, not a single thing. He never for one moment thought that he was mad. If he had he would never have done it. He would still be alive.'

'In other words, your report, this business of nervous troubles, is a fabrication.'

'Of course.'

'Why not write the truth?'

'Why?' he repeated.

A long silence followed. It was true that I was still completely in the dark. I had been under the impression that I had overcome his doubts and that we were going to pool our resources to solve the enigma. Why, then, was he refusing to talk?

'Where are the robots?'

'In the store-rooms. We've locked them all away; only the reception robots are operational.'

'Why?'

Once more, he refused to answer.

'You don't want to talk about it?'

'I can't.'

He seemed constantly on the point of unburdening himself, only to pull himself up at the last moment. Perhaps I would do better to tackle Sartorius. Then I remembered the letter and, as I thought of it, realized how important it was.

'Do you intend continuing with the experiments?'

He gave a contemptuous shrug:

'What good would that do?'

'Oh – in that case, what do *you* suggest we do?'

He was silent. In the distance, there was a faint noise of bare feet padding over the floor. The muffled echo of these shuffling steps reverberated eerily among the nickel-plated and laminated equipment and the tall shafts, furrowed with glass tubes, which encased the complicated electronic installations.

Unable to control myself any longer, I stood up. As I listened to the approaching footsteps, I watched Snow. Behind the drooping lids, his eyes showed no fear. Was he not afraid of her, then?

42

'Where does she come from?' I asked.

'I don't know.'

The sound of the footsteps faded, then died away.

'Don't you believe me?' he said. 'I swear to you that I don't know.'

In the silence that followed, I opened a locker, pushed the clumsy atmosphere-suits aside and found, as I expected, hanging at the back, the gas pistols used for manoeuvering in space. I took one out, checked the charge, and slung the harness over my shoulder. It was not, strictly speaking, a weapon, but it was better than nothing.

As I was adjusting a strap, Snow showed his yellow teeth in a mocking grin.

'Good hunting!' he said.

I turned towards the door.

'Thanks.'

He dragged himself out of his chair.

'Kelvin!'

I looked at him. He was no longer smiling. I have never seen such an expression of weariness on anyone's face.

He mumbled:

'Kelvin, it isn't that . . . Really, I . . . I can't . . .'

I waited; his lips moved, but uttered no sound. I turned on my heel and went out.

4

SARTORIUS

I followed a long, empty corridor, then forked right. I had never lived on the Station, but during my training on Earth I had spent six weeks in an exact replica of it; when I reached a short aluminium stairway, I knew where it led.

The library was in darkness, and I had to fumble for the light switch. I first consulted the index, then dialled the coordinates for the first volume of the *Solarist Annual* and its Supplement. A red light came on. I turned to the register: the two books were marked out to Gibarian, together with *The Little Apocrypha*. I switched the lights off and returned to the lower deck.

In spite of having heard the footsteps receding, I was afraid to re-enter Gibarian's room. *She* might return. I hesitated for some time outside the door; finally, pressing down the handle, I forced myself to go in.

There was no one in the room. I began rummaging through the books scattered beneath the window, interrupting my search only to close the locker door: I could not bear the sight of the empty space among the work-suits.

The supplement was not in the first pile, so, one by one, I started methodically picking up the rest of the books around the room. When I reached the final pile, between the bed and the wardrobe, I found the volume I was looking for.

I was hoping to find some sort of clue and, sure enough, a book-marker had been slipped between the pages of the index. A name, unfamiliar to me, had been underlined in red: André Berton. The corresponding page numbers indicated two different chapters; glancing at the first, I learnt that Berton was a reserve pilot on Shannahan's ship. The second reference appeared about a hundred pages further on.

At first, it seemed, Shannahan's expedition had proceeded with extreme caution. When, however, after sixteen days, the plasmatic ocean had not only shown no signs of aggression, but appeared to shun any direct contact with men and machines, recoiling whenever anything approached its surface, Shannahan and his deputy, Timolis, discontinued some of the precautions which were hindering the progress of their work. The force fences which had been used to demarcate and protect the working areas were taken back to base, and the expedition split up into groups of two or three men, some groups making reconnaissance flights over a radius of some several hundred miles.

Apart from some unexpected damage to the oxygen-supply systems – the atmosphere had an unusually corrosive effect on the valves, which had to be replaced almost daily – four days passed without mishap. On the morning of the fifth day – twenty-one days after the arrival of the expedition – two scientists, Carucci and Fechner (the first a radiobiologist, the second a physicist), left on a mission aboard a hovercraft. Six hours later, the explorers were overdue. Timolis, who was in charge of the base in Shannahan's absence, raised the alarm and diverted every available man into search-parties.

By a fatal combination of circumstances, long-range radio contact had been cut that morning an hour after the departure of the exploration groups – a large spot had appeared on the red sun, producing a heavy bombardment of charged particles in the upper atmosphere. Only the ultra-shortwave transmitters continued to function, and contact was restricted to a radius of about twenty miles. As a crowning stroke of bad luck, a thick fog descended just before sunset and the search had to be called off.

The rescue teams were returning to base when the hovercraft was spotted by a flitter, barely twenty-four miles from the commandship. The engine was running and the machine, at first sight undamaged, was hovering above the waves. Carucci alone could be seen, semi-conscious, in the glass-domed cockpit.

The hovercraft was escorted back to base. After treatment, Carucci quickly regained consciousness, but could throw no light on Fechner's disappearance. Just after they had decided to return to base a valve in his oxygen-gear had failed and a small amount of unfiltered gas had penetrated his atmosphere-suit. In an attempt to repair the valve, Fechner had been forced to undo his safely belt and stand up. That was the last thing Carucci could remember.

According to the experts who reconstructed the sequence of events, Fechner must have opened the cabin roof because it impeded his movements – a perfectly legitimate thing to do since the cabins of these vehicles were not air-tight, the glass dome merely providing some protection against infiltration and turbulence. While Fechner was occupied with his colleague, his own oxygen supply had probably been damaged and, no longer realizing what he was doing, he had pulled himself up on to the superstructure, from which he had fallen into the ocean.

Fechner thus became the ocean's first victim. Although the atmosphere-suit was buoyant, they searched for his body without success. It was, of course, possible that it was still floating somewhere on the surface, but the expedition was not equipped for a thorough search of this immense, undulating desert, covered with patches of dense fog.

By dusk, all but one of the search craft had returned to base; only a big supply helicopter piloted by André Berton was still missing. Just as they were about to raise the alarm, the aircraft appeared. Berton was obviously suffering from nervous shock; after struggling out of his suit, he ran round in circles like a madman. He had to be over-powered, but went on shouting and sobbing. It was rather surprising behaviour, to put it mildly, on the part of a man who had been flying for seventeen years and was well used to the hazards of cosmic navigation. The doctors assumed that he too was suffering from the effects of unfiltered gases.

Having more or less recovered his senses, Berton nevertheless refused to leave the base, or even to go near the window overlooking the ocean. Two days later, he asked for permission to dictate a flight-report, stressing the importance of what he was about to reveal. This report was studied by the expeditionary council, who concluded that it was the morbid creation of a mind under the influence of poisonous gases from the atmosphere. As for the supposed revelations, they were evidently regarded as part of Berton's clinical history rather than that of the expedition itself, and they were not described.

So much for the supplement. It seemed to me that Berton's report

46

must at any rate provide a key to the mystery. What strange happening could have had such a shattering effect on a veteran space-pilot? I began to search through the books once more, but *The Little Apocrypha* was not to be found. I was growing more and more exhausted and left the room, having decided to postpone the search until the following day.

As I was passing the foot of the stairway, I noticed that the aluminium treads were streaked with light falling from above. Sartorius was still at work. I decided to go up and see him.

It was hotter on the upper deck, but the paper strips still fluttered frenziedly at the air vents. The corridor was wide and low-ceilinged. The main laboratory was enclosed by a thick panel of opaque glass in a chrome embrasure. A dark curtain screened the door on the inside, and the light was coming from windows let in above the lintel. I pressed down the handle, but, as I expected, the door refused to budge. The only sound from the laboratory was an intermittent whine like that of a defective gas jet. I knocked. No reply. I called:

'Sartorius! Dr Sartorius! I'm the new man, Kelvin. I must see you, it's very important. Please let me in!'

There was a rustling of papers.

'It's me, Kelvin. You must have heard of me. I arrived off the *Prometheus* a few hours ago.'

I was shouting, my lips glued to the angle where the door joined the metal frame.

'Dr Sartorius, I'm alone. Please open the door!'

Not a word. Then the same rustling as before, followed by the clink of metal instruments on a tray. Then . . . I could scarcely believe my ears . . . there came a succession of little short footsteps, like the rapid drumming of a pair of tiny feet, or remarkably agile fingers tapping out the rhythm of steps on the lid of an empty tin box.

I yelled:

'Dr Sartorius, are you going to open this door, yes or no?'

No answer. Nothing but the pattering, and, simultaneously, the sound of a man walking on tiptoe. But, if the man was moving about, he could not at the same time be tapping out an imitation of a child's footsteps.

47

No longer able to control my growing fury, I burst out:

'Dr Sartorius, I have not made a sixteen-month journey just to come here and play games! I'll count up to ten. If you don't let me in, I shall break down the door!'

In fact, I was doubtful whether it would be easy to force this particular door, and the discharge of a gas pistol is not very powerful. Nevertheless, I was determined somehow or other to carry out my threat, even if it meant resorting to explosives, which I could probably find in the munition store. I could not draw back now; I could not go on playing an insane game with all the cards stacked against me.

There was the sound of a struggle – or was it simply objects being thrust aside? The curtain was pulled back, and an elongated shadow was projected on to the glass.

A hoarse, high-pitched voice spoke:

'If I open the door, you must give me your word not to come in.'

'In that case, why open it?'

'I'll come out.'

'Very well, I promise.'

The silhouette vanished and the curtain was carefully replaced.

Obscure noises came from inside the laboratory. I heard a scraping – a table being dragged across the floor? At last, the lock clicked back, and the glass panel opened just enough to allow Sartorius to slip through into the corridor.

He stood with his back against the door, very tall and thin, all bones under his white sweater. He had a black scarf knotted around his neck, and over his arm he was carrying a laboratory smock, covered with chemical burns. His head, which was unusually narrow, was cocked to one side. I could not see his eyes: he wore curved dark glasses, which covered up half his face. His lower jaw was elongated; he had bluish lips and enormous, blue-tinged ears. He was unshaven. Red anti-radiation gloves hung by their laces from his wrists.

For a moment we looked at one another with undisguised aversion. His shaggy hair (he had obviously cut it himself) was the colour of lead, his beard grizzled. Like Snow, his forehead was burnt, but the lower half only; above, it was pallid. He must have worn some kind of cap when exposed to the sun.

'Well, I'm listening,' he said.

I had the impression that he did not care what I had to say to him. Standing there, tense, still pressed against the door panel, his attention was mainly directed to what was going on behind him.

Disconcerted, I hardly knew how to begin.

'My name is Kelvin,' I said, 'You must have heard about me. I am, or rather I was, a colleague of Gibarian's.'

His thin face, entirely composed of vertical planes, exactly as I had always imagined Don Quixote's, was quite expressionless. This blank mask did not help me to find the right words.

'I heard that Gibarian was dead . . .' I broke off.

'Yes. Go on, I'm listening.' His voice betrayed his impatience.

'Did he commit suicide? Who found the body, you or Snow?'

'Why ask me? Didn't Dr Snow tell you what happened?'

'I wanted to hear your own account.'

'You've studied psychology, haven't you, Dr Kelvin?'

'Yes. What of it?'

'You think of yourself as a servant of science?'

'Yes, of course. What has that to do with . . .'

'You are not an officer of the law. At this hour of the day, you should be at work, but instead of doing the job you were sent here for, you not only threaten to force the door of my laboratory, you question me as though I were a criminal suspect.'

His forehead was dripping with sweat. I controlled myself with an effort. I was determined to get through to him. I gritted my teeth and said:

'You *are* suspect, Dr Sartorius. What is more, you're well aware of it!'

'Kelvin, unless you either retract or apologize, I shall lodge a complaint against you.'

'Why should I apologize? You're the one who barricaded himself in this laboratory instead of coming out to meet me, instead of telling me the truth about what is going on here. Have you gone completely mad? What are you – a scientist, or a miserable coward?'

I don't know what other insults I hurled at him. He did not even flinch. Globules of sweat trickled down over the enlarged pores of his cheeks. Suddenly I realized that he had not heard a word I was saying. Both hands behind his back, he was holding the door in position with all his strength; it was rattling as though someone inside were firing bursts from a machine-gun at the panel.

In a strange, high-pitched voice, he moaned:

'Go away. For God's sake, leave me. Go downstairs, I'll join you later. I'll do whatever you want, only please go away now.'

His voice betrayed such exhaustion that instinctively I put out my arms to help him control the door. At this, he uttered a cry of horror, as though I had pointed a knife at him. As I retreated, he was shouting in his falsetto voice: 'Go away! Go away! I'm coming, I'm coming, I'm coming! No! No!' He opened the door and shot inside. I thought I saw a shining yellow disc flash across his chest.

Now a muffled clamour rose from the laboratory; a huge shadow appeared, as the curtain was brushed momentarily aside; then it fell back into place and I could see nothing more. What was happening inside that room? I heard running footsteps, as though a mad chase were in progress, followed by a terrifying crash of broken glass and the sound of a child's laugh.

My legs were trembling, and I stared at the door, appalled. The din had subsided, giving way to an uneasy silence. I sat down on a window ledge, too stunned to move; my head was splitting.

From where I was, I could see only a part of the corridor encircling the laboratory. I was at the summit of the Station, beneath the actual shell of the superstructure; the walls were concave and sloping, with oblong windows a few yards apart. The blue day was ending, and, as the shutters grated upwards, a blinding light shone through the thick glass. Every metal fitting, every latch and joint, blazed, and the great glass panel of the laboratory door glittered with pale coruscations. My hands looked grey in the spectral light. I noticed that I was holding the gas pistol; I had not realized that I had taken it out of its holster, and replaced it. What use could I have made of it – or even of a gamma pistol, had I had one? I could hardly have taken the laboratory by force.

I got up. The disc of the sun, reminiscent of a hydrogen explosion, was sinking into the ocean, and as I descended the stairway I was pierced by a jet of horizontal rays which was almost tangible. Halfway downstairs I paused to think, then went back up the steps and followed the corridor round the laboratory. Soon, I came across a second glass door, exactly like the first; I made no attempt to open it, knowing that it would be locked.

I was looking for an opening or vent of some sort. The idea of spying on Sartorius had come to me quite naturally, without the least sense of shame. I was determined to have done with conjecture and discover the truth, even if, as I imagined it would, the truth proved incomprehensible. It struck me that the laboratory must be lit from above by windows let into the dome. It should be possible, therefore, to spy on Sartorius from the outside. But first I should have to equip myself with an atmosphere-suit and oxygen gear.

When I reached the deck below, I found the door of the radio-cabin ajar. Snow, sunk in his armchair, was asleep. At the sound of my footsteps, he opened his eyes with a start.

'Hello, Kelvin!' he croaked. 'Well, did you discover anything?'

'Yes . . . he's not alone.'

Snow grinned sourly.

'Oh, really? Well, that's something. Has he got visitors?'

'I can't understand why you won't tell me what's going on,' I retorted impulsively. 'Since I have to remain here, I'm bound to find out the truth sooner or later. Why the mystery?'

'When you've received some visitors yourself, you'll understand.'

I had the impression that my presence annoyed him and he had no desire to prolong the conversation.

I turned to go.

'Where are you off to?'

I did not answer.

The hangar-deck was just as I had left it. My burnt-out capsule still stood there, gaping open, on its platform. On my way to select an atmosphere-suit, I suddenly realized that the skylights through which I hoped to observe Sartorius would probably be made of slabs of opaque glass, and I lost interest in my venture on to the outer hull.

Instead, I descended the spiral stairway which led to the lower-deck store rooms. The cramped passage at the bottom contained the usual litter of crates and cylinders. The walls were sheeted in bare metal which had a bluish glint. A little further on, the frosted pipes of the refrigeration plant appeared beneath a vault and I followed them to the far end of the corridor where they vanished into a cooling-jacket with a wide, plastic collar. The door to the cold store was two inches thick and lagged with an insulating compound. When I opened it, the icy cold gripped me. I stood, shivering, on the threshold of a cave carved out of an iceberg; the huge coils, like sculptured reliefs, were hung with stalactites. Here, too, buried beneath a covering of snow, there were crates and cylinders, and shelves laden with boxes and transparent bags containing a yellow, oily substance. The vault sloped downwards to where a curtain of ice hid the back of the cave. I broke through it. An elongated figure, covered with a sheet of canvas, lay stretched out on an aluminium rack.

I lifted a corner of the canvas and recognized the stiff features of Gibarian. His glossy black hair clung tightly to his skull. The sinews of his throat stood out like bones. His glazed eyes stared up at the vault, a tear of opaque ice hanging from the corner of each lid. The cold was so intense that I had to clench my teeth to prevent them from chattering. I touched Gibarian's cheek; it was like touching a block of petrified wood, bristling with black prickly hairs. The curve of the lips seemed to express an infinite, disdainful patience.

As I let the canvas fall, I noticed, peeping out from beneath folds at the foot, five round, shiny objects, like black pearls, ranged in order of size. I stiffened with horror.

What I had seen were the round pads of five bare toes. Under the shroud, flattened against Gibarian's body, lay the Negress. Slowly, I pulled back the canvas. Her head, covered in frizzy hair twisted up into little tufts, was resting in the hollow of one massive arm. Her back glistened, the skin stretched taut over the spinal column. The huge body gave no sign of life. I looked again at the soles of her naked feet; they had not been flattened or deformed in any way by the weight which they had had to carry. Walking had not calloused the skin, which was as unblemished as that of her shoulders.

With a far greater effort than it had taken to touch Gibarian's corpse, I forced myself to touch one of the bare feet. Then I made a second bewildering discovery: this body, abandoned in a deep freeze, this apparent corpse, lived and moved. The woman had withdrawn her foot, like a sleeping dog when you try to take its paw.

'She'll freeze,' I thought confusedly, but her flesh had been warm to the touch, and I even imagined I had felt the regular beating of her pulse. I backed out and fled.

As I emerged from the white cave, the heat seemed suffocating. I climbed the spiral stairway back to the hangar-deck.

I sat on the hoops of a rolled-up parachute and put my head in my hands. I was stunned. My thoughts ran wild. What was happening to me? If my reason was giving way, the sooner I lost consciousness the better. The idea of sudden extinction aroused an inexpressible, unrealistic hope.

Useless to go and find Snow or Sartorius: no one could fully understand what I had just experienced, what I had seen, what I had touched with my own hands. There was only one possible explanation, one possible conclusion: madness. Yes, that was it, I had gone mad as soon as I arrived here. Emanations from the ocean had attacked my brain, and hallucination had followed hallucination. Rather than exhaust myself trying to solve these illusory riddles, I would do better to ask for medical assistance, to radio the *Prometheus* or some other vessel, to send out an S O S.

Then a curious change came over me: at the thought that I had gone mad, I calmed down.

And yet . . . I had heard Snow's words quite clearly. If, that is, Snow existed and I had ever spoken to him. The hallucinations might have begun much earlier. Perhaps I was still on board the *Prometheus*; perhaps I had been stricken with a sudden mental illness and was now confronting the creations of my own inflamed brain. Assuming that I was ill, there was reason to believe that I would get better, which gave me some hope of deliverance – a hope irreconcilable with a belief in the reality of the tangled nightmares through which I had just lived.

If only I could think up some experiment in logic – a key experiment – which would reveal whether I had really gone mad and was a helpless prey to the figments of my imagination, or whether, in spite of their ludicrous improbability, I had been experiencing real events.

As I turned all this over in my mind, I was looking at the monorail which led to the launching-pad. It was a steel girder, painted pale green, a yard above the ground. Here and there, the paint was chipped, worn by the friction of the rocket trolleys. I touched the steel, feeling it grow warm beneath my fingers, and rapped the metal plating with my knuckles. Could madness attain such a degree of reality? Yes, I answered myself. After all, it was my own subject, I knew what I was talking about.

But was it possible to work out a controlled experiment? At first I told myself that it was not, since my sick brain (if it really was sick) would create the illusions I demanded of it. Even while dreaming, when we are in perfectly good health, we talk to strangers, put questions to them and hear their replies. Moreover, although our interlocutors are in fact the creations of our own psychic activity, evolved by a pseudo-independent process, until they have spoken to us we do not know what words will emerge from their lips. And yet these words have been formulated by a separate part of our own minds; we should therefore be aware of them at the very moment that we think them up in order to put them into the mouths of imaginary beings. Consequently, whatever form my proposed test were to take, and whatever method I used to put it into execution, there was always the possibility that I was behaving exactly as in a dream. Neither Snow nor Sartorius having any real existence, it would be pointless to put questions to them.

I thought of taking some powerful drug, peyotl for example, or another preparation inducing vivid hallucinations. If visions ensued, this would prove that I had really experienced these recent events and that they were part and parcel of the surrounding material reality. But then, no, I thought, this would not constitute the proof I needed, since I knew the effects of the drug (which I should have chosen for myself) and my imagination could suggest to me the double illusion of having taken the drug and of experiencing its effects.

I was going around in circles; there seemed to be no escape. It was not possible to think except with one's brain, no one could stand outside himself in order to check the functioning of his inner processes. Suddenly an idea struck me, as simple as it was effective.

I leapt to my feet and ran to the radio-cabin. The room was deserted. I glanced at the electric clock on the wall. Nearly four o'clock, the fourth hour of the Station's artificial night-time. Outside, the red sun was shining. I quickly plugged in the long-range transmitter, and, while the valves warmed up, I went over in my mind the principal stages of the experiment.

I could not remember the call-sign for the automatic station on the satellite, but I found it on a card hanging above the main instrument panel, sent it out in Morse, and received the answering signal eight seconds later. The satellite, or rather its electronic brain, identified itself by a rhythmic pulse.

I instructed the satellite to give me the figures for the galactic meridians it was traversing at twenty-two-second intervals while orbiting Solaris, and I specified an answer to five decimal points.

Then I sat and waited for the reply. Ten minutes later, it arrived. I tore off the strip of freshly printed paper and hid it in a drawer, taking care not to look at it. I went to the bookcase and took out the big galactic charts, the logarithm tables, a calendar giving the daily path of the satellite, and various other textbooks. Then I sat down to work out for myself the answer to the question I had posed. For an hour or more, I integrated the equations. It was a long time since I had tackled such elaborate calculations. My last major effort in this direction must have been my practical astronomy exam.

I worked at the problem with the help of the Station's giant computer. My reasoning went as follows: by making my calculations from the galactic charts, I would obtain an approximate cross-check with the results provided by the satellite. Approximate because the path of the satellite was subject to very complex variations due to the effects of the gravitational forces of Solaris and its two suns, as well as to the local variations in gravity caused by the ocean. When I had the two series of figures, one furnished by the satellite and the other calculated theoretically on the basis of the galactic charts, I would make the necessary adjustments and the two groups would then coincide up to the fourth decimal point, discrepancies due to the unforeseeable influence of the ocean arising only at the fifth.

If the figures obtained from the satellite were simply the product of my deranged mind, they could not possibly coincide with the second series. My brain might be unhinged, but it could not conceivably compete with the Station's giant computer and secretly perform calculations requiring several months' work. Therefore if the figures corresponded, it would follow that the Station's computer really existed, that I had really used it, and that I was not delirious.

My hands trembled as I took the telegraphic tape out of the drawer and laid it alongside the wide band of paper from the computer. As I had predicted, the two series of numbers corresponded up to the fourth decimal point.

I put all the papers away in the drawer. So the computer existed independently of me; that meant that the Station and its inhabitants really existed too.

As I was closing the drawer, I noticed that it was stuffed with sheets of paper covered with hastily scribbled sums. A single glance told me that someone had already attempted an experiment similar to mine and had asked the satellite, not for information about the galactic meridians, but for the measurements of Solaris's albedo at intervals of forty seconds.

I was not mad. The last ray of hope was extinguished. I unplugged the transmitter, drank the remains of the soup in the vacuum flask, and went to bed.

5

RHEYA

Desperation and a sort of dumb rage had sustained me while working with the computer. Now, overcome with exhaustion, I could not even remember how to let down a mechanical bed. Forgetting to push back the clamps, I hung on to the handle with all my weight and the mattress tumbled down on top of me.

I tore off my clothes and flung them away from me, then collapsed on to the pillow, without even taking the trouble to inflate it properly. I fell asleep with the lights on.

I reopened my eyes with the impression of having dozed off for only a few minutes. The room was bathed in a dim red light. It was cooler, and I felt refreshed.

I lay there, the bedclothes pushed back, completely naked. The curtains were half drawn, and there, opposite me, beside the window-pane lit by the red sun, someone was sitting. It was Rheya. She was wearing a white beach dress, the material stretched tightly over her breasts. She sat with her legs crossed; her feet were bare. Motionless, leaning on her sun-tanned arms, she gazed at me from beneath her black lashes: Rheya, with her dark hair brushed back. For a long time, I lay there peacefully gazing back at her. My first thought was re-assuring: I was dreaming and I was aware that I was dreaming. Nevertheless, I would have preferred her not to be there. I closed my eyes and tried to shake off the dream. When I opened them again, Rheya was still sitting opposite me. Her lips were pouting slightly – a habit of hers – as though she were about to whistle; but her expression was serious. I thought of my recent speculations on the subject of dreams.

She had not changed since the day I had seen her for the last time; she was then a girl of nineteen. Today, she would be twenty-nine. But, evidently, the dead do not change; they remain eternally young. She went on gazing at me, an expression of surprise on her face. I thought of throwing something at her, but, even in a dream, I could not bring myself to harm a dead person.

I murmured: 'Poor little thing, have you come to visit me?'

The sound of my voice frightened me; the room, Rheya, everything seemed extraordinarily real. A three-dimensional dream, coloured in half-tones . . . etc. I saw several objects on the floor which I had not noticed when I went to bed. When I wake up, I told myself, I shall check whether these things are still there or whether, like Rheya, I only saw them in a dream.

'Do you mean to stay for long?' I asked. I realized that I was speaking very softly, like someone afraid of being overheard. Why worry about eavesdroppers in a dream?

The sun was rising over the horizon. A good sign. I had gone to bed during a red day, which should have been succeeded by a blue day, followed by another red day. I had not slept for fifteen hours at a stretch. So it *was* a dream!

Reassured, I looked closely at Rheya. She was silhouetted against the sun. The scarlet rays cast a glow over the smooth skin of her left cheek and the shadows of her eyelashes fell across her face. How pretty she was! Even in my sleep my memory of her was uncannily precise. I watched the movements of the sun, waiting to see the dimple appear in that unusual place slightly below the corner of the lips. All the same, I would have preferred to wake up. It was time I did some work. I closed my eyelids tightly.

I heard a metallic noise, and opened my eyes again. Rheya was sitting beside me on the bed, still looking at me gravely. I smiled at her. She smiled back at me and leant forward. We kissed. First a timid, childish kiss, then more prolonged ones. I held her for a long time. Was it possible to feel so much in a dream, I wondered. I was not betraying her memory, for it was of her that I was dreaming, only her. It had never happened to me before . . .

Was it then that I began to have doubts? I went on telling myself that it was a dream, but my heart tightened.

I tensed my muscles, ready to leap out of bed. I was half-expecting to fail, for often, in dreams, your sluggish body refuses to respond. I hoped that the effort would drag me out of sleep. But I did not wake;

I sat on the edge of the bed, my legs dangling. There was nothing for it, I should have to endure this dream right to the bitter end. My feeling of well-being had vanished. I was afraid.

'What . . .' I asked. I cleared my throat. 'What do you want?'

I felt around the floor with my bare feet, searching for a pair of slippers. I stubbed my toe against a sharp edge, and stifled a cry of pain. That'll wake me up, I thought with satisfaction, at the same time remembering that I had no slippers.

But still it went on. Rheya had drawn back and was leaning against the end of the bed. Her dress rose and fell lightly with her breathing. She watched me with quiet interest.

Quick, I thought, a shower! But then I realized that in a dream a shower would not interrupt my sleep.

'Where have you come from?'

She seized my hand and, with a gesture I knew well, threw it up and caught it again, then played with my fingers.

'I don't know,' she replied. 'Are you angry?'

It was her voice, that familiar, low-pitched, slightly far-away voice, and that air of not caring much about what she was saying, of already being preoccupied with something else. People used to think her off-hand, even rude, because the expression on her face rarely changed from one of vague astonishment.

'Did . . . did anyone see you?'

'I don't know. I got here without any trouble. Why, Kris, is it important?'

She was still playing with my fingers, but her face now wore a slight frown.

'Rheya.'

'What, my darling?'

'How did you know where I was?'

She pondered. A broad smile revealed her teeth.

'I haven't the faintest idea. Isn't it funny? When I came in you were asleep. I didn't wake you up because you get cross so easily. You have a very bad temper.'

She squeezed my hand.

'Did you go down below?'

'Yes. It was all frozen. I ran away.'

She let go of my hand and lay back. With her hair falling to one side, she looked at me with the half-smile that had irritated me before it had captivated me.

'But, Rheya . . .' I stammered.

I leaned over her and turned back the short sleeve of her dress. There, just above her vaccination scar, was a red dot, the mark of a hypodermic needle. I was not really surprised, but my heart gave a lurch.

I touched the red spot with my finger. For years now I had dreamt of it, over and over again, always waking with a shudder to find myself in the same position, doubled up between the crumpled sheets – just as I had found *her*, already growing cold. It was as though, in my sleep, I tried to relive what she had gone through; as though I hoped to turn back the clock and ask her forgiveness, or keep her company during those final minutes when she was feeling the effects of the injection and was overcome by terror. She, who dreaded the least scratch, who hated pain or the sight of blood, had deliberately done this horrible thing, leaving nothing but a few scribbled words addressed to me. I had kept her note in my wallet. By now it was soiled and creased, but I had never had the heart to throw it away.

Time and time again I had imagined her tracing those words and making her final preparations. I persuaded myself that she had only been play-acting, that she had wanted to frighten me and had taken an overdose by mistake. Everyone told me that it must have happened like that, or else it had been a spontaneous decision, the result of a sudden depression. But people knew nothing of what I had said to her five days earlier; they did not know that, in order to twist the knife more cruelly, I had taken away my belongings and that she, as I was closing my suitcases, had said, very calmly: 'I suppose you know what this means?' And I had pretended not to understand, even though I knew quite well what she meant; I thought her too much of a coward, and had even told her as much . . . And now she was lying across the bed, looking at me attentively, as though she did not know that it was I who had killed her.

'Well?' she asked. Her eyes reflected the red sun. The entire room was red. Rheya looked at her arm with interest, because I had been examining it for so long, and when I drew back she laid her smooth, cool cheek in the palm of my hand.

'Rheya,' I stammered, 'it's not possible . . .'

'Hush!'

I could sense the movement of her eyes beneath their closed lids.

'Where are we, Rheya?'

'At home.'

'Where's that?'

One eye opened and shut again instantly. The long lashes tickled my palm.

'Kris.'

'What?'

'I'm happy.'

Raising my head, I could see part of the bed in the washbasin mirror: a cascade of soft hair – Rheya's hair – and my bare knees. I pulled towards me with my foot one of the misshapen objects I had found in the box and picked it up with my free hand. It was a spindle, one end of which had melted to a needle-point. I held the point to my skin and dug it in, just beside a small pink scar. The pain shot through my whole body. I watched the blood run down the inside of my thigh and drip noiselessly on to the floor.

What was the use? Terrifying thoughts assailed me, thoughts which were taking a definite shape. I no longer told myself: 'It's a dream.' I had ceased to believe that. Now I was thinking: 'I must be ready to defend myself.'

I examined her shoulders, her hip under the close-fitting white dress, and her dangling naked feet. Leaning forward, I took hold of one of her ankles and ran my fingers over the sole of her foot.

The skin was soft, like that of a newborn child.

I knew then that it was not Rheya, and I was almost certain that she herself did not know it.

The bare foot wriggled and Rheya's lips parted in silent laughter.

'Stop it,' she murmured.

Cautiously I withdrew my hand from under the cheek and stood up. Then I dressed quickly. She sat up and watched me.

'Where are your things?' I asked her. Immediately, I regretted my question.

'My things?'

'Don't you have anything except that dress?'

From now on, I would pursue the game with my eyes open. I tried to appear unconcerned, indifferent, as though we had parted only yesterday, as though we had never parted.

She stood up. With a familiar gesture, she tugged at her skirt to smooth out the creases. My words had worried her, but she said nothing. For the first time, she examined the room with an inquiring, scrutinizing gaze. Then, puzzled, she replied:

'I don't know.' She opened the locker door. 'In here, perhaps?'

'No, there's nothing but work-suits in there.'

I found an electric point by the basin and began to shave, careful not to take my eyes off her.

She went to and fro, rummaging everywhere. Eventually, she came up to me and said:

'Kris, I have the feeling that something's happened . . .'

She broke off. I unplugged the razor, and waited.

'I have the feeling that I've forgotten something,' she went on, 'that I've forgotten a lot of things. I can only remember you. I . . . I can't remember anything else.'

I listened to her, forcing myself to look unconcerned.

'Have I . . . Have I been ill?' she asked.

'Yes . . . in a way. Yes, you've been slightly ill.'

'There you are then. That explains my lapses of memory.'

She had brightened up again. Never shall I be able to describe how I felt then. As I watched her moving about the room, now smiling, now serious, talkative one moment, silent the next, sitting down and then getting up again, my terror was gradually overcome by the conviction that it was the real Rheya there in the room with me, even though my reason told me that she seemed somehow stylized, reduced to certain characteristic expressions, gestures and movements.

Suddenly, she clung to me.

'What's happening to us, Kris?' She pressed her fists against my chest. 'Is everything all right? Is there something wrong?'

'Things couldn't be better.'

She smiled wanly.

'When you answer me like that, it means things could hardly be worse.'

'What nonsense!' I said hurriedly. 'Rheya, my darling, I must leave you. Wait here for me.' And, because I was becoming extremely hungry, I added: 'Would you like something to eat?'

'To eat?' She shook her head. 'No. Will I have to wait long for you?'

'Only an hour.'

'I'm coming with you.'

'You can't come with me. I've got work to do.'

'I'm coming with you.'

She had changed. This was not Rheya at all; the real Rheya never imposed herself, would never have forced her presence on me.

'It's impossible, my sweet.'

She looked me up and down. Then suddenly she seized my hand. And my hand lingered, moved up her warm, rounded arm. In spite of myself I was caressing her. My body recognized her body; my body desired her, my body was attracted towards hers beyond reason, beyond thought, beyond fear.

Desperately trying to remain calm, I repeated:

'Rheya, it's out of the question. You must stay here.'

A single word echoed round the room:

'No.'

'Why?'

'I . . . I don't know.' She looked around her, then, once more, raised her eyes to mine. 'I can't,' she whispered.

'But why?'

'I don't know. I can't. It's as though . . . as though . . .' She searched for the answer, which, as she uttered it, seemed to come to her like a revelation. 'It's as though I mustn't let you out of my sight.'

The resolute tone of her voice scarcely suggested an avowal of affection; it implied something quite different. With this realization, the manner in which I was embracing Rheya underwent an abrupt, though not immediately noticeable, change.

I was holding her in my arms and gazing into her eyes.

Imperceptibly, almost instinctively, I began to pull her hands together behind her back at the same time searching the room with my eyes: I needed something with which to tie her hands.

Suddenly she jerked her elbows together, and there followed a powerful recoil. I resisted for barely a second. Thrown backwards and almost lifted off my feet, even had I been an athlete I could not have freed myself. Rheya straightened up and dropped her arms to her sides. Her face, lit by an uncertain smile, had played no part in the struggle.

She was gazing at me with the same calm interest as when I had first awakened – as though she was utterly unmoved by my desperate ploy, as though she was quite unaware that anything had happened, and had not noticed my sudden panic. She stood before me, waiting – grave, passive, mildly surprised.

Leaving Rheya in the middle of the room, I went over to the wash-basin. I was a prisoner, caught in an absurd trap from which at all costs I was determined to escape. I would have been incapable of putting into words the meaning of what had happened or what was going through my mind; but now I realized that my situation was identical with that of the other inhabitants of the Station, that everything I had experienced, discovered or guessed at was part of a single whole, terrifying and incomprehensible. Meanwhile, I was racking my brain to think up some ruse, to work out some means of escape. Without turning round, I could feel Rheya's eyes following me. There was a medicine chest above the basin. Quickly I went through its contents, and found a bottle of sleeping pills. I shook out four tablets – the maximum dose – into a glass, and filled it with hot water. I made little effort to conceal my actions from Rheya. Why? I did not even bother to ask myself.

When the tablets had dissolved, I returned to Rheya, who was still standing in the same place.

'Are you angry with me?' she asked, in a low voice.

'No. Drink this.'

Unconsciously, I had known all along that she would obey me. She took the glass without a word and drank the scalding mixture in one gulp. Putting down the empty glass on a stool, I went and sat in a chair in the corner of the room.

Rheya joined me, squatting on the floor in her accustomed manner with her legs folded under her, and tossing back her hair. I was no longer under any illusion: this was not Rheya – and yet I recognized her every habitual gesture. Horror gripped me by the throat; and what was most horrible was that I must go on tricking her, pretending to take her for Rheya, while she herself sincerely believed that she *was* Rheya – of that I was certain, if one could be certain of anything any longer.

She was leaning against my knees, her hair brushing my hand. We remained thus for some while. From time to time, I glanced at my watch. Half-an-hour went by; the sleeping tablets should have started to work. Rheya murmured something:

'What did you say?'

There was no reply.

Although I attributed her silence to the onset of sleep, secretly I doubted the effectiveness of the pills. Once again, I did not ask myself why. Perhaps it was because my subterfuge seemed too simple.

Slowly her head slid across my knees, her dark hair falling over her face. Her breathing grew deeper and more regular; she was asleep. I stooped in order to lift her on to the bed. As I did so, her eyes opened; she put her arms round my neck and burst into shrill laughter.

I was dumbfounded. Rheya could hardly contain her mirth. With an expression that was at once ingenuous and sly, she observed me through half-closed eyelids. I sat down again, tense, stupefied, at a loss. With a final burst of laughter, she snuggled against my legs.

In an expressionless voice, I asked:

'Why are you laughing?'

Once again, a look of anxiety and surprise came over her face. It was clear that she wanted to give me an honest explanation. She sighed, and rubbed her nose like a child.

'I don't know,' she said at last, with genuine puzzlement. 'I'm behaving like an idiot, aren't I? But so are you . . . you look idiotic, all stiff and pompous like . . . like Pelvis.'

I could hardly believe my ears.

'Like who?'

'Like Pelvis. You know who I mean, that fat man . . .'

Rheya could not possibly have known Pelvis, or even heard me mention him, for the simple reason that he had returned from an expedition three years after her death. I had not known him previously and was therefore unaware of his inveterate habit, when presiding over meetings at the Institute, of letting sessions drag on indefinitely.

Moreover, his name was Pelle Villis and until his return I did not know that he had been nicknamed Pelvis.

Rheya leaned her elbows on my knees and looked me in the eyes. I put out my hand and stroked her arms, her shoulders and the base of her bare neck, which pulsed beneath my fingers. While it looked as though I was caressing her (and indeed, judging by her expression, that was how she interpreted the touch of my hands) in reality I was verifying once again that her body was warm to the touch, an ordinary human body, with muscles, bones, joints. Gazing calmly into her eyes, I felt a hideous desire to tighten my grip.

Suddenly I remembered Snow's bloodstained hands, and let go.

'How you stare at me,' Rheya said, placidly.

My heart was beating so furiously that I was incapable of speech. I closed my eyes. In that very instant, complete in every detail, a plan of action sprang to my mind. There was not a second to lose. I stood up.

'I must go out, Rheya. If you absolutely insist on coming with me, I'll take you.'

'Good.'

She jumped to her feet.

I opened the locker and selected a suit for each of us. Then I asked:

'Why are you bare-foot?'

She answered hesitantly:

'I don't know . . . I must have left my shoes somewhere.'

I did not pursue the matter.

'You'll have to take your dress off to put this on.'

'Flying-overalls? What for?'

As she tried to take off her dress, an extraordinary fact became apparent: there were no zips, or fastenings of any sort; the red buttons down the front were merely decorative. Rheya smiled, embarrassed.

As though it were the most normal way of going about it, I picked up some kind of scalpel from the floor and slit the dress down the back from neck to waist, so that she could pull it over her head.

When she had put on the flying-overalls (which were slightly too large for her) and we were about to leave, she asked:

'Are we going on a flight?'

66

I merely nodded. I was afraid of running into Snow. But the dome was empty and the door leading to the radio cabin was shut.

A deathly silence still hung over the hangar-deck. Rheya followed my movements attentively. I opened a stall and examined the shuttle vehicle inside. I checked, one after another, the micro-reactor, the controls and the diffusers. Then, having removed the empty capsule from its stand, I aimed the electric trolley towards the sloping runway.

I had chosen a small shuttle used for ferrying stores between the Station and the satellite, one that did not normally carry personnel since it did not open from the inside. The choice was carefully calculated in accordance with my plan. Of course, I had no intention of launching it, but I simulated the preparations for an actual departure. Rheya, who had so often accompanied me on my space-flights, was familiar with the preliminary routine. Inside the cockpit, I checked that the climatization and oxygen-supply systems were functioning. I switched in the main circuit and the indicators on the instrument panel lit up. I climbed out and said to Rheya, who was waiting at the foot of the ladder:

'Get in.'

'What about you?'

'I'll follow you. I have to close the hatch behind us.'

She gave no sign that she suspected any trickery. When she had disappeared inside, I stuck my head into the opening and asked:

'Are you comfortable?'

I heard a muffled 'yes' from inside the confined cockpit. I withdrew my head and slammed the hatch to with all my strength. I slid home the two bolts and tightened the five safety screws with the special spanner I had brought with me. The slender metal cigar stood there, pointing upwards, as though it were really about to take off into space.

Its captive was in no danger: the oxygen-tanks were full and there were food supplies in the cockpit. In any case, I did not intend to keep her prisoner indefinitely. I desperately needed two hours of freedom in order to concentrate on the decisions which had to be taken and to work out a joint plan of action with Snow.

As I was tightening the last screw but one, I felt a vibration in the three-pronged clamp which held the base of the shuttle. I thought I must have loosened the support in my over-eager handling of the heavy spanner, but when I stepped back to take a look, I was greeted by a spectacle which I hope I shall never have to see again.

The whole vehicle trembled, shaken from the inside as though by some superhuman force. Not even a steel robot could have imparted such a convulsive tremor to an 8-ton mass, and yet the cabin contained only a frail, dark-haired girl.

The reflections from the lights quivered on the shuttle's gleaming sides. I could not hear the blows; there was no sound whatever from inside the vehicle. But the outspread struts vibrated like taut wires. The violence of the shockwaves was such that I was afraid the entire scaffolding would collapse.

I tightened the final screw with a trembling hand, threw down the spanner and jumped off the ladder. As I slowly retreated, I noticed that the shock-absorbers, designed to resist a continuous pressure, were vibrating furiously. It looked to me as though the shuttle's outer skin was wrinkling.

Frenziedly, I rushed to the control panel and with both hands lifted the starting lever. As I did so the intercom connected to the shuttle's interior gave out a piercing sound – not a cry, but a sound which bore not the slightest resemblance to the human voice, in which I could nevertheless just make out my name, repeated over and over again: 'Kris! Kris! Kris!'

I had attacked the controls so violently, fumbling in my haste, that my fingers were torn and bleeding.

A bluish glimmer, like that of a ghostly dawn, lit up the walls. Swirling clouds of vaporous dust eddied round the launching pad: the dust turned into a column of fierce sparks and the echoes of a thunderous roar drowned all other noise. Three flames, merging instantly into a single pillar of fire, lifted the craft, which rose up through the open hatch in the dome, leaving behind a glowing trail which rippled as it gradually subsided. Shutters slid over the hatch, and the automatic ventilators began to suck in the acrid smoke which billowed round the room.

It was only later that I remembered all these details; at the time, I hardly knew what I was seeing. Clinging to the control panel, the fierce heat burning my face and singeing my hair, I gulped the acrid air, which smelt of a mixture of burning fuel and the ozone given off by ionization. I had instinctively closed my eyes at the moment of lift-off, but the glare had penetrated my eyelids. For some time, I saw nothing but black, red and gold spirals which slowly died away. The ventilators continued to hum; the smoke and the dust were gradually clearing.

The green glow of the radar-screen caught my eye. My hands flew across its controls as I began to search for the shuttle. By the time I had located it, it was already flying above the atmosphere. I had never launched a vehicle in such a blind and unthinking way, with no pre-set speed or direction. I did not even know its range and was afraid of causing some unpredictable disaster. I judged that the easiest thing to do would be to place it in a stationary orbit around Solaris and then cut the engines. I verified from the tables that the required altitude was 725 miles. It was no guarantee, of course, but I could see no other way out.

I did not have the heart to switch on the intercom, which had been disconnected at lift-off. I could not bear to expose myself again to the sound of that horrifying voice, which was no longer even remotely human.

I felt I was justified in thinking that I had defeated the 'simulacra', and that behind the illusion, contrary to all expectation, I had found the real Rheya again – the Rheya of my memories, whom the hypothesis of madness would have destroyed.

At one o'clock, I left the hangar-deck.

6

'THE LITTLE APOCRYPHA'

My face and hands were badly burnt. I remembered noticing a jar of anti-burn ointment when I was looking for sleeping pills for Rheya (I was in no mood to laugh at my naïveté), so I went back to my room.

I opened the door. The room was glowing in the red twilight. Someone was sitting in the armchair where Rheya had knelt. For a second or two, I was paralysed with terror, filled with an overwhelming desire to turn and run. Then the seated figure raised its head: it was Snow. His legs crossed, still wearing the acid-stained trousers, he was looking through some papers, a pile of which lay on a small table beside him. He put down those he was holding in his hand, let his glasses slide down his nose, and scowled up at me.

Without saying a word, I went to the basin, took the ointment out of the medicine chest and applied it to my forehead and cheeks. Fortunately my face was not too swollen and my eyes, which I had closed instinctively, did not seem to be inflamed. I lanced some large blisters on my temples and cheekbones with a sterilized needle; they exuded a serous liquid, which I mopped up with an antiseptic pad. Then I applied some gauze dressing.

Snow watched me throughout these first-aid operations, but I paid no attention to him. When at last I had finished (and my burns had become even more painful), I sat myself down in the other chair. I had first to remove Rheya's dress – that apparently quite normal dress which was nevertheless devoid of fastenings.

Snow, his hands clasped around one bony knee, continued to observe me with a critical air.

'Well, are you ready to have a chat?' he asked.

I did not answer; I was busy replacing a piece of gauze which had slipped down one cheek.

'You've had a visitor, haven't you?'

'Yes,' I answered curtly.

He had begun the conversation on a note which I found displeasing.

'And you've rid yourself of it already? Well, well! That was quick!'

He touched his forehead, which was still peeling and mottled with pink patches of new skin. I was thunderstruck. Why had I not realized before the implications of Snow's and Sartorius's 'sunburn'? No one exposed himself to the sun here.

Without noticing my sudden change of expression he went on:

'I imagine you didn't try extreme methods straight away. What did you use first – drugs, poison, judo?'

'Do you want to discuss the thing seriously or play the fool? If you don't want to help, you can leave me in peace.'

He half-closed his eyes.

'Sometimes one plays the fool in spite of oneself. Did you try the rope, or the hammer? Or the well-aimed ink-bottle, like Luther? No?' He grimaced. 'Aren't you a fast worker! The basin is still intact, you haven't banged your head against the walls, you haven't even turned the room upside down. One, two and into the rocket, just like that!' He looked at his watch. 'Consequently, we have two or three hours at our disposal ... Am I getting on your nerves?' he added, with a disagreeable smile.

'Yes,' I said curtly.

'Really? Well, if I tell you a little story, will you believe me?'

I said nothing.

Still with that hideous smile, he went on:

'It started with Gibarian. He locked himself in his cabin and refused to talk to us except through the door. And can you guess what we thought?'

I remained silent.

'Naturally, we thought he had gone mad. He let a bit of it out – through the locked door – but not everything. You may wonder why he didn't tell us that there was someone with him. Oh, *suum cuique!* But he was a true scientist. He begged us to let him take his chance!'

'What chance?'

'He was obviously doing his damnedest to solve the problem, to get to the bottom of it. He worked day and night. You know what he was doing? You must know.'

'Those calculations, in the drawer of the radio cabin – were they his?'

'Yes.'

'How long did it go on?'

'This visit? About a week ... We thought he was suffering from hallucinations, or having a nervous breakdown. I gave him some scopolamine.'

'Gave him?'

'Yes. He took it, but not for himself. He tried it out on someone else.'

'What did you do?'

'On the third day we had decided, if all else failed, to break down the door, maybe injuring his self-esteem, but at least curing him.'

'Ah ...'

'Yes.'

'So, in that locker ...'

'Yes, my friend, quite. But in the meantime, we too had received visitors. We had our hands full, and didn't have a chance to tell him what was going on. Now it's ... it's become a routine.'

He spoke so softly that I guessed rather than heard the last few words.

'I still don't understand!' I exclaimed. 'If you listened at his door, you must have heard two voices.'

'No, we heard only his voice. There were strange noises, but we thought they came from him too.'

'Only his voice! But how is it that you didn't hear ... her?'

'I don't know. I have the rudiments of a theory about it, but I've dropped it for the moment. No point getting bogged down in details. But what about you? You must already have seen something yesterday, otherwise you would have taken us for lunatics.'

'I thought it was I who had gone mad.'

'So you didn't see anyone?'

'I saw someone.'

'Who?'

I gave him a long look – he no longer wore even the semblance of a smile – and answered:

'That ... that black woman ...' He was leaning forward, and as I spoke his body almost imperceptibly relaxed. 'You might have warned me.'

'I did warn you.'

'You could have chosen a better way!'

'It was the only way possible. I didn't know what you would see. No one could know, no one ever knows . . .'

'Listen, Snow, I want to ask you something. You've had some experience of this . . . phenomenon. Will she . . . will the person who visited me today . . .?'

'Will she come back, do you mean?'

I nodded.

'Yes and no,' he said.

'What does that mean?'

'She . . . this person will come back as though nothing had happened, just as she was at the beginning of her first visit. More precisely, she will appear not to realize what you did to get rid of her. If you abide by the rules, she won't be aggressive.'

'What rules?'

'That depends on the circumstances.'

'Snow!'

'What?'

'Don't let's waste time talking in riddles.'

'In riddles? Kelvin, I'm afraid you still don't understand.' His eyes glittered. 'All right, then!' he went on, brutally. 'Can you tell me who your visitor was?'

I swallowed my saliva and turned away. I did not want to look at him. I would have preferred to be dealing with anyone else but him; but I had no choice. A piece of gauze came unstuck and fell on my hand. I gave a start.

'A woman who . . .' I stopped. 'She died. An injection . . .'

'Suicide?'

'Yes.'

'Is that all?'

He waited. Seeing that I remained silent, he murmured:

'No, it's not all . . .'

I looked up quickly; he was not looking at me.

'How did you guess?' He said nothing. 'It's true, there's more to it than that.' I moistened my lips. 'We quarrelled. Or rather, I lost my temper and said a lot of things I didn't mean. I packed my bags and cleared out. She had given me to understand ... not in so many words – when one's lived together for years it's not necessary. I was certain she didn't mean it, that she wouldn't dare, she'd be too afraid, and I told her so. Next day, I remembered I'd left these ... these ampoules in a drawer. She knew they were there. I'd brought them back from the laboratory because I needed them, and I had explained to her that the effect of a heavy dose would be lethal. I was a bit worried. I wanted to go back and get them, but I thought that would give the impression that I'd taken her remarks seriously. By the third day I was really worried and made up my mind to go back. When I arrived, she was dead.'

'You poor innocent!'

I looked up with a start. But Snow was not making fun of me. It seemed to me that I was seeing him now for the first time. His face was grey, and the deep lines between cheek and nose were evidence of an unutterable exhaustion: he looked a sick man.

Curiously awed, I asked him:

'Why did you say that?'

'Because it's a tragic story.' Seeing that I was upset, he added, hastily: 'No, no, you still don't understand. Of course it's a terrible burden to carry around, and you must feel like a murderer, but ... there are worse things.'

'Oh, really?'

'Yes, really. And I'm almost glad that you refuse to believe me. Certain events, which have actually happened, are horrible, but what is more horrible still is what hasn't happened, what has never existed.'

'What are you saying?' I asked, my voice faltering.

He shook his head from side to side.

'A normal man,' he said. 'What is a normal man? A man who has never committed a disgraceful act? Maybe, but has he never had uncontrollable thoughts? Perhaps he hasn't. But perhaps something, a phantasm, rose up from somewhere within him, ten or thirty years ago, something which he suppressed and then forgot about, which he doesn't fear since he knows he will never allow it to develop and so lead to any action on his part. And now, suddenly, in broad daylight, he comes across this thing . . . this thought, embodied, riveted to him, indestructible. He wonders where he is . . . Do you know where he is?'

'Where?'

'Here,' whispered Snow, 'on Solaris.'

'But what does it mean? After all, you and Sartorius aren't criminals . . .'

'And you call yourself a psychologist, Kelvin! Who hasn't had, at some moment in his life, a crazy daydream, an obsession? Imagine . . . imagine a fetishist who becomes infatuated with, let's say, a grubby piece of cloth, and who threatens and entreats and defies every risk in order to acquire this beloved bit of rag. A peculiar idea, isn't it? A man who at one and the same time is ashamed of the object of his desire and cherishes it above everything else, a man who is ready to sacrifice his life for his love, since the feeling he has for it is perhaps as overwhelming as Romeo's feeling for Juliet. Such cases exist, as you know. So, in the same way, there are things, situations, that no one has dared to externalize, but which the mind has produced by accident in a moment of aberration, of madness, call it what you will. At the next stage, the idea becomes flesh and blood. That's all.'

Stupefied, my mouth dry, I repeated:

'That's all?' My head was spinning. 'And what about the Station? What has it got to do with the Station?'

'It's almost as if you're purposely refusing to understand,' he groaned. 'I've been talking about Solaris the whole time, solely about Solaris. If the truth is hard to swallow, it's not my fault. Anyhow, after what you've already been through, you ought to be able to hear me out! We take off into the cosmos, ready for anything: for solitude, for hardship, for exhaustion, death. Modesty forbids us to say so, but there are times when we think pretty well of ourselves. And yet, if we examine it more closely, our enthusiasm turns out to be all sham. We don't want to conquer the cosmos, we simply want to extend the boundaries of Earth to the frontiers of the cosmos. For us, such and such a planet is as arid as the Sahara, another as frozen as the North Pole, yet another as lush as the Amazon basin. We are humanitarian and chivalrous; we don't want to enslave other races, we simply want to bequeath them our values and take over their heritage in exchange.

We think of ourselves as the Knights of the Holy Contact. This is another lie. We are only seeking Man. We have no need of other worlds. We need mirrors. We don't know what to do with other worlds. A single world, our own, suffices us; but we can't accept it for what it is. We are searching for an ideal image of our own world: we go in quest of a planet, of a civilization superior to our own but developed on the basis of a prototype of our primeval past. At the same time, there is something inside us which we don't like to face up to, from which we try to protect ourselves, but which nevertheless remains, since we don't leave Earth in a state of primal innocence. We arrive here as we are in reality, and when the page is turned and that reality is revealed to us – that part of our reality which we would prefer to pass over in silence – then we don't like it any more.'

I had listened to him patiently.

'But what on earth are you talking about?'

'I'm talking about what we all wanted: contact with another civilization. Now we've got it! And we can observe, through a microscope, as it were, our own monstrous ugliness, our folly, our shame!' His voice shook with rage.

'So . . . you think it's . . . the ocean? That the ocean is responsible for it all? But why? I'm not asking how, I'm simply asking why? Do you seriously think that it wants to toy with us, or punish us – a sort of elementary demonomania? A planet dominated by a huge devil, who satisfies the demands of his satanic humour by sending succubi to haunt the members of a scientific expedition . . .? Snow, you can't believe anything so absurd!'

He muttered under his breath.

'This devil isn't such a fool as all that . . .'

I looked at him in amazement. Perhaps what had happened, assuming that we had experienced it in our right minds, had finally driven him over the edge? A reaction psychosis?

He was laughing to himself.

'Making your diagnosis? Don't be in too much of a hurry! You've only been through one ordeal – and that a reasonably mild one.'

'Oh, so the devil had pity on me!'

I was beginning to weary of this conversation.

'What is it you want exactly?' Snow went on. 'Do you want me to tell you what this mass of metamorphic plasma – x-billion tons of meta-morphic plasma – is scheming against us? Perhaps nothing.'

'What do you mean, nothing?'

Snow smiled.

'You must know that science is concerned with phenomena rather than causes. The phenomena here began to manifest themselves eight or nine days after that X-ray experiment. Perhaps the ocean reacted to the irradiation with a counter-irradiation, perhaps it probed our brains and penetrated to some kind of psychic tumour.'

I pricked up my ears.

'Tumour?'

'Yes, isolated psychic processes, enclosed, stifled, encysted – foci smouldering under the ashes of memory. It deciphered them and made use of them, in the same way as one uses a recipe or a blue-print. You know how alike the asymmetric crystalline structures of a chromosome are to those of the DNA molecule, one of the constituents of the cere-brosides which constitute the substratum of the memory-processes? This genetic substance is a plasma which "remembers". The ocean has "read" us by this means, registering the minutest details, with the result that . . . well, you know the result. But for what purpose? Bah! At any rate, not for the purpose of destroying us. It could have anni-hilated us much more easily. As far as one can tell, given its techno-logical resources, it could have done anything it wished – confronted me with your double, and you with mine, for example.'

'So that's why you were so alarmed when I arrived, the first even-ing?'

'Yes. In fact, how do you know it hasn't done so? How do you know I'm really the same old Ratface who landed here two years ago?'

He went on laughing silently, enjoying my discomfiture, then he growled:

'No, no, that's enough of that! We're two happy mortals; I could kill you, you could kill me.'

'And the others, can't they be killed?'

'I don't advise you to try – a horrible sight!'

'Is there no means of killing them?'

'I don't know. Certainly not with poison, or a weapon, or by injec-tion . . .'

'What about a gamma pistol?'

'Would you risk it?'

'Since we know they're not human . . .'

'In a certain subjective sense, they *are* human. They know nothing whatsoever about their origins. You must have noticed that?'

'Yes. But then, how do you explain . . .?'

'They . . . the whole thing is regenerated with extraordinary rapidity, at an incredible speed – in the twinkling of an eye. Then they start behaving again as . . .'

'As?'

'As we remember them, as they are engraved on our memories, following which . . .'

'Did Gibarian know?' I interrupted.

'As much as we do, you mean?'

'Yes.'

'Very probably.'

'Did he say anything to you?'

'No. I found a book in his room . . .'

I leapt to my feet.

'*The Little Apocrypha!*'

'Yes.' He looked at me suspiciously. 'Who could have told you about that?'

I shook my head.

'Don't worry, you can see that I've burnt my skin and that it's not exactly renewing itself. No, Gibarian left a letter addressed to me in his cabin.'

'A letter? What did it say?'

'Nothing much. It was more of a note than a letter, with bibliographic references – allusions to the Supplement to the *Annual* and to the *Apocrypha*. What is this *Apocrypha*?'

'An antique which seems to have some relevance to our situation. Here!' He drew from his pocket a small, leatherbound volume, scuffed at the edges, and handed it to me.

I grabbed the little book.

'And what about Sartorius?'

'Him! Everyone has his own way of coping. Sartorius is trying to remain normal – that is, to preserve his respectability as an envoy on an official mission.'

78

'You're joking!'

'No, I'm quite serious. We were together on another occasion. I won't bother you with the details, but there were eight of us and we were down to our last 1,000 pounds of oxygen. One after another, we gave up our chores, and by the end we all had beards except Sartorius. He was the only one who shaved and polished his shoes. He's like that. Now, of course, he can only pretend, act a part – or else commit a crime.'

'A crime?'

'Perhaps that isn't quite the right word. "Divorce by ejection!" Does that sound better?'

'Very funny!'

'Suggest something else if you don't like it.'

'Oh, leave me alone!'

'No, let's discuss the thing seriously. You know pretty well as much as I do by now. Have you got a plan?'

'No, none. I haven't the least idea what I'll do when . . . when she comes back. She will return, if I've understood you correctly?'

'It's on the cards.'

'How do they get in? The Station is hermetically sealed. Perhaps the layer on the outer hull . . .'

He shook his head.

'The outer hull is in perfect condition. I don't know where they get in. Usually, they're there when you wake up, and you have to sleep eventually!'

'Could you barricade yourself securely inside a cabin?'

'The barricades wouldn't survive for long. There's only one solution, and you can guess what that is . . .'

We both stood up.

'Just a minute, Snow! You're suggesting we liquidate the Station and you expect me to take the initiative and accept the responsibility?'

'It's not as simple as that. Obviously, we could get out, if only as far as the satellite, and send an SOS from there. Of course, we'll be regarded as lunatics; we'll be shut up in a mad-house on Earth – unless we have the sense to retract. A distant planet, isolation, collective derangement – our case won't seem at all out of the ordinary. But at least we'd be better off in a mental home than we are here: a quiet garden, little white cells, nurses, supervised walks . . .'

Hands in his pockets, staring fixedly at a corner of the room, he spoke with the utmost seriousness.

The red sun had disappeared over the horizon and the ocean was a sombre desert, mottled with dying gleams, the last rays lingering among the long tresses of the waves. The sky was ablaze. Purple-edged clouds drifted across this dismal red and black world.

'Well, do you want to get out, yes or no? Or not yet?'

'Always the fighter! If you knew the full implications of what you're asking, you wouldn't be so insistent. It's not a matter of what I want, it's a matter of what's possible.'

'Such as what?'

'That's the point, I don't know.'

'We stay here then? Do you think we'll find some way . . .?'

Thin, sickly-looking, his peeling face deeply lined, he turned towards me:

'It might be worth our while to stay. We're unlikely to learn anything about *it*, but about ourselves . . .'

He turned, picked up his papers, and went out. I opened my mouth to detain him, but no sound escaped my lips.

There was nothing I could do now except wait. I went to the window and ran my eyes absently over the dark-red glimmer of the shadowed ocean. For a moment, I thought of locking myself inside one of the capsules on the hangar-deck, but it was not an idea worth considering for long: sooner or later, I should have to come out again.

I sat by the window, and began to leaf through the book Snow had given me. The glowing twilight lit up the room and coloured the pages. It was a collection of articles and treatises edited by an Otho Ravintzer, Ph.D., and its general level was immediately obvious. Every science engenders some pseudo-science, inspiring eccentrics to explore freakish by-ways; astronomy has its parodists in astrology, chemistry used to have them in alchemy. It was not surprising, therefore, that Solaristics, in its early days, had set off an explosion of marginal cogitations. Ravintzer's book was full of this sort of intellectual speculation, prefaced, it is only fair to add, by an introduction in which the editor dissociated himself from some of the texts reproduced. He considered, with some justice, that such a collection could provide an invaluable period document as much for the historian as for the psychologist of science.

Berton's report, divided into two parts and complete with a summary of his log, occupied the place of honour in the book.

From 14.00 hours to 16.40 hours, by expedition time, the entries in the log were laconic and negative.

'Altitude 3,000 – or 3,500–2,500 feet; nothing visible; ocean empty.' The same words recurred over and over again.

Then, at 16.40 hours: 'A red mist rising. Visibility 700 yards. Ocean empty.

'17.00 hours: fog thickening; visibility 400 yards, with clear patches. Descending to 600 feet.

'17.20 hours: in fog. Altitude 600. Visibility 20–40 yards. Climbing to 1,200.

'17.45: altitude 1,500. Pall of fog to horizon. Funnel-shaped openings through which I can see ocean surface. Attempting to enter one of these clearings; something is moving.

'17.52: have spotted what appears to be a waterspout; it is throwing up a yellow foam. Surrounded by a wall of fog. Altitude 300. Descending to 60 feet.'

The extract from Berton's log stopped at this point. There followed his case-history, or, more precisely, the statement dictated by Berton and interrupted at intervals by questions from the members of the Commission of Enquiry.

BERTON: When I reached 100 feet it became very difficult to maintain altitude because of the violent gusts of wind inside the cone. I had to hang on to the controls and for a short period – about ten or fifteen minutes – I did not look outside. I realized too late that a powerful under-tow was dragging me back into the fog. It wasn't like an ordinary fog, it was a thick colloidal substance which coated my windows. I had a lot of trouble cleaning them; that fog – or glue rather – was obstinate stuff. Due to this resistance, the speed of my rotor-blades was reduced by thirty percent and I began losing height. I was afraid of capsizing on the waves; but, even at full power, I could maintain altitude but not increase it. I still had four booster-rockets left but felt the situation was not yet desperate enough to use them. The aircraft was shaken by shuddering vibrations that grew more and more violent. Thinking my rotor blades must have become coated with the gluey substance, I glanced at the overload indicator, but to my surprise it read zero. Since entering the fog, I had not seen the sun – only a red glow. I continued to fly around in the hope of emerging into one of the funnels, which, after half an hour, was what happened. I found myself in a new 'well', perfectly cylindrical in shape, and several hundred yards in diameter. The walls of the cylinder were formed by an enormous whirlpool of fog, spiralling upwards. I struggled to keep in the middle, where the wind was less violent. It was then that I noticed a change in the ocean's surface. The waves had almost completely disappeared, and the upper layer of the fluid – or whatever the ocean is made of – was becoming transparent, with murky streaks here and there which gradually dissolved until, finally, it was perfectly clear. I could see distinctly to a depth of several yards. I saw a sort of yellow sludge which was sprouting vertical filaments. When these filaments emerged above the surface, they had a glassy sheen. Then they began to exude foam – they frothed – until the foam solidified; it was like a very thick treacle. These glutinous filaments merged and became intertwined; great bubbles swelled up on the surface and slowly began to change shape. Suddenly I realized that my machine was being driven towards the wall of fog. I had to manoeuvre against the wind, and when I was able to look down again, I saw something which looked like a garden. Yes, a garden. Trees, hedges, paths – but it wasn't a real garden; it was all made of the same substance, which had hardened and by now looked like yellow plaster. Beneath this garden, the ocean glittered. I came down as low as I dared in order to take a closer look.

QUESTION: Did the trees and plants you saw have leaves on them?

BERTON: No, the shapes were only approximate, like a model garden. That's exactly what it was like: a model, but lifesize. All of a sudden, it began to crack; it broke up and split into dark crevices; a thick white liquid ran out and collected into pools, or else drained away. The 'earthquake' became more violent, the whole thing boiled over and was buried beneath the foam. At the same time, the walls of the fog began to close in. I gained height rapidly and came clear at 1,000 feet.

QUESTION: Are you absolutely sure that what you saw resembled a garden – there was no other possible interpretation?

BERTON: Yes. I noticed several details. For example, I remember seeing a place where there were some boxes in a row. I realized later that they were probably beehives.

QUESTION: You realized later? But not at the time, not at the moment when you actually saw them?

BERTON: No, because everything looked at though it were made of plaster. But I saw something else.

QUESTION: When was that?

BERTON: I saw things which I can't put a name to, because I didn't have time to examine them carefully. Under some bushes I thought I saw tools, long objects with prongs. They might have been plaster models of garden tools. But I'm not absolutely certain. Whereas I'm sure, quite certain, that I recognized an apiary.

QUESTION: It didn't occur to you that it might be an hallucination?

BERTON: No. I thought it was a mirage. It never occurred to me that it was an hallucination because I felt perfectly well, and I had never seen anything like it before. When I reached 1,000 feet and took another look at the fog, it was pitted with more irregularly-shaped holes, rather like a piece of cheese. Some of these holes were completely hollow, and I could see the ocean waves; others were only shallow saucers in which something was bubbling. I descended another well and saw – the altimeter read 120 feet – I saw a wall lying beneath the ocean surface. It wasn't very deep and I could see it clearly beneath the waves. It seemed to be the wall of a huge building, pierced with rectangular openings, like windows. I even thought I could see something moving behind them, but I couldn't be absolutely certain of that. The wall slowly broke the surface and a mucous bubbling liquid streamed down its sides. Then it suddenly broke in half and disappeared into the depths.

I regained height and continued to fly above the fog, the machine almost touching it, until I discovered another clearing, much larger than the previous one.

While I was still some distance away, I noticed a pale, almost white, object floating on the surface. My first thought was that it was Fechner's flying-suit, especially as it looked vaguely human in form. I brought the aircraft round sharply, afraid of losing my way and being unable to find the same spot again. The shape, the body, was moving; sometimes it seemed to be standing upright in the trough of the waves. I accelerated and went down so low that the machine bounced gently. I must have hit the crest of a huge wave I was overflying. The body – yes, it was a human body, not an atmosphere-suit – the body was moving.

QUESTION: Did you see its face?

BERTON: Yes.

QUESTION: Who was it?

BERTON: A child.

QUESTION: What child? Did you recognize it?

BERTON: No. At any rate, I don't remember having seen it before. Besides, when I got closer – when I was forty yards away, or even sooner – I realized that it was no ordinary child.

QUESTION: What do you mean?

BERTON: I'll explain. At first, I couldn't understand what worried me about it; it was only after a minute or two that I realized: this child was extraordinarily large. Enormous, in fact. Stretched out horizontally, its body rose twelve feet above the surface of the ocean, I swear. I remembered that when I touched the wave, its face was a little higher than mine, even though my cockpit must have been at least ten feet above the ocean.

QUESTION: If it was as big as that, what makes you say it was a child?

BERTON: Because it was a tiny child.

QUESTION: Do you realize, Berton, that your answer doesn't make sense?

BERTON: On the contrary. I could see its face, and it was a very young child. Besides, its proportions corresponded exactly to the proportions of a child's body. It was a . . . babe in arms. No, I exaggerate. It was probably two or three years old. It had black hair and blue eyes – enormous blue eyes! It was naked – completely naked – like a new-born baby. It was wet, or I should say glossy; its skin was shiny. I was shattered. I no longer thought it was a

84

mirage. I could see this child so distinctly. It rose and fell with the waves; but apart from this general motion, it was making other movements, and they were horrible!

QUESTION: Why? What was it doing?

BERTON: It was more like a doll in a museum, only a living doll. It opened and closed its mouth, it made various gestures, horrible gestures.

QUESTION: What do you mean?

BERTON: I was watching it from about twenty yards away – I don't suppose I went any closer. But, as I've already told you, it was enormous. I could see very clearly. Its eyes sparkled and you really would have thought it was a living child, if it hadn't been for the movements, the gestures, as though someone was trying . . . It was as though someone else was responsible for the gestures . . .

QUESTION: Try to be more explicit.

BERTON: It's difficult. I'm talking of an impression, more of an intuition. I didn't analyse it, but I knew that those gestures weren't natural.

QUESTION: Do you mean, for example, that the hands didn't move as human hands would move, because the joints were not sufficiently supple?

BERTON: No, not at all. But . . . these movements had no meaning. Each of our movements means something, more or less, serves some purpose . . .

QUESTION: Do you think so? The movements of an infant don't have much meaning!

BERTON: I know. But an infant's movements are confused, random, uncoordinated. The movements I saw were . . . er . . . yes, that's it, they were *methodical* movements. They were performed one after another, like a series of exercises; as though someone had wanted to make a study of what this child was capable of doing with its hands, its torso, its mouth. The face was more horrifying than the rest, because the human face has an expression, and this face . . . I don't know how to describe it. It was alive, yes, but it wasn't human. Or rather, the features as a whole, the eyes, the complexion, were, but the expression, the movements of the face, were certainly not.

QUESTION: Were they grimaces? Do you know what happens to a person's face during an epileptic fit?

BERTON: Yes. I've watched an epileptic fit. I know what you mean. No, it was something quite different. Epilepsy provokes spasms, convulsions. The movements I'm talking about were fluid, continuous, graceful . . . melodious, if one can say that of a movement. It's the nearest definition I can think of. But this face . . . a face can't divide itself into two – one half gay, the other sad, one half scowling and the other amiable, one half frightened and the other triumphant. But that's how it was with this child's face. In addition to that, all these movements and changes of expression succeeded one another with unbelievable rapidity. I stayed down there a very short time, perhaps ten seconds, perhaps less.

QUESTION: And you claim to have seen all that in such a short time? Besides, how do you know how long you were there? Did you check your chronometer?

BERTON: No, but I've been flying for seventeen years and, in my job, one can measure instinctively, to the nearest second, the duration of what would be called an instant of time. It's an acquired faculty, and essential for successful navigation. A pilot isn't worth his salt if he can't tell whether a particular phenomenon lasts five or ten seconds, whatever the circumstances. It's the same with observation. We learn, over the years, to take in everything at a glance.

QUESTION: Is that all you saw?

BERTON: No, but I don't remember the rest so precisely. I suppose I must already have seen more than enough; my attention faltered. The fog began to close in, and I had to climb. I climbed, and for the first time in my life I all but capsized. My hands were shaking so much that I had difficulty in handling the controls. I think I shouted something, called up the base, even though I knew we were not in radio contact.

QUESTION: Did you then try and get back?

BERTON: No. In the end, having gained height, I thought to myself that Fechner was probably in the bottom of one of the wells. I know it sounds crazy, but that's what I thought. I told myself that everything was possible, and that it would also be possible for me to find Fechner. I decided to investigate every clearing I came across along my route. At the third attempt I gave up. When I had regained height, I knew it was useless to persist after what I had just seen on this, the third, occasion. I couldn't go on any longer. I should add, as you already know, that I was suffering from bouts of nausea and that I vomited in the cockpit. I couldn't understand it; I have never been sick in my life.

COMMENT: It was a symptom of poisoning.

BERTON: Perhaps. I don't know. But what I saw on this third occasion I did not imagine. That was not the effect of poisoning.

QUESTION: How can you possibly know?

BERTON: It wasn't an hallucination. An hallucination is created by one's own brain, wouldn't you say?

COMMENT: Yes.

BERTON: Well, my brain couldn't have created what I saw. I'll never believe that. My brain wouldn't have been capable of it.

COMMENT: Get on with describing what it was!

BERTON: Before I do so, I should like to know how the statements I've already made will be interpreted.

QUESTION: What does that matter?

BERTON: For me, it matters very much indeed. I have said that I saw things which I shall never forget. If the Commission recognizes, even with certain reservations, that my testimony is credible, and that a study of the ocean must be undertaken — I mean a study orientated in the light of my statements — then I'll tell everything. But if the Commission considers that it is all delusions, then I refuse to say anything more.

QUESTION: Why?

BERTON: Because the contents of my hallucinations belong to me and I don't have to give an account of them, whereas I am obliged to give an account of what I saw on Solaris.

QUESTION: Does that mean that you refuse to answer any more questions until the expedition authorities have announced their findings? You realize, of course, that the Commission isn't empowered to take an immediate decision?

BERTON: Yes.

The first minute ended here. There followed a fragment of the second minute drawn up eleven days later.

PRESIDENT: ... after due consideration, the Commission, composed of three doctors, three biologists, a physicist, a mechanical engineer and the deputy head of the expedition, has reached the conclusion that Berton's report is symptomatic of hallucinations caused by atmospheric poisoning, consequent upon inflammation of the associative zone of the cerebral cortex, and that Berton's account bears no, or at any rate no appreciable, relation to reality.

BERTON: Excuse me, what does 'no appreciable relation' mean? In what proportion is reality appreciable or not?

PRESIDENT: I haven't finished. Independently of these conclusions, the Commission has duly registered a dissenting vote from Dr Archibald Messenger, who considers the phenomena described by Berton to be objectively possible and declares himself in favour of a scrupulous investigation.

BERTON: I repeat my question.

PRESIDENT: The answer is simple. 'No appreciable relation to reality' means that phenomena actually observed may have formed the basis of your hallucinations. In the course of a nocturnal stroll, a perfectly sane man can imagine he sees a living creature in a bush stirred by the wind. Such illusions are all the more likely to affect an explorer lost on a strange planet and breathing a poisonous atmosphere. This verdict is in no way prejudicial to you, Berton. Will you now be good enough to let us know your decision?

BERTON: First of all, I should like to know the possible consequences of this dissenting vote of Dr Messenger's.

PRESIDENT: Virtually none. We shall carry on our work along the lines originally laid down.

BERTON: Is our interview on record?

PRESIDENT: Yes.

BERTON: In that case, I should like to say that although the Commission's decision may not be prejudicial to me personally, it is prejudicial to the spirit of the expedition itself. Consequently, as I have already stated, I refuse to answer any further questions.

PRESIDENT: Is that all?

BERTON: Yes. Except that I should like to meet Dr Messenger. Is that possible?

PRESIDENT: Of course.

That was the end of the second minute. At the bottom of the page there was a note in minuscule handwriting to the effect that, the following day, Dr Messenger had talked to Berton for nearly three hours. As a result of this conversation, Messenger had once more begged the expedition Council to undertake further investigations in order to check the pilot's statements. Berton had produced some new and extremely convincing revelations, which Messenger could not divulge unless the Council reversed its negative decision. The Council – Shannahan, Timolis and Trahier – rejected the motion and the affair was closed.

The book also reproduced a photocopy of the last page of a letter, or rather, the draft of a letter, found by Messenger's executors after his death. Ravintzer, in spite of his researches, had been unable to discover if this letter had ever been sent.

'. . . obtuse minds, a pyramid of stupidity,' – the text began. 'Anxious to preserve its authority, the Council – more precisely Shannahan and Timolis (Trahier's vote doesn't count) – has rejected my recommendations. Now I am taking the matter up directly with the Institute; but, as you can well imagine, my protestations won't convince anybody. Bound as I am by oath, I can't, alas, reveal to you what Berton told me. If the Council disregarded Berton's testimony, it was basically because Berton has no scientific training, although any scientist would envy the presence of mind and the gift of observation shown by this pilot. I should be grateful if you could send me the following information by return post:
i) Fechner's biography, in particular details about his childhood.
ii) Everything you know about his family, facts and dates – he probably lost his parents while still a child.
iii) The topography of the place where he was brought up.
I should like once more to tell you what I think about all this. As you know, some time after the departure of Fechner and Carucci, a spot appeared in the centre of the red sun. This chromospheric eruption caused a magnetic storm chiefly over the southern hemisphere, where our base was situated, according to the information

provided by the satellite, and the radio links were cut. The other parties were scouring the planet's surface over a relatively restricted area, whereas Fechner and Carucci had travelled a considerable distance from the base.

Never, since our arrival on the planet, had we observed such a persistent fog or such an unremitting silence.

I imagine that what Berton saw was one of the phases of a kind of "Operation Man" which this viscous monster was engaged in. The source of all the various forms observed by Berton is Fechner – or rather, Fechner's brain, subjected to an unimaginable 'psychic dissection' for the purposes of a sort of re-creation, an experimental reconstruction, based on impressions (undoubtedly the most durable ones) engraved on his memory.

I know this sounds fantastic; I know that I may be mistaken. But do please help me. At the moment, I am on the *Alaric*, where I look forward to receiving your reply.

Yours,

A.'

It was growing dark, and I could scarcely make out the blurred print at the top of the grey page – the last page describing Berton's adventure. For my part, my own experience led me to regard Berton as a trustworthy witness.

I turned towards the window. A few clouds still glowed like dying embers above the horizon. The ocean was invisible, blanketed by the purple darkness.

The strips of paper fluttered idly beneath the air-vents. There was a whiff of ozone in the still, warm air.

There was nothing heroic in our decision to remain on the Station. The time for heroism was over, vanished with the era of the great interplanetary triumphs, of daring expeditions and sacrifices. Fechner, the ocean's first victim, belonged to a distant past. I had almost stopped caring about the identity of Snow's and Sartorius's visitors. Soon, I told myself, we would cease to be ashamed, to keep ourselves apart. If we could not get rid of our visitors, we would accustom ourselves to their presence, learn to live with them. If their Creator altered the rules of the game, we would adapt ourselves to the new rules, even if at first we jibbed or rebelled, even if one of us despaired and killed himself. Eventually, a certain equilibrium would be re-established.

Night had come; no different from many nights on Earth. Now I could make out only the white contours of the basin and the smooth surface of the mirror.

I stood up. Groping my way to the basin, I fumbled among the objects which cluttered up the shelf, and found the packet of cotton wool. I washed my face with a damp wad and stretched out on the bed.

A moth fluttered its wings . . . no, it was the ventilator-strip. The whirring stopped, then started up again. I could no longer see the window; everything had merged into darkness. A mysterious ray of light pierced the blackness and lingered in front of me – against the wall, or the black sky? I remembered how the blank stare of the night had frightened me the day before, and I smiled at the thought. I was no longer afraid of the night; I was not afraid of anything. I raised my wrist and looked at the ring of phosphorescent figures; another hour, and the blue day would dawn.

I breathed deeply, savouring the darkness, my mind empty and at rest.

Shifting my position, I felt the flat shape of the tape-recorder against my hip: Gibarian, his voice immortalized on the spools of tape. I had forgotten to resurrect him, to listen to him – the only thing I could do for him any more. I took the tape-recorder out of my pocket in order to hide it under the bed.

I heard a rustling sound; the door opened.

'Kris?' An anxious voice whispered my name. 'Kris, are you there? It's so dark . . .'

I answered:

'Yes, I'm here. Don't be frightened, come!'

7

THE CONFERENCE

I was lying on my back, with Rheya's head resting on my shoulder.

The darkness was peopled now. I could hear footsteps. Something was piling up above me, higher and higher, infinitely high. The night transfixed me; the night took possession of me, enveloped and penetrated me, impalpable, insubstantial. Turned to stone, I had ceased breathing, there was no air to breathe. As though from a distance, I heard the beating of my heart. I summoned up all my remaining strength, straining every nerve, and waited for death. I went on waiting ... I seemed to be growing smaller, and the invisible sky, horizonless, the formless immensity of space, without clouds, without stars, receded, extended and grew bigger all round me. I tried to crawl out of bed, but there was no bed; beneath the cover of darkness there was a void. I pressed my hands to my face. I no longer had any fingers or any hands. I wanted to scream ...

The room floated in a blue penumbra, which outlined the furniture and the laden bookshelves, and drained everything of colour. A pearly whiteness flooded the window.

I was drenched with sweat. I glanced to one side. Rheya was gazing at me.

She raised her head.

'Has your arm gone to sleep?'

Her eyes too had been drained of colour; they were grey, but luminous, beneath the black lashes.

'What?' Her murmured words had seemed like a caress even before I understood their meaning. 'No. Ah, yes!' I said, at last.

I put my hand on her shoulder; I had pins and needles in my fingers.

'Did you have a bad dream?' she asked.

I drew her to me with my other hand.

'A dream? Yes, I was dreaming. And you, didn't you sleep?'

'I don't know. I don't think so. I'm sleepy. But that mustn't stop you from sleeping . . . Why are you looking at me like that?'

I closed my eyes. Her heart was beating against mine. Her heart? A mere appendage, I told myself. But nothing surprised me any longer, not even my own indifference. I had crossed the frontiers of fear and despair. I had come a long way – further than anyone had ever come before.

I raised myself on my elbow. Daybreak . . . and the peace that comes with dawn? A silent storm had set the cloudless horizon ablaze. A streak of light, the first ray of the blue sun, penetrated the room and broke up into sharp-edged reflections; there was a crossfire of sparks, which coruscated off the mirror, the door-handles, the nickel pipes. The light scattered, falling on to every smooth surface as though it wanted to conquer ever more space, to set the room alight. I looked at Rheya; the pupils of her grey eyes had contracted.

She asked in an expressionless voice, 'Is the night over already?'

'Night never lasts long here.'

'And us?'

'What about us?'

'Are we going to stay here long?'

Coming from her, the question had its comic side; but when I spoke, my voice held no trace of gaiety.

'Quite a long time, probably. Why, don't you want to stay here?'

Her eyes did not blink. She was looking at me inquiringly. Did I see her blink? I was not sure. She drew back the blanket and I saw the little pink scar on her arm.

'Why are you looking at me like that?'

'Because you're very beautiful.'

She smiled, without a trace of mischief, modestly acknowledging my compliment.

'Really? It's as though . . . as though . . .'

'What?'

'As though you were doubtful of something.'

'What nonsense!'

'As though you didn't trust me and I were hiding something from you . . .'

'Rubbish!'

'By the way you're denying it, I can tell I'm right.'

The light became blinding. Shading my eyes with my hand, I looked for my dark glasses. They were on the table. When I was back by her side, Rheya smiled.

'What about me?'

It took me a minute to understand what she meant.

'Dark glasses?'

I got up and began to hunt through drawers and shelves, pushing aside books and instruments. I found two pairs of glasses, which I gave to Rheya. They were too big; they fell half way down her nose.

The shutters slid over the window; it was dark once more. Groping, I helped Rheya remove her glasses and put both pairs down under the bed.

'What shall we do now?' she asked.

'At night-time, one sleeps!'

'Kris . . .'

'Yes?'

'Do you want a compress for your forehead?'

'No, thanks. Thank you . . . my darling.'

I don't know why I had added those two words. In the darkness, I took her by her graceful shoulders. I felt them tremble, and I knew, without the least shadow of doubt, that I held Rheya in my arms. Or rather, I understood in that moment that she was not trying to deceive me; it was I who was deceiving her, since she sincerely believed herself to be Rheya.

I dropped off several times after that, and each time an anguished start jolted me awake. Panting, exhausted, I pressed myself closer to her; my heart gradually growing calmer. She touched me cautiously on the cheeks and forehead with the tips of her fingers, to see whether or not I was feverish. It was Rheya, the real Rheya, the one and only Rheya.

A change came over me; I ceased to struggle and almost at once I fell asleep.

I was awakened by an agreeable sensation of coolness. My face was covered by a damp cloth. I pulled it off and found Rheya leaning over me. She was smiling and squeezing out a second cloth over a bowl.

'What a sleep!' she said, laying another compress on my forehead. 'Are you ill?'

'No.'

I wrinkled my forehead; the skin was supple once again. Rheya sat on the edge of my bed, her black hair brushed back over the collar of a bathrobe – a man's bathrobe, with orange and black stripes, the sleeves turned back to the elbow.

I was terribly hungry; it was at least twenty hours since my last meal. When Rheya had finished her ministrations I got up. Two dresses, draped over the back of a chair, caught my eye – two absolutely identical white dresses, each decorated with a row of red buttons. I myself had helped Rheya out of one of them, and she had reappeared, yesterday evening, dressed in the second.

She followed my glance.

'I had to cut the seam open with scissors,' she said. 'I think the zip fastener must have got stuck.'

The sight of the two identical dresses filled me with a horror which exceeded anything I had felt hitherto. Rheya was busy tidying up the medicine chest. I turned my back and bit my knuckles. Unable to take my eyes off the two dresses – or rather the original dress and its double – I backed towards the door. The basin tap was running noisily. I opened the door and, slipping out of the room, cautiously closed it behind me. I heard the sound of running water, the clinking of bottles; then, suddenly, all sound ceased. I waited, my jaw clenched, my hands gripping the door handle, but with little hope of holding it shut. It was nearly torn from my grasp by a savage jerk. But the door did not open; it shook and vibrated from top to bottom. Dazed, I let go of the handle and stepped back. The panel, made of some plastic material, caved in as though an invisible person at my side had tried to break into the room. The steel frame bent further and further inwards and the paint was cracking. Suddenly I understood: instead of pushing the door, which opened outwards, Rheya was trying to open it by pulling it towards her. The reflection of the lighting strip in the ceiling was distorted in the white-painted door-panel; there was a resounding crack and the panel, forced beyond its limits, gave way. Simultaneously the handle vanished, torn from its mounting. Two bloodstained hands appeared, thrusting through the opening and smearing the white paint with blood. The door split in two, the broken halves hanging askew on their hinges. First a face appeared, deathly pale, then a wild-looking apparition, dressed in an orange and black bathrobe, flung itself sobbing upon my chest.

I wanted to escape, but it was too late, and I was rooted to the spot. Rheya was breathing convulsively, her dishevelled head drumming against my chest. Before I could put my arms round her to hold her up, Rheya collapsed.

Avoiding the ragged edges of the broken panel, I carried her into the room and laid her on the bed. Her fingertips were grazed and the nails torn. When her hands turned upwards, I saw that the palms were cut to the bone. I examined her face; her glazed eyes showed no sign of recognition.

'Rheya.'

The only answer was an inarticulate groan.

I went over to the medicine chest. The bed creaked; I turned round; Rheya was sitting up, looking at her bleeding hands with astonishment.

'Kris,' she sobbed, 'I . . . I . . . what happened to me?'

'You hurt yourself trying to break down the door,' I answered curtly.

My lips were twitching convulsively, and I had to bite the lower one to keep it under control.

Rheya's glance took in the pieces of door-panel hanging from the steel frame, then she turned her eyes back towards me. She was doing her best to hide her terror, but I could see her chin trembling.

I cut off some squares of gauze, picked up a pot of antiseptic powder and returned to the bedside. The glass jar slipped through my hands and shattered – but I no longer needed it.

I lifted one of Rheya's hands. The nails, still surrounded by traces of clotted blood, had regrown. There was a pink scar in the hollow of her palm, but even this scar was healing, disappearing in front of my eyes.

I sat beside her and stroked her face, trying to smile without much success.

'What did you do that for, Rheya?'

'I did . . . that?'

96

With her eyes, she indicated the door.

'Yes . . . Don't you remember?'

'No . . . that is, I saw you weren't there, I was very frightened, and . . .'

'And what?'

'I looked for you. I thought that perhaps you were in the bathroom . . .'

Only then did I notice that the sliding door covering the entrance to the bathroom had been pushed back.

'And then?'

'I ran to the door.'

'And after that?'

'I can't remember . . . Something must have happened . . .'

'What?'

'I don't know.'

'What do you remember?'

'I was sitting here, on the bed.'

She swung her legs over the edge of the bed, got up and went over to the shattered door.

'Kris!'

Walking up behind her, I took her by the shoulders; she was shaking. She suddenly turned and whispered:

'Kris, Kris . . .'

'Calm yourself!'

'Kris, if it's me . . . Kris, am I an epileptic?'

'What an extraordinary idea, my sweet. The doors in this place are rather special . . .'

We left the room as the shutter was grinding its way up the window; the blue sun was sinking into the ocean.

I guided Rheya to the small kitchen on the other side of the dome. Together we raided the cupboards and the refrigerators. I soon noticed that Rheya was scarcely better than I was at cooking or even at opening tins. I devoured the contents of two tins and drank innumerable cups of coffee. Rheya also ate, but as children eat when they are not hungry and do not want to displease their parents; on the other hand, she was not forcing herself, simply taking in nourishment automatically, indifferently.

After our meal, we went into the sick bay, next to the radio cabin. I had had an idea. I told Rheya that I wanted to give her a medical examination – a straightforward check-up, sat her in a mechanical chair, and took a syringe and some needles out of the sterilizer. I knew exactly where each object was to be found; as far as the model of the Station's interior was concerned, the instructors had not overlooked a single detail during my training course. Rheya held out her fingers; I took a sample of blood. I smeared the blood on to a slide which I laid in the suction pipe, introduced it into the vacuum tank and bombarded it with silver ions.

Performing a familiar task had a soothing effect, and I felt better. Rheya, leaning back on the cushions in the mechanical chair, gazed around at the instruments in the sick bay.

The buzzing of the videophone broke the silence; I lifted the receiver:

'Kelvin.'

I looked at Rheya; she was still quiet, apparently exhausted by her recent efforts.

I heard a sigh of relief.

'At last.'

It was Snow. I waited, the receiver pressed close to my ear.

'You've had a visit, haven't you?'

'Yes.'

'Are you busy?'

'Yes.'

'A little auscultation, eh?'

'I suppose you've got a better suggestion – a game of chess maybe?'

'Don't be so touchy, Kelvin! Sartorius wants to meet you, he wants all three of us to meet.'

'Very kind of him!' I answered, taken aback. 'But . . .' I stopped, then went on: 'Is he alone?'

'No. I haven't explained properly. He wants to have a talk with us. We'll set up a three-way videophone link, but with the telescreen lenses covered.'

'I see. Why didn't he contact me himself? Is he frightened of me?'

'Quite possibly,' grunted Snow. 'What do you say?'

'A conference. In an hour's time. Will that suit you?'

'That's fine.'

I could see him on the screen – just his face, about the size of a fist. For a moment, he looked at me attentively; I could hear the crackling of the electric current. Then he said, hesitantly:

'Are you getting on all right?'

'Not too bad. How about you?'

'Not so well as you, I dare say. May I . . .?'

'Do you want to come over here?'

I glanced at Rheya over my shoulder. She was leaning back, legs crossed, her head bent. With a morose air, she was fiddling mechanically with the little chrome ball on the end of a chain fixed to the arm-rest.

Snow's voice erupted:

'Stop that, do you hear? I told you to stop it!'

I could see his profile on the screen, but I could no longer hear him although his lips were moving – he had put his hand over the microphone.

'No, I can't come,' he said quickly. 'Later perhaps; in any case, I'll contact you in an hour.'

The screen went blank; I replaced the receiver.

'Who was it?' asked Rheya indifferently.

'Snow, a cybernetician. You don't know him.'

'Is this going on much longer?'

'Are you bored?'

I put the first of the series of slides into the neutron microscope, and, one after another, I pressed the different-coloured switches; the magnetic fields rumbled hollowly.

'There's not much to do in here, and if my humble company isn't enough for you . . .'

I was talking distractedly, with long gaps between my words.

I pulled the big black hood round the eye-piece of the microscope towards me, and leaned my forehead against the resilient foam-rubber viewer. I could hear Rheya's voice, but without taking in what she was saying. Beneath my gaze, sharply foreshortened, was a vast desert flooded with silvery light, and strewn with rounded boulders – red corpuscles – which trembled and wriggled behind a veil of mist. I focused the eye-piece and penetrated further into the depths of the silvery landscape. Without taking my eyes away from the viewer, I turned the view-finder; when a boulder, a single corpuscle, detached itself and appeared at the junction of the cross-hairs, I enlarged the image. The lens had apparently picked up a deformed erythrocyte, sunken in the centre, whose uneven edges projected sharp shadows over the depths of a circular crater. The crater, bristling with silver ion deposits, extended beyond the microscope's field of vision. The nebulous outlines of threads of albumen, distorted and atrophied, appeared in the midst of an opalescent liquid. A worm of albumen twisted and turned beneath the cross-hairs of the lens. Gradually I increased the enlargement. At any moment, I should reach the limit of this exploration of the depths; the shadow of a molecule occupied the whole of the space; then the image became fuzzy.

There was nothing to be seen. There should have been the ferment of a quivering cloud of atoms, but I saw nothing. A dazzling light filled the screen, which was flawlessly clear. I pushed the lever to its utmost. The angry, whirring noise grew louder, but the screen remained a blank. An alarm signal sounded once, then was repeated; the circuit was overloaded. I took a final look at the silvery desert, then I cut the current.

I looked at Rheya. She was in the middle of a yawn which she changed adroitly into a smile.

'Am I in good health?' she asked.

'Excellent. Couldn't be better.'

I continued to look at her and once more I felt as though something was crawling along my lower lip. What had happened exactly? What was the meaning of it? Was this body, frail and weak in appearance but indestructible in reality, actually made of nothing? I gave the microscope cylinder a blow with my fist. Was the instrument out of order? No, I knew that it was working perfectly. I had followed the procedure faithfully: first the cells, then the albumen, then the molecules; and everything was just as I was accustomed to seeing it in the course of examining thousands of slides. But the final step, into the heart of the matter, had taken me nowhere.

I put a ligature on Rheya, took some blood from a median vein and transferred it to a graduated glass, then divided it between several test-tubes and began the analyses. These took longer than usual; I was rather out of practice. The reactions were normal, every one of them.

I dropped some congealed acid on to a coral-tinted pearl. Smoke. The blood turned grey and a dirty foam rose to the surface. Disintegration, decomposition, faster and faster! I turned my back to get another test-tube; when I looked again at the experiment, I nearly dropped the slim glass phial.

Beneath the skin of dirty foam, a dark coral was rising. The blood, destroyed by the acid, was re-creating itself. It was crazy, impossible!

'Kris.' I heard my name called, as though from a great distance. 'Kris, the videophone!'

'What? Oh, thanks.'

The instrument had been buzzing for some time, but I had only just noticed it.

I picked up the receiver:

'Kelvin.'

'Snow. We are now all three plugged into the same circuit.'

The high-pitched voice of Sartorius came over the receiver:

'Greetings, Dr Kelvin!' It was the wary tone of voice, full of false assurance, of the lecturer who knows he is on tenuous ground.

'Good-day to you, Dr Sartorius!'

I wanted to laugh; but in the circumstances I hardly felt I could yield to a mood of hilarity. After all, which of us was the laughing stock? In my hand I held a test-tube containing some blood. I shook it. The blood coagulated. Had I been the victim of an illusion a moment ago? Had I, perhaps, been mistaken?

'I should like to set forth, gentlemen, certain questions concerning the . . . the phantoms.'

I listened to Sartorius, but my mind refused to take in his words. I was pondering the coagulated blood and shutting out this distracting voice.

'Let's call them Phi-creatures,' Snow interjected.

'Very well, agreed.'

A vertical line, bisecting the screen and barely perceptible, showed that I was linked to two channels: on either side of this line, I should have seen two images – Snow and Sartorius. But the light-rimmed screen remained dark. Both my interlocutors had covered the lenses of their sets.

'Each of us has made various experiments.' The nasal voice still held the same wariness. There was a pause.

'I suggest first of all that we pool such knowledge as we have acquired so far,' Sartorius went on. 'Afterwards, I shall venture to communicate to you the conclusions that I, personally, have reached. If you would be so good as to begin, Dr Kelvin . . .'

'Me?'

All of a sudden, I sensed Rheya watching me. I put my hand on the table and rolled the test-tube under the instrument racks. Then I perched myself on a stool which I dragged up with my foot. I was about to decline to give an opinion when, to my surprise, I heard myself answer:

'Right. A little talk? I haven't done much, but I can tell you about it. A histological sample . . . certain reactions. Micro-reactions. I have the impression that . . .' I did not know how to go on. Suddenly I found my tongue and continued: 'Everything looks normal, but it's a camouflage. A cover. In a way, it's a super-copy, a reproduction which is superior to the original. I'll explain what I mean: there exists, in man, an absolute limit – a term to structural divisibility – whereas here, the frontiers have been pushed back. We are dealing with a sub-atomic structure.'

'Just a minute, just a minute! Kindly be more precise!' Sartorius interrupted.

Snow said nothing. Did I catch an echo of his rapid breathing? Rheya was looking at me again. I realized that, in my excitement, I had almost shouted the last words. Calmer, I settled myself on my uncomfortable perch and closed my eyes. How could I be more precise?

'The atom is the ultimate constituent element of our bodies. My guess is that the Phi-beings are constituted of units smaller than ordinary atoms, much smaller.'

'Mesons,' put in Sartorius. He did not sound in the least surprised.

'No, not mesons . . . I would have seen them. The power of this instrument here is between a tenth to a twentieth of an angstrom, isn't it? But nothing is visible, nothing whatsoever. So it can't be mesons. More likely neutrinos.'

'How do you account for that theory? Conglomerations of neutrinos are unstable . . .'

'I don't know. I'm not a physicist. Perhaps a magnetic field could stabilize them. It's not my province. In any event, if my observations are correct, the structure is made up of particles at least ten thousand times smaller than atoms. Wait a minute, I haven't finished! If the albuminous molecules and the cells were directly constructed from micro-atoms, they must be proportionally even smaller. This applies to the corpuscles, the micro-organisms, everything. Now, the dimensions are those of atomic structures. Consequently, the albumen, the cell and the nucleus of the cell are nothing but camouflage. The real structure, which determines the functions of the visitor, remains concealed.'

'Kelvin!'

Snow had uttered a stifled cry. I stopped, horrified. I had said 'visitor'.

Rheya had not overheard. At any rate, she had not understood. Her head in her hand, she was staring out of the window, her delicate profile etched against the purple dawn.

My distant interlocutors were silent: I could hear their breathing.

'There's something in what he says,' Snow muttered.

'Yes,' remarked Sartorius, 'but for one fact: Kelvin's hypothetical particles have nothing to do with the structure of the ocean. The ocean is composed of atoms.'

'Perhaps it's capable of producing neutrinos,' I replied.

Suddenly I was bored with all their talk. The conversation was pointless, and not even amusing.

'Kelvin's hypothesis explains this extraordinary resistance and the speed of regeneration,' Snow growled. 'They probably carry their own energy source as well; they don't need food . . .'

'I believe I have the chair,' Sartorius interrupted. The self-designated chairman of the debate was clinging exasperatingly to his role. 'I should like to raise the question of the motivation behind the appearance of the Phi-creatures. I put it to you as follows: what are the Phi-creatures? They are not autonomous individuals, nor copies of actual persons. They are merely projections materializing from our brains, based on a given individual.'

I was struck by the soundness of this description; Sartorius might not be very sympathetic, but he was certainly no fool.

I rejoined the conversation:

'I think you're right. Your definition explains why a particular per . . . creation appears rather than another. The origin of the materialization lies in the most durable imprints of memory, those which are especially well-defined, but no single imprint can be completely isolated, and in the course of the reproduction, fragments of related imprints are absorbed. Thus the new arrival sometimes reveals a more extensive knowledge than that of the individual of whom it is a copy . . .'

'Kelvin!' shouted Snow once more.

It was only Snow who reacted to my lapses; Sartorius did not seem to be affected by them. Did this mean that Sartorius's visitor was less perspicacious than Snow's? For a moment, I imagined the scholarly Sartorius cohabiting with a cretinous dwarf.

'Indeed, that corresponds with our observations,' Sartorius said. 'Now, let us consider the motivation behind the apparition! It is natural enough to assume, in the first instance, that we are the object of an experiment. When I examine this proposition, the experiment seems to me badly designed. When we carry out an experiment, we profit by the results and, above all, we carefully note the defects of our methods. As a result, we introduce modifications in our future procedure. But, in the case with which we are concerned, not a single modification has occurred. The Phi-creatures reappear exactly as they were, down to the last detail . . . as vulnerable as before, each time we attempt to . . . to rid ourselves of them . . .'

'Exactly,' I broke in, 'a recoil, with no compensating mechanism, as Dr Snow would say. Conclusions?'

'Simply that the thesis of experimentation is inconsistent with this . . . this unbelievable bungling. The ocean is . . . precise. The dual-level structure of the Phi-creatures testifies to this precision. Within the prescribed limits, the Phi-creatures behave in the same way as the real . . . the . . . er . . .'

He could not disentangle himself.

'The originals,' said Snow, in a loud whisper.

'Yes, the originals. But when the situation no longer corresponds to the normal faculties of . . . er . . . the original, the Phi-creature suffers a sort of "disconnection of consciousness", followed immediately by unusual, non-human manifestations . . .'

'It's true,' I said, 'and we can amuse ourselves drawing up a catalogue of the behaviour of . . . of these creatures – a totally frivolous occupation!'

'I'm not so sure of that,' protested Sartorius. I suddenly realized why he irritated me so much: he didn't talk, he lectured, as though he were in the chair at the Institute. He seemed to be incapable of expressing himself in any other way. 'Here we come to the question of individuality,' he went on, 'of which, I am quite sure, the ocean has not the smallest inkling. I think that the . . . er . . . delicate or shocking aspect of our present situation is completely beyond its comprehension.'

'You think its activities are unpremeditated?'

I was somewhat bewildered by Sartorius's point of view, but on second thought, I realized that it could not be dismissed.

'No, unlike our colleague Snow, I don't believe there is malice, or deliberate cruelty . . .'

Snow broke in:

'I'm not suggesting it has human feelings, I'm merely trying to find an explanation for these continual reappearances.'

With a secret desire to nag poor Sartorius, I said:

'Perhaps they are plugged into a contrivance which goes round and round, endlessly repeating itself, like a gramophone record . . .'

'Gentlemen, I beg you, let us not waste time! I haven't yet finished. In normal circumstances, I would have felt it premature to present a report, even a provisional one, on the progress of my research; in view of the prevailing situation, however, I think I may allow myself to speak out. I have the impression – only an impression, mark you – that Dr Kelvin's hypothesis is not without validity. I am alluding to the hypothesis of a neutrino structure . . . Our knowledge in this field is purely theoretical. We did not know if there was any possibility of stabilizing such structures. Now a clearly defined solution offers itself to us. A means of neutralizing the magnetic field that maintains the stability of the structure . . .'

A few moments previously, I had noticed that the screen was flickering with light. Now a split appeared from top to bottom of the left-hand side. I saw something pink move slowly out of view. Then the lens-cover slipped again, disclosing the screen.

Sartorius gave an anguished cry:

'Go away! Go away!'

I saw his hands flapping and struggling, then his forearms, covered by the wide sleeves of the laboratory gown. A bright golden disc shone out for an instant, then everything went dark. Only then did I realize that this golden disc was a straw hat . . .

I took a deep breath.

'Snow?'

An exhausted voice replied:

'Yes, Kelvin . . .' Hearing his voice, I realized that I had become quite fond of him, and that I preferred not to know who or what his companion was. 'That's enough for now, don't you think?' he said.

'I agree.' Before he could cut off, I added quickly: 'Listen, if you can, come and see me, either in the operating room or in my cabin.'

'OK, but I don't know when.'

The conference was over.

8

THE MONSTERS

I woke up in the middle of the night to find the light on and Rheya crouched at the end of the bed, wrapped in a sheet, her shoulders shaking with silent tears. I called her name and asked her what was wrong, but she only curled up tighter.

Still half asleep, and barely emerged from the nightmare which had been tormenting me only a moment before, I pulled myself up to a sitting position and shielded my eyes against the glare to look at her. The trembling continued, and I stretched out my arms, but Rheya pushed me away and hid her face.

'Rheya . . .'

'Don't talk to me!'

'Rheya, what's the matter?'

I caught a glimpse of her tear-stained face, contorted with emotion. The big childish tears streamed down her face, glistened in the dimple above her chin and fell on to the sheet.

'You don't want me.'

'What are you talking about?'

'I heard . . .'

My jaw tightened; 'Heard what? You don't understand . . .'

'Yes I do. You said I wasn't Rheya. You wanted me to go, and I would, I really would . . . but I can't. I don't know why. I've tried to go, but I couldn't do it. I'm such a coward.'

'Come on now . . .' I put my arms round her and held her with all my strength. Nothing mattered to me except her: everything else was meaningless. I kissed her hands, talked, begged, excused myself and made promise after promise, saying that she had been having some silly, terrible dream. Gradually she grew calmer, and at last she stopped crying and her eyes glazed, like a woman walking in her sleep. She turned her face away from me.

'No,' she said at last, 'be quiet, don't talk like that. It's no good, you're not the same person any more.' I started to protest, but she went on: 'No, you don't want me. I knew it before, but I pretended not to notice. I thought perhaps I was imagining everything, but it was true . . . you've changed. You're not being honest with me. You talk about dreams, but it was you who were dreaming, and it was to do with me. You spoke my name as if it repelled you. Why? Just tell me why.'

'Rheya, my little . . .'

'I won't have you talking to me like that, do you hear? I won't let you. I'm not your little anything, I'm not a child. I'm . . .'

She burst into tears and buried her face in the pillow. I got up. The ventilation hummed quietly. It was cold, and I pulled a dressing-gown over my shoulders before sitting next to her and taking her arm: 'Listen to me, I'm going to tell you something. I'm going to tell you the truth.'

She pushed herself upright again. I could see the veins throbbing beneath the delicate skin of her neck. My jaw tightened once more. The air seemed to be colder still, and my head was completely empty.

'The truth?' she said. 'Word of honour?'

I opened my mouth to speak, but no sound came. 'Word of honour' . . . it was our special catch-phrase, our old way of making an unconditional promise. Once these words had been spoken, neither of us was permitted to lie, or even to take refuge behind a half-truth. I remembered the period when we used to torture each other in an exaggerated striving for sincerity, convinced that this ingenuous honesty was the precondition of our relationship.

'Word of honour, Rheya,' I answered gravely, and she waited for me to continue. 'You have changed too – we all change. But that is not what I wanted to say. For some reason that neither of us understands, it seems that . . . you are forced to stay near me. And that's fine with me, because I can't leave you either . . .'

'No, Kris. The change is not in you,' Rheya whispered. 'It's me. Something is wrong. Perhaps it has to do with the accident?'

She looked at the dark, empty rectangle of the door. The previous evening, I had removed the shattered remains – a new one would have to be fitted. Another thought struck me:

'Have you been managing to sleep?'

'I don't know.'

'What do you mean?'

'I have dreams . . . I don't know whether they really are dreams. Perhaps I'm ill. I lie there and think, and . . .'

'What?'

'I have strange thoughts. I don't know where they come from.'

It took all my self-control to steady my voice and tell her to go on, and I found myself tensing for her answer as if for a blow in the face.

'They are thoughts . . .' She shook her head helplessly, '. . . all around me.'

'I don't understand.'

'I get a feeling as if they were not from inside myself, but somewhere further away. I can't explain it, can't put words to it . . .'

I broke in almost involuntarily: 'It must be some kind of dream.' Then, back in control again: 'And now, we put the light out and we forget our problems until morning. Tomorrow we can invent some new ones if you like. OK?'

She pressed the switch, and darkness fell between us. Stretched out on the bed, I felt her warm breathing beside me, and put my arms round her.

'Harder!' she whispered, and then, after a long pause:

'Kris!'

'What?'

'I love you.'

I almost screamed.

In the red morning, the sun's swollen disc was rising over the horizon.

An envelope lay in the doorway, and I tore it open. I could hear Rheya humming to herself in the bath, and from time to time she looked into the room and I would see her face, half hidden by her wet hair.

I went to the window, and read:

Kelvin, things are looking up. Sartorius has decided that it may be possible to use some form of energy to destabilize the neutrino structure. He wants to examine some Phi plasma in orbit. He suggests that you make a reconnaissance flight and take a certain quantity of plasma in the capsule. It's up to you, but let me know what you decide. I have no opinion. I feel as if I no longer have anything. If I am more in favour of your going, it's because we would at least be making some show of progress. Otherwise, we can only envy G.

Snow

PS All I ask is for you to stay outside the cabin. You can call me on the videophone.

I felt a stir of apprehension as I read the letter, and went over it again carefully before tearing it up and throwing the pieces into the disposal unit.

I went through the same terrible charade that I had begun the previous day, and made up a story for Rheya's benefit. She did not notice the deception, and when I told her that I had to make an inspection and suggested that she come with me she was delighted. We stopped at the kitchen for breakfast – Rheya ate very little – and then made for the library.

Before venturing on the mission suggested by Sartorius, I wanted to glance through the literature dealing with magnetic fields and neutrino structures. I did not yet have any clear idea of how I would set about it, but I had made up my mind to make an independent check on Sartorius's activities. Not that I would prevent Snow and Sartorius from 'liberating' themselves when the annihilator was completed: I meant to take Rheya out of the Station and wait for the conclusion of the operation in the cabin of an aircraft. I set to work with the automatic librarian. Sometimes it answered my queries by ejecting a card with the laconic inscription 'Not on file', sometimes it practically submerged me under such a spate of specialist physics textbooks that I hesitated to use its advice. Yet I had no desire to leave the big circular chamber. I felt at ease in my egg, among the rows of cabinets crammed with tape and microfilm. Situated right at the centre of the Station, the library had no windows: it was the most isolated area in the great steel shell, and made me feel relaxed in spite of finding my researches held up.

Wandering across the vast room, I stopped at a set of shelves as high as the ceiling, and holding about six hundred volumes – all classics on the history of Solaris, starting with the nine volumes of Giese's monumental and already relatively obsolescent monograph. Display for its own sake was a respectful tribute to the memory of the pioneers. I took down the massive volumes of Giese and sat leafing through them. Rheya had also located some reading matter. Looking over her shoulder, I saw that she had picked one of the many books brought out by the first expedition, the *Interplanetary Cookery Book*, which could have been the personal property of Giese himself. She was poring over the recipes adapted to the arduous conditions of interstellar flight. I said nothing, and returned to the book resting on my knees. *Solaris – Ten Years of Exploration* had appeared as volumes four–twelve of the Solariana collection, whose most recent additions were numbered in the thousands.

Giese was an unemotional man, but then in the study of Solaris emotion is a hindrance to the explorer. Imagination and premature theorizing are positive disadvantages in approaching a planet where – as has become clear – anything is possible. It is almost certain that the unlikely descriptions of the 'plasmatic' metamorphoses of the ocean are faithful accounts of the phenomena observed, although these descriptions are unverifiable, since the ocean seldom repeats itself. The freakish character and gigantic scale of these phenomena go too far outside the experience of man to be grasped by anybody observing them for the first time, and who would consider analogous occurrences as 'sports of nature', accidental manifestations of blind forces, if he saw them on a reduced scale, say in a mud-volcano on Earth.

Genius and mediocrity alike are dumbfounded by the teeming diversity of the oceanic formations of Solaris; no man has ever become genuinely conversant with them. Giese was by no means a mediocrity, but nor was he a genius. He was a scholarly classifier, the type whose compulsive application to their work utterly divorces them from the pressures of everyday life. Giese devised a plain descriptive terminology, supplemented by terms of his own invention, and although these were inadequate, and sometimes clumsy, it has to be admitted that no semantic system is as yet available to illustrate the behaviour of the ocean. The 'tree-mountains', 'extensors', 'fungoids', 'mimoids', 'symmetriads' and 'asymmetriads', 'vertebrids' and 'agilus' are artificial, linguistically awkward terms, but they do give some impression of Solaris to anyone who has only seen the planet in blurred photographs and incomplete films. The fact is that in spite of his cautious nature the scrupulous Giese more than once jumped to premature conclusions. Even when on their guard, human beings inevitably theorize. Giese, who thought himself immune to temptation, decided that the 'extensors' came into the category of basic forms. He compared them to accumulations of gigantic waves, similar to the tidal movements of our Terran oceans. In the first edition of his work, we find them originally named as 'tides'. This geocentrism might be considered amusing if it did not underline the dilemma in which he found himself.

As soon as the question of comparisons with Earth arises, it must be understood that the 'extensors' are formations that dwarf the Grand Canyon, that they are produced in a substance which externally resembles a yeasty colloid (during this fantastic 'fermentation', the yeast sets into festoons of starched open-work lace; some experts refer to 'ossified tumours'), and that deeper down the substance becomes increasingly resistant, like a tensed muscle which fifty feet below the surface is as hard as rock but retains its flexibility. The 'extensor' appears to be an independent creation, stretching for miles between membranous walls swollen with 'ossified growths', like some colossal python which after swallowing a mountain is sluggishly digesting the meal, while a slow shudder occasionally ripples along its creeping body. The 'extensor' only looks like a lethargic reptile from overhead. At close quarters, when the two 'canyon walls' loom hundreds of yards above the exploring aircraft, it can be seen that this inflated cylinder, reaching from one side of the horizon to the other, is bewilderingly alive with movement. First you notice the continual rotating motion of a greyish-green, oily sludge which reflects blinding sunlight, but skimming just above the 'back of the python' (the 'ravine' sheltering the 'extensor' now resembles the sides of a geological fault), you realize that the motion is in fact far more complex, and consists of concentric fluctuations traversed by darker currents. Occasionally this mantle turns into a shining crust that reflects sky and clouds and then is riddled by explosive eruptions of the internal gases and fluids. The observer slowly realizes that he is looking at the guiding forces that are thrusting outward and upward the two gradually crystallizing gelatinous walls. Science does not accept the obvious without further proof, however, and virulent controversies have reverberated down the years on the key question of the exact sequence of events in the interior of the 'extensors' that furrow the vast living ocean in their millions.

Various organic functions have been ascribed to the 'extensors'. Some experts have argued that their purpose is the transformation of matter; others suggested respiratory processes; still others claimed that they conveyed alimentary materials. An infinite variety of hypotheses now moulder in library basements, eliminated by ingenious, sometimes dangerous experiments. Today, the scientists will go no further than to refer to the 'extensors' as relatively simple, stable formations whose duration is measurable in weeks – an exceptional characteristic among the recorded phenomena of the planet.

The 'mimoid' formations are considerably more complex and bizarre, and elicit a more vehement response from the observer, an instinctive response, I mean. It can be stated without exaggeration that Giese fell in love with the 'mimoids' and was soon devoting all his time to them. For the rest of his life, he studied and described them and brought all his ingenuity to bear on defining their nature. The name he gave them indicates their most astonishing characteristic, the imitation of objects, near or far, external to the ocean itself.

Concealed at first beneath the ocean surface, a large flattened disc appears, ragged, with tar-like coating. After a few hours, it begins to separate into flat sheets which rise slowly. The observer now becomes a spectator at what looks like a fight to the death, as massed ranks of waves converge from all directions like contorted, fleshy mouths which snap greedily around the tattered, fluttering leaf, then plunge into the depths. As each ring of waves breaks and sinks, the fall of this mass of hundreds of thousands of tons is accompanied for an instant by a viscous rumbling, an immense thunderclap. The tarry leaf is overwhelmed, battered and torn apart; with every fresh assault, circular fragments scatter and drift like feebly fluttering wings below the ocean surface. They bunch into pear-shaped clusters or long strings, merge and rise again, and drag with them an undertow of coagulated shreds of the base of the primal disc. The encircling waves continue to break around the steadily expanding crater. This phenomenon may persist for a day or linger on for a month, and sometimes there are no further developments. The conscientious Giese dubbed this first variation a 'stillbirth', convinced that each of these upheavals aspired towards an ultimate condition, the 'major mimoid', like a polyp colony (only covering an area greater than a town) of pale outcroppings with the faculty of imitating foreign bodies. Uyvens, on the other hand, saw this final stage as constituting a degeneration or necrosis: according to him, the appearance of the 'copies' corresponded to a localized dissipation of the life energies of the ocean, which was no longer in control of the original forms it created.

Giese would not abandon his account of the various phases of the process as a sustained progression towards perfection, with a conviction which is particularly surprising coming from a man of such a moderate, cautious turn of mind in advancing the most trivial hypothesis on the other creations of the ocean. Normally he had all the boldness of an ant crawling up a glacier.

Viewed from above, the mimoid resembles a town, an illusion produced by our compulsion to superimpose analogies with what we know. When the sky is clear, a shimmering heat-haze covers the pliant structures of the clustered polyps surmounted by membranous palisades. The first cloud passing overhead wakens the mimoid. All the outcrops suddenly sprout new shoots, then the mass of polyps ejects a thick tegument which dilates, puffs out, changes colour and in the space of a few minutes has produced an astonishing imitation of the volutes of a cloud. The enormous 'object' casts a reddish shadow over the mimoid, whose peaks ripple and bend together, always in the opposite direction to the movement of the real cloud. I imagine that Giese would have been ready to give his right hand to discover what made the mimoids behave in this way, but these 'isolated' productions are nothing in comparison to the frantic activity the mimoid displays when 'stimulated' by objects of human origin.

The reproduction process embraces every object inside a radius of eight or nine miles. Usually the facsimile is an enlargement of the original, whose forms are sometimes only roughly copied. The reproduction of machines, in particular, elicits simplifications that might be considered grotesque – practically caricatures. The copy is always modelled in the same colourless tegument, which hovers above the outcrops, linked to its base by flimsy umbilical cords; it slides, creeps, curls back on itself, shrinks or swells and finally assumes the most complicated forms. An aircraft, a net or a pole are all reproduced at the same speed. The mimoid is not stimulated by human beings themselves, and in fact it does not react to any living matter, and has never copied, for example, the plants imported for experimental purposes. On the other hand, it will readily reproduce a puppet or a doll, a carving of a dog, or a tree sculpted in any material.

The observer must bear in mind that the 'obedience' of the mimoid does not constitute evidence of cooperation, since it is not consistent. The most highly-evolved mimoid has its off-days, when it 'lives' in slow-motion, or its pulsation weakens. (This pulsation is invisible to the naked eye, and was only discovered after close examination of rapid-motion film of the mimoid, which revealed that each 'beat' took two hours.)

During these 'off-days', it is easy to explore the mimoid, especially if it is old, for the base anchored in the ocean, like the protuberances growing out of it, is relatively solid, and provides a firm footing for a man. It is equally possible to remain inside the mimoid during periods of activity, except that visibility is close to nil because of the whitish colloidal dust continually emitted through tears in the tegument above. In any case, at close range it is impossible to distinguish what forms the tegument is assuming, on account of their vast size – the smallest 'copy' is the size of a mountain. In addition, a thick layer of colloidal snow quickly covers the base of the mimoid: this spongy carpet takes several hours to solidify (the 'frozen' crust will take the weight of a man, though its composition is much lighter than pumice stone). The problem is that without special equipment there is a risk of being lost in the maze of tangled structures and crevasses, sometimes reminiscent of jumbled colonnades, sometimes of petrified geysers. Even in day-light it is easy to lose one's direction, for the sun's rays cannot pierce the white ceiling ejected into the atmosphere by the 'imitative explosions'.

On gala days (for the scientist as well as for the mimoid), an un-forgettable spectacle develops as the mimoid goes into hyperproduction and performs wild flights of fancy. It plays variations on the theme of a given object and embroiders 'formal extensions' that amuse it for hours on end, to the delight of the non-figurative artist and the despair of the scientist, who is at a loss to grasp any common theme in the performance. The mimoid can produce 'primitive' simplifications, but is just as likely to indulge in 'baroque' deviations, paroxysms of extravagant brilliance. Old mimoids tend to manufacture extremely comic forms. Looking at the photographs, I have never been moved to laughter; the riddle they set is too disquieting to be funny.

During the early years of exploration, the scientists literally threw themselves upon the mimoids, which were spoken of as open windows on the ocean and the best opportunity to establish the hoped-for contact between the two civilizations. They were soon forced to admit that there was not the slightest prospect of communication, and that the entire process began and ended with the reproduction of forms. The mimoids were a dead end.

Giving way to the temptations of a latent anthropomorphism or zoomorphism, there were many schools of thought which saw various other oceanic formations as 'sensory organs', even as 'limbs', which was how experts like Maartens and Ekkonai classified Giese's 'vertebrids' and 'agilus' for a time. Anyone who is rash enough to see protuberances that reach as far as two miles into the atmosphere as limbs, might just as well claim that earthquakes are the gymnastics of the Earth's crust!

Three hundred chapters of Giese catalogue the standard formations which occur on the surface of the living ocean and which can be seen in dozens, even hundreds, in the course of any day. The symmetriads – to continue using the terminology and definitions of the Giese school – are the least 'human' formations, which is to say that they bear no resemblance whatsoever to anything on Earth. By the time the symmetriads were being investigated, it was already clear that the ocean was not aggressive, and that its plasmatic eddies would not swallow any but the most foolhardy explorer (of course I am not including accidents resulting from mechanical failures). It is possible to fly in complete safety from one part to another of the cylindrical body of an extensor, or of the vertebrids, Jacob's ladders oscillating among the clouds: the plasma retreats at the speed of sound in the planet's atmosphere to make way for any foreign body. Deep funnels will open even beneath the surface of the ocean (at a prodigious expenditure of energy, calculated by Scriabin at around 10^{19} ergs). Nevertheless, the first venture into the interior of a symmetriad was undertaken with the utmost caution and discipline, and involved a host of what turned out to be unnecessary safety measures. Every schoolboy on Earth knows the names of these pioneers.

It is not their nightmare appearance that makes the gigantic symmetriad formations dangerous, but the total instability and capriciousness of their structure, in which even the laws of physics do not hold. The theory that the living ocean is endowed with intelligence has found its firmest adherents among those scientists who have ventured into their unpredictable depths.

The birth of a symmetriad comes like a sudden eruption. About an hour beforehand, an area of tens of square miles of ocean vitrifies and begins to shine. It remains fluid, and there is no alteration in the rhythm of the waves. Occasionally the phenomenon of vitrification occurs in the neighbourhood of the funnel left by an agilus. The gleaming sheath of the ocean heaves upwards to form a vast ball that reflects sky, sun, clouds and the entire horizon in a medley of changing, variegated images. Diffracted light creates a kaleidoscopic play of colour.

The effects of light on a symmetriad are especially striking during the blue day and the red sunset. The planet appears to be giving birth to a twin that increases in volume from one moment to the next. The immense flaming globe has scarcely reached its maximum expansion above the ocean when it bursts at the summit and cracks vertically. It is not breaking up; this is the second phase, which goes under the clumsy name of the 'floral calyx phase' and lasts only a few seconds. The membranous arches soaring into the sky now fold inwards and merge to produce a thick-set trunk enclosing a scene of teeming activity. At the centre of the trunk, which was explored for the first time by the seventy-man Hamalei expedition, a process of polycrystallization on a giant scale erects an axis commonly referred to as the 'backbone', a term which I consider ill-chosen. The mind-bending architecture of this central pillar is held in place by vertical shafts of a gelatinous, almost liquid consistency, constantly gushing upwards out of wide crevasses. Meanwhile, the entire trunk is surrounded by a belt of snowy foam, seething with great bubbles of gas, and the whole process is accompanied by a perpetual dull roar of sound. From the centre towards the periphery, powerful buttresses spin out and are coated with streams of ductile matter rising out of the ocean depths. Simultaneously the gelatinous geysers are converted into mobile columns that proceed to extrude tendrils that reach out in clusters towards points rigorously predetermined by the overall dynamics of the entire structure: they call to mind the gills of an embryo, except that they are revolving at fantastic speed and ooze trickles of pinkish 'blood' and a dark green secretion.

The symmetriad now begins to display its most exotic characteristic – the property of 'illustrating', sometimes contradicting, various laws of physics. (Bear in mind that no two symmetriads are alike, and that the geometry of each one is a unique 'invention' of the living ocean.) The interior of the symmetriad becomes a factory for the production of 'monumental machines', as these constructs are sometimes called, although they resemble no machine which it is within the power of mankind to build: the designation is applied because all this activity has finite ends, and is therefore in some sense 'mechanical'.

When the geysers of oceanic matter have solidified into pillars or into three-dimensional networks of galleries and passages, and the 'membranes' are set into an inextricable pattern of storeys, panels and vaults, the symmetriad justifies its name, for the entire structure is divided into two segments each mirroring the other to the most infinitesimal detail.

After twenty or thirty minutes, when the axis may have tilted as much as eight to ten degrees from the horizontal, the giant begins slowly to subside. (Symmetriads vary in size, but as the base begins to submerge even the smallest reach a height of half a mile, and are visible from miles away.) At last, the structure stabilizes itself, and the partly submerged symmetriad ceases its activity. It is now possible to explore it in complete safety by making an entry near the summit, through one of the many syphons which emerge from the dome. The completed symmetriad represents a spatial analogue of some transcendental equation.

It is a commonplace that any equation can be expressed in the figurative language of non-Euclidean geometry and represented in three dimensions. This interpretation relates the symmetriad to Lobachevsky's cones and Riemann's negative curves, although its unimaginable complexity makes the relationship highly tenuous. The eventual form occupies an area of several cubic miles and extends far beyond our whole system of mathematics. In addition, this extension is four-dimensional, for the fundamental terms of the equations use a temporal symbolism expressed in the internal changes over a given period.

It would be only natural, clearly, to suppose that the symmetriad is a 'computer' of the living ocean, performing calculations for a purpose that we are not able to grasp. This was Fremont's theory, now generally discounted. The hypothesis was a tempting one, but it proved impossible to sustain the concept that the living ocean examined problems of matter, the cosmos and existence through the medium of titanic eruptions, in which every particle had an indispensable function as a controlled element in an analytical system of infinite purity. In fact, numerous phenomena contradict this over-simplified (some say childishly naïve) concept.

Any number of attempts have been made to transpose and 'illustrate' the symmetriad, and Averian's demonstration was particularly well received. Let us imagine, he said, an edifice dating from the great days of Babylon, but built of some living, sensitive substance with the capacity to evolve: the architectonics of this edifice passes through a series of phases, and we see it adopt the forms of a Greek, then of a Roman building. The columns sprout like branches and become narrower, the roof grows lighter, rises, curves, the arch describes an abrupt parabola then breaks down into an arrow shape: the Gothic is born, comes to maturity and gives way in time to new forms. Austerity of line gives way to a riot of exploding lines and shapes, and the Baroque runs wild. If the progression continues – and the successive mutations are to be seen as stages in the life of an evolving organism – we finally arrive at the architecture of the space age, and perhaps too at some understanding of the symmetriad.

Unfortunately, no matter how this demonstration may be expanded and improved (there have been attempts to visualize it with the aid of models and films), the comparison remains superficial. It is evasive and illusory, and side-steps the central fact that the symmetriad is quite unlike anything Earth has ever produced.

The human mind is only capable of absorbing a few things at a time. We see what is taking place in front of us in the here and now, and cannot envisage simultaneously a succession of processes, no matter how integrated and complementary. Our faculties of perception are consequently limited even as regards fairly simple phenomena. The fate of a single man can be rich with significance, that of a few hundred less so, but the history of thousands and millions of men does not mean anything at all, in any adequate sense of the word. The symmetriad is a million – a billion, rather – raised to the power of N: it is incomprehensible. We pass through vast halls, each with a capacity of ten Kronecker units, and creep like so many ants clinging to the folds of breathing vaults and craning to watch the flight of soaring girders, opalescent in the glare of searchlights, and elastic domes which criss-cross and balance each other unerringly, the perfection of a moment, since everything here passes and fades. The essence of this architecture is movement synchronized towards a precise objective. We observe a fraction of the process, like hearing the vibration of a single string in an orchestra of supergiants. We know, but cannot grasp, that above and below, beyond the limits of perception or imagination, thousands and millions of simultaneous transformations are at work, interlinked like a musical score by mathematical counterpoint. It has been described as a symphony in geometry, but we lack the ears to hear it.

Only a long-distance view would reveal the entire process, but the outer covering of the symmetriad conceals the colossal inner matrix where creation is unceasing, the created becomes the creator, and absolutely identical 'twins' are born at opposite poles, separated by towering structures and miles of distance. The symphony creates itself, and writes its own conclusion, which is terrible to watch. Every observer feels like a spectator at a tragedy or a public massacre, when after two or three hours – never longer – the living ocean stages its assault. The polished surface of the ocean swirls and crumples, the desiccated foam liquefies again, begins to seethe, and legions of waves pour inwards from every point of the horizon, their gaping mouths far more massive than the greedy lips that surround the embryonic mimoid. The submerged base of the symmetriad is compressed, and the colossus rises as if on the point of being shot out of the planet's gravitational pull. The upper layers of the ocean redouble their activity, and the waves surge higher and higher to lick against the sides of the symmetriad. They envelop it, harden and plug the orifices, but their attack is nothing compared to the scene in the interior. First the process of creation freezes momentarily; then there is 'panic'. The smooth interpenetration of moving forms and the harmonious play of planes and lines accelerates, and the impression is inescapable that the symmetriad is hurrying to complete some task in the face of danger. The awe inspired by the metamorphosis and dynamics of the symmetriad intensifies as the proud sweep of the domes falters, vaults sag and droop, and 'wrong notes' – incomplete, mangled forms – make their appearance. A powerful moaning roar issues from the invisible depths like a sigh of agony, reverberates through the narrow funnels and booms through the collapsing domes. In spite of the growing destructive violence of these convulsions, the spectator is rooted to the spot. Only the force of the hurricane streaming out of the depths and howling through the thousands of galleries keeps the great structure erect. Soon it subsides and starts to disintegrate. There are final flutterings, contortions, and blind, random spasms. Gnawed and undermined, the giant sinks slowly and disappears, and the space where it stood is covered with whirlpools of foam.

So what does all this mean?

I remembered an incident dating from my spell as assistant to Gibarian. A group of schoolchildren visiting the Solarist Institute in Aden were making their way through the main hall of the library and looking at the racks of microfilm that occupied the entire left-hand side of the hall. The guide explained that among other phenomena immortalized by the image, these contained fragmentary glimpses of symmetriads long since vanished – not single shots, but whole reels, more than ninety thousand of them!

One plump schoolgirl (she looked about fifteen, peering inquisitively over her spectacles) abruptly asked: 'And what is it for?'

In the ensuing embarrassed silence, the school mistress was content to dart a reproving look at her wayward pupil. Among the Solarists whose job was to act as guides (I was one of them), no one would produce an answer. Each symmetriad is unique, and the developments in its heart are, generally speaking, unpredictable. Sometimes there is no sound. Sometimes the index of refraction increases or diminishes. Sometimes, rhythmic pulsations are accompanied by local changes in gravitation, as if the heart of the symmetriad were beating by gravitating. Sometimes the compasses of the observers spin wildly, and ionized layers spring up and disappear. The catalogue could go on indefinitely. In any case, even if we did ever succeed in solving the riddle of the symmetriads, we would still have to contend with the asymmetriads!

The asymmetriads are born in the same manner as the symmetriads but finish differently, and nothing can be seen of their internal processes except tremors, vibrations and flickering. We do know, however, that the interior houses bewildering operations performed at a speed that defies the laws of physics and which are dubbed 'giant quantic phenomena'. The mathematical analogy with certain three-dimensional models of the atom is so unstable and transitory that some commentators dismiss the resemblance as of secondary importance, if not purely accidental. The asymmetriads have a very short life-span of fifteen to twenty minutes, and their death is even more appalling than that of the symmetriads: with the howling gale that screams through its fabric, a thick fluid gushes out, gurgles hideously, and submerges everything beneath a foul, bubbling foam. Then an explosion, coinciding with a muddy eruption, hurls up a spout of debris which rains slowly down into the seething ocean. This debris is sometimes found scores of miles from the focus of the explosion, dried up, yellow and flattened, like flakes of cartilage.

Some other creations of the ocean, which are much more rare and of very variable duration, part company with the parent body entirely. The first traces of these 'independents' were identified – wrongly, it was later proved – as the remains of creatures inhabiting the ocean deeps. The free-ranging forms are often reminiscent of many-winged birds, darting away from the moving trunks of the agilus, but the preconceptions of Earth offer no assistance in unravelling the mysteries of Solaris. Strange, seal-like bodies appear now and then on the rocky outcrop of an island, sprawling in the sun or dragging themselves lazily back to merge with the ocean.

There was no escaping the impressions that grew out of man's experience on Earth. The prospects of Contact receded.

Explorers travelled hundreds of miles in the depths of symmetriads, and installed measuring instruments and remote-control cameras. Artificial satellites captured the birth of mimoids and extensors, and faithfully reproduced their images of growth and destruction. The libraries overflowed, the archives grew, and the price paid for all this documentation was often very heavy. One notorious disaster cost one hundred and six people their lives, among them Giese himself: while studying what was undoubtedly a symmetriad, the expedition was suddenly destroyed by a process peculiar to the asymmetriads. In two seconds, an eruption of glutinous mud swallowed up seventy-nine men and all their equipment. Another twenty-seven observers surveying the area from aircraft and helicopters were also caught in the eruption.

Following the Eruption of the Hundred and Six, and for the first time in Solarist studies, there were petitions demanding a thermonuclear attack on the ocean. Such a response would have been more cruelty than revenge, since it would have meant destroying what we did not understand. Tsanken's ultimatum, which was never officially acknowledged, probably influenced the negative outcome of the vote. He was in command of Giese's reserve team, and had survived owing to a transmission error that took him off his course, to arrive in the disaster area a few minutes after the explosion, when the black mushroom cloud was still visible. Informed of the proposal for a nuclear strike, he threatened to blow up the Station, together with the nineteen survivors sheltering inside it.

Today, there are only three of us in the Station. Its construction was controlled by satellites, and was a technical feat on which the human race has a right to pride itself, even if the ocean builds far more impressive structures in the space of a few seconds. The Station is a disc of one hundred yards radius, and contains four decks at the centre and two at the circumference. It is maintained at a height of from five to fifteen hundred yards above the ocean by gravitors programmed to compensate for the ocean's own field of attraction. In addition to all the machines available to ordinary Stations and the large artificial satellites that orbit other planets, the Solaris Station is equipped with specialized radar apparatus sensitive to the smallest fluctuations of the ocean surface, which trips auxiliary power-circuits capable of thrusting the steel disc into the stratosphere at the first indication of new plasmatic upheavals.

But today, in spite of the presence of our faithful 'visitors', the Station was strangely deserted. Ever since the robots had been locked away in the lower-deck storerooms – for a reason I had still not discovered – it had been possible to walk around without meeting a single member of the crew of our ghost ship.

As I replaced the ninth volume of Giese on the shelf, the plastic-coated steel floor seemed to shudder under my feet. I stood still, but the vibration had stopped. The library was completely isolated from the other rooms, and the only possible source of vibration must be a shuttle leaving the Station. This thought jerked me back to reality. I had not yet decided to accept Sartorius's suggestion and leave the Station. By feigning approval of his plan, I had been more or less postponing the outbreak of hostilities, for I was determined to save Rheya. All the same, Sartorius might have some chance of success. He certainly had the advantage of being a qualified physicist, while I was in the ironic position of having to count on the superiority of the ocean. I pored over microfilm texts for an hour, and made myself wrestle with the unfamiliar language of neutrino physics. The undertaking seemed hopeless at first: there were no less than five current theories dealing with neutrino fields, an obvious indication that none was definitive. Eventually I struck promising ground, and was busily copying down equations when there was a knock at the door. I got up quickly and opened it a few inches, to see Snow's perspiring face, and behind him an empty corridor.

'Yes, it's me.' His voice was hoarse, and there were dark pouches under the bloodshot eyes. He wore an anti-radiation apron of shiny rubber, and the same worn old trousers held up by elastic braces.

Snow's gaze flickered round the circular chamber and alighted on Rheya where she stood by an armchair at the other end. Then it returned to me, and I lowered my eyelids imperceptibly. He nodded, and I spoke casually:

'Rheya, come and meet Dr Snow . . . Snow – my wife.'

'I ... I'm just a minor member of the crew. Don't get about much . . .' He faltered, but managed to blurt out: 'That's why I haven't had the pleasure of meeting you before . . .'

Rheya smiled and held out her hand, which he shook in some surprise. He blinked several times and stood looking at her, tongue-tied, until I took him by the arm.

'Excuse me,' he said to Rheya. 'I wanted a word with you, Kelvin . . .'

'Of course.' (My composure was an ugly charade, but what else could I do?) 'Take no notice of us, Rheya. We'll be talking shop . . .'

I guided Snow over to the chairs on the far side of the room, and Rheya sat in the armchair I had occupied earlier, swivelling it so that she could glance up at us from her book. I lowered my voice:

'Any news?'

'I'm divorced,' he whispered. If anybody had quoted this to me as the opening of a conversation a few days before, I would have burst out laughing, but the Station had blunted my sense of humour. 'It feels like years since yesterday morning,' he went on. 'And you?'

'Nothing.' I was at a loss for words. I liked Snow, but I distrusted him, or rather I distrusted the purpose of his visit.

'Nothing? Surely . . .'

'What?' I pretended not to understand.

Eyes half shut, he leaned so close to me that I could feel his breath on my face:

'This business has all of us confused, Kelvin. I can't make contact with Sartorius. All I know is what I wrote to you, which is what he told me after our little conference . . .'

'Has he disconnected his videophone?'

'No, there's been a short-circuit at his end. He could have done it on purpose, but there's also . . .' He clenched his fist and mimed somebody aiming a punch, curling his lips in an unpleasant grin. 'Kelvin, I came here to . . . What do you intend doing?'

'You want my answer to your letter. All right, I'll go on the trip, there's no reason for me to refuse. I've only been getting ready . . .'

'No,' he interrupted. 'It isn't that.'

'What then? Go on.'

'Sartorius thinks he may be on the right track,' Snow muttered. His eyes never left me, and I had to stay still and try to look casual. 'It all started with that X-ray experiment that he and Gibarian arranged, you remember. That could have produced some alteration . . .'

'What kind of alteration?'

'They beamed the rays directly into the ocean. The intensity was only modulated according to a pre-set program.'

'I know. It's already been done by Nilin and a lot of others.'

'Yes, but the others worked on low power. This time they used everything we had.'

'That could lead to trouble . . . violating the four-power convention, and the United Nations . . .'

'Come on, Kelvin, you know as well as I do that it doesn't matter now. Gibarian is dead.'

'So Sartorius makes him the scapegoat?'

'I don't know. We haven't talked about that. Sartorius is intrigued by the visiting hours. They only come as we wake up, which suggests that the ocean is especially interested in our sleeping hours, and that that is when it locates its patterns. Sartorius wants to send our waking selves – our conscious thoughts. You see?'

'By mail?'

'Keep the jokes to yourself. The idea is to modulate the X-rays by hooking in an electro-encephalograph taken from one of us.'

'Ah!' Light was beginning to dawn. 'And that one of us is me?'

'Yes, Sartorius had you in mind.'

'Tell him I'm flattered.'

'Will you do it?'

I hesitated. Snow darted a look at Rheya, who seemed absorbed in her book. I felt my face turn pale.

'Well?'

'The idea of using X-rays to preach sermons on the greatness of mankind seems absolutely ridiculous to me. Don't you think so?'

'You mean it?'

'Yes.'

'Right,' he said, smiling as if I had fallen in with some idea of his own, 'then you're opposed to the plan?'

His expression told me that he had somehow been a step ahead of me all the time.

'Okay,' he went on. 'There is a second plan – to construct a Roche apparatus.'

'An annihilator?'

'Yes. Sartorius has already made the preliminary calculations. It is feasible, and it won't even require any great expenditure of energy. The apparatus will generate a negative field twenty-four hours a day, and for an unlimited period.'

'And its effect?'

'Simple. It will be a negative neutrino field. Ordinary matter will not be affected at all. Only the . . . neutrino structures will be destroyed. You see?'

Snow gave me a satisfied grin. I stood stock-still and gaping, so that he stopped smiling, looked at me with a frown, and waited a moment before speaking:

'We abandon the first plan then, the "Brainwave" plan? Sartorius is working on the other one right now. We'll call it "Project Liberation".'

I had to make a quick decision. Snow was no physicist, and Sartorius's videophone was disconnected or smashed. I took the chance:

'I'd rather call the second idea "Operation Slaughterhouse".'

'And you ought to know! Don't tell me you haven't had some practice lately. Only there'll be a radical difference this time – no more visitors, no more Phi creatures – they will disintegrate as soon as they appear.'

I nodded, and managed what I hoped was a convincing smile:

'You haven't got the point. Morality is one thing, but self-preservation . . . I just don't want to get us all killed, Snow.'

He stared back at me suspiciously, as I showed him my scribbled equations:

'I've been working along the same lines. Don't look so surprised. The neutrino theory was my idea in the first place, remember? Look. Negative fields can be generated all right. And ordinary matter is unaffected. But what happens to the energy that maintains the neutrino structure when it disintegrates? There must be a considerable release of that energy. Assuming a kilogram of ordinary matter represents 10^8 ergs, for a Phi creation we get 5^7 multiplied by 10^8. That means the equivalent of a small atomic bomb exploding inside the Station.'

'You mean to tell me Sartorius won't have been over all this?'

It was my turn to grin maliciously:

'Not necessarily. Sartorius follows the Frazer–Cajolla school. Their theories would indicate that the energy potential would be given off in the form of light – powerful, yes, but not destructive. But that isn't the only theory of neutrino fields. According to Cayatte, and Avalov, and Sion, the radiation-spectrum would be much broader. At its maximum, there would be a strong burst of gamma radiation. Sartorius has faith in his tutors. I don't say we can't respect that, but there are other tutors, and other theories. And another thing, Snow,' – I could see him beginning to waver – 'we have to bear in mind the ocean itself! It is bound to have used the optimum means of designing its creations. It seems to me that we can't afford to back Sartorius against the ocean as well as the other theories.'

'Give me that paper, Kelvin.'

I passed it to him, and he pored over my equations.

'What's this?' He pointed to a line of calculations.

'That? The transformation tensor of the magnetic field.'

'Give it here.'

'Why?' (I already knew his reply.)

'I'll have to show Sartorius.'

'If you say so,' I shrugged. 'You're welcome to it, naturally, provided you realize that these theories have never been tested experimentally: neutrino structures have been abstractions until now. Sartorius is relying on Frazer, and I've followed Sion's theory. He'll say I'm no physicist, or Sion either, not from his point of view, at least. He will dispute my figures, and I'm not going to get into the kind of argument where he tries to browbeat me for his own satisfaction. You, I can convince. I couldn't begin to convince Sartorius, and I have no intention of trying.'

'Then what *do* you want to do? He's already started work . . .'

All his earlier animation had subsided, and he spoke in a monotone. I did not know if he trusted me, and I did not much care:

'What do I want to do? Whatever a man does when his life is in danger.'

'I'll try to contact him. Maybe he can develop some kind of safety device . . . And then there's the first plan. Would you cooperate? Sartorius would agree, I'm sure of it. At least it's worth a try.'

'You think so?'

'No,' he snapped back. 'But what have we got to lose?'

I was in no hurry to accept. It was time that I needed, and Snow could help me to prolong the delay:

'I'll think about it.'

'Okay, I'm going.' His bones creaked as he got up. 'We'll have to begin with the encephalogram,' he said, rubbing at his overall as if to get rid of some invisible stain.

Without a word to Rheya, he walked to the door, and after it had closed behind him I got up and crumpled the sheet of paper in my hand. I had not falsified the equations, but I doubted whether Sion would have agreed with my extensions of his theory. I started abruptly, as Rheya's hand touched my shoulder.

'Kris, who is he?'

'I told you, Dr Snow.'

'What's he like?'

'I don't know him very well . . . why?'

'He was giving me such a strange look.'

'So, you're an attractive woman . . .'

'No, this was a different sort of look . . . as if . . .' She trembled, looked up at me momentarily, then lowered her eyes. 'Let's go back to the cabin.'

9

THE LIQUID OXYGEN

I have no idea how long I had been lying in the dark, staring at the luminous dial of my wristwatch. Hearing myself breathing, I felt a vague surprise, but my underlying feeling was one of profound indifference both to this ring of phosphorescent figures and to my own surprise. I told myself that the feeling was caused by fatigue. When I turned over, the bed seemed wider than usual. I held my breath; no sound broke the silence. Rheya's breathing should have been audible. I reached out, but felt nothing. I was alone.

I was about to call her name, when I heard the tread of heavy footsteps coming towards me. A numb calm descended:

'Gibarian?'

'Yes, it's me. Don't switch the light on.'

'No?'

'There's no need, and it's better for us to stay in the dark.'

'But you are dead . . .'

'Don't let that worry you. You recognize my voice, don't you?'

'Yes. Why did you kill yourself?'

'I had no choice. You arrived four days late. If you had come earlier, I would not have been forced to kill myself. Don't worry about it, though, I don't regret anything.'

'You really are there? I'm not asleep?'

'Oh, you think you're dreaming about me? As you did with Rheya?'

'Where is she?'

'How should I know?'

'I have a feeling that you do.'

'Keep your feelings for yourself. Let's say I'm deputizing for her.'

'I want her here too!'

'Not possible.'

'Why not? You know very well that it isn't the real you, just my . . .'

'No, I am the real Gibarian – just a new incarnation. But let's not waste time on useless chatter.'

'You'll be leaving again?'

'Yes.'

'And then she'll come back?'

'Why should you care about that?'

'She belongs to me.'

'You are afraid of her.'

'No.'

'She disgusts you.'

'What do you want with me?'

'Save your pity for yourself – you have a right to it – but not for her. She will always be twenty years old. You must know that.'

I felt suddenly at ease again, for no apparent reason, and ready to hear him out. He seemed to have come closer, though I could not see him in the dark.

'What do you want?'

'Sartorius has convinced Snow that you have been deceiving him. Right now they are trying to give you the same treatment. Building the X-ray beamer is a cover for constructing a magnetic field disruptor.'

'Where is she?'

'Didn't you hear me? I came to warn you.'

'Where is she?'

'I don't know. Be careful. You must find some kind of weapon. You can't trust anyone.'

'I can trust Rheya.'

He stifled a laugh: 'Of course, you can trust Rheya – to some extent. And you can always follow my example, if all else fails.'

'You are not Gibarian.'

'No? Then who am I? A dream?'

'No, you are only a puppet. But you don't realize that you are.'

'And how do you know what *you* are?'

I tried to stand up, but could not stir. Although Gibarian was still speaking, I could not understand his words; there was only the drone of his voice. I struggled to regain control of my body, felt a sudden wrench and . . . I woke up, and drew down great gulps of air. It was dark, and I had been having a nightmare. And now I heard a distant, monotonous voice: '. . . a dilemma that we are not equipped to solve. We are the cause of our own sufferings. The polytheres behave strictly as a kind of amplifier of our own thoughts. Any attempt to understand the motivation of these occurrences is blocked by our own anthropomorphism. Where there are no men, there cannot be motives accessible to men. Before we can proceed with our research, either our own thoughts or their materialized forms must be destroyed. It is not within our power to destroy our thoughts. As for destroying their material forms, that could be like committing murder.'

I had recognized Gibarian's voice at once. When I stretched out my arm, I found myself alone. I had fallen asleep again. This was another dream. I called Gibarian's name, and the voice stopped in mid-sentence. There was the sound of a faint gasp, then a gust of air.

'Well, Gibarian,' I yawned, 'you seem to be following me out of one dream and into the next . . .'

There was a rustling sound from somewhere close, and I called his name again. The bed-springs creaked, and a voice whispered in my ear: 'Kris . . . it's me . . .'

'Rheya? Is it you? What about Gibarian?'

'But . . . you said he was dead, Kris.'

'He can be alive in a dream,' I told her dejectedly, although I was not completely sure that it had been a dream. 'He spoke to me . . . He was here . . .'

My head sank back on to the pillow. Rheya said something, but I was already drifting into sleep.

In the red light of morning, the events of the previous night returned. I had dreamt that I was talking to Gibarian. But afterwards, I could swear that I had heard his voice, although I had no clear recall of what he had said, and it had not been a conversation – more like a speech.

Rheya was splashing about in the bathroom. I looked under the bed, where I had hidden the tape-recorder a few days earlier. It was no longer there.

'Rheya!' She put her face round the door. 'Did you see a tape-recorder under the bed, a little pocket one?'

'There was a pile of stuff under the bed. I put it all over there.' She pointed to a shelf by the medicine cabinet, and disappeared back into the bathroom.

There was no tape-recorder on the shelf, and when Rheya emerged from the bathroom I asked her to think again. She sat combing her hair, and did not answer. It was not until now that I noticed how pale she was, and how closely she was watching me in the mirror. I returned to the attack:

'The tape-recorder is missing, Rheya.'

'Is that all you have to tell me?'

'I'm sorry. You're right, it's silly to get so worked up about a tape-recorder.'

Anything to avoid a quarrel.

Later, over breakfast, the change in Rheya's behaviour was obvious, yet I could not define it. She did not meet my eyes, and was frequently so lost in thought that she did not hear me. Once, when she looked up, her cheeks were damp.

'Is anything the matter? You're crying.'

'Leave me alone,' Rheya blurted. 'They aren't real tears.'

Perhaps I ought not to have let her answer so, but 'straight talking' was the last thing I wanted. In any case, I had other problems on my mind; I had dreamt that Snow and Sartorius were plotting against me, and although I was certain that it had been nothing more than a dream, I was wondering if there was anything in the Station that I might be able to use to defend myself. My thinking had not progressed to the point of deciding what to do with a weapon once I had it. I told Rheya that I had to make an inspection of the store-rooms, and she trailed behind me silently.

I ransacked packing-cases and capsules, and when we reached the lower deck I was unable to resist looking into the cold store. Not wanting Rheya to go in, I put my head inside the door and looked around. The recumbent figure was still covered by its dark shroud, but from my position in the doorway I could not make out whether the black woman was still sleeping by Gibarian's body. I had the impression that she was no longer there.

I wandered from one store-room to another, unable to locate anything that might serve as a weapon, and with a rising feeling of depression. All at once I noticed that Rheya was not with me. Then she reappeared; she had been hanging back in the corridor. In spite of the pain she suffered when she could not see me, she had been trying to keep away. I should have been astonished: instead, I went on acting as if I had been offended – but then, who had offended me? – and sulking like a child.

My head was throbbing, and I rifled the entire contents of the medicine-cabinet without finding so much as an aspirin. I did not want to do anything. I had never been in a blacker temper. Rheya tiptoed about the cabin like a shadow. Now and then she went off somewhere. I don't know where, I was paying her no attention; then she would creep back inside.

That afternoon, in the kitchen (we had just eaten, but in fact Rheya had not touched her food, and I had not attempted to persuade her), Rheya got up and came to sit next to me. I felt her hand on my sleeve, and grunted: 'What's the matter?'

I had been meaning to go up to the deck above, as the pipes were carrying the sharp crackling sound of high-voltage apparatus in use, but Rheya would have had to come with me. It had been hard enough to justify her presence in the library; among the machinery, there was a chance that Snow might drop some clumsy remark. I gave up the idea of going to investigate.

'Kris,' she whispered, 'what's happening to us?'

I gave an involuntary sigh of frustration with everything that had been happening since the previous night: 'Everything is fine. Why?'

'I want to talk.'

'All right, I'm listening.'

'Not like this.'

'What? You know I have a headache, and that's not the least of my worries . . .'

'You're not being fair.'

I forced myself to smile; it must have been a poor imitation: 'Go ahead and talk, darling, please.'

'Will you tell me the truth?'

'Why should I lie?' This was an ominous beginning.

'You might have your reasons . . . it might be necessary . . . But if you want . . . Look, I am going to tell you something, and then it will be your turn – only no half-truths. Promise!' I could not meet her gaze. 'I've already told you that I don't know how I came to be here. Perhaps you do. Wait! – perhaps you don't. But if you do know, and you can't tell me now, will you tell me one day, later on? I couldn't be any the worse for it, and you would at least be giving me a chance.'

'What are you talking about, child,' I stammered. 'What chance?'

'Kris, whatever I may be, I'm certainly not a child. You promised me an answer.'

Whatever I may be . . . my throat tightened, and I stared at Rheya shaking my head like an imbecile, as if forbidding myself to hear any more.

'I'm not asking for explanations. You only need to tell me that you are not allowed to say.'

'I'm not hiding anything,' I croaked.

'All right.'

She stood up. I wanted to say something. We could not leave it at that. But no words would come.

'Rheya . . .'

She was standing at the window, with her back turned. The blue-black ocean stretched out under a cloudless sky.

'Rheya, if you believe . . . You know very well I love you . . .'

'Me?'

I went to put my arms round her, but she pulled away.

'You're too kind,' she said. 'You say you love me? I'd rather you beat me.'

'Rheya, darling!'

'No, no, don't say any more.'

She went back to the table and began to clear away the plates. I gazed out at the ocean. The sun was setting, and the Station cast a lengthening shadow that danced on the waves. Rheya dropped a plate on the floor. Water splashed in the sink. A tarnished golden halo ringed the horizon. If I only knew what to do . . . if only . . . Suddenly there was silence. Rheya was standing behind me.

'No, don't turn round,' she murmured. 'It isn't your fault, I know. Don't torment yourself.'

I reached out, but she slipped away to the far side of the room and picked up a stack of plates: 'It's a shame they're unbreakable. I'd like to smash them, all of them.'

I thought for a moment that she really was going to dash them to the floor, but she looked across at me and smiled: 'Don't worry, I'm not going to make scenes.'

In the middle of the night, I was suddenly wide awake. The room was in darkness and the door was ajar, with a faint light shining from the corridor. There was a shrill hissing noise, interspersed with heavy, muffled thudding, as if some heavy object was pounding against a wall. A meteor had pierced the shell of the Station! No, not a meteor, a shuttle, for I could hear a dreadful laboured whining . . .

I shook myself. It was not a meteor, nor was it a shuttle. The sound was coming from somebody at the end of the corridor. I ran down to where light was pouring from the door of the little work-room, and rushed inside. A freezing vapour filled the room, my breath fell like snow, and white flakes swirled over a body covered by a dressing-gown, stirring feebly then striking the floor again. I could hardly see through the freezing mist. I snatched her up and folded her in my arms, and the dressing-gown burnt my skin. Rheya kept on making the same harsh gasping sound as I stumbled along the corridor, no longer feeling the cold, only her breath on my neck, burning like fire.

I lowered Rheya on to the operating-table and pulled the dressing-gown open. Her face was contorted with pain, the lips covered by a thick, black layer of frozen blood, the tongue a mass of sparkling ice crystals.

Liquid oxygen . . . The Dewar bottles in the workroom contained liquid oxygen. Splinters of glass had crunched underfoot as I carried Rheya out. How much of it had she swallowed? It didn't matter. Her trachea, throat and lungs must be burnt away – liquid oxygen corrodes flesh more effectively than strong acids. Her breathing was more and more laboured, with a dry sound like tearing paper. Her eyes were closed. She was dying.

I looked across at the big, glass-fronted cabinets, crammed with instruments and drugs. Tracheotomy? Intubation? She had no lungs! I stared at shelves full of coloured bottles and cartons. She went on gasping hoarsely, and a wisp of vapour drifted out of her open mouth.

Thermophores . . .

I started looking for them, then changed my mind, ran to another cupboard and turned out boxes of ampoules. Now a hypodermic – where are they? – here – needs sterilizing. I fumbled with the lid of the sterilizer, but my numb fingers had lost all sensation and would not bend.

The harsh rattle grew louder, and Rheya's eyes were open when I reached the table. I opened my mouth to say her name but my voice had gone and my lips would not obey me. My face did not belong to me; it was a plaster mask.

Rheya's ribs were heaving under the white skin. The ice-crystals had melted and her wet hair was entangled in the headrest. And she was looking at me.

'Rheya!' It was all I could say. I stood paralysed, my hands dangling uselessly, until a burning sensation mounted from my legs and attacked my lips and eyelids.

A drop of blood melted and slanted down her cheek. Her tongue quivered and receded. The laboured panting went on.

I could feel no pulse in her wrist, and put my ear against her frozen breast. Faintly, behind the raging blizzard, her heart was beating so fast that I could not count the beats, and I remained crouched over her, with my eyes closed. Something brushed my head – Rheya's hand in my hair. I stood up.

'Kris!' A harsh gasp.

I took her hand, and the answering pressure made my bones creak. Then her face screwed up with agony, and she lost consciousness again. Her eyes turned up, a guttural rattle tore at her throat, and her body arched with convulsions. It was all I could do to keep her on the operating table; she broke free and her head cracked against a porcelain basin. I dragged her back, and struggled to hold her down, but violent spasms kept jerking her out of my grasp. I was pouring with sweat, and my legs were like jelly. When the convulsions abated, I tried to make her lie flat, but her chest thrust out to gulp at the air. Suddenly her eyes were staring out at me from behind the frightful blood-stained mask of her face.

'Kris . . . how long . . . how long?'

She choked. Pink foam appeared at her mouth, and the convulsions racked her again. With my last reserves of strength I bore down on her shoulders, and she fell back. Her teeth chattered loudly.

'No, no, no,' she whimpered suddenly, and I thought that death was near.

But the spasms resumed, and again I had to hold her down. Now and then she swallowed drily, and her ribs heaved. Then the eyelids half closed over the unseeing eyes, and she stiffened. This must be the end. I did not even try to wipe the foam from her mouth. A distant ringing throbbed in my head. I was waiting for her final breath before my strength failed and I collapsed to the ground.

She went on breathing, and the rasp was now only a light sigh. Her chest, which had stopped heaving, moved again to the rapid rhythm of her heartbeat. Colour was returning to her cheeks. Still I did not realize what was happening. My hands were clammy, and I heard as if through layers of cotton wool, yet the ringing sound continued.

Rheya's eye-lids moved, and our eyes met.

I could not speak her name from behind the mask of my face. All I could do was look at her.

She turned her head and looked round the room. Somewhere behind me, in another world, a tap dripped. Rheya levered herself up on her elbow. I recoiled, and again our eyes met.

'It . . . it didn't work,' she stammered. 'Why are you looking at me like that?' Then she screamed out loud: 'Why are you looking at me like that?'

Still I could say nothing. She examined her hands, moved her fingers . . .

'Is this me?'

My lips formed her name, and she repeated it as a question – 'Rheya?'

She let herself slide off the operating table, staggered, regained her balance and took a few steps. She was moving in a daze, and looking at me without appearing to see me.

'Rheya? But . . . I am not Rheya. Who am I then? And you, what about you?' Her eyes widened and sparkled, and an astonished smile lit up her face. 'And you, Kris. Perhaps you too . . .'

I had backed away until I came up against the wall. The smile vanished.

'No. You are afraid. I can't take any more of this, I can't . . . I didn't know, I still don't understand. It's not possible.' Her clenched fists struck her chest. 'What else could I think, except that I was Rheya! Maybe you believe this is all an act? It isn't, I swear it isn't.'

Something snapped in my mind, and I went to put my arms round her, but she fought free:

'Don't touch me! Leave me alone! I disgust you, I know I do. Keep away! I'm not Rheya . . .'

We screamed at each other and Rheya tried to keep me at arm's length. I would not let her go, and at last she let her head fall to my shoulder. We were on our knees, breathless and exhausted.

'Kris . . . what do I have to do to put a stop to this?'

'Be quiet!'

'You don't know!' She lifted her head and stared at me. 'It can't be done, can it?'

'Please . . .'

'I really tried . . . No, go away. I disgust you – and myself, I disgust myself. If I only knew how . . .'

'You would kill yourself.'

'Yes.'

'But I want you to stay alive. I want you here, more than anything.'

'You're lying.'

'Tell me what I have to do to convince you. You are here. You exist. I can't see any further than that.'

'It can't possibly be true, because I am not Rheya.'

'Then who are you?'

There was a long silence. Then she bowed her head and murmured:

'Rheya . . . But I know that I am not the woman you once loved.'

'Yes. But that was a long time ago. That past does not exist, but you do, here and now. Don't you see?'

She shook her head:

'I know that it was kindness that made you behave as you did, but there is nothing to be done. That first morning when I found myself waiting by your bed for you to wake up, I knew nothing. I can hardly believe it was only three days ago. I behaved like a lunatic. Everything was misty. I didn't remember anything, wasn't surprised by anything. It was like recovering from a drugged sleep, or a long illness. It even occurred to me that I might have been ill and you didn't want to tell me. Then a few things happened to set me thinking – you know what I mean. So after you met that man in the library and you refused to tell me anything, I made up my mind to listen to that tape. That was the only time I have lied to you, Kris. When you were looking for the tape-recorder, I knew where it was. I'd hidden it. The man who recorded the tape – what was his name?'

'Gibarian.'

'Yes, Gibarian – he explained everything. Although I still don't understand. The only thing missing was that I can't . . . that there is no end. He didn't mention that, or if he did it was after you woke up and I had to switch off. But I heard enough to realize that I am not a human being, only an instrument.'

'What are you talking about?'

'That's what I am. To study your reactions – something of that sort. Each one of you has a . . . an instrument like me. We emerge from your memory or your imagination, I can't say exactly – anyway you know better than I. He talks about such terrible things . . . so far fetched . . . if it did not fit in with everything else I would certainly have refused to believe him.'

'The rest?'

'Oh, things like not needing sleep, and being compelled to go wherever you go. When I think that only yesterday I was miserable because I thought you detested me. How stupid! But how could I have imagined the truth? He – Gibarian – didn't hate that woman, the one who came to him, but he refers to her in such a dreadful way. It wasn't until then that I realized that I was helpless whatever I did, and that I couldn't avoid torturing you. More than that though, an instrument of torture is passive, like the stone that falls on somebody and kills them. But an instrument of torture which loves you and wishes you nothing but good – it was too much for me. I wanted to tell you the little that I *had* understood. I told myself that it might be useful to you. I even tried to make notes . . .'

'That time when you had the light switched on?'

'Yes. But I couldn't write anything. I searched myself for . . . you know, some sign of "influence" . . . I was going mad. I felt as if there was no body underneath my skin and there was something else instead: as if I was just an illusion meant to mislead you. You see?'

'I see.'

'When you can't sleep at night and your mind keeps spinning for hours on end, it can take you far away; you find yourself moving in strange directions . . .'

'I know what you mean.'

'But I could feel my heart beating. And then I remembered that you had made an analysis of my blood. What did you find? You can tell me the truth now.'

'Your blood is like my own.'

'Truly?'

'I give you my word.'

'What does that indicate? I had been telling myself that the . . . unknown force might be concealed somewhere inside me, and that it might not occupy very much space. But I did not know whereabouts it was. I think now that I was evading the real issue because I didn't have the nerve to make a decision. I was afraid, and I looked for a way out. But Kris, if my blood is like yours . . . if I really . . . no, it's impossible. I would already be dead, wouldn't I? That means there really is something different – but where? In the mind? Yet it seems to me that I think as any human being does . . . and I know nothing! If that alien thing was thinking in my head, I would know everything. And I would not love you. I would be pretending, and aware that I was pretending. Kris, you've got to tell me everything you know. Perhaps we could work out a solution between us.'

'What kind of solution?' She fell silent. 'Is it death you want?'

'Yes, I think it is.'

Again silence. Rheya sat on the floor, her knees drawn up under her chin. I looked around at the white-enamelled fittings and gleaming instruments, perhaps looking for some unsuspected clue to suddenly materialize.

'Rheya, I have something to say, too.' She waited quietly. 'It is true that we are not exactly alike. But there is nothing wrong with that. In any case, whatever else we might think about it, that . . . difference . . . saved your life.'

A painful smile flickered over her face: 'Does that mean that I am . . . immortal?'

'I don't know. At any rate, you're far less vulnerable than I am.'

'It's horrible . . .'

'Perhaps not as horrible as you think.'

'But you don't envy me.'

'Rheya, I don't know what your fate will be. It cannot be predicted, any more than my own or any other members' of the Station's personnel. The experiment will go on, and anything can happen . . .'

'Or nothing.'

'Or nothing. And I have to confess that nothing is what I would prefer. Not because I'm frightened – though fear is undeniably an

element of this business – but because there can't be any final outcome. I'm quite sure of that.'

'Outcome? You mean the ocean?'

'Yes, contact with the ocean. As I see it, the problem is basically
very simple. Contact means the exchange of specific knowledge, ideas,
or at least of findings, definite facts. But what if no exchange is
possible? If an elephant is not a giant microbe, the ocean is not a giant
brain. Obviously there can be various approaches, and the consequence
of one of them is that you are here, now, with me. And I am trying
my hardest to make you realize that I love you. Just your being here
cancels out the twelve years of my life that went into the study of
Solaris, and I want to keep you.

'You may have been sent to torment me, or to make my life happier,
or as an instrument ignorant of its function, used like a microscope
with me on the slide. Possibly you are here as a token of friendship,
or a subtle punishment, or even as a joke. It could be all of those at
once, or – which is more probable – something else completely. If you
say that our future depends on the ocean's intentions, I can't deny it. I
can't tell the future any more than you can. I can't even swear that I
shall always love you. After what has happened already, we can expect
anything. Suppose tomorrow it turns me into a green jellyfish! It's out
of our hands. But the decision we make today is in our hands. Let's
decide to stay together. What do you say?'

'Listen Kris, there's something else I must ask you . . . Am I . . . do
I look very like her?'

'You did at first. Now I don't know.'

'I don't understand.'

'Now all I see is you.'

'You're sure?'

'Yes. If you really were her, I might not be able to love you.'

'Why?'

'Because of what I did.'

'Did you treat her badly?'

'Yes, when we . . .'

'Don't say any more.'

'Why not?'

'So that you won't forget that I am the one who is here, not her.'

10

CONVERSATION

The following morning, I received another note from Snow: Sartorius had left off working on the disruptor and was getting ready for a final experiment with high-power X-rays.

'Rheya, darling, I have to pay a visit to Snow.'

The red dawn blazing through the window divided the room in two. We were in an area of blue shadow. Everything outside this shadow-zone was burnished copper: if a book had fallen from a shelf, my ear would have listened instinctively for a metallic clang.

'It's to do with the experiment. Only I don't know what to do about it. Please understand, I'd rather . . .'

'You needn't justify yourself, Kris. If only it doesn't go on too long.'

'It's bound to take a while. Look, do you think you could wait in the corridor?'

'I can try. But what if I lose control?'

'What does it feel like? I'm not asking just out of curiosity, believe me, but if we can discuss how it works you might find some way of keeping it in check.'

Rheya had turned pale, but she tried to explain:

'I feel afraid, not of some thing or some person – there's no focus, only a sense of being lost. And I am terribly ashamed of myself. Then, when you come back, it stops. That's what made me think I might have been ill.'

'Perhaps it's only inside this damned Station that it works. I'll make arrangements for us to get out as soon as possible.'

'Do you think you can?'

'Why not? I'm not a prisoner here. I'll have to talk it over with Snow. Have you any idea how long you could manage to remain by yourself?'

'That depends . . . If I could hear your voice, I think I might be able to hold out.'

'I'd rather you weren't listening. Not that I have anything to hide, but there's no telling what Snow might say.'

'You needn't go on. I understand. I'll just stand close enough to hear the sound of your voice.'

'I'm going to the operating room to phone him. The doors will be open.'

Rheya nodded agreement.

I crossed the red zone. The corridor seemed dark by contrast, in spite of the lighting. Inside the open door of the operating room, fragments of the Dewar bottle, the last traces of the previous night's events, gleamed from under a row of liquid oxygen containers. When I took the phone off the hook, the little screen lit up, and I tapped out the number of the radio cabin. Behind the dull glass, a spot of bluish light grew, burst, and Snow was looking at me, perched on the edge of his chair.

'I got your note and I want to talk to you. Can I come over?'

'Yes. Right away?'

'Yes.'

'Excuse me, but are you coming alone or . . . accompanied?'

'Alone.'

His creased forehead and thin, tanned face filled the screen as he leant forward to scrutinize me through the convex glass. Then he appeared to reach an abrupt decision:

'Fine, fine, I'll be expecting you.'

I went back to the cabin, where I could barely make out the shape of Rheya behind the curtain of red sunlight. She was sitting in an armchair, with her hands clutching the armrests. She must have failed to hear my footsteps, and I saw her for a moment fighting the inexplicable compulsion that possessed her and wrestling with the fierce contractions of her entire body, which stopped immediately she saw me. I choked back a feeling of blind rage and pity.

We walked in silence down the long corridor with its polychromed walls; the designers had intended the variations in colour to make life more tolerable inside the armoured shell of the Station. A shaft of red light ahead of us meant the door of the radio cabin was ajar, and I looked at Rheya. She made no attempt to return my smile, totally absorbed in her preparations for the coming battle with herself. Now that the ordeal was about to begin, her face was pinched and white. Fifteen paces from the door, she stopped, pushing me forward gently with her fingertips as I started to turn around. Suddenly I felt that Snow, the experiment, even the Station itself were not worth the agonizing price that Rheya was ready to pay, with myself as assistant torturer. I would have retraced my steps, but a shadow fell across the cabin doorway, and I hurried inside.

Snow stood facing me with the red sun behind him making a halo of purple light out of his grey hair. We confronted one another without speaking, and he was able to examine me at his leisure in the sunlight that dazzled me so that I could hardly see him.

I walked past him and leaned against a tall desk bristling with microphones on their flexible stalks. Snow pivoted slowly and went on staring at me with his habitual cheerless smile, in which there was no amusement, only overpowering fatigue. Still with his eyes on mine, he picked his way through the piles of objects littered about the cabin – thermic cells, instruments, spare parts for the electronic equipment – pulled a stool up against the door of a steel cabinet, and sat down.

I listened anxiously, but no sound came from the corridor. Why did Snow not speak? The prolonged silence was becoming exasperating.

I cleared my throat:

'When will you and Sartorius be ready?'

'We can start today, but the recording will take some time.'

'Recording? You mean the encephalogram?'

'Yes, you agreed. Is anything wrong?'

'No, nothing.'

Another lengthening silence. Snow broke it:

'Did you have something to tell me?'

'She knows,' I whispered.

He frowned, but I had the impression that he was not really surprised. Then why pretend? I lost all desire to confide in him. All the same, I had to be honest:

'She started to suspect after our meeting in the library. My behaviour, various other indications. Then she found Gibarian's tape-recorder and played back the tape.'

145

Snow sat intent and unmoving. Standing by the desk, my view of the corridor was blocked by the half-open door. I lowered my voice again:

'Last night, while I was asleep, she tried to kill herself. She drank liquid oxygen . . .' There was a sound of rustling, like papers stirred by the wind. I stopped and listened for something in the corridor, but the noise did not come from there. A mouse in the cabin? Out of the question, this was Solaris. I stole a glance at Snow.

'Go on,' he said calmly.

'It didn't work, of course. Anyway, she knows who she is.'

'Why tell me?'

I was taken aback for an instant, then I stammered out:

'So as to inform you, to keep you up to date on the situation . . .'

'I warned you.'

'You mean you knew?' My voice rose involuntarily.

'What you have just told me? Of course not. But I explained the position. When it arrives, the visitor is almost blank – only a ghost made up of memories and vague images dredged out of its . . . source. The longer it stays with you, the more human it becomes. It also becomes more independent, up to a certain point. And the longer that goes on, the more difficult it gets . . .' Snow broke off, looked me up and down, and went on reluctantly: 'Does she know everything?'

'Yes, I've just told you.'

'Everything? Does she know that she came once before, and that you . . .'

'No!'

'Listen Kelvin,' he smiled ruefully, 'if that's how it is, what do you want to do – leave the Station?'

'Yes.'

'With her?'

'Yes.'

The silence while he considered his reply also revealed something else. Again, from somewhere close, and without being able to pin it down, I heard the same faint rustling in the cabin, as if through a thin partition.

Snow shifted on his stool.

'All right. Why look at me like that? Did you think I would stand in your way? You can do as you like, Kelvin. We're in enough trouble already without putting pressure on each other. I know it will be a hopeless job to convince you, but there's something I have to say: you are doing all you can to stay human in an inhuman situation. Noble it may be, but it isn't going to get you anywhere. And I'm not so sure about it being noble – not if it's idiotic at the same time. But that's your affair. Let's get back to the point. You renege on the experiment and take her away with you. Has it struck you that you'll only be embarking on a different kind of experiment?'

'What do you mean? If you want to know whether she can manage it, as long as I'm with her, I don't see . . .' I trailed to a halt.

Snow sighed:

'All of us have our heads in the sand, Kelvin, and we know it. There's no need to put on airs.'

'I'm not putting anything on.'

'I'm sorry, I didn't want to offend you. I take back the airs, but I still think that you are playing the ostrich game – and a particularly dangerous version. You deceive yourself, you deceive her, and you chase your own tail. Do you know the necessary conditions for stabilizing a neutrino field?'

'No, and nor do you. Nor does anyone.'

'Exactly. All we know is that the structure is inherently unstable, and can only be maintained by means of a continuous energy input. Sartorius told me that. This energy creates a rotating stabilization field. Now, does that energy come from outside the "visitor", or is it generated internally? You see the difference?'

'Yes. If it is external, she . . .'

Snow finished the sentence for me:

'Away from Solaris, the structure disintegrates. It's only a theory, of course, but one that you can verify, since you have already set up an experiment. The vehicle you launched is still in orbit. In my spare moments, I've even calculated its trajectory. You can take off, intercept, and find out what happened to the passenger . . .'

'You're out of your mind,' I yelled.

'You think so? And what if we brought the shuttle down again? No problem – it's on remote control. We'll bring it out of orbit, and . . .'

'Shut up!'

'That won't do either? There's another method, a very simple one. It doesn't involve bringing the shuttle down, only establishing radio contact. If she's alive, she'll reply, and . . .'

'The oxygen would have run out days ago.'

'She may not need it. Shall we try?'

'Snow . . . Snow . . .'

He mimicked my intonation angrily:

'Kelvin . . . Kelvin . . . Think, just a little. Are you a man or not? Who are you trying to please? Who do you want to save? Yourself? Her? And which version of her? This one or that one? Haven't you got the guts to face them both? Surely you realize that you haven't thought it through. Let me tell you one last time, we are in a situation that is beyond morality.'

The rustling noise returned, and this time it sounded like nails scraping on a wall. All at once I was filled with a dull indifference. I saw myself, I saw both of us, from a long way off, as if through the wrong end of a telescope, and everything looked meaningless, trivial and slightly ridiculous.

'So what do you suggest? Send up another shuttle? She would be back tomorrow. And the day after, and the day after that. How long do you want it to go on? What's the good of disposing of her if she keeps returning? How would it help me, or you, or Sartorius, or the Station?'

'No, here's my suggestion: leave with her. You'll witness the transformation. After a few minutes, you'll see . . .'

'What? A monster, a demon?'

'No, you'll see her die, that's all. Don't think that they are immortal – I promise you that they die. And then what will you do? Come back . . . for a fresh sample?' He stared at me with bantering condescension.

'That's enough!' I burst out, clenching my fists.

'Oh, I'm the one who has to be quiet? Look, I didn't start this conversation, and as far as I'm concerned it has gone on long enough. Let me just suggest some ways for you to amuse yourself. You could scourge the ocean with rods, for instance. You've got it into your head that you're a traitor if you . . .' He waved his hand in farewell, and raised his head as if to watch an imaginary ship in flight. '. . . and a good man if you keep her. Smiling when you feel like screaming, and shamming cheerful when you want to beat your head against a wall, isn't that being a traitor? What if it is not possible, here, to be anything but a traitor? What will you do? Take it out on that bastard Snow, who is the cause of it all? In that case, Kelvin, you just put the lid on the rest of your troubles by acting like a complete idiot!'

'You are talking from your own point of view. I love this girl.'

'Her memory, you mean?'

'No, herself. I told you what she tried to do. How many "real" human beings would have that much courage?'

'So you admit . . .'

'Don't quibble.'

'Right. So she loves you. And you want to love her. It isn't the same thing.'

'You're wrong.'

'I'm sorry, Kelvin, but it was your idea to spill all this. You don't love her. You do love her. She is willing to give her life. So are you. It's touching, it's magnificent, anything you like, but it's out of place here – it's the wrong setting. Don't you see? No, you don't want to. You are going around in circles to satisfy the curiosity of a power we don't understand and can't control, and she is an aspect, a periodic manifestation of that power. If she was . . . if you were being pestered by some infatuated hag, you wouldn't think twice about packing her off, right?'

'I suppose so.'

'Well then, that probably explains why she is not a hag! You feel as if your hands are tied? That's just it, they are!'

'All you are doing is adding one more theory to the millions of theories in the library. Leave me alone, Snow, she is . . . No, I won't say any more.'

'It's up to you. But remember that she is a mirror that reflects a part of your mind. If she is beautiful, it's because your memories are. You provide the formula. You can only finish where you started, don't forget that.'

'What do you expect me to do? Send her away? I've already asked you why, and you don't answer.'

'I'll give you an answer. It was you who wanted this conversation, not me. I haven't meddled with your affairs, and I'm not telling you what to do or what not to do. Even if I had the right, I would not. You come here of your own free will, and you dump it all on me. You know why? To take the weight off your own back. Well, I've experienced that weight – don't try to shut me up – and I leave you free to find your own solution. But you *want* opposition. If I got in your way, you could fight me, something tangible, a man just like you, with the same flesh and blood. Fight me, and you could feel that you too were a man. When I don't give you the excuse to fight, you quarrel with me, or rather with yourself. The one thing you've left out is telling me you'd die of grief if *she* suddenly disappeared . . . No, please, I've heard enough!'

I countered clumsily:

'I came to tell you, because I thought you ought to know, that I intend leaving the Station with her.'

'Still on the same tack,' Snow shrugged. 'I only offered my opinion because I realized that you were losing touch with reality. And the further you go, the harder you fall. Can you come and see Sartorius around nine tomorrow morning?'

'Sartorius? I thought he wasn't letting anybody in. You told me you couldn't even phone him.'

'He seems to have reached some kind of settlement. We never discuss our domestic troubles. With you, it's another matter. Will you come tomorrow morning?'

'All right,' I grunted.

I noticed that Snow had slipped his left hand inside the cabinet. How long had the door been ajar? Probably for some time, but in the heat of the encounter I had not registered that the position of his hand was not natural. It was as if he was concealing something – or holding somebody's hand.

I licked my lips:

'Snow, what have you . . .'

'You'd better leave now,' he said evenly.

I closed the door in the final glow of the red twilight. Rheya was huddled against the wall a few paces down the corridor. She sprang to her feet at once:

'You see? I did it, Kris. I feel so much better . . . Perhaps it will be easier and easier . . .'

'Yes, of course . . .' I answered absently.

We went back to my quarters. I was still speculating about that cabinet, and what had been hiding there, perhaps overhearing our entire conversation. My cheeks started to burn so hard that I involuntarily passed the back of my hand over them. What an idiotic meeting! And where did it get us? Nowhere. But there was tomorrow morning . . .

An abrupt thrill of fear ran through me. My encephalogram, a complete record of the workings of my brain, was to be beamed into the ocean in the form of radiation. What was it Snow had said – would I suffer terribly if Rheya departed? An encephalogram records every mental process, conscious and unconscious. If I want her to disappear, will it happen? But if I wanted to get rid of her would I also be appalled at the thought of her imminent destruction? Am I responsible for my unconscious? No one else is, if not myself. How stupid to agree to let them do it. Obviously I can examine the recording before it is used, but I won't be able to decode it. Nobody could. The experts can only identify general mental tendencies. For instance, they will say that the subject is thinking about some mathematical problem, but they are unable to specify its precise terms. They claim that they have to stick to generalizations because the encephalogram cannot discriminate among the stream of simultaneous impulses, only some of which have any psychological 'counterpart', and they refuse pointblank to hazard any comment on the unconscious processes. So how could they be expected to decipher memories which have been more or less repressed?

Then why was I so afraid? I had told Rheya only that morning that the experiment could not work. If Terran neurophysiologists were incapable of decoding the recording, what chance was there for that great alien creature . . .?

Yet it had infiltrated my mind without my knowledge, surveyed my memory, and laid bare my most vulnerable point. That was undeniable. Without any assistance or radiation transmissions, it had found its way through the armoured shell of the Station, located me, and come away with its spoils . . .

'Kris?' Rheya whispered.

Standing at the window with unseeing eyes, I had not noticed the coming of darkness. A thin ceiling of high cloud glowed a dim silver in the light of the vanished sun, and obscured the stars.

If she disappears after the experiment, that will mean that I wanted her to disappear – that I killed her. No, I will not see Sartorius. They can't force me to cooperate. But I can't tell them the truth, I'll have to dissemble and lie, and keep on doing it . . . Because there may be thoughts, intentions and cruel hopes in my mind of which I know nothing, because I am a murderer unawares. Man has gone out to explore other worlds and other civilizations without having explored his own labyrinth of dark passages and secret chambers, and without finding what lies behind doorways that he himself has sealed. Was I to abandon Rheya there out of false shame, or because I lacked the courage?

'Kris,' said Rheya, more softly still.

She was standing quite close to me now. I pretended not to hear. At that moment, I wanted to isolate myself. I had not yet resolved anything, or reached any decision. I stood motionless, looking at the dark sky and the cold stars, pale ghosts of the stars that shone on Earth. My mind was a blank. All I had was the grim certainty of having crossed some point of no return. I refused to admit that I was travelling towards what I could not reach. Apathy robbed me of the strength even to despise myself.

II

THE THINKERS

'Kris, is it the experiment that's on your mind?'

The sound of her voice made me start with surprise. I had been lying in the dark for hours with my eyes open, unable to sleep. Not hearing Rheya's breathing, I had forgotten her, letting myself drift in a tide of aimless speculation. The waking dream had lured me out of sight of the measure and meaning of reality.

'How did you know I wasn't asleep?'

'Your breathing changes when you are asleep,' she said gently, as if to apologize for her question. 'I didn't want to interfere ... If you can't answer, don't.'

'Why would I not tell you? Anyway you've guessed right, it is the experiment.'

'What do they expect to achieve?'

'They don't know themselves. Something. Anything. It isn't "Operation Brainwave", it's "Operation Desperation". Really, one of us ought to have the courage to call the experiment off and shoulder the responsibility for the decision, but the majority reckons that that kind of courage would be a sign of cowardice, and the first step in a retreat. They think it would mean an undignified surrender for mankind — as if there was any dignity in floundering and drowning in what we don't understand and never will.' I stopped, but a new access of rage quickly built up. 'Needless to say they're not short of arguments. They claim that even if we fail to establish contact we won't have been wasting our time investigating the plasma, and that we shall eventually uncover the secret of matter. They know very well that they are deceiving themselves. It's like wandering about in a library where all the books are written in an indecipherable language. The only thing that's familiar is the colour of the bindings!'

'Are there no other planets like this?'

'It's possible. This is the only one we've come across. In any case, it's in an extremely rare category, not like Earth. Earth is a common type – the grass of the universe! And we pride ourselves on this universality. There's nowhere we can't go; in that belief we set out for other worlds, all brimming with confidence. And what were we going to do with them? Rule them or be ruled by them: that was the only idea in our pathetic minds! What a useless waste . . .'

I got out of bed and fumbled in the medicine cabinet. My fingers recognized the shape of the big bottle of sleeping pills, and I turned around in the darkness:

'I'm going to sleep, darling.' Up in the ceiling, the ventilator hummed. 'I must get some sleep . . .'

In the morning, I woke up feeling calm and refreshed. The experiment seemed a petty matter, and I could not understand how I had managed to take the encephalogram so seriously. Nor was I much bothered by having to bring Rheya into the laboratory. In spite of all her exertions, she could not bear to stay out of sight and earshot for longer than five minutes, so I had abandoned my idea of further tests (she was even prepared to let herself be locked up somewhere), asked her to come with me, and advised her to bring something to read.

I was especially curious about what I would find in the laboratory. There was nothing unusual about the appearance of the big, blue and white-painted room, except that the shelves and cupboards meant to contain glass instruments seemed bare. The glass panel in one door was starred, and in some doors it was missing altogether, suggesting that there had been a struggle here recently, and that someone had done his best to remove the traces.

Snow busied himself with the equipment, and behaved quite civilly, showing no surprise at the sight of Rheya, and greeting her with a quick nod of the head.

I was lying down, and Snow was swabbing my temples and forehead with saline solution, when a narrow door opened and Sartorius emerged from an unlighted room. He was wearing a white smock and a black anti-radiation overall that came down to his ankles, and his greeting was authoritative and very professional in manner. We might have been two researchers in some great institute on Earth, continuing from where we had left off the day before. He was not wearing his dark glasses, but I noticed that he had on contact lenses, which I took to be the explanation of his lack of expression.

Sartorius looked on with arms folded as Snow attached the electrodes and wrapped a bandage around my head. He looked around the room several times, ignoring Rheya, who sat on a stool with her back against the wall, pretending to read.

Snow stepped back, and I moved my head, which was bulging with metal discs and wires, to watch him switch on. At this point Sartorius raised his hand and launched into a flowery speech:

'Dr Kelvin, may I have your attention and concentration for a moment. I do not intend to dictate any precise sequence of thought to you, for that would invalidate the experiment, but I do insist that you cease thinking of yourself, of me, our colleague Snow, or anybody else. Make an effort to eliminate any intrusion of individual personalities, and concentrate on the matter in hand. Earth and Solaris; the body of scientists considered as a single entity, although generations succeed each other and man as an individual has a limited span; our aspirations, and our perseverance in the attempt to establish an intellectual contact; the long historic march of humanity, our own certitude of furthering that advance, and our determination to renounce all personal feelings in order to accomplish our mission; the sacrifices that we are prepared to make, and the hardships we stand ready to overcome . . . These are the themes that might properly occupy your awareness. The association of ideas does not depend entirely on your own will. However, the very fact of your presence here bears out the authenticity of the progression I have drawn to your attention. If you are unsure that you have acquitted yourself of your task, say so, I beg you, and our colleague Snow will make another recording. We have plenty of time.'

A dry little smile flickered over his face as he spoke these last words, but his expression remained morose. I was still trying to unravel the pompous phraseology which he had spun out with the utmost gravity.

Snow broke the lengthening silence:

'Ready, Kris?'

He was leaning with one elbow on the control panel of the electroencephalograph, looking completely relaxed. His confident tone reassured me, and I was grateful to him for calling me by my first name.

'Let's get started.' I closed my eyes.

A sudden panic had overwhelmed me after Snow had fixed the electrodes and walked over to the controls: now it disappeared just as suddenly. Through half-closed lids, I could see the red lights winking on the black control-panel. I was no longer aware of the damp, unpleasant touch of the crown of clammy electrodes. My mind was an empty grey arena ringed by a crowd of invisible onlookers massed on tiers of seats, attentive, silent, and emanating in their silence an ironic contempt for Sartorius and the Mission. What should I improvise for these spectators? . . . Rheya . . . I introduced her name cautiously, ready to withdraw it at once, but no protest came, and I kept going. I was drunk with grief and tenderness, ready to suffer prolonged sacrifices patiently. My mind was pervaded with Rheya, without a body or a face, but alive inside me, real and imperceptible. Suddenly, as if printed over that despairing presence, I saw in the grey shadow the learned, professorial face of Giese, the father of Solarist studies and of Solarists. I was not visualizing the nauseating mud-eruption which had swallowed up the gold-rimmed spectacles and carefully brushed moustache. I was seeing the engraving on the title-page of his classic work, and the close-hatched strokes against which the artist had made his head stand out – so like my father's, that head, not in its features but in its expression of old-fashioned wisdom and honesty, that I was finally no longer able to tell which of them was looking at me, my father or Giese. They were dead, and neither of them buried, but then deaths without burial are not uncommon in our time.

The image of Giese vanished, and I momentarily forgot the Station, the experiment, Rheya and the ocean. Recent memories were obliterated by the overwhelming conviction that these two men, my father and Giese, nothing but ashes now, had once faced up to the totality of their existence, and this conviction afforded a profound calm which annihilated the formless assembly clustered around the grey arena in the expectation of my defeat.

I heard the click of circuit-breakers, and light penetrated my eyelids, which blinked open. Sartorius had not budged from his previous position, and was looking at me. Snow had his back turned to operate the control-panel. I had the impression that he was amusing himself by making his sandals slap on the floor.

'Do you think that stage one has been successful, Dr Kelvin?' Sartorius inquired, in the nasal voice which I had come to detest.

'Yes.'

'Are you sure?' he persisted, obviously rather surprised, and perhaps even suspicious.

'Yes.'

My assurance and the bluntness of my answers made him lose his composure briefly.

'Oh . . . good,' he stammered.

Snow came over to me and started to unwrap the bandage from my head. Sartorius stepped back, hesitated, then disappeared into the dark-room.

I was rubbing the circulation back into my legs when he came out again, holding the developed film. Zigzag lines traced a lacy pattern along fifty feet of glistening black ribbon. My presence was no longer necessary, but I stayed, and Snow fed the ribbon into the modulator. Sartorius made a final suspicious examination of the last few feet of the spool, as if trying to decipher the content of the wavering lines.

The experiment proceeded with a minimum of fuss. Snow and Sartorius each sat at a bank of controls and pushed buttons. Through the reinforced floor, I heard the whine of power building up in the turbines. Lights moved downward inside glass-fronted indicators in time with the descent of the great X-ray beamer to the bottom of its housing. They came to a stop at the low limit of the indicators.

Snow stepped up the power, and the white needle of the voltmeter described a left-to-right semicircle. The hum of current was barely audible now, as the film unwound, invisible behind the two round caps. Numbers clicked through the footage indicator.

I went over to Rheya, who was watching us over her book. She glanced up at me inquiringly. The experiment was over, and Sartorius was walking towards the heavy conical head of the machine.

'Can we go?' Rheya mouthed silently.

I replied with a nod, Rheya stood up, and we left the room without taking leave of my colleagues.

A superb sunset was blazing through the windows of the upper-deck corridor. Usually the horizon was reddish and gloomy at this hour. This time it was a shimmering pink, laced with silver. Under the soft glow of the light, the sombre foothills of the ocean shone pale violet. The sky was red only at the zenith.

We came to the bottom of the stairway, and I stopped, reluctant to wall myself up again in the prison cell of the cabin.

'Rheya, I want to look something up in the library. Do you mind?'

'Of course not,' she exclaimed, in a forced attempt at cheerfulness. 'I can find myself something to read . . .'

I knew only too well that a gulf had opened between us since the previous day. I should have behaved more considerately, and tried to master my apathy, but I could not summon the strength.

We walked down the ramp leading to the library. There were three doors giving on to the little entrance hall, and crystal globes containing flowers were spaced out along the walls. I opened the middle door, which was lined with synthetic leather on either side. I always avoided contact with this upholstery when entering the library. We were greeted by a pleasant gust of fresh air. In spite of the stylized sun painted on the ceiling, the great circular hall had remained cool.

Idly running a finger along the spines of the books, I was on the point of choosing, out of all the Solarist classics, the first volume of Giese, so as to refresh my memory of the portrait on the title-page, when I came upon a book I had not noticed before, an octavo volume with a cracked binding. It was Gravinsky's *Compendium*, used mostly by students, as a crib.

Sitting in an armchair, with Rheya at my side, I leafed through Gravinsky's alphabetical classification of the various Solarist theories. The compiler, who had never set foot on Solaris, had combed through every monograph, expedition report, fragmentary outline and provisional account, even making excerpts of incidental comments about Solaris in planetological works dealing with other worlds. He had drawn up an inventory crammed with simplistic formulations, which grossly diminished the subtlety of the ideas it resumed. Originally intended as an all-embracing account, Gravinsky's book was little more than a curiosity now. It had only been published twenty years before, but since that time such a mass of new theories had accumulated that there would not have been room for them in a single volume. I glanced through the index – practically an obituary list, for few of the authors cited were still alive, and among the survivors none was still playing an active part in Solarist studies. Reading all these names, and adding up the sum of the intellectual efforts they represented in every field of research, it was tempting to think that surely one of the theories quoted must be correct, and that the thousands of listed hypotheses must each contain some grain of truth, could not be totally unrelated to the reality.

In his introduction, Gravinsky divided the first sixty years of Solarist studies into periods. During the initial period, which began with the scouting ship that studied the planet from orbit, nobody had produced theories in the strict sense. 'Common sense' suggested that the ocean was a lifeless chemical conglomerate, a gelatinous mass which through its 'quasi-volcanic' activity produced marvellous creations and stabilized its eccentric orbit by virtue of a self-generated mechanical process, as a pendulum keeps itself on a fixed path once it is set in motion. To be precise, Magenon had come up with the idea that the 'colloidal machine' was alive three years after the first expedition, but according to the *Compendium* the period of biological hypotheses does not begin until nine years later, when Magenon's idea had acquired numerous supporters. The following years teemed with theoretical accounts of the living ocean, extremely complex, and supported by biomathematical analysis. During the third period, scientific opinion, hitherto practically unanimous, became divided.

What followed was internecine warfare between scores of new schools of thought. It was the age of Panmaller, Strobel, Freyus, Le Greuille and Osipowicz: the entire legacy of Giese was submitted to a merciless examination. The first atlases and inventories appeared, and new techniques in remote control enabled instruments to transmit stereophotographs from the interior of the asymmetriads, once considered impossible to explore. In the hubbub of controversy, the 'minimal' hypotheses were contemptuously dismissed: even if the long-awaited contact with the 'reasoning monster' did not materialize, it was argued that it was still worth investigating the cartilaginous cities of the mimoids and the ballooning mountains that rose above the ocean because we would gain valuable chemical and physio-chemical information, and enlarge our understanding of the structure of giant molecules. Nobody bothered even to refute the adherents of this defeatist line of reasoning. Scientists devoted themselves to drawing up catalogues of the typical metamorphoses which are still standard works, and Frank developed his bioplasmatic theory of the mimoids, which has since been shown to be inaccurate, but remains a superb example of intellectual audacity and logical construction.

The thirty or so years of the first three 'Gravinsky periods', with their open assurance and irresistibly optimistic romanticism, constitute the infancy of Solarist studies. Already a growing scepticism heralded the age of maturity. Towards the end of the first quarter-century the early colloido-mechanistic theories had found a distant descendant in the concept of the 'apsychic ocean', a new and almost unanimous orthodoxy which threw overboard the view of that entire generation of scientists who believed that their observations were evidence of a conscious will, teleological processes, and activity motivated by some inner need of the ocean. This point of view was now overwhelmingly repudiated, and the ground was cleared for the team headed by Holden, Ionides and Stoliva, whose lucid, analytically-based speculations concentrated on scrupulous examination of a growing body of data. It was the golden age of the archivists. Microfilm libraries burst at the seams with documents; expeditions, some of them more than a thousand strong, were equipped with the most lavish apparatus Earth could provide – robot recorders, sonar and radar, and the entire range of spectrometers, radiation counters and so on. Material was being accumulated at an accelerating tempo, but the essential spirit of the research flagged, and in the course of this period, still an optimistic one in spite of everything, a decline set in.

The first phase of Solaristics had been shaped by the personality of men like Giese, Strobel and Sevada, who had remained adventurous whether they were asserting or attacking a theoretical position. Sevada, the last of the great Solarists, disappeared near the south pole of the planet, and his death was never satisfactorily explained. He fell victim to a mistake which not even a novice would have made. Flying at low altitude, in full view of scores of observers, his aircraft had plunged into the interior of an agilus which was not even directly in its path. There was speculation about a sudden heart attack or fainting fit, or a mechanical failure, but I have always believed that this was in fact the first suicide, brought on by the first abrupt crisis of despair.

There were other 'crises', not mentioned in Gravinsky, whose details I was able to fill in out of my own knowledge as I stared at the yellowed, closely-printed pages.

The later expressions of despair were in any case less dramatic, just as outstanding personalities became rarer. The recruitment of scientists to any particular field of study in a given age has never been studied as a phenomenon in its own right. Every generation throws up a fairly constant number of brilliant and determined men; the only difference lies in the direction they choose to take. The absence or presence of such individuals in a particular field of study is probably explicable in terms of the new perspectives offered. Opinions may differ about the researchers of the classical age of Solarist studies, but nobody can deny their stature, even their genius. For several decades, the mysterious ocean had attracted the best mathematicians and physicists, and the top specialists in biophysics, information theory and electro-physiology. Now, without warning, the army of researchers found itself leaderless. There remained a faceless mass of industrious collectors and compilers. The occasional original experiment might be devised, but the succession of vast expeditions mounted on a worldwide scale petered out, and the scientific world no longer echoed with ambitious, controversial theories.

The machinery of Solaristics fell into disrepair, and rusted over with hypotheses differentiated only in minor details, and unanimous in their concentration on the theme of the ocean's degeneration, regression and introversion. Now and then a bolder, more interesting concept might emerge, but it always amounted to a kind of indictment of the ocean, viewed as the end-product of a development which long ago, thousands of years before, had gone through a phase of superior organization, and now had nothing more than a physical unity. The argument went that its many useless, absurd creations were its death-throes – impressive enough, nonetheless – which had been going on for centuries. Thus, for instance, the extensors and mimoids were seen as tumours, and all the surface processes of the huge fluid body as expressions of chaos and anarchy. This approach to the problem became an obsession. For seven or eight years, the academic literature produced a spate of assertions which, although framed in polite, cautious terms, amounted to little more than insults, the revenge of a rabble of leaderless suitors when they realized that the object of their most pressing attentions was indifferent to the point of obstinately ignoring all their advances.

A group of European psychologists once carried out a public opinion poll spread over a period of several years. Their report had no direct bearing on Solarist studies, and was not included in the library collection, but I had read it, and retained a clear memory of its findings. The investigators had strikingly demonstrated that the changes in lay opinion were closely correlated to the fluctuations of opinion recorded in scientific circles.

That change was expressed even in the coordinating committee of the Institute of Planetology, which controls the financial appropriations for research, by means of a progressive reduction in the budgets of institutes and appointments devoted to Solarist studies, as well as by restrictions on the size of the exploration teams.

Some scientists adopted a position at the other extreme, and agitated for more vigorous steps to be taken. The administrative director of the Universal Cosmological Institute ventured to assert that the living ocean did not despise men in the least, but had not noticed them, as an elephant neither feels nor sees the ants crawling on its back. To attract and hold the ocean's attention, it would be necessary to devise more powerful stimuli, and gigantic machines tailored to the dimensions of the entire planet. Malicious commentators were not slow to point out that the director could well afford to be generous, since it was the Institute of Planetology which would have had to foot the bill.

Still the hypotheses rained down – old, 'resurrected' hypotheses, superficially modified, simplified, or complicated to the extreme – and Solaristics, a relatively well-defined discipline in spite of its scope, became an increasingly tangled maze where every apparent exit led to a dead end. In the climate of general indifference, stagnation and despondency, the ocean of Solaris was submerging under an ocean of printed paper.

Two years before I began the stint in Gibarian's laboratory which ended when I obtained the diploma of the Institute, the Mett-Irving Foundation offered a huge prize to anybody who could find a viable method of tapping the energy of the ocean. The idea was not a new one. Several cargoes of the plasmatic jelly had been shipped back to Earth in the past, and various methods of preservation had been patiently tested: high and low temperatures, artificial micro-atmospheres and micro-climates, and prolonged irradiation. The whole gamut of physical and chemical processes had been run, only to end with the same outcome, a gradual process of decomposition which passed through well-defined stages, starting with wasting, maceration, then first-degree (primary) and late (secondary) liquefaction. The samples removed from the plasmatic growths and creations met with the same fate, with certain variations in the phases of decomposition. The end-product was always a light metallic ash.

Once the scientists recognized that it was impossible to keep alive, or even in a 'vegetative' state, any fragment of the ocean, large or small, in dissociation from the entire organism, a growing tendency developed (under the influence of the Meunier-Proroch school) to isolate this problem as the key to the mystery. It was seen as a matter of interpretation – solve it, and the back of the problem would be broken.

The quest for this key, the philosopher's stone of Solarist studies, had absorbed the time and energy of all kinds of people with little or no scientific training. During the fourth decade of Solaristics the craze spread like an epidemic, and provided a fertile ground for the psychologists. An unknown number of cranks and ignorant fanatics toiled at their fumbling researches with a greater enthusiasm than any which had animated the old prophets of perpetual motion, or the squaring of the circle. The craze fizzled out in only a few years, and by the time I was ready to leave for Solaris it had vanished from the headlines and from conversation, and the ocean itself was practically forgotten by the public.

I took care to replace the *Compendium* in its correct alphabetical position, and in doing so dislodged a slim pamphlet by Grastrom, one of the most eccentric authors in Solarist literature. I had read the pamphlet, which was dictated by the urge to understand what lies beyond the grasp of mankind, and aimed in particular against the individual, man, and the human species. It was the abstract, acidulous work of an autodidact who had previously made a series of unusual contributions to various marginal and rarefied branches of quantum physics. In this fifteen-page booklet (his magnum opus!), Grastrom set out to demonstrate that the most abstract achievements of science, the most advanced theories and victories of mathematics represented nothing more than a stumbling, one- or two-step progression from our rude, prehistoric, anthropomorphic understanding of the universe around us. He pointed out correspondences with the human body – the projections of our senses, the structure of our physical organization, and the physiological limitations of man – in the equations of the theory of relativity, the theorem of magnetic fields and the various unified field theories. Grastrom's conclusion was that there neither was, nor could be, any question of 'contact' between mankind and any nonhuman civilization. This broadside against humanity made no specific mention of the living ocean, but its constant presence and scornful, victorious silence could be felt between every line, at any rate such had been my own impression. It was Gibarian who drew it to my attention, and it must have been Gibarian who had added it to the Station's collection, on his own authority, since Grastrom's pamphlet was regarded more as a curiosity than a true contribution to Solarist literature.

With a strange feeling almost of respect, I carefully slid the slim pamphlet back into the crowded bookshelf, then stroked the green bronze binding of the *Solaris Annual* with my fingertips. In the space of a few days, we had unquestionably gained positive information about a number of basic questions, which had made seas of ink flow and fed innumerable controversies, yet had remained sterile for lack of arguments. Today the mystery practically had us under siege, and we had powerful arguments.

Was the ocean a living creature? It could hardly be doubted any longer by any but lovers of paradox or obstinacy. It was no longer possible to deny the 'psychic' functions of the ocean, no matter how that term might be defined. Certainly it was only too obvious that the ocean had 'noticed' us. This fact alone invalidated that category of Solarist theories which claimed that the ocean was an 'introverted' world, a 'hermit entity', deprived by a process of degeneration of the thinking organs it once possessed, unaware of the existence of external objects and events, the prisoner of a gigantic vortex of mental currents created and confined in the depths of this monster revolving between two suns.

Not only that, we had discovered that the ocean was capable of reproducing what we ourselves had never succeeded in creating artificially – a perfect human body, modified in its sub-atomic structure for purposes we could not guess.

The ocean lived, thought and acted. The 'Solaris problem' had not been annihilated by its very absurdity. We were truly dealing with a living creature. The 'lost' faculty was not lost at all. All this now seemed proved beyond doubt. Like it or not, men must pay attention to this neighbour, light years away, but nevertheless a neighbour situated inside our sphere of expansion, and more disquieting than all the rest of the universe.

Perhaps we had arrived at a turning-point. What would the high-level decision be? Would we be ordered to give up and return to Earth, immediately or in the near future? Was it even possible that we would be ordered to liquidate the Station? It was at least not improbable. But I did not favour the solution by retreat. The existence of the thinking colossus was bound to go on haunting men's minds. Even when man had explored every corner of the cosmos, and established relations with other civilizations founded by creatures similar to ourselves, Solaris would remain an eternal challenge.

Misplaced among the thick volumes of the *Annual*, I discovered a small calf-bound book, and scanned its scuffed, worn cover for a moment. It was Muntius's *Introduction to Solaristics*, published many years before. I had read it in a single night, after Gibarian had smilingly lent me his personal copy; and when I had turned the final page the light of a new Earth dawn was shining through my window. According to Muntius, Solaristics is the space era's equivalent of religion: faith disguised as science. Contact, the stated aim of Solaristics, is no less vague and obscure than the communion of the saints, or the second coming of the Messiah. Exploration is a liturgy using the language of methodology; the drudgery of the Solarists is carried out only in the expectation of fulfilment, of an Annunciation, for there are not and cannot be any bridges between Solaris and Earth. The comparison is reinforced by obvious parallels: Solarists reject arguments – no experiences in common, no communicable notions – just as the faithful rejected the arguments that undermined the foundations of their belief. Then again, what can mankind expect or hope for out of a joint 'pooling of information' with the living ocean? A catalogue of the vicissitudes associated with an existence of such infinite duration that it probably has no memory of its origins? A description of the aspirations, passions and sufferings that find expression in the perpetual creation of living mountains? The apotheosis of mathematics, the revelation of plenitude in isolation and renunciation? But all this represents a body of incommunicable knowledge. Transposed into any human language, the values and meanings involved lose all substance; they cannot be brought intact through the barrier. In any case, the 'adepts' do not expect such revelations – of the order of poetry, rather than science – since unconsciously it is Revelation itself that they expect, and this revelation is to explain to them the meaning of the destiny of man! Solaristics is a revival of long-vanished myths, the expression of mystical nostalgias which men are unwilling to confess openly. The cornerstone is deeply entrenched in the foundations of the edifice: it is the hope of Redemption.

Solarists are incapable of recognizing this truth, and consequently take care to avoid any interpretation of Contact, which is presented in their writings as an ultimate goal, whereas originally it had been considered as a beginning, and as a step on to a new path, among many other possible paths. Over the years, Contact has become sanctified. It has become the heaven of eternity.

Muntius analyses this 'heresy' of planetology very simply and trenchantly. He brilliantly dismantles the Solarist myth, or rather the myth of the Mission of Mankind.

Muntius's had been the first voice raised in protest, and had encountered the contemptuous silence of the experts, at a time when they still retained a romantic confidence in the development of Solaristics. After all, how could they have accepted a thesis that struck at the foundations of their achievements?

Solaristics went on waiting for the man who would re-establish it on a firm foundation and define its frontiers with precision. Five years after the death of Muntius, when his pamphlet had become a rare collectors' piece, a group of Norwegian researchers founded a school named after him. In contact with the personalities of his various spiritual heirs, the quiet thought of the master went through profound transformations; it led to the corrosive irony of Erle Ennesson and, on a more mundane plane, the 'utilitarian' or 'utilitarianistic' Solaristics of Fa-leng, who argued that science should settle for the immediate advantages offered by exploration, and not concern itself with any intellectual communion of two civilizations, or some illusory contact. Compared with the ruthless, lucid analysis of Muntius, the works of his disciples are hardly more than compilations and sometimes vulgarizations, with the exception of Ennesson's essays and perhaps the studies of Takata. Muntius himself had already defined the complete development of Solarist concepts. He called the first phase the era of the 'prophets', among whom he included Giese, Holden and Sevada; the second, the 'great schism' – the fragmentation of the one Solarist church into a number of warring sects; and he anticipated a third phase, which would set in when there was nothing left to investigate, and manifest itself in a crabbed, academic dogmatism. This prophecy was to prove inaccurate, however. In my opinion, Gibarian was right to characterize Muntius's strictures as a monumental simplification which ignored all the aspects of Solarist studies that had nothing in common with a creed, since the work of interpretation based itself only on the concrete evidence of a globe orbiting two suns.

Slipped between two pages of Muntius's pamphlet, I discovered an off-print of the quarterly review *Parerga Solariana*, which turned out to be one of the first articles written by Gibarian, even before he was appointed director of the Institute. The article was called 'Why I am a Solarist' and began with a concise account of all the material phenomena which confirmed the possibility of contact. Gibarian belonged to that generation of researchers who had been daring and optimistic enough to hark back to the golden age, and who did not disown their own version of a faith that overstepped the frontiers imposed by science, and yet remained concrete, since it pre-supposed the success of perseverance.

Gibarian had been influenced by the classical work in bio-electronics for which the Eurasian school of Cho Enmin, Ngyalla and Kawakadze is famous. Their studies established an analogy between the charted electrical activity of the brain and certain discharges occurring deep in the plasma before the appearance, for example, of elementary polymorphs or twin solarids. Gibarian was opposed to anthropomorphizing interpretations, and the mystifications of the psychoanalytic, psychiatric and neurophysiological schools which attempted to endow the ocean with the symptoms of human illnesses, epilepsy among them (supposed to correspond with the spasmodic eruptions of the asymmetriads). He was one of the most cautious and logical proponents of Contact, and saw no advantage in the kind of sensationalism which was in any case becoming more and more rare as applied to Solaris.

My own doctoral thesis received a fair amount of attention, not all of it welcome. It was based on the discoveries of Bergmann and Reynolds, who had succeeded in isolating and 'filtering' the elements of the most powerful emotions – despair, grief and pleasure – out of the mass of general mental processes. Systematically comparing their recordings with the electrical discharges from the ocean, I had observed oscillations in certain parts of symmetriads and at the bases of nascent mimoids which were sufficiently analogous to deserve further investigation. The journalists pounced on my thesis, and in some newspapers my name was coupled with grotesque headlines – 'The Despairing Jelly', 'The Planet in Orgasm'. But this dubious fame did have the fortunate consequence (or so I had thought a few days previously) of attracting the attention of Gibarian, who naturally could not read every new publication dealing with Solaris. The letter he sent me ended a chapter of my life, and began a new one . . .

12

THE DREAMS

When six days passed with no reaction from the ocean, we decided to repeat the experiment. Until now, the Station had been located at the intersection of the forty-third parallel and the 116th meridian. We moved south, maintaining a constant altitude of 1200 feet above the ocean – our radar confirmed automatic observations relayed by the artificial satellite which indicated a build-up of activity in the plasma of the southern hemisphere.

Forty-eight hours later, a beam of X-rays modulated by my own brain-patterns was bombarding the almost motionless surface of the ocean at regular intervals.

At the end of this two-day journey we had reached the outskirts of the polar region. The disc of the blue sun was setting to one side of the horizon, while on the opposite side billowing purple clouds announced the dawn of the red sun. In the sky, blinding flames and showers of green sparks clashed with the dull purple glow. Even the ocean participated in the battle between the two stars, here glittering with mercurial flashes, there with crimson reflections. The smallest cloud passing overhead brightened the shining foam on the wave-crests with iridescence. The blue sun had barely set when, at the meeting of ocean and sky, indistinct and drowned in blood-red mist (but signalled immediately by the detectors), a symmetriad blossomed like a gigantic crystal flower. The Station held its course, and after fifteen minutes the colossal ruby throbbing with dying gleams was once again hidden beneath the horizon. Some minutes later, a thin column spouted thousands of yards upwards into the atmosphere, its base obscured from view by the curvature of the planet. This fantastic tree, which went on growing and gushing blood and quicksilver, marked the end of the symmetriad: the tangled branches at the top of the column melted into a huge mushroom shape, illuminated by both suns simultaneously, and carried on the wind, while the lower part bulged, broke up into heavy clusters, and slowly sank. The death-throes lasted well over an hour.

Another two days passed. Our X-rays had irradiated a vast stretch of the ocean, and we made a final repetition of the experiment. From our observation post we spotted a chain of islets two hundred and fifty miles to the south – six rocky promontories encrusted with a snowy substance which was in fact a deposit of organic origin, proving that the mountainous formation had once been part of the ocean bed.

We then moved south-west, and skirted a chain of mountains capped by clouds which gathered during the red day, and then disappeared. Ten days had elapsed since the first experiment.

On the surface, not much was happening in the Station. Sartorius had programmed the experiment for automatic repetition at set intervals. I did not even know whether anybody was checking the apparatus for correct function. In fact, the calm was not as complete as it seemed, but not because of any human activity.

I was afraid that Sartorius had no real intention of abandoning the construction of the disruptor. And how would Snow react when he found out that I had kept information from him and exaggerated the dangers we might run in the attempt to annihilate neutrino structures? Yet neither of the two said anything further about the project, and I kept wondering why they were so silent. I vaguely suspected them of keeping something from me – perhaps they had been working in secret – and every day I inspected the room which housed the disruptor, a windowless cell situated directly underneath the main laboratory. I never found anybody in the room, and the layer of dust over the armatures and cables of the apparatus proved that it had not been touched for weeks.

As a matter of fact, I did not meet anybody anywhere, and could not get through to Snow any more: nobody answered when I tried to call the radio cabin. Somebody had to be controlling the Station's movements, but who? I had no idea, and oddly enough I considered the question was out of my province. The absence of response from the ocean left me equally indifferent, so much so that after two or three days I had stopped being either hopeful or apprehensive, and had completely written off the experiment and its possible results.

For days on end, I remained sitting in the library or in my cabin, accompanied by the silent shadow of Rheya. I was aware that there was an unease between us, and that my state of mindless suspension could not go on for ever. Obviously it was up to me to break the stalemate, but I resisted the very idea of any kind of change: I was incapable of making the most trivial decision. Everything inside the Station, and my relationship with Rheya in particular, felt fragile and insubstantial, as if the slightest alteration could shatter the perilous equilibrium and bring down ruin. I could not tell where this feeling originated, and the strangest thing of all is that Rheya too had a similar experience. When I look back on those moments today, I have a strong conviction that this atmosphere of uncertainty and suspense, and my presentiment of impending disaster, was provoked by an invisible presence which had taken possession of the Station. I believe too that I can claim that this presence manifested itself just as powerfully in dreams. I have never had visions of that kind before or since, so I decided to note them down and to transcribe them approximately, in so far as my vocabulary permits, given that I can convey only fragmentary glimpses almost entirely denuded of an incommunicable horror.

A blurred region, in the heart of vastness, far from earth and heaven, with no ground underfoot, no vault of sky overhead, nothing. I am the prisoner of an alien matter and my body is clothed in a dead, formless substance – or rather I have no body, I *am* that alien matter. Nebulous pale pink globules surround me, suspended in a medium more opaque than air, for objects only become clear at very close range, although when they do approach they are abnormally distinct, and their presence comes home to me with a preternatural vividness. The conviction of its substantial, tangible reality is now so overwhelming that later, when I wake up, I have the impression that I have just left a state of true perception, and everything I see after opening my eyes seems hazy and unreal

That is how the dream begins. All around me, something is awaiting my consent, my inner acquiescence, and I know, or rather the knowledge exists, that I must not give way to an unknown temptation, for the more the silence seems to promise, the more terrible the outcome will be. Yet I essentially know no such thing, because I would be afraid if I knew, and I never felt the slightest fear.

I wait. Out of the enveloping pink mist, an invisible object emerges, and touches me. Inert, locked in the alien matter that encloses me, I can neither retreat nor turn away, and still I am being touched, my prison is being probed, and I feel this contact like a hand, and the hand recreates me. Until now, I thought I saw, but had no eyes: now I have eyes! Under the caress of the hesitant fingers, my lips and cheeks emerge from the void, and as the caress goes further I have a face, breath stirs in my chest – I exist. And recreated, I in my turn create: a face appears before me that I have never seen until now, at once mysterious and known. I strain to meet its gaze, but I cannot impose any direction on my own, and we discover one another mutually, beyond any effort of will, in an absorbed silence. I have become alive again, and I feel as if there is no limitation on my powers. This creature – a woman? – stays near me, and we are motionless. The beat of our hearts combines, and all at once, out of the surrounding void where nothing exists or can exist, steals a presence of indefinable, unimaginable cruelty. The caress that created us and which wrapped us in a golden cloak becomes the crawling of innumerable fingers. Our white, naked bodies dissolve into a swarm of black creeping things, and I am – we are – a mass of glutinous coiling worms, endless, and in that infinity, no, I am infinite, and I howl soundlessly, begging for death and for an end. But simultaneously I am dispersed in all directions, and my grief expands in a suffering more acute than any waking state, a pervasive, scattered pain piercing the distant blacks and reds, hard as rock and ever-increasing, a mountain of grief visible in the dazzling light of another world.

That dream was one of the simplest. I cannot describe the others, for lack of language to convey their dread. In those dreams, I was unaware of the existence of Rheya, nor was there any echo of past or recent events.

There were also visionless dreams, where in an unmoving, clotted silence I felt myself being slowly and minutely explored, although no instrument or hand touched me. Yet I felt myself being invaded through and through, I crumbled, disintegrated, and only emptiness remained. Total annihilation was succeeded by such terror that its memory alone makes my heart beat faster today.

So the days passed, each one like the next. I was indifferent to everything, fearing only the night and unable to find a means of escape from the dreams. Rheya never slept. I lay beside her, fighting against sleep, and the tenderness with which I clung to her was only a pretext, a way of avoiding the moment when I would be compelled to close my eyes. I had not mentioned these nightmares to her, but she must have guessed, for her attitude involuntarily betrayed a sense of deep humiliation.

As I say, I had not seen Snow or Sartorius for some time, yet Snow gave occasional signs of life. He would leave a note at my door, or call me on the videophone, asking whether I had noticed any new event or change, or anything at all which could be interpreted as a response to the repeated X-ray bombardments. I told him No, and asked him the same question, but there in the little screen Snow only shook his head.

On the fifteenth day after the conclusion of the experiment, I woke up earlier than usual, exhausted by the previous night's dreams. All my limbs were numbed, as if emerging from the effects of a powerful narcotic. The first rays of the red sun shone through the window, a blanket of red flame rippled over the surface of the ocean, and I realized that the vast expanse, which had not been disturbed by the slightest movement in the past four days, was beginning to stir. The dark ocean was abruptly covered by a thin veil of mist which seemed at the same time to have a very palpable consistency. Here and there the mist shook, and tremors spread out to the horizon in all directions. Now the ocean disappeared altogether beneath thick, corrugated membranes with pink swellings and pearly depressions, and these strange waves suspended above the ocean swirled suddenly and coalesced into great balls of blue-green foam. A tempest of wind hurled them upwards to the height of the Station, and wherever I looked, immense membranous wings were soaring in the red sky. Some of these wings of foam, which blotted out the sun, were pitch-black, and others shone with highlights of purple as they were exposed obliquely to the sunlight. Still the phenomenon continued, as if the ocean were mutating, or shedding an old scaly skin. Now and again the dark surface of the ocean could be glimpsed through a gap that the foam filled in an instant. Wings of foam planed all around me, only a few yards from the window, and one swooped to rub against the window pane like a silken scarf. As the ocean went on giving birth to these fantastic birds, the first flights were already dissipating high above, decomposing at their zenith into transparent filaments.

The Station remained motionless as long as the spectacle lasted – about three hours, until night intervened. And even after the sun had set and the shadows had spread over the ocean, the lurid glow of myriads of wings could still be discerned rising into the sky, hovering in massed ranks, and climbing effortlessly towards the light.

This performance had terrified Rheya, but it was no less disconcerting for me, although its novelty ought not to have been disturbing, since two or three times a year, and oftener when luck smiled on them, Solarists observed forms and creations never previously recorded.

The following night, an hour before the blue sunrise, we witnessed another effect: the ocean was becoming phosphorescent. Pools of grey light were rising and falling to the rhythm of invisible waves. Isolated at first, these grey patches quickly spread and joined together, and soon made up a carpet of spectral light extending as far as the eye could see. The intensity of the light grew progressively for some fifteen to twenty minutes, then the phenomenon came to a surprising end. A pall of shadow approached from the west, stretching along a front several hundred miles wide. When this moving shadow had overtaken the Station, the phosphorescent part of the ocean, retreating eastward, seemed to be trying to escape from the vast extinguisher. It was like an aurora put to flight, and retreating as far as the horizon, which was edged by a fading glow before the darkness conquered. Shortly afterwards, the sun rose above the ocean wastes, which were furrowed by a few solidified waves, whose mercurial reflections played on my window.

The phosphorescence was a recorded effect, sometimes observed before the eruption of an asymmetriad, but always indicative of a local increase in the activity of the plasma. Nevertheless, in the course of the next two weeks nothing happened either inside or outside the Station, except on one occasion when in the middle of the night I heard the sound of a piercing scream which came from no human throat. The shrill, protracted howling woke me out of a nightmare, and at first I thought that it was the beginning of another. Before falling asleep, I had heard dull noises coming from the direction of the laboratory, part of which lay directly over my cabin. It sounded like heavy objects and machinery being shifted. When I realized that I was not dreaming, I decided that the scream also came from above, but could not understand how it managed to penetrate the sound-proof ceiling. The terrible sounds went on for almost half an hour, until my nerves jangled and I was pouring with sweat. I was about to go up and investigate when the screaming stopped, to be replaced by more muffled sounds as of objects being dragged across the floor.

Rheya and I were sitting in the kitchen two days later when Snow came in. He was dressed as people dress on Earth after their day's work, and looked like a different person, taller and older. He did not look at us, or pull up a chair, but stood at the table, opened a can of meat and began cramming it down between mouthfuls of bread. His jacket sleeve brushed against the greasy top of the can.

'Look out, Snow, your sleeve!'

'What?' he grunted, then went on stuffing himself with food as if he had not eaten for days. He poured out a glass of wine, drank it at a gulp, sighed, and wiped his lips. Then he looked at me with bloodshot eyes, and mumbled:

'So you've stopped shaving? Ah . . .'

Rheya cleared the table. Snow swayed on his heels, then pulled a face and sucked his teeth noisily, deliberately exaggerating the action. He stared at me insistently:

'So you've decided not to shave?' I made no reply. 'Believe me,' he went on, 'you're making a mistake. That was how it started with him too . . .'

'Go and lie down.'

'What? Just when I feel like talking? Listen, Kelvin, perhaps it wishes well . . . perhaps it wants to please us but doesn't quite know how to set about the job. It spies out desires in our brains, and only two per cent of mental processes are conscious. That means it knows us better than we know ourselves. We've got to reach an understanding with it. Are you listening? Don't you want to? Why' – he was sobbing by now – 'why don't you shave?'

'Shut up! . . . you're drunk.'

'Me, drunk? And what if I am? Just because I drift about from one end of space to another and poke my nose into the cosmos, does that

mean I'm not allowed to get drunk? Why not? You believe in the
mission of mankind, don't you, Kelvin? Gibarian told me about you
before he started letting his beard grow . . . It was a very good description. Just don't go to the lab, if you don't want to lose your faith.
It belongs to Sartorius – Faust in reverse . . . he's looking for a cure
for immortality! He is the last knight of the Holy Contact, the man
we need. His latest discovery is pretty good too . . . prolonged dying.
Not bad, eh? *Agonia perpetua* . . . of the straw . . . the straw hats . . .
and still you don't drink, Kelvin?'

He raised his swollen eyelids and looked at Rheya, who was standing
quite still with her back to the wall. Then he began chanting:

'O fair Aphrodite, child of Ocean, your divine hand . . .' He choked
with laughter. 'It fits, eh, Kel . . . vin . . .'

He broke off in a fit of coughing.

'Shut up! Shut up and get out!' I grated through clenched teeth.

'You're chucking me out? You too? You don't shave and you chuck
me out? What about my warnings, and my advice? Interstellar colleagues ought to help each other! Listen Kelvin, let's go down and
open the traps and call out. It might hear us. But what's its name? We
have named all the stars and all the planets, even though they might
already have had names of their own. What a nerve! Come on, let's go
down. We'll shout it such a description of the trick it's played us that
it will be touched. It will make us silver symmetriads, pray to us in
calculus, send us its blood-stained angels. It will share our troubles
and terrors, and beg us to help it die. It is already begging us, imploring
us. It implores us to help it die with every one of its creations. You're
not amused . . . but you know I'm just a joker. If man had more of a
sense of humour, things might have turned out differently. Do you
know what he wants to do? He wants to punish this ocean, hear it
screaming out of all its mountains at once. If you think he'll never
have the nerve to submit his plan to that bunch of doddering ancients
who sent us here to redeem sins we haven't committed, you're right –
he is afraid. But he is only afraid of the little hat. He won't let
anybody see the little hat, he won't dare, not Faust . . .'

I said nothing. Snow's swaying increased. Tears were streaming
down his cheeks and on to his clothes. He went on:

'Who is responsible? Who is responsible for this situation? Gibarian?

Giese? Einstein? Plato? All criminals . . . Just you think, in a rocket a man takes the risk of bursting like a balloon, or freezing, or roasting, or sweating all his blood out in a single gush, before he can even cry out, and all that remains is bits of bone floating inside armoured hulls, in accordance with the laws of Newton as corrected by Einstein, those two milestones in our progress. Down the road we go, all in good faith, and see where it gets us. Think about our success, Kelvin; think about our cabins, the unbreakable plates, the immortal sinks, legions of faithful wardrobes, devoted cupboards . . . I wouldn't be talking this way if I weren't drunk, but sooner or later somebody was bound to say it, weren't they? You sit there like a baby in a slaughter-house, and you let your beard grow . . . Who's to blame? Find out for yourself.'

He turned slowly and went out, putting an arm out against the doorpost to steady himself. Then his footsteps died away along the corridor.

I tried not to look at Rheya, but my eyes were drawn to hers in spite of myself. I wanted to get up, take her in my arms and stroke her hair. I did not move.

13

VICTORY

Another three weeks. The shutters rose and fell on time. I was still a prisoner in my nightmares, and every morning the play began again. But was it a play? I put on a feigned composure, and Rheya played the same game. The deception was mutual and deliberate, and our agreement only contributed to our ultimate evasion. We talked about the future, and our life on Earth on the outskirts of some great city. We would spend the rest of our lives among green trees and under a blue sky, and never leave Earth again. Together we planned the lay-out of our house and garden and argued over details like the location of a hedge or a bench.

I do not believe that I was sincere for a single instant. Our plans were impossible, and I knew it, for even if Rheya could leave the Station and survive the voyage, how could I have got through the immigration checks with my clandestine passenger? Earth admits only human beings, and even then only when they carry the necessary papers. Rheya would be detained for an identity check at the first barrier, we would be separated, and she would give herself away at once. The Station was the one place where we could live together. Rheya must have known that, or found it out.

One night I heard Rheya get out of bed silently. I wanted to stop her; in the darkness and silence we occasionally managed to throw off our despair for a while by making each other forget. Rheya did not notice that I had already woken up. When I stretched my hand out, she was already out of bed, and walking bare-foot towards the door. Without daring to raise my voice, I whispered her name, but she was outside, and a narrow shaft of light shone through the doorway from the corridor.

There was a sound of whispering. Rheya was talking to somebody . . . but who? Panic overtook me when I tried to stand up, and my legs would not move. I listened, but heard nothing. The blood hammered through my temples. I started counting, and was approaching a thousand when there was a movement in the doorway and Rheya returned. She stood there for a second without moving, and I made myself breathe evenly.

'Kris?' she whispered.

I did not answer.

She slid quickly into bed and lay down, taking care not to disturb me. Questions buzzed in my mind, but I would not let myself be the first to speak, and made no move. The silent questioning went on for an hour, maybe more. Then I fell asleep.

The morning was like any other. I watched Rheya furtively, but could not see any change in her behaviour. After breakfast, we sat at the big panoramic window. The Station was hovering among purple clouds. Rheya was reading, and as I stared out I suddenly noticed that by holding my head at a certain angle I could see us both reflected in the window. I took my hand off the rail. Rheya had no idea that I was watching her. She glanced at me, obviously decided from my posture that I was looking at the ocean, then bent to kiss the place where my hand had rested. In a moment she was reading her book again.

'Rheya,' I asked gently, 'where did you go last night?'

'Last night?'

'Yes.'

'You ... you must have been dreaming, Kris. I didn't go anywhere.'

'You didn't leave the cabin?'

'No. It must have been a dream.'

'Perhaps ... yes, perhaps I dreamt it.'

The same evening, I started talking about our return to Earth again, but Rheya stopped me:

'Don't talk to me about the journey again, Kris. I don't want to hear any more about it, you know very well ...'

'What?'

'No, nothing.'

After we went to bed, she said that she was thirsty:

'There's a glass of fruit-juice on the table over there. Could you give it to me?' She drank half of it then handed it to me.

'I'm not thirsty.'

'Drink to my health then,' she smiled.

It tasted slightly bitter, but my mind was on other things. She switched the light off.

'Rheya ... If you won't talk about the voyage, let's talk about something else.'

'If I did not exist, would you marry?'

'No.'

'Never?'

'Never.'

'Why not?'

'I don't know. I was by myself for ten years and I didn't marry again. Let's not talk about that . . .' My head was spinning as if I had been drinking too much.

'No, let's talk about it. What if I begged you to?'

'To marry again? Don't be silly, Rheya. I don't need anybody except you.'

I felt her breath on my face and her arms holding me:

'Say it another way.'

'I love you.'

Her head fell to my shoulder, and I felt tears.

'Rheya, what's the matter?'

'Nothing . . . nothing . . . nothing . . .' Her voice echoed into silence, and my eyes closed.

The red dawn woke me with a splitting head and a neck so stiff that I felt as if the bones were welded together. My tongue was swollen, and my mouth felt foul. Then I reached out for Rheya, and my hand touched a cold sheet.

I sat up with a start.

I was alone − alone in bed and in the cabin. The concave window reflected a row of red suns. I dragged myself out of bed and staggered over to the bathroom, reeling like a drunkard and propping myself up on the furniture. It was empty. So was the workshop.

'Rheya!'

Calling, running up and down the corridor.

'Rheya!' I screamed, one last time, then my voice gave out. I already knew the truth . . .

I do not remember the exact sequence of events after that, as I stumbled half naked through all the length and breadth of the Station. It seems to me that I even went into the refrigeration section, searched through the storage rooms, hammered with my fists on bolted doors then came back again to throw myself against doors which had already resisted me. I half-fell down flights of steps, picked myself up and hurried onwards. When I reached the double armoured doors which opened into the ocean I was still calling, still hoping that it was a dream. Somebody was standing by me. Hands took hold of me and pulled me away.

I came to my senses again lying on a metal table in the little workshop and gasping for breath. My throat and nostrils were burning with some alcoholic vapour, my shirt was soaked in water, and my hair plastered over my skull.

Snow was busy at a medicine cupboard, shifting instruments and glass vessels which clattered with an unbearable din. Then his face appeared, looking gravely down into my eyes.

'Where is she?'

'She is not here.'

'But . . . Rheya . . .'

He bent over me, brought his face closer, and spoke very slowly and clearly:

'Rheya is dead.'

'She will come back.' I whispered.

Instead of dreading her return, I wanted it. I did not attempt to remind myself why I myself had once tried to drive her away, and why I had been so afraid of her return.

'Drink this.'

Snow held out a glass, and I threw it in his face. He staggered back, rubbing his eyes, and by the time he opened them again I was on my feet and standing over him. How small he was . . .

'It was you.'

'What do you mean?'

'Come on, Snow, you know what I mean. It was you who met her the other night. You told her to give me a sleeping pill . . . What has happened to her? Tell me!'

He felt in his shirt-pocket and took out an envelope. I snatched it out of his hand. It was sealed, and there was no inscription. Inside was a sheet of paper folded twice, and I recognized the sprawling, rather childish handwriting:

My darling, I was the one who asked him. He is a good man. I am sorry I had to lie to you. I beg you to give me this one wish – hear him out, and do nothing to harm yourself. You have been marvellous.

There was one more word, which she had crossed out, but I could see that she had signed 'Rheya'.

My mind was now absolutely clear. Even if I had wanted to scream hysterically, my voice had gone, and I did not even have the strength to groan.

'How . . . ?'

'Later, Kelvin. You've got to calm down.'

'I'm calm now. Tell me how.'

'Disintegration.'

'But . . . what did you use?'

'The Roche apparatus was unsuitable. Sartorius built something else, a new destabilizer. A miniature instrument, with a range of a few yards.'

'And she . . .'

'She disappeared. A pop, and a puff of air. That's all.'

'A short-range instrument . . .'

'Yes, we didn't have the resources for anything bigger.'

The walls loomed over me, and I shut my eyes.

'She will come back.'

'No.'

'What do you know about it?'

'You remember the wings of foam? Since that day, they do not come back.'

'You killed her,' I whispered.

'Yes . . . In my place, what else would you have done?'

I turned away from him and began pacing up and down the room. Nine steps to the corner. About turn. Nine more rapid steps, and I was facing Snow again.

'Listen, we'll write a report. We'll ask for an immediate link with the Council. It's feasible, and they'll accept – they must. The planet will no longer be subject to the four-power convention. We'll be authorized to use any means at our disposal. We can send for anti-matter generators. Nothing can stand up against them, nothing . . .' I was shouting now, and blinded with tears.

'You want to destroy it? Why?'

'Get out, leave me alone!'

'No, I won't get out.'

'Snow!' I glared at him, and he shook his head. 'What do you want? What am I supposed to do?'

He walked back to the table.

'Fine, we'll draw up a report.'

I started pacing again.

'Sit down!'

'I'll do what I like!'

'There are two distinct questions. One, the facts. Two, our recommendations.'

'Do we have to talk about it now?'

'Yes, now.'

'I won't listen, you hear? I'm not interested in your distinctions.'

'We sent our last message about two months ago, before Gibarian's death. We'll have to establish exactly how the "visitor" phenomena function . . .'

I grabbed his arm:

'Will you shut up!'

'Hit me if you like, but I will not shut up.'

'Oh, talk away, if it gives you pleasure . . .' I let him go.

'Good, listen. Sartorius will want to conceal certain facts. I'm almost certain of it.'

'And what about you? Won't you conceal anything?'

'No. Not now. This business goes further than individual responsibilities. You know that as well as I do. "It" has given a demonstration of considered activity. It is capable of carrying out organic synthesis on the most complex level, a synthesis we ourselves have never managed to achieve. It knows the structure, micro-structure and metabolism of our bodies . . .'

'All right . . . But why stop there? It has performed a series of . . .

experiments on us. Psychic vivisection. It has used knowledge which it stole from our minds without our consent.'

'Those are not facts, Kelvin. They are not even propositions. They are theories. You could say that it has taken account of desires locked into secret recesses of our brains. Perhaps it was sending us . . . presents.'

'Presents! My God!' I shook with a fit of uncontrollable laughter.

'Take it easy!' Snow took hold of my hand, and I tightened my grip until I heard bones cracking. He went on looking at me without any change of expression. I let go, and walked over to a corner of the workshop:

'I'll try to get hold of myself.'

'Yes, of course. I understand. What do we ask them?'

'I leave it to you . . . I can't think straight right now. Did she say anything – before?'

'No, nothing. If you want my opinion, from now on we stand a chance.'

'A chance? What chance?' I stared at him, and light suddenly dawned. 'Contact? Still Contact? Haven't you had enough of this madhouse? What more do you need? No, it's out of the question. Count me out!'

'Why not?' he asked quietly. 'You yourself instinctively treat it like a human being, now more than ever. You hate it.'

'And you don't?'

'No, Kelvin. It is blind' – I thought that I might not have heard him correctly – '. . . or rather it "sees" in a different way from ourselves. We do not exist for it in the same sense that we can exist for each other. We recognize one another by the appearance of the face and the body. That appearance is a transparent window to the ocean. It introduces itself directly into the brain.'

'Right, what if it does? What are you driving at? It succeeded in recreating a human being who exists only in my memory, and so accurately that her eyes, her gestures, her voice . . .'

'Don't stop. Talk.'

'I'm talking . . . Her voice . . . because it is able to read us like a book. You see what I mean?'

'Yes, that it could make itself understood.'

'Doesn't that follow?'

'No, not necessarily. Perhaps it used a formula which is not expressed in verbal terms. It may be taken from a recording imprinted on our minds, but a man's memory is stored in terms of nucleic acids etching asynchronous large-moleculed crystals. "It" removed the deepest, most isolated imprint, the most "assimilated" structure, without necessarily knowing what it meant to us. Suppose I'm capable of reproducing the architecture of a symmetriad, and I know its composition and have the requisite technology . . . I create a symmetriad and I drop it into the ocean. But I don't know why I'm doing so, I don't know its function, and I don't know what the symmetriad means to the ocean . . .'

'Yes. You may be right. In that case it wished us no harm, and it was not trying to destroy us. Yes, it's possible . . . and with no intention . . .'

My mouth began to tremble.

'Kelvin!'

'All right, don't get worried. You are kind, the ocean is kind. Everybody is kind. But why? Explain that. Why has it done this? What did you say . . . to her?'

'The truth.'

'I asked you what you said.'

'You know very well. Come back to my cabin and we'll write out the report. Come on.'

'Wait. What exactly do you want? You can't be intending to remain in the Station.'

'Yes, I want to stay.'

14

THE OLD MIMOID

I sat by the panoramic window, looking at the ocean. There was nothing to do now that the report, which had taken five days to compile, was only a pattern of waves in space. It would be months before a similar pattern would leave earth to create its own line of disturbance in the gravitational field of the galaxy towards the twin suns of Solaris.

Under the red sun, the ocean was darker than ever, and the horizon was obscured by a reddish mist. The weather was unusually close, and seemed to be building up towards one of the terrible hurricanes which broke out two or three times a year on the surface of the planet, whose sole inhabitant, it is reasonable to suppose, controlled the climate and willed its storms.

There were several months to go before I could leave. From my vantage point in the observatory I would watch the birth of the days – a disc of pale gold or faded purple. Now and then I would come upon the light of dawn playing among the fluid forms of some edifice risen from the ocean, watch the sun reflected on the silver sphere of a symmetriad, follow the oscillations of the graceful agiluses that curve in the wind, and linger to examine old powdery mimoids.

And eventually, the screens of all the videophones would start to blink and all the communications equipment would spring to life again, revived by an impulse originating billions of miles away and announcing the arrival of a metal colossus. The *Ulysses*, or it might be the *Prometheus*, would land on the Station to the piercing whine of its gravitators, and I would go out on to the flat roof to watch the squads of white, heavy-duty robots which proceed in all innocence with their tasks, not hesitating to destroy themselves or to destroy the unforeseen obstacle, in strict obedience to the orders etched into the crystals of their memory. Then the ship would rise noiselessly, faster than sound, leaving a sonic boom far behind over the ocean, and every passenger's face would light up at the thought of going home.

What did the word mean to me? Earth? I thought of the great bustling cities where I would wander and lose myself, and I thought of them as I had thought of the ocean on the second or third night, when I had wanted to throw myself upon the dark waves. I shall immerse myself among men. I shall be silent and attentive, an appreciative companion. There will be many acquaintances, friends, women – and perhaps even a wife. For a while, I shall have to make a conscious effort to smile, nod, stand and perform the thousands of little gestures which constitute life on Earth, and then those gestures will become reflexes again. I shall find new interests and occupations; and I shall not give myself completely to them, as I shall never again give myself completely to anything or anybody. Perhaps at night I shall stare up at the dark nebula that cuts off the light of the twin suns, and remember everything, even what I am thinking now. With a condescending, slightly rueful smile I shall remember my follies and my hopes. And this future Kelvin will be no less worthy a man than the Kelvin of the past, who was prepared for anything in the name of an ambitious enterprise called Contact. Nor will any man have the right to judge me.

Snow came into the cabin, glanced around, then looked at me again. I went over to the table:

'You wanted me?'

'Haven't you got anything to do? I could give you some work . . . calculations. Not a particularly urgent job . . .'

'Thanks,' I smiled, 'you needn't have bothered.'

'Are you sure?'

'Yes, I was thinking a few things over, and . . .'

'I wish you'd think a little less.'

'But you don't know what I was thinking about! Tell me something. Do you believe in God?'

Snow darted an apprehensive glance in my direction:

'What? Who still believes nowadays . . .'

'It isn't that simple. I don't mean the traditional God of Earth religion. I'm no expert in the history of religions, and perhaps this is nothing new – do you happen to know if there was ever a belief in an . . . imperfect god?'

'What do you mean by imperfect?' Snow frowned. 'In a way all the gods of the old religions were imperfect, considering that their attributes were amplified human ones. The God of the Old Testament, for instance, required humble submission and sacrifices, and was jealous of other gods. The Greek gods had fits of sulks and family quarrels, and they were just as imperfect as mortals . . .'

'No,' I interrupted. 'I'm not thinking of a god whose imperfection arises out of the candour of his human creators, but one whose imperfection represents his essential characteristic: a god limited in his omniscience and power, fallible, incapable of foreseeing the consequences of his acts, and creating things that lead to horror. He is a . . . sick god, whose ambitions exceed his powers and who does not realize it at first. A god who has created clocks, but not the time they measure. He has created systems or mechanisms that served specific ends but have now overstepped and betrayed them. And he has created eternity, which was to have measured his power, and which measures his unending defeat.'

Snow hesitated, but his attitude no longer showed any of the wary reserve of recent weeks:

'There was Manicheanism . . .'

'Nothing at all to do with the principle of Good and Evil,' I broke in immediately. 'This god has no existence outside of matter. He would like to free himself from matter, but he cannot . . .'

Snow pondered for a while:

'I don't know of any religion that answers your description. That kind of religion has never been . . . necessary. If I understand you, and I'm afraid I do, what you have in mind is an evolving god, who develops in the course of time, grows, and keeps increasing in power while remaining aware of his powerlessness. For your god, the divine condition is a situation without a goal. And understanding that, he despairs. But isn't this despairing god of yours mankind, Kelvin? It is a man you are talking about, and that is a fallacy, not just philosophically but also mystically speaking.'

I kept on:

'No, it's nothing to do with man. Man may correspond to my provisional definition from some points of view, but that is because the definition has a lot of gaps. Man does not create gods, in spite of appearances. The times, the age, impose them on him. Man can serve his age or rebel against it, but the target of his cooperation or rebellion comes to him from outside. If there was only a single human being in existence, he would apparently be able to attempt the experiment of creating his own goals in complete freedom – apparently, because a man not brought up among other human beings cannot become a man. And the being – the being I have in mind – cannot exist in the plural, you see?'

'Oh, then in that case . . .' He pointed out of the window.

'No, not the ocean either. Somewhere in its development it has probably come close to the divine state, but it turned back into itself too soon. It is more like an anchorite, a hermit of the cosmos, not a god. It repeats itself, Snow, and the being I'm thinking of would never do that. Perhaps he has already been born somewhere, in some corner of the galaxy, and soon he will have some childish enthusiasm that will set him putting out one star and lighting another. We will notice him after a while . . .'

'We already have,' Snow said sarcastically. 'Novas and supernovas. According to you they are the candles on his altar.'

'If you're going to take what I say literally . . .'

'And perhaps Solaris is the cradle of your divine child,' Snow went on, with a widening grin that increased the number of lines round his eyes. 'Solaris could be the first phase of the despairing God. Perhaps its intelligence will grow enormously. All the contents of our Solarist libraries could be just a record of his teething troubles . . .'

'. . . and we will have been the baby's toys for a while. It is possible. And do you know what you have just done? You've produced a completely new hypothesis about Solaris – congratulations! Everything suddenly falls into place: the failure to achieve contact, the absence of responses, various . . . let's say various peculiarities in its behaviour towards ourselves. Everything is explicable in terms of the behaviour of a small child.'

'I renounce paternity of the theory,' Snow grunted, standing at the window.

For a long instant, we stood staring out at the dark waves. A long pale patch was coming into view to the east, in the mist obscuring the horizon.

Without taking his eyes off the shimmering waste, Snow asked abruptly:

'What gave you this idea of an imperfect god?'

'I don't know. It seems quite feasible to me. That is the only god I could imagine believing in, a god whose passion is not a redemption, who saves nothing, fulfils no purpose – a god who simply is.'

'A mimoid,' Snow breathed.

'What's that? Oh yes, I'd noticed it. A very old mimoid.'

We both looked towards the misty horizon.

'I'm going outside,' I said abruptly. 'I've never yet been off the Station, and this is a good opportunity. I'll be back in half an hour.'

Snow raised his eyebrows:

'What? You're going out? Where are you going?'

I pointed towards the flesh-coloured patch half-hidden by the mist:

'Over there. What is there to stop me? I'll take a small helicopter. When I get back to Earth I don't want to have to confess that I'm a Solarist who has never set foot on Solaris!'

I opened a locker and started rummaging through the atmosphere-suits, while Snow looked on silently. Finally he said:

'I don't like it.'

I had selected a suit. Now I turned towards him:

'What?' I had not felt so excited for a long time. 'What are you worrying about? Out with it! You're afraid that I . . . I promise you I have no intention . . . it never entered my mind, honestly.'

'I'll go with you.'

'Thanks, but I'd rather go alone.' I pulled on the suit. 'Do you realize this will be my first flight over the ocean?'

Snow muttered something, but I could not make out what. I was in a hurry to get the rest of the gear together.

He accompanied me to the hangar deck, and helped me drag the flitter out on to the elevator disc. As I was checking my suit, he asked me abruptly:

'Can I rely on your word?'

'Still fretting? Yes, you can. Where are the oxygen tanks?'

We exchanged no further words. I slid the transparent canopy shut, gave him the signal, and he set the lift going. I emerged on to the Station roof; the motor burst into life; the three blades turned and the machine rose – strangely light – into the air. Soon the Station had fallen far behind.

Alone over the ocean, I saw it with a different eye. I was flying quite low, at about a hundred feet, and for the first time I felt a sensation often described by the explorers but which I had never noticed from the height of the Station: the alternating motion of the gleaming waves was not at all like the undulation of the sea or the billowing of clouds. It was like the crawling skin of an animal – the incessant, slow-motion contractions of muscular flesh secreting a crimson foam.

When I started to bank towards the drifting mimoid, the sun shone into my eyes and blood-red flashes struck the curved canopy. The dark ocean, flickering with sombre flames, was tinged with blue.

The flitter came around too wide, and I was carried a long way down wind from the mimoid, a long irregular silhouette looming out of the ocean. Emerging from the mist, the mimoid was no longer pink, but a yellowish grey. I lost sight of it momentarily, and glimpsed the Station, which seemed to be sitting on the horizon, and whose outline was reminiscent of an ancient zeppelin. I changed course, and the sheer mass of the mimoid grew in my line of vision – a baroque sculpture. I was afraid of crashing into the bulbous swellings, and pulled the flitter up so brutally that it lost speed and started to lurch; but my caution was unnecessary, for the rounded peaks of those fantastic towers were subsiding.

I flew past the island; and slowly, yard by yard, I descended to the level of the eroded peaks. The mimoid was not large. It measured about three quarters of a mile from end to end, and was a few hundred yards wide. In some places, it was close to splitting apart. This mimoid was obviously a fragment of a far larger formation. On the scale of Solaris it was only a tiny splinter, weeks or perhaps months old.

Among the mottled crags overhanging the ocean, I found a kind of beach, a sloping, fairly even surface a few yards square, and steered towards it. The rotors almost hit a cliff that reared up suddenly in my path, but I landed safely, cut the motor and slid back the canopy. Standing on the fuselage I made sure that there was no chance of the flitter sliding into the ocean. Waves were licking at the jagged bank about fifteen paces away, but the machine rested solidly on its legs, and I jumped to the 'ground'.

The cliff I had almost hit was a huge bony membrane pierced with holes, and full of knotty swellings. A crack several yards wide split this wall diagonally and enabled me to examine the interior of the island, already glimpsed through the apertures in the membrane. I edged warily on to the nearest ledge, but my boots showed no tendency to slide and the suit did not impede my movements, and I went on climbing until I had reached a height of about four storeys above the ocean, and could see a broad stretch of petrified landscape stretching back until it was lost from sight in the depths of the mimoid.

It was like looking at the ruins of an ancient town, a Moroccan city tens of centuries old, convulsed by an earthquake or some other disaster. I made out a tangled web of winding sidestreets choked with debris, and alleyways which fell abruptly towards the oily foam that floated close to the shore. In the middle distance, great battlements stood intact, sustained by ossified buttresses. There were dark openings in the swollen, sunken walls – traces of windows or loop-holes. The whole of this floating town canted to one side or another like a foundering ship, pitched and turned slowly, and the sun cast continually moving shadows, which crept among the ruined alleys. Now and again a polished surface caught and reflected the light. I took the risk of climbing higher, then stopped; rivulets of fine sand were beginning to trickle down the rocks above my head, cascading into ravines and alleyways and rebounding in swirling clouds of dust. The mimoid is not made of stone, and to dispel the illusion one only has to pick up a piece of it: it is lighter than pumice, and composed of small, very porous cells.

Now I was high enough to feel the swaying of the mimoid. It was moving forward, propelled by the dark muscles of the ocean towards an unknown destination, but its inclination varied. It rolled from side to side, and the languid oscillation was accompanied by the gentle rustling sound of the yellow and grey foam which streamed off the emerging shore. The mimoid had acquired its swinging motion long before, probably at its birth, and even while it grew and broke up it had retained its initial pattern.

Only now did I realize that I was not in the least concerned with the mimoid, and that I had flown here not to explore the formation but to acquaint myself with the ocean.

With the flitter a few paces behind me, I sat on the rough, fissured beach. A heavy black wave broke over the edge of the bank and spread out, not black, but a dirty green. The ebbing wave left viscous streamlets behind, which flowed back quivering towards the ocean. I went closer, and when the next wave came I held out my hand. What followed was a faithful reproduction of a phenomenon which had been analysed a century before: the wave hesitated, recoiled, then enveloped my hand without touching it, so that a thin covering of 'air' separated my glove inside a cavity which had been fluid a moment previously, and now had a fleshy consistency. I raised my hand slowly, and the wave, or rather an outcrop of the wave, rose at the same time, enfolding my hand in a translucent cyst with greenish reflections. I stood up, so as to raise my hand still higher, and the gelatinous substance stretched like a rope, but did not break. The main body of the wave remained motionless on the shore, surrounding my feet without touching them, like some strange beast patiently waiting for the experiment to finish. A flower had grown out of the ocean, and its calyx was moulded to my fingers. I stepped back. The stem trembled, stirred uncertainly and fell back into the wave, which gathered it and receded.

I repeated the game several times, until – as the first experimenter had observed – a wave arrived which avoided me indifferently, as if bored with a too familiar sensation. I knew that to revive the 'curiosity' of the ocean I would have to wait several hours. Disturbed by the phenomenon I had stimulated, I sat down again. Although I had read numerous accounts of it, none of them had prepared me for the experience as I had lived it, and I felt somehow changed.

In all their movements, taken together or singly, each of these branches reaching out of the ocean seemed to display a kind of cautious but not feral alertness, a curiosity avid for quick apprehension of a new, unexpected form, and regretful at having to retreat, unable to exceed the limits set by a mysterious law. The contrast was inexpressible between that lively curiosity and the shimmering immensity of the ocean that stretched away out of sight . . . I had never felt its gigantic presence so strongly, or its powerful changeless silence, or the secret forces that gave the waves their regular rise and fall. I sat unseeing, and sank into a universe of inertia, glided down an irresistible slope and identified myself with the dumb, fluid colossus; it was as if I had forgiven it everything, without the slightest effort of word or thought.

During that last week, I had been behaving so normally that Snow had stopped keeping a watchful eye on me. On the surface, I was calm: in secret, without really admitting it, I was waiting for something. Her return? How could I have been waiting for that? We all know that we are material creatures, subject to the laws of physiology and physics, and not even the power of all our feelings combined can defeat those laws. All we can do is detest them. The age-old faith of lovers and poets in the power of love, stronger than death, that *finis vitae sed non amoris*, is a lie, useless and not even funny. So must one be resigned to being a clock that measures the passage of time, now out of order, now repaired, and whose mechanism generates despair and love as soon as its maker sets it going? Are we to grow used to the idea that every man relives ancient torments, which are all the more profound because they grow comic with repetition? That human existence should repeat itself, well and good, but that it should repeat itself like a hackneyed tune, or a record a drunkard keeps playing as he feeds coins into the jukebox . . .

That liquid giant had been the death of hundreds of men. The entire human race had tried in vain to establish even the most tenuous links with it, and it bore my weight without noticing me any more than it would notice a speck of dust. I did not believe that it could respond to the tragedy of two human beings. Yet its activities did have a purpose ... True, I was not absolutely certain, but leaving would mean giving up a chance, perhaps an infinitesimal one, perhaps only imaginary ... Must I go on living here then, among the objects we both had touched, in the air she had breathed? In the name of what? In the hope of her return? I hoped for nothing. And yet I lived in expectation. Since she had gone, that was all that remained. I did not know what achievements, what mockery, even what tortures still awaited me. I knew nothing, and I persisted in the faith that the time of cruel miracles was not past.

The Chain of Chance

The last day was by far the longest and most drawn out. Not that I was nervous or scared; I had no reason to be. Surrounded by a multi-lingual crowd, I felt lonely the whole time. No one took any notice of me; even my escorts kept out of sight. Besides, they were total strangers to me. I should actually have felt relieved knowing that by tomorrow I would be shedding my false skin, because not for a moment did I believe I was tempting fate by sleeping in Adams's pyjamas, shaving with his razor, and retracing his steps around the bay. Nor was I expecting an ambush along the way – not the slightest harm had come to him on the highway – and during my one night in Rome I was to be given special protection. I was just anxious to get it over with, I told myself, now that the mission had proved a failure anyway. I told myself a lot of other sensible things, but that didn't stop me from continually upsetting my daily schedule.

After a trip to the baths I was scheduled to be back at the Vesuvio by three o'clock. But at twenty past two I was already heading towards the hotel as if hounded there by something. There was no chance of anything happening in my room, so I walked up and down the street for a while. I knew the neighbourhood inside out – the barbershop on the corner, the tobacconist's a few doors down, the travel agency, followed by the hotel parking lot set back in a row of houses. If you walked uphill past the hotel, you passed the boot shop where Adams had left the suitcase with the broken handle for repair – and a small, round-the-clock movie house. The first evening I almost ducked inside, after mistaking the rosy-pink spheres on the posters for planets. Not until I was standing in front of the box office did I notice my mistake: displayed on the poster was an enormous fanny. The stagnant heat was starting to get to me, so I hurried back to the corner and turned, to find a street vendor peddling his almonds – last year's supply of chestnuts had already run out. After scanning the selection of pipes in the window, I stepped into the tobacconist's and bought a pack of Kools, even though I was not in the habit of smoking menthols. The hoarse guttural sounds from the movie loudspeakers carried above the noisy traffic, reminding me of a slaughterhouse. Meanwhile the almond vendor had pushed his cart into the shade of the Vesuvio's sheltered driveway.

Everything testified to the gradual decline of what must have been an elegant hotel at one time. The lobby was practically deserted, and the inside of the elevator was cooler than my room. I scrutinized my surroundings. Packing in this heat would mean working up a good sweat, in which case the sensors wouldn't stick. I decided to pack in the bathroom, which in this old hotel was nearly as big as my room. The air in the bathroom was just as stuffy, but at least there was a marble floor. I took a shower in a tub supported by lions' paws; then, without drying off completely, standing barefoot to savour the coolness beneath my feet, I began stuffing things into my suitcases. While I was filling my toilet kit, I came across something solid. The automatic. It had completely slipped my mind. At that moment I would have liked nothing better than to ditch it under the bathtub; instead I buried it in the larger suitcase, under my shirts, then carefully dried off the skin around my chest and stood before the mirror to attach the sensors. There had been a time when my body used to show marks in these places, but they were gone now. To attach the first electrode I located my heart's apex beat between my ribs, but the other electrode refused to stick in the region of the clavicular fossa. I dried off the skin a second time and fixed some tape on either side, so the sensor wouldn't stick out beyond the collarbone. I was new at this game; I'd never had to do it on my own before. Next: shirt, pants and suspenders. I'd started wearing suspenders after my return trip to earth. I was more comfortable that way, because I didn't have to keep reaching for my pants, which always felt as if they were on the verge of falling. When you're in orbit your clothes are weightless, but as soon as you're back on earth the 'trousers reflex' sets in; hence the suspenders.

I was ready. I had the whole plan down pat. Three-quarters of an hour for lunch, taking care of the bill, and picking up the car keys; a half hour to reach the highway, which allowed for rush-hour traffic with ten minutes to spare. I checked the chest of drawers, set my luggage down by the door, splashed some cold water on my face, made a final inspection in the mirror to make sure the sensors weren't visible, and took the elevator downstairs. The restaurant was already packed. A waiter dripping with sweat set a bottle of chianti down in front of me, and I ordered a spaghetti dish with a basil sauce, and a Thermos of coffee. I'd just finished my meal and was checking the time when a garbled message came over the loudspeaker: 'Telephone call for Mr Adams!' I watched as the tiny bristles lining the back of my hands stood on end. Should I go to the phone, or shouldn't I? A barrel-bellied man in a peacock-blue shirt got up from a small table by the window and headed for the telephone booth. Somebody else with the same name. Adams was certainly a common enough name. I realized now it was a false alarm, but I was still annoyed with myself: it turned out my composure was only skin deep. I wiped my mouth to get rid of the olive oil, swallowed a bitter-tasting pill, washed it down with the rest of the wine, and got up to go to the reception desk. The hotel still prided itself on its plush furniture, stucco ornaments, and velvet coverings, though it wasn't hard to detect various kitchen odours coming from the back. The hotel. an aristocrat belching with sauerkraut.

That was the extent of my farewell. A porter carried out my bags, and I followed him into the stubborn heat. A Hertz rental car was waiting, with two wheels rolled up on to the kerb. A Hornet, black as a hearse. I stopped the porter just in time from loading my luggage into the trunk, where I had a hunch the transmitter was stored, and sent him on his way with a tip. Climbing into the car was like climbing into an oven. I immediately broke out in a sweat and reached into my pocket for the gloves. Unnecessary, since the steering wheel was up-holstered with leather. The trunk turned out to be empty — so where could they have put the amplifier? It was lying on the floorboard on the passenger's side, hidden underneath a magazine that was spread out in such a way that a naked blonde on the cover lay staring up at me passively, with her moist and shiny tongue hanging out. I made no sound, but something inside me quietly groaned as I began merging with the heavy traffic. A solid line from one light to the next. Even though I'd slept enough, I felt moody and on edge, first grouchy and then a little giddy. That's what I got for eating all that damned spaghetti, which I normally couldn't stand. It was always the same: the greater the danger, the more weight I'd put on. At the next intersection I turned on the blower, which immediately began bubbling with exhaust fumes. I switched it off. Cars were lined up bumper to bumper, Italian style. A detour. In both mirrors nothing but car roofs and automobile hoods, *la potente benzina italiana* stank of carbon monoxide, and I was stalled behind a bus, trapped in its smelly exhaust fumes. Some kids, all wearing the same green caps, sat gawking at me through the rear window. My stomach felt like a lump of dough, my head was on fire, and stuck to my heart was a sensor that caught on my suspenders every time I turned the wheel. I broke open a package of Kleenex and stuck a few tissues on top of the steering column. My nose was starting to tickle the way it always did before a storm. I sneezed once, twice, and soon was so busy sneezing I lost track of ever having left Naples, now fading in the azure coastal sky. I was cruising along the Strada del Sole now. Traffic was pretty light for the rush hour, but it was as if I'd never taken the Plimasine: my eyes were tingling and my nose was running, though my mouth was dry. I could have used some coffee, though I'd already drunk two cappuccinos back at the hotel, but the first coffee break wasn't till Magdalena. The *Herald* wasn't on the stands again because of some strike or other. While I was boxed in between some smoking Fiats and a Mercedes, I turned on the radio. It was a news broadcast, though most of it was lost on me. Some demonstrators had set fire to a building. One of the security guards was interviewed. The feminist underground promised more demonstrations in the future; then a woman, speaking in a deep alto, read a proclamation by the terrorists condemning the Pope, followed by various voices of the press . . .

A women's underground. Nothing took one by surprise any more. People had lost all capacity to be surprised. What were they fighting against, anyhow? The tyranny of men? I didn't feel like a tyrant, any more than others did. Woe to the playboys! What were they planning to do to them? Would they wind up kidnapping the clergy, too? I shut off the radio as if slamming shut a garbage chute.

To have been in Naples and not seen Vesuvius – it was almost unforgivable of me. All the more so since I'd always been amiably disposed towards volcanoes. Half a century ago my father used to tell me bedtime stories about them. I'm turning into an old man, I thought, and was as stunned by this last thought as if I'd said I was on the verge of becoming a cow. Volcanoes were something solid, something that inspired trust. The earth erupts, lava spills, houses collapse. Everything looks so marvellous and simple to a five-year-old. I was sure you could reach the centre of the earth by climbing down a crater, though my father had disputed that. Too bad he died when he did; he'd have been so proud of me. You don't have time to contemplate the terrifying silence of those infinite expanses when you're listening to the marvellous sound of the couplers as they moor the space vehicle to the module. Granted, my career had been a short one, and all because I'd proved myself unworthy of Mars. He'd have taken the news a lot harder than I did. What the hell – would you rather have had him die right after your first flight, so he could have closed his eyes still believing in you? Now, was that cynical or just plain petty of me? Better keep your eyes on the road.

As I was squeezing in behind a psychedelic-painted Lancia, I glanced in the mirror. Not a sign of the Hertz-rented Chrysler. Something had flashed back in the vicinity of Marianelli, but I couldn't be sure, because the other car had dropped out of sight again. On me alone did this short and monotonous highway, now teeming with an energetic mob on wheels, bestow the privilege of its secret, a secret that had uncannily eluded the police of both the old and new worlds combined. I alone had in my car trunk an air mattress, a surfboard and a badminton racket intended not for sport and recreation but for inviting a treacherous blow from out of the unknown. I tried to get a little worked up, but the whole affair had ceased to be an adventure, had lost its charm. My thoughts were no longer on the mystery of the deadly conspiracy, only on whether it was time for another Plimasine to stop my constantly runny nose. I didn't care any more where the Chrysler was; besides, the transmitter had a hundred-mile range. My grandmother once had had a pair of bloomers on the attic line matching the colour of that Lancia.

At six-twenty I began stepping on the gas. For a while I stayed behind a Volkswagen with a pair of sheep's eyes painted on the back that kept staring at me in tender reproach. The car is an amplifier of the personality. Later I cut in behind a fellow countryman from Arizona with a bumper sticker that read: HAVE A NICE DAY. In front and in back of me were cars piled high with outboards, water skis, golf bags, fishing gear, paddle boards, and bundles in all shapes and colours including orange and raspberry-red: Europe was doing its damnedest to 'have a nice day'. I held up my right hand and then my left one, as I'd done so many times in the past, and examined my outstretched fingers. Not one of them was shaking. They say that's the first sign. But who's to say for sure? No one can claim to be an authority in such matters. If I held my breath for a whole minute, Randy would certainly panic. What a half-assed idea!

A viaduct. The air made a flapping noise along the concrete uprights. I stole a glance at the scenery, a marvellous panorama of desolate green stretching all the way to the mountains that framed the horizon. A Ferrari as flat as a bedbug chased me out of the fast lane, and I broke out in another fit of sneezing that sounded more like swearing. My windshield was dotted with the remains of flies, my pant legs were sticking to my calves and the glare from the wipers was killing my eyes. As I went to blow my nose, the package of Kleenex slipped down into the gap between the front seats and made a rustling noise. Who can describe that still-life spectacle that takes place in orbit? Just when you think you've got everything tied, secured, magnetized, and taped down with adhesive, the real show begins – that whirling swarm of felt-tip pencils, eyeglasses and the loose ends of cables writhing about in space like lizards. Worst of all were the crumbs, hunting for crumbs with a vacuum cleaner . . .

Or dandruff. The hidden background of mankind's cosmic steps was usually passed over in silence. Only children would dare to ask how you pee on the moon.

The mountains loomed up brown and sturdy, serene and somehow familiar. One of earth's more scenic spots. When the road later changed direction, the sun started shifting around the car's interior in a rectangular pattern, reminding me of the silent and majestic rotation of light inside the cabin. Day lurking within night, the one merging with the other as before the creation of the world, and then man's dream of flying becomes a reality, and the body's confusion, its dismay when the impossible becomes possible . . .

Although I'd attended a number of lectures on motion sickness, I had my own thoughts on the subject. Motion sickness was no ordinary attack of nausea, but a panic of the intestines and the spleen; though not usually conspicuous, they protested. Their bewilderment evoked only pity in me. All the time we were enjoying the cosmos, it was making them sick. They couldn't take it from the start. When we insisted on dragging them there, they revolted, though training obviously helped. But even if a bear can be taught to ride a bicycle, that doesn't mean he's cut out for it. The whole thing was ridiculous. We kept at it till the cerebral congestion and hardening of the intestines went away, but that was only postponing the inevitable: sooner or later we had to come back down. After landing on earth we had to put up with the excruciating pressure, the painful ordeal of having to unbend our knees and backs, and the sensation of having our heads spin around like bullets. I was fully aware of the effects, because I'd often seen athletically trained men made so uncomfortable by their inability to move that they would have to be lowered into tubs where they could be momentarily freed of bodily weight. Damned if I know what made me think it'd be any different with me.

According to that bearded psychologist, my own case was not exceptional. But even after you regained your sense of gravity, the experience of orbital weightlessness would come back to haunt you as a kind of nostalgia. We're not meant for the cosmos, and for that very reason we'll never give up.

A flashing red signal travelled straight to my foot, short-circuiting my brain. My tyres made a crunching sound as they rolled over something like spilled rice, only bigger, like hailstones, which turned out to be glass. Traffic was slowing down to a crawl; the right lane was blocked off with traffic cones. I tried to get a glimpse beyond the line-up of cars and caught sight of a yellow helicopter in the process of making a slow landing in a field, the dust swirling under its fuselage like flour. On the ground lay two metal hulks, their hoods up and their front ends rammed into each other. But why so far off the road? And why were there no people around? Again the sound of glass crunching under tyres as we drove at a snail's pace past a line of policemen waving us on with the words 'Faster, faster!' Police helmets, ambulances, stretchers, an overturned car with one wheel still spinning and its directional signal still blinking . . . The highway was under a cloud of smoke. From burning asphalt? More likely gasoline. Cars began switching back to the right lane, and breathing became easier as soon as traffic started picking up speed. A death toll of forty had been predicted. Soon an elevated restaurant came into view. Next door the sparks of a welder's torch lit up the dark interior of the car repair shops located inside the sprawling *area di servizio*. Judging by my odometer, Cassino was the next exit. At the first bend in the road, my nose suddenly stopped tickling: the Plimasine had finally worked its way through the spaghetti.

Another curve. At one point I had the chilling sensation of being stared at from below, as if someone were lying on his back and watching my every move from underneath the car seat. The sun had fallen on the magazine cover featuring the blonde with the tongue on display. Without taking my eyes from the road I leaned forward and flipped the magazine over. For an astronaut you lead a pretty rich inner life – I was told by the psychologist after the Rorschach test. I couldn't remember which of us had started up the conversation, he or I. There were two kinds of anxiety, he claimed – one high, the other low, the first coming from the imagination, the second straight from the guts. Was he serious, or was he just trying to console me by implying I was too sensitive?

A hazy, washed-out film was all that was left of the clouds. Gradually a gas station drew near. I was just slowing down when some crazy old sport, his long hair blowing in the wind, raced ahead of me with a lot of racket and show in a broken-down Votan. I branched off towards the pumps, and while the tank was being filled I finished the rest of the Thermos, with its yellowish-brown residue of sugar at the bottom. No one bothered to wipe off the oil and blood spots on the window. After pulling up next to a construction site, I climbed out of the driver's seat and stretched my bones. Not far from where I was parked stood the glass-walled shopping pavilion where Adams had stopped to buy a deck of cards, imitation of Italian tarot cards dating from the eighteenth or nineteenth century. The station was in the process of being expanded; a mound of white, unlaid gravel stood surrounding a trench that had been dug out for a new gas pump. A glass door parted and I went inside the shop, which turned out to be deserted. Was it siesta time, I wondered? No, it was too late in the day for that. I wandered in and out of stacks of gaudy boxes and artificial fruit. A white escalator going to the second floor started moving whenever I came near it but stopped the moment I walked away. I saw a profile of myself on the television monitor installed near the front windows. The black-and-white picture flickered in the sunlight and made me look paler than usual. Not a clerk in sight. The shelves were piled high with cheap souvenirs and stacks of postcards all of the same variety. I reached into my pocket for some change. While looking around for a clerk, I heard the crunching of gravel under tyres. A white Opel skidded to a halt, and out stepped a blonde in a pair of jeans who made her way around the ditches and into the shop. Though my back was turned, I could see her on the television monitor. She was standing perfectly still, only a dozen or so steps in back of me. From the counter I picked up a facsimile of an ancient woodcut showing a smoking Vesuvius towering above the bay. On the same counter were some cards featuring reproductions of Pompeian frescoes of the sort that would have shocked our fathers. The blonde took a few steps towards me as if trying to make up her mind whether I was a salesclerk. The escalator began moving without a sound, but the tiny figure in pants kept her distance.

I turned around and started for the exit. So far nothing out of the ordinary. She had a childlike face, a blank expression in the eyes, a delicate little mouth. Only once did I slow down while passing her; it was when she fixed me with those gaping eyes of hers, at the same time scratching the neck of her blouse with her fingernail; then she keeled over backward without uttering a sound or batting an eyelash. I was so unprepared for this reaction that before I could lunge towards her she slumped to the floor. Unable to catch her, I managed only to break her fall by grabbing hold of her bare arms as if helping her stretch out on her back of her own free will. She lay there, stiff as a doll. Anyone looking in from the outside would have thought I was kneeling beside an overturned dummy, several of which stood in the windows on either side of me, dressed in Neapolitan costumes. I grabbed her wrist; her pulse was weak but steady. Her teeth were partly showing, and the whites of her eyes were visible as if she were sleeping on her back with her eyelids half open. Less than a hundred metres away, cars were pulling up to the pumps, then wheeling around again and rejoining the steady stream of traffic roaring along the del Sole. Only two cars were parked out in front – mine and the girl's. Slowly I got up and gazed down at the figure stretched out on the floor. Her forearm, the one whose slender wrist I had just let go of, swung limply to one side; as it pulled the rest of the arm along with it and exposed the light-blonde hairs lining her armpit, I noticed two tiny marks resembling scratches or a miniature tattoo. I had seen similar marks once before, on concentration-camp prisoners – runic signs of the SS. But these looked more like an ordinary birthmark. I had the urge to kneel down again but checked the impulse and headed for the exit instead. As if to emphasize the fact that the scene was over, the escalator suddenly came to a stop. On my way out I threw a final backward glance. A bunch of brightly coloured balloons stood in the way, but I could still see her prostrate body on the far television screen. The picture jiggled, but I could have sworn it was she who moved. I waited two or three seconds more, but nothing happened. The glass door obligingly let me pass; I jumped across the mounds, climbed into the Hornet and backed up so I could make out the Opel's licence plate. It was a German plate. A golf club was sticking up out of a motley pile of junk crammed into the back seat.

After merging with the traffic, I found I now had other thoughts to occupy me. The whole thing had the appearance of a quiet epileptic fit, *un petit mal*. Such attacks were not uncommon, even without convulsions. She might have felt the first symptoms coming on, decided to stop the car, then once inside the pavilion suddenly fainted. That would explain the blank stare and that insectlike movement of the fingers as she went to scratch the neck of her blouse. Then again, there was always the possibility of a simulation. I couldn't recall having seen her Opel along the way, but then I hadn't been that observant; besides, there was no telling how many Opels I'd come across with the same white finish and rectangular lines. I went over every detail in my mind, re-examining each as if through a magnifying glass. A shop like that must have had at least two if not three attendants on duty. Had they all gone out for a drink at the same time? Strange. Though nowadays even that was possible. Maybe they'd ducked out to a café, knowing that no customer would drop in at the pavilion at that time of day. And the girl must have thought it better to have the attack there, rather than at the station, where she had no intention of creating a scene for the benefit of those fellows in the Supercortemaggiori overalls. That all seemed logical enough, maybe even a bit too logical. She was travelling alone. Now what person in her condition would risk travelling alone? Even if she'd pulled out of it, I wouldn't have let her get behind the wheel again; I'd have advised her to leave the Opel parked where it was and to climb into my car. Anyone in my shoes would have done the same. That's exactly what I would have done if I had been just a tourist.

The heat was beginning to get to me. I should have stayed behind and let myself fall into the trap – assuming it *was* a trap. That's what I was here for, damn it! The more convinced I became that her fainting spell had been real, the less sure I was of it. And not only where her fainting spell was concerned. People just don't leave a shopping pavilion unattended like that, not when it's nearly the size of a department store. At least there should have been a cashier behind the register. But even the cashier's desk had been empty. True, the inside of the store was clearly visible from the little café that stood facing it across the ditches. But who could have guessed that I would be going in there? No one. Anyway, it wasn't I they were after – unless I was singled out as an anonymous victim. If so, then whose victim? Unless they were all in on it together – the attendants, the cashier, the girl. But that struck me as being too far-fetched. A pure coincidence, then. So we were back where we'd started. Adams had driven all the way to Rome without incident. Alone, too. But what about the others? Suddenly I remembered the golf club in the Opel. Good Lord, those were the same kind of clubs that . . .

I was determined to get a firm grip on myself, even if I'd already made a fool of myself. Like a bad but stubborn actor, I went back to playing the role I'd flubbed so miserably. At the next gas station I asked for an inner tube without getting out of the car. A handsome, dark-haired man inspected my tyres. 'You're driving tubeless, sir.' But I was adamant. While I paid for the tube, I kept one eye on the highway so I wouldn't miss the Chrysler. Not a sign of it. Fourteen kilometres down the road I replaced one of the good tyres with the spare. I did it because Adams had made a tyre change. As I crouched down beside the jack, the heat finally caught up with me. The jack needed oiling and squeaked. Overhead the sky was rent by the screeching roar of invisible jets, reminding me of the barrage of ship artillery covering the Normandy bridgehead. What made me think of that now? Later I had made another trip to Europe, this time as an official showpiece, as one of the crew from the Mars mission – though, as a backup pilot, only a second-rate, make-believe one. In those days Europe had shown me its more flattering side, whereas only now was I getting to know it if not better then at least more informally: the pissy back streets of Naples, the gruesome-looking prostitutes, even the hotel still boasting of its starlets but inwardly decayed and infested with street hustlers; the porno house, which once upon a time would have been unthinkable alongside such a shrine. But maybe it was the other way around. Maybe there was some truth to the rumour that Europe was rotting from above, from the top.

The metal panelling and tool kit were blazing hot. I cleaned my hands with some cleansing cream, wiped them dry with Kleenex, then climbed back into the car. At the last station I'd bought a bottle of Schweppes, but it took me a while to open it, because I couldn't lay my hands on the pocketknife with the bottle opener. As I swallowed the bitter liquid I thought of Randy, who was listening to me drink while driving along somewhere on the highway. The headrest was scorching hot from the sun's rays, and the back of my neck felt baked to a crisp. A metallic sheen lay shimmering on the asphalt near the horizon like a pool of water. Was that thunder in the distance? Sure enough, a thunderstorm. Most likely it was thundering that time the jets had roared across the sky, and the constant drone of the highway had drowned out the storm's fainter rumblings. Now everything was drowned out by the thunder, which cracked through the yellow-gold clouds till a pall of strident yellow hung over the mountains.

Some road signs announced the approach of Frosinone. Sweat was trickling down my back as if someone were running a feather between my shoulder blades. The storm, displaying all the theatricality of the Italians, rumbled menacingly without shedding a drop of rain, while grey tufts of cloud drifted across the landscape like an autumnal haze. Once, as I was starting around a winding curve, I could see where a long diagonal column was trying to pull a cloud down to the road. The sound of the first heavy drops splattering on the windshield was a welcome relief. Suddenly I was caught in a furious downpour.

By this time my windshield had become a battlefield. I waited a while before turning on the wipers. When the last of the insect debris had been washed away, I switched off the wipers and pulled over to the shoulder of the road, where I was supposed to stay parked for a full hour. The rain came in sheets and pounded on the roof, and the passing cars left blurry streaks of iridescent drops and billowing sprays of water in their tracks, while I just sat back and relaxed. Soon the water came trickling through the side vent on to my knee. I lit a cigarette, cupping it with my palm to keep it dry. The menthol left a bad taste in my mouth. A silver-coloured Chrysler drove by, but the windshield was so flooded with water I couldn't be sure it was the right one. The sky was turning darker. First came the lightning, then peals of thunder cracking like sheet metal that was being ripped apart. To pass the time I counted the seconds between a bolt of lightning and a clap of thunder. The highway rumbled and roared; nothing could silence it. The hands on my watch showed it was past seven: it was time. I got out reluctantly. At first the cold rain shower was uncomfortable, but after a while it felt invigorating. All the time I pretended to be fixing the windshield wipers, I kept glancing out on to the road. No one seemed to take any notice of me; not one patrol car came my way. Soaked to my skin, I got back into the car and drove off.

Even though the storm was starting to ease up, it was getting darker by the moment. Past Frosinone the rain let up completely, the road was drier, and the puddles lying on either side of the road gave off a low white steam that mingled with the headlight beams. Finally, as if the land were eager to show itself in a new light before nightfall, the sun came out from behind the clouds. With everything cast in an eerie pink glow, I drove the car into the parking lot of a Pavesi restaurant arching above the highway. After unsticking my shirt from my body to make the sensors less noticeable, I went upstairs. I hadn't noticed the Chrysler in the lot. Upstairs, people were babbling away in ten different languages and eating without so much as a glance at the cars shooting by down below like bowling balls. At some point, though I couldn't say exactly when, a sudden calm came over me, and I gave up worrying. It was as if the incident with the girl had taken place years ago. I relaxed over a couple of cups of coffee and a glass of Schweppes with lemon, and might have gone on relaxing if it hadn't dawned on me that the building was made of reinforced concrete: the interference might have made them lose track of my heartbeat. When you're transmitting between Houston and the moon, you don't have to worry about such problems. On my way out I washed my hands and face in the rest room, smoothed my hair in front of the mirror with a look of self-annoyance, then drove off again.

I still had some time to kill, so I drove as though the horse knew the way and all I had to do was to let up on the reins. I neither wandered in my thoughts nor passed the time daydreaming, but just switched off and pretended I wasn't there – 'the vegetable life', I used to call it. Still, I must have been somewhat alert, because I managed to stop the car right on schedule. It was a good place to park, situated just below the summit of a gentle rise where the highway knifed through the top of the ridge like a perfect geometric incision. Through this slitlike opening I could see all the way to the horizon, where, with resolute energy, the asphalt strip cut straight across the next sloping hump. The one closest to me looked like a sighting notch, the one farthest like a rifle bead. Before cleaning the windshield I first had to open the trunk, because I'd already used up the last of the Kleenex. I touched the suitcase's soft bottom, where the weapon was resting peacefully. As though by some unconscious design, practically all the headlights went on at the same time. I scanned the broad expanse below. The route to Naples was streaked with patches of white that turned progressively redder as one approached Rome, where the road was now a bed of glowing coals. At the bottom of the grade, drivers were having to use their brakes, transforming that particular stretch into a vibrant strip of shimmering red – a pretty example of a stationary wave. If the road had been three times as wide, it could have been a road in Texas or Montana. Though standing only a few steps away from the edge of the road, I felt so alone I was overcome by a serene calm. People need grass every bit as much as goats do, and no one knows that better than the goats. As soon as I heard a helicopter churning through the invisible sky, I tossed my cigarette away and got into the car, whose warm interior still preserved traces of the afternoon heat.

Stark neon lights beyond the hills announced the approach of Rome. I still had some driving ahead of me, because my instructions were to circle the city first. The growing darkness obscured the faces of the people in the other cars, and the things piled high on the roofs took on weird and mysterious shapes. Everything was assuming a grave and impersonal aspect, full of hidden implications, as if matters of an extremely urgent nature were waiting at the road's end. Every backup astronaut has to be a little bit of a bastard, because something in him is always waiting for the regulars to slip up, and if not, then he's a stupid ass. I had to make another stop. The coffee in combination with the Plimasine, Schweppes and ice water did the trick. I left the side of the road on foot and was struck by the surroundings. Not only the traffic but time along with it seemed to fade. Standing with my back to the highway, and despite the exhaust fumes, I could make out the scent of flowers in the gently fluttering breeze. What would I have done now if I were thirty? No sense brooding over such questions; better to button your fly and get behind the wheel again. The ignition key slipped between my fingers, and I fumbled around in the dark for it between the pedals, not wanting to switch on the interior light. As I drove along, I felt neither drowsy nor alert, neither edgy nor relaxed, but somehow strange, vulnerable, even a little astonished. The light from the lampposts streamed through the front windshield, turning my hands on the steering wheel white, then gradually retreated to the back of the car. Billboards came and went like phantoms, the concrete road joints drummed softly underneath. Now to the right, to pick up the city bypass that would bring me out on to the same northern route Adams had used to enter the city. He no longer meant anything to me now. He was just one case out of eleven. It was just a fluke that I'd inherited his things. Randy had insisted on it, and he was right: if you're going to do a job, then do it properly. The fact that I was using a dead man's shirts and luggage didn't faze me in the slightest, and if it was a little hard going at first, then it was only because these things belonged to a stranger, not because their owner was dead. While driving down a lonely and deserted stretch, I kept feeling that something was missing. The windows were rolled down, and the breeze brought the smell of flowers in bloom. Luckily the grasses had already retired for the night. Not once did I have the sniffles. They could talk all they liked about psychology; in the end it was the hay fever that had been the deciding factor. Of that I was sure, even though they'd tried to make me believe otherwise. What they'd said made sense, I suppose, because since when does grass grow on Mars? Besides, being allergic to dust is not a defect. Even so, somewhere in my files, in the space reserved for comments, they must have written the word 'allergic' – in other words, defective. Because of that diagnosis I became a backup astronaut – a pencil sharpened with the best possible instruments so that in the end it couldn't be used to make a single dot. A backup Christopher Columbus, as it were.

I was being blinded now by a steady stream of oncoming traffic; I tried closing one eye and then the other. Had I taken the wrong route? I couldn't find a single exit. A mood of apathy came over me: I had no choice but to keep driving through the night. A towering billboard sign lit at an angle read ROMA TIBERINA. So I was headed in the right direction, after all. The closer I got to the downtown area, the more congested were the lights and traffic. Luckily all the hotels on my itinerary were located close to one another. At each of them I was greeted by the same gesture of outstretched hands – 'The season! No vacancy!' – forcing me to get behind the wheel again. At the last hotel there was a vacancy, but I asked for a quiet room in one of the side wings. The porter gave me an inquisitive look; I shook my head with regret and walked back to the car.

The empty sidewalk in front of the Hilton was flooded with light. As I climbed out of the car I couldn't see the Chrysler anywhere, and it occurred to me that they might have had an accident, which would have explained why I hadn't seen them on the road. I routinely slammed the car door shut, and as I did I caught a glimpse of the Chrysler's front end in a fleeting reflection in the window. It was parked just outside the lot in the shadows, between the chains and a NO PARKING sign. On my way back into the hotel I could make out the car's dark interior, which looked to be deserted, though one of its windows was rolled down. When I came to within five paces of the car, the head of a cigarette lit up the interior. I felt an impulse to wave but resisted, giving my hand only a slight jerk before sticking it back into my pocket and entering the lobby. This was just a minor incident, magnified by the fact that one chapter was over and another was beginning. The cold night air lent everything a marvellous clarity – the car trunks in the parking lot, the sound of my footsteps, the sidewalk markings – which made my inability to wave even more frustrating. Till now I'd stuck to my timetable as faithfully as a school kid, not giving a single thought to the guy who'd driven the same route before me, stopped off at the same places, taken the same number of coffee breaks and made the same rounds of the hotels so that he could wind up here, at the Hilton, which he would never leave again alive. At that moment my assumed role struck me as something of a mockery, a wilful defiance of fate.

A young punk, swaggering with self-importance, or perhaps only disguising his drowsiness, followed me out to the car, where he grabbed hold of the dusty suitcases with gloved hands while I smiled absently at his shiny buttons. The lobby was deserted. Another bruiser loaded my luggage into the elevator, which travelled upstairs to the sounds of piped music. I was still feeling the rhythm of the road, which, like a haunting tune, I couldn't shake off. The bellboy stopped, opened a set of double doors, switched on the wall light and overhead lamp, and turned on the living-room and bedroom lights; as soon as he was finished arranging my bags, I was alone again. Though Naples and Rome were no farther than a handshake away from each other, I felt tired, but it was a tiredness of a different kind, more tense, and that came as the next surprise. It was as if I'd polished off a can of beer in spoonfuls – a kind of stupefying sobriety. I made a tour of the rooms. The bed reached all the way to the floor, so there was no point in playing hide-and-seek. I opened all the closet doors, knowing ahead of time I wouldn't surprise any assassins because that would have been too easy, but I did my duty anyway. I lifted the sheets, the double mattress and then the headrest, though I didn't seriously believe I'd never get up out of this bed again. Oh, yeah? Man is an undemocratic institution. His brain centre, those voices from the right and the left, are nothing but a sham legislature, because there are also the catacombs, which bully him. The gospel according to Freud. I checked the air conditioner, then tested the blinds by raising and lowering them a few times. The room ceilings were plain and cheerful, unlike those at the Three Witches Inn, where the element of danger was so grimly conspicuous and where the bed canopy looked as if any moment it might collapse and smother you. Here there was no canopy, none of that syrupy, romantic atmosphere. Here everything – armchairs, desk, carpets – was neatly arranged in the usual display of comfort. Had I turned off the headlights?

The windows faced the other way, so I couldn't see the car. I was pretty sure I'd switched them off, and if not, well . . . let Hertz worry about it. I closed the curtains and started getting undressed, not caring where my shirt and pants landed. When I was completely stripped, I carefully detached the sensors. After taking a shower I'd have to stick them on again. I opened the larger suitcase, the one with the Band-Aid box lying on top, but I couldn't find the scissors. Standing in the middle of the room, I could feel a slight pressure in my head and the soft carpet pile beneath my feet. Then I remembered – I'd slipped them into my briefcase. Impatiently I yanked at the clasp, and out fell the scissors, along with a relic of the past – a photo of Sinus Aurorae, mounted in a Plexiglass frame and looking as yellow as the Sahara: landing site number 1, the one I never made it to. On the carpet, next to my bare feet, it looked embarrassing, silly, full of nasty innuendo. I picked it up and studied it in the white light of the overhead lamp: ten degrees north latitude by fifty-two degrees east longitude, the patch of Bosporus Gemmatus at the top and the tropical formation below. The places I was to have reconnoitred on foot. I stood there with the photo in my hand, but instead of putting it back into my suitcase, I laid it down on the nightstand, next to the telephone, and went into the bathroom.

It was a jewel of a shower; the water came shooting out in a hundred hot streams. Civilization began with the invention of running water, with the lavatories of King Minos on Crete. For his tombstone one of the Pharaohs ordered a brick made of all the dirt that had been scraped from his skin over the period of a lifetime. And there has always been something vaguely symbolic about washing the body. When I was a teenager, if there was anything wrong with my car I used to put off washing it till after some work had been done to it, restoring its honour with a good wax job. For what could I have known then about the symbolic rites of purity and impurity and the fact that they had survived in all religions? In expensive apartments the only things I care about are the bathrooms. A person feels only as good as his skin. In the full-length mirror I caught a glimpse of my soap-covered body still showing the imprint left by the electrode, almost as if I were back in Houston. My hips were still white from the swimming trunks. When I turned up the water, the pipes let out a mournful howl. The computation of turbulent flow that causes no resonances is still one of the seemingly unsolvable problems of hydraulics. What a lot of useless facts.

When I had finished drying off, not being too choosy which towel I used, I walked back into the bedroom stark naked, leaving a trail of wet footprints as I went. I taped on the heart electrode, but instead of lying down I sat on the edge of the bed and did some quick calculations: seven cups of coffee, counting what was in the Thermos. I never used to have any trouble going to sleep, but lately I'd acquired the habit of tossing from side to side. In one of my suitcases, unknown to Randy, I'd stashed some Seconal, a medicine prescribed for astronauts. Adams had never used the stuff, being apparently a sound sleeper. For me to take it now would have been an act of disloyalty. I'd forgotten to switch off the light in the bathroom. Though my bones were unwilling, I climbed out of bed. My hotel suite seemed to expand in the dark. Standing there naked, with my back to the bed, I hesitated. Oh, yes – I was supposed to lock the door and leave the key in the lock. Room 303. They'd even seen to it that I was given the same room number. So what the hell. I looked for some sign of fear in myself but was conscious only of something vague and undefined, of something bordering on shame. But I couldn't tell whether my anxiety came from the prospect of a sleepless night or from that of my own death. Everyone is superstitious, though not everyone is aware of it. I again surveyed my surroundings in the glare of the night light, only this time with genuine suspicion. My suitcases were half open, my clothes were scattered all over the armchairs. A real dress rehearsal. Should I get out the automatic? Nonsense. I shook the self-pity out of my head, then lay down and turned off the night light, relaxing my muscles until my breathing became more regular.

Knowing how to fall asleep on schedule was an essential part of the mission. Especially when two people were sitting down below in a car and watching an oscilloscope as a luminous white line recorded every move of my heart and lungs. If the door was locked from the inside and the windows hermetically sealed, what difference did it make if he'd gone to sleep in the same bed and at the same time?

There was a world of difference between the Hilton and the Three Witches Inn. I tried to picture my homecoming; I saw myself pulling up to the house unannounced, or better yet, parking the car by the drugstore and walking the rest of the way on foot, as if on my way back from a stroll. The boys would be home from school already; as soon as they saw me coming, the stairs would reverberate with their footsteps. It suddenly dawned on me that I was supposed to take another shot of gin. For a moment I lay there undecided, sitting up on one elbow. The bottle was still in the suitcase. I dragged myself out of bed, groped my way over to the table, located the flat bottle under my shirts, then filled the cap till the stuff started dripping down my fingers. While emptying the small metal tumbler, I again had the sensation of being an actor in an amateur play. A job's a job, I said by way of self-justification. As I walked back to the bed, my suntanned trunk, arms and legs merged with the darkness, and my hips stood out like a white girdle. I lay down on the bed, the slug of gin gradually warming my stomach, and slammed my fist into the pillow: so this is what you've come to, you backup man! OK, pull up the covers and get some sleep.

Then I fell into the sort of drowse where the final flickerings of consciousness can be extinguished only by a state of total relaxation. A vision. I was sailing through space. Strangely enough, it was the same dream I'd had just before my trip to the orbital station. It was as if the stubborn catacombs of my mind refused to acknowledge any corrections dictated by experience. Flying in dreams is deceptive, because the body never really loses its normal sense of direction and the arms and legs can be manipulated as easily as in reality, though with greater facility. The real thing is another story. The muscles are thrown completely out of whack; if you try to push something away, you can find yourself getting shoved backward; if you try to sit up straight, you find yourself tucking your knees under your chin. One careless move and you can knock yourself out. The body goes wild the moment it's liberated from earth's beneficial resistance.

I woke up with a choking sensation. Something soft but unyielding was interfering with my breathing. I bolted upright with my arms stretched out as if trying to grab the person who was choking me. Sitting up in bed, I tried to clear my mind, but it was like peeling some horribly sticky wrapper from my brain. A quicksilver glare from outside was streaming into the room through a crack between the curtains; in its shimmering brightness I saw that I was alone. I could hardly breathe any more: my nose felt cemented together, my mouth was caked, and my tongue was all dried up. I must have been snoring dreadfully. It was the snoring that had reached me towards the tail end, just as I was waking up.

I got up, still a little shaky on my feet because even though I was awake my dream kept weighing me down like motionless gravity. Carefully I bent over my suitcase, groping blindly in the side pocket for the elastic band holding the tube of Pyribenzamine in place. The blooming season had reached Rome. The spore capsules in the south are the first to turn reddish-brown, and then gradually the fading process spreads to higher regions, a fact well known to anyone who suffers from chronic hay fever. It was two in the morning. I was a little worried that my escorts might jump out of the car when they saw my heart playing funny tricks on the oscilloscope, so I lay down again and turned my head sideways on the pillow, this being the fastest way to relieve a congested nose. I lay there with one ear tuned to the corridor to make sure no unwanted help was on the way, but all was quiet. My heart resumed its normal rhythm again.

I gave up trying to picture the house. I was no longer in the mood for it, or maybe I realized it was wrong of me to drag the kids into this. A hell of a thing if you couldn't go to sleep without the help of the kids! The yoga would have to do, the kind adapted especially for astronauts by Dr Sharp and his assistants. I knew it backward and forward like the Lord's Prayer. The exercises worked so well that before long my nose began to make a soft whistling sound as the passages opened up to let the air through, and the Pyribenzamine, once it lost its effect as a stimulant, trickled into my brain and induced its familiar but somehow impure sleepiness, so that before I knew it I was sound asleep.

ROME – PARIS

At eight the next morning I went to see Randy. I was in a fairly decent mood, because I'd started the day with Plimasine and despite the dry heat my nose wasn't bothering me. Randy's hotel was nowhere near my hotel; it was located on a crowded back street paved in the Roman style, not far from the Spanish Steps. I'd forgotten the name of the street. While I waited for Randy in a narrow passageway containing lobby, reception desk and coffee shop, I browsed through a copy of the *Herald* I'd picked up on the way to the hotel. I was interested in negotiations under way between Air France and the government, because I didn't relish the thought of being stranded at Orly. A strike had been declared by the airport's auxiliary crew, but Paris was still open to incoming flights.

It wasn't long before Randy showed up. Considering he'd been up most of the night he was in pretty good shape, except for being a little down in the mouth, but then by now it was obvious the mission had been a flop. Paris was our last resort, our last refuge. Randy offered to drive me to the airport, but I didn't let him; I thought it was better he got some sleep. He insisted it was impossible to sleep in his hotel room, so I followed him upstairs. As a matter of fact, his room was bright as day, and from the bathroom came the smell of hot suds instead of cool air.

Luckily we were in a high-pressure area. Relying on my professional knowledge, I drew the curtains, dampened them underneath to improve the air circulation, and left all the faucets running slightly. Having done my Samaritan duty, I said good-bye, promising to give him a call as soon as I came up with something concrete. I took a taxi out to the airport, stopping off at the Hilton for my things, and shortly before eleven was already pushing my luggage cart towards the departure area. It was my first trip to the new airport terminal in

Rome, and I kept my eyes peeled for the wonders of its technical security system, which had been publicized in all the papers, never suspecting I would become something of an expert on it.

The press had greeted the opening of the new terminal as an event signalling the end of all terrorist attacks. The glassed-in departure area was the only thing that looked somehow familiar. Viewed from above, the building resembled a drum, traversed by a network of escalators and ramps that discreetly filtered the boarding passengers. Lately people had begun smuggling aboard weapons and explosives in parts, later assembling them in the airport toilets, which was why the Italians were the first to stop using magnetometers. The screening was now conducted by means of ultrasonic detection devices while the passengers were being transported on the escalators; the data obtained from this invisible search was then instantly evaluated by a computer programmed to identify smuggling suspects. It was reported that these ultrasonic waves were able to sense every tooth filling and suspender clasp, that not even a non-metallic explosive could escape detection.

The new terminal was known unofficially as the Labyrinth. During a trial run lasting several weeks, intelligence experts armed with the most ingeniously concealed weapons had crammed the escalators, and not one of these smuggling attempts was known to have succeeded. The Labyrinth had been operating since April without any serious incidents; the only ones caught were those having in their possession objects as harmless as they were strange: a toy cap pistol, for example, or a metalized plastic replica of a gun. Some of the experts argued that such incidents amounted to a kind of psychological diversion on the part of frustrated terrorists, while others claimed they were merely meant to test the system's effectiveness. These pseudo smugglers posed something of a problem for the legal experts because, although their motives were unmistakable, they could not be considered punishable by law. So far the only serious incident had taken place on the day of my departure from Naples. An Asian passenger, after being detected by the sensors, had unloaded a live bomb on the Bridge of Sighs, which spanned the entire width of the Labyrinth. Hurled straight down into the hall, it caused an explosion that did little damage except to the nerves of the other passengers. In retrospect, I now believe these minor incidents were staged in preparation for an operation aimed at penetrating the new security system with a new type of offence.

My Alitalia flight was delayed an hour because of the uncertainty over whether we were to land at Orly or De Gaulle. Since the forecast was for thirty degress Celsius in Paris, I decided to change clothes. I couldn't remember which suitcase I'd packed my summer shirts in, so I set out for the rest room with my luggage cart, which was too big for the escalator. I wandered in and out of the lower-level ramps until a rajah finally showed me the way – he was on his way to the rest room, too. I couldn't tell whether he was really a rajah, because although he wore a turban he had a very weak command of English. I was curious to see if he would take off his turban in the rest room. My little excursion with the cart had consumed so much time that I had to shower in a hurry and change quickly into my cotton summer suit and laced canvas sneakers. By sticking my toilet kit into a suitcase I was able to free my hands to make my way back to departures and to check in all my things as luggage. As it turned out this was a smart move, since I doubt whether the rolls of microfilm – they were stashed in the toilet kit – would have survived 'the massacre of the steps'.

The terminal's air-conditioning system was on the blink, blowing ice-cold air in some places and warm air in others. At the Paris gate it was warm, so I slung my jacket over my shoulder, which also turned out to be a lucky move. Each of us was handed an Ariadne Pass – a plastic pouch equipped with an electronic resonator – without which it was impossible to board any of the planes. On the other side of the turnstile was an escalator so narrow it could only be boarded single file. The ride was a little reminiscent of Tivoli and a little of Disneyland. The escalator climbed straight up till it gradually levelled off into a moving ramp that spanned the hall in a flood of fluorescent lights while the ground floor remained dark, though how they managed to achieve such a lighting effect was beyond me. Once past the Bridge of Sighs, the ramp swerved around and became an escalator again, cutting back at a steep angle across the same hall, which was now recognizable only by the openwork ceiling, as both sides of the ramp were lined with aluminium panels decorated with mythological scenes. I never did find out what the rest of it looked like. The idea was simple: any passenger having something suspicious in his possession was reported by means of an uninterrupted sound transmitted by the plastic pouch. The suspect had no possible escape, since the conveyor ramp was too narrow, and the constant repetition of passageways was designed to weaken him psychologically and force him to dispose of his weapon. The departure area was posted with signs in twenty different languages warning that anyone attempting to smuggle weapons or explosives aboard would place his own life in jeopardy if he tried to commit an act of terrorism against his fellow passengers. This cryptic warning was variously interpreted. There were even rumours that a team of sharpshooters was kept concealed behind the aluminium walls, but I didn't believe a word of it.

The flight had originally been a charter, but because the Boeing made available turned out to be larger than the number of passengers, the remaining seats were sold over the counter. Those who eventually landed in trouble were those like myself who bought their tickets at the last minute. The Boeing had been rented by a bank consortium, though the people standing closest to me hardly looked like bankers. The first to step on the escalator was an elderly lady with a cane; then came a blonde woman carrying a small dog, then myself, a little girl and a Japanese. Glancing back down the stairs, I noticed that a couple of men had unfolded their newspapers. Since I was more in the mood for sightseeing, I tucked my *Herald* under the top of my suspenders like a fatigue cap.

The blonde, whose pearl-trimmed pants fitted so snugly you could see the outline of her panties on her fanny, turned out to be carrying a stuffed animal; it was the way it blinked that made it seem alive. I was reminded of the blonde on the magazine cover who had accompanied me on my trip to Rome. In her white outfit and with her quick eyes, the little girl looked more like a doll. The Japanese, who wasn't much taller than the girl, was dressed to perfection and had all the mannerisms of an avid tourist. Crisscrossing the top of his buttoned-up checkered suit were the straps of a transistor radio, a pair of binoculars and a powerful Nikon Six. While I happened to be looking around, he was in the process of opening the camera case to get a shot of the Labyrinth and the wonders of its interior. At the point where the stairs levelled off to form a ramp, I heard a shrill, drawn-out whistle; I spun around. It was coming from the direction of the Japanese.

The little girl could be seen backing anxiously away from him, hugging her purse, which contained the ticket pouch. With a deadpan expression the Japanese turned up the volume on his radio, naïvely mistaken if he thought he could drown out the whistle: it was only the first warning.

We were gliding over the hall's vast interior. Looming up in the fluorescent light on either side of the bridge ramp were Romulus, Remus and the she-wolf. By this time the whining noise coming from the ticket pouch of the Japanese had reached a piercing intensity. A tremor passed through the crowd, but no one dared to raise his voice. The only one who didn't bat an eyelash was the Japanese, who stood there expressionless, with only a few beads of sweat visible on his forehead. All of a sudden he yanked the pouch from his pocket and started wrestling with it like a madman, before a crowd of speechless onlookers – not a single woman cried out. As for me, I was only waiting to see how they would yank him out of the crowd. As the Bridge of Sighs came to an end and the ramp veered around a corner, the Japanese crouched down so suddenly and so low it looked as if he'd vanished from sight. It took me a while to realize what he was doing down there. Pulling the Nikon out of its case, he opened it just as the escalator was straightening out and beginning to climb again; it was now obvious that this second Bridge of Sighs was nothing more than an escalator moving back across the main hall at an angle. As soon as he was back on his feet again, there emerged from his Nikon a rounded, cylindrical object that glittered like a Christmas-tree ornament and that would barely have fitted into the palm of my hand. A non-metallic corundum grenade with a notched casing and no stem. The plastic pouch stopped whining. Using both hands, the Japanese pressed the bottom of the grenade to his mouth in the manner of a kiss; not until he removed it did I realize he'd pulled out the pin with his teeth and it was now sticking out between his lips. I made a dive for the grenade but only brushed it because the Japanese suddenly lunged backward with such force that he knocked those behind him off their feet and kicked me in the knee. My elbow landed in the girl's face; the impact sent me reeling against the railing. I banged into her again and this time took her with me as we both cleared the railing and went sailing through the air. Then something solid hit me in the back, and I passed from light into darkness.

I was expecting to land on sand. Though the papers hadn't mentioned explicitly what covered the floor, they were quite emphatic about the fact that no damage had resulted from the previous bomb explosion. Anticipating sand, I tried to get my legs into position while I was still in the air. But instead I encountered something soft and wet that gave way under me like foam until I landed in a freezing liquid. Simultaneously the blast of the explosion rocked my insides. I lost sight of the girl as my legs sank into some kind of sticky slime or mud; deeper and deeper I sank, fighting desperately with my hands, until a sudden calm took hold of me. I had about a minute, maybe a bit longer, to scramble out. First think – then act. It must have been a tank designed to soften the impact of a shock wave – a tank shaped more like a funnel than a bowl, spread with a layer of some sticky substance, filled with water, and then covered with a thick coating of an asphyxiating foam. There was no way I could charge uphill – I was knee-deep in the stuff – so I crouched down like a frog and began groping around on the bottom with my hands spread out; it was sloped to the right. Using the palms of my hands like shovels and pulling my feet out of the muck one at a time, I started crawling in that direction with all my strength. I kept it up, sometimes sliding back down the sloping incline and having to start all over again, using my hands to hoist myself up like a mountain climber trying to scale a snowy cliff without any handholds – but at least one can breathe in the snow.

I worked my way up high enough so that the big blistery bubbles on my face began to pop; half asphyxiated and gasping for air, I emerged into a shadowy penumbra filled with the concerted howls of those directly above me. With my head barely sticking out above the surface of tossing foam, I looked around. The girl was gone. I took a deep breath and dived below. I had to keep my eyes closed; something in the water made them burn like hell. Three times I surfaced and went below, getting noticeably weaker after each dive: since there was no way to bounce back up from the slime, I had to keep swimming over it to avoid being sucked under. Just when I'd given up hope, my hand accidentally touched her long hair. The foam had left it slippery as a fish. While I was trying to tie a knot in her blouse as a grip, the blouse ripped.

How we made it to the surface again I'll never know. All I can remember is the frantic struggle, the huge bubbles I kept wiping from her face, the awful metallic taste of the water, how I kept swearing under my breath, and how I managed to shove her over the edge of the funnel – a thick, rubberlike embankment. When she was safely on the other side, I hung there for a while before getting out, standing up to my neck in the softly hissing foam and trying to get my breath while the howling continued in the background. I had the illusion that it was raining – a warm, fine sort of rain. I could even feel a few drops falling on me. You're hallucinating, I thought. Rain? In here? Arching back my head I caught sight of the bridge: aluminium sheets were dangling from it like rags, the floor was riddled like a sieve, and the stairs looked like a honeycomb cast in metal, deliberately perforated to filter the air blast and catch any flying debris.

I heaved myself up over the curved embankment in the gentle downpour and laid the girl face down across my knee. She was not as far gone as I thought, because she was starting to vomit. As I rhythmically massaged her back and sides, I could feel her labouring with all her little bones. She was still choking and gasping, but at least she was breathing normally again. I felt like vomiting, so I helped it along with my finger. Though it left me feeling better, I still didn't have the nerve to get up. For the first time I was able to make out where I was, though the poor visibility was made even worse by the blowout of a section of the fluorescent lighting. The howling overhead was giving way to sounds of groaning and gurgling. People are dying up there, I thought – why isn't anyone coming to their aid? There was a lot of racket near by, mostly clanking, as if someone was trying to get the stalled escalator in service again. I could hear people crying out – healthy people, uninjured people. I couldn't figure out what was happening up there. The entire length of the escalator was jammed with people who had piled on top of one another out of panic. There was no way of reaching the dying without first removing those in a state of shock. Shoes and articles of clothing had become wedged between the steps. There was no access from the side: the bridge had turned out to be a trap.

Meanwhile I looked after myself and the girl. She was obviously conscious now and sitting up. I told her not to worry, that everything would be O K, that we'd be out of there in no time. And sure enough, once my eyes got accustomed to the dark it wasn't long before I spotted an exit: a hatchway that had inadvertently been left open. If it hadn't been for someone's negligence, we might have been stranded there like a couple of trapped mice. The hatchway opened up on to a sewerlike tunnel in which another hatchway, or, rather, a convex shield, also stood ajar. A corridor lined with recessed-light cages led us into a squat, bunkerlike basement full of cables, pipes and plumbing installations.

'These pipes might lead to the rest rooms.'

I turned to the girl, but she was gone.

'Hey . . . where are you?' I yelled, at the same time scouting the entire length and width of the basement. I caught sight of her as she was running barefoot from one concrete pillar to another. Backache or no backache, I caught up with her in a couple of leaps, grabbed her by the hand, and said in a stern voice:

'What's the big idea, honey? You and I have to stick together, or we'll both get lost.'

She tagged along after me in silence. It was starting to get brighter up ahead: a ramp flanked by white-tiled walls. We came out and found ourselves standing on a higher level. One glance at our surroundings and I knew where we were. A short distance away was the very same ramp I'd pushed my luggage cart down an hour ago. Around the corner was a corridor lined with doors. I took some change from my pocket, dropped a coin in the first door, and grabbed the little girl's hand on the hunch she was planning to run away again. She still looked to be in a state of shock. Small wonder. I dragged her into the bathroom. She said nothing, and when I saw in the light how she was covered all over with blood I stopped talking, too: I knew now what the warm rain was. I must have looked a sight, too. After stripping both of us down, I dumped all our things into the tub, turned on the faucet, and, dressed only in my underwear, I shoved her under the shower. The hot water had a soothing effect on my backache and ran off our bodies in red streams. I rubbed her small back and sides. Not only to wash off the blood, but also to revive her. She submitted willingly, even passively, while I rinsed her hair as best I could.

When we came out of the shower, I asked her casually what her name was.

'Annabella.'

'English?'

'French.'

'From Paris?'

'No, from Clermont.'

I switched to French, and started fishing our things out of the tub one by one to give them a rinse.

'If you feel up to it,' I suggested, 'would you mind rinsing out your dress?' She bent over the tub obediently.

While I was wringing out my pants and shirt, I contemplated our next move. By this time the airport would be shut down and crawling with police. So now what? Go merrily on our way till we got stopped somewhere? The Italian authorities weren't wise to my little game yet. The only other person in the know was du Bois Fenner, the embassy's first secretary. My airplane ticket was made out to a different name from the one on the hotel bill, and *it* was somewhere back in the hall along with my jacket. The automatic and the electrodes were still at the Hilton, all packaged and ready to be picked up by Randy that same evening. If they intercepted the package, I'd make a damned nice suspect, which I probably was anyway after making such a slick getaway and after going to such trouble to get rid of the blood. They might even accuse me of being an accomplice. No one was above suspicion, not since respectable lawyers and a few other big shots had been caught in the act of smuggling bombs out of ideological sympathy. Eventually I'd be cleared of everything, but only after landing behind bars. Nothing like being helpless to get the police all excited. I gave Annabella a thorough inspection. A black eye, wet hair hanging down in strands, dress drying under the hand dryer; a bright kid. I started formulating a plan.

'Listen, honey,' I said, 'do you know who I am? An American astronaut, and I'm here incognito on a very important mission. Follow me? I've got to be in Paris by today at the latest, but if we stick around we'll be interrogated and that'll mean a delay. So I have to phone the embassy right away to get the first secretary to come down. He's going to help us. The airport's shut down, but there are other planes besides the normal ones, special planes they use for taking out the embassy mail. That's the kind we'll be flying on. You and me. Wouldn't you like that?'

She just stood there and stared. Not yet recovered, I thought. I started getting dressed. Thanks to the laces I still had my shoes, but Annabella had lost her sandals, though nowadays it was nothing to see girls running around barefoot in the street, and if worst came to worst her slip could pass for a blouse. I helped her straighten the pleats on her dress, now almost dry.

'Now we're going to play father and daughter,' I said. 'That way we won't have any trouble getting to a telephone. OK?'

She nodded, and off we went, hand in hand, to face the world. We ran into the first barricade the moment we stepped off the ramp. Some reporters armed with cameras were being forced back outside by the *carabinieri*; firemen, their helmets already on, were charging in the other direction. No one took any notice of us. One of the *carabinieri* – the one I happened to be talking to – could even get along in English. I fed him a story about how we'd been swimming, but without listening to a word I said, he told us to take escalator B upstairs to the European section, where all the passengers were being assembled. We started for the escalator, but the moment it blocked us from view I turned down a side corridor, leaving all the commotion behind. We entered a deserted waiting room where passengers came to claim their luggage. A row of telephone booths stood on the other side of some conveyor belts now moving quietly along. I took Annabella with me into one of the booths and dialled Randy's number. My call jolted him out of his sleep. Standing in a yellow glare, with my hand cupped around the receiver, I told him the whole story. He interrupted me only once, thinking possibly he'd misunderstood me. Then all I could hear was his heavy breathing, followed by a long pause as if he'd suddenly gone numb.

'Still there?' I asked when I was finished.

'Man!' he said. Then a second time: 'Man!' Nothing else.

Then I came to the most critical part. He was to get Fenner from the embassy and drive down in the car with him right away. They'd have to make it fast; otherwise we'd be caught between two barricades. The airport would be shut down, but Fenner would find a way to get through. The girl would be right here with me. In the left wing of the building, next to luggage claim counter E10, right by the telephone booths. In case we weren't there, they could find us together with the other passengers in the European section, or else, for sure, in the custody of the police. I got him to recapitulate, then hung up, hoping the girl would acknowledge our success with a smile, or at least a look of relief, but she remained just as remote and tight-lipped as before. Several times I caught her spying on me, as if she were expecting something. An upholstered bench stood between the booths. We sat down. Through the plate-glass walls in the distance, the airport's approach ramps could be seen. Ambulance after ambulance kept pulling up in front; the continual racket of sirens and alarms was punctuated by women's spasmodic cries coming from inside the building. To make conversation I inquired about the girl's parents, about her trip, about who had brought her out to the airport. Her answers were evasive, monosyllabic; not even her Clermont address could I pry out of her. It was starting to get on my nerves. It was 1.40 by my watch. A half hour had gone by since my talk with Randy on the phone. Some guys dressed in overalls and wheeling what looked like an electric welding machine came trotting through the waiting room, but without so much as a glance in our direction. Again the sound of footsteps. A technician wearing earphones came in and started moving down the row of telephone booths, holding the little round plate attached to the mine detector up close to the doors as he went. He stopped in his tracks the moment he saw us. Two policemen closed in from behind till we were surrounded by all three.

'What are you doing here?'

'We're waiting.'

I was telling the truth.

One of the *carabinieri* rushed off somewhere and came back a few minutes later accompanied by a tall man in civilian clothes. When I was asked the same question again, I replied that we were waiting for a representative from the American embassy. The plainclothesman asked to see my papers. As I was reaching for my wallet, the technician pointed to the booth adjacent to us. Its glass panels were fogged up on the inside – the steam left by our wet clothes. They were all eyes. The other *carabiniere* touched my pants.

'Wet!'

'Right!' I snapped back. 'Sopping wet!'

They pointed their rifles at us.

'Don't worry,' I whispered to Annabella.

The man in civilian clothes took a pair of handcuffs out of his pocket. Without wasting any time on formalities, he handcuffed me to himself while one of the other policemen looked after Annabella, who kept giving me a funny look. The plainclothesman had a walkie-talkie strapped over his shoulder; lifting it up close to his mouth, he said something in Italian, but so fast I couldn't catch a word of it. He seemed pleased with the reply. Then we were escorted through a side exit, where three more *carabinieri* joined the procession. The escalator was still out of order. A generous flight of stairs brought us out into the departure area. On the way I caught a glimpse of the patrol cars lined up outside, and had just begun pondering our fate when a black Continental bearing the embassy banner pulled up in front. I can't remember when the sight of the Stars and Stripes has ever given me such a thrill. The scene that followed could only have happened on stage: just as we were making our way downstairs towards a glass door, du Bois, Randy and one of the embassy interpreters entered the building. They were a strange sight – Randy in his Levis, the others in their dinner jackets. Randy started when he saw me and leaned over to Fenner, who turned to the interpreter, and it was he who approached us first.

Both groups halted, and a short, picturesque scene followed. The spokesman for the rescue team started up a conversation with the plainclothesman, the one I was chained to. The talking was done in a staccato manner; forgetting he was impeded by the handcuffs, my Italian escort kept yanking my hand up every time he made a gesture. I didn't understand a thing except '*astronauto americano*' and '*presto, presto!*' When my escort appeared satisfied, he again resorted to the portable radio. Even Fenner was granted the privilege of talking into it. Then the agent spoke a few more words into the set, which responded in a way that made him snap to attention; the situation was becoming more farcical by the moment. The cuffs were taken off, there was an about-face, and, falling into the same formation as before, only now with the roles completely reversed – those arrested were now acting as honorary escort – we headed upstairs to the first floor. On the way we passed a waiting room filled with passengers bivouacked on whatever was at hand, crossed a line of uniforms, filed through two leather-upholstered doors, and finally wound up in a crowded office.

With our arrival an apoplectic-looking giant started chasing people out the door. All but about ten people actually left the room. The hoarse, apoplectic-looking man turned out to be a deputy police chief. Someone offered me an armchair; Annabella was already seated. Despite the fact that it was broad daylight outside, all the lights in the room were on. Cross sections of the Labyrinth on the wall, a model of same on a portable stand next to the desk, glistening wet photos in the process of drying on the desk top. It wasn't hard to guess what was in the photos. Fenner, who was sitting behind me, gave my arm a slight squeeze: things had gone so well because he'd phoned the police chief directly from the embassy. There were a few people huddled around the desk, some others perched on the window sill, and the deputy police chief paced the floor in silent concentration. A teary-eyed secretary was ushered in from the next room. The interpreter kept shifting his head back and forth between me and the girl, ready to come to our rescue, but somehow my Italian improved significantly. I learned that my jacket, along with Annabella's purse, had been salvaged by a team of frogmen, thanks to which I was now a chief suspect, because in the meantime they'd already got in touch with the Hilton. I was suspected of being an accomplice of the Japanese. After releasing the grenade, we had planned to make a getaway towards the front, which was why we'd been among the first to board the escalator. But somehow there must have been a mixup in plans: the Japanese was killed in the explosion, while I saved myself by jumping over the bridge. On this point there was a difference of opinion. Some took Annabella to be a terrorist, others claimed I'd taken her as a hostage.

All this was passed on to me confidentially; they were still waiting for the arrival of the head of airport security before starting the interrogation. As soon as the latter had appeared, Randy, acting as self-appointed spokesman for the Americans, began briefing everyone on the nature of our mission. I listened, at the same time discreetly freeing my wet pant legs from my calves. He included in his report only what was absolutely necessary. Fenner was no less sparing in details, confirming that the embassy had been informed of our mission and that Interpol, which had also been briefed, was supposed to have notified the Italian authorities. This was a shrewd move on Fenner's part, because now the burden of responsibility had been shifted to an international organization. The Italians were not the least bit interested in our operation; they were much keener to know what had happened on the escalator. An engineer from the airport's staff said it was inconceivable that I could have escaped from either the tank or the hall without being familiar with the technical layout of the place. To which Randy replied that one shouldn't underestimate the sort of commando training administered by the USAF to people like me. He neglected to mention that my training days had been over thirty years ago. The sound of hammering vibrated through the walls. The rescue operation was still under way, they were cutting away a part of the bridge, the section torn apart by the explosion. So far they had dug out a total of nine bodies from the rubble, plus twenty-two wounded, seven of them critically. A commotion was heard outside the door; the deputy police chief motioned to one of his officers to investigate. As he was leaving the room I had a chance to observe, through a gap in the gathering, a little side table where my jacket was lying, with all the seams ripped open, and right beside it Annabella's purse, likewise demolished. The contents of her purse were neatly arranged, like stacks of poker chips, on little squares of white paper. The officer returned and, wringing his hands, said, 'Newspaper reporters!' A few of the more enterprising reporters had managed to get this far before being turned back. Meanwhile another officer introduced himself to me.

'Lieutenant Canetti. What can you tell us about the explosive used? How was it smuggled in?'

'The camera had a false bottom. He opened it and the back popped out – film and all – like a jack-in-the-box. All he had to do then was to pull out the hand grenade.'

'Are you familiar with this type of grenade?'

'I've come across something like it in the States. Part of the primer is located in the handle. As soon as I saw the handle was missing, I realized the primer was a modified one. A highly explosive anti-personnel bomb, metal content almost nil, with a casing made of solidified silicon carbide.'

'And you just happened to be standing in that particular place on the escalator? Is that it?'

'Not quite.'

I took advantage of the pause, a nerve-racking pause interrupted only by the hammering outside, to select my words carefully.

'It wasn't just by accident that I was standing there. The Japanese let the girl go ahead of him because he figured a kid would be the least likely to cramp his style. The girl' – I nodded in her direction – 'was at the head of the line because she was intrigued by a stuffed dog. That's my impression, anyway. Am I right, Annabella?'

'Yes.' She was visibly surprised.

I smiled at her.

'And as for me . . . I was in a hurry. It's irrational, I agree, but when you're in a hurry you automatically want to be the first to board the plane. And that goes for the boarding ramp as well . . . It wasn't deliberate on my part, it just happened that way.'

Everyone sighed. Canetti murmured something to the deputy police chief, who nodded.

'We would like to spare you, young lady . . . certain details of the inquiry. Would you mind stepping outside for a while?'

I glanced over at Annabella. A girlish smile – her first – just for me. She got up. Someone opened the door for her. As soon as she was out of the room, Canetti went at it again.

'Now for the next question. When did you begin to suspect the Japanese?'

'I never suspected him for a moment; he was so totally convincing in that tourist getup of his. Till the moment he crouched down, that is. At first I thought he was out of his mind. But as soon as I saw he'd triggered the grenade, I figured I had about three seconds, more or less.'

'How many did you have exactly?'

'Hard to say. The grenade didn't explode right away when he pulled the pin, it must have had a delay mechanism. My guess is two, maybe two and a half seconds.'

'That would coincide with our own estimate,' said one of the men over by the window.

'You seem to have trouble walking. Were you injured?'

'Yes, but not by the explosion. The blast came just as I was landing in the water. How high up is the bridge? About five metres?'

'Four and a half.'

'That would account for one second. My reaching for the grenade and clearing the railing would account for another. You asked if I was injured. I banged my back against something while I was in the air. I once fractured my tail bone.'

'You hit a deflector,' explained the man seated on the window sill. 'A boom equipped with a diagonal shield designed to deflect an object into the centre of the funnel. You've never heard of such a deflector?'

'No.'

'I beg your pardon, but it's still my turn!' protested Canetti. 'Did that man – that Japanese – actually throw the grenade?'

'No. He held on to it till the very end.'

'Didn't he try to escape?'

'Nope.'

'Poltrinelli, head of airport security.' The newcomer was leaning against the desk, dressed in a pair of grease-stained overalls. 'Are you absolutely sure the man wanted to die?'

'Did he *want* to die? Yes. He made no attempt to save his own skin. He could have unloaded the whole camera if he'd wanted to.'

'Excuse me, but this is an important point for us. Isn't it possible he planned to jump over the bridge after throwing the grenade but was prevented from doing so by your surprise attack?'

'Impossible. Though I could be wrong,' I conceded. 'For one thing, I didn't attack him. I was only trying to get the grenade out of his hands after he pulled it away from his face; I could see the pin sticking out between his teeth. It was made of nylon instead of metal. He was using both hands to hold the thing. That's not how you throw a hand grenade.'

'How did you attack him? From above?'

'That's how I would have attacked if the stairs had been empty or if we'd been last in line. That's why he knew better than to stand at the back. Any hand grenade can be knocked loose by a straight jab from above, in which case it would just have gone sailing down the stairs. If I'd only poked it out of his hand, it would have landed close by. Even though it's against regulations, people still put their hand luggage on the steps. In which case the grenade wouldn't have rolled very far. That's why I swung from the left, and that's what took him by surprise.'

'From the left, you say? Are you left-handed?'

'Yes. He wasn't expecting that. He ducked the wrong way. The guy was a real pro. He stuck out his elbow to guard from the right.'

'Then what happened?'

'After that he kicked me in the knee and threw himself backward. He must have been extremely well trained; even if you're willing to die, it's hard as hell to throw yourself backward down a flight of stairs. Most of us would rather die facing forward.'

'But the stairs were crowded.'

'Right! And yet there was no one standing behind him. Everyone was trying to move back out of the way.'

'He wasn't counting on that.'

'I know, but nothing was left to chance. He was too slick, he had every move down pat.'

The security chief squeezed the desk top till his knuckles turned white. He fired away with his questions as if conducting a cross-examination.

'I wish to emphasize that as far as we're concerned your behaviour is beyond reproach. But I repeat: it is of vital importance to us that we get at the facts in this case. You understand why, don't you?'

'The question is whether they have people ready to face certain death.'

'Precisely. That's why I must ask you to reconsider the exact sequence of events that took place during that one second. Let me put myself in his place. I release the safety catch. Next I plan to jump over the bridge. If I stick to my plan, you intercept the grenade and throw it back at me as I'm going down. I hesitate, and it's that split second of hesitation that proves decisive. Couldn't that have been the way it happened?'

'No. A person planning to throw a hand grenade doesn't hold it with both hands.'

'But you shoved him as you were going for the grenade.'

'No. If my fingers hadn't slipped I would've pulled him towards me. I couldn't get a grip on him; he got away from me by keeling over backward. That was a deliberate move on his part. I confess I underestimated him. I should have just grabbed him and dumped him over the railing along with the grenade. That's what I would have done if I hadn't been so startled.'

'He might have dropped the grenade by your feet.'

'Then I'd have gone over the railing with him. Or tried to, at least. Of course it's easy to say afterwards, but I think I would have gambled. I weighed twice as much as he did, and his arms were no bigger than a kid's.'

'Thank you. No further questions.'

'Scarron, engineer.' The man introducing himself was young looking but prematurely grey; he wore civilian clothes and a pair of horn-rimmed glasses. 'Can you think of any security measures that might have prevented such an attack?'

'You're asking too much of me. It looks to me as if you've taken care of everything.'

They were prepared for many things, he said, but not everything. They'd even found a way of counteracting the so-called Lod Type Operation. At the push of a button, isolated sections of the escalator could be converted into a sloping plane capable of depositing people in a water tank.

'One equipped with the same kind of foam?'

'No. That's an anti-detonation tank designed strictly for under the bridge. No, I had other kinds in mind.'

'Well, then . . . what was stopping you? Not that it would have mattered, really . . .'

'Exactly. His execution was too fast.'

He pointed to the interior of the Labyrinth shown on the display map. The entire route was in fact conceived as a kind of firing zone, one that could be flooded from above with water released at a pressure great enough to sweep away everything in its path. The funnel was thought to be escape-proof; the failure to secure the escape hatches had been a serious oversight. He offered to take me over to the model, but I declined.

The engineer looked flustered. He was dying to show me the results of his farsightedness, even though he must have realized it was a waste of time. He had solicited my opinion hoping I wouldn't be able to offer any.

Just when I thought the interrogation was over, an elderly man sitting in the chair left vacant by Annabella raised his hand.

'Dr Torcelli. I have only one question. Can you explain how you were able to save the girl?'

I gave it a moment's thought.

'It was a lucky coincidence, that's all. She was standing between us. To get at the Japanese I had to shove her out of the way; the impact of his fall made me collide with her. It was a low railing; if she'd been an adult I would never have got her over. I doubt whether I would've even attempted it.'

'What if it had been a woman?'

'There *was* a woman,' I said, meeting his gaze. 'In front of me. A blonde in pearl-trimmed pants, the one with the stuffed dog. What ever happened to her?'

'She bled to death.' The comment came from the head of security. 'She had both legs torn off by the explosion.'

There was a lapse in the conversation. Those seated on the window sill stood up, and there was a shuffling of chairs, but my thoughts kept going back to that moment on the escalator. One thing I knew: I hadn't wasted any time in going over the railing. Grabbing hold of it with my right arm, I'd taken off from the step with my other arm wrapped around the girl. By hurdling the railing in the manner of a side vault, I'd forced her to accompany me on my way down. Whether I'd put my arm around her deliberately or because she just happened to be standing there, I couldn't say.

Although they were through with me, I wanted some assurance I would be spared any publicity. This was interpreted as an expression of undue modesty, something I refused to admit. It had nothing to do with modesty. I simply had no desire to become personally implicated in the 'massacre on the steps'. The only one who guessed my real motive was Randy.

Fenner suggested I stay overnight in Rome as a guest of the embassy. But on this point I was equally adamant: I insisted on taking the next available flight to Paris, which turned out to be a Cessna carrying a shipment of materials used at a conference that had ended that afternoon with a cocktail reception; this explained why Fenner and the interpreter had arrived in dinner jackets. We were drifting towards the door in small groups, still engaged in conversation, when a woman with magnificent dark eyes, whose presence I had overlooked till now, took me aside. She turned out to be a psychologist, the one who'd been looking after Annabella. She asked if I was serious about wanting to take the girl along with me to Paris.

'Why, yes. She must have told you about my promise.'

A smile. She asked whether I had any children of my own.

'No. Well . . . let's say not quite. I have two nephews.'

'And are they very fond of you?'

'You bet they are.'

She then revealed Annabella's secret. The girl had been worried sick. Even though I'd saved her life she had a very low opinion of me, taking me for an accomplice of the Japanese or something very close to it. That's why she'd tried to run away. In the rest room I gave her an even worse scare.

'How, for God's sake?'

Not for a moment did she fall for the story about the astronaut. Nor for the one about the embassy. The telephone conversation she took to be with another accomplice. And since her father owned a winery, she assumed I was inquiring about her Clermont address as part of a plan to kidnap her in exchange for a ransom. The psychologist made me swear not to breathe a word of this to Annabella.

'Maybe she'll feel like telling me herself,' I said.

'Never, or perhaps ten years from now. You may know something about boys, but girls are different.'

Another smile, and she was gone. I went to take care of our flight reservations. Only one seat left; I insisted there had to be two. Negotiations by telephone. Finally some VIP was persuaded to give up his seat. To Annabella. Fenner was in a hurry but offered to cancel some important meeting if I agreed to join him for lunch. I declined a second time. After Randy and the others had driven off, I inquired whether the girl and I could get a bite to eat in one of the airport facilities. The bars and cafeterias had all been closed down, but an exception was made in our case: we were now above the law. A man – dark-featured, bushy-haired, an undercover agent – escorted us to a small restaurant located on the other side of the departure area. Annabella's eyes were red and swollen: she'd been crying. Before long she started getting prissy. While the waiter was taking our order and I was debating what she should have to drink, she commented in a rather brisk, matter-of-fact tone that at home she was always served wine. She had on a blouse that was a couple of sizes too big, with rolled-up sleeves, and a pair of shoes that also looked a size too large. I was just beginning to enjoy the comfort of dry pants and the fact that I didn't have to stick to a diet of spaghetti any more, when I suddenly remembered her parents. There was a chance the news story might make the afternoon edition. We quickly drafted a telegram message, but when I got up from the table our cicerone sprang out of nowhere and offered to take care of it. When it came time to pay, we were treated as guests of the management. I tipped the waiter with the sort of generosity Annabella might have expected of a real astronaut. In her eyes I had suddenly become a celebrity and a hero – and a confidant, to the point where she even told me how she was dying to change clothes. Our chaperon escorted us to the Alitalia Hotel, where our luggage was already waiting for us in our room.

I had to hurry her along a little. At last, looking very prim and proper, she was ready, and with due decorum we embarked for the airplane. We were picked up by the airport's acting managing director – the managing director was temporarily indisposed, owing to a slight nervous breakdown – and driven out to the Cessna in one of the little Fiats used by the air controllers. At the foot of the ladder a rather courtly young Italian apologized for intruding and asked whether I cared for any souvenir photos of the recent drama. The photos would be forwarded to any address requested. I thought of the blonde woman and thanked him anyway. A round of farewell handshakes. In the flurry of handshakes I could have sworn that I shook the same hand that had held me captive a short while ago.

I enjoyed flying in small planes. After a birdlike takeoff our Cessna veered northward. We landed at Orly shortly after seven. Annabella's father was there to meet her. Before landing we exchanged addresses, and to this day I still have fond memories of her. I wish I could say the same about her father. He was profusely grateful, even paying me a farewell compliment inspired no doubt by his having watched the television coverage of the 'massacre on the steps'. He said I had *l'esprit de l'escalier*.

PARIS
(Orly – Garges – Orly)

I spent the night at Orly, at the Hotel Air France, since by now my contact had already left the Centre National de Recherche Scientifique and I didn't particularly feel like bothering him at home. Before going to sleep I had to get up and close the windows, because my nose was starting to act up again. It was then I realized I'd gone the whole day without sneezing once.

As it turned out I could have taken Fenner up on his offer, but then I'd been in such a hurry to reach Paris.

The next morning, the first thing after breakfast, I called the CNRS only to find out that my contact was on vacation, moving into a new house, but that he could still be reached. I then placed a call to his house in Garges, but it turned out he was just having his new phone connected. Announced or unannounced, I decided to pay him a visit. At the Gare du Nord the suburban trains were not in service, due to a strike. Seeing the mile-long line-up in front of the cabstand, I inquired about the nearest car rental agency – it turned out to be another Hertz – and settled for a Peugeot compact.

Trying to get around Paris, especially when you're unsure of your destination, is sheer hell. Not far from the Opéra – it wasn't on my itinerary; I wound up there quite by accident – a delivery van rammed into my bumper; the damage was so minor I kept on going, my mind now conjuring up visions of Canadian lakes and glacial waters as a distraction from the downpour of blazing-hot sun, unseasonable for this time of year. By mistake I wound up in a place called Sarcelles, one of those ugly, nondescript little settlements; then later I got stuck in front of a railway crossing, sweated, and pined after an air conditioner. Dr Philippe Barth, my contact, was a well-known French computer scientist who also served as a scientific consultant for the Sûreté. The team he headed was in the process of programming a computer capable of solving multifactorial problems in which the number of case-related facts exceeded the storage capacity of the human memory.

The exterior of the house had just been freshly stuccoed. Surrounding the house was an old-fashioned garden: one wing shaded by stately elms, a gravel driveway, a flower bed in the centre – marigolds, if I'm not mistaken (botany is the only subject astronauts are spared). Parked in front of a shed serving temporarily as a garage was a 2 CV, mud-spattered from the windows down, and right beside it a cream-coloured Peugeot 604, its doors wide open, floormats spread out on the lawn, and dripping all over with soapsuds. Some kids were washing the car, but with such bustle and teamwork I had trouble counting them at first. They were all Barth's kids. The oldest two, a boy and a girl, greeted me in collective English: as soon as one began to falter, the other would fill in the missing word. How did they know they were supposed to speak English? A telegram had come from Randy announcing the arrival of an American astronaut. How could they tell I was the astronaut? No one else was in the habit of wearing suspenders. Good old Randy. While I was talking with the older kids, the younger one – I couldn't tell whether it was a boy or a girl – kept circling around me, hands folded behind its back, as if hunting for the spot that presented me in the most interesting light. I was told their father was very busy, and just as I was debating whether to go inside the house or to join the car-washing party, Dr Barth leaned out of the ground-floor window. He looked surprisingly young, but then I was still not accustomed to my own age. I was given a polite but restrained welcome, which made me wonder if I hadn't made a mistake in approaching him by way of the Sûreté, rather than the CNRS. But Randy was on friendlier terms with the police than with the scientific community.

Barth showed me into the library – his study was still in a state of chaos following the move – and then briefly excused himself while he went to change out of his varnish-stained smock. The house had been made to look like new already; rows of books stood freshly arrayed on the shelves, the smell of wax and varnish was everywhere. On the wall I noticed a blowup of Barth and his kids mounted on an elephant. Judging from the face in the photo I would never have guessed he was the promise of French computer science, but then I'd already had occasion to observe that people in the exact sciences tend to be less conspicuous in appearance than those in the humanities.

Barth came back into the room, frowning at his hands, which still showed traces of varnish, prompting me to suggest various ways of getting rid of the stains. We sat down by the window. I started out by saying I was neither a detective nor a criminologist, but that I had become involved in a rather bizarre and morbid case, and that I had come to him as a last resort. He was impressed by my fluent but not very European French. I explained that I was of French Canadian origin.

Randy had more confidence in my personal charm than I did. I was so anxious to gain this man's favour that I was somewhat embarrassed by the situation. The Sûreté was not a reference that he seemed to hold in particularly high esteem. Then, too, the attitude prevailing in academic circles is a decidedly anti-militaristic one. In such circles it's widely believed that astronauts are recruited from the armed forces, which was not always so, at least not in my case. But then I could hardly confide in him my whole life history. I was in doubt, therefore, as to what course I should take to break the ice. It wasn't till much later that he confessed to having been somewhat moved by the look of utter desperation on my face. My guess had been right: the colonel Randy had got to introduce me was in Barth's eyes a clown; nor was Barth exactly on the best of terms with the Sûreté. But sitting there in the library, I had no way of knowing that this indecision of mine was the best possible strategy.

He agreed to hear my story. I'd been involved with the case for so long I could have recited every detail from memory. I'd also brought along a set of microfilms containing all the documentation needed to illustrate my lecture, and Barth had just finished unpacking his projector. We plugged it in, leaving the windows and curtains open since the trees were already suffusing the room with a greenish half-light.

'It's a jigsaw puzzle,' I began, feeding the first reel into the projector. 'A puzzle consisting of numerous pieces; each of them is distinct enough on its own, but when fitted together they make for an indistinct whole. Not even Interpol has been able to crack the case. Just recently we conducted a simulation mission, the details of which I'll save till later on. The results were negative.'

I was aware that his computer program was still in the experimental stage, that it had never been tested in the field, and that it was the subject of conflicting reports; but I was anxious to arouse his curiosity, and so I decided to give him a succinct version of the whole affair.

On June 27 of last year, the management of the Savoy Hotel in Naples notified the police that Robert T. Coburn, an American, aged fifty, had failed to return after setting out for the beach on the previous morning. His disappearance was all the more suspicious in that Coburn, a guest of the hotel for the past ten days, had been in the habit of going to the beach every morning, even walking the hundred-metre distance in his beach robe. That same evening his robe was found in his cabin by the beach attendant.

Coburn had the reputation of being an excellent swimmer. Twenty years ago he had been a member of the American crawling team, and though he had a tendency to gain weight, he had managed to keep reasonably fit for a man his age. Since the beach was crowded, his disappearance went unnoticed. Five days later his body was washed ashore by the waves of a passing storm. His death would have been attributed to accidental drowning, a not unusual occurrence on every major beach, were it not for several minor details that later prompted an investigation. The dead man, a real-estate broker from Illinois, had no wife. Since he had died of unnatural causes an autopsy was performed, the results of which indicated that he had drowned on an empty stomach. Yet the hotel management claimed he had left for the beach right after breakfast. A minor discrepancy, perhaps, but the police commission was not on the best of terms with a group of city aldermen who had invested money in the renovation of certain hotels – among them the Savoy, which had recently been the scene of another incident, to be discussed later on. The police commission took a special interest in those hotels in which guests had met with accidents. A young assistant was put in charge of conducting a secret investigation, and he immediately placed the hotel and its guests under close surveillance. Being a freshly minted detective, he was anxious to sparkle in the eyes of his superior, and, thanks to his zealous enthusiasm, some very odd things were revealed. Coburn's daily routine had consisted of mornings at the beach, naps in the afternoon, then early-evening visits to the Vittorini brothers' health spa for the mineral-bath treatment that a local doctor, Dr Gioni, had prescribed for him – Coburn was being treated for the early stages of rheumatism. It also developed that during the week before his death Coburn had been involved in three car accidents, always on his way back from the Vittorini resort and each time under similar circumstances, namely, while trying to run a red light at an intersection. In every case the damage was minor, amounting to no more than dented fenders, and Coburn got off with only a fine and a warning. It was also around this time that he began eating supper in his room, rather than in the hotel dining room – before letting the waiter in, Coburn would first check through the door to make sure he was an employee of the hotel – and he soon gave up taking his daily stroll around the bay at sunset. These were indications that he felt harassed, even personally threatened – running a red light is a well-known method for shaking a tailing car – and such an interpretation would also explain why the deceased man had taken precautionary steps inside the hotel. But the investigation failed to turn up any further evidence. Coburn, whose childless marriage had ended in divorce fourteen years earlier, had made no friends either in the Savoy or downtown. It was later discovered that on the day before his death he had tried to buy a revolver from a local gun dealer, not realizing that by Italian law he was required to have a gun licence. Since he didn't have one, he bought an imitation fountain pen designed to spray an attacker with a mixture of tear gas and an indelible dye. The pen was later found, not yet unwrapped, among his personal belongings, and so they were able to trace it back to the local retailer. Coburn had known no Italian, and the gun dealer had only a weak command of English. All that was learned was that Coburn had asked for a weapon capable of repelling a dangerous attacker, and not just some petty thief.

After establishing that all the accidents had occurred while Coburn was on his way back from the health spa, the assistant then proceeded to the Vittorinis. Because of the American's generosity towards the staff, they had no trouble remembering him. There had been nothing extraordinary about his behaviour except that lately he had seemed more pressed for time, frequently ignoring the bath attendant's warning to wait ten minutes and dry off before going outside. Such meagre findings failed to satisfy the investigating officer, who, in a fit of enthusiasm and inspiration, undertook a review of the establishment's books, which contained a record of payments made by all its bathing customers as well as those requiring hydrotherapeutic treatment.

Since the middle of May a total of ten Americans had visited the Vittorini spa, four of whom, like Coburn, had paid for a season pass (one could buy a one-, two-, three- or four-week pass) but failed to show up after the eighth or ninth day. Not that there was anything particularly unusual about that, since any one of them might have been called away unexpectedly and thus had to forgo whatever refund he had coming. But now that the assistant knew their names, he decided to follow up his investigation. When later asked why he had limited himself to American citizens, he was not able to give a clear-cut answer. At one point he claimed he had hit on the idea of an American connection after learning that the police had recently smashed a narcotics ring trafficking in heroin between Naples and the States; on another occasion he said he had restricted himself to Americans for the simple reason that Coburn had been an American.

Of the four who failed to take full advantage of their subscriptions, the first, Arthur J. Holler, an attorney from New York, had suddenly left town after being notified of his brother's death. He was now back in his native city. Married and thirty-six years of age, he was employed as legal consultant for a large advertising agency.

The remaining three showed a certain physical resemblance to Coburn. In each case the person involved was a single male, between forty and fifty years of age, reasonably well-to-do, and invariably a patient of Dr Giono. One of the Americans, Ross Brunner, Jr, had stayed at the same hotel as Coburn, the Savoy; the other two, Nelson C. Emmings and Adam Osborn, at boarding-houses that offered more modest accommodation but were also situated by the bay. Photos obtained from the States established beyond any doubt the physical resemblances of the missing: athletic builds, a tendency towards obesity, signs of balding, obvious attempts to camouflage same. Though Coburn's body was subjected to a thorough examination in the Institute of Forensic Medicine and showed no traces of violence, and though the cause of death was attributed to accidental drowning due to a muscle cramp or physical exhaustion, the police commission recommended in favour of continuing the investigation. Further inquiry was made into the fate of the other three Americans, and it was soon learned that Osborn had left Rome without notice, that Emmings had flown to Paris, and that Brunner had gone insane. Brunner's case was already a matter of police record. Though originally a guest of the Savoy, he had been lying in the city hospital since early May. He was an automobile designer from Detroit. During the first week of his stay in Naples he was a model of good behaviour, spending mornings at the solarium and evenings at the Vittorini spa, except on Sundays, when he made a habit of going on various sightseeing tours. Since his trips were all arranged through a local travel agency, a branch of which was located in the Savoy, it was easy to establish his itineraries. Among the places he visited were Pompeii and Herculaneum; he took no sea baths, since his doctor had advised against it because of his kidney stones. Even though he had paid in advance, he cancelled a trip to Anzio on the day before it was scheduled to leave; for the preceding two days his behaviour had also been somewhat erratic. He gave up walking altogether, demanding his car even when his destination was only two blocks away, which turned out to be a nuisance because a new parking lot was then under construction and cars belonging to the guests had to be squeezed into a neighbouring lot.

Brunner refused to pick up the car himself and insisted that it be brought around by one of the hotel staff; this gave rise to several altercations. That Sunday, he not only passed up the sightseeing tour but also failed to show up for supper, ordering through room service instead. No sooner did the waiter set foot inside the door than Brunner jumped him from behind and tried to strangle him. In the scuffle he broke one of the waiter's fingers before jumping out the window, suffering a broken leg and a fractured pelvis in the two-storey fall. At the hospital he was diagnosed as having suffered – in addition to the multiple fractures – a mental blackout caused by an attack of schizophrenia. The hotel management was understandably anxious to hush up the whole affair. It was this incident in particular that prompted the commission's decision – following the death of Coburn – to widen the scope of the inquiry. The case now came under general review. The question arose whether Brunner had in fact jumped from the window, or whether he had been pushed. Yet no evidence could be found to challenge the waiter's credibility. He happened to be an elderly man with no criminal record.

Brunner remained in the hospital, not because of his mental

condition, which gradually improved, but because of complications arising from the mending of his hip bone, while a relative who was supposed to come for him from the States kept postponing his visit. Finally, a prominent physician diagnosed Brunner's illness as insanity caused by an acute psychotic seizure of unknown aetiology: the investigation had reached a dead end.

The second American, Adam Osborn, a middle-aged bachelor with a degree in economics, had driven an Avis rental car from Naples to Rome on June 5. In his hurry to leave the hotel, he had left behind such personal items as an electric razor, several brushes, a chest expander and a pair of slippers. The management of the Savoy, wishing to forward his things, phoned the hotel in Rome where Osborn had made a reservation but was told that no one had checked in under that name. The hotel soon gave up trying to track down its capricious guest, but a more thorough investigation revealed that Osborn had never reached his destination. At the Avis rental agency the detective learned that the rental car, an Opel Record, had been found parked in the emergency lane of Zagarolo, just outside Rome – in perfect running condition and with Osborn's luggage still intact. Since the Opel belonged to and was registered with the firm's fleet in Rome – it had been delivered to Naples by a French tourist en route from Rome – the agency notified the Rome police. Osborn's things were seized, and the police in Rome decided to launch a separate investigation of their own when Osborn was found at dawn the following day – dead. He had been run over by a car on the Strada del Sole, at the Palestrina exit, roughly nine kilometres from where the rental car had been abandoned.

The assumption was that for no apparent reason he had climbed out of his car and started walking along the shoulder of the road until reaching the first exit, where he became the victim of a hit-and-run accident. The police were able to reconstruct the exact sequence of events, because Osborn had accidentally spilled some eau de cologne on the car's rubber matting; a police dog had little trouble in following the scent, even though it had rained during the night. It seems Osborn had kept to the side of the road the whole time except when the highway cut through a hill, at which point he had left the concrete road and climbed to the top of the nearest knoll. After a while he returned to the road and resumed hiking. When he came to the exit ramp, he went zigzagging down the road like a drunk. He died instantly of a fractured skull. The road was spotted with blood and strewn with splinters of headlight glass when they found the body. So far the police in Rome had been unable to track down the hit-and-run driver. The most curious thing of all was that, despite the heavy afternoon traffic, Osborn had been able to walk a distance of nine kilometres on the highway without being noticed. If nothing else, he should have attracted the attention of a highway patrol car, since pedestrians are not allowed on the highway. The explanation came a few days later, when a golf bag was found dumped early one morning in front of a police station and identified as Osborn's through the name engraved on the handgrips. This led to speculation that he might have been carrying the golf bag over his shoulder and that, because the clubs were covered by a hood and he himself was wearing a pair of jeans and a short-sleeved shirt, the passing drivers might have mistaken him for a member of the road crew. The clubs were probably left lying at the scene of the accident; whoever picked them up must have read about the investigation in the papers, panicked at the thought of becoming personally implicated in a criminal matter, and got rid of them.

Osborn's motive for abandoning the car and taking off with the golf clubs was still not known. The empty cologne bottle and traces of spilled cologne found on the floorboard suggested that he might have splashed the cologne on his face to ward off an attack of nausea or even a fainting spell. The autopsy failed to turn up any traces of alcohol or toxins in his blood. Before leaving the hotel Osborn had set fire to several sheets of hand-written stationery in a wastebasket. Though nothing could be salvaged from the ashes, they found among the items left behind an empty envelope addressed to the police, suggesting that at one point he had considered notifying the police but later changed his mind.

The third American, Emmings, was a press correspondent for United Press International. On a return trip from the Far East, where he had been on a recent assignment, he decided to stop over in Naples. He made a two-week reservation when he registered at the hotel but then unexpectedly left town on the tenth day of his stay. At the British European Airways agency he booked a seat on a Naples–London flight, and it took only one phone call to establish that immediately after landing in London he had committed suicide in one of the airport rest rooms. He shot himself in the mouth, and died three days later in the hospital without ever regaining consciousness.

The reason for his abrupt departure was completely legitimate: he had received a cable from UPI instructing him to conduct a series of interviews in connection with rumours of a new scandal in Parliament. Emmings had the reputation of being a courageous and well-balanced man. He had served as a war correspondent in Vietnam, and before that as an apprentice reporter in Nagasaki following the Japanese surrender, where one of his eyewitness accounts had brought him instant fame.

Confronted with such facts, the assistant was eager to follow up his investigation by flying to London, the Far East, and even Japan, but instead he was instructed to interrogate those persons associated with Emmings during his stopover in Naples. Emmings had travelled alone, so they again had to rely on the testimony of hotel personnel. His behaviour revealed nothing out of the ordinary. But the maid recalled that while cleaning his room after his departure she had come across traces of blood in the washbasin and bathtub, as well as a bloody bandage on the floor. According to the autopsy report in London, Emmings had suffered a laceration on his left wrist. The cut was covered with a bandage and had a fresh scab. The conclusion reached was that Emmings had tried to commit suicide in the hotel by slashing his wrists but had then bandaged the wound before riding out to the airport. He, too, had taken the mineral baths, made daily trips to the beach, and toured the bay in a rented motorboat – in other words, had behaved in a most normal fashion.

Three days before he died, Emmings had gone to Rome to see a press attaché at the American embassy, an old acquaintance of his. The attaché later testified that Emmings had been in high spirits, but that on the way back to the airport he had never stopped glancing out the rear window, to the point where it became obvious. Jokingly he had asked Emmings if he'd made any enemies in Al Fatah. In reply Emmings had smiled and hinted he was on to something else, something he couldn't leak to anyone, not even to his friend, though it didn't really matter since it would soon be all over the front pages. Four days later he was dead.

Enlisting the help of several agents, the assistant went back to the health spa, this time to review the records of previous years. His presence at the Vittorini spa was becoming less and less welcome, since these constant invasions by the police were jeopardizing the establishment's good name. But when all the books were finally brought out into the open, eight new leads were uncovered.

Even though the pattern of events remained a mystery, the assistant began focusing his attention on men who were middle-aged foreigners and whose daily routine was suddenly interrupted some time between the second and third weeks of their stay.

Two of them turned out to be false leads. Both involved American citizens who had unexpectedly cut short their stay in Naples – one because a strike had been declared at his company, the other because he had to appear in court as a plaintiff in a suit filed against a construction company accused of installing a defective drainage system on his property. The date of the hearing had been inexplicably moved up.

In the case of the owner whose company had been struck, the investigation was finally called off when it was learned that the owner had died and that a separate inquest was already under way as a matter of course. Eventually the police in the States reported the man had died of a cerebral haemorrhage exactly two months after his return trip to America. For years the deceased man had suffered from a cerebral vascular disease.

The next lead, the third, involved an actual criminal case that was never included in the official file because this American's 'disappearance' was caused by his having been arrested by the local police. Acting on a tip from Interpol, the police uncovered a large amount of heroin on the suspect. He was presently awaiting trial in a Naples prison.

Three of the eight leads were thus eliminated. Two of the others seemed questionable. One involved a forty-year-old American who had come to the Vittorini spa for hydrotherapeutic treatment but who had stopped coming after injuring his spine in a water-skiing accident. The accident occurred while he was wearing a sailing kite harnessed to his back that allowed him to manoeuvre up and down on the towline; when the motorboat suddenly made an abrupt turn, the man came crashing down from a height of more than a dozen metres. Because of his injury he was laid up in a cast for a long time. The driver of the motorboat was also an American, a close friend of the victim; the incident still wasn't considered closed, because while convalescing in the hospital the man with the back injury developed a fever and began raving in delirium. The diagnosis wavered between some exotic disease contracted in the tropics and a delayed case of food poisoning.

The other questionable lead concerned a pensioner in his sixties, a naturalized American from Italy who had gone to Naples to collect his pension in dollars. He had been taking the mineral baths for his rheumatism when he suddenly interrupted the treatments, claiming they were bad for his heart. He was found drowned in the bathtub in his own apartment, exactly one week after his last visit to the spa. The autopsy ascribed the death to congestive heart failure and sudden cardiac arrest. Although the coroner uncovered nothing suspicious, the chief investigator, who had only stumbled on the case while checking the Vittorini records, ordered it reopened. Speculation arose that the pensioner might actually have been pushed under water: the bathroom door had been unlocked from the inside. An interrogation of the dead man's relatives failed to confirm any of these suspicions; not even a material motive could be established, since the pension was only a lifetime annuity.

Of the original eight leads only the last three led to the discovery of new victims, victims whose fates were typical of the evolving pattern. Again it was a matter of single men just past their prime, only now it was no longer restricted to Americans. The first was Ivar Olaf Leyge, an engineer from Malmö. The second was Karl Heinz Schimmelreiter, an Austrian from Graz. The third was James Brigg, a free-lance screenwriter identifying himself as an author, who, on his way over from Washington, had stopped off in Paris and contacted Olympia Press, a publisher that specialized in erotic and pornographic literature. During his stay in Naples he boarded with an Italian family. His landlord and landlady knew nothing about him except what he himself had declared when he introduced himself, namely, that he was interested in exploring the 'outer fringes of life'; it later came as news to them that he had been a regular visitor to the spa. On the fifth day he failed to return for the night. He was never again seen alive. Before notifying the police, the owners entered his room with a spare key to see what their tenant had left behind, only to discover that all his things were missing except an empty suitcase. They then recalled having seen their tenant leave the house every day with his briefcase full, only to return later with it empty. There was little reason to doubt their testimony, since the same family had been renting out rooms for years and enjoyed a spotless reputation. Brigg had been a bald man, of athletic build, with a face showing the scars of a harelip operation. He left no survivors, at least none who could be located. When he was later questioned, the publisher in Paris testified that Brigg had proposed writing a book exposing the seamier side of American beauty contests, a proposal the publisher had rejected as being too conventional. These statements could be neither confirmed nor denied. Brigg's disappearance had been so complete that no one could be found who had seen him since the day he vacated his room. Random inquiries among the city's prostitutes, pimps and junkies led nowhere. That was why the Brigg case was still classified as questionable; and, strange as it might sound, the only reason it was being kept on active file was that the man suffered from hay fever.

Not so the Swede and the Austrian, whose fates were never open to doubt. Leyge, a long-time member of the Himalaya Club and conqueror of Nepal's seventeen-thousand-foot range, had landed in Naples after divorcing his wife. He stayed at the Hotel Roma downtown, never went swimming, stayed away from the beach, made use of the solarium, took mineral baths and made the rounds of the museums. Late in the evening of May 19 he left for Rome, even though he had originally intended to spend the entire summer in Naples. In Rome he left all his things in the car and headed straight for the Colosseum, where he climbed his way up to the highest tier and plunged down the outer wall. The coroner's verdict was 'death due to suicide or accident as a result of a sudden mental blackout'. A tall and well-proportioned blond, the Swede looked young for his age and was extremely fussy about his outward appearance and about keeping fit: tennis every morning at six, no drinking, no smoking – in short, a fanatic when it came to physical fitness. The divorce had been settled by mutual consent, with incompatibility as the reason. These facts were established with the help of the Swedish police to rule out sudden depression as a possible suicide motive following the breakup of a long marriage. It was later revealed that the couple had actually been separated for a number of years and had filed for divorce to make everything legal.

The story of the Austrian Schimmelreiter turned out to be more complicated. Although present in Naples since the middle of winter, he had not started the mineral bath treatment until April. Noticing a definite improvement in his condition, he had his ticket extended for the month of May. A week later he couldn't sleep, turned grumpy and irritable, and went around claiming that people were rummaging through his things; when his spare pair of gold-rimmed glasses disappeared and later turned up behind the sofa, he insisted it was the work of a thief. He had been living in a small boarding-house and had been on friendly terms with his Italian landlady up to the time of his personality change, and so it was possible to get an exact description of his habits. On May 10 Schimmelreiter tripped on the stairs and had to spend some time in bed recuperating from a bruised knee. Within the space of two days he became more sociable, made up with his landlady, and, when his rheumatism refused to go away even after the pain in his knee subsided, resumed his trips to the baths. A few days later he had the whole boarding-house on its feet with screams for help. Possibly imagining that someone was hiding behind the mirror – unlikely, since it was a wall mirror – he shattered it with his fist and tried to escape out of the window. The landlady, unable to cope with the hysterical Schimmelreiter, called in a doctor acquaintance who made a diagnosis of coronary artery disease, a condition often leading to a minor stroke. The landlady insisted that the Austrian be transferred to the hospital. But while still at the boarding-house he managed to smash the bathroom mirror and another one on the landing before being relieved of his walking stick. At the hospital he was given to fits of anxiety and crying spells and would try to hide under the bed, while frequent attacks of asthma – he was also an asthmatic – only made his condition worse. To one of the interns in charge of him he secretly confided that on two occasions an attendant at the Vittorini spa had tried to kill him by slipping poison into the bathing water and that this was surely the work of an Israeli secret agent. The intern debated whether he should include this information in the patient's medical chart. The ward doctor interpreted it as a symptom of a persecution complex arising from presenile dementia. Towards the end of May Schimmelreiter died of lung cancer. Not having any next of kin, he was buried in Naples at public expense, since his stay in the hospital had exhausted his funds. His case therefore represented an exception to the rule; in contrast to all the other victims, this one involved a foreigner who was financially destitute. Subsequent investigation revealed that during the war Schimmelreiter had served as a clerk in the concentration camp at Mauthausen and that he had stood trial following Germany's defeat but had escaped sentencing when the majority of witnesses, all of them former inmates of the camp, testified on his behalf. Although there were those who accused him of having beaten prisoners, their testimony was treated as third-hand evidence, and he was finally acquitted. And despite the apparent coincidence that his health had twice taken a turn for the worse following visits to the Vittorini establishment, the dead man's suspicions proved unwarranted, since there is no known poison capable of affecting the brain once it has been dissolved in bathing water.

The bathing attendant accused of having tried to poison the Austrian turned out to be a Sicilian, and not a Jew, and was in no way connected with Israeli intelligence.

Not counting the missing Brigg, the file now included the cases of six persons who had all met sudden deaths from random causes. Invariably the trail led back to the Vittorini health spa; and since there were a number of such spas in Naples it was decided to check their records as well. The investigation began to avalanche: the number of cases that had to be checked soon jumped to twenty-six, since it was quite common for people to discontinue the baths without demanding a refund, especially as the amount of money involved was usually quite small. The investigation proceeded slowly, because each and every lead had to be fully explored. Only when the subject turned up in good health was the case dropped.

Herbert Heyne, a forty-nine-year-old naturalized American of German origin and owner of a drugstore chain in Baltimore, landed in Naples around the middle of May. An asthmatic, he had been undergoing treatment for years in a number of sanatoria when a lung specialist prescribed sulphur baths as a precaution against rheumatic complications. He began his treatment in a small place located not far from his hotel on the Piazza Municipale, taking all his meals in the hotel restaurant where, nine days later, he created a scene by insisting the food tasted vilely bitter. After the episode in the restaurant he checked out of the hotel and travelled to Salerno, where he registered at a seaside resort. Late that same evening he decided to go for a swim. When the porter tried to talk him out of it because of the strong tide and poor visibility, Heyne insisted he would die not from drowning but from a vampire's kiss. He even showed him where the kiss of death would come – on the wrist. The porter, a Tirolese who began treating the guest as a fellow countryman the moment the conversation switched to German, went down to the beach when he heard Heyne crying for help. A lifeguard was found and the German was rescued, but when he began showing signs of madness – such as biting the lifeguard – they decided to have him transferred by ambulance to the hospital; there, in the middle of the night, he got up out of bed, smashed the windowpane, and started slashing his wrists with a sliver of broken glass. The nurse on duty alerted the staff just in time to save him from bleeding to death, but he came down with a severe attack of bronchial pneumonia and died three days later, without regaining consciousness. The inquest ascribed his suicide attempt to the state of shock caused by his near-drowning, which was also cited as the cause of his pneumonia. Two months later Interpol was brought into the case, when Heyne's Baltimore lawyer received a letter mailed by Heyne shortly before his departure from Naples stating that in the event of his sudden death the police should be notified at once because he suspected someone was plotting to kill him. The letter gave no other details except that the suspected killer was staying at the same hotel. The letter was sprinkled with a number of glaring Germanisms, although Heyne, a resident of the United States for twenty years, had a perfect command of English. This fact, along with certain discrepancies in the handwriting, made the lawyer dubious of the letter's authenticity – it had been written on hotel stationery – and after learning of his client's death, he went ahead and notified the authorities. The handwriting expert's report confirmed that Heyne had written the letter himself but in great haste and a state of extreme agitation. At this point the case was dropped.

The next case to come under review was that of Ian E. Swift, English-born, US citizen, fifty-two, manager of a large furniture company in Boston, who landed by ship in Naples in early May, paid for a series of baths at the Adriatica, and stopped showing up after a week of visits; he stayed for a while at a cheaper hotel called the Livorno, then moved into the more luxurious Excelsior the same day he quit the baths. Witnesses were questioned in each of the hotels, but the testimony seemed to revolve around two different persons. The Swift at the Livorno spent most of the time in his room slaving over business correspondence, was an all-day boarder because it was cheaper, and occasionally went to the movies at night. The Swift at the Excelsior toured the local nightclubs in a hired, chauffeured car, travelled around in the company of a private detective, insisted on having his bed changed every day, had flowers sent to his hotel room, accosted girls on the street with invitations to join him for a ride and for supper, and went on periodic shopping sprees. He kept up this boisterous routine for four days. On the fifth day he left a note for the detective at the reception desk. When the detective finished reading the note in astonishment, he tried to reach Swift on the phone, but Swift refused to answer, even though he was in his room. He kept to his room the whole day, skipped lunch, and ordered dinner through room service. When the waiter appeared at the door, he found the room empty and heard Swift talking to him through a crack in the bathroom door. The same scene was repeated the following day – as if he couldn't stand the sight of the waiter. He kept up these antics until one day another man checked into the hotel, a man named Harold Kahn, an old friend and former business partner of Swift's who happened to be en route to the States after a long stay in Japan. Learning by chance that Swift was registered in the same hotel, he decided to pay him a visit, and forty-eight hours later they were both aboard a Pan Am jet bound for New York.

Though it lacked a fatal epilogue and therefore seemed to be an exception, Swift's case was none the less included in the series, since Swift really had Kahn to thank for his lucky trip home. The private detective testified that Swift had struck him as being not all there, that he was constantly talking about his negotiations with a terrorist organization called 'The Terror of the Night', which he said he was prepared to finance if he was promised protection against a killer hired by one of his competitors in Boston. The detective was supposed to be a witness to these negotiations and act as a bodyguard. The whole thing sounded so preposterous that the detective's first impression was that his client must be on drugs. Swift's laconic note, in which a hundred-dollar bill had been enclosed, was in effect a letter of dismissal. He made no mention of his enemies except to say that they had come to pay him a visit at the Livorno, though in fact he had not received a single visitor there.

It was extremely hard to get any information out of Kahn concerning his meeting with Swift in Naples. Nor did the Americans have any reason to launch an investigation, since neither Swift nor Kahn had committed any crime. Both had returned to the States without incident, and Swift had gone back to his manager's job. Still the Italians persisted, in the hope that Kahn was in possession of certain facts that could possibly shed light on recent events. At first Kahn refused to talk; not until he was briefed on the case and given assurance of absolute confidentiality did he agree to make a deposition. His testimony proved disappointing to the Italians. It seems that Swift had welcomed Kahn in the most cordial manner but only after checking through the door to make sure it was he. He admitted with some embarrassment to having played a few 'gags' and blamed it on the fact that he'd been drugged. Though outwardly calm and rational in his behaviour, he refused to leave his room, because he said he'd lost all confidence in his detective and suspected him of having 'gone over to the enemy'. He had shown Kahn part of a letter in which someone had threatened to poison him unless a demand for twenty thousand dollars was met. When the letter was first sent to Swift at the Livorno, he had ignored the death threat, though rashly so, because the day after the deadline he felt so weak he could hardly get out of bed. For the better part of the day he was bothered by hallucinations and dizzy spells, so he wasted no time in packing and moving into the Excelsior. Realizing there was no easy way out of the extortion plot, he hired a private investigator, though without immediately divulging the purpose, because he first wanted to look him over and test him while living it up in the manner already described. The whole thing was somehow beginning to make sense, though it still didn't explain why Swift simply hadn't left town, especially when there was nothing keeping him in Naples. As Swift explained it, the mineral baths had proved so beneficial for his rheumatism that he was eager to complete the treatment.

At first Kahn was inclined to believe him, but after thinking over everything Swift had told him he began finding his friend's story less and less credible. The stories he had heard earlier from the hotel staff

only confirmed his doubts. Had Swift been testing the detective that
time he fired a gun at some flies during an orgy with several ladies of
the night? – Kahn asked him straight out. Swift admitted it was true
but repeated that the poison had left him temporarily deranged.
Almost certain now that his friend had been stricken with some mental
illness, Kahn decided to get him back to the States as fast as he possibly
could. He settled Swift's hotel bill, bought plane tickets, and didn't
leave Swift's side until they were both packed and on their way to the
airport. Certain inconsistencies in the record suggest that Swift did
not accept his friend's Samaritan kindness passively. The hotel staff
testified that shortly before their departure the two Americans had
had a serious quarrel. Whether or not Kahn had used physical force
as well as verbal arguments, he would not volunteer any further information helpful to the inquiry, and the only solid piece of evidence,
the letter, had disappeared. Kahn had seen only the first page, which
had been typewritten – the illegible type made it look like one of a
number of carbon copies – and full of grammatical mistakes in English. Back in the States, when he asked Swift what had happened to
the letter, Swift broke out laughing and started opening a desk drawer
as if he meant to show it to him, only to find it gone. The experts
treated this latest evidence as a combination of the plausible and the
implausible. Typing an extortion letter through several sheets of thick
paper is a common practice, since once the individual letter traits have
been obliterated in this way, it is next to impossible to trace the
machine used. The fact that this was still a relatively recent practice
unknown to most laymen seemed to argue in favour of the letter's
authenticity. On the other hand, Swift's behaviour all seemed in-
appropriate. A man who is being extorted doesn't react the way Swift
did, not if he believes that the threats made on his life are actually
going to be carried out. The experts finally concluded they were dealing with two overlapping factors: real coercion in the form of a shake-
down attempt, apparently the work of a local resident (judging at least
by the letter's poor English), and Swift's temporary insanity. If that
was so, then the Swift case, when viewed within the context of the
investigation's previous findings, only confused matters, since his
apparent insanity otherwise conformed to the typical pattern.

The next one involved a Swiss by the name of Mittelhorn who

arrived in Naples on May 27. His case differed from the others in that he was a familiar sight at the hotel, where he was an annual guest. The owner of a large secondhand bookshop in Lausanne and a well-to-do bachelor, he was a man given to certain eccentricities of behaviour that were tolerated because he was considered such a desirable guest. He always occupied two adjoining rooms – one serving as an office, the other as a bedroom. Because of a food allergy, he always ordered specially prepared dishes and would carefully inspect the tableware before every meal. Whenever his face showed signs of swelling, a symptom commonly associated with Quincke's oedema, he would summon the cook into the dining room and reprimand him severely. Yet the waiters claimed he was in the habit of eating between meals in some of the cheaper places downtown, where, although it was strictly against his diet, he would indulge his craving for fish soup, and then later take it out on the people at the hotel. During his most recent stay he had revised his habits somewhat. On his doctor's advice he had begun taking mud baths at the Vittorini spa, after suffering all winter long from rheumatism. In Naples he had his own private barber come regularly to the hotel, using no tools but those supplied by Mittelhorn himself, who refused to be touched by any blade or comb that had already been used on someone else. When hearing on his arrival this time that his barber had gone out of business, he became furious and never stopped complaining until he finally found another one he could trust.

On June 7 he requested that the fireplace in his room be lit. The fireplace served as a decorative piece and had never been used before, yet no one dared to question his order. His request was granted, although the temperature outdoors was quite high. The fireplace smoked a bit, but this did not seem to disturb him. That afternoon he locked himself in his room and skipped lunch, which was unprecedented, since he never missed a meal otherwise and was always so concerned about being punctual that he carried two watches, one on his wrist and another in his pocket. When he failed to answer either the telephone or the door, they had to force their way into his room – the lock had been jammed from the inside with a broken nail-file. They found him unconscious in the smoke-filled room. An empty bottle of sleeping pills suggested he had taken an overdose, so he was rushed to the hospital by ambulance. As he had been scheduled to go to Rome at the end of June to attend an auction, Mittelhorn had brought along a trunk containing rare and old prints. This was now empty, and the fireplace was full of charred sheets of paper. Folios of parchment not damaged by the fire had been cut into little strips with a pair of barber's scissors, and frames for mounting woodcuts had been completely demolished. None of the hotel property had been damaged except for a curtain cord that had been ripped out and made into a noose, indicating he had tried to hang himself but failed when the cord wasn't strong enough to support his weight. A stool placed next to the window provided still further evidence.

When Mittelhorn finally regained consciousness, after spending two days in a coma, his doctor, suspecting the early stages of congestive heart failure, asked for X-rays. That night Mittelhorn became restless and delirious. At one point he started screaming that he was innocent, that he was someone else; then he began making threatening gestures, as though he were fighting with someone, until he finally tried to jump out of bed. Unable to control him, the nurse ran to get the doctor. Mittelhorn, taking advantage of her momentary absence, slipped into the orderly room next to his isolation ward, smashed his fist through a windowpane in the medicine chest, and drank a whole bottle of iodine. He died three days later from severe internal burns.

The coroner's ruling was suicide caused by a sudden fit of depression. But when the investigation was later reopened and the hotel staff was subjected to a more thorough interrogation, the night porter referred to a curious incident that had taken place the evening before the crucial day. A box of stationery and envelopes was kept on the reception-desk counter for the convenience of guests and visitors. After dinner a messenger came to deliver an opera ticket to Mittelhorn's next-door neighbour, a German, who was out. The porter slipped the ticket into an envelope and stuck it into Mittelhorn's box by mistake. Stopping off for his key on the way to his room, Mittelhorn was given the envelope, opened it, and took it over to a lamp in the lobby to read it. He collapsed into an armchair and covered his eyes. After a while, he glanced down again at the slip of paper in his hand, then hurried back to his room almost at a run. At that point the porter remembered the messenger with the ticket and, recalling having ordered the ticket himself over the phone, he realized it had been meant for the German and not for Mittelhorn. The sight of the German's empty box confirmed his mistake, and he decided to go directly to Mittelhorn's room. He knocked on the door but, getting no answer, went inside. The room was deserted. Lying on the table were the torn envelope and a crumpled piece of paper. The porter peeked into the envelope and found the ticket, which Mittelhorn had evidently overlooked. He took the ticket and, out of curiosity, smoothed out the sheet of stationery that had made such an impression on the Swiss. It was completely blank. The porter left the room, thoroughly bewildered, but said nothing when he later ran into Mittelhorn, who was on his way back from the refrigerator with a bottle of mineral water.

Since by now the investigation had reached the point of desperation, the detail of the blank sheet of paper began to acquire a special significance, all the more so as Mittelhorn had spent all of the following day burning his precious prints in the fireplace, coming downstairs only for lunch. Either the blank piece of paper had been a secret message or signal, or else he had experienced an hallucination in the hotel lobby and only imagined having read a non-existent letter. The first possibility seemed highly implausible, smacking of some cheap movie thriller, and was not at all consistent with Mittelhorn's reputation as a man of unimpeachable honesty, a respected antiquarian, and an authority in his field. An audit of his business transactions turned up nothing the least bit shady or suspicious. As they probed deeper into the past, however, the investigation uncovered certain facts dating from the last world war. During it, Mittelhorn had been manager of one of Germany's largest secondhand bookshops, located in Munich. The owner of the shop was a rich and elderly Jew. When the Nuremberg laws went into effect, Mittelhorn was appointed sole trustee of the shop, and its former owner was shipped off to Dachau, where he eventually perished. After the war, Mittelhorn took legal possession of the shop, supporting his claim with a document designating him as sole heir and executor of the dead man's estate. But there were rumours that the document had been signed under duress and that Mittelhorn had had a hand in it. Two years later, even though these were only rumours, Mittelhorn transferred his business to Switzerland and settled permanently in Lausanne. Speculation arose that his mental breakdown was somehow connected with these events that had transpired some forty years ago, that, owing perhaps to an optical illusion, he mistook the blank sheet of paper for some communication reminding him of past sins, became so disturbed that he decided to destroy his most valuable possessions, and was eventually driven to the point of attempting suicide. On regaining consciousness in the hospital, he may have had a vision of the deceased; helpless against the dead man's reproaches, he was driven again to suicide. However plausible it may have been, such a hypothesis appeared too ingenious; above all it did nothing to explain how such a well-balanced man could suffer a sudden mental breakdown. When they interviewed Mittelhorn's former neighbour at the hotel, he merely confirmed the porter's testimony, namely, that he had failed to get the opera ticket and that by the time he did receive it the following day it was too late. The case of the eccentric antiquarian thus reached an impasse, like all the others.

The file now included nine cases, all following the same mysterious pattern and all ending in tragedy. Despite their all-too-obvious similarity, there were still insufficient grounds for launching a criminal investigation aimed at prosecuting the guilty, since there was not the slightest hint as to their whereabouts or whether in fact they even existed. One very curious incident took place soon after the Mittelhorn case was officially closed; the hotel turned over to the police a letter recently addressed to the deceased man, even though he had been dead for more than a year. Postmarked Lausanne and bearing a typewritten address, the letter contained a blank sheet of paper. Efforts to trace the letter failed. Nor could it have been someone's idea of a practical joke, since the press had never made any mention of the first letter. I had my own thoughts on the matter, though I preferred not to reveal them for the time being.

Of the two remaining cases, the first dated from some time ago, the second was more recent. To start with the older one, some years ago, in May, a German from Hanover, Johann Titz, took a room in Portici, not far from Herculaneum. He chose a small boarding-house with a spectacular view of Vesuvius, because as a postcard manufacturer he was interested in producing a series of cards devoted to Vesuvius. But he was also there for medical reasons: he had suffered from asthma since his childhood. After too much exposure to the sun, he came down with a severe case of heat blisters. A dermatologist whom he consulted in Naples advised against any more sunbathing. To the doctor's astonishment, his patient vehemently objected, insisting that the sunbathing was absolutely indispensable for clearing up his asthma and that it had been recommended by his doctor in Hanover. Titz was taking mud baths in a small spa to which he commuted every day from Herculaneum – he had driven down from Germany in his own car. On May 9 he began having dizzy spells and attributed them to food poisoning. He accused his landlady of serving him contaminated fish and threatened not to pay his bill. But in the end he paid it and drove off. When the landlady later went to clean his room, she found a message inscribed on the wall in red India ink: 'I was poisoned here.' The ink had penetrated so deeply into the plaster that there was no getting rid of it except by repainting the walls, so the owner of the boarding-house filed a complaint against her former tenant.

On his way north, however, somewhere in the vicinity of Milan, Titz suddenly swerved to the left on a straight stretch of highway, cut across a grass island, and, disregarding the blinking lights and honking horns of the other drivers, started driving down the opposite lane into the path of the oncoming traffic. Astonishingly enough, he was able to drive like this for a distance of four kilometres, forcing the oncoming cars into the most desperate tactical manoeuvres. Some of these drivers later testified that he seemed to be aiming for the 'right' car. To avoid a long-haul Intratrans truck blocking his path, he swerved on to the island, waited till the truck had passed, then moved back into the wrong lane, where, less than a kilometre down the road, he collided with a small Simca carrying a young couple and a child. The child, though critically injured, was the sole survivor. Titz, who had been driving at high speed without a safety belt, died behind the wheel. There was speculation in the press that this was a new form of suicide in which the suicide victim tried to take others with him. In a collision involving the huge tractor-trailer he would probably have been the sole fatality, which explained why he had passed up the 'chance'. The case was classified as definitely belonging to the series when reports came in concerning certain incidents that had taken place immediately prior to the accident. Just outside Rome, Titz had pulled in at a service station because of apparent engine trouble and pleaded with the mechanics to hurry because he said the 'red bandit' was on his tail. At first the mechanics thought he was joking, but they changed their minds when he promised each of them ten thousand lire if they could fix his engine in fifteen minutes, and then actually kept his promise. When he gave all of the nine mechanics on duty the same 'bonus', they decided he was not all there. He might have gone un-identified had it not been that while he was backing out of the garage the German put a dent in one of the cars parked outside and drove off without stopping, though not before they were able to take down his licence-plate number.

The last case dealt with Arthur T. Adams II, who checked into the Hotel Vesuvio in Naples, bought a three-week pass to the mineral baths, then dropped out a few days later when he discovered he was allergic to sulphur. At forty-nine, he was a tall and easygoing man, always on the move and something of a restless type, having tried his hand at some ten different jobs. At one time or another he had been a bank officer, a Medicare official, a piano salesman; he had taught correspondence courses in banking, worked as a judo and later as a karate instructor, and actively pursued a number of hobbies: he was a licensed parachutist and an amateur astronomer, and for the past year or so he had been publishing on an irregular basis *The Arthur T. Adams II Newsletter*, featuring editorials on a wide range of subjects of personal concern to its publisher. Copies of the newsletter were run off on a duplicating machine at his own expense and distributed free of charge to several dozen acquaintances. He was also a member of a number of different societies, ranging from a dianetics circle to an organization for hay-fever sufferers.

Adams first began acting suspiciously on his return trip to Rome by barrelling along at high speed, then pulling over in deserted places; buying an inner tube when his car used tubeless tyres; sitting out a storm in a parked car just outside Rome; and telling a highway patrol-man his windshield wipers were broken when there was actually nothing wrong with them. That night he arrived in Rome and made the rounds of the hotels, looking for a vacancy – even though he had already reserved a room at the Hilton – returning to the Hilton only when he failed to find any. The next morning he was found lying dead in his bed. The autopsy disclosed early emphysema, enlargement of the heart, and generalized hyperaemia typical of death due to suffocation. The actual cause of death was never determined. The coroner's report suggested either overstimulation of the parasympathetic nervous system or suffocation caused by cardiac arrest precipitated by a severe asthmatic attack. For a while the case came under discussion in various medical journals, where the coroner's ruling was attacked as erroneous. It was argued that only infants have been known to die of pillow suffocation, whereas an adult will immediately awaken if his nose and mouth are obstructed. Nor was there any evidence to substantiate the claim that he had suffered an asthmatic attack. Finally, there was the position of the body: Adams was found lying on his stomach, with both arms wrapped around his pillow and the pillow pressed flat against his face. But if it was a suicide, then it had no precedent in the records of forensic medicine. Some tried to attribute his death to extreme fright, but, although such cases have been known to occur, no one has yet proved nightmares to be a cause of death. After a long delay, Interpol finally decided to intervene when two letters turned up in the States, both mailed by the deceased to his former wife, with whom he remained on friendly terms following their divorce. The letters had been mailed three days apart, but they arrived at the same time because of the backlog of mail created by a postal strike. In the first letter Adams wrote he was depressed and that he was having hallucinations of the 'sugar cube' variety. This was a reference to the period preceding their divorce, when Adams and his wife had been in the habit of taking psilocibin dished up in sugar cubes. Now, five years later, he had no idea what was causing these 'freaky' hallucinations, which occurred mainly at night. The second letter was altogether different in both tone and content. He was still having hallucinations, but he was no longer alarmed now that he knew what was causing them.

A detail you'd never suspect as being important has led me to the most incredible discovery. I've managed to get my hands on some material for a series of articles dealing with a completely new type of crime, a crime that's not only unmotivated but also indiscriminate, in the same way that scattering nails all over the road is an indiscriminate crime. You know I'm the last person to exaggerate, but the press won't be the only ones to sit up and take notice when I start publishing this stuff. But I've got to be careful. This material is too hot to keep around here. Don't worry, though; I've got it stored someplace where it's good and safe. Not another word till I get back. Will write from Rome as soon as I can. This is the sort of bonanza every journalist dreams about. And what a lethal one it is.

There's no need for me to elaborate on the intensive search that was made into the whereabouts of Adams's secret hiding place. The search proved to be a waste of time. Either he didn't know anything and the letter was just another one of his hallucinations, or he had done too good a job of hiding the material.

Adams's death brings to a close the list of tragic events originating in and around Naples. Besides the Italians, the investigation involved the law-enforcement agencies of Sweden, Germany, Austria, Switzerland and the United States, who were drawn into the case because of the victims' nationality. Interpol, which was supervising and coordinating the case, revealed a number of irregularities and minor omissions in the course of their investigation – such as failing to report missing hotel guests right away, or neglecting to perform an autopsy despite indications of a violent death – but in no instance were they able to establish any criminal motives, attributing the mistakes either to sloppiness, to negligence, or to self-interest.

Interpol was the first to resign from the case, with all the other agencies – including the Italian – following suit. It was re-opened only on the initiative of Mrs Ursula Barbour, Adams's chief executor. Adams had left an estate worth ninety thousand dollars in stocks and bonds, and Mrs Barbour, a woman in her eighties who had been Adams's foster mother, decided to use a part of the estate for apprehending the murderers of the man she regarded as her son. After familiarizing herself with the circumstances of his death, in particular with that last letter addressed to his former wife, she became thoroughly convinced that he was the victim of a crime so cunningly executed it had defied the efforts of all the various international agencies combined.

Mrs Barbour turned the matter over to Elgin, Elgin and Thorn, a respectable agency headed by Samuel Ohlin-Gaar, a lawyer and former friend of my father's. This was around the time when the end of my career as an astronaut was already inevitable. After Ohlin-Gaar's people had reviewed all the files, checked every possible lead, and gone to considerable expense to consult the most eminent authorities in criminology and forensic medicine, and still failed to make any progress, Ohlin-Gaar, acting on the advice of one of his oldest associates – a man by the name of Randolph Loers, better known to his friends as Randy – decided, more out of desperation than hope, to mount a simulation mission, that is, to send to Naples an unmarried American matching the type of victim in every possible way. At that time I was a frequent guest at old man Ohlin's place, and one day he began filling me in on the case in a casual sort of way, insisting it was not a violation of professional secrecy to do so since by now the only alternative to carrying out a simulation mission was to wash one's hands of the whole affair.

At first I didn't take the thought of my eligibility too seriously, but then it turned out the job was mine for the asking. It so happened that I was fifty and – except for an occasional touch of rheumatism and of course my hay fever – in top physical condition. Since it looked so tempting from across the ocean, I volunteered for the mission. Three weeks ago, using the alias of George L. Simpson, a broker from Boston, I landed by plane in Naples, where I checked in at the Vesuvio, bought a pass to the Vittorini spa, got a suntan, and played lots of volleyball. To make it look as authentic as possible, I used some of Adams's personal things, which Mrs Barbour had been saving. During the time I was in Naples, a six-man team kept me under constant surveillance – two men to a shift, plus two technicians to monitor my blood, heart and lungs. I wore electronic sensors wherever I went, except on the beach, where a pair of well-hidden binoculars was deployed. As soon as I arrived I put nineteen thousand dollars in the hotel safe: five days later I picked up the money, and kept it in my room from then on. I wasn't shy about making friends; I visited the same museums as Adams, went to the opera as he had, followed his footsteps around the bay, and drove to Rome in the exact same Hornet. To increase the range of the sensors, the car was equipped with an amplifier. A specialist in forensic medicine, Dr Sidney Fox, was waiting for me in Rome. His job was to examine all the medical data recorded on the tapes, which he did, and that's how the mission ended – a complete flop.

What I had given Barth was an abbreviated version of the case, the one we always used when it became necessary to enlist the services of an outsider. We called it 'the panoramic variant'.

The windows of the study faced the north, and the shade thrown by the giant elms made the room even darker. I disconnected the projector, Barth switched on the desk lamp, and the room was immediately transformed. He said nothing, with only his eyebrows registering mild astonishment, and suddenly I realized the utter futility of my having intruded on a complete stranger. I was afraid he was going to ask how I thought he could be of help – assuming he didn't simply dismiss the whole thing out of hand. Instead he got up, paced up and down the room, then came to a stop behind a handsome antique chair, placed his hands on its carved back rest, and said:

'You know what you should have done? Sent a whole group of simulators down there. No fewer than five.'

'You think so?' I asked with some bewilderment.

'Of course. If we conceive of your mission in terms of a scientific experiment, then you failed to fulfil either the preliminary or the accessory conditions. Either *you* were deficient or your environment was. In case you were the cause, then you should have selected men having the same characteristic variability ratio as that exhibited by the victims.'

'Aptly put!' The words slipped out of my mouth.

He smiled.

'You're not accustomed to our language, I see. That's because you associate with people who have a policeman's mentality. That mentality is all right for prosecuting criminals but not for proving whether in fact a criminal exists. I suspect if your life had been in danger you wouldn't have noticed it. Up to a point, of course. Later you'd have been aware of the accompanying circumstances but not of the causality itself.'

'Aren't they one and the same?'

'They can but need not be.'

'But I was ready for that. I was supposed to record anything that looked the least bit suspicious.'

'And what did you record?'

I smiled in embarrassment.

'Nothing. Oh, once or twice I was tempted to, but then I realized it was a case of too much introspection.'

'Have you ever used hallucinogens?'

'In the States, before joining the mission, LSD, psilocibin, mescalin – all under medical supervision.'

'I see ... part of your training. And would you mind telling me what you hoped to achieve by taking on the part? You personally.'

'Hoped to achieve? I was fairly optimistic. I thought we could at least prove whether it was a crime or just a matter of coincidence.'

'You *were* optimistic, weren't you. Naples is a trap, there's no doubt about that. But one that operates like a lottery, not like a machine. The symptoms tend to fluctuate, to behave erratically. They can subside or disappear altogether, right?'

'Absolutely correct.'

'All right, suppose now we take a firing zone as a model. You can be killed either by someone deliberately aiming at you or by the sheer density of fire. But either way someone on the other end is anxious to see a lot of people dead.'

'Oh, I see what you're driving at. The element of chance doesn't rule out the possibility of a crime, is that it?'

'Precisely. You mean to say that was never considered?'

'Not really. Someone once raised the possibility, but the reply was that if that were the case it would mean having to revise the whole method of investigation . . .'

'Either a wicked man or a wicked fate, is that it? But even the expression *corriger la fortune* has become proverbial. Why didn't you hook up a two-way transmission?'

'Too much of a bother. I couldn't go around loaded down with a lot of electronic equipment. Besides, there was another catch, one that came up in connection with the Swift case – Swift was the one rescued by the friend who had registered at the same hotel. Swift made his hallucinations sound so convincing he almost had his friend believing them.'

'I see what you mean. *Folie à deux*. In other words, you didn't want to risk having your shadow fall for any of your hallucinations, is that it?'

'Exactly.'

'Correct me if I'm wrong. Of the eleven victims, two escaped alive, and then there's another who is still missing. The missing man's name is Brigg. Am I right?'

'Correct. Brigg would have been the twelfth. He hasn't been definitely classified yet.'

'Due to insufficient evidence, I suppose. Now we come to their chronological order. In this respect your summary is misleading. It presents the individual cases in the order of their discovery, which is something completely incidental, rather than in the order of their occurrence. What was the time span involved? Two years?'

'Yes. Titz, Coburn and Osborn passed away two years ago. Brigg disappeared around the same time. The rest date from last year.'

'Any this year?'

'If there have been any, we wouldn't know about them till the fall. Especially since the original investigation has been discontinued.'

'Assuming your facts are correct, then it would seem to be an expanding series. Three in the first set, eight in the second. Well, well . . . I see you weren't acting as a decoy only in Italy.'

'Meaning?'

'That you've been trying to bait me, too. And I have to admit it's tempting! Your version makes everything seem crystal clear. The pattern is all too obvious. But the fact that it has everybody stumped leads me to believe there's more to it than meets the eye. Although the more one hears of the case histories, the more one begins to suspect some form of unmotivated insanity. Wouldn't you agree?'

'Yes. On that point there's general agreement. Otherwise they wouldn't have called off the investigation.'

'So why should there be any doubt that a crime has been committed?'

'How should I put it . . . it's like looking at a photo – I'm thinking now of a halftone. The naked eye can make out the general outline but not the details. A magnifying glass will make some things stand out more clearly, but the image will remain blurred. If we take it to the microscope we find the picture gets lost, that it disintegrates into tiny dots. Each dot is something distinct; they no longer combine to a meaningful picture.'

'Are you suggesting that once you've accepted the hypothesis of a random series of poisonings, the more detailed the examination the flimsier the hypothesis?'

'Precisely.'

'And the same thing applies if you assume the existence of a culprit?'

'The same thing applies. The conclusion is almost always the same: not one of the victims was poisoned by someone else, and not one of them had the means to do it himself. But the fact still remains . . .'

I shrugged my shoulders.

'So then why do you always insist on its being either a crime or a coincidence?'

'What alternative is there?'

'Maybe there is one.' He picked up a copy of *France-Soir* from his desk. 'Have you read today's papers?'

He showed me the headlines in bold print: BOMB EXPLODES IN THE LABYRINTH – MASSACRE ON THE STEPS – TEENAGED GIRL RESCUED BY UNIDENTIFIED MAN.

'Yes,' I replied. 'I'm familiar with what happened.'

'There you have it. The classic example of a modern crime. Premeditated and at the same time accidental. Anyone standing in the vicinity automatically became a victim.'

'But that's not quite the same thing!'

'Granted, it's not. The victims in Naples were predestined for death because of certain personality traits, but not those at the airport. Fair enough. But what about the case of that man Adams, who wrote his wife about the possibility of a random crime, and who compared it to covering a road with nails. Obviously it was a crude analogy. But it's just as obvious that whoever's behind these deaths is anxious to create the impression he doesn't exist.'

I withheld comment. Barth gave me a quick glance, stood up, paced around the room, then sat down again and asked:

'What's your own personal opinion?'

'I can only tell you what struck me most. Suppose the cause of death was poisoning; wouldn't you expect the symptoms to be the same in every case?'

'Well, weren't they? I was of the impression they all followed a pattern. First the phase of excitement and aggression, then the hallucinating phase, most often associated with a persecution mania, and finally the withdrawal phase – withdrawal either from Naples or from life itself. Either they tried to escape by car, plane, or on foot, or they resorted to a piece of glass, a razor blade, a cord, a bullet in the mouth, a bottle of iodine . . .'

I had the suspicion he was trying to impress me with the power of his memory.

'I'll admit they were similar. But when you start looking into the backgrounds . . .'

'Go on.'

'Well, as a rule, the manner of death has nothing to do with the personality of the deceased. Whether a person dies of pneumonia, cancer, or in a car accident is not something determined by his personality. Of course there are exceptions, as in the case of a test pilot's occupational death, but as a rule there's no correlation between the way a person dies and the way he lives.'

'In short, death is unrelated to personality type. Go on.'

'But here it is related.'

'Ah, now you're feeding me demonology! Just what are you implying?'

'Exactly what I said. A champion swimmer dies in a drowning accident. A mountain climber falls to his death. A car fiend gets killed in a head-on collision.'

'Hold on! Which one was the car fiend – Titz?'

'Yes. He owned three cars, two of them sports cars. To continue: a coward is killed while running away . . .'

'Who was that?'

'Osborn. The one who abandoned his car and was taken for a member of the road gang.'

'You didn't mention anything about his being a coward.'

'I'm sorry. The version I gave you left out many details. Osborn was in the insurance business, was heavily insured himself, and was known as a man who avoided taking any risks. The first time he felt threatened he sat down and wrote a letter to the police, then lost his nerve and took off. Adams, the eccentric, died as he lived – in an unconventional manner. The heroic reporter stuck it out till the end and then shot himself . . .'

'Wasn't he trying to escape, too?'

'I don't think so. He had orders to fly to London. He suffered a momentary breakdown, tried to slash his wrists, then patched himself up and flew off on his new assignment. When he saw he wasn't up to it, he shot himself. He must have been a very proud man. I have no idea how Swift would have died. As a young man he was known for being wishy-washy, a typical prodigal son, a dreamer, always in need of someone stronger than himself. A wife, a friend. It was the same way in Naples.'

Barth sat there with wrinkled brow, tapping his chin, and stared absently into space.

'Well, that's easy enough to explain. A case of regression, of reversion to an earlier time period . . . I'm not a specialist in this area, but I believe that some hallucinogens . . . What was the consensus of the toxicologists? Of the psychiatrists?'

'Certain symptomatic analogues with LSD, except that LSD does not have such individualized effects. Pharmacology has no record of such a drug. The deeper I delved into their individual backgrounds, the more I saw that not one of them had acted contrary to his nature – quite the opposite, that each had revealed it in grotesquely exaggerated form. A man who's careful with money becomes a penny pincher. A pedant – I'm referring now to the rare-book dealer – spends the whole day cutting up a trunkful of papers into little strips. Examples abound. If I could leave you the files, you'd see for yourself.'

'By all means. So this factor X would have to be something in the order of a "personality drug". Right . . . But such an approach won't bring us any closer to a solution. Psychological analysis can tell us how the factor behaves, but not how it infiltrates the victim.'

He was leaning forward in his chair, his head lowered and his eyes fixed on his hands, which were cupped around his knees. Suddenly he looked me straight in the eye.

'I'd like to ask you a personal question. May I?'

I nodded.

'What was it like during the simulation? Were you confident the whole time?'

'No. It was altogether an awkward situation, not at all as I had imagined it would be. Not because I was using a dead man's things – I got used to that in a very short time. Because of my profession, I was considered tailor-made for the mission.'

'Is that so?' His eyebrows shot up.

'The public imagines it to be fascinating, but except for a few brief moments of excitement it's all routine – boring and monotonous routine.'

'I see. In much the same way as in Naples, right?'

'Yes, especially since we're also trained in the art of self-analysis. If instruments are always subject to error, then the final indicator has to be man.'

'Monotonous routine, you say. In what ways were you excited in Naples? When and where?'

'When I was afraid.'

'Afraid?'

'At least twice. And each time it gave me something of a thrill.'

The words did not come easily, for I was dealing in intangibles. He never took his eyes off me.

'Did you enjoy being afraid?'

'I can't give you a yes or no answer. It's best when a person's abilities coincide with his ambitions. My ambitions have always tended towards the impossible. There's an infinite variety of risks, but I personally have never been attracted by such ordinary risks as, say, Russian roulette. That sort of test strikes me as jejune. On the other hand, I've always had a great attraction for the unknown, the unpredictable, the undefinable.'

'Is that why you decided to become an astronaut?'

'I don't know. Maybe that's the reason. People think of us as clever chimpanzees guided by a remote-control computer. The highest order, the symbol of our civilization, whose opposite pole you see before you.' I pointed to the paper featuring a front-page photo of the escalator. 'I don't believe that's necessarily true. And even if it were true, we'd have been all alone on Mars, completely on our own. I knew all along my physical disability would hang over me like the sword of Damocles. For six weeks out of the year, during the blooming season, I'm totally worthless. Still, I was counting on the fact that since no vegetation grew on Mars, which everybody, including my superiors, took for granted . . . but anyhow it was the hay fever that got me demoted to the backup crew, where I knew I didn't stand a chance.'

'Of flying to Mars?'

'That's right.'

'And did you go on being a backup member?'

'No.'

'*Aut Caesar aut nihil.*'

'That's one way of putting it.'

He unclasped his hands and sank deeper into his armchair. Sitting there with eyelids half open, he seemed to be digesting my words. Then a twitch of the eyebrows and a flicker of a smile.

'Let's return to earth. Did all the victims have allergies?'

'Just about, though in one case it was never substantiated. The allergies varied, dust allergy being the most common, followed by asthma . . .'

'And when was it you were afraid? A moment ago you mentioned . . .'

'I remember two different occasions. The first time was in the hotel restaurant, when another Adams was paged to the phone. I knew it was a popular name, I knew they were paging someone else; still, for a moment I had the feeling it wasn't just a coincidence.'

'You had the feeling they were paging a dead man, is that it?'

'Not at all. I thought it was the start of something. That it was a code word being used so none of the other customers would be the wiser.'

'Did it ever occur to you it might have been someone from your own team?'

'Out of the question. Under no circumstances were they to get in touch with me. Only in the event of a catastrophe, say, a declaration of war, was Randy, our leader, supposed to approach me directly. But only under such conditions.'

'Excuse me for being so inquisitive, but this strikes me as important. So Adams was paged. But what if the caller really had you in mind; wouldn't that mean he saw through your disguise and was telling you as much?'

'That's exactly why I was so scared. I was even tempted to go to the phone.'

'What for?'

'To make contact with the other side. Better that than nothing at all.'

'I see. But you didn't go, did you?'

'No. The real Adams beat me to it.'

'And the second time?'

'That was during my one night in Rome, at the hotel. I was staying in the room where Adams had died in his sleep. Oh yes, there's something else I should explain. You see, various simulation roles were considered. I didn't have to pose as Adams, there were alternate roles, but I sat in on the meetings and tipped the scale in favour of Adams – '

I broke off, seeing Barth's eyes momentarily light up.

'Let me guess. It wasn't the temporary insanity, it wasn't the seaside, and it wasn't the highway. It was just the thought of that safe and secluded hotel room – the solitude, the comfort, and death. Am I right?'

'Possibly, though I wasn't aware of it at the time. I guess they thought I was hoping to find the secret disclosures he was supposed to have stashed away somewhere, but that wasn't it at all. The truth was, I found the man somehow likeable.'

Even though he'd stung me a moment ago with his '*Aut Caesar aut nihil*', I found myself being a lot more talkative than usual, so dependent was I on this man's help. Exactly when this whole affair had become an obsession with me I couldn't say. At first I'd treated the impersonation as just another routine exercise, as a necessary part of the game. I don't know at what point it had pulled me in so completely that at the same time it pushed me away. I was looking forward to the danger, counting on it; I knew it wasn't my imagination; but just when I seemed to be on the verge of it, it turned out to be an illusion. I was barred from it. I'd done everything Adams had done – everything except share the same fate, and that's why I had nothing to show for it. Maybe Barth's remark had offended me so much because it touched on the truth. One of Fitzpatrick's medical colleagues on the Mars project, Kerr, a Freudian, would have said I was trying to force a showdown, that I preferred death to defeat; in other words, he'd have explained my choice of Adams, the mission itself, in terms of a Freudian death wish. You can bet that's what he would have said. But who cares. Asking for this Frenchman's help was tantamount to violating the mountain climber's code: I was giving him the lead so he could pull me up on the rope. But better that than total disaster: I had no intention of winding up a loser.

'Let's talk about methodology.' Barth's voice roused me from my thoughts. 'First of all, the class of victims, the mode of differentiation. In this regard you proceeded far too arbitrarily.'

'What makes you think so?'

'The fact that the incidents didn't form categories of their own but were arbitrarily categorized as relevant or irrelevant. Your criteria were death and insanity, or at least insanity, even when the latter failed to result in death. Compare the behaviour of Swift and Adams. Swift, you might say, went publicly insane, whereas if it hadn't been for Adams's letter to his wife, you never would have found out about his hallucinations. And there's no telling how many other cases there were like that.'

'Excuse me,' I said, 'but that's inevitable. What you've just accused us of is the classic dilemma of every investigation into the unknown. Before its limits can be defined the agent of causality must be identified, but before the agent of causality can be identified one must first of all define the subject under investigation.'

He looked at me with undisguised approval.

'Well, well, I see you're well versed in the language, too. But it surely wasn't the detectives who taught it to you, now was it?'

I said nothing in reply. He sat rubbing his chin.

'Yes, that is indeed the classic dilemma of induction. But let's turn to some of the discarded facts, to the false clues. Were there any promising leads that in the end proved useless?'

Now it was my turn to look at him with approval.

'Yes, one very interesting one. We really had our hopes pinned on it. Before leaving for Italy all of the American victims had been patients at one of Dr Stella's clinics. You've heard of Dr Stella, I suppose?'

'No, I haven't.'

'People say different things about him – some consider him to be one of the best, others claim he's a quack. Whenever one of his patients was suffering from rheumatism, he would prescribe the mineral baths in Naples.'

'What!'

'I jumped, too, when I heard that, but it turned out to be a false lead. He considered the baths around Vesuvius to be far and away the best, even though we have more than our share in the States. The ones who were talked into making the trip were in the minority, for it isn't true that all Americans are spendthrifts. If a patient said he couldn't afford a trip to Vesuvius, Stella would send him to an American health spa. We tracked down these people – they numbered about a hundred – and found them all safe and sound. Some of the patients were just as handicapped as before, but in any case we didn't come across a single fatality of the Italian type. Most of them died of natural causes – heart disease, cancer . . .'

'I assume they were married, had families of their own,' said Barth, distracted by some thought or other.

I couldn't help smiling.

'Doctor, now you're resorting to the same kind of crazy parlance, the same clichés, as those people in the agency . . . As a matter of fact, most of them did have families, but then there was no shortage of widowers and old bachelors among them, either. Besides, since when are wives and children an antidote? And an antidote against what?'

'You can't reach the truth without crossing a sea of mistakes,' Barth said sententiously but with a wry look in his eye. 'And do you happen to know how many patients this Dr Stella sent to Naples?'

'Yes, I do know. And this is one of the most bizarre coincidences of all. Every time I think about it I feel like I'm on the verge of cracking the case. Altogether he sent twenty-nine rheumatic patients, including five of our Americans: Osborn, Brunner, Coburn, Heyne and Swift.'

'Five of the seven Americans?'

'That's right. Neither Emmings nor Adams had gone to Stella's clinic for treatment. Nor had Brigg, but then, as you know, he was never classified as a victim.'

'This is all extremely relevant. And the other twenty-four patients?'

'I know the statistics by heart. Sixteen of them had been sent before any of the incidents in question had taken place. All returned safely to the States. Last year he sent thirteen. Five of the victims came from this group.'

'Five of the thirteen? And of the eight who survived, were there any conforming to the "model victim"?'

'Three of them, in fact. All single men, financially well off, and in their fifties. All safely returned. All alive.'

'Only men? Didn't Stella ever treat women?'

'He did treat women. Prior to the deaths in question he sent four women to Italy, two just last year. None this year.'

'How do you explain this disproportion between the sexes?'

'Stella's clinics first became famous as treatment centres for men. Potency disorders, falling hair . . . Later this was played down, but

Stella still has the image of being a man's doctor. So there's a very logical explanation for the disproportion.'

'Still, the fact remains . . . not a single woman was included among the victims, even though Europe has its share of elderly ladies, too. Does Stella operate any clinics in Europe?'

'No. The European victims never came into contact with Stella. That's pretty safe to assume, since none of them had visited the States within the previous five years.'

'Did you ever consider the possibility that there might be two separate operations – one for the Americans, another for the Europeans?'

'We did consider that. We compared both groups within the same set, but nothing came of it.'

'Why did he insist on sending his patients to Naples and not somewhere else?'

'Very simple. He's a second-generation Italian, his family comes from somewhere around Naples, and he probably stood to make a profit through his connections with some of the local balneologists, such as Dr Giono. Medical confidentiality prevented our gaining access to the correspondence, but it's only logical that a doctor on the other side of the ocean would recommend patients to his Italian colleagues. At any rate, we didn't uncover anything suspicious in their relationship. I suppose that for every patient he recommended he received a certain percentage.'

'How do you explain that mysterious blank letter delivered after Mittelhorn's death?'

'I suspect it was sent by a member of Mittelhorn's own family, someone who was familiar with the circumstances of his death and who was as eager as Mrs Barbour to see the investigation continued but who, for one reason or another, couldn't or didn't want to intervene as openly as she did. Someone who had good reason to believe a crime had been committed and was trying to stir up suspicion so the police would keep the case open. The letter was postmarked Switzerland, where Mittelhorn had a number of relatives . . .'

'Were there any drug addicts among Dr Stella's patients?'

'Two, neither of them heavy users and both of them elderly men – one a widower, the other a bachelor. Arrived last year around the end of May, beginning of June, took the baths, sunbathed regularly – in short, did everything that according to the statistics should have exposed them to the maximum danger. But the fact is both returned safe and sound. And I shouldn't forget to mention that one was allergic to pollen and the other to strawberries!'

'How disastrous!' exclaimed Barth, but neither of us was in the mood to laugh.

'You figured it was the allergy, didn't you? So did I.'

'What kind of drugs were they taking?'

'Marijuana in the case of the one with the strawberry allergy. The one with hay fever was taking LSD, but only once in a while. His supply ran out just before he flew back to the States; that's probably why he quit the baths and left ahead of schedule. In Naples he couldn't get his hands on the stuff. The police had just busted up a huge Middle Eastern ring based in Italy, trafficking had stopped, and the suppliers who hadn't been arrested were lying low.'

'And the one with the strawberry allergy . . .' mumbled Barth. 'Well, that takes care of that. What about those with mental problems?'

'Negative. Oh, you know as well as I do there's bound to be something in everyone's family closet, but that would be stretching it too far. All the patients in question – victims as well as survivors – were mentally sound. A few neurotics and insomniacs, but that's about it. Among the men, that is. Among the women patients we found one case of melancholia, one case of depression associated with menopause, and one suicide attempt.'

'A suicide attempt, you say?'

'One of those false alarms on the part of a typical neurotic. Poisoned herself under circumstances where she was sure to be saved. With the others it was just the opposite: not one of them had gone around proclaiming a suicidal mania. On the contrary, the repeated attempts give evidence of a ruthless determination.'

'Why only in Naples?' Barth asked. 'Weren't there any cases reported in places like Messina or Etna?'

'No. Naturally we wouldn't check out every sulphur spring in the world, but a special group was assigned to investigate the ones in Italy. An absolute blank. There was a case of someone dying of a shark attack, another in a drowning accident.'

'Coburn died in a drowning accident, too, didn't he?'

'Yes, but while temporarily deranged.'

'Has that definitely been proved?'

'Almost. We know relatively little about the man. Only that when he was served breakfast that time in his room, he hid his toast, butter and eggs in an empty cigar box, and later put some food on the window sill before going out.'

'Of course! He suspected poison and wanted to see if the birds . . .'

'And he probably wanted to take the box to a toxicologist but drowned before he had a chance to do so.'

'What about the experts' reports?'

'Two thick, typewritten volumes. We even resorted to the Delphi method of polling the experts.'

'Well?'

'The majority argued in favour of some unknown psychotropic drug similar in its effect to LSD, though not necessarily having a similar chemical composition.'

'An unknown drug? What a strange diagnosis.'

'Not necessarily unknown. These same experts believe it might be a combination of several known substances, since the symptoms of a synergy can seldom be deduced from the effects of its individual ingredients.'

'What was the minority opinion?'

'An acute psychosis of unknown aetiology. You know how loquacious doctors and specialists can be when they're in the dark about something.'

'Only too well. Would you mind giving me another rundown based on the typology of cause of death?'

'Not in the least. Coburn died an accidental or premeditated death by drowning. Brunner jumped from a window but survived it –'

'Excuse me, but whatever became of him?'

'He's back in the States, in bad health but still alive. He has a vague recollection of certain things but doesn't like to be reminded of them. All he can remember is having taken a waiter for a member of the Mafia and the feeling of being constantly shadowed. Shall I go on?'

'Please do.'

'Osborn was the victim of a hit-and-run accident. The driver of the car has never been found. Emmings twice tried to commit suicide. Died of a self-inflicted gun wound. Leyge, the Swede, drove to Rome and fell from the Colosseum. Schimmelreiter died in the hospital of natural cases, of a lung tumour, after going berserk. Heyne nearly drowned, then slashed his wrists in the hospital. Pulled through but later died of pneumonia. Swift escaped injury. Mittelhorn also tried to commit suicide twice – once with an overdose of sleeping pills, the second time by consuming iodine. Died of internal burns. Titz was killed in a highway accident. Lastly, Adams died in his hotel room at the Hilton in Rome, apparently from suffocation of unknown cause. The Brigg case is still a mystery.'

'Thank you. Of those who escaped alive, do any remember the initial symptoms?'

'Yes. One symptom was a trembling of the hands and a noticeable change in the taste of food. We found that out from Swift. Brunner definitely recalls the food's having an "off taste" but remembers nothing about any trembling of the hands. His testimony is probably the result of a residual psychic effect. At least that was the opinion of the medical experts.'

'The cause of death covers quite a spectrum, and the suicide victims always seemed to resort to whatever means was available at the time. Did you conduct an investigation based on the *cui prodest* principle?'

'You mean did we investigate those who stood to gain financially? That would have been pointless, since there was nothing in the way of evidence to connect any of the heirs with the individual deaths.'

'Any press coverage?'

'A total news blackout. Of course the local papers ran obituaries on each of the fatalities, but these got lost among all the other accident reports. We were worried they might interfere with the investigation. Only one paper in the States, the name of which escapes me, made any mention of the tragic fates met by the patients of Dr Stella. Stella himself insisted it was the work of some unscrupulous competitor. Even so, last year he didn't send a single patient to Naples.'

'So he stopped! Doesn't that look suspicious?'

'Not necessarily. One more incident and the publicity could have cost him more than he stood to make on the deal. He couldn't have been making very much on the kickbacks.'

'I now propose we play the following game,' suggested Barth. 'We'll call it "How to die a mysterious death in Naples". The purpose of the game will be to find out how one qualifies for such a death. Will you help me out?'

'By all means. The list of qualifications will include a person's sex, age, build, physical disabilities, financial status, plus some other characteristics that I'll try to specify. To qualify one would have to be a male in his fifties, rather tall, the athletic or the pyknic type, a bachelor, a widower or divorced, but in any case single during the time spent in Naples. As is evident from the Schimmelreiter case, financial prosperity is not an absolute requirement. Nor should one know any Italian, or if so, only a smattering.'

'None of the victims was fluent in Italian?'

'Not one. Now for the more specific characteristics. To be a candidate one should not be a diabetic.'

'Is that so?'

'There wasn't a single diabetic in the whole series. On the other hand, there were five known diabetics among the rheumatic patients sent to Naples by Dr Stella, all of whom returned home safely.'

'How do your experts explain that?'

'I'm not really sure I can answer that. Some ascribed it to the patient's metabolism, to the formation of acetone derivatives that might possibly have acted as an antidote, though this was challenged by some of the less distinguished – but in my opinion more honest – experts. Acetone derivatives form in the blood when an organism begins to suffer the effects of an insulin deficiency. But nowadays every diabetic is warned to take his prescribed medicine regularly. The next requirement is an allergy. Hypersensitivity to grass, hay fever, asthma. But then there were people who met all of the above conditions and still managed to escape unharmed. Take the patient with the strawberry allergy, or the one with hay fever.'

'Single, well-to-do men who took the mineral baths, were athletic in build, suffered from an allergy, and didn't know Italian?'

'They even used the same antihistamines as the others, in addition to Plimasine.'

'What's that?'

'An antihistamine with the added ingredient Ritalin. Ritalin is α-phenyl-α-piperidineacetic acid methyl ester hydrochloride. The first substance in Plimasine, Pyribenzamine, neutralizes the symptoms of allergic reaction but causes drowsiness and a diminution of the reflexes. That's why drivers are advised to take it in combination with Ritalin, which is classified as a stimulant.'

'You're quite a chemist, I see!'

'I've been taking Plimasine for years. Anyone who has an allergy is to some extent his own doctor. In the States I used to take an equivalent medication, since Plimasine is manufactured in Switzerland. Charles Decker, the man with the hay fever, was also on Plimasine, yet no one touched a hair on his head – Wait a moment.'

I sat there with gaping mouth like a moron. Barth stared at me in silence.

'They all showed signs of baldness,' I said at last.

'Baldness?'

'The beginning stages, at least. Wait a minute. Right, Decker had a bald spot, too . . . at the back of the head. But that still doesn't . . . oh, never mind.'

'But you're not exactly bald,' observed Barth.

'Sorry? Oh, right – I'm not. That was an oversight. But if Decker escaped injury . . . even though he showed signs of baldness . . . But what connection could there be between baldness and insanity?'

'Or between insanity and diabetes?'

'You're right, doctor, that's not a valid question.'

'Was the question of baldness completely overlooked?'

'The situation was like this. We compared those who died with those who left Naples unharmed. The question of baldness certainly came up. The problem was that verification was possible only in the case of the victims, since most of the survivors would have been reluctant to admit they were wearing a toupee. Human pride being what it is, this is one area where people tend to be extremely sensitive, and getting people to submit willingly to an on-the-spot examination would have been tricky. Also, it would have meant trying to locate the place where the wig or hair transplant had been ordered, and we simply had neither the time nor the staff for that.'

'Wasn't it considered very relevant?'

'People were divided. Some thought it was a waste of time trying to establish whether any of the survivors was anxious to conceal his baldness, and didn't see what connection that would have with the tragic fates of the others.'

'Well, then, if you had taken the hair factor into consideration, why did you act so startled a moment ago?'

'It was a negative correlation, I'm afraid. What startled me was that none of the deceased had tried to conceal his baldness. Not one of them had worn a toupee or undergone a hair transplant. There are such operations, you know.'

'So I've heard. Anything else?'

'Nothing – except that all the victims were in the process of going bald and made no effort to conceal it, whereas the survivors included both those who were balding and those with a normal head of hair. A minute ago I was reminded of Decker's bald spot, that's all. For a moment I thought I'd stumbled on to something. It wouldn't have been the first time, either. You see, I've been at this for so long that now and then I begin seeing things, phantoms . . .'

'Oh, that smacks of magic spells, spirits from the other world . . . But maybe there's something to it.'

'Do you believe in the existence of spirits?' A long and hard stare.

'It's probably enough if *they* believed in them, isn't it? Let's suppose some fortune-teller was operating in Naples, someone who went after rich foreign clients . . .'

'All right. Supposing there was such a person,' I said, sitting up in my chair, 'what then?'

'Let's assume this fortune-teller tries to win people's confidence through various kinds of tricks and séances, gives away samples of some miraculous elixir imported from Tibet, some type of narcotic that makes the client totally dependent on him or is passed off as a cure-all for every conceivable ailment . . . Now let's suppose that out of a hundred such cases there are some ten or eleven who rashly consume an overdose of the stuff . . .'

'Right!' I exclaimed. 'But in that case wouldn't the Italians have been wise to his little game? The Italian police, I mean? The fact is that in some cases we were so familiar with the victim's routine we knew exactly when he left the hotel, what he liked to wear, which were his favourite news-stands and even which papers he bought, which cabin he used for changing clothes at the beach, what and where he ate, which opera performances he saw . . . Now we might have missed such a quack or guru in one or two instances, but not in every single case. No, there never was any such person. Besides, the whole thing sounds too far-fetched. It's not just that none of them knew Italian; but would a Swede with a university education, a rare-book dealer, and a respectable businessman be likely to visit an Italian fortune-teller? Besides, none of them would have had the time . . .'

'Refuted but not defeated. Here goes another wild shot.' He sat up in his chair. 'If something had them hooked, then it must have strung them along gently and without leaving a trace. Right?'

'Right.'

'Now what else could have hooked them in a purely private, inti-mate, and casual sort of way but – sex!'

I hesitated before answering.

'No. Granted, there were a few brief erotic encounters, but that's hardly the same thing. Believe me, we did such a thorough background check we couldn't possibly have overlooked anything as "big" as a woman, a sex orgy, or a brothel. No, it must have been something else, something utterly banal . . .'

I was a little surprised by these last words of mine, since I'd never thought of it in such terms before. But it turned out to be grist for Barth's mill.

'Banal but lethal . . . Yes, why not! Some shameful and hidden desire, some secret lust that had to be satisfied . . . Not shameful to us, perhaps, but something that might have meant a horrible scandal for others if it were ever made public . . .'

'The circle has closed,' I said. 'Because now you've come around to the very same position you forced me to abandon a while ago, namely, psychology . . .'

Someone honked outside. Looking very young at that moment, the doctor stood up, peered down below, and shook his finger threaten-ingly. The honking stopped. I was surprised to notice it had already grown dark. I consulted my watch and was shocked to discover that I'd taken up three hours of Barth's time. I stood up to say good-bye, but he refused to hear anything of the sort.

'Oh, no, you don't. First of all, you'll stay with us for dinner. Second, we didn't settle anything. And third, or, rather, first and foremost, I'd like to apologize for reversing the roles and grilling you like some examining magistrate. I'll admit I had an ulterior motive, one not exactly worthy of a host . . . I wanted to find out certain things – both about you and from you – things I couldn't get from the files. It's always been my feeling that only a person can convey the atmosphere of a case. At times I was even out to provoke you a little, to needle you, but I must say you took it very well, though you haven't nearly as good a poker face as you imagine you do ... If there's anything that can redeem me in your eyes, then let it be my good intentions, because I'm ready to offer you my services. But let's sit down until dinner's served. They'll ring when it's ready.'

We sat down again. I felt enormously relieved.

'I'll work on the case,' he continued, 'though I don't believe we'll have much luck ... May I ask exactly how you envision my role?'

'This is a case lending itself to a multifactorial analysis,' I began cautiously, selecting my words with care. 'I'm not familiar with your program but I am familiar with a number of GPSS-type programs, and I assume your computer is somewhat analogous. The problem is not so much a criminal as an intellectual one. Obviously the computer won't be able to identify the culprit, but it might be able to eliminate the culprit as an unknown factor. Solving the case would mean positing a theory to account for the fatalities, a law governing these deaths ...'

Dr Barth looked at me almost with sympathy. Or perhaps it was only the way the light fell from above, gently modulating his features every time he made the slightest movement.

'When I said *we* I had in mind a team of men, not electrons. I've assembled a brilliant interdisciplinary team, including some of the best minds of France, and I'm sure they'd jump at the chance ... But as for the computer ... True, we've managed to program one, and so far the test results have been satisfactory, but with such a case – never ...' He shook his head.

'Why not?'

'Very simple. The computer won't work without hard data.' He spread out his arms. 'And what are we supposed to use as hard data in this case? Let's suppose a new narcotics ring is operating in Naples, that a hotel is being used as a drop, and they are delivering the stuff by substituting it for the salt in certain salt shakers. Now isn't it possible for the salt shakers to get switched around occasionally on the dining-room tables? In that case wouldn't only those who like salt on their food run the risk of getting drugged? And how, may I ask, is a computer supposed to process this if the processing data include nothing about the salt shakers, the drugs, or the culinary habits of the victims?'

I looked at him with admiration. How adept he was at manipulating such ideas. The dinner bell rang, louder and louder till it reached a shrill intensity, then suddenly stopped, and a woman's voice could be heard scolding a child.

'It's time for us to go downstairs . . . We always eat on schedule.'

The dining room was lit by a long row of pink candles on the table. On the way down Barth whispered that his grandmother would be joining them for dinner, adding that for a ninety-year-old woman she was still extremely fit, if a little on the eccentric side. I took this as a warning of sorts, but before I had a chance to reply I found myself being introduced to the other members of the family. Besides the three children whom I'd already met, and Mrs Barth, who was already seated across the table in a hand-carved chair identical to the one in the library, I saw an elderly lady dressed in a gown of royal purple. An old-fashioned lorgnette trimmed with diamonds glittered on her chest, and her small black eyes transfixed me like a couple of shiny pebbles. She held out her hand, but so high and with such enthusiasm that I kissed it, something I otherwise never do; and in a surprisingly deep and masculine voice, one that sounded as false as a voice in a poorly dubbed film, she said:

'So you're an astronaut, are you? I've never sat at the same table with an astronaut before.'

Even the doctor was taken by surprise. Mrs Barth was quick to remark that the children had announced my arrival. The old lady told me to sit down next to her and to speak in a loud voice, as she was hard of hearing. Next to her table setting was a kidney-shaped hearing aid, but at no time during the meal did she use it.

'You can keep me entertained,' she said. 'I doubt whether I shall have a similar occasion so soon again. Please, be so kind as to tell me how the earth *really* looks from up there? I don't trust the photographs.'

'And rightly so,' I said, passing her the salad bowl, secretly charmed by her blunt and unceremonious manner. 'No photo can ever match it, especially not when the orbital path is close and the earth gradually takes the place of the sky. It doesn't block the sky, it *becomes* the sky. That's the impression one gets.'

'Is it really as beautiful as they say?' Her voice expressed doubt.

'It was to me, anyhow. What impressed me most was the emptiness of it, the desolation. Not a sign of any cities, highways or seaports – nothing but oceans, continents and clouds. By the way, the oceans and continents look much the same as we were taught at school. But the clouds . . . I found the clouds to be the most uncanny thing of all, maybe because they didn't look like clouds.'

'What *did* they look like?'

'That depends on the altitude. From very far away they look like the old and wrinkly hide of a rhinoceros, all cracked and bluish-grey. But the closer you get, the more they look like different shades of sheep's wool after it's been combed out.'

'Were you ever on the moon?'

'I'm sorry to say I never was.'

I was preparing myself for more questions of a cosmological nature when she abruptly changed the subject.

'You speak French so fluently, but with a strange accent and a slightly different vocabulary. You're not from Canada, are you?'

'My family was Canadian; I was born in the States.'

'Just as I thought: then your mother is French?'

'*Was* French.'

I could see that both husband and wife were trying to dampen the old lady's curiosity by means of glances from across the table, but she simply ignored them.

'And did your mother speak French with you?'

'Yes, she did.'

'Your first name is John. So she must have called you Jean.'

'She did.'

'Then I shall call you that. Please take away the asparagus, Jean – I'm not supposed to eat it. The secret of growing old, Jean, is having lots of experience you can no longer use. They're right' – she said, indicating the rest of the family – 'not to pay me any attention. You're still too young to know, but there's quite a difference between being seventy and being ninety. A *fundamental* difference,' she added for emphasis. She stopped talking and began eating her meal, and came to life again only when the table was being cleared in preparation for the next course.

'How many times did you travel to outer space?'

'Twice. But I didn't travel very far from earth. If you compare it to an apple, then only as far as the peel is thick.'

'Aren't you being modest?'

'Not really.'

The conversation had taken a somewhat strange turn, but I can't say I found it awkward, especially since the old lady had a special charm about her. And so I was not the least bit irritated when she went on with her interrogation.

'Are you in favour of letting women travel in outer space?'

'I really haven't given it much thought,' I answered honestly. 'If that's their ambition, then why not?'

'You're the ones who started that whole crazy movement, aren't you? That women's liberation business. It's so childish, so tasteless, though it certainly is convenient.'

'Do you think so? Why convenient?'

'It's always convenient to know who's to blame for everything. Everything's the fault of men, say the ladies. They're the only ones who can straighten out the world. They want to take your place. As preposterous as it may sound, they do have a definite goal in mind, which is more than can be said of you men.'

After a dessert of rhubarb sprinkled with sugar, the kids sneaked out of the dining room and I got ready to leave. But when the doctor heard I was staying at Orly, he insisted I move in with him. I had no desire to take advantage of him, but I was sorely tempted. To put it bluntly, I wanted to pester the hell out of him.

Mrs Barth seconded her husband's invitation and showed me their still-empty guest book, saying it would bring good luck if an astronaut were the first to sign it. After a round or two of polite exchanges, I finally gave in. It was decided that I would move in with them the following day. Dr Barth accompanied me to my car and after I was behind the wheel confided that his grandmother had taken a distinct liking to me, adding that this was no small honour. He was still standing in the gateway as I drove off and plunged into a Parisian night.

To avoid the traffic I swung around the centre of the city and headed for the boulevards along the Seine, where the midnight traffic was sure to be lighter. I was tired but contented. My conversation with Barth had left me feeling extremely hopeful. I took it easy on the road, not trusting myself after drinking all that white wine. Ahead of me a small 2 CV was nervously hugging the curb. The road was deserted. Warehouses loomed high above the railings that ran along the opposite bank of the Seine, but I hardly noticed them: my mind was wandering. Suddenly a pair of car lights blazed in the rear-view mirror like a couple of suns. I was right in the middle of passing the 2 CV and was a little too far over to the left, so I decided to make way for the night racer and drop back into the slow lane, but it was too late. His headlights flooded the inside of my car, and a second later a flattened-out shape came shooting through the gap. By the time I recovered from the air blast, he was gone. Something was missing from the right front fender. All that was left of the mirror was the stem. Cut off. A little farther down the road it occurred to me that if it hadn't been for the wine I would have blocked its path and might now be lying underneath the wreckage of my own car. Now *that* would have given Randy food for thought. How beautifully my death would have fit the Naples pattern. How sure Randy would have been it was connected with the simulation mission. But it seems I wasn't fated to be the twelfth victim: I made it back to the hotel safely.

On the fourth day of my visit, on a Sunday, in order to put his team's involvement in the case on a more personal basis, and also perhaps to show off his new house, Barth held a little get-together at his place to which more than twenty people were invited. Since I hadn't been prepared for any formal affairs, I decided to drive to Paris on Saturday to pick up something more appropriate for the occasion, but Barth talked me out of it. So, dressed as I was in a pair of faded jeans and a scraggly sweater – all my better clothes had been ruined by the Italian police – I stood at the entrance along with the Barths. The walls on the ground floor had been opened up, converting the downstairs area into a spacious drawing room. It was a rather strange situation: surrounded by a crowd of bearded neophytes and periwigged bluestockings, I felt a little like a crasher and a little like a host, inasmuch as I was Barth's houseguest and was even sharing the honours of the house. Being neatly trimmed and shaven, I must have made the impression of an overaged Boy Scout.

Curiously absent from the party was that atmosphere of courtly formality, or even worse that revolutionary clowning so characteristic of intellectuals: ever since the latest events in China, the Maoists had gone into hiding. I made an effort to socialize with all the guests because I knew they had come expressly to meet an allergic astronaut, a roaming detective ad interim. Nonchalantly the conversation turned to the tribulations of the world. Not nonchalantly, really, but in a mood of surrender now that Europe's eternal mission had come to an end, a fact that these graduates of Nanterre and l'École Supérieure seemed to grasp better than their compatriots. Europe had survived, but only in an economic sense. Prosperity had been restored, but not the feeling of self-confidence. It was not the cancer patient's fear of malignancy, but the awareness that the spirit of history had moved on, and that if it ever returned it would not be here. France had lost its power and influence, and now that it had been moved from the stage into the audience it was at liberty to show concern for the sufferings of the world. McLuhan's prophecies were coming true, but in an inverse sort of way, as prophecies have a habit of doing. His 'global village' was already here, but split into two halves. The poorer half was suffering, while the wealthier half was importing that suffering via television and commiserating from a distance. That it wouldn't go on like this was everywhere taken for granted, but it went on just the same. No one asked for my opinion on the State Department's new 'wait and see' policy within the economic buffer zone, nor did I venture to offer any.

The conversation then switched from the trials of the world to its follies. Among other things, I learned that a famous French film director was planning to make a film about the 'massacre on the steps'. The part of the mysterious hero was to be played by Jean-Paul Belmondo; the little girl would be played not by a child actress – since bedding down with a kid would have been considered in bad taste – but by a famous British movie star. Being just recently married, this same actress had invited a number of prominent personalities to her public wedding night – such pastimes were now the vogue – in order to take up a collection around the nuptial bed for the benefit of the airport casualties in Rome. Ever since reading about those Belgian nuns who indulged in charitable prostitution in order to redeem the hypocrisy of the Church, I'm no longer appalled by such things. And of course there was a lot of talk about politics. The latest news item was that members of an Argentine movement of national patriots had been exposed as government stooges. Various people expressed the fear that something like that couldn't be ruled out even in a country like France. Fascism had survived, along with the most ruthless dictatorships – at least in Europe – whereas the only way to deal effectively with extremist terror was to exterminate the activists. Although a democracy refused to condone 'preventive murders', it none the less looked the other way when it came to pro-government assassinations carried out under discreet supervision and with limited liability. This was not to be confused with the old-fashioned type of political execution or repression instituted by the State, but was, rather, a form of constructive terror *per procurationem*. I once heard of a philosophy that advocated the total legalization of violence, which even de Sade regarded as the epitome of true freedom. It would have constitutionally sanctioned every sort of activity – revolutionary as well as reactionary; and since the supporters of the *status quo* far outnumbered the subversives, the established order was sure to emerge intact in a violent confrontation of both extremes, should it ever come to something like a civil war.

Around eleven Barth began showing the more curious guests around the house, leaving only a handful of people downstairs. I decided to join three of the guests who were sitting around an open patio door. Two were mathematicians belonging to rival camps: Saussure, a relative of Lagrange, was specializing in analysis, that is, in pure mathematics; the other was in applied mathematics, being a programmer and statistician by profession. Even their outward appearance offered an amusing contrast. Saussure looked as if he might have stepped out of a daguerreotype – lean, dark-haired, with chiselled features, bushy sideburns, a gold pince-nez dangling on a ribbon – and wore a Japanese transistorized calculator around his neck like a medal, which was obviously meant as a joke. The statistician, a burly, curly-headed blond, was a double for the slouchy Boche featured in French postcards from the time of the First World War, and was in fact of German origin. His name was Mayer, and not Mailleux, as I thought at first after hearing it pronounced that way. The mathematicians were in no hurry to make conversation, unlike the third man, a pharmacologist named Dr Lapidus. Sporting a full-length beard, he looked as if he'd just returned from an uninhabited island. He asked me whether the investigation had turned up any abortive cases, that is, cases where the outward signs of insanity had simply come and gone. I answered that all the files were on microfilm, and that unless one wanted to classify the Swift case as abortive, there were none falling into that category.

'That's amazing!' he exclaimed.

'Why amazing?'

'The symptoms varied in their intensity, but the moment any of the victims was hospitalized, like that man who jumped out the window, they immediately subsided. If one assumes the psychosis was chemically induced, that would mean the dose taken had a strange kind of cumulative effect. Didn't anyone notice this?'

'I don't really see your point.'

'There's no psychotropic compound known to have such a delayed effect that, say, if it were taken on Monday it could begin producing the first symptoms on Tuesday, cause hallucinations on Wednesday, and reach a maximum intensity on Saturday. Of course it might be possible to build up a supply by using a hypodermic injection that it would take several weeks to absorb; but such a procedure would leave traces in the body, and I found nothing in the autopsy reports to indicate this.'

'You didn't find anything because nothing like that was ever reported.'

'That's what I find amazing!'

'But they might have taken the stuff more than once, which would explain the cumulative effect . . .'

He shook his head with disapproval.

'How? Between the change in routine and the appearance of the first symptoms there was always a time lapse of six to eight days on the average, nine in one case. And no chemical agent is capable of having such a delayed or cumulative effect. Let's assume they started taking this chemical substance the first or second day after their arrival; then the initial symptoms would have had to occur within the next forty-eight hours. In the case of patients with kidney or liver diseases that's debatable, but then there weren't any such patients.'

'So what's your opinion?'

'The case histories would indicate they were drugged on a *steady*, *gradual* and *continual* basis.'

'So you believe it was a case of premeditated poisoning?'

He broke out in a smile, revealing his gold teeth.

'No. Who knows, maybe the goblins are to blame, or maybe some flies were on their way back from raiding a pharmaceutical lab and happened to land on the victims' toast after tramping around in the latest derivatives of lysergic acid. But I do know that the process of accretion took place *gradually*.'

'But what if it were an unknown compound?'

'Unknown to *us*?'

He said it in such a way that I couldn't help smiling.

'Yes. Unknown to you. To chemistry. Would that be impossible?'

He made a wry grimace and flashed the gold in his mouth.

'There are more unknown compounds than there are stars in the sky. But you can't have any that are both resistant and non-resistant to tissue metabolism. There are many circles, but there is no such thing as a squared circle.'

'I don't follow you.'

'Very simple. Chemical agents known to cause acute reactions act by binding irreversibly to the body's haemoglobin to form insoluble compounds with carbon monoxide or cyanide. An autopsy will always be able to detect the presence of such agents, especially if micromethods are used – chromatography, for example. But even with the help of chromatography they couldn't find any traces! That means the chemical agent involved must be easily degradable. If it's easily degradable, then it would have to be administered in a number of small doses or else in one massive dose. But if it were administered in a single dose, then the symptoms would start becoming noticeable in a matter of hours and not days. Now do you follow me?'

'Yes. Do you see any other possibilities?'

'There is one other. And that is if it involved some basically innocuous substance that began developing psychotropic properties the moment it started distributing itself in the blood or tissue. In the liver, for instance. To expel this substance the liver might convert it into a toxic agent. The result would be an interesting biochemical trap, though a completely hypothetical one, since nothing like that has ever been known to happen and I doubt whether it ever could.'

'How can you be so sure?'

'Because pharmacology has no record of such a toxin, of such a

"Trojan horse". And if something has never been known to happen, the chances are slim that it ever will.'

'So where does that leave us?'

'I don't know.'

'Is *that* all you have to say?'

I was being impolite, but the man was beginning to get on my nerves. Even so, he didn't seem to take offence.

'No, that's not all. The effect could be the result of something else.'

'A combination of different substances? Of different toxins?'

'Yes.'

'But that would definitely make it a case of premeditated murder, wouldn't it?'

The answer came unexpectedly from Saussure.

'A girl from Lombardy was working as a housemaid for a certain Parisian lawyer living at 48 Rue St-Pierre, on the third floor. One day her sister came to visit her but forgot the name of the street, confusing it with St-Michel. When she came to 48 Boulevard St-Michel, she went upstairs, found a doctor's nameplate, rang the doorbell, and asked for her sister, Maria Duval. By sheer coincidence it turned out that a woman with the exact same name – Maria Duval – was working for another doctor, on another street, but was in fact somebody else entirely. Now in trying to determine the a priori probability of such a coincidence, we find it impossible to offer a rational, that is to say, mathematically valid explanation. The example may appear trivial, but, believe me, it opens up an endless void. The only model for the theory of probability is Gibbs' world of recurrent events. When it comes to unique and statistically unclassifiable events, the theory of probability is inapplicable.'

'There are no such things as unique events,' said Mayer, who all this time had been standing there in amusement, grinning wryly.

'Of course there are,' countered Saussure.

'At least not as a set.'

'You happen to be a unique set of events yourself. Everyone is.'

'Distributively or collectively speaking?'

Just when it looked as if we were in for a duel of abstractions, Lapidus placed a hand on each man's knee and said:

'Gentlemen!'

Both men smiled. Mayer went on smirking with tongue in cheek while Saussure tried to pick up where he had left off.

'One can easily run a frequency analysis on the name Duval or the residences of Parisian doctors. But what's the ratio between confusing Rue St-Pierre with Boulevard St-Michel, and the frequency of these names as street names throughout France? And what numerical value do you assign to a situation in which the woman finds a house with an occupant named Duval but on the fourth, rather than the third floor? In short, the set of possibilities is limitless.'

'But not infinite,' interjected Mayer.

'I can prove it's infinite in both the classical and the transfinite sense.'

'Excuse me,' I interrupted, wishing to pick up the thread. 'Dr Saussure, I'm sure your story had a moral to it. What exactly was the moral?'

Mayer gave me a sympathetic glance and strode out onto the patio. Saussure seemed somewhat startled by my lack of perspicacity.

'Have you been out in the garden behind the summerhouse, out where the strawberry patch is?'

'Why, yes.'

'Did you happen to notice the round wooden table standing there, the one trimmed with copper nails?'

'Yes.'

'Do you think it would be possible to take an eyedropper and squeeze out as many drops as there are nails so that each drop hits a nail head?'

'Well . . . if a person were to take careful aim, why not?'

'But not if a person just started firing away at random?'

'Then obviously not.'

'But five minutes of a steady downpour and each nail would be *sure* to get hit by a drop of water.'

'You mean to say . . .' I was beginning to see his point.

'Yes, yes! My position is an extreme one: there's no such thing as a mysterious event. It all depends on the magnitude of the set. The greater the set, the greater the chance of improbable events occurring within it.'

'Then the victims do not really form a set . . .?'

'The victims were the result of a random causality. Out of that realm of infinite possibilities I mentioned earlier, you chose a certain fraction of cases that exhibited a multifactorial similarity. You then treated these as an entire set, and that's why they seem mysterious.'

'So you would agree with Mr Lapidus that we should investigate the abortive cases?'

'No. For the simple reason that they would be impossible to find. The class of soldiers stationed at the front includes the subclass of both killed and wounded. While these two groups can be differentiated easily, you'll never be able to differentiate those soldiers who came within an inch of being hit from those who missed being hit by a kilometre. That's why you'll never find out anything except by sheer accident. An adversary who relies on a strategy of chance can only be defeated by the same strategy.'

'Are you at it again, Dr Saussure?' came a voice from behind us. It was Barth, accompanied by a lean, grizzly-haired man whose name I failed to catch when we were introduced. Barth treated Saussure not as a member of his team but more as a curiosity. I later found out that until a year ago Saussure had been working for Futuribles before joining up with the French CETI investigating the possibility of extraterrestrial civilizations, but that he had always been something of a drifter. I asked him whether he believed such civilizations existed.

'That's not so simple,' he said, rising to his feet. 'Other civilizations exist and at the same time do not exist.'

'Meaning?'

'They do not exist as projections of our own concept of civilization, from which it follows that man is incapable of defining what makes these civilizations be civilizations.'

'Perhaps,' I conceded. 'Still, it must be possible to define our place in the cosmos, don't you think? Either we're nothing but a drab mediocrity, or we're an exception, and a glaring one at that.'

Our listeners broke out laughing, and I was surprised to learn that it was precisely this line of reasoning that had persuaded Saussure to quit the CETI. At the moment he was the only one not laughing; he just stood there, fingering his calculator as if it were a pendant. After luring him away from the others and manoeuvring him over to the table, I offered him a glass of wine, poured myself one, and, while drinking to his version of civilization, asked him to share his views with me.

This was a shrewd tactic, one I'd learned from Fitzpatrick: affecting an air of seriousness bordering on parody. Saussure began by explaining that the progress of human knowledge was a gradual renunciation of the *simplicity* of the world. 'Man wanted everything to be simple, even if mysterious: one God – in the singular, of course; one form of natural law; one principle of reason in the universe, and so on. Astronomy, for example, held that the totality of existence was made up of stars – past, present and future – and their debris in the form of planets. But gradually astronomy had to concede that a number of cosmic phenomena couldn't be contained within its scheme of things. Man's hunger for simplicity paved the way for Ockham's razor, the principle stating that no entity, no category can be multiplied unnecessarily. But the complexity that we refused to acknowledge finally overcame our prejudices. Modern physics has turned Ockham's maxim upside down by positing that everything is possible. Everything in physics, that is; the complexity of civilizations is far greater than that of physics.'

I could have gone on listening to him, but just then Lapidus insisted on introducing me to a group of doctors and biologists. All were of the same opinion: not enough data. The consensus was that one should start with the hypothesis that the deaths were caused by a congenitally determined reaction to certain unknown elements in the microbiosphere. Two groups should be singled out for study – forty in each, all men in their fifties, all having an athletic or a pyknic build, all randomly selected – and made to undergo a steady programme of sulphur baths, sunbathing, body massages, sudorifics, ultraviolet lamps, horror films and some titillating pornography, until one of them showed signs of cracking. A genealogical study would then have to be made of their hereditary backgrounds for any sudden or unexplained deaths, which is where the computer would come in handy. They had gone on to discuss the chemical composition of the bathing water and the air, the subject of adrenochromes, the possibility of a chemogenic schizophrenia of metabolic origin – when Dr Barth came to my rescue and began introducing me to the legal experts on the team. Some of the lawyers argued in favour of the Mafia, others in favour of some new and hitherto undisclosed organization that was in no hurry to claim responsibility for the mysterious deaths. Their motive? But, then, what motive did that Japanese have for slaughtering all those Serbs, Dutchmen and Germans in Rome? And had I seen today's papers? A New Zealand tourist had tried to protest the kidnapping of an Australian diplomat in Bolivia by hijacking a charter plane in Helsinki that was carrying pilgrims bound for the Vatican. That principle of Roman law which said '*id fecit cui prodest*' was no longer valid. No, it had to be the Mafia, since any one of the Italians could have been a mafioso: the street vendor, the hotel porter, the bath attendant, the taxicab driver . . . And the acute psychosis would suggest the presence of hallucinogens; although slipping someone a hallucinogen in a restaurant might have been tricky, where else would a person be apt to gulp down a cool, refreshing drink if not in a health spa after a hot and sweaty bath? The lawyers were then surrounded by the doctors, whose company I had just left, and an argument broke out on the subject of baldness, but without resolving anything. The whole scene was rather comical. Around one o'clock the smaller groups began merging to form a fairly animated crowd, and while champagne was being served the subject of sex came up. All were convinced that the list of drugs and medications found on the victims was incomplete. Why was that? Because it didn't include any of the latest sex stimulants or aphrodisiacs, and you could be sure the older men were using them. Topcraft, Bios 6, Dulong, Antipraecox, Orkasfluid, Sex Tonicum, Sanurex Erecta, Elixire d'Égypte, Erectovite, Topform, Action Cream – the market was flooded with them. I was overwhelmed by this display of erudition, and also a little embarrassed, since they'd managed to reveal a flaw in the investigation: at no time had anyone bothered to investigate the psychotropic effects of such medications. I was advised to look into it. You mean to say that not one of these medications was found on the victims? That in itself was suspicious. A younger man wouldn't make any bones about it, but then we all know how older men are apt to be secretive, prudish and self-conscious when it comes to such matters. They had probably used the stuff and got rid of the wrappers . . .

The party was getting noisy; windows were thrown open; corks went flying; a smiling Barth kept popping in and out of different doorways; Spanish girls made the rounds with trays; a platinum blonde – Lapidus's wife, I guessed – not bad-looking in the dark, said I reminded her of an ex-boyfriend . . . The party was a grand success. And yet I was in such a blue, melancholic mood, mellowed by the champagne: I felt cheated. Not one of these rather amiable hotshots had any of that flair, that special flash of illumination which in art went by the name of inspiration, that ability to sniff out what's relevant from a pile of facts. They didn't care about finding a solution to the problem; they only wanted to complicate it by inventing new ones. Randy had the gift but was short on the sort of erudition of which the Barth house was chock full – full but unfired.

I stuck around till the very end, joined my hosts in seeing off the last of the guests, watched as car after car went down the driveway till it was empty, gazed up at the house ablaze with lights, then went upstairs feeling defeated and disaffected. More with myself than with anyone else. Outside, a refulgent Paris loomed beyond the dark stretch of gardens and suburban clutter, but its refulgence was not enough to eclipse the planet Mars, now radiantly ascendant above the horizon: a yellow sphere someone had put there as the final dot.

There are friends with whom we share neither interests nor any particular experiences, friends with whom we never correspond, whom we seldom meet and then only by chance, but whose existence none-the-less has for us a special if uncanny meaning. For me the Eiffel Tower is just such a friend, and not merely because it happens to be the symbol of a city, for Paris leaves me neither hot nor cold. I first became aware of this attachment of mine when reading in the paper about plans for its demolition, the mere thought of which filled me with alarm.

Whenever I'm in Paris I make a point of going to see it. To look and see, that's all. Towards the end of my visit I like to step under its foundation, to station myself between its four iron pylons and gaze up at its interlacing arches, the intricate trusswork outlined against the sky, and the grand, old-fashioned wheels used to propel the elevator. The day after the get-together at Barth's was no exception. Though it was now completely hemmed in by high-rise boxes, the tower was just as impressive as ever.

It was a bright and sunny day. Sitting on a bench, I thought about how I might back out of the whole affair – I'd already made up my mind the moment I woke up that morning. After all that effort, the mission now seemed to me so phony and irrelevant and misguided. Especially misguided was my enthusiasm. It was like a moment of self-revelation: behind all the major decisions in my life I saw the same impulsiveness, the same infantile thinking. On impulse I had enlisted in the commandos as an eighteen-year-old and wound up a spectator of the Normandy invasion – from a stretcher, that is; my glider, after taking enemy flak, had crash-landed off target, with me and a crew of thirty on board, right on top of some German bunkers, and the next day I found myself in an English field hospital with a broken tailbone. Mars was just a repeat performance. Even if I'd made it up there and back I couldn't have gone on reminiscing about it for ever; otherwise I might have gone the route of that astronaut who wound up contemplating suicide because everything else seemed so anticlimactic by comparison, including offers to sit on the board of directors of several large corporations. One of my fellow astronauts had been made managing director of a Florida beer-distributing company; and now, every time I reach for a can of beer, I always see him stepping into the elevator in his angel-white spacesuit. That's why I'd joined the Naples mission: I had no intention of following in their footsteps.

Now, as I stood looking up at the Eiffel Tower, it all seemed so clear to me. It was a frustrating profession, so tempting with its promise of that 'big step for mankind' which was, at the same time, in Armstrong's words, a 'small step for men'; but in reality it was a high point, an apogee (and not only in the astronomical sense); a position in danger of being lost, a symbolic image of human life in which the lust for the unattainable consumes all of man's powers and hopes. Only up there hours take the place of years, and a man's best years at that. Aldrin knew that the prints left by his space boots would survive not only the Apollo programme but mankind as well, that they would be eroded only when the sun expanded into the earth's orbit one and a half billion years from now. So how could a man who'd been so close to eternity settle for a beer distributor's job? To know that from then on it was all downhill, and to have experienced it in such an intense and irrevocable manner, that's more than a letdown; that's a mockery. As I sat there admiring this iron monument erected to the last century by a master engineer, I wondered even more at my own fanaticism, at my own stubborn persistence, and it was now only a feeling of shame that kept me from racing back to Garges and packing my things on the sly. Shame and a sense of loyalty.

That afternoon Barth dropped by my guestroom in the attic. He seemed a little on edge. News. Inspector Pingaud, the Sûreté's liaison with the Barth team, had invited both of us to his office. To brief us about a past investigation headed by one of Pingaud's colleagues, Superintendent Leclerc. Pingaud felt that the case merited our attention. Naturally I agreed to the interview, and we drove off to Paris together.

Pingaud was expecting us. The moment I saw him I recognized him as the quiet, grey-haired man I'd seen at Barth's side the night before, though he was much older than I'd taken him to be. He greeted us in a little side room, and as he stood up I noticed a tape recorder lying on his desk. Dispensing with any preliminaries, he told us the superintendent had been to see him the day before yesterday – though retired, the superintendent was in the habit of dropping in on old friends. During their conversation Leclerc had made reference to a case that he couldn't brief me on personally but that the inspector persuaded him to record on tape. Because it was a rather lengthy story, he invited us to make ourselves comfortable, then left us alone in the room. He did this seemingly as a matter of courtesy, not wishing to disturb us perhaps, but the whole thing struck me as fishy.

I wasn't accustomed to police hospitality, much less from the French police. Then again, maybe it was too little. Not that I detected any outright discrepancies in Pingaud's version; I had no reason to believe it was a fake investigation or that the superintendent wasn't really retired. Still, nothing would have been easier than to set up a private meeting somewhere. I could understand it if they were reluctant to drag out the files – the files being something sacrosanct for these people – but the tape recorder alone implied they were anxious to avoid any sort of discussion. The briefing was to take place without commentary: you can't very well pump a tape recorder. But why the elaborate cover? Barth was either thrown just as far off balance as I, or else he wanted – was obliged? – to keep any doubts he may have had to himself. My mind was still mulling over such thoughts when a rather low, self-assured, asthmatic voice came on the tape recorder.

'Monsieur, just so there won't be any misunderstandings : I will tell you as much of the story as discretion will allow. Inspector Pingaud has vouched for you; still, there are certain matters that are better left undiscussed. The dossier you brought with you to Paris is something

I've known about for a long time, longer than you, and I'll give you
my honest opinion: this case doesn't warrant an investigation. Don't
take me wrong. It's just that I have no professional interest in anything
that doesn't come under the penal code. The world's full of mind-
baffling things – flying saucers, exorcisms, guys on TV who can
bend forks from a distance – but none of that means anything to me
as a policeman. Oh, when I read about such things in *France-Soir*, I
can scratch my head and say, "Well, I'll be damned!". I may be wrong
in saying the Italian affair doesn't call for an investigation; then again,
I've put in a good thirty years on the force. You may disagree with
me; that's your privilege. Inspector Pingaud had asked me to brief
you on a case I handled a couple of years ago. When I'm finished
you'll see why it was never publicized. At the risk of being rude, I
must warn you that if you ever try to publish any of this material I
shall categorically deny everything. You'll see why. It's a question of
raison d'état, and I am, after all, a member of the French police force.
Please don't take it personally; it's a matter of professional loyalty.
What I'm telling you is standard procedure.

'The case has now been shelved, though at one time the police, the
Sûreté, and even French counter-intelligence were all in on it. Well,
to start with, the subject's name was Dieudonné Proque. Proque is not
really a French name; originally it was Procke. He was a German Jew
who, as a young boy, emigrated to France with his parents during the
Hitler regime, in 1937. His parents belonged to the middle class, thought
of themselves – till the time of the Nazis, that is – as German patriots, and
had distant relatives in Strasbourg whose ancestors had settled in France
in the eighteenth century. I'm going so far back in time because this was
one of those cases calling for a thorough background investigation. The
tougher the case, the more widely the net has to be thrown.

'His father left him nothing when he died, and Proque later became
an optician. He spent the occupation years in Marseilles, in the un-
occupied zone, where he stayed with relatives. Except for the war
years, he lived the whole time in Paris, in my *arrondissement*, where he
ran a little optical shop out of his apartment on Rue Amélie. Since he
didn't have the resources to compete with the more established firms,
business was bad, and he barely made ends meet. He made very little
from sales, mostly from repairs – replacing lenses, fixing broken toys,

that sort of thing. An optician for the poor. He lived with his mother, a woman going on ninety. A bachelor, he was sixty-one at the time in question. His record was clean: not one court conviction, though we knew the photo lab he'd fixed up at the back of the shop was far from being the innocent little hobby he said it was. There are people who specialize in risqué pictures – not necessarily pornography – but who are unable or unwilling to do their own developing, in which case they need someone else to handle it, someone reliable who won't make extra prints for himself. Within limits, there's not even anything illegal about it. Then there are those who lure people into tricky situations and take pictures for blackmail. We keep most of the blackmailers on file, and it's not advisable for them to have their own darkroom or camera equipment or to hire a photographer who's already had a conviction. Proque was running that kind of racket, but only as a sideline. We knew that he was developing pictures and that he usually did it when he was hard pressed financially. But that was still no reason to move in on him. And frankly, these aren't the only things that get by the police nowadays. Not enough full-time staff, not enough funds, and not enough manpower. Besides, we knew Proque wasn't making a bundle on the deal. He didn't have the nerve to use extortion against any of his clients. He was the cautious type, a coward by nature, completely dominated by his mother. Every July they'd make the same trip to Normandy; they lived always in the same cluttered apartment above the shop, in the same building, with the same neighbours they'd known since before the war. A brief physical description of the man, since that's important for you: short, thin, prematurely stooped, with a tic in his left eye and a constantly drooping eyelid. To those who didn't know him, and especially in the afternoon hours, he gave the impression of being hard of hearing and a bit of a crank. But he was completely in his right mind, except for periodic drowsy spells – usually in the afternoon – caused by low blood pressure. That's why he always kept a Thermos of coffee on his workbench, to help keep him awake on the job. As the years went by, these spells grew worse, to the point where he was constantly yawning and on the verge of fainting or collapsing. Finally his mother made him go to see a doctor. He saw two doctors, both of whom prescribed harmless stimulants, which actually helped for a while.

'What I'm telling you isn't a secret; every tenant in the building knew about it. People even knew about his shady business deals in the darkroom. The guy was so easy to see through. And in the end these pictures were nothing compared to your bread-and-butter sort of stuff. The fact is, I'm in Homicide; morals offences are not my department. Anyway, what happened later had nothing to do with morals offences. What else should I tell you to complete the picture? He was a collector of old postcards, used to grumble a lot about having hypersensitive skin – too much exposure to the sun made him break out all over, though he didn't seem like the sort of man who'd go out of his way to get a suntan. But that fall his complexion started to change, became sort of coppery, the way it does when it's been exposed to a sun lamp, and some of his regular customers, friends of his, started saying, "Tch, tch, Monsieur Proque, don't tell me you've been going to a sunroom?!" And, blushing like a little girl, he'd explain that he had a bad case of boils – in the most sensitive spot, he said – so bad that his doctor had prescribed radiation plus vitamins and a special skin ointment. Apparently the treatment worked.

'That October was especially cold and rainy. Fall was also the time of year the optician was most susceptible to attacks of dizziness and fainting spells, so again he went to see the doctor, and again the doctor prescribed some pep pills. Around the end of the month, while he and his mother were eating dinner one night, he became very excited and began telling her about how he stood to make a killing on a big order for developing and enlarging lots of prints, in colour and in large format. He figured on netting sixteen hundred francs on the deal, a small fortune for a man like Proque. At seven that evening he lowered the shutter and, after telling his mother he wouldn't be back till late, shut himself up in his darkroom. Around one in the morning his mother was awakened by a noise coming from her son's room. She found him sitting on the floor and crying "worse than any man has ever cried before", to quote the transcript. In a sobbing voice he kept screaming that he'd wasted his whole life and that suicide was the only way out, started ripping up his favourite postcards, knocking over the furniture . . . and there was nothing his mother could do to stop him. Though normally obedient, he completely ignored her. It was like some cheap melodrama. She kept trailing him around the room and yanking at his clothes; he kept looking for some rope, ripped off the curtain cord but was so weak his mother had no trouble getting it away from him; he went for a knife in the kitchen, and as a last resort threatened to go down to the darkroom, where he always kept a supply of lethal chemicals on hand. But then he suddenly went limp, slumped to the floor, and before long was snoring and whining in his sleep. His mother wasn't strong enough to lift him into bed, so she slipped a pillow under his head and let him sleep like that through the night.

'The next morning he was his normal self again, though extremely demoralized. He complained of a bad headache, said he felt as if he'd been drinking the whole night, though in fact all he'd had to drink was a quarter of a bottle of wine at lunch, and a weak table wine at that. After taking a couple of aspirin tablets, he went down to the shop, where he spent a routine day. He had very few customers as an optician, and since he spent most of his time in the back polishing lenses or in the darkroom developing photos, the shop was usually empty. That afternoon he waited on a total of four customers. He kept a record of every order, even the most minor repair job done on the spot. If the customer was a stranger, he'd merely jot down the order. Needless to say, he didn't keep a record of his photographic work.

'The next two days were also uneventful. On the third day he got an advance for the enlargements and prints, though of course he was shrewd enough not to enter this amount in the cash receipts. That night he and his mother ate more extravagantly than usual, at least by their standards: an elegant wine, a special fish dish – oh, I can't remember all the dishes any more, though there was a time when I knew all of them by heart, even what kind of cheese they ate for dessert. The following day he received another batch of undeveloped film, from the same client. During lunch he was in an excellent mood, telling his mother all about his plans for building a house, then, in the evening, he shut himself up in his darkroom again. Around midnight his mother heard a terrible commotion, went downstairs, stood in the hallway, and knocked on the back door of the darkroom. Through the plywood partition she listened to him ranting and raving, breaking things, turning the place upside down ... Panic-stricken, she ran to get her neighbour, an engraver whose workshop was just down the street. The neighbour, an easygoing old widower, used a chisel to pry open the bolt on the partition door.

'It was dark inside, hardly any noise. They found Proque lying on the floor; scattered all around him were the partially developed and still sticky negatives of pornographic photos. They were everywhere, many of them torn and others still glued together. The linoleum floor was covered with chemicals, all the reagent bottles had been smashed to smithereens, the enlarger lay damaged on the floor, there were acid burns on Proque's hands and holes in his clothes, the faucet was running full blast, and he was soaked from head to foot – apparently after trying to revive himself by sticking his head under the faucet. From the looks of it, he'd tried to poison himself, by mistake grabbed some bromide instead of cyanide, and went into a narcotic stupor. He put up no resistance when his neighbour practically carried him back to his apartment. His mother testified that after the neighbour left, Proque tried to go on another rampage but was too worn out physically. The scene that followed was again straight out of some second-rate comedy: he flopped around in his bed, tried to rip up his top sheet to hang himself, stuffed his pillowcase into his mouth, and all the time kept shrieking, crying, swearing. As soon as he tried to get to his feet he collapsed and fell asleep on the floor, as he had the time before.

'He woke up the next day feeling miserable as hell. The sight of all the damage he'd caused only made him feel guiltier and more despondent, so he spent the whole morning picking up the pieces, rinsing things off, trying to salvage what was left of the negatives, and mopping up the mess. When he was finished cleaning up the darkroom, he took his cane – he was having another one of his dizzy spells – and went out to stock up on a new supply of chemicals. That evening he complained about having some sort of mental illness, asked his mother if she knew of any cases of insanity in the family, and refused to believe her when she said she didn't. The very fact that he could accuse her of lying convinced her that he wasn't fully recovered yet, since in the past he wouldn't have dared even to raise his voice to her. Never before had he acted so aggressively, but then she could understand how a person might lose his self-control after two consecutive attacks of hysteria, which would've been enough to make anybody think he was going insane. He promised his mother that if it ever happened again he'd go straight to a psychiatrist. It wasn't like him to make such rash decisions; it had taken him weeks to go to see a dermatologist, and then not until his boils were really killing him. Not because he was tightfisted – he had no need to be, since he was medically insured – but because he couldn't put up with the slightest change in his routine.

'Not long after that he had a falling out with his client because several of the pictures turned up missing. We still don't know what transpired between them; it's the only major dark spot in the whole affair.

'The following week passed quietly. Proque became more subdued and never brought up the subject of his mental illness again. That Sunday he and his mother went to see a movie. Then on Monday he went completely berserk. It happened like this. Around eleven in the morning he walked out of the shop without bothering to close the door behind him. Nor did he bother to return his friend's greeting – an Italian who ran a little candy store on the corner – when the man called out to him from in front of the shop. The Italian later testified that Proque looked "somehow funny". Proque went straight inside the shop, bought some candy, said he'd pay for it on his way back – which wasn't like him at all – because by then he'd be "rolling in dough", climbed into a taxi even though it was a good ten years since he'd last taken one, and told the driver to take him to Avenue de l'Opéra. There he made the driver wait and came back fifteen minutes later yelling and waving an envelope full of cash, gave holy hell to some street tramp who tried to make off with the money, climbed back into the taxi, and told the driver this time to take him to Notre Dame. When he reached the island, he paid the fare with a hundred-franc note – the cabby said he saw only hundred-franc notes inside the envelope – and before the cab had even pulled away from the kerb, started to climb over the bridge railing. A passer-by grabbed hold of his leg, there was a scuffle, the cabby jumped out of the car, but not even the two of them could handle him. A gendarme showed up, and together they managed to shove him into the taxi, leaving the hundred-franc notes lying on the sidewalk. When Proque wouldn't stop being hysterical, the gendarme handcuffed him, and they headed straight for the hospital. On the way there, Proque pulled a fast one. After the car drove off he collapsed on the seat, went completely limp, then suddenly lunged forward, and before the gendarme could stop him – they were driving in heavy traffic now – grabbed hold of the steering wheel. The cab rammed straight into a Citroën's front door, pinning the driver's arm between the steering wheel and the door. The gendarme managed to get Proque to the hospital in another taxi. At first the hospital didn't treat his case too seriously, since all he did was stand there in a daze, whimper a little, and refuse to answer any questions. Finally he was admitted for observation, but later, when the chief physician was making his rounds, Proque turned up missing. He was found under the bed, wrapped in a blanket pulled out from under his sheet, and huddled up so close to the wall that it was a while before he was even noticed. He was unconscious from loss of blood, having slashed both wrists with a razor blade smuggled from his clothes into his hospital gown. It took three blood transfusions, but they pulled him through, though he later developed complications due to his poor heart condition.

'I was assigned to the case the day after the incident on the Île St-Louis. Though there was nothing to warrant an investigation by the Sûreté, the lawyer representing the owner of the Citroën, figuring this was a good chance to milk the police, came up with a version charging the police official on duty with criminal negligence. Having in his custody a deranged criminal, the lawyer claimed, the policeman was responsible for allowing the taxicab to collide with his client's car, causing bodily and property damage as well as severe psychological shock to his client. Since the police were criminally liable, any compensation for damages would have to come out of government funds.

'Hoping to gain an advantage, the lawyer leaked his version to the press, which had the effect of escalating the whole affair, since now it was the prestige of the Police Judiciaire that was at stake. It was at this point that I was called in to make an investigation.

'The preliminary medical report indicated Proque had suffered an acute psychosis caused by a delayed attack of schizophrenia, but the longer he was kept under observation after his suicide attempt, the less this diagnosis seemed to hold up. In the space of just six days he had become a thoroughly broken and wasted old man, but he was completely sane in all other respects. On the seventh day of his stay in the hospital he made a deposition. He testified that instead of paying him the sixteen hundred francs they had agreed upon, his client had paid him less than one hundred fifty, for failing to deliver all the prints. That Monday, while he was grinding some lenses for a new fitting, he suddenly became so furious he dropped everything and left the shop, "to get what he had coming to him". He had no recollection of going into the candy store or of anything that happened on the bridge, only that his client had come up with the balance of the money after Proque went to his apartment and made a stink. Later that night, after making his deposition, Proque suddenly took a turn for the worse. He died early the next morning of heart failure. The doctors were unanimous in ascribing it to a reactive psychosis.

'Though Proque's death was only indirectly related to Monday's attack, the case was becoming more serious. Nothing like having a corpse for a trump card. The day before he died, I had gone to pay Proque's mother a visit. For a woman her age she turned out to be very cooperative and obliging. On my way out to Rue Amélie I picked up a man from Narcotics to examine the darkroom and the photo-lab chemicals. I was tied up for quite a while with Madame Proque, because once she got started on something there was nothing I could do but sit and listen patiently. Near the end of my visit, I thought I heard the shop's doorbell ring through a crack in the window. I found my helper behind the counter going through the work ledger.

' "Find anything?" I asked.

' "Nothing to speak of."

'His voice betrayed uncertainty.

' "Did someone come in?"

' "Yes. How did you know?"

'He then told me what had happened. When the bell rang, he had been standing on a chair searching an electrical cable box, so it was a few seconds before he was able to enter the shop. The customer heard him tinkering around in the back and, thinking it was Proque, called out in a loud voice, "How are you feeling today, Dieudonné?"

'Just then my assistant came into the shop and spotted a bareheaded, middle-aged man who, the moment he saw him, instinctively made a move for the door. The reason was purely accidental. Normally the Narcotics Squad wore civilian clothes on the job, but that afternoon they were obliged to appear in full uniform for a small decoration ceremony being held in honour of one of their superiors. Since it wasn't scheduled to begin until four, my assistant had decided to wear his uniform to work so he wouldn't have to go home again to change clothes.

'It was obviously the sight of the uniform that had startled the intruder. He said he had come for his glasses and showed the agent his repair tag. The agent explained that the owner of the shop had been incapacitated and that therefore he would have to wait for his glasses. It looked as if there was nothing left to be said, but the stranger refused to leave. Then he asked in a low voice if Proque had suddenly been taken ill. The agent said he had.

' "Seriously ill?"

' "Fairly seriously, yes."

' "I . . . desperately need those glasses," the stranger said quite unexpectedly, apparently unable to ask the question uppermost in his mind.

' "Is he . . . is he still alive?" he blurted out suddenly.

'By now my assistant was getting suspicious. Without giving a reply, he placed his hand on the counter top's hinged lid with the idea of checking the man's identification, but just then the man spun around and left the shop. By the time the agent lifted the counter top and ran outside, the stranger was gone. It was the start of the four o'clock rush hour, a light drizzle was falling, and the sidewalks were packed.

'I was upset that he'd let him get away, but I postponed giving him a reprimand. Besides, we now had the optician's work ledger. I asked the agent whether he could recall the number on the man's repair tag, but it had escaped his notice. The ledger included a number of recent entries, but only the customers' initials were given, which didn't look too promising. Our only other lead was the missing stranger, who knew Proque well enough to call him by his first name. I jotted down the most recent entries, though I wasn't very optimistic. Was the repair tag a pretext or cover? I wondered. But any drugs that well hidden would have meant it was the work of professionals. I didn't know what to make of Proque any more. But even if I'd misjudged the man and his shop *was* being used as a drop, it seemed pretty absurd to think Proque would have helped himself to a dose, much less taken an overdose. The stuff could have been counterfeit, which was often the case, but it was unusual for dealers and middlemen to use narcotics themselves: they're too well acquainted with the after-effects to be tempted. I was nearly at the end of my wits when my assistant suddenly recalled that, even though it had been raining, the stranger had been without an umbrella or a hat, and that his mohair coat was almost completely dry. We knew he couldn't have come by car, because the street had been blocked off for repairs, so chances were that he lived somewhere in the neighbourhood. It took us five days to track him down. How did we find him? Very simple. Based on the agent's description a composite sketch was made of the missing man and circulated among all the concierges on Rue Amélie. The man identified was a prominent scientist, a doctor of chemistry by the name of Dunant. Jérôme Dunant. While going through the ledger I'd noticed something unusual: the initials J. D. were listed on each of the three days preceding Proque's attacks. The doctor lived a few doors down the street, so early one afternoon I went to call on him. When he met me at the door, I recognized him at once from the sketch.

' "Oh, yes," he said. "Come right in." '

' "It looks as if you were expecting me," I said as I followed him inside. '

' "I was. Is Proque still alive?" '

' "I beg your pardon, but it was *I* who wanted to ask *you* a few questions, not vice versa. What makes you think Proque might not be alive?" '

' "Now it's my turn not to answer. You see, inspector, it's absolutely essential there be no publicity about this. It *must* be kept out of the press. Otherwise the consequences could be disastrous." '

' "Disastrous for whom? For yourself?" '

' "For France." '

'I ignored this last comment but couldn't get any more out of him.

' "I'm sorry," he said, "but any statement I make will have to be to the head of the Sûreté, and then not before I have special clearance from my superiors." '

'He volunteered no other information, afraid I might be one of those policemen who like to pass on sensational news stories to the media. That I found out only afterwards. He gave us quite a hard time, but in the end he got his way. My superior got in touch with his superior, and two ministries had to approve before he was allowed to testify.

'It's a well-known fact that every nation loves peace and makes plans for war. France is no exception. Chemical warfare is always treated with moral indignation, but still the research goes on. It just so happened that Dr Dunant was working on a project aimed at developing chemical compounds known as psychotropic depressants, which in pill or gas form would be capable of paralysing the enemy's will and morale. Under the seal of secrecy we were told that for over four years Dr Dunant had been trying to synthesize such a depressant. By working with a certain chemical compound, he had obtained a number of derivatives, one of which proved to be capable of producing the desired effect on the brain but only when administered in massive doses. Only when taken by the spoonful did it produce the symptomatic effects of hyperexcitability and aggression, followed by depression, and culminating in an acute suicidal mania. Finding the right compound is very often a matter of luck, arrived at by substituting various chemical groups in the original compound and then analysing the derivatives for their pharmacological properties. Sometimes it can take years of research to find the right combination; other times one can achieve instantaneous results, the latter being of course the exception, rather than the rule.

'Since he was extremely nearsighted, Dr Dunant was forced to wear his glasses at all times. For the past several years he had been a steady customer of Proque's. Since he was severely handicapped without his glasses, he made it a point always to keep three pairs on hand. He would wear one pair, carry the second pair around with him as a spare, and keep the third pair at home. He'd begun taking these precautions after breaking a pair of glasses in the lab and having to interrupt his work as a result. And just before his last visit to the shop – three weeks before, to be exact – he had had another accident. Dunant worked in a maximum-security laboratory. Before entering the lab he would have to change into a new set of clothes, including special shoes and underwear, and deposit all his personal items in a changing room separated from the work area by a pressure chamber. While he worked he was required to wear a transparent plastic hood equipped with its own air supply system. At no time was his body or glasses allowed to come into contact with any of the chemical substances under investigation. To avoid any further possible inconvenience, he had got into the habit of putting his extra pair of glasses on one of the reagent shelves before going to work. One day, as he was reaching for a reagent, he accidentally knocked them to the floor, shattering one lens and damaging the frame by stepping on it with his foot. He immediately took them to Proque for repair, but two days later, when he went to pick them up, he hardly recognized the optician, who had the tired and haggard look of someone who's just recovered from a serious illness. Proque told him he suspected having been poisoned, because the night before he'd been overcome by a strange attack that for some reason made him feel like crying even now.

'Dunant quickly forgot about Proque and his troubles, but he was far from satisfied with the repair job: not only did one of the stems pinch, but also one of the newly fitted lenses came loose from its plastic frame and finally popped out and broke on the laboratory's tiled floor. Dunant brought the glasses back a second time, but when he stopped by for them the following day Proque seemed to have aged overnight. Casually he began inquiring about the details of this latest "attack". Proque's description sounded like an acute depression caused by a chemically induced psychosis, very similar, in fact, to the symptoms produced by the compound X he had been working on. But since it would have taken a hefty dose of at least ten grams in pure form to provoke such a violent reaction, he failed to see what connection this could have with the glasses. Twice he had brought for repair the pair that usually lay on the reagent shelf located above the Bunsen burner. Then he began wondering whether the chemical fumes might have travelled through the air and settled on the glasses in microscopic amounts. He decided to run a test on them. By subjecting the glasses to a chemical analysis, he established that traces of the compound were indeed present on the lenses and frame stems, but in amounts measurable in gammas – in other words, in micrograms. The story of how LSD was discovered is a familiar one among chemists. Like everyone else at the time, the chemist experimenting with it was completely unaware of its hallucinogenic effects. But after returning home from work one night, he started experiencing all the symptoms of a "trip" – visions, psychic manifestations, and the like – though before leaving the lab he had washed his hands as thoroughly as he always did. But the infinitesimal amount lodged under his fingernails had been enough to induce the symptoms while he was making dinner.

'Dunant began thinking how an optician goes about installing a new set of lenses and adjusting the stems. He recalled that the synthetically made stems are passed quickly back and forth over a gas flame. Could the heat have altered the chemical composition of the compound, in a way that it made its effect a million times more potent? Taking samples of the compound, Dunant tried heating them by every means possible – with burners, spirit lamps, candle flame – but with no results. At that point he decided to perform the *experimentum crucis*. He deliberately bent one of the stems and bathed it with a thin enough solution of compound X so that a residue amounting to one-millionth of a gram remained on the frame after the solvent had evaporated. He then brought the glasses back to the optician for the third time. This was the pair he had come to pick up when he saw the agent behind the counter.

'There you have the whole story, monsieur, a story without a solution or an end. Dr Dunant theorized that the chemical alteration was caused by something in the optician's workshop and that the resulting catalytic reaction made the chemical's effect a million times more powerful. But since nothing was found to corroborate his theory, we decided to drop the case: if you have to chase after atoms instead of people, then it's time to call off the investigation. No crime was committed, since the amount smeared by Dr Dunant on the glasses was barely enough to kill a fly, much less the optician. I later heard that Dunant – or someone acting on his behalf – acquired the contents of the darkroom from Madame Proque and tested all the reagents for their effect on compound X, but without any results.

'Madame Proque died before Christmas that same year. In the department it was rumoured that after her death Dunant spent the whole winter in the abandoned shop and during that time took samples of everything – the plywood partition, the grinding stone, the varnish on the wall, the dust on the floor – but found nothing. It was Inspector Pingaud who insisted I tell you the whole story. I suspect your Naples case falls into the same category. Now that the world has reached a state of scientific perfection, such things are bound to happen. That's all I have to say.'

Because of the traffic, it took us nearly an hour to drive back to Garges. Neither of us said very much along the way. The story of Proque's gradual insanity was as familiar to me as the back of my own hand. All that was missing was the hallucination phase, but, then, who knows what sort of visions the poor bastard might have had. Funny, all along I'd been treating the other victims like the pieces of a puzzle, but Proque was different. I felt sorry for him. Thanks to Dunant. Oh, I could understand that mice weren't enough. Mice couldn't be driven to suicide. For that he needed a human being. He wasn't taking any risks, either: the moment he saw a cop at the door, he could always use France as an alibi. Even that I could understand. But what made me so furious was that 'How are you feeling today, Dieudonné?' of his. If that Japanese assassin in Rome was a criminal, then what was Dunant? I bet Dunant wasn't even his real name. Why had the inspector let me listen to the story? I wondered. Not out of sympathy, that's for sure. And what was the *real* story behind all this? The ending could have been faked, too. If that was the case, then the whole thing could have been staged as a harmless pretext for relaying information to the Pentagon about a new type of chemical weapon.

The more I thought about it, the more plausible this seemed. They'd shown their hand so well that if worst came to worst, they could always deny everything. Even *they* had said they came away empty-handed, and how the hell was I to tell whether they were telling the truth. If I'd been your ordinary private detective, you can be sure they wouldn't have bothered with such a show; but an astronaut, even a second-string one, has ties with NASA, and NASA has ties with the Pentagon. If the whole thing was planned by the higher-ups, then Pingaud was merely carrying out orders, and Barth's confusion wasn't to be taken at face value, either. Barth was in a far trickier situation than I. He, too, must have detected an element of big-league politics in this unexpected 'generosity' of theirs, but he didn't feel it was worth telling me about because it must have taken him by surprise. I was sure he hadn't been tipped off in advance; I knew enough about the rules of the game to know that. They couldn't very well take him aside and say, 'OK, all we have to do is show that Yank one of our high cards and he's bound to pass it on.' That's just not the way it's done. And it would have looked funny as hell if they'd clued me in and not Barth, especially when they knew he'd already promised me the use of his team. No, they could afford neither to leave him out nor to bring him in, so they did the next most sensible thing: they let him hear exactly what I heard and then left him to worry about the implications on his own. I would have bet he was sorry he ever offered me his help. Then I started meditating on what all this meant in terms of the investigation. It didn't present a very rosy picture. From the Italian series we'd deduced a number of qualifying factors: the mineral baths, men past the age of fifty, sturdy physique, bachelors, sun, allergy, and here was someone well over sixty, skinny, not allergic to anything, living with his mother, who never took sulphur baths, never got a tan, and hardly ever left the house! In fact, he couldn't have been a more dissimilar type. In a fit of magnanimity I suggested to Barth that each of us digest this latest bit of news on his own, to avoid influencing the other, and compare notes later on that evening. He was all for it.

Around three I went into the garden, where little Pierre was waiting for me. This meeting was our very own secret. He showed me the parts of his rocket. The first stage was a washtub. No one is more sensitive than a child, so I did not mention that a washtub wasn't exactly cut out to be a booster rocket, and I drew for him on the sand the various stages of a Saturn V and IX.

At five I went to keep my appointment with Barth in the library. He took me somewhat by surprise when he led off by saying that since France was doing research on factor X, it was safe to assume that other countries were engaged in similar research. Such work, he said, was always carried out on a parallel basis, in which case even the Italians might have . . . Maybe it was time to re-examine the whole affair. The compound wouldn't have had to come from a government lab; it could also have originated in a private company. It might have been developed by a chemist connected with the extremists, or, as seemed more likely, some of it might have been pirated. Perhaps the people in charge of administering it did not know how to exploit it to its maximal effect, and so they decided to conduct some experiments. But, then, why were the victims all foreigners, all in the same age group, all rheumatics, and so on?

He had an answer for that as well.

'Put yourself in the place of the group's leader. You've heard about the chemical's powerful reaction, but you're not exactly sure *what* kind of effect it has. Since you're a man without any moral scruples, you decide to try it out on various people. But which people? You can't very well test it out on your own members. So who? On just anyone? That would mean an Italian, with a family. But since the initial symptoms would be interpreted as a personality change, an Italian would very soon wind up under a doctor's care or as a patient in a clinic. A single man, however, can do just about anything before anyone will take notice, especially in hotels, where every sort of whim is indulged. And the better the hotel, the greater the isolation. At a third-class boarding-house, the landlady is likely to keep a watchful eye on her tenants' every move, whereas at the Hilton you can walk around on your hands and still not attract any attention. Neither the management nor the employees will bat an eyelash as long as it doesn't involve a criminal offence. Speaking a foreign language is another isolating factor. So far so good?'

'What about the other factors – age, allergy, rheumatism, the sulphur treatments?'

'The greater the difference in behaviour before and after the chemical agent has been administered, the more meaningful the test results. A young man is always on the go; one day he's in Naples, the next day he's in Sicily. An older man makes an ideal subject, especially if he's a patient at a health spa, where all his movements – from the doctor's office to the baths, from the sunroom to the hotel – are likely to be according to schedule, in which case the drug's effects will be more noticeable . . .'

'What about the sex factor?'

'It wasn't a coincidence that all the victims were men. Why? Because they were out to get only men in the first place. This seems crucial to me, because it would seem to point to an underlying political motive. If it's high-ranking politicians you're after, then it's only logical for you to choose men . . . What do you think?'

'You might have something there . . .' I admitted, suddenly awed by the prospect. 'So you think they might have had people planted in the hotels and selected a certain type of guest matching in age those politicians they were planning to assassinate as part of a *coup d'état*? Is that what you had in mind?'

'I'm not one for jumping to conclusions. It's better not to limit the scope of the inquiry . . . Well now, fifteen or twenty years ago such an idea would have smacked of a gimmicky potboiler or thriller, but today . . . You see what I mean?'

I saw what he meant, and sighed: I didn't enjoy the prospect of reopening the investigation. I quickly weighed the pros and cons.

'I have to admit I'm speechless . . . But there are still quite a few things to be explained. Why only people with allergies? And what about the baldness? Or the time of year – the end of May, beginning of June? Have you got an explanation for these as well?'

'No. At least not an immediate one. In my opinion one should start from the other end, by classifying not the "experimental" victims but the *real* victims, the ones actually intended. That would mean going down the list of Italy's political élite. If it turned out that there were a few allergy problems . . .'

'I see! In other words, you're sending me back to Rome. And I'm afraid I'll have to go; this could be the hottest lead so far . . .'

'There's no need for you to leave right away, is there?'

'Tomorrow or the next day at the latest. These are things that can't be handled over the phone.'

We left it at that. The more I thought over Barth's theory in my room, the more ingenious I found it. Not only had he put forward a plausible hypothesis, but he'd also managed to get himself off the hook by referring the matter to Rome and side-stepped the whole issue of France's involvement with compound X. This way it no longer mattered whether Dunant actually succeeded in reconstructing the chemical in the darkroom on Rue Amélie. The more I thought about it, the more positive I became that Barth's version was right on target. Compound X not only existed but also worked. I was sure of it, just as I was sure that such a method for political assassination couldn't help but have a tremendous impact – and not only in Italy – an impact even greater than that of a 'classic' *coup d'état*.

I now began to view the case of the eleven with an antipathy bordering on disgust. What was once an inscrutable mystery had now been turned into a struggle for power as crass as it was bloody. Behind all the bizarre appearances was something as trite as political murder.

The next day I headed straight for Rue Amélie. I don't really know why. But around eleven there I was, walking down the sidewalk and browsing in the shop-windows, though even as I was leaving Garges I was still debating whether I shouldn't reconsider and go by the Eiffel Tower to bid farewell to Paris. But once I reached the boulevards it was too late for that. I didn't know my way around this part of Paris, so I had trouble finding the street, and it took me a while to find a parking place. I recognized Proque's apartment even before I could make out the number. It looked more or less as I'd imagined it would, an old apartment building with closed shutters and that old-fashioned trim around the gables with which architects of the last century used to lend their buildings a touch of individuality. The optician's shop was defunct, the shutter lowered and padlocked. On my way back I stopped in front of a toy store. It was time to shop around for some souvenirs, because I had no intention of taking part in a new investigation; I'd pass on all the information to Randy and then head back to the States. My mind made up, I went inside to buy something for my sister's boys – as a way of justifying this latest lark of mine. On the shelves our whole civilization was gaudily arrayed in miniature. I looked around for toys I remembered from childhood but found only electronic gadgets, rocket launchers, and miniature supermen shown in judo or karate attack positions. You dope, I told myself, who are the toys for, anyway?

I decided on a couple of plumed parade helmets – the kind worn by the French Guard – and a Marianne puppet, because these were toys you couldn't get in Detroit. As I was heading back to the car with my packages, I spotted a candy store with white curtains on the corner. In the display window was a bronze-coloured Vesuvius covered with roasted almonds; I was reminded of the almond peddler I used to pass on my way from the hotel to the beach. I wasn't sure the boys would like the bitter-tasting almonds, but I went in and bought a couple of bags anyway. How strange, I thought, that of all places Naples should be saying good-bye to me here. Grudgingly I made my way back to the car, as if I still hadn't given up – given *what* up? I didn't know; maybe it was the purity that all along I'd unconsciously attached to the mystery. I threw the packages down on the back seat and, standing there with one hand on the open car door, said good-bye to Rue Amélie. Was there any more reason to doubt Leclerc's words or Barth's hypothesis? All my wildest, most private conjectures vanished. But had I ever really believed I would make some startling discovery, that I would splice together all the details in a way no one had ever done before and by some stroke of genius arrive at the hitherto undisclosed truth? Here and there vestiges of the old Paris were still to be seen, but they were destined to be obliterated, wiped out by that army of Molochs at Défense. I had lost all desire to visit the Eiffel Tower. By now Dr Dunant would already be at work in his porcelain and nickel-plated labs. I had visions of him wrapped in his synthetic turban, eyes aglitter over the distilling apparatus, the coiled air hose trailing behind his plastic cocoon. I was more than familiar with that world: in Houston I had seen the most exquisite labs, the sterile church naves of rocket domes.

I no longer felt like taking in the scenery as I used to do before takeoff, moments before everything collapsed below me. I had such a bad feeling that I jumped behind the wheel, but before I had a chance to start the car my nose began tickling. Angrily I held my breath for a moment; then the sneezing started. Thunder rumbled across the rooftops, the sky was turning darker, and a cloudburst hung overhead. I blew my nose and went on sneezing, but now I was laughing at myself. The blooming season was catching up with me in Paris, and the worst time was always just before a storm. I reached into the glove compartment, but the Plimasine got stuck in my throat and fell apart into bitter-tasting pieces. For lack of anything better, I tore open the bag of almonds and munched on them all the way back to Garges.

I like driving in the rain, so I took my time. On the highway the steam given off by the rain was turned a dirty shade of silver by the headlights. It was a fierce but short storm, so that by the time I climbed out of the car in front of the house, the rain had stopped. I wasn't meant to leave town that day, I guess, because on my way down to the dining room I slipped on the stairs – they'd just been freshly polished by the Spanish maid – leaving me doubled up and with an aching tail bone. At the dinner table I tried to play it down and chatted with the old lady, who was sure I'd injured a disc and said that there was no better cure for that than flowers of sulphur, the universal remedy for every sort of rheumatic ailment, and that all I had to do was to sprinkle it under my shirt. I thanked her for the sulphur powder and, realizing it was impossible for me to fly to Rome in this condition, willingly accepted Barth's offer to take me to a famous Parisian chiropractor.

Accompanied by expressions of sympathy, I dragged myself upstairs and crawled into bed like a cripple. I managed to fall asleep after finding the least painful position, but later woke up sneezing, having inhaled some sort of acrid powder coming from underneath my pillow. I jumped out of bed and let out a howl: I had forgotten about my back. At first I thought the Spanish maid, in an excess of zeal, had sprinkled the sheets with an insecticide, but it turned out to be that infallible remedy for rheumatism that good old Pierre had secretly administered while I was at the dinner table. I shook the yellow dust out of the sheet, pulled the cover over my head, and dozed off to the steady patter of raindrops pounding on the roof.

At breakfast time, I descended the stairs as if lowering myself down an icy rope ladder on a whaler caught in an arctic storm: a belated precaution. The chiropractor recommended by Barth turned out to be an American black; after taking X-rays and hanging the films on a viewer above the examining table, he went to work on me with hands like paddles. I experienced a sharp but fleeting pain, crawled down from the table under my own power, and discovered that I really did feel a lot better. I had to lie on my back in the office for another half hour, but after that I headed for the nearest Air France office and booked an evening flight. I tried to reach Randy by phone, but he wasn't in his hotel, so I left a message for him.

Back at Barth's house it occurred to me that I had nothing for Pierre, so I promised to send him my space helmet from the States, said good-bye to the whole family, then left for Orly. There I went straight to a Fleurop shop, ordered some flowers for Mrs Barth, and settled down in a waiting room filled with American newspapers. I sat and sat, but still there was no boarding announcement. I now looked on the case as if it were a thing of the past. Still undecided about the future, I tried – but without success – to glamorize this indecision of mine. Meanwhile our departure time passed, and a steady but indistinct stream of apologies came over the loudspeaker. Then a stewardess stepped out of an office and regretfully announced that Rome was no longer taking any incoming flights.

There was a lot of running around and a flurry of phone calls until it was finally confirmed that in fact Rome was accepting only American planes, Alitalia and BEA, whereas Swiss-air, SAS and my Air France were cancelling all departures until further notice. It seems a selective strike had been called by ground personnel, though the reason for the strike was lost in the stampede to exchange tickets and reservations for those airlines that had been given landing clearance. Before I could even fight my way through to the ticket counter, all the seats had been snatched up by the more enlightened passengers. The next available flight was on BEA, scheduled to leave the following day at a God-awful time – at 5.40 a.m. I had little choice: I had my ticket rewritten for the BEA flight, loaded my bags on to a cart, and headed for the Hotel Air France, where I'd spent the first night after my arrival from Rome. There I was in for another surprise. The hotel was filled to capacity with passengers stranded in the same way I was. I was now faced with the prospect of spending the night in Paris and getting up at four o'clock in the morning to make my 5.40 flight. There was no point in going back to Garges, either, since it was situated to the north of Paris and Orly to the south. I shoved my way through the crowd of disappointed passengers, reached the exit, and debated my next move. I could always postpone my departure a day, but that was the last thing I felt like doing: there's nothing worse than a long delay.

I was still deliberating what to do when a man carrying a stack of magazines stepped out of a kiosk and began arranging them on the news-stand. My attention was caught by the latest edition of *Paris-Match*. Staring at me from the black front cover was a man shown suspended in midair like a gymnast executing a side vault. He was wearing suspenders and holding against his chest a child with streaming hair whose head was tilted back in the manner of a trapeze artist. Not believing my own eyes, I walked up to the news-stand. It was a picture taken of Annabella and me. I bought a copy of the magazine, which automatically flipped open to the page featuring the exclusive cover story. Stretched across the entire page in bold letters above a picture of the demolished and body-strewn escalator was the following headline: WE'D RATHER DIE FACING FORWARD. I skimmed through the report. They'd tracked down Annabella, and on the next page was a picture of her with her family – but nowhere was my name mentioned. The photos came from the video tape used by the airport to photograph all those passing through the Labyrinth. I hadn't counted on the publicity. I was relying on their promises of strict confidentiality. I ran through the text again; it was accompanied by a sketch of the escalator and the detonation tank, with arrows indicating the path of my escape, and an enlarged detail from the cover photo showing a checkered sleeve situated between my pant legs and the landing. The caption underneath described it as the arm of the assassin blown off by the explosion. What I'd have given to buttonhole the author of that article! What was stopping him from mentioning me by name? Oh, I figured in it, all right – as 'the astronaut'. But Annabella's name was there, that 'lovely teen-aged girl' who was still waiting for a letter from her rescuer. Though it wasn't made explicit, there were sly insinuations that the airport disaster had given rise to a love affair. A cold fury took hold of me; I wheeled around, elbowed my way through the crowd in the lobby, and barged into the manager's office, where people were all talking at the same time. Cashing in on my recent heroism, I threw the *Paris-Match* down on the manager's desk and started outshouting everyone. I still blush with shame whenever I think back on that scene, but I got my way. The manager, unaccustomed to dealing with heroic astronauts, finally broke down and gave me his last vacancy, swearing up and down that it really was his last when the other passengers suddenly pounced on him like a pack of hounds let off their leashes.

I started to go for my bags but was told the room wouldn't be ready till eleven o'clock; it was still only eight. I left my luggage at the reception desk and found myself in command of three hours' leisure. I regretted having made a spectacle of myself, and since there could have been serious repercussions if a member of the press had happened to be present, I decided to keep a safe distance from the hotel till eleven. I wasn't in the mood for going to a movie or eating out, so on a whim I decided to do something I'd once thought of doing in Quebec when my plane was grounded by a blizzard. I headed for the other end of the terminal, strolled into a barbershop, and ordered the works. The barber was a Gascon, so much of what he said was lost on me, but, sticking to my decision, I agreed to all the frills in order not to risk being hustled out of the chair. After a fairly routine haircut and shampoo, he shifted into high gear. Tuning in some rock-and-roll music on a transistor standing between the mirrors, he turned up the volume, rolled up his sleeves, and, tapping his foot to the music, started to go to town. He patted my face, pulled my cheeks, tweaked my chin, slapped a steaming compress over my eyes and nose, now and then made a small air hole in the burning-hot towel to keep me from suffocating, and asked me a question that I didn't catch because my ears were still plugged with the cotton wads

he'd put there before cutting my hair. My '*ça va, bien*' sent him
scurrying to his cabinet for more bottles and lotions. Altogether I
spent about an hour in the barber's chair. Towards the end he combed
and evened out my eyebrows, stepped back, and examined me with a
critical frown; then he changed my apron, took out of a separate
compartment a small, gold-covered bottle that he held up for my
inspection as if it were some classy wine, smeared some green jelly on
his fingers, and began rubbing it into my scalp. All this was accompanied by a steady stream of uninterrupted patter, the gist of which
was that my worrying days were over now: I would never grow bald.
After brushing my hair with a series of brisk strokes, he took away all
the hand towels and compresses, pulled the cotton out of my ears,
blew into each ear in a way that was both gentle and intimate, showered
me with powder, snapped his towel in front of my face, then stepped
back and made a dignified bow. He was pleased with himself. With
tightened scalp and cheeks aglow, I got up from the chair in a daze,
tipped him ten francs, and walked out of the shop.

With some time to go before my room would be ready, I started
heading for the observation deck to take in the airport at night but
somehow got lost. They were doing some repair work inside the terminal; one section of the escalator was roped off, and mechanics were
making a lot of racket in the shafts below. Somehow I drifted into a
crowd of people racing towards the departure area. Soldiers in foreign
uniforms, nuns in starched bonnets, long-legged blacks who looked to
be members of a men's basketball team . . . Bringing up the rear was a
stewardess pushing a wheelchair in which a grey-haired man in dark
glasses sat holding a furry bundle in his lap; suddenly the bundle
jumped down and started crawling towards me on all fours. A monkey
dressed in a green jacket and a tiny skullcap stared up at me with
darting black eyes, then pirouetted around and started hopping after
the moving wheelchair. The rock-and-roll music coming from the
barbershop was so infectious I could hear it reverberating in peoples'
footsteps and voices. Standing alongside the wall under some neon
lights was a TV hockey game; I dropped in a coin and batted the
luminous dot around till my eyes began to hurt, then got up and left
before my turn was up. Passengers were still streaming towards departures. Among them was a peacock; it stood calmly with its tail

lowered, narrowly missing getting hit, and its head tilted to one side as if it were trying to decide whose leg to peck first. Somebody must have lost a peacock, I thought. Unable to fight the crowd, I circled around, but by the time I reached the spot where the peacock had been it was gone.

I thought again of the observation deck but took the wrong corridor by mistake and wound up downstairs in a maze of jewellers, fur shops, foreign-exchange offices and myriad other little shops. Pausing idly in front of the shop windows, I had the sensation of standing on top of a frozen lake and looking down into its deepest, blackest part. It was much as if the terminal had its own mute and murky negative counterpart underneath. To be more exact, I was conscious of the abyss without actually seeing or feeling anything. I took the escalator upstairs but wound up in another wing, in a hall full of golf carts, dune buggies and beach cars that stood in narrow rows waiting to be loaded. Squeezing my way through the aisles, I had fun with the fluorescent sheen given off by their luminous bodies, an effect I attributed to the lighting and to the new enamel finish. I paused in front of one buggy that was glazed a metallic gold and caught a glimpse of my own reflection – a quivering mass of yellow with a face that kept stretching vertically and then horizontally; when I held my head in a certain position, my eyes became dark holes secreting black metal beetles; when I leaned forward, another, darker, and more imposing reflection would appear behind my own. I glanced around – no one – but the figure mirrored in gold refused to go away. An uncanny optical illusion. The hall was sealed off by a sliding door at the other end, so I went back the way I came, my every movement and gesture mockingly reflected by my surroundings as in a hall of mirrors. I was somehow disturbed by this proliferation of images. Then I realized it was because the reflections were mimicking me but with a slight delay in time, even though that would have been impossible. To drown out the rock-and-roll tune banging away in my head, I started whistling 'John Brown's Body'.

I wasn't having any luck finding the observation deck, so I took a side exit and went outside. Despite the proximity of the streetlights, the night was so black and palpably thick you could have squeezed it with your hands: a real African night. It occurred to me that I might have been coming down with night blindness, that something might have been wrong with my rhodopsin, but gradually my vision improved. Must have been that excursion through the gold-plated gallery, I thought – my old eyes can't adjust to the change of light the way they used to.

A huge building was under construction in a lighted area beyond the parking lots. Bulldozers crawled in and out of the columns of light, pushing their loads of shimmering gold sand. A flat cloud of fiery quicksilver hung over this nocturnal Sahara like the Milky Way, while time and again flashes of lightning stitched the backdrop in slow motion – the headlights of cars turning off the highway for the airport. There was something strangely magical in this otherwise ordinary spectacle. It was then that my return trip through the terminal began to take on an aura of anticipation – not of the hotel room, though I hadn't forgotten about it, but of something more important. The fateful moment was approaching. It had the mark of absolute certainty, but, like a man struggling with a name on the tip of his tongue, I couldn't put my finger on it, on what it was I was expecting.

At the main entrance I started mingling with the crowd, or, rather, I was swept up and flung inside. I decided it was time to get a bite to eat at a snack bar. My hot dog tasted as bland as paper; I tossed the half-eaten hot dog and its plastic plate into the trash can and went into a café with a peacock stationed over the entrance in full array. It was much too big to have been stuffed. A week ago Annabella and I had sat under the very same peacock while waiting for her father. There were others in the café. I sat down with my coffee at a corner table, my back to the wall: while standing at the counter I had been conscious of someone staring at me from the rear. No one was looking my way now – to the point where it was blatantly obvious. The distant whine of the jet engines now seemed to come from another, more important world. I sat there using my spoon to break up the sugar lumps at the bottom of my cup. A magazine with a black cover and a red band running across the top lay on the table next to me – a copy of *Paris-Match*, I guessed – but a woman sitting with her dark-haired Romeo had managed to cover the title with her purse. On purpose, probably. Someone had spotted me, but who? An autograph hound? Some passing reporter? I dropped a copper ashtray on the floor, pretending it was an accident. Despite the noise, no one turned around. Suspicions confirmed. Not wanting to be harassed, I gulped down the rest of my coffee and walked out. I was in a bad way: legs like a couple of hollow pipes, an aching tail bone that served as a painful reminder of the recent past . . .

Suddenly I was fed up with all the stalling around, so I made my way past the glittering shop-windows and aimed for the escalator marked AIR FRANCE in big sky-blue letters. It was a short-cut to the hotel. I held on tightly to the railing: the combed treads on the steps were slippery, and I wasn't about to take any chances. Halfway between levels I noticed that standing in front of me was a woman with a dog in her arms. I winced: her hair was the exact same shade of blonde. Slowly I glanced back over my shoulder, though I had a pretty good hunch who would be standing behind me. A flat face, a complexion made livid by the fluorescent lighting, sunglasses. I shoved my way past the blonde and worked my way up the escalator, but I couldn't just walk off without satisfying my curiosity. So I stood by the railing and inspected the passengers as the escalator dropped them off one by one on the landing. The blonde gave me the once-over as she strolled by. She was carrying a folded shawl with a knotted fringe, the same fringe I'd taken for a dog's tail. The guy in back of me turned out to be fat and pasty-looking. Not a trace of Mongol blood. *Esprit de l'escalier*, I thought – but a week later?! Man, are you ever in bad shape – what you need is a good night's sleep!

Along the way I picked up a bottle of Schweppes, slipped it into my coat pocket, and glanced at the clock above the reception desk with a sigh of relief: my room would be ready. My bellboy went ahead of me with my bags, set the smaller one down on top of the larger one in the hallway, pocketed a ten-franc tip, and was on his way. The hotel breathed a quiet sort of intimacy that made the whining roar of a landing aeroplane seem incongruous. Good thing I'd remembered to pick up a Schweppes. I was thirsty now, but, not having a bottle opener, I peeked into the corridor to see if there was a refrigerator where I might be able to lay my hands on one. The warm colours of the hallway carpet and walls caught my eye, filling me with respect and admiration for French interior decorators. I found a refrigerator, opened the bottle of Schweppes, and was already heading back to my room when who should come around the corner but

Annabella. In a dark dress she looked taller than I'd remembered her, but she had the same white ribbon in her hair; and when she came towards me, swinging her shoulder bag at her side, it was with the same serious look in her dark eyes. I recognized the purse, too, though the last time I'd seen it, it had been ripped open at the seams. I'd left the door open on my way out, and she slipped into the doorway.

'Annabella, what're you doing here?' I wanted to say, being as shocked as I was glad to see her, but all I could muster was a faint 'Aa –' before she went inside the room, with such an inviting toss of the head and with such an unequivocal glance of the eyes that I stopped dead in my tracks. She left the inner door open, and in my momentary panic I thought maybe she wanted to confide in me, but before I was even in the room I distinctly heard both her shoes fall to the floor and the bed squeak. With these sounds still fresh in my ears, feeling morally indignant, I went in and gasped: the room was empty.

'Annabella!' I yelled. The bed was untouched. 'Annabella!' Silence. In the bathroom, maybe? I opened the door, but it was dark inside; I waited in the doorway till the light blinked on. Bathtub, bidet, towel rack, washbasin, my own reflection in the mirror . . . I went back into the room, not daring to call out any more. Though it was unlikely she would have had time to hide in the wardrobe cabinet, I opened it anyway. Empty. My knees began to buckle, so I slumped into an armchair. Even now I could describe exactly the way she walked, the kind of clothes she wore . . . Then I realized why she'd seemed taller: she was wearing high heels instead of sandals. I could still see that expression in her eyes as she passed through the doorway, the way her hair spilled over her shoulder when she motioned with her head. I could still hear her naughtily kicking off her shoes and the sound made by the creaking bedsprings, and I remembered my jabbing, stinging sensation at hearing those sounds . . . Was it all just a fantasy? A hallucination?

I touched my knees, my chest and my face, as if this were the sequence in which I had to examine them, ran my hands over the chair's rough upholstery, walked across the room and banged my fist against the wardrobe's half-open door; everything felt solid, stationary, immutable, well defined, and yet somehow ambiguous. I paused in front of the television set and saw a reduced reflection of the bed and a pair of girls' shoes carelessly flung down on the carpet. I spun around in horror.

There was nothing on the floor, nothing anywhere. Next to the television set was a telephone. I picked up the receiver, heard the dial tone, but stopped short of dialling. What was I to tell Barth – that I was in a hotel fantasizing about some girl and was afraid to be left alone? I hung up the receiver, took my toilet kit out of my suitcase, went into the bathroom; as I leaned over the basin, I suddenly froze. Everything I was doing had its immediate and familiar precedent. Like Proque I splashed my face with cold water. Like Osborn I rubbed my temples with cologne. Then I went back into the room, not knowing what to do next. Nothing happened to me. The most sensible thing would have been to climb into bed and go to sleep. On the other hand, I was afraid of undressing, as if my clothes were somehow a protection. Moving quietly in order not to rouse the evil spirit, I took off my pants, shoes and shirt, and after switching off the overhead light, pressed my head against the pillow. Now the threat seemed to come from outside – from the hazy ambiguity of the objects standing in the penumbra of the night light. I switched off the lamp. A feeling of inertia came over me; I forced myself to take long and even breaths. There was a knock at the door; I didn't move a muscle. There was another knock, and someone – a man – opened the door and stepped into the passageway. The figure, silhouetted against the corridor's brightness, started advancing towards my bed.

'Monsieur . . .'

I didn't make a sound. Now so close that he stood over me, he laid something down on the table and quietly withdrew. The lock on the door clicked; I was alone again. I dragged myself out of bed – more beat than dazed – and switched on the wall light. Lying on the table was a telegram. With a pounding heart and wobbly legs I picked it up. It was addressed to me, care of the Hotel Air France. I glanced down at the sender's name, and my blood ran cold. I pressed my eyelids together, opened the telegram, and again read the name of the man who had been buried long enough to be a rotting corpse.

WAITING ROME HILTON RM 303

ADAMS

I must have read and reread the message ten times, examining the telegram up close and from every angle. It had left Rome at 10.40, thus well over an hour ago. It was probably just a slip of the pen. Randy might have moved into the Hilton – he had settled for the little hotel near the Spanish Steps for lack of anything better – and this was his way of letting me know. Or he might have received my message, given up waiting for me, then heard about the flight cancellations and decided to wire me. But why the switch in names? And of all names, why that one? I sat down by the wall and considered whether the whole thing wasn't just a dream. The wall light was burning right over my head. Everything around me was taking on a new appearance. The window curtain, the television set and the outline of the shadows had all become portents of something inscrutable. Everything was becoming dependent on me, subject to my will. I decided to eliminate the wardrobe cabinet. Its lacquer finish suddenly turned dull, the outline of the door became blurred, the rear wall burst open, and an unshapely black hole was soon crawling with writhing, slithering shapes. I tried to restore the cabinet but couldn't. The centre of the room was gradually being enveloped by the shadows in the corners. I could only rescue those objects that still remained in the light. I reached for the phone; the receiver, which had taken on a perverse and mocking shape, slipped out of my hand. The telephone became a grey rock with a rough surface, the dial a hole. My fingers penetrated the surface and touched something cold. There was a ball-point pen lying on the table. Exerting all my powers of concentration to keep the pen from disappearing, I scrawled a message across the telegram in large letters:

11.00 NAUSEA
11.50 ILLUSIONS AND DELUSIONS

But while I was writing I lost all control over my surroundings and at any moment I expected the room to collapse. Then the unexpected happened: I noticed something was going on in my immediate vicinity. I realized that the immediate vicinity was my own body. It was stretching; my hands and feet were moving farther away from me. Afraid that I might bang my head against the ceiling, I made a dive for the bed. I lay on my back but had trouble breathing; my chest swelled like the dome of Saint Peter's; my hands became big enough to scoop up several pieces of furniture, if not the whole room. A night-mare, I told myself. Just ignore it! By then I had stretched so far my extremities were dissolving into darkness. They were so distant from me that I'd lost all sensation in them. Only my interior was left. A vast and labyrinthine region, a gulf lying between my mind and the world, which in fact had ceased to exist. I leaned out breathlessly over my own abyss. Where I once had had a pair of lungs, intestines and veins, I now saw only thoughts – gigantic thoughts; and in those thoughts, my life, my tangled and splintered life, as it glowed, turned to charcoal and finally into ashes. I watched it disintegrate into a fiery dust, a black Sahara. The black Sahara was my life. The room in which I was lying like a fish on the ocean floor had shrunk to the size of a grain of sand; it, too, was a part of me. The more I kept expanding beyond the limits of my body, the more terrified I became. Little by little I was being consumed by an awesome power, by the power of my expanding mass, which was devouring everything in a greedy surge. I groaned in despair as I found myself sucked into the depths; I tried raising myself up by supporting my elbows on the mattress, now located somewhere in the middle of the earth. I was afraid that with one jerk of my hand I might cave in the walls. It can't be, I kept telling myself, but I could feel it in every nerve and fibre of my body. In a senseless attempt to escape, I crawled out of bed, got down on my knees, and groped along the wall for the light switch. The room was inundated by a razor-sharp whiteness. I saw the table oozing with an iridescent film; the telephone bleached bone-white; and in the mirror my own face glistening with sweat. I recognized the face, but everything else had changed. I tried to understand what was happening to me, to get at the force that was bursting to get out. Was I that force? I was and I wasn't. My swollen hand was still mine. But what if it turned into a mountain of flesh and tried to crush me with its seething, bubbling mass? Could I then still claim it as my own and not the force expanding it? Whenever I tried to resist the metamorphosis, I was too late; by then the change had already taken place. With a mere glance I could remove the ceiling; under my gaze everything buckled, caved in, collapsed — melted like a house of wax on fire. You're hallucinating! I kept telling myself, and the words would bounce back like an echo from a well. I shoved myself away from the wall, spread out my feet, watched as they kept sinking into the mushy parquet flooring, turned my head like the dome of some lofty cathedral, and spotted my watch lying on the night stand. The dial was the bottom of a luminous crater; the second hand was ticking off the seconds in eerie slow motion, leaving behind it a trail more white than the dial's enamel finish, while the dial expanded to become a battlefield traversed by military columns. The chalky ground between the marching ranks was ripped apart by explosions, the smoke assumed the shape of faces – malleable masks of mute agony. Swarms of antlike soldiers congealed into a vitreous mass; their blood ran out to form round pools of red mud, but they marched on, dust-covered and bloodied, to the steady accompaniment of a drum roll. The battle gradually diminished in scale as I put down the watch, but never ceased. Suddenly the room became tilted, began rotating in slow motion, and hurled me towards the ceiling. Something broke my fall. I dropped down on my hands and knees and lay by the bed as the room gradually came to a stop and everything settled back into place. Stretched out with my head on the floor like a dog, I glanced up at the watch leaning against the lamp on the night stand; it was a quarter to one.

All was quiet again; the second hand crept along like an ant. I sat up on the floor and was braced by its coolness. In the austere light the room assumed the appearance of a solid crystal filled with a faint ringing and a blinding refulgence. In this atmosphere of extreme clarity the furniture, the folds in the window curtain, the shadows cast by the table stood out with unspeakable perfection. I paid little attention to the beauty of my surroundings; I was like an off-duty fireman who, continually on the lookout for smoke in a theatre auditorium, is oblivious of the beauty on stage. I stood up, feeling woozy, and, overcoming the estrangement in my fingers, scribbled a few more notes on the telegram:

12.50 RELIEF
PLIMASINE IN THE MORNING
ORLY – BARBERSHOP

More I didn't know. While I was bent over the table I felt another change coming on. The reflection on the table top began fluttering like dragonfly wings; then the whole table rose up and flapped its grey-ribbed bat wings in my face till it completely shrouded the milky glow of the night light. The edge of the table turned limp as soon as I grabbed it with my hands. I could neither escape this rush of transformations nor catch up with it – they were becoming more accelerated now, more monstrous, more majestic, more mocking – they passed through me like a breeze – I closed my eyelids – I didn't need eyes to see them. I recall making a vague but determined effort to expel the foreign element, to puke it out; it was no use. I tried to defend myself as best I could; I was becoming less a spectator and more a part of these teeming visions – their quivering, shuddering flaw.

Some time after one o'clock I managed to surface again. It came in waves now, like the process of peristalsis; at each stage it promised to be over, only to become more intense during the sequel. The visions began to let up between two and three, which proved to be even worse than before because now everything assumed its normal appearance again, only this time on a different level of consciousness. How to describe it? The furniture and walls became petrified in the middle of some horrible transition; time came to a halt, leaving only the surrounding world, which suddenly stopped advancing towards me like an avalanche and became frozen in a prolonged flash of magnesium. The whole room was like a gasp between two successive screams; its intended target was manifested and undisguised malice in the intricacies of the wallpaper design, in the picture of the Loire castle hanging above the bed, and in the castle's green lawns. This greenery was my sentence; I stared up at it from a kneeling position and realized that I had to lose. Then I began attacking the room – yes, the room; I ripped the cords off the curtains and blinds, yanked the drapes down from their hooks, pulled off the bedcovers, and threw the whole lethal pile into the bathtub. Then I shut the bathroom door and broke the key while trying to jam it into the door's outerlock. Out of breath, I leaned against the doorframe and surveyed the battlefield. I realized it was all a waste of time: it was impossible to remove the windows and walls. I dumped the contents of my bags out on to the floor and dug my way through to the flat metal rings connected by a short rod; Randy had given them to me back in Naples so I could handcuff the murderer when the time came. Now I had him. A bunch of tiny dark objects spilled out from between my shirts – almonds that had fallen out of the package – but I didn't have time to record them, I was afraid I wouldn't make it; so I threw a handful on top of the telegram, pulled an armchair up to the radiator, made myself comfortable in it, and leaned my back against the upholstery; then I pressed my feet down on the floor, handcuffed myself to the radiator pipe, and in a state of unbelievable tension waited for IT to happen, as in the moments before a takeoff. I was propelled neither upward nor downward, however, but inward, into a hot and reddish fog, surrounded by whirling walls, shackled and chained. Straining like a dog on a leash, I could reach only as far as one of the bedposts. I pulled the bed towards me, buried my face in the mattress as if trying to smother a fire, chewed my way through to the foam rubber; but it was too porous to suffocate me, so I grabbed my windpipe with my free hand and squeezed it with all my might. Despair: I still couldn't kill myself. Just before losing consciousness, I remember hearing explosions in my head: I must have banged it against the pipes. I also recall experiencing one final, faint glimmer of hope that this time I would bring it off. Then nothing; I died, and I didn't even find anything strange about the fact that I was conscious of dying. Later I had the sensation of swimming through black waterfalls of unknown grottoes, where the water's roar was so loud it was as if only my sense of hearing had survived. I could hear bells chiming. The black colour turned pink. I opened my eyes and beheld a large, strange, pale, and incredibly calm face bent over me. The face belonged to Dr Barth. I recognized him at once and was about to tell him something to that effect when I suddenly fainted in a most jejune manner.

They found me around four in the morning, handcuffed to the radiator, after some Italians next door had alerted the hotel staff. Since it gave the appearance of being an attack of frenzy, I was given a tranquillizing shot before being rushed to the hospital. After learning of the flight cancellation the following day, Barth had telephoned Orly, been told what had happened to me, and driven straight to the hospital, where I was still lying unconscious. It was thirty hours before I finally regained consciousness. I wound up with several broken ribs, a lacerated tongue, a head full of stitches, and a badly swollen wrist caused by my chafing on the handcuffs. Luckily the radiator to which I had been handcuffed was made of cast iron; one made of synthetic material would have broken, and I would have jumped out the window.

A Canadian biologist has proved that people resistant to balding have the same nucleic acid in their skin tissue as catarrhine monkeys, which are also immune to balding. This substance, which goes by the name of 'monkey's hormone', has been proved effective in the treatment of baldness. In Europe, the manufacture of a hormone ointment was begun three years ago by a Swiss company operating under licence from the American firm of Pfizer. The Swiss succeeded in modifying the hormone's chemical structure in a way that made it more effective but also more sensitive to heat, a factor resulting in its rapid degradation.

When the skin is exposed to the sun, the hormone undergoes a chemical alteration; if it is then combined with Ritalin it can be converted into Dr Dunant's compound X, a depressant, though only when administered in large doses does it produce any toxic effects. Ritalin is present in the blood stream of those who use it, while the hormone is applied topically in the form of an ointment that contains the added ingredient hyaluronidase to enable the medication to be absorbed through the skin and to enter the circulation. But in order to produce a psychotropic reaction, one would have to apply at least two hundred grams of the ointment daily and exceed the recommended dosage of Ritalin.

Certain compounds, such as cyanide plus sulphur – or thiocyanates – act as catalysts that can increase the psychotropic toxicity a million times. The chemical symbols – C N S – provide the key to the riddle. Cyanide is one of the chemical constituents of bitter almonds; it is what gives them their distinctively bitter and pungent taste. Some time ago a number of almond factories in Naples became infested with cockroaches. The disinfectant used to exterminate them contained sulphur, traces of which found their way into the emulsion used to coat the almonds before they were placed in the oven. As long as the oven temperature remained low, nothing happened; but as soon as the temperature rose high enough to allow the sugar to caramelize, the cyanide combined with the sulphur to form cyanogen sulphide, or a thiocyanate. But when introduced into the body by itself, cyanogen sulphide is incapable of having a catalytic effect on factor X; ionic sulphur must also be present in the reacting bodies. Ions in the form of sulphates and sulphites were traced back to the mineral baths. Therefore, a person would die if he used the hormone ointment, took

338

Ritalin and mineral baths, and ate the Neapolitan-style sugar-roasted almonds. The catalytic reaction triggered by the thiocyanates involved such negligible amounts as to be undetectable except by chromatography. A prerequisite for involuntary self-destruction was a fondness for sweets. Those who couldn't eat sweets because of diabetes, or who weren't partial to sweets, escaped unharmed. The Swiss version of the ointment had been available on the European market for two years, which explained why no cases had been reported before that. No cases were reported in the States, because the only product available there was Pfizer's, which was not nearly so sensitive to heat as the European variety. And since the product was intended exclusively for men, it was only natural that women were not included among the victims.

Proque also fell into the trap, but by a different route. Though he had never had any need of the scalp ointment, gone to the beach, or taken mineral baths, the sulphur ions entered his circulation through inhalation of sulphur dioxide from hypo used in developing photos; the Ritalin came from the stimulant prescribed for his lethargy; and the compound X, from Dr Dunant's glasses. All the time the learned and patient doctor was busy running tests on every scrap, every speck of dust inside Proque's shop, taking specimens of the plywood partition and the grinding powder, little did he realize that the mystery substance was located approximately four metres above his head – in a bag of sugar-coated almonds lying at the bottom of a dresser drawer.

What had alerted Barth's chemists and provided them with the missing link were the almonds found with my notes on the table.

One incidental though rather amusing detail: after my return to the States, I was told by a chemist friend of mine that the flowers of sulphur sprinkled in my bed by little Pierre could not have acted as a chemical agent, for the reason that elemental sulphur, obtained as a solid through sublimation, is monionic and insoluble in water. My friend came up with the hypothesis that the ionic sulphur found in my blood must have come from wine that had been allowed to sulphurize. Following the French custom, I was in the habit of drinking wine with every meal; this last time, however, I had drunk exclusively at Barth's place, since I never ate any meals out. The chemists from the CNRS must have been aware of this but preferred not to embarrass their boss by insinuating he was serving his guests bad wine.

I was later asked whether the almonds had been my great discovery. Nothing would have been easier than to give a yes or no answer, but the truth was I didn't know. During my rampage, when I'd gone around destroying everything within reach, dumping everything that seemed lethal into the bathtub, I had certainly acted like a madman, but in this madness of mine there was an element of self-preservation. It might have been similar with the almonds. I'd wanted to make a note of them, that much I know, though this reflex of mine could have been the result of many years of practice. I had been trained to record things under conditions of maximum stress, to assess the relevance of something regardless of my own personal opinion. It might have been just a flash of intuition that led me to connect the thunderstorm, my sneezing fit, the pill stuck in my throat, the almonds, and the image of Proque making that last trip into the corner candy store on Rue Amélie. But that strikes me as too good to be true. I might have associated the almonds with the Naples affair at the sight of the miniature Vesuvius displayed in the shop-window. Though not directly related to the case, Vesuvius turned out to be the magic link that put me on the right trail. Though if you look back carefully over my report, you will see there were many times during the investigation when I thought I was on the right trail, and yet nothing came of it. Barth was on the right track, too, though he was wrong in suspecting a political motive. He was right in questioning the method of selection – the 'group of eleven' – and also in saying the victims included only unmarried foreigners because the latter were more apt to be isolated from their Italian surroundings by their unfamiliarity with the language and the absence of any dependents. The first sign of a toxic reaction was always a change in disposition, which only someone close to the victim would have been able to detect in the early stages. Subsequent investigation revealed several 'abortive cases' involving Italians and foreigners who had come to Naples with their wives. In every case the pattern was identical; alarmed by her husband's erratic behaviour, the wife would start to keep a closer eye on him, and the moment he started having hallucinations she would do her utmost to persuade him to leave the country. This impulse to return home was an instinctive reaction in the face of an unknown danger. The Italians, on the other hand, would immediately be put under a psychiatrist's care – usually under family pressure – at which time they would be advised to stop driving, to discontinue the Plimasine, and to interrupt their bathing treatment; as a result of this abrupt change, the symptoms would rapidly disappear. A chance circumstance kept the investigation from uncovering these 'abortive cases' earlier. In each and every instance someone from the victim's immediate family would come to claim the prepaid subscription, but since the books of the various spas recorded only the financial transactions, and not the reason for the cancellation, there was absolutely no way the persons in question could be traced.

There were a number of other factors impeding the investigation. No one likes to brag about using an ointment as a preventive against baldness. Those who made no fuss about going bald, or who preferred wearing a wig to using an ointment, escaped unharmed, though there was no way investigators could know this at the time. Those who avoided the hormone had no reason to testify, since they were safe and sound, while those who did use it died. No packages containing the Swiss ointment were ever found among the victims' personal belongings because the medication was supposed to be kept stored in the refrigerator. This was easy enough to do at home, but not in a hotel, so rather than take the medication along with them on their travels, the more conscientious among the older men would rely on the local barbers. The directions called for one application every ten days, which meant that only one application was needed during the time spent in Naples. And of course during the investigation it never occurred to anyone to canvass the local barbershops to find out what they were rubbing into the scalps of certain customers.

And lastly, just as all the victims shared a definite physical resemblance, so, too, they all had certain psychological traits in common. All were men well past their prime, still very conscious of their appearance, struggling with old age but reluctant to admit it. Those men who were already in their sixties and completely bald had given up trying to look younger than their age and had stopped shopping around for miraculous cures, whereas those who were thirty and had grown prematurely bald were not likely to require any bathing treatment for advanced rheumatism. Therefore the ones who were exposed to the greatest danger were those who had already crossed the shadow line.

In retrospect, the more closely one examined the facts, the more inter-related they became. For example, the chemical poisonings all took place during the blooming season, when drivers were more apt to use Plimasine, and since patients with acute asthma were physically unable to drive, they would have had no need for a drug intended for drivers.

Barth was gracious enough to keep me company during my stay in the hospital, so I decided to pay him a farewell visit before flying back to the States. Pierre was keeping a lookout by the stairs but ducked out of sight the moment he saw me coming. I knew what was on his mind and promised him I wouldn't forget about his helmet. Barth had another visitor, Dr Saussure, now wearing a shirt with frilled cuffs instead of a frock coat, with a pocket watch dangling from his neck instead of a calculator. While he browsed through some books in the library, Barth spoke to me about one of the supreme ironies of the case: even though it had been inoperative and un-programmed the whole time, the computer had proved enormously beneficial to the investigation. Because if I hadn't flown to Paris with the idea of using the computer, I never would have stayed at Barth's place, never would have aroused the sympathy of his grandmother, and little Pierre never would have come to my rescue with the flowers of sulphur after my fall on the stairs . . . In short, the computer played an undisputed role in unravelling the mystery, though in a purely abstract sort of way. With a laugh I commented that the whole com-bination of fortuitous events leading up to the solving of the mystery now seemed to me more amazing than the mystery itself.

'Now you're committing the egocentrist fallacy!' Saussure exclaimed as he turned around to face us from the bookcase. 'This series of yours is not as much a sign of the times as a portent of tomorrow. A vague premonition of things to come . . .'

'Do you understand it?'

'I see only the warning signs. Mankind has multiplied to such an extent that it's now starting to be governed by atomic laws. The movement of gas atoms is chaotic, but out of this chaos are born such things as stable pressure, temperature, specific gravity and so on. Your accidental success looks like a long series of extraordinary coincidences. But it only *seems* that way to you. You will probably argue that besides your falling down Barth's stairs and accidentally inhaling sulphur, a number of other factors were necessary to trigger the chain reaction: your scouting trip to Rue Amélie, your sneezing fit, the decision to buy some almonds for your nephews, the flight cancellation, the crowded hotel, the barber, and even the fact that the barber was a Gascon . . .'

'Oh, why stop there,' I intruded. 'If I hadn't broken my tail bone in the liberation of France, I wouldn't have had a relapse on the escalator in Rome, or here, either, for that matter. And if I hadn't wound up in front of the assassin on the escalator, my picture wouldn't have landed on the cover of *Paris-Match*. And if it hadn't been for the picture, I would have spent the night in Paris instead of fighting for a room at the Hotel Air France, and that would have been the end of it. The chances of my being there at all during the explosion were astronomically small. I could have booked another flight; I could have been standing on another step . . . Not to mention all the other astronomical improbabilities that came before and after! For instance, if I hadn't heard about the Proque affair, I wouldn't have decided to fly back to Rome just when the flights were being cancelled . . . and in a way that was the purest coincidence of all.'

'You mean your finding out about the Proque affair? I don't believe it was a coincidence. The doctor and I were just talking about it before you came in. You were briefed because of the political infighting going on between Sûreté and Défense. Someone was out to discredit a certain military official who was playing politics to promote Dr Dunant. You were caught in a billiard game.'

'Was I supposed to be a ball or a cue?'

'Our guess is that they were using you to get the Proque case reopened so they could damage Dunant's reputation . . .'

'But I still don't see what my coming to Paris had to do with all this political infighting.'

'It had absolutely nothing to do with it. That's why the large number of coincidences strikes you as being contrary to common sense. But I say to hell with common sense! By itself each segment of your experience is plausible enough, but the trajectory resulting from the aggregate of these segments borders on being a miracle. That's what you thought, wasn't it?'

'Yes.'

'But meanwhile the very thing I was telling you about three weeks ago has happened. Imagine a firing range where a postage stamp is set up as a target a half mile away. Let's make it a ten-centime stamp, with a picture of Marianne on it. Along comes a fly and leaves a speck the size of a dot. Now let several sharpshooters start firing away at the dot. They will surely miss it, because at that distance they won't even be able to see it. But now suppose a hundred mediocre marksmen were to start firing for weeks on end. You can bet that one of their bullets will eventually hit its target. Not because the man who fired it was a phenomenal marksman, but because of the sheer density of fire. Wouldn't you agree?'

'Yes, but that still doesn't explain – '

'Wait, I'm not finished yet. It's summer now, and the range is crawling with flies. The probability of hitting the dot was extremely small. But the probability of simultaneously hitting both the dot and a fly that happens to wander into the bullet's path is even smaller. The probability of hitting the dot and *three* flies with the same bullet would be – to use your words – astronomically small. And yet I assure you that such a coincidence would come to pass as long as the firing was kept up long enough.'

'Excuse me, but you're talking about a whole barrage, while I was just one of a series . . .'

'That's an illusion. At the precise moment the bullet hits both the dot and the three flies, then it, too, is only one of a series. The lucky marksman will be just as amazed as you were, even though there would be nothing so terribly miraculous or unusual about the fact that *he* hit it, because, you see, *somebody would have had to hit it*. See what I mean? Common sense isn't worth a damn here. My prediction came true. The Naples mystery was the result of a random causality, and it was the same random causality that solved it. The law of probability applies to both members of the proposition. Needless to say, if only one of the set of necessary conditions had gone unfulfilled, you never would have been drugged, but sooner or later someone would have met all the conditions. One, three, five years from now. And that is so because we now live in such a dense world of random chance, in a molecular and chaotic gas whose "improbabilities" are amazing only to the individual human atoms. It's a world where yesterday's rarity becomes today's cliché, and where today's exception becomes tomorrow's rule.'

'OK, but I was the one – '

He didn't let me finish. Barth, who knew Saussure, looked at both of us with twinkling eyes, as if trying his best not to laugh.

'Excuse me, but if it hadn't been you, it would have been someone else.'

'Who? Some other detective?'

'I don't know and I don't care. Someone, that's all. By the way, is it true you're planning to write a book about the case?'

'As a matter of fact, I am. I even have a publisher . . . but why do you ask?'

'Because that's also related. Just as some bullet is bound to hit its target, someone was bound to crack the case. And if that's so, then regardless of the publisher or author, the publication of this book was also a mathematical certainty.'

A Perfect Vacuum

CONTENTS

S. Lem

A PERFECT VACUUM

(*Czytelnik, Warsaw*)

Reviewing non-existent books is not Lem's invention; we find such experiments not only in a contemporary writer, Jorge Luis Borges (for example, his 'Investigations of the Writings of Herbert Quaine'), but the idea goes further back – and even Rabelais was not the first to make use of it. *A Perfect Vacuum* is unusual in that it purports to be an anthology made up entirely of such critiques. Pedantry or a joke, this methodicalness? We suspect the author intends a joke; nor is this impression weakened by the Introduction – long-winded and theoretical – in which we read: 'The writing of a novel is a form of the loss of creative liberty . . . In turn, the reviewing of books is a servitude still less noble. Of the writer one can at least say that he has enslaved himself – by the theme selected. The critic is in a worse position: as the convict is chained to his wheelbarrow, so the reviewer is chained to the work reviewed. The writer loses his freedom in his own book, the critic in another's.'

The overstatement of these simplifications is too patent to be taken seriously. In the next section of the Introduction ('Auto-Momus') we read: 'Literature to date has told us of fictitious *characters*. We shall go further: we shall depict fictitious *books*. Here is a chance to regain creative liberty, and at the same time to wed two opposing spirits – that of the belletrist and that of the critic.'

'Auto-Momus' – Lem explains – is to be free creation 'squared', because the critic of the text, if placed within that very text, will have more possibilities for manoeuvring than the narrator of traditional or non-traditional literature. One might go along with this, for in fact literature nowadays fights for greater distance from the thing created, like a runner on his second wind. The trouble is, Lem's erudite Introduction doesn't seem to want to end. In it he discourses on the positive aspects of nothingness, on ideal objects in mathematics, and on new metalevels of language. It is all a bit drawn out, as if in jest. What is more, with this overture Lem is leading the reader (and perhaps himself as well?) afield. For there are pseudo-reviews in *A Perfect Vacuum* that are not merely a collection of anecdotes. I would divide the reviews, in opposition to the author, into the following three groups:

(1) Parodies, pastiches, gibes: here belong 'The Robinsonad', 'Nothing, or the Consequence' (both texts, in different ways, poke fun at the *nouveau roman*), and perhaps also 'You' and 'Gigamesh'. It's true that 'You' is a somewhat chancy entry, because to invent a *bad* book, which one can then lambaste because it is bad, is rather cheap. The most original formally is 'Nothing, or the Consequence', since no one could possibly have written that novel, and therefore the device of the pseudo-review permits an acrobatic trick: a critique of a book that not only does not exist but also cannot. 'Gigamesh' was the least to my taste. The idea is to give the show away; yet is it really right to dispose of a masterpiece with *those* kinds of jokes? Perhaps, if one does not pen them oneself.

(2) Drafts and outlines (for they actually are, in their own way, outlines): 'Gruppenführer Louis XVI', for instance, or 'The Idiot', and 'A Question of the Rate'. Each of these could – who knows – become the embryo of a decent novel. Even so, one ought to write the novels first. A synopsis, critical or otherwise, only amounts to an hors d'oeuvre that whets our appetite for a course not found in the kitchen. Why not found? Criticism *ad hominem* is not 'cricket', but this once I will indulge in it. The author had ideas that he was unable to realize in full form; he could not write, but regretted not writing – and there you have the whole genesis of this aspect of *A Perfect Vacuum*. Lem, sufficiently clever to foresee precisely such a charge, decided to protect himself – with an introduction. That is why in 'Auto-Momus' he speaks of the poverty of the craft of prose, of how one must, as an artisan at his workbench, whittle descriptions to say that the Marquise left the house at five. But good craft is not impoverishment. Lem took fright at the difficulties presented by each of these three titles, which I have mentioned only by way of example. He preferred not to risk it, preferred to duck the issue, to take the coward's way out. In stating, 'Every book is a grave of countless others, it deprives them of life by supplanting them,' he gives us to understand that he has more

ideas than biological time (*Ars longa, vita brevis*). However, there are not all that many significant, highly promising ideas in *A Perfect Vacuum*. There are displays of agility, to which I alluded, but there we are speaking of jokes. Yet I suspect a matter of more importance – namely, a longing that cannot be satisfied.

The last group of works in the volume convinces me that I am not mistaken: 'De Impossibilitate Vitae', 'Civilization as Error' and – most of all! – 'The New Cosmogony'.

'Civilization as Error' stands on their head the views which Lem has more than once expounded in his books both belletristic and discursive. The technology explosion, there condemned as the destroyer of culture, here is put in the role of the saviour of humanity. And for a second time Lem plays apostate in 'De Impossibilitate Vitae'. Let us not be misled by the amusing absurdity of the long causal chains of the family chronicle. The purpose lies not in these comic anecdotes; what is taking place is an attack on Lem's Holy of Holies – on the theory of probability, i.e., of chance, i.e., of that category on which he built and developed so many of his voluminous conceptions. The attack is carried out in a clownish setting, and this is meant to blunt its edge. Was it, then, if only for a moment, conceived not as satire?

Doubts like these are dispelled by 'The New Cosmogony', the true *pièce de résistance* of the book, hidden in its pages like a Trojan horse. If not a joke, not a fictional review, then what precisely is it? A bit heavy for a joke, loaded down as it is with such massive scientific argumentation – we know that Lem has devoured encyclopaedias; shake him and out come logarithms and formulas. 'The New Cosmogony' is the fictional oration of a Nobel Prize laureate that presents a revolutionary new model of the Universe. If I did not know any other book of Lem's I might conclude that the thing was meant to be a gag for the benefit of some thirty initiates – that is, physicists and other relativists – in the entire world. That, however, seems unlikely. What then? I suspect, again, that there was an idea, any idea that burst upon the author – and from which he shrank. Of course he will never admit to this, and neither I nor anyone else will be able to prove to him that he has taken seriously the model of the Universe as a game. He can always plead the facetiousness of the context, and point to the very title of the book (*A Perfect Vacuum* – that is to say, a book 'about nothing'). And besides, the best refuge and excuse is *licentia poetica.*

All the same, I believe that behind these texts there hides a certain gravity. The Universe as a game? An Intentional Physics? Being a worshipper of science, having prostrated himself before its sacred methodology, Lem could not well assume the role of its foremost heresiarch and dissenter. Therefore, he could not place this thought within any discursive exposition. On the other hand, to make the idea of a 'game of Universe' the pivot of a story plot would have meant writing yet another work, the umpteenth, of 'normal science fiction'.

What then remained? For a sound mind, nothing but to keep silent. Books that the writer does not write, that he will certainly never undertake, come what may, and that can be attributed to fictitious authors – are not such books, by virtue of their non-existence, re-markably like silence? Could one place oneself at any safer distance from heterodox thoughts? To speak of these books, of these treatises, as belonging to others, is practically the same as to speak – without speaking. Particularly when this takes place within the scenario of a joke.

And so, from long years of secret hungering for the nourishment of realism, from notions too bold with regard to one's own views for them to be voiced outright, from all that one dreams of and dreams in vain, arose *A Perfect Vacuum.* The theoretical Introduction, which ostensibly makes the case for a 'new genre of literature', is a manoeuvre to divert attention, the deliberately exhibitory gesture of the prestidigitator who wishes to draw our eyes from what he is actually doing. We are to believe that feats of dexterity are being performed, when it is otherwise. It is not the trick of the 'pseudo-review' that gave birth to these works; rather, they, demanding – in vain – to be expressed, used this trick as an excuse and a pretext. In the absence of the trick all would have remained in the realm of the unsaid. For we have here the betrayal of fantasy to the cause of well-grounded realism, and defection in empiricism, and heresy in science. Did Lem really think he would not be seen through in his machination? It is simplicity itself: to shout out, with laughter, what one would dare not whisper in earnest. Contrary to what the Introduction says, the critic does not have to be chained to the book 'as the convict is . . . to his wheelbarrow': the critic's freedom does not lie in raising up or tearing down the book, but lies in this, that through the book, as through a microscope, he may observe the author; and in that case *A Perfect Vacuum* turns out to be a tale of what is desired but is not to be had. It is a book of ungranted wishes. And the only subterfuge the evasive Lem might still avail himself of would be a counterattack: in the assertion that it was not I, the critic, but he himself, the author, who wrote the present review and added it to − and made it part of − *A Perfect Vacuum*.

Marcel Coscat

LES ROBINSONADES

(*Editions du Seuil, Paris*)

After Defoe's Robinson came, watered down for the kiddies, the Swiss Robinson and a whole slew of further infantilized versions of the life on the desert island; then a few years ago the Paris Olympia published, in step with the times, *The Sex Life of Robinson Crusoe*, a trivial thing whose author there is no point even in naming, because he hid under one of those pseudonyms that are the property of the publisher himself, who hires toilers of the pen for well-known ends. But for *The Robinsonad* of Marcel Coscat it has been worth waiting. This is the social life of Robinson Crusoe, his social-welfare work, his arduous, hard and overcrowded existence, for what is dealt with here is the sociology of isolation – the mass culture of an unpopulated island that, by the end of the novel, is packed solid.

Monsieur Coscat has not written, as the reader will quickly observe, a work of a plagiaristic or commercial nature. He goes into neither the sensational nor the pornographic aspect of the desert island; he does not direct the lust of the castaway to the palm trees with their hairy coconuts, to the fish, the goats, the axes, the mushrooms and the pork salvaged from the shattered ship. In this book, to spite Olympia, Robinson is no longer the male in rut who, like a phallic unicorn trampling the shrubbery, the groves of sugar cane and bamboo, violates the sands of the beach, the mountaintops, the waters of the bay, the screeches of the seagulls, the lofty shadows of the albatross, or the sharks washed ashore in a storm. He who craves such material will not find in this book food for the inflamed imagination. The Robinson of Marcel Coscat is a logician in the pure state, an extreme conventionalist, a philosopher who took the conclusions of his doctrine as far as possible; and the shipwreck – of the three-master *Patricia* – was for him only the opening of the gates, the severing of the ties, the preparation of the laboratory for the experiment, for it enabled him to reach into his own being uncontaminated by the presence of Others.

Sergius N., sizing up his situation, does not meekly resign himself but determines to become a true Robinson, beginning with the voluntary assumption of that very name, which is rational, inasmuch as from his past, his existence till now, he will no longer be able to derive any advantage.

The castaway's life, in its sum total of hardship and vicissitude, is unpleasant enough already and needs no further ministration by the futile exertions of a memory nostalgic for what is lost. The world, exactly as it is found, must be put to rights, and in a civilized fashion; and so the former Sergius N. resolves to form both the island and himself – from zero. The New Robinson of Monsieur Coscat has no illusions; he knows that Defoe's hero was a fiction whose real-life model – the sailor Selkirk – turned out to be, when found accidentally years later by some brig, a creature grown so completely brutish as to be bereft of speech. Defoe's Robinson saved himself not thanks to Friday – Friday appeared too late – but because he scrupulously counted on the company – stern, perhaps, but the best possible for a Puritan – of the Lord God Himself. It was this Companion who imposed upon him the severe pedanticism of behaviour, the obstinate industry, the examination of conscience, and especially that fastidious modesty which so exasperated the author of the Paris Olympia that the latter attacked it head on with the lowered horns of obscenity.

Sergius N., or the New Robinson, feeling within himself some measure of creative power, knows ahead of time that there is one thing he will definitely never produce: the Supreme Being is sure to be beyond him. He is a rationalist, and it is as a rationalist that he sets about his task. He wishes to consider everything, and therefore begins with the question of whether the most sensible thing might not be to do nothing at all. This, of a certainty, will lead to madness, but who knows if madness may not be an altogether convenient condition? Tush, if one could but select the type of insanity, like matching a tie to a shirt; hypomanic euphoria, with its constant joy, Robinson would be perfectly willing to develop in himself; but how can he be sure it will not drift into a depression that ends with suicide attempts? This thought repels him, particularly out of aesthetic considerations, and besides, passivity does not lie in his nature. For either hanging himself or drowning he will always have time, and therefore he postpones such a variant ad acta.

The world of dream – he says to himself, in one of the first pages of the novel – is the Nowhere that can be absolutely perfect; it is a utopia, though weakened in clarity, being but feebly fleshed out, submerged in the nocturnal workings of the mind, the mind which does not at that time (at night) measure up to the requirements of reality. 'In my sleep,' declares Robinson, 'I am visited by various persons, and they put questions to me, to which I know not the answer till it falls from their lips. Is this to signify that these persons are fragments untying themselves from my being, that they are, as it were, its umbilical continuation? To speak thus is to fall into great error. Just as I do not know whether those grubs, *already* appetizing to me, those juicy little white worms, are to be found beneath this flat stone, here, which I begin gingerly to pry at with the big toe of my bare foot, so, too, I do not know what is hidden in the minds of the persons who come to me in my sleep. Thus in relation to my *I* these persons are as external as the grubs. The idea is not at all to erase the distinction between dream and reality – that is the way to madness! – but to create a new, a better order. What in a dream succeeds only now and then, with mixed results, in muddled fashion, waveringly and by chance, must be straightened, tightened, fitted together, and made secure; a dream, when moored in reality, when brought out into the light of reality *as a method*, and serving reality, and peopling reality, packing it with the very finest goods, ceases to be a dream, and reality, under the influence of such curative treatment, becomes both as clear as before and shaped as never before. Since I am alone, I need take no one into account; however, since at the same time the knowledge that I am alone is poison to me, I will therefore not be alone. The Lord God I cannot manage, it is true, but that does not mean I cannot manage Anyone!'

And our logical Robinson says further: 'A man without Others is a fish without water, but just as most water is murky and turbid, so, too, my medium was a rubbish heap. My relatives, parents, superiors, teachers I did not choose myself; this applies even to my mistresses, for they came my way at random: throughout, I took (if it can be said

I took at all) what chance provided. If, like any other mortal, I was condemned to the accidents of birth and family and friends, then there is nothing for which I need mourn. And therefore – let there resound the first words of Genesis: Away with this clutter!'

He speaks these words, we see, with a solemnity to match that of the Maker: 'Let there be . . .' For in fact Robinson prepares to create himself a world from zero. It is not now merely through his liberation from people due to a fortuitous calamity that he embarks upon creation whole hog, but by design. And thus the logically perfect hero of Marcel Coscat outlines a plan that later will destroy and mock him – can it be, as the human world has done to *its* Creator?

Robinson does not know where to begin. Ought he to surround himself with ideal beings? Angels? Winged horses? (For a moment he has a yen for a centaur.) But, stripped of illusions, he understands that the presence of beings in any respect perfect will be difficult to stomach. Therefore, for a start, he supplies himself with one about whom before, till now, he could only dream: a loyal servant, a butler, valet and footman in one person – the fat (no lean and hungry look!) Snibbins. In the course of this first Robinsonad our apprentice Demiurge reflects upon democracy, which, like any man (of this he is certain), he had put up with only out of necessity. When yet a boy, before dropping off to sleep, he imagined how lovely it would be to be born a mighty lord in some medieval time. Now at last that fantasy can be realized. Snibbins is properly stupid, for thereby he automatically elevates his master; nothing original ever enters his head, hence he will never give notice; he performs everything in a twinkling, even that which his master has not yet had time to ask.

The author does not at all explain whether – and how – Robinson does the work *for* Snibbins, because the story is told in the first (Robinson's) person; but even if Robinson (and how can it be otherwise?) does do everything himself on the sly and afterwards attributes it to the servant's offices, he acts at that time totally without awareness, and thus only the results of those exertions are visible. Hardly has Robinson rubbed the sleep from his eyes in the morning when there at his bedside lie the carefully prepared little oysters of which he is so fond – salted lightly with sea water, seasoned to taste with the sour tang of sorrel herbs – and, for an appetizer, soft grubs, white as butter, on dainty saucer-stones; and behold, near by are his shoes polished to a high shine with coconut fibre, and his clothes all laid out, pressed by a rock hot from the sun, and the trousers creased, and a fresh flower in the lapel of the jacket. But even so the master usually grumbles a little as he eats and dresses. For lunch he will have roast tern, for supper coconut milk, but well chilled. Snibbins, as befits a good butler, receives his orders – of course – in submissive silence.

The Master grumbles, the Servant listens; the Master orders, the Servant does as bid. It is a pleasant life, quiet, a little like a vacation in the country. Robinson goes for walks, pockets interesting pebbles, even builds up a collection of them; Snibbins, in the meantime, prepares the meals – but eats nothing at all himself: how easy on the budget and how convenient! But by and by in the relations of Master and Servant there appear the first sands of discord. The existence of Snibbins is beyond question: to doubt it is to doubt that the trees stand and the clouds float when no one is watching them. But the stiff formality of the footman, his meticulousness, obedience, submission, grow downright wearisome. The shoes are *always* waiting for Robinson polished, the oysters give off their smell each morning by his hard bed; Snibbins holds his tongue – and a good thing, too, the Master can't abide servants' ifs, ands and buts – but from this it is evident that Snibbins *as a person* is not in any way present on the island. Robinson decides to add something that will make the situation – too simple, primitive really – more refined. To give Snibbins slothfulness, contrariness, an inclination to mischief, cannot be done: the way he is, is the way he is; he has by now too solidly established himself in existence. Robinson therefore engages, as a scullery boy and helper, the little Boomer. This is a filthy but good-looking urchin, foot-loose, you might say, somewhat of a loafer, but sharp-witted, full of shenanigans, and now it is not the Master but the Servant who begins to have more and more work – not in attendance on the Master, but to conceal from the Master's eye all the things that that young whippersnapper thinks up. The result is that Snibbins, because he is constantly occupied with thrashing Boomer, is absent to an even higher degree than before; from time to time Robinson can hear, inadvertently, the sounds of Snibbins's dressing-downs, carried in his direction by the ocean wind (the shrill voice of Snibbins is amazingly like the voice of the big gulls), but he is not about to involve himself in the bickering of servants! What, Boomer is pulling Snibbins away from the Master? Boomer will be dismissed – has already been sent packing, scattered to the winds. Had even helped himself to the oysters! The Master is willing to forget this little episode, but then Snibbins cannot, try as he might; he falls down on the job; scolding does not help; the servant maintains his silence, still waters run deep, and it's clear now that he's started thinking. The Master disdains to interrogate a servant or demand frankness – to whom is he to be confessor?! Nothing goes smoothly, a sharp word has no effect – very well then, you too, old fool, out of my sight! Here's three months' wages – and to hell with you!

Robinson, haughty as any master, wastes an entire day in the throwing together of a raft, with it reaches the deck of the *Patricia*, which lies wrecked upon a reef: the money, fortunately, has not been carried off by the waves. Accounts squared, Snibbins vanishes – except that he has left behind the counted-out money. Robinson, insulted thus by the servant, does not know what to do. He feels that he has committed an error, though as yet feels this by intuition only. What has gone wrong?!

I am Master here, I can do anything! – he says to himself immediately, for courage, and takes on Wendy Mae. She is, we conjecture, an allusion to the paradigm of Man Friday. But this young, really rather simple girl might lead the Master into temptation. He might easily perish in her marvellous – since unattainable – embraces, he might lose himself in a fever of rut and lusting, go mad on the point of her pale, mysterious smile, her fleeting profile, her bare little feet bitter from the ashes of the campfire and reeking with the grease of barbecued mutton. Therefore, from the very first, in a moment of true inspiration, he makes Wendy Mae . . . three-legged. In a more ordinary, that is, a tritely objective reality, he would not have been able to do this! But here he is Lord of Creation. He acts as one who, having a cask of methyl alcohol, poisonous yet inviting him to drink and be merry, plugs it up himself, against himself, for he will be living with a temptation he must never indulge; at the same time he will be kept on his toes, for his appetite will constantly be removing from the cask, lewdly, its hermetic bung. And thus Robinson will live, from now on, cheek by jowl with a three-legged maid, always able – of course – to imagine her *without* the middle leg, but that is all. He becomes wealthy in emotions unspent, in endearments unsquandered (for what point would there be in wasting them on such a person?). Little Wendy Mae, associated in his mind with both Wednesday and Wedding Day (note: Wednesday, *Mitt-woch*, the middle of the week – an obvious symbolization of sex; perhaps, too, Wendy – Wench – Window), and also with a poor orphan ('Wednesday's child is full of woe'), becomes his Beatrice. Did that silly little chit of a fourteen-year-old know anything whatever about Dante's infernal spasms of desire? Robinson is indeed pleased with himself. He created her and by that very act – her three-leggedness – barricaded her from himself. Nevertheless, before long the whole thing begins to come apart at the seams. While concentrating on a problem important in some respects, Robinson neglected so many other important facets of Wendy Mae!

It begins innocently enough. He would like, now and then, to take a peek at the little one but has pride enough to resist this urge. Later, however, various thoughts run through his brain. The girl does what formerly was Snibbins's job. Gathering the oysters – no problem there; but taking care of the Master's wardrobe, even his personal linen? Here already one can detect an element of ambiguity – no! – it is all too unambiguous! So he gets up surreptitiously, in the dead of night, when she is sure to be still sleeping, and washes his unmentionables in the bay. But since he has begun to rise so early, why couldn't he – just once – you know – for fun (but only his own, Master's, solitary fun) – wash *her* things? Didn't he give them to her? By himself, in spite of the sharks, he went out several times to penetrate the hull of the *Patricia* and found some ladies' frippery, shifts, pinafores, petticoats, panties. Yes, but when he washes them, won't he have to hang everything on a line, between the trunks of two palms? A dangerous game! Particularly dangerous in that, though Snibbins is no longer on the island as a servant, he has not dropped completely out of the picture. Robinson can almost hear his heavy breathing, can guess what he is thinking: Your Lordship, begging your pardon, never washed anything for *me*. While he existed, Snibbins never would have dared utter words so audaciously insinuating, but, missing, he turns out to be devilishly loose of tongue! Snibbins is gone, that is true; but he has left his absence. He is not to be seen in any concrete place, but even when he served he modestly lay low, kept out of the Master's way and dared not show himself. Now, Snibbins haunts: his pathologically obsequious, goggle-eyed stare, his screechy voice, it all returns; the distant quarrels with Boomer shrill through the screams of the least gull; and now Snibbins bares his hairy chest among the ripe coconuts (to what leads the shamelessness of such hints?!), he bends to the curve of the scaled palm trunks and with fisheyes (the goggle!) looks at Robinson like a drowned man from beneath the waves. Where? There, over there, where that rock is, on the point – for he had his own little hobby, did Snibbins: he loved to sit on the promontory and hurl croaking curses at the aged and infirm whales, who loose their spouts sedately, within the confines of their families, on the bounding main.

If only it were possible to come to an understanding with Wendy Mae and thereby make the relationship, already very unbusinesslike, more settled, more restricted, more decorous as regards obedience and command, with the sternness and the maturity of the masculine Master! Ah, but it's really such a simple-minded girl; she's never heard of Snibbins; to speak to her is like talking to a wall. Even if she actually thinks some thought of her own, it's certain that she'll never say a word. This, it would seem, out of simplicity, timidity (she's a servant, after all!), but in fact such little-girlishness is instinctively crafty: she knows perfectly well for what – no, *against* what – the Master is dry, calm, controlled and high-flown! Moreover she vanishes for hours on end, nowhere to be seen till nightfall. Could it be Boomer? Because it couldn't be Snibbins – no, that's out of the question! Snibbins definitely isn't on the island!

The naïve reader (alas, there are many such) will by now probably have concluded that Robinson is suffering hallucinations, that he is slipping into insanity. Nothing of the sort! If he is a prisoner, it is only of his own creation. For he may not say to himself the one thing that would act upon him, in a radical way, therapeutically – namely, that Snibbins never existed at all, and likewise Boomer. In the first place, should he say it, she who now *is* – Wendy Mae – would succumb, a helpless victim, to the destructive flood of such manifest negation. And furthermore, this explanation, once made, would completely and permanently paralyse Robinson as Creator. Therefore, regardless of what may yet happen, he can no more admit to himself the *nothingness* of his handiwork than the real Creator can ever admit to the creation – in His handiwork – of *spite*. Such an admission would mean, in both cases, total defeat. God has not created evil; nor does Robinson, by analogy, work in any kind of void. Each being, as it were, a captive of his own myth.

So Robinson is delivered up, defenceless, to Snibbins. Snibbins exists, but always beyond the reach of a stone or a club, and it does not help to set out Wendy Mae, tied in the dark to a stake, for him as bait (already Robinson has resorted to this!). The dismissed servant is nowhere, and therefore everywhere. Poor Robinson, who wanted so to avoid shoddiness, who intended to surround himself with chosen ones, has befouled his nest, for he has ensnibbined the entire island.

Our hero suffers the torments of the damned. Particularly good are the descriptions of the quarrels at night with Wendy Mae, those dialogues, conversations rhythmically punctuated by her sullen, female, seductively swollen silences, in which Robinson throws all moderation, restraint, to the winds. His lordliness falls from him; he has become simply her chattel – dependent on her least nod, wink, smile. And through the darkness he feels that small, faint smile of the girl; however, when, fatigued and covered with sweat, he turns over on his hard bed to face the dawn, dissolute and mad thoughts come to him; he begins to imagine what else he might do with Wendy Mae ... something paradisiacal, perhaps? From this we get – in his threshing out of the matter – allusions, through feather stoles and boas, to the Biblical serpent (note, too: servant – serpent), and we have the attempted anagrammatic mutilation of birds to obtain Adam's rib, which is Eve (note, too: *Aves* – Eva). Robinson, naturally, would be her Adam. But he well knows that if he cannot rid himself of Snibbins, in whom he took no personal interest whatever during the latter's tenure as lackey, then surely a scheme to put Wendy Mae out of the way must spell disaster. Her presence in any form is preferable to parting with her: that much is clear.

What follows is a tale of degeneration. The nightly washing of the fluffs and frills becomes a sort of sacramental rite. Awakened in the middle of the night, he listens intently for her breathing. At the same time he knows that now he can at least struggle with himself *not* to leave his place, *not* to stretch his hand forth in that direction – but if he were to drive away the little tormentor, ah, that would be the end! In the first rays of the sun her underthings, scrubbed so, bleached by the sun, full of holes (oh, the locality of those holes!), flap frivolously in the wind; Robinson comes to know all the possibilities of those most hackneyed agonies which are the privilege of the lovelorn. And her chipped hand mirror, and her little comb . . . Robinson begins to flee his cave-home, no more does he spurn the reef from which Snibbins abused the old, phlegmatic whales. But things cannot go on like this much longer, and so: let them not. There he is now, hastening to the beach to wait for the great white hulk of the *Caryatid*, a transatlantic steamer which a storm (very likely also conveniently invented) will be casting up on the leaden, foot-scorching sand covered with the gleam of dying chambered nautili. But what does it mean, that some of the chambered nautili contain within them bobby pins, while others in a soft-slimy slurp spit out – at Robinson's feet – soaked butts of Camels? Do not such signs clearly indicate that even the beach, the sand, the trembling water, and its sheets of foam sliding back into the deep, are likewise no longer part of the material world? But whether this is the case or not, surely the drama that begins upon the beach, where the wreck of the *Caryatid*, ripped open on the reef with a monstrous rumble, spills its unbelievable contents before the dancing Robinson – that drama is entirely real, it is the wail of feelings unrequited . . .

From this point on, we must confess, the book grows more and more difficult to understand and demands no little effort on the part of the reader. The line of development, precise till now, becomes entangled and doubles back upon itself. Can it be that the author deliberately sought to disturb the eloquence of the romance with dissonances? What purpose is served by the pair of barstools to which Wendy Mae has given birth? We assume that their three-leggedness is a simple family trait – that's clear, fine; but who was the father of those stools? Can it be that we are faced with the immaculate conception of furniture?? Why does Snibbins, who previously only spat at the whales, turn out to be their ardent admirer, even to the point of requesting metamorphosis (Robinson says of him, to Wendy Mae,

'He wants whaling')? And further: at the beginning of the second volume Robinson has from three to five children. The uncertainty of the number we can understand. It is one of the characteristics of a hallucinated world that has grown too complicated: the Creator is no longer able to keep straight in his memory all the details of the creation simultaneously. Well and good. But with whom did Robinson have these children? Did he create them by a pure act of will, as previously he did Snibbins, Wendy Mae, Boomer, or – instead – did he beget them in an act imagined indirectly, i.e., with a woman? There is not one word in the second volume that refers to Wendy Mae's third leg. Might this amount to a kind of anti-creational deletion? In Chapter Eight our suspicions would appear to be confirmed by a fragment of conversation with the tomcat of the *Caryatid*, in which the latter says to Robinson, 'You're a great one for pulling legs.' But since Robinson neither found the tomcat on the ship nor in any other way created it, the animal having been thought up by that aunt of Snibbins's whom Snibbins's wife refers to as the '*accoucheuse* of the Hyperboreans', it is not known, unfortunately, whether Wendy Mae had any children in addition to the stools or not. Wendy Mae does not admit to children, or at least she does not answer any of Robinson's questions during the great jealousy scene, in which the poor devil goes so far as to weave himself a noose out of coconut fibres.

'Cock Robinson' is what the hero calls himself in this scene, ironically, and then, 'Mock Robinson'. How are we to understand this? That Wendy Mae is 'killing' him? And that he holds all that he has done (created) to be counterfeit? Why, too, does Robinson say that although he is not nearly so three-legged as Wendy Mae, still in this regard he is, to some extent, similar to her? This may more or less allow of an explanation, but the remark, closing the first volume, has no continuation in the second, neither anatomically nor artistically. Furthermore, the story of the aunt from the Hyperboreans seems rather tasteless, as does the children's chorus which accompanies her metamorphosis: 'There are three of us here, there are four and a half, Old Fried Eggs.' Fried Eggs, incidentally, is Wendy Mae's uncle (Friday?); the fish gurgle about him in Chapter Three, and again we have some allusions to a leg (via fillet of sole), but it is not known whose.

The deeper we get into the second volume, the more perplexing it becomes. In the second half of it, Robinson no longer speaks to Wendy Mae directly: the last act of communication is a letter, at night, in the cave, written by her in the ashes of the fireplace, by feel, a letter to Robinson, who will read it at the crack of dawn – but he trembles in advance, able to guess its message in the darkness when he passes his fingers over the cold cinders . . . 'Do leave me be!' she wrote, and he, not daring to reply, fled with his tail between his legs. To do what? To organize a Miss Chambered Nautilus Pageant, to belabour the palm trees with a cudgel, reviling them in the most opprobrious terms, to shout out, on the promenade of the beach, his programme for harnessing the island to the tails of the whales! And then, in the course of one morning, arise those throngs which Robinson calls into existence off the cuff, carelessly, writing names, first and last, and nicknames, on whatever comes to hand. After this, complete chaos, it seems, is ushered in: e.g., the scenes of the putting together of the raft and the tearing asunder of the raft, of the raising up of the house for Wendy Mae and the pulling of it down, of the arms that fatten as the legs grow thin, of the impossible orgy without beets, where the hero cannot tell black eyes from peas or blood from bortsch!

All this – nearly 170 pages, not counting the epilogue – produces the impression that either Robinson abandoned his original plans, or else the author himself lost his way in the book. Jules Nefastes, in *Figaro Littéraire*, states that the work is 'plainly clinical'. Sergius N., in spite of his praxiological plan of Creation, *could not avoid* madness. The result of any truly consistent solipsistic creation *must be* schizophrenia. The book attempts to illustrate this truism. Therefore, Nefastes considers it intellectually barren, albeit entertaining in places, owing to the author's inventiveness.

Anatole Fauche, on the other hand, in *La Nouvelle Critique*, disputes the verdict of his colleague from *Figaro Littéraire*, saying – in our opinion, entirely to the point – that Nefastes, quite aside from what *The Robinsonad* propounds, is not qualified as a psychiatrist (following which there is a long argument on the lack of any connection between solipsism and schizophrenia, but we, considering the question to be wholly immaterial to the book, refer the reader to *The New Criticism* in this regard). Fauche sets forth the philosophy of the novel thus: the work shows that the act of creation is *asymmetrical*, for in fact anything may be created in thought, but not everything (almost nothing) may then be erased. This is rendered impossible by the memory of the one creating, and memory is not subject to the will. According to Fauche the novel has nothing in common with a clinical case history (of a particular form of insanity on a desert island) but, rather, exemplifies the principle of aberrance in creation. Robinson's actions (in the second volume) are senseless only in that he personally gains nothing by them, but psychologically they are quite easily explained. Such flailing about is characteristic of a man who has got himself into a situation he only partially anticipated; the situation, taking on solidity in accordance with laws of its own, holds him captive. From real situations – emphasizes Fauche – one may in reality escape; from those imagined, however, there is no exit. Thus *The Robinsonad* shows only that for a man the true world is indispensable ('the true external world is the true internal world'). Monsieur Coscat's Robinson was not in the least mad; it was only that his scheme to build himself a synthetic universe on the uninhabited island was, in its very inception, doomed to failure.

On the strength of these conclusions Fauche goes on to deny *The Robinsonad* any underlying value, for, thus interpreted, the work indeed appears to offer little. In the opinion of this reviewer, both critics here cited went wide of the mark; they failed to read the book's contents properly.

The author has, in our opinion, set forth an idea far less banal than, on the one hand, the history of a madness on a desert island, or, on the other, a polemic against the thesis of the creative omnipotence of solipsism. (A polemic of the latter type would in any case be an absurdity, since in formal philosophy no one has ever promulgated the notion that solipsism grants creative omnipotence; each to his own, but in philosophy there is no percentage in tilting at windmills.)

To our mind, what Robinson does when he 'goes mad' is no derangement – and neither is it some sort of polemical foolishness. The original intention of the novel's hero is sane and rational. He knows that the limitation of every man is Others; the idea, too hastily drawn from this, which says that the elimination of Others provides the self with unlimited freedom, is psychologically false, corresponding to the physical falsehood which would have us believe that since shape is given to water by the shape of the vessel that contains it, the breaking of all vessels provides that water with 'absolute freedom'. Whereas, just as water, when deprived of a vessel, will spread out into a puddle, so, too, will a totally isolated man explode, that explosion taking the form of a complete deculturalization. If there is no God and if, more-over, there are neither Others nor the hope of their return, one must save oneself through the construction of a system of some faith, a system that, with respect to the one creating it, *must* be external. The Robinson of Monsieur Coscat understood this simple precept.

And further: for the common man the beings who are the most desired, and at the same time entirely real, are beings *beyond reach*. Everyone knows of the Queen of England, of her sister the Princess, of the former wife of the President of the United States, of the famous movie stars; that is to say, no one who is normal doubts for a minute the actual existence of such persons, even though he cannot directly (by touch) substantiate their existence. In turn, he who can boast of a direct acquaintance with such persons will no longer see in them phenomenal paragons of wealth, femininity, power, beauty, etc., because, in entering into contact with them, he experiences – by dint of everyday things – their completely ordinary, normal, human im-perfection. For such persons, up close, are not in the least godlike beings or otherwise extraordinary. Beings that are truly at the pinnacle of perfection, that are therefore truly boundlessly desired, yearned for, longed after, must be *remote* even to full unattainability. It is their elevation above the masses that lends them their magnetic glam-our; it is not qualities of body or soul but an unbridgeable social distance that accounts for their seductive halo.

This characteristic of the real world, then, Robinson attempts to reproduce on his island, within the realm of beings of his own inven-tion. Immediately he errs, because he *physically* turns his back on the creation, the Snibbinses, Boomers, et al., and that distance, natural enough between Master and Servant, he is only too willing to break down when he acquires a woman. Snibbins he could not, nor did he wish to, take into his arms; now – with a woman – he only *cannot*. The point is not (for this is no intellectual problem!) that he was unable to embrace a woman not there. Of course he was unable! The thing was to create *mentally* a situation whose own natural *law* would forever stand in the way of erotic contact – and at the same time it had to be a law that would totally ignore the *non-existence* of the girl. This *law* was to restrain Robinson, and not the banal, crude fact of the female partner's non-existence! For to take simple cognizance of her non-existence would have been to ruin everything.

And so Robinson, seeing what must be done, sets to work – that is, the establishment on the island of an entire, imaginary society. It is this that will stand between him and the girl; this that will throw up a system of obstacles and thus provide that impassable distance from which he will be able to love her, to desire her continually – no longer exposed to any mundane circumstance, as, for example, the urge to stretch out his hand and feel her body. He realizes – he must – that if he yields but once in the struggle waged against himself, if he attempts to feel her, the whole world that he has created will, in that bat of an eye, crumble. And this is the reason he begins to 'go mad', in a frenzied scramble to pull multitudes out of the hat of his imagination – thinking up and writing in the sand all those names, cognomens and sobriquets, ranting and raving about the wives of Snibbins, the Hyperborean aunts, the Old Fried Eggses and so on and so forth. And since this swarm is necessary to him *only* as a certain insurmountable space (to lie between Him and Her), he creates indifferently, sloppily, chaotically; he works in haste, and that haste discredits the thing created, lays bare its incoherence, its lack of thought, its cheapness.

Had he succeeded, he would have become the eternal lover, a Dante, a Don Quixote, a Werther, and in so doing would have had his way. Wendy Mae – is it not obvious? – would then have been a woman no less real than Beatrice, than Lotte, than any queen or princess. Being completely real, she would have been at the same time unattainable. And this would have allowed him to live and dream of her, for there is a profound difference between a situation in which a man from reality pines after his own dream, and one in which reality lures reality – precisely by its inaccessibility. Only in this second case is it still possible to cherish hope, since now it is the social distance alone, or other, similar barriers, that rule out the chance for the love to be consummated. Robinson's relationship to Wendy Mae could therefore have undergone normalization only if she at one and the same time had taken on *realness* and *inapproachability* for him.

To the classic tale of the star-crossed lovers united in the end, Marcel Coscat has thus opposed an ontological tale of the necessity of permanent separation, this being the only guarantee of a plighting of the spirits that is permanent. Comprehending the full boorishness of the blunder of the 'third leg', Robinson (and not the author, that's plain!) quietly 'forgets' about it in the second volume. Mistress of her world, princess of the ice mountain, untouchable inamorata – this is what he wished to make of Wendy Mae, that same Wendy Mae who began her education with him as a simple little servant girl, a domestic to replace the uncouth Snibbins . . . And it was precisely in this that he failed. Do you know now, have you guessed why? The answer could not be simpler: because Wendy Mae, unlike any queen, *knew* of Robinson and loved him. She had no desire to become the vestal goddess, and this division drove the hero to his ruin. If it were only *he* that loved *her*, bah! But she returned his feelings . . . Whoever does not understand this simple truth, whoever believes, as our grandfathers were instructed by their Victorian governesses, that we are able to love others, but not ourselves in those others, would do better not to open this mournful romance that Monsieur Coscat has vouchsafed us. Coscat's Robinson dreamed himself a girl whom he did not wish to give up completely to reality, since *she* was *he*, since from that reality that never releases its hold on us, there is – other than death – no awakening.

Patrick Hannahan

GIGAMESH

(*Transworld Publishers, London*)

Here is an author who covets the laurels of James Joyce. *Ulysses* condensed the *Odyssey* into a single Dublin day, made Circe's infernal palace from the dirty laundry of *la belle époque*, tied the bloomers of Gerty McDowell into a hangman's noose for Bloom the travelling salesman, and with an army of four hundred thousand words descended upon Victorianism, which was demolished with all the stylistics that lay at the disposal of the pen, from stream of consciousness to trial deposition. Was this not already the culmination of the novel, and at the same time the monumental laying of it to rest in the family sepulchre of the arts (in *Ulysses* there is music, too!)? Apparently not; apparently Joyce himself did not think so, inasmuch as he decided to go further, writing a book that is supposed to be not only the focusing of civilization into a single language, but also an *omnilinguistic* lens, a descent to the foundations of the Tower of Babel. As to the brilliance of *Ulysses* and *Finnegans Wake*, which attempts the infinite with double-barrelled audacity, we neither affirm it here nor deny it. A solitary review can now be nothing but a grain cast upon that mountain of homages and imprecations that has grown over both books. It is certain, however, that Patrick Hannahan, Joyce's countryman, never would have written his *Gigamesh* if not for the great example, which he took as a challenge.

One would think that such an idea would be doomed to failure from the beginning. Doing a second *Ulysses* is as worthless as doing a second *Finnegan*. At the summits of art only the first achievements count, just as, in the history of mountain climbing, it is only the first surmounting of walls unscaled.

Hannahan, tolerant enough of *Finnegans Wake*, thinks little of *Ulysses*. 'What an idea,' he says, 'packing the nineteenth century of Europe, and Ireland, into the sarcophagal form of the *Odyssey*!

Homer's original itself is of doubtful value. Why, it is your comic book of antiquity, with Ulysses as Superman, and the happy end. *Ex ungue leonem*: in the choice of his model we see the calibre of the writer. The *Odyssey* is a pirating of *Gilgamesh*, and bastardized to suit the tastes of the Greek hoi polloi. What in the Babylonian epic represented the tragedy of a struggle crowned with defeat, the Greeks turn into a picturesque adventure tour of the Mediterranean. *"Navigare necesse est,"* "life is a journey" – great gems of wisdom, these. The *Odyssey* is a *dégringolade* in plagiarism; it ruins all the greatness of the fight of Gilgamesh.'

One has to admit that *Gilgamesh*, as Sumerology teaches us, did in fact contain themes that Homer used – the themes of Odysseus, of Circe, of Charon – and is perhaps the oldest version we have of a tragic ontology, because it manifests what Rainer Maria Rilke, thirty-six centuries later, was to call a growing, which consists in this: *'der Tiefbesiegte von immer Grösserem zu sein.'* Man's fate as a battle that leads inescapably to defeat – this is the final sense of *Gilgamesh*.

It was on the Babylonian cycle, then, that Patrick Hannahan decided to spread his epic canvas – a curious enough canvas, let us note, because his *Gigamesh* is a story extremely limited in time and space. The notorious gangster, hired killer and American soldier (of the time of the last world war) 'GI Joe' Maesch, unmasked in his criminal activity by an informer, one N. Kiddy, is to be hanged – by sentence of the military tribunal – in a small town in Norfolk County, where his unit is stationed. The whole action takes thirty-six minutes, the time required to transport the condemned man from his cell to the place of execution. The story ends with the image of the noose, whose black loop, seen against the sky, falls upon the neck of the calmly standing Maesch. This Maesch is of course Gilgamesh, the semi-divine hero of the Babylonian epos, and the one who sends him to the gallows – his old buddy N. Kiddy – is Gilgamesh's closest friend, Enkidu, created by the gods in order to bring about the hero's downfall. When we present it thus, the similarity in creative method between *Ulysses* and *Gigamesh* becomes immediately apparent. But justice demands that we concentrate on the differences between these two works. Our task is made easier in that Hannahan – unlike Joyce! – provided his book with a commentary, which is twice the size of the

373

novel itself (to be exact, *Gigamesh* runs 395 pages, the Commentary 847). We learn at once how Hannahan's method works: the first, seventy-page chapter of the Commentary explains to us all the divergent allusions that emanate from a single, solitary word – namely, the title. Gigamesh derives first, obviously, from Gilgamesh: with this is revealed the mythic prototype, just as in Joyce, for his *Ulysses* also supplies the classical referent before the reader comes to the first word of the text. The omission of the letter L in the name Gigamesh is no accident; L is Lucifer, Lucipherus, the Prince of Darkness, present in the work although he puts in no personal appearance. Thus the letter (L) is to the name (Gigamesh) as Lucifer is to the events of the novel: he is there, but *invisibly*. Through 'Logos' L indicates the Beginning (the Causative Word of Genesis); through Laocoön, the End (for Laocoön's end is brought about by serpents: he was *strangled*, as will be strangled – by the rope – the hero of *Gigamesh*). L has ninety-seven further connections, but we cannot expound them here.

To continue, Gigamesh is a GIGAntic MESS; the hero is in a mess indeed, one hell of a mess, with a death sentence hanging over his head. The word also contains: GIG, a kind of rowboat (Maesch would drown his victims in a gig, after pouring cement on them); GIGgle (Maesch's diabolical giggle is a reference – reference No. 1 – to the musical leitmotif of the descent to hell in *Klage Dr Fausti* [more on this later]); GIGA, which is (a) in Italian, 'fiddle', again tying in with the musical substrates of the novel, and (b) a prefix signifying the magnitude of a billion (as in the word GIGAwatts), but here the magnitude of *evil* in a technological civilization. *Geegh* is Old Celtic for 'avaunt' or 'scram'. From the Italian *giga* through the French *gigue* we arrive at *geigen*, a slang expression in German for copulation. For lack of space we must forgo any further etymological exposition. A different partitioning of the name, in the form of Gi-GAME-sh, foreshadows other aspects of the work: GAME is a game played, but also the quarry of a hunt (in Maesch's case, we have a manhunt). This is not all. In his youth Maesch was a GIGolo; AME suggests the Old German *Amme*, a wet nurse; and MESH, in turn, is a net – for instance, the one in which Mars caught his goddess wife with her lover – and therefore a gin, a snare, a *trap* (under the scaffold), and, moreover, the engagement of gear teeth (e.g., 'synchroMESH').

A separate section is devoted to the title read backward, because during the ride to the place of execution Maesch in his thoughts reaches *back*, seeking the memory of a crime so monstrous that it will *redeem* the hanging. In his mind, then, he plays a game (!) for the highest stakes: if he can recall an act infinitely vile, this will match the infinite Sacrifice of the Redemption; that is, he will become the Anti-saviour. This – on the metaphysical level; obviously Maesch does not consciously undertake any such anti-theodicy; rather – psychologically – he seeks some heinousness that will render him impassive in the face of the hangman. G I J. Maesch is therefore a Gilgamesh who in defeat attains perfection – *negative* perfection. We have here a high symmetry of asymmetry with regard to the Babylonian hero.

So, then, when read in reverse, 'Gigamesh' becomes 'Shemagig'. *Shema* is the ancient Hebraic injunction taken from the Pentateuch ('*Shema Yisrael!*' – 'Hear O Israel, the Lord our God, the Lord is One!'). Because it is in reverse, we are dealing here with the Antigod, that is, the personification of evil. 'Gig' is of course now seen to be 'Gog' (Gog and Magog). From *Shema* derives the name 'Simeon' (Hebrew Shimeon), and immediately we think of Simeon Stylites; but if the Saint sits atop the pillar, the halter hangs down from it; therefore Maesch, dangling beneath, will become a stylite *à rebours*. This is a further step in the antisymmetry. Enumerating in this fashion, in his exegesis, 2,912 expressions from the Old Sumerian, Babylonian, Chaldean, Greek, Church Slavonic, Hottentot, Bantu, South Kurile, Sephardic, the dialect of the Apaches (the Apaches, as everyone knows, commonly exclaim 'Igh' or 'Ugh'), along with their Sanskrit roots and references to underworld argot, Hannahan stresses that this is no haphazard rummage, but a precise semantic wind rose, a multidimensional compass card and map of the work, its cartography – for the object is the plotting of all those ties and links which the novel will realize polyphonically.

In order to go beyond what Joyce did – to go Joyce one better – Hannahan decides to make the book an intersecting point (nexus – node – *nodus* – knot – noose!) not only of all cultures, *ethoi* and *ethnoi*, but also of all languages. Such analysis is necessary (the letter M in 'GigaMesh', for instance, directs us to the history of the Mayans, to the god Vitzi-Putzli, to the entire Aztec cosmogony, and also their

375

irrigation system), but it is by no means sufficient! For the book is woven out of the *sum total* of human knowledge. And again, involved here is not only current knowledge, but also the history of science, and therefore the cuneiform arithmetics of the Babylonians, the models of the world – now extinct, reduced to ashes – of the Chaldeans and the Egyptians, and those from the Ptolemaic to the Einsteinian, and the abacus and the calculus, algebras of groups and of tensors, the methods of firing Ming Dynasty vases, the flying machines of Lilienthal, Hieronymus, Leonardo, the suicide balloon of André and the balloon of General Nobile. (The incidence of cannibalism during Nobile's expedition has its own deep, special significance in the novel; it represents, as it were, a place in which a certain fatal weight has fallen into water and disturbed the mirror surface; so, then, the spreading concentric circles of the waves surrounding *Gigamesh* are the 'sum total' of man's existence on Earth, going back to Homo javanensis and the Palaeopithecus.) All this information lies inside *Gigamesh*, concealed, but retrievable, as in the real world.

We understand the compositional idea of Hannahan thus: with an eye towards outdoing his great countryman and predecessor, he wishes to encompass in a belletristic work not only the accumulated linguistic-cultural wealth of the past, but in addition its universal-cognitive and universal-instrumental heritage (pangnosis).

The preposterousness of such an objective would appear to be self-evident; it smacks of the pretensions of an idiot, for how can a single novel, the story of the hanging of some gangster, possibly become the distillation, the matrix, the key, and the repository of that which swells the libraries of the globe?! Perfectly aware of this cold, even sneering scepticism on the part of the reader, Hannahan does not confine himself to making claims, but proves his case in the Commentary.

It is impossible to summarize it; we can only demonstrate Hannahan's method of creation with a small, rather peripheral example. The first chapter of *Gigamesh* consists of eight pages, wherein the condemned man relieves himself in the latrine of the military prison, reading – over the urinal – the countless graffiti with which other soldiers, before him, have ornamented the walls of that sanctuary. His attention rests on the inscriptions only in passing. Their extreme obscenity turns out to be, precisely through his intermittent awareness of them, a false bottom, since we pass through them straight into the sordid, hot, enormous bowels of the human race, into the inferno of its coprolalia and physiological symbolism, which goes back, through the Kama Sutra and the Chinese 'war of flowers', to the dark caves, with the steatopygous Aphrodites of primitive peoples, for it is *their* naked parts that look out from underneath the filthy acts scrawled awkwardly across the wall. At the same time, the phallic explicitness of some of the drawings points to the East, with its ritual sanctification of Phallos–Lingam, while the East denotes the place of the primeval Paradise, revealed to be a thin lie incapable of hiding the truth – that in the beginning there was poor information. Yes, exactly: for sex and 'sin' arose when the protoamoebas lost their virgin unisexuality; because the equipollence and bipolarity of sex must be derived directly from the Information Theory of Shannon; and now the purpose of the last two letters (SH) in the name of the epic becomes apparent! And thus the path leads from the walls of the latrine to the depths of natural evolution . . . for which countless cultures have served as a fig leaf. Yet this is but a drop in the bucket, because in the chapter we also find:

(a) The Pythagorean quantity pi, symbolizing the feminine principle $(3.14159265359787 \ldots)$, is expressed by the number of letters to be found in the thousand words of the chapter.

(b) When we take the numbers designating the dates of birth of Weismann, Mendel and Darwin and apply them to the text as a key to a code, it turns out that the seeming chaos of that lavatory scatology is an exposition of sexual mechanics, where pairs of colliding bodies are replaced by pairs of copulating bodies; meanwhile this entire sequence of meanings now begins to interlock (synchroMESH!) with other sections of the work, and so through Chapter III (the Trinity!) it relates to Chapter X (pregnancy lasts ten lunar months!), and the latter, if read backward, turns out to be Freudianism explained *in Aramaic*. That is not all: as is shown by Chapter III – if we overlay it on IV and turn the book upside down – Freudianism, that is, the doctrine of psychoanalysis, constitutes a naturalistically secularized version of Christianity. The state prior to the Neurosis equals Paradise; the Trauma of Childhood is the Fall; the Neurotic is the Sinner, the Psychoanalyst the Saviour, and Freudian treatment Salvation through Grace.

(c) Leaving the latrine at the end of Chapter I, J. Maesch whistles a sixteen-bar tune (sixteen being the age of the girl he raped and strangled in the rowboat); its words – extremely vulgar – he only thinks to himself. This excess has psychological justification at the particular moment; in addition, the song, when considered syllabo-tonically, gives us an orthogonal matrix of transformations for the next chapter (it has two different meanings, depending on whether or not we apply the matrix to it).

Chapter II is the development of the blasphemous song whistled by Maesch in the first, but upon application of the matrix the blas-phemies are transformed into hosannas. The entirety has three refer-ents: (1) the *Faust* of Marlowe (Act II, Scene 6 ff.), (2) the *Faust* of Goethe ('*Alles Vergängliche ist nur ein Gleichnis*'), and (3) the *Doctor Faustus* of Thomas Mann. The allusion to Mann's *Faustus* is a master stroke! Because the whole second chapter, when to each and all of the *letters* of its words we assign notes according to the Old Gregorian clef, turns out to be a musical composition, into which Hannahan has translated *back* (going by Mann's description) the *Apocalypsis cum Figuris*, a work attributed, as we know, from Mann, to the composer Adrian Leverkühn. That diabolical music is in Hannahan's novel both present and absent (obvious it certainly is not), like Lucifer (the letter L, left out in the title). Chapters IX, X and XI (the descent from the van, spiritual comfort, the preparation of the gallows) also have a musical subtext (the *Klage Dr Fausti*), but only, so to speak, inci-dentally. Because, when treated as an adiabatic system à la Sadi–Carnot, they prove to be a cathedral (built based on Boltzmann's con-stant) in which is celebrated a Black Mass. (The silent meditations are Maesch's reminiscences in the prison van, concluded with a curse whose suspended glissandi cut short Chapter VIII.) These chapters are truly a cathedral, since the interclausal and phraseological propor-tions of the prose have a syntactic skeleton that is a *blueprint* – in a Monge projection on to an imaginary plane – of the Notre Dame Cathedral with all its pinnacles, cantilevers, buttresses, with its monu-mental portal and the famous Gothic rose window, and so forth. So, then, in *Gigamesh* we also have architecture, inspired by a theodicy. In the Commentary the reader will find (p. 397 et seq.) a complete dia-gram of the cathedral as it is contained in the text of the afore-mentioned chapters, on a scale of 1:1000. If, however, instead of a stereometric Monge projection we use a projection that is non-orthogonal, with an initial displacement according to the matrix from Chapter I, we obtain Circe's Palace, and at the same time the Black Mass changes into a caricature of a lecture on the Augustinian doctrine (again, iconoclasm: Augustinianism in Circe's Palace, while in the cathedral, the Black Mass). The cathedral and Augustinianism are thus not mechanically inserted into the work; they constitute elements of the argument.

This single example may serve to explain how the author, with true Irish pertinacity, united in one novel the entire world of man, man's myths, symphonies, churches and physics, and the annals of world history. The example returns us once more to the title, because – to take that path of meanings – the 'gigantic mess' of *Gigamesh* acquires an unexpectedly profound sense. The Cosmos, after all, is tending, according to the Second Law of Thermodynamics, to ultimate chaos. Entropy *must* increase, and for that reason the end of each and every being is failure. And so 'a gigantic mess' is not only what happens to some former gangster; 'a gigantic mess' is the Universe itself (the 'disorder' of the Cosmos is symbolized by all the 'disorderly houses', the brothels, which Maesch remembers on the way to the gibbet). But at the same time there is the celebration of 'a Gigantic Mass' – in German, *Messe* – of the transubstantiation of Form into final Void. Hence the connection between Sadi–Carnot and the cathedral, hence the embodiment, in it, of Boltzmann's constant: Hannahan *had to* do this, for *chaos* will be the Last Judgement! Of course the Gilgamesh myth itself finds full expression in the work, but this fidelity of Hannahan's – to the Babylonian model – is child's play compared to the interpretational chasms that open up beneath each of the 241,000 words of the novel. The betrayal that N. Kiddy (Enkidu) commits against Maesch–Gilgamesh is a cumulative massing of all the betrayals in history; N. Kiddy is *also* Judas, G I Joe Maesch is *also* the Redeemer (and MESSiah!), and so on, and so on.

Opening the book at random, we find on page 131, fourth line from the top, the exclamation 'Bah!' With it Maesch refuses the Camel offered him by the driver. In the index of the Commentary we find twenty-seven different *bahs*, but to the one from page 131 corresponds the following sequence: Baal, Bahai, Baobab, Bahleda (one might think that Hannahan was in error here, giving us an incorrect spelling of the name of the Polish mountaineer, but no, not at all! The omission of the *c* in that name refers, by the principle already known to us, to the Cantorian *c* as a symbol of the Continuum in its transfiniteness!), Baphomet, Babelisks (Babylonian obelisks – a neologism typical of the author), Babel (Isaac), Abraham, Jacob, ladder, hook and ladder, fire department, hose, riot, Hippies (*h*!), badminton, racket, rocket, moon, mountains, Berchtesgaden – the last, since the *h* in 'Bah' also signifies a worshipper of the Black Mass, as was, in the twentieth century, Hitler. [*Berchtesgaden was Hitler's mountain retreat in Bavaria.* – ED.]

So functions on every height and breadth *one single* word, a common exclamation, so innocent enthymematically, one would have thought! Consider, then, what vast semantic labyrinths await us on the upper levels of the linguistic edifice that is *Gigamesh*! Theories of preformation do battle there with theories of epigenesis (Ch. III, p. 240 ff.); the hand movements of the hangman who ties the loop of the noose have as syntactic accompaniment the Hoyle–Milne hypothesis of the *looping* of two time scales in spiral galaxies. Maesch's reminiscences – his crimes – are a complete register of all the villainies of mankind (the Commentary shows how against his transgressions are marshalled the Crusades, the empire of Charles the Hammer, the slaughter of the Albigenses, the slaughter of the Armenians, the burning at the stake of Giordano Bruno, the witch trials, mass hysteria (Mass!), Flagellantism, the Plague (Black!), Holbein's dances of death, Noah's ark, Arkansas, *ad calendas graecas*, *ad nauseam*, etc.). The gynaecologist whom Maesch stomps in Cincinnati is called Andrew B. Cross: acronymically alphabetic (atomic, biological and chemical warfare), the name is a conglomeration of allusions – to the Passion, anthropomorphism (android), the BAHamas (the island Andros), and Ulysses (Johnson preceding Grant as president) – while the middle initial, again, is the key of B minor, 'The Lament of Dr Faust', which this passage of the text incorporates.

Indeed yes: this novel is a bottomless pit; in whatever place you touch it, roads open up, no end of roads (the pattern of the commas in Chapter VI is an analogue of the map of Rome!), and roads not every which way, for they all, with their innumerable outbranchings, interweave harmoniously to form a single whole (which Hannahan proves employing topological algebra – see the Commentary, the Metamathematical Appendix, p. 811 ff.). And thus everything achieves its realization.

Only one doubt arises, and that is: has Patrick Hannahan reached the mark of his great predecessor, or has he overshot that mark, thereby calling into question not only himself – but his predecessor as well! – in the realm of Art? There are rumours to the effect that Hannahan was assisted in his creation by a battery of computers furnished him by IBM. And even if this be true, I see no offence in it; these days composers make common use of computers – why should writers be denied? Some say that books so fashioned can be read only, in turn, by other digital machines, since no man is capable of encompassing, in his mind, such an ocean of facts and their correlations. Permit me one question: does the man exist who is able thus to encompass *Finnegans Wake* or even *Ulysses*? I do not mean on the literal level, but all the allusions, all the associations and cultural-mythic symbolisms, all the combined paradigms and archetypes on which these works stand and grow in glory? Certainly no one could manage it alone. No one, for that matter, could wade through the entire body of criticism that the prose of James Joyce has accumulated to date! And therefore the question as to the validity of computer participation in fiction is wholly immaterial.

Hostile reviewers say that Hannahan has produced the largest logogriph in literature, a semantic monster rebus, a truly infernal charade or crossword puzzle. They say that the cramming of those million or billion allusions into a work of belles-lettres, that the flaunting play with etymological, phraseological and hermeneutic complications, that the piling up of layers of never-ending, perversely antinomial meanings, is not literary creativity, but the composing of brain teasers for peculiarly paranoiac hobbyists, for enthusiasts and collectors fanatically given to bibliographical digging. That this is, in a word, utter perversion, the pathology of a culture and not its healthy development.

Excuse me, gentlemen – but where exactly is one to draw the line between the multiplicity of meaning that marks the integration of a genius, and the sort of enriching of a work with meanings that represents the pure schizophrenia of a culture? I suspect that the anti-Hannahan group of literary experts fears being put out of work. For Joyce provided brilliant charades but did not tack on to them any explanation of his own; consequently the critic who contributes commentary to *Ulysses* and *Finnegan* is able to display his intellectual biceps, his far-reaching perspicacity, or his imitative genius. Hannahan, on the other hand, did everything *himself*. Not content merely to create the work, he added reference materials, an *apparatus criticus* twice its size. In this lies the crucial difference, and not in such circumstances as, for example, the fact that Joyce 'thought up everything on his own', whereas Hannahan relied on computers hooked up to the Library of Congress (twenty-three million volumes). So, I see no way out of the trap into which we have been driven by the murderously meticulous Irishman: either *Gigamesh* is the crowning achievement of modern literature, or else neither it nor the tale of Finnegan together with the Joycean Odyssey can be granted admission to literary Olympus.

Simon Merrill

SEXPLOSION

(Walker & Company, New York)

If one is to believe the author – and more and more they tell us to believe the authors of science fiction! – the current surge of sex will become a deluge in the 1980s. But the action of the novel *Sexplosion* begins twenty years later, in a New York buried in snowdrifts during a severe winter. An old man of unknown name, wading through the drifts, bumping into the hulks of snow-covered cars, reaches a lifeless office building; he pulls a key from his breast pocket, warm with the last of his body heat, opens the iron gate, and goes down to the basement. His roaming there and the snatches of memory that intrude upon it – this is the whole novel.

The silent vaults of the basement, through which wanders the beam of the flashlight unsteady in the old man's hand, may have been a museum once, or the shipping division of a powerful concern in the years when America once again carried out the successful invasion of Europe. The still half-handmade trade of the Europeans had clashed with the implacable march of conveyor-belt production, and the scientific-technological-postindustrial colossus instantly emerged the victor.

On the field of battle remained three corporations – General Sexotics, Cybordelics and Intercourse International. When the production of these giants was at its peak, sex, from a private amusement, a spectator sport, group gymnastics, a hobby and a collector's market, turned into a philosophy of civilization. McLuhan, who as a hale and hearty old codger had lived to see these times, argued in his *Genitocracy* that this precisely was the destiny of mankind from the moment it entered on the path of technology; that even the ancient rowers, chained to the galleys, and the woodsmen of the North with their saws, and the steam engine of Stephenson with its cylinder and piston, all traced the rhythm, the shape and the meaning of the movements of which the sex of man – that is to say, the sense of man – consists. The impersonal industry of the USA, having appropriated the situational wisdoms of East and West, took the fetters of the Middle Ages and made of them unchastity belts, harnessed Art to the designing of sexercisers, incubunks, copul cots, push-button clitters, porn cones and phallophones, set in motion antiseptic assembly lines from which began to roll sadomobiles, succubuses, sodomy sofas for the home, and public gomorrarcades, and at the same time it established research institutes and science foundations to take up the fight to liberate sex from the servitude of the perpetuation of the species. Sex ceased to be a fashion, for it had become a faith; the orgasm was regarded as a constant duty, and its meters, with their red needles, took the place of telephones in the office and on the street.

But who, then, is this old man prowling the passageways of the basement halls? The legal adviser of General Sexotics? For he recalls the celebrated cases brought before the Supreme Court, the battle for the right to duplicate with manikins the physical appearance of famous people, beginning with the First Lady. General Sexotics had won, at the cost of twenty million dollars – and now the wandering beam of the flashlight plays on the dusty plastic bell jars under which stand frozen the leading film stars and the world's foremost women of society, princesses and queens in splendid dress, for by the decision of the courts it was forbidden to exhibit them otherwise.

In the course of the decade, synthetic sex came a long way from the first models, the inflatables and the hand-windups, to the prototypes with thermostats and feedback. The originals of these copies are long dead, or else are now decrepit crones, but teflon, nylon, dralon and Sexofix have withstood the wear of time; like waxwork figures in a museum, leaping from the darkness into the light, elegant ladies smile immobilely at the old man, and they hold in their raised hands cassettes, each with its siren text (by Supreme Court ruling, the seller was not permitted to place the tape inside the manikin, but the buyer, of course, could do so in the privacy of his home).

The slow, shaky step of the old hermit raises clouds of dust, through which glimmer from across the room, in pale pinks, scenes of group erotica, some of them thirty-membered, resembling giant pretzels or intricately braided breads. Could this be the president of General

Sexotics himself who walks the aisles among these high gomorrarcades and cosy sodomy sofas, or perhaps the chief designer of the company, the man who made all America, and then the world, crotch-aware? Here are videos ('viewrinals') with their controls and programmes, and with that lead seal of the censor over which lawsuits ran through six courts; and here are stacks of containers ready for shipment overseas, filled with Japanese spheres, dildos, precoital creams, and a thousand similar articles, complete with instructions and service manuals.

That was the era of democracy come true at last: one could do anything – with anyone. Heeding the advice of their own futurologists, the corporations, having quietly divided up among themselves the global market in contravention of the antitrust act, went into specialization. General Sexotics worked on equal rights for deviants, and the remaining two companies invested in automation. Flagellashes, batterabusers, black-n-blues appeared as prototypes, to assure the public that there could be no talk of a glut on the market, for a great industry – if it be truly a great industry – does not simply meet needs: it creates them! The old methods of home fornication – the time had come for them to be laid to rest alongside the flints and clubs of the Neanderthals. Scholarly bodies offered six- and eight-year courses of study, then graduate work and advanced degrees in the higher and lower eroticisms; the neurosexator was developed, then throttles, mufflers, insulating materials and special sound absorbers, in order that one tenant not disturb another's peace or pleasure with uncontrolled outcries.

But they had to go on, further, fearlessly and ever forward, because stagnation is the death of production. Already in the works was an Olympus for individual use; already the first androids in the shape of Greek gods and goddesses were being fashioned out of plastic in the blazing ateliers of Cybordelics. There was talk, too, of angels, and a financial reserve was set up for legal battles with the churches. However, certain technical problems still had to be ironed out: what should the wings be made of; feathers might irritate the nose; should they be moveable, or would that get in the way; how about the halo, what sort of switch to turn it on, where to put the switch, etc. And then the lightning struck.

A chemical substance – code name Nosex – had been synthesized some time before, possibly as early as the 1970s. Only a small group of experts, security-cleared, knew of its existence. The drug was immediately recognized to be a type of secret weapon, and was manufactured by the laboratories of a small firm connected with the Pentagon. The use of Nosex in aerosol form could in fact decimate the population of any country, because the drug, taken in quantities of fractions of a milligram, eliminated all sensation accompanying the sex act. The act, true, continued to be possible, but only as a variety of physical labour, fairly fatiguing, like wringing out clothes, scouring pots, scrubbing floors. Later on, consideration was given to the idea of using Nosex to check the population explosion in the Third World, but the plan was thought to be dangerous.

No one knows how the world-wide catastrophe came about. Was it true, as some said, that a stockpile of Nosex blew up as the result of a short circuit, a fire and a tank of ether? Or did there come into play here a move on the part of the industrial enemies of the three corporations that controlled the market? Or, then again, did some subversive organization – reactionary or religious – possibly have a hand in it? We are not told.

Wearied by his trek through the miles of vaults, the old man takes a seat on the smooth knees of a plastic Cleopatra, but not before pulling her brake, and his thoughts travel back, as to the edge of a precipice, to the Crash of 1998. Overnight, in an instinctive feeling of revulsion, the public turned its back on all the products then flooding the market. That which yesterday enticed, today was what an axe is to a tired logger, a washboard to a laundress. The eternal (it had seemed) enchantment, the spell cast by biology on the human race, was broken. Thereafter, breasts brought to mind only the fact that people are mammalian; legs, that they have with what to walk; buttocks, that there is something also with which to sit. Nothing more, but nothing more! How lucky McLuhan, that he did not live to witness this catastrophe, he who in his later works had interpreted the cathedral and the spaceship, the jet engine, the turbine, the windmill, the saltcellar, the hat, the theory of relativity, the brackets in mathematical equations, zeros and exclamation points as surrogates and substitutes for that single function which alone is the experiencing of existence in the pure state.

This line of reasoning lost its validity in a matter of hours. The spectre of extinction hung over humanity. It began with an economic crisis compared to which the one of 1929 was as nothing. The entire editorial staff of *Playboy*, in the forefront as ever, set fire to itself and died in flames; employees of striptease clubs and topless bars went hungry, and many leaped from windows; magazine publishers, film producers, huge advertising combines, beauty schools went bankrupt; the entire cosmetic–perfume industry was shaken, as was lingerie. In the year 1999, there were thirty-two million jobless in America.

What now was still capable of exciting the public's interest? Trusses, fake humps, grey wigs, a palsied figure in a wheelchair, for only these did not suggest the strain of sex, that onus, that curse, that grind; only these seemed to guarantee protection from the erotic threat, hence respite and peace. The governments, aware of the danger, were mobilizing all their forces to save the species. In newspaper columns there were appeals to reason, to a sense of responsibility; clergymen of every faith appeared on television with sublime exhortations and admonitions, reminding their flocks of higher ideals, but this chorus of authorities was listened to by the general public with little enthusiasm. Nor did the sounding of the official trumpets help, the proclamations enjoining people to get a grip on themselves. The results were negligible; only one unusually law-abiding nation, Japan, gritted its teeth and followed these injunctions. Then special material incentives began to be instituted, honorary degrees and distinctions, prizes, awards, citations, medals and fornication competitions (the trophies were loving cups); when this tack also failed, repressive measures were taken. But then the populations of whole provinces began to evade their procreative obligation, teen-age draft dodgers lay low in the surrounding forests, older men presented forged certificates of impotence, and the public boards of enforcement and supervision became riddled with graft, for everyone was ready – if need be – to keep tabs on his neighbour, to see that he wasn't shirking, though he himself avoided that dreary labour as much as he could.

The time of the catastrophe is now only a memory sifting through the mind of the lonely old man as he sits on Cleopatra's knees in the basement. Mankind has not perished; fertilization now takes place in a way that is sanitary and hygienic; it is not unlike inoculation; after years of ordeal a stabilization of sorts has taken over. But culture abhors a vacuum, and the terrifying suction óf that emptiness caused by the implosion of sex has drawn, into the vacated place, food. The gastronomy of the day is divided into normal and obscene; there exist perversions of gluttony, glossy restaurant publications with centrefolds, and the partaking of meals in certain positions is considered unspeakably depraved. It is not permitted, for example, to consume fruit while kneeling (but for this very freedom a sect of knee deviates is fighting); it is not permitted to eat spinach or scrambled eggs with one's feet propped up. But there exist – of course! – private clubs in which connoisseurs and epicures are treated to indecent floor shows; before the eyes of the spectators special champions gorge themselves, and the drool trickles down the audience's collective chin. From Denmark are smuggled pornoculinary magazines containing things unbelievably gross. One picture shows the ingestion of scrambled eggs through a straw, during which the ingester, sinking his fingers into heavily garlicked spinach and at the same time sniffing paprika goulash, lies on the table, wrapped in the tablecloth, his feet bound with a cord hooked up to a percolator which in this orgy serves as the chandelier. The Prix Femina that year went to a novel about a character who first smeared the floor with truffle paste, then licked it clean, after having wallowed his fill in spaghetti. The ideal of beauty also has changed: the thing now is to be a two-hundred-and-ninety-pound butterball, for this attests to uncommon ability on the part of the alimentary canal. Changes have taken place in fashion as well, and it is generally impossible to distinguish women from men by their dress. In the parliaments of the more enlightened countries, however, the question is being debated whether or not schoolchildren should be instructed in the facts of life, i.e., the digestive processes. So far, this subject, because it is indecent, has been placed under a strict taboo.

And at last the biological sciences are nearing the complete elimination of sexual reproduction, that superfluous and prehistoric relic. Embryos will be conceived synthetically and grown according to programmes of genetic engineering. From them will come neuter individuals, and this finally will put an end to the terrible memories that linger· in the minds of all who have lived through the catastrophe of sex. In bright laboratories, those temples of progress, there will arise the magnificent hermaphrodite or, rather, the neutrone, and then humanity, cut free of its former disgrace, will be able, with ever-increasing relish, to bite into every fruit – now only gastronomically forbidden.

Alfred Zellermann

GRUPPENFÜHRER LOUIS XVI

(Suhrkampf Verlag, Frankfurt)

Gruppenführer Louis XVI (or *Nazi Squad Leader Louis the Sixteenth*) is the fiction debut of Alfred Zellermann. Zellermann, practically in his sixties, is a well-known literary historian and a doctor of anthropology. He spent the *regnum Hitlerianum* in Germany, in the country with his wife's parents, having at the time been relieved of his university position; therefore, he was a passive observer of the life of the Third Reich. We venture to call this novel an excellent work, and add that probably only such a German, with such a fund of practical experience – and with such theoretical knowledge of literature! – could have written it.

Despite the title, it is no work of fantasy we have before us. The setting: Argentina in the first decade after the conclusion of the war. The fifty-year-old Gruppenführer Siegfried Taudlitz, a fugitive from the crushed and occupied Reich, makes his way to South America, carrying with him a part of the 'treasure' amassed by the notorious Academy of the S S ('*Ahnenerbe*'), a trunk bound with steel bands and filled with dollar bills. Gathering about himself a group of other fugitives from Germany, including various drifters and adventurers, and moreover having taken on a dozen or so women of doubtful character for services unspecified for the time being (some of these women Taudlitz himself buys out of brothels in Rio de Janeiro), the former S S General organizes an expedition deep into the Argentine interior. This, with a skill that reveals his talents as a staff officer.

In a region several hundred miles removed from the last outposts of civilization, the expedition comes upon ruins that are at least twelve centuries old, ruins of buildings that were raised in all likelihood by Aztecan crews; the expedition takes up residence in these. Attracted by the possibility of earning money, Indians and mestizos of the area show up at this site, which has been immediately named by Taudlitz (for reasons not yet disclosed) 'Parisia'. The former Gruppenführer makes efficient work brigades out of them and sets his armed men over them as taskmasters. Several years pass, and from such activity emerges the shape of the realm that Taudlitz had envisioned for himself. In his person he combines a ruthlessness that stops at nothing with the addled idea of re-creating – in the heart of the jungle – the French State in its heyday of monarchical splendour, for he himself is to be the reincarnation of none other than Louis XVI.

An aside here. The above does not summarize the novel, nor does what follows, for the progression of the action in the novel does not conform to the calendar chronology given in our account. We are well aware of the demands of artistic composition that governed the author; however, we wish to reconstruct in chronicle fashion, as it were, the train of events, so that the central concept, the idea of the work, will stand out clearly and with particular force. At the same time, we are passing over, in our 'chronologized' recapitulation of the work, a multitude of side issues and minor episodes, because it is plainly impossible to contain in any capsule form a whole, when that whole runs to two volumes of over 670 pages. But we will attempt in the present discussion to deal as well with the sequence of events that Alfred Zellermann implements in his epic.

Thus is created – to return to the story – a royal court, with a host of courtiers, knights, clergy, lackeys, and a palace chapel and ballrooms amid the fortress battlements, into which have been transformed the venerable ruins of the Aztec buildings, their rubble rebuilt in a manner architecturally absurd. Having at his side three men blindly loyal to him – Hans Mehrer, Johann Wieland and Erich Palatzky (soon they become Cardinal Richelieu, the Duc de Rohan and the Duc de Montbazon) – the 'new Louis' manages not only to maintain himself on his bogus throne, but also to shape the life going on about him in accordance with his own designs. At the same time – and this is important in the novel – the historical knowledge of the former Gruppenführer is fragmentary at best and full of gaps. One can hardly say he possesses such knowledge at all; his head is filled not so much with bits and pieces of the history of seventeenth-century France as with tripe carried over from his boyhood days, when he would lose himself in the adventures of Dumas, beginning with *The Three Musketeers*, and later, as an adolescent with 'monarchistic' leanings (that is what he called them; in fact they were merely sadistic), would pore over the books of Karl May. And since on to the memories of this reading cheap romances were afterwards added, voraciously devoured and thumbed, it is not the history of France that he is able to bring to life, but only the brutally primitivized, outright imbecilic hodgepodge that in his mind stands for it, and that has become for him a profession of faith.

Actually – as far as one can gather from the numerous details and references scattered throughout the work – Hitlerism was for Taudlitz only a choice of necessity, the alternative that, relatively speaking, suited him the most, being the closest to his 'monarchistic' fantasies. Hitlerism, in his eyes, came close to the Middle Ages – granted, not half so close as he would have liked! But it was, in any event, more welcome than any form of institutional democracy. On the other hand, having his own private, secret 'dream of the crown' in the Third Reich, Taudlitz never succumbed to Hitler's magnetism; he never believed in Hitler's doctrine, and for this reason was not obliged to mourn the fall of 'Great Germany'. Instead, having wit enough to see it coming, particularly since he had never identified himself with the élite of the Third Reich (though belonging to it), he prepared himself for the disaster appropriately. His cult of Hitler, universally known, was not even the product of self-deception; for ten years Taudlitz played a cynical comedy, for he had his own myth, which gave him a resistance to Hitler's, and this proved especially convenient for him, because those disciples of *Mein Kampf* who made even a small attempt to take the doctrine seriously, more than once – as in the case of Albert Speer – felt themselves alienated from Hitler later on, whereas Taudlitz, as a man who only outwardly professed each day the views prescribed for that day, was immune to any heresy.

Taudlitz believes implicitly and without reservation only in the power of money and force; he knows that with material goods people can be persuaded to go along with any plan of a sufficiently open-handed master, provided that master be also duly resolute and un-compromising in the carrying out of commitments once made. Taudlitz does not in the least trouble himself about whether his 'courtiers', that many-coloured throng made up of Germans, Indians, mestizos and Portuguese, really take seriously the vast spectacle imposed over many years, which he has staged in a manner that is – would be, to an outside observer – unspeakably insipid, uninspired, crass, or whether any of the actors believe in the reasonableness of the court of the Louis, or are instead only playing a comedy, reckoning on the payment, possibly also on making off with the 'King's bundle' after the death of the ruler. The problem does not appear to exist for Taudlitz.

The life of the court community is so patent a forgery, and a clumsy one at that, it is such a piece of unauthenticity, that at least the more clearheaded of the people, those who came later to Parisia, as well as all who with their own eyes saw the origination of the pseudo-monarch and the pseudo-princes, cannot – even for a minute – have any doubt in this regard. And therefore, particularly in its early days, the kingdom resembles, as it were, a person schizo-phrenically split in two: one speaks one way at the palace audiences and balls, especially in the vicinity of Taudlitz, and quite another way in the absence of the monarch and his three confidants, who ensure in a most ruthless manner (with torture, even) the continuation of the imposed game. And it is a game decked out in rare splendour, bathed in a glitter now not false, for a stream of caravan supplies, paid for with hard currency, has in the space of twenty months raised castle walls, covered them with frescoes and Gobelins, dressed the parquet floors with elegant carpeting, set out endless pieces of furniture, mir-rors, gilt clocks, commodes, built secret doors and hiding places in the walls, alcoves, pergolas, terraces, encircled the castle with an enormous, magnificent park, and, beyond, with a palisade and a moat. Every German is an overseer and keeps the Indian slaves under thumb (it is by Indian sweat and toil that the artificial kingdom comes into being); he parades attired like a true seventeenth-century knight, but wears on his gold belt a military handgun of the 'Parabellum' make, the final argument in all disputes between feudal capital and labour.

But the monarch and his confidants slowly, and at the same time systematically, eliminate from their surroundings every manifestation, every sign that would immediately unmask the fictitiousness of the court and the kingdom. So first a special language comes into use; in it may be worded any news that makes its way – roundabout, to be sure – in from the outside world, such as the possibility that the 'nation' may be threatened by intervention on the part of the Argentine government; meanwhile these wordings, conveyed to the King by his high officials, dare not lay bare – that is, state point-blank – the unsovereignty of the monarch and the throne. Argentina, for example, is always called 'Spain' and treated as a neighbouring country. Gradually they all become so much at home inside their artificial skins, and learn to move about so naturally in splendid robes, to wield the sword and the tongue with such address, that the lie sinks deeper – into the very warp and woof of this fabric, this living picture. The picture remains a humbug, but a humbug now that throbs with the blood of authentic desires, hatreds, quarrels, rivalries; for at the unreal court are hatched real intrigues, courtiers strive to undo others, to draw nearer the throne over the bodies of their rivals, that they may receive from the hands of the King the high ranks and honours of the toppled; therefore the innuendo, the cup of poison, the informer's whisper, the dagger, begin their hidden, altogether genuine work; yet only so much of the monarchistic and feudal element continues to inhere in all of this as Taudlitz, the new Louis XVI, is able to breathe into it from his own dream of absolute power, a dream dramatized by a pack of former SS men.

Taudlitz believes that somewhere in Germany lives his nephew, the last of the line, Bertrand Gülsenhirn, whose age was thirteen at the time of the fall of Germany. To seek out this youth (now twenty-one) Louis XVI sends the Duc de Rohan, or Johann Wieland, the only 'intellectual' among his men, for Wieland had been a physician in the Waffen SS and had carried out, in the camp at Mauthausen, 'scientific studies'. The scene where the King entrusts the Duc with the secret mission to find the boy and bring him to the court as the Infante is among the finest in the novel. First the monarch is gracious enough to explain how he is much troubled by his own childlessness, out of consideration for the good of the throne, that is, the succession; these opening phrases help him continue in this vein; the insane savour of the scene lies in this, that now the King cannot admit even to himself that he is not a real king. He does not, in fact, know French, but, employing German, which prevails at court, he maintains – as does everyone after him, when the subject arises – that it is French he is speaking, seventeenth-century French.

This is not madness, for madness would be – now – to admit to Germanness, even if only in language; Germany does not exist, inasmuch as France's only neighbour is Spain (that is, Argentina)! Anyone who dares utter words in German, letting it be understood that he is speaking *thus*, stands in peril of his life: from the conversation between the Archbishop of Paris and the Duc de Salignac (Vol. I, p. 311), it may be inferred that the Prince de Chartreuse, beheaded for 'high treason', in reality had drunkenly called the palace not simply a 'whorehouse', but a 'German whorehouse'. *Nota bene*: the abundance of French names in the novel, which bear a striking similarity to the names of cognacs and wines – take, for example, the 'Marquis Châteauneuf du Pape', the master of ceremonies! – undoubtedly derives from the fact (though nowhere does the author say it) that in the brain of Taudlitz there clamour, for readily understandable reasons, far more names of liquors and liqueurs than those of the French aristocracy.

In addressing his emissary, then, Taudlitz speaks as he imagines King Louis might speak to a trusted agent being sent on such a mission. He does not tell Monsieur le Duc to put aside his sham apparel, but, on the contrary, to 'disguise himself as an Englishman or a Dutchman', which simply means to try for a normal, up-to-date appearance. The word 'up-to-date', however, may not be uttered – it belongs among those expressions that would dangerously weaken the fiction of the kingdom. Even dollars are called, always, 'thalers'.

Provided with a considerable amount of ready money, Wieland goes to Rio, where the commercial agent of the 'court' operates; after acquiring good false identity papers, Taudlitz's emissary sails for Europe. The book passes in silence over the peregrinations of his search. We know only that they are crowned with success after eleven months, and the novel, in its actual form, characteristically opens with the second conversation between Wieland and the young Gülsenhirn, who is working as a waiter in a large Hamburg hotel. Bertrand (he will be allowed to keep the name: it has, in the opinion of his uncle Taudlitz, a good ring) is first told only of his millionaire uncle who is prepared to adopt him as a son, and for Bertrand this is reason enough to leave his job and go off with Wieland. The journey of this curious pair serves as an introduction to the novel and performs its function brilliantly, because we have here a moving forward in space which at the same time is, as it were, a retreating back into historical time: the travellers change from a transcontinental jet to a train, later to an automobile, from the automobile to a horse-drawn wagon, and finally cover the last 145 miles on horseback.

As Bertrand's clothes wear out piece by piece, his spare things 'vanish', and in their place appear archaic garments, providently supplied and laid out for such occasions by Wieland; meanwhile, the latter is turning into the Duc de Rohan. This metamorphosis is by no means Machiavellian; it takes place, from stopping point to stopping point, with strange simplicity. One gathers (later on, this is confirmed) that Wieland has gone through such costume changes (only not quite in these instalments) numerous times as the factotum envoy of Taudlitz. And so, while Wieland, who embarked for Europe as Mr Heinz Karl Müller, becomes the armed and mounted Duc de Rohan, an analogous transformation – at least externally – is undergone by Bertrand.

Bertrand is flabbergasted, stupefied. He is going to his uncle, the owner – so he has been informed – of a vast estate; he has forsaken the life of a waiter to become heir to millions, and now they lead him into the circle of some costume comedy or farce he cannot comprehend. The instructions Wieland-Müller-de Rohan gives him on the way only serve to increase the muddle in his head. Sometimes it seems to him that his companion is merely pulling his leg; sometimes, that he is leading him to his doom, or on the other hand that he, Bertrand, is being let in on some unimaginable skulduggery, whose entirety cannot be revealed all at once. There will be moments in which he will feel he has gone mad. The instructions, of course, never call a thing by its name; this instinctive wisdom is the common property of the court.

'You must,' de Rohan tells him, 'observe the formalities your uncle requires' ('your uncle', then 'His Lordship', finally 'His Highness'!); 'his name is "Louis", not "Siegfried" – it is not permitted *ever* to say the latter. He has put it aside – such is his will!' declares Müller, becoming *le duc*. 'His estate' is altered to 'his latifundium', then to 'his realm'; thus Bertrand, little by little, during the long days spent in the saddle, riding through the jungle, and then, in the final hours, inside a gilded sedan chair borne by eight naked, muscular mestizos, and observing from its window a retinue of mounted knights in casques – thus Bertrand is convinced of the truth of the words of his enigmatic companion. Then he shifts his suspicions of insanity from himself to the companion and places all his hope on the meeting with his uncle, whom, however, he hardly remembers – he saw him last as a nine-year-old boy. But the meeting is the centre of a magnificent, impressive celebration, which represents an amalgam of all the ceremonies, rituals and customs Taudlitz was able to recall. So the choir sings and silver fanfares are played, the King enters in his crown, but first the footmen cry drawlingly, 'The King! The King!' as they open the carved double doors; Taudlitz is surrounded by twelve 'Peers of the Realm' (which he borrowed by error, from the wrong source), and the sublime moment arrives – Louis greets his nephew with the sign of the cross, names him his Infante, and permits him to kiss his ring, his hand and his sceptre. But when they are alone together at breakfast, where they are waited on by Indians in tails, with a marvellous panorama spread out before them from the heights of the castle down to the park and its sparkling, spouting rows of fountains, Bertrand, looking upon that splendour, and again upon the distant belt of jungle that surrounds the entire estate with its glimmering of cruel green, simply cannot find the courage to ask his uncle anything. When the latter gently admonishes him to speak, Bertrand begins: 'Your Majesty . . .' 'Yes, that is the way . . . higher reasons require it . . . my welfare lies in this, and yours . . .' kindly says to him the former SS Gruppenführer in the crown.

The unusualness of this book stems from the fact that it unites elements that would appear to be totally irreconcilable. Either something is authentic or it is unauthentic, it is either false or true, make-believe or spontaneous life; yet here we are faced with a prevaricated truth and an authentic fake, hence a thing that is at once the truth and a lie. Had the courtiers of old Taudlitz merely played their roles, stammering out their conned lines, we would have had before us a lifeless puppet pageant; but they assimilated the form, each in his own way growing into it, and have grown so at home with it over the years that when, shortly after Bertrand's arrival, they begin conspiring against Taudlitz, they are unable entirely to shake off the imposed patterns, so that the conspiracy itself is also a grotesque potpourri of psychologies, like a layer cake with jelly, lumps of dough, macaroni and the corpses of mice that have choked to death on the nuts. For it was an *authentic* passion, an honest lust for ruling, that the Gruppen-führer clothed in a conglomeration of garbled memories pertaining to the history of the French Louis, a history taken thirdhand – from penny dreadfuls and dime novels. At the beginning he did not insist on obedience to his mania – he could not – but simply paid for it, and during that time had to pretend not to hear what the former chauf-feurs, noncoms and sentries of the SS were saying about him, and about the whole 'production', behind his back; but he possessed enough sense to bear it all patiently until the moment when finally it became easy for him to achieve discipline through fear, compulsion, torture; that was also when dollars, hitherto the only lure, became 'thalers' . . .

This primitive phase (in a manner of speaking, the prehistory of the kingdom) is shown in the novel only in snatches of incidental conversation, and it should be kept in mind that for such references to the past one can pay dearly. The action begins in Europe, when an unknown emissary wins the confidence of the young waiter Bertrand, but it is only in the second part of the novel that the narrative allows us to figure out what, until then, we were struggling to reconstruct. Obviously, to have former MPs, camp guards, camp doctors, the drivers and the gunners of the SS panzer division *Grossdeutschland*, as courtiers, nobles and priests of the court of Louis XVI, is as ghastly and insane a hash, a mismatching of roles, as ever there could be. On the other hand, they are not so much playing well-defined roles poorly – for such roles never existed – as they are doing their best, in their own way, often moronically, to cope with a difficult task, since they can do nothing else . . . That which was false in its very inception is now played by them falsely and dully; the result should therefore be a miscellany that turns the book into a pile of nonsense.

However, it is not that way at all. Those Hitlerite butchers may once have felt ridiculous wriggling into the cardinal's scarlet, the bishop's violet and gilt plates of armour, but then they felt less ridiculous – for it was amusing – taking prostitutes from seaport brothels and renaming them consorts (in the case of the secular lords) or princesses and countess-concubines (in the case of the priesthood of King Louis). And these roles captured the fancy of the prostitutes themselves; immersed in spurious stateliness, each such creature luxuriated and put on airs, but at the same time would improve herself, emulating whatever ideal of the great lady she was capable of imagining. Thus the passages of the novel where the former thugs in ecclesiastical hats and lace throat-ruffles are given the floor are simply incredible exhibitions of the author's psychological skill. The wretches derive from their positions a pleasure alien to true aristocrats, for it is enhanced twofold by what might be most simply described as an ennobling or outright legalizing of crime. A scoundrel consumes the fruits of evil with the greatest delight only when he does so in the majesty of the law; the professionals in concentration-camp sadism are provided a distinct satisfaction by the possibility of repeating more than one of the old practices now in the aura and glory of the court's splendour, in its light, which seems to magnify every filthy act. It is for this reason that, while doing disgraceful things, they all of them, now of their own free will, try, at least in their words, not to step out of character, out of the bishop's or the prince's role. For thus they are able to disgrace as well the whole majestic symbolism of those high honours with which they have bedecked themselves. This is why, too, the slow-witted among them, such as Mehrer, envy the Duc de Rohan, who can so adroitly justify his weakness for abusing Indian children, who has turned the torturing of them into an activity in all respects 'courtly', that is to say, to the highest degree seemly. (Note, by the way, that the Indians are routinely called 'Negroes', for Negroes as slaves are 'in better taste'.)

We can understand, too, Wieland's (the Duc de Rohan's) exertions to obtain the cardinal's hat: this is now the only thing he lacks; it will enable him to play his degenerate little games as one of God's vicars on earth. But Taudlitz denies him the privilege, as if aware of the chasm of villainy that lies behind this ambition of Wieland's. Because Taudlitz, in that game, fancies differently: he does not wish to be conscious of *both* the present eminence *and* the old past of the Schutzstaffeln, because he has 'another dream, another myth'; he craves the royal purple in earnest and therefore spurns with true indignation the Wieland method of exploiting the situation. The author's

mastery lies in showing the extraordinary variety of human knavish-
ness, that wealth, that multifariousness of evil which cannot be
reduced to any single, simple formula. For Taudlitz is not one whit
'better' than Wieland; he is merely taken up with something else, for
he aspires to an impossible – for a total – transfiguration. Hence his
'puritanism', which his closest associates hold so much against him.

As for the courtiers, we have seen that they strove to be courtiers
indeed – for different reasons . . . But later, when ten of them took to
plotting against the monarch-Gruppenführer, with the idea of robbing
him of his chest full of dollars and of murdering him besides, they
none the less regretted having to part with the senatorial chairs, titles,
decorations, distinctions, and thus found themselves in a true quan-
dary. They did not want to cut the old man's throat and flee with the
loot; they did not and yet they did; and it was not merely the matter
of appearances that interfered with their plotting. There were
moments now when they themselves believed in the possibility of
their eminence, for that possibility answered their needs to the highest
degree. What hampered them the most (and this is madness indeed,
but perfectly logical, psychologically consistent) was no longer the
recognition, in the form of memory, that they were not what they
pretended to be, but the arbitrary cruelty of Taudlitz-as-monarch:
had not the monarch been so much – every inch – the SS Gruppenführer, had he not made it so very clear to them – silently! – that they
were his creatures, existing by the act of his will and momentary
favour, then the France of the Angevins in the Argentine interior
would definitely have proved more stable, viable. And so, in truth, the
actors now held against the impresario of the show . . . his insufficient
authenticity. That band of thieves desired to be *plus monarchique* than
the monarch himself would allow.

Of course, they were in error, for they could not compare themselves, in these roles, with the true, better authenticity of a magnificent
court; unable to raise themselves befittingly to the level of the roles,
they nevertheless made those roles their own, and brought life to
them; each put into his own what he had and could, what his heart
dictated. There is no affectation or stiltedness here; we see, after all,
and more than once, how these *ducs* address their *duchesses*, how the
Marquis de Beaujolais (the onetime Hans Wehrholz) pounds his spouse

and how he throws up to her her whorish past. In such scenes the aim of the writer is to make credible that which seems so incredible when only summarized. True, the wretches sometimes weary of the performances they must give, but what tops everything are those who play the high clergy of the Roman Catholic Church.

There are no Catholics whatever in the colony, and it is impossible to speak of any sort of religious feeling among the former SS men; it becomes generally accepted, then, for the so-called services held in the palace chapel to be extremely brief, and they are reduced to the chanting of a few verses from the Bible; one or two people, in fact, suggest to the monarch that even these divine duties could really be dispensed with, but Taudlitz is unbending. On the other hand, both cardinals, the Archbishop of Paris, and the other bishops in this way 'justify' their high titles, because those few minutes each week – an atrocious parody of Mass – legitimize primarily in their own eyes their rank in the church hierarchy; thus they put up with it all and remain at their altars for minutes on end, in order later to reward themselves with hours spent at the banquet tables and beneath the canopies of sumptuous beds. Therefore, too, the idea of the projector smuggled into the palace (without the King's knowledge!) from Montevideo, and used to show stag films in the castle cellar – where the Archbishop of Paris (the quondam Gestapo chauffeur Hans Schaeffert) does the honours as projectionist, and Cardinal du Sauterne (excommissary) helps change the reels – that idea has at one and the same time a macabre humour and a verisimilitude, as do all the other elements of this tragicomedy, which continues because nothing is able to challenge it from within.

To these people all things are now reconcilable with all things, to them everything goes with everything else, and it should come as no surprise when, for example, mention is made of the dreams of some of them – for did not the commandant of Block III at Mauthausen have 'the biggest collection of canaries in all Bavaria', which he recalls wistfully, and did he not try feeding these canaries according to the advice of a certain camp foreman who assured him that canaries sang best when fed on human flesh? This, then, is criminality taken to such a degree of self-ignorance that we would be dealing with *innocent* former murderers, were the criterion of criminality in man to be based exclusively on autodiagnosis, on the individual's independent recognition of sin. It is possible that in some sense Cardinal du Sauterne knows that a real cardinal does not behave thus, that a real cardinal believes in God and most probably does not go about raping the Indian boys who assist at Mass in surplices, but since within a radius of four hundred miles there are no other cardinals, such a thought does not trouble him unduly.

Falsehood feeding on falsehood produces in consequence this proliferating fertility of form, which surpasses any authentic court as a mirror of human behaviour, for it is true to life in two ways at once. The author does not permit himself the least exaggeration, and the realism of the subject remains uncompromised; when the general drunkenness goes beyond a certain point, the royal Gruppenführer always retires to his chambers, for he knows the old prison-guard ways will win out over the veneer of refinement and from drunken hiccupping there will soon escape those grotesque and gruesome locutions whose power derives from the boggling contrast between the adopted mentality and the real. The whole genius of Taudlitz – if one may use that term – lies in his having the courage and the consequentiality to 'close' the system he created.

This system, frightfully crippled, functions thanks only to its insularity; one puff from the real world would topple it. And just such a potential toppler is young Bertrand, though he does not feel in himself the strength to speak out with that genuine voice of dismay that calls things by their name. The simplest possibility, which explains the totality of the situation, Bertrand dares not contemplate. What, only a vulgar lie, kept going for years, maintained methodically, thumbing its nose at common sense – a lie and nothing more? No, never; sooner a communal paranoia or some inconceivable, secret game of unknown purpose, yet rational at core, complete with bona fide and fully cogent motives; anything, anything but simple lying, lying enamoured of itself, self-absorbed, self-inflated without bound. The thesis we have been presenting is beyond his grasp.

Bertrand, then, capitulates at once: he lets them dress him in the garments of the heir to the throne, lets them instruct him in court etiquette – that is to say, in that rudimentary repertoire of bows, gestures and words which all seem strangely familiar to him. There is nothing strange about it; he, too, has read the cheap romances and pseudo-historical rubbish that were the inspiration of the King and his master of ceremonies. Bertrand, however, is recalcitrant, unaware that his inertness, his passivity – which aggravates not merely the courtiers but the King himself – is an instinctive resistance to a situation that forces on him submissive idiocy. Bertrand does not want to be buried in lies, though he himself does not know the source of his opposition; therefore he limits himself to making gibes, ironical remarks, those lordly half-witted utterances of honoured guests. During the second big banquet, it happens that the King, stung by an insinuation behind Bertrand's seemingly casual words – words whose hidden malice the boy himself does not immediately realize – in a fit of genuine rage begins hurling at him scraps of a partly eaten roast, whereat half the hall seconds the fury with a gleeful howl of approbation, throwing at the poor wretch greasy bones off their silver plates, while the rest preserve an uneasy silence, wondering whether Taudlitz might not be laying a trap of some sort for those present, as he is fond of doing, whether he might not be acting in concert with the Infante.

The most difficult thing for us to convey here is that, for all the obtuseness of the game, for all the flatness of the performance, which, put on at one time indifferently, now has grown so in power that it does not want to end, and does not want to because it cannot, and cannot because beyond it there awaits now only utter *nothingness* (they cannot quit being bishops, princes of the blood, marquises, since they cannot go back to their former posts of Gestapo chauffeur, crematorium guard, camp commandant, just as the King, even if he wished, could not become again SS Gruppenführer Taudlitz) – for all the banal and atrocious flatness (to repeat) of this kingdom and this court, there vibrates in it at the same time, like a single vigilant, taut nerve, a ceaseless cunning, a mutual suspicion, which permits one to conduct, albeit in counterfeit forms, real battles and campaigns, to undercut the favourites of the throne, and write denunciations, and in silence wrest for oneself the favour of the lord. In fact it is not the cardinals' hats, not ribbons and medals, laces, ruffs, suits of armour that warrant such underground labour, these tunnellings of intrigue – for what, really, do veterans of a hundred battles and a thousand murders want with the trappings of fictitious glory? It is the ambushes themselves, the machinations, the traps set for one's foes so that they will betray themselves before the King, falling flat on their faces from their strutting roles – that constitute the greatest common passion . . .

So this jockeying for position, seeking the right moves on the court parquet, in the shining halls whose mirrors reflect their decked-out silhouettes, this incessant yet bloodless warfare (not always bloodless in the cellars of the castle) is their reason for being; it gives meaning to what would be, otherwise, only a children's carnival, suitable perhaps for beardless youths, not for men who know the taste of blood . . . Poor Bertrand meanwhile can no longer endure being alone with his unuttered dilemma; as a drowning man grasps at straws he seeks a kindred spirit, one to whom he can unburden himself of the purpose that is growing within him.

Because – and this is another of the author's merits – Bertrand gradually becomes the Hamlet of this mad court. He is here, by instinct, the last righteous man (he never read *Hamlet*!), and hence concludes that his duty is to go mad. He does not suspect them all of cynicism – for that he has indeed too little intellectual courage. Bertrand, not knowing this himself, wishes to do something that would be realistic, certainly, at a less sordid court: his desire is to say what constantly rushes to his lips and burns his tongue, but he knows by now that as a normal person he cannot do so with impunity. But if he were to go insane, ah, that is quite a different matter! He begins, then, not to simulate madness cold-bloodedly, like Shakespeare's Hamlet: no, as a simpleton, naïve, a bit of a hysteric, he simply tries to go insane, with all good faith in the necessity for his own madness! Thus he will utter the words of truth that oppress him . . . But the Duchesse de Clicot, an old prostitute from Rio, having taken a fancy to the young man, gets him into bed with her and there, educating him in the ways remembered from the time of her unhighborn past, ways learned at the hand of a certain madam, adjures him sternly not to say things that might cost him his neck. For she knows well that such a thing as respect for the unaccountability of mental illness has no place here; at heart, as we can see, the old woman wishes Bertrand well. But that conversation between the sheets, in which the Duchesse proves a truly accomplished whore, though at the same time she is no longer completely able to address the youth as a whore (because her limited intellect has been steeped in the court seven years and taken on a good deal of pseudo-polish and etiquette) – that conversation does not succeed in changing Bertrand's mind. He is beyond caring now. He will either go mad or run away. A dissection of the subconscious of the others would probably reveal that their awareness of the outside world, which awaits them with sentences *in absentia*, prison terms and tribunals, is an invisible force spurring them to continue with the game; but Bertrand, who has nothing in common with such a past, has no wish to.

Meanwhile, the conspiracy enters the phase of action: now not ten, but fourteen courtiers, ready for anything, having gained an accomplice in the captain of the palace guard, break into the royal bedroom after midnight. Their main objective is torpedoed at the culminating moment: it turns out that the good dollars have long since been spent, and all that remain, in the famous 'second compartment of the trunk', are the counterfeit. The King knew this well. Therefore there is really nothing to fight for, but they have burned their bridges: they must kill the King, who so far has only been watching from his bonds on the bed as they turn upside down the 'treasury' hidden underneath it. They were going to have beaten him to death out of practical considerations, in order that he not be able to pursue them; now they kill him out of hatred, because he has enticed them with false treasure.

Execrable as it sounds, I must say that the murder scene is marvellous; in the unerring strokes of the brush one recognizes the master. For in order to get at the old man as painfully as possible, before he is quite strangled with the cord, the conspirators begin to roar at him in the language of camp cooks and Gestapo chauffeurs, the language that had been anathematized, banished eternally from the kingdom. But then, as the body of the victim still is twitching on the floor (the brilliant motif of the towel!), the murderers, regaining their composure, *return* to the language of the court, indeed without design, it is only that they now have no alternative: the dollars are counterfeit, there is nothing with which to flee, nor any reason, Taudlitz has bound and tied them; though lifeless himself, he will let no one leave his State! They must consent, then, to the continuation of the game, in keeping with the motto '*Le roi est mort, vive le roi!*' – and there, at once, over the corpse, they must choose a new king.

The next chapter (Bertrand in hiding at his 'Duchesse's') is much weaker. But the final one, in which a patrol of mounted police comes knocking at the castle gate, that great, silent scene, the last in the novel, is a magnificent close. The drawbridge, the policemen in rumpled uniforms with Colts in shoulder holsters, wearing wide hats turned up on one side, and opposite them guards in half armour, with halberds, each side staring at the other in amazement, like two times, two worlds impossibly brought to a single place . . . on either side of the portcullis, which slowly, heavily begins to lift, with an infernal grinding sound . . . a finale worthy of the work! But unfortunately the author lost sight of his Hamlet, Bertrand; he did not make use of the tremendous opportunity that lay within that character. I will not say he should have had him killed off – Shakespeare's play need not serve here as a paradigm – but it is a shame, this lost chance, this greatness oblivious of itself but present in the everyday, well-meaning heart of man. A shame.

Solange Marriot

RIEN DU TOUT,
OU LA CONSÉQUENCE

(Editions du Midi, Paris)

Nothing, or the Consequence is not only Mme Solange Marriot's first book; it is also the first novel ever to have reached the limit of what writing can do. Not that it is a masterpiece of art; if I had to call it anything, I would call it a masterpiece of decency. The need for decency is the thorn in the side of all our literature today. Because our literature's main malaise is the disgrace that one cannot be a writer and at the same time a man who is completely, that is, in full seriousness, decent. The initiation into the true essence of literature brings about a malaise quite similar to that which afflicts a sensitive child when it is for the first time informed of the facts of life. The child's shock is a form of internal rebellion against the genital biology of our bodies, which seems to call for condemnation from the standpoint of good taste, and the shame and shock of the writer come from the realization of the inevitable lie that one commits in writing. There exist necessary lies, e.g., those that are morally defensible (thus the doctor lies to his terminally ill patient), but literary lies do not belong in this category. Someone has to be a doctor, consequently someone has to lie as a doctor, but no necessity brings the pen into proximity with the clean page. The past knew not this embarrassment, for it was not free; literature in an age of faith does not lie, it only serves. Its emancipation from what was necessary service gave rise to a crisis whose manifestations today are often pitiful, if not outright obscene.

Pitiful, because a novel that depicts its own origination is half confession and half humbug. It, too, contains a residue, and even a good amount, of the lie. Sensing this, the next literati wrote gradually more and more about *how* one writes, to the detriment of the thing written, the story, and this method followed a falling curve down to works, finally, that were manifestoes of epic impotence. And so the novel invited us to step into its dressing room. But such invitations must always be suspect – if they do not actually amount to propositioning, then they turn out to be coquetry, and to flirt instead of lie – it is like going from the frying pan to the fire.

The anti-novel strove to become more radical; that is, it made every effort to demonstrate that it was no illusion of anything. While the 'self-novel' was like a magician who reveals to the public all that he is holding up his sleeve, the anti-novel was to become a pretence of nothing, not even of the self-unmasking magician. What then? It promised to communicate nothing, to tell of nothing, to signify not a thing, but merely *to be*, as a cloud is, a table, a tree. Fine in theory. It failed, however, because not everyone can be Lord God *tout court*, a creator of autonomous worlds, and a writer most certainly cannot. What decides the defeat is the issue of contexts: on them – on that which is completely *inexpressible* – depends the sense of what we say. The world of the Lord God has no contexts, hence it can be successfully replaced only by a world that is equally self-sufficient. You may stand on your head if you like, but it will never work – not in language.

What then was left to literature after the fatal knowledge of its own indecency? The self-novel is a partial striptease; the anti-novel, ipso facto, is (alas) a form of autocastration. Like the Skoptsi who, outraged in their moral conscience by their own genitality, performed upon themselves horrid operations, the anti-novel has mutilated the unfortunate body of traditional literature. What then was left? Nothing except a romance with nothingness. For he who lies (and, as we know, a writer must lie) about *nothing* surely ceases to be a liar.

It was necessary, then – and herein is the consequence – to write *nothing*. But can such a task make sense? To write *nothing* – is it not the same as to write nothing? What then . . .?

Roland Barthes, the author of the now not-so-new essay 'Le Degré zéro de l'écriture', had not an inkling of this (but for all its famous wit, his is a shallow intellect). He did not comprehend that literature always is parasitic on the mind of the reader. Love, a tree, a park, a sigh, an earache – the reader understands, because the reader has experienced it. It is possible, of course, with a book to rearrange the furniture inside a reader's head, but only to the extent that there is some furniture there already, before the reading.

He is no parasite on anything, whose work is real: a mechanic, a doctor, a builder, a tailor, a dishwasher. What, in comparison, does a writer produce? Semblances. This is a serious occupation? The anti-novel wished to pattern itself after mathematics; mathematics, surely, yields nothing real! Yes, but mathematics does not lie, for it does only what it must. It operates under the constraint of necessities that it does not invent on the spur of the moment; the method is given to it, which is why the discoveries of mathematicians are genuine, and why, too, their horror is genuine when the method leads them to a contradiction. The writer, because he does not operate under such necessity, because he is free, can only enter into his quiet negotiations with the reader; he urges the reader kindly to assume . . . to believe . . . to accept as good coin . . . but this is a game, and not the blessed bondage in which mathematics thrives. Total freedom is total paralysis in literature.

Of what are we speaking? Of Mme Solange's novel. Let us begin with the observation that this pretty name may be read variously, depending on the context in which it is placed. In French it can be Sun and Angel (*Sol, Ange*). In German it will be merely the name of an interval of time (*so lange* – so long). The absolute autonomy of language is arrant nonsense; humanists have believed it out of naïveté – to which naïveté, however, the cybernetics people had no right. Machines to translate faithfully, indeed! No word, no whole sentence has meaning in itself, within its own trench and boundary. Borges came close to this state of affairs when, in his story 'Pierre Menard, the Author of *Don Quixote*', he described a literary fanatic, the eccentric Menard, who after a great number of intellectual preparations wrote *Don Quixote a second time*, word for word, not copying down Cervantes but – as it were – immersing himself totally in the latter's creative milieu. But the place in which Borges's short story touches on the secret is this following passage:

'A comparison of the pages of Menard and Cervantes is highly revealing. The latter, for example, wrote (*Don Quixote*, Part One, Chapter XIX): ". . . truth, whose mother is history, who is the rival of time, the repository of deeds, the witness of the past, the pattern and the caution for the present day, and the lesson for future ages."

'This catalogue, published in the seventeenth century, penned by the "layman genius" Cervantes, is simply a rhetorical encomium to history. Menard, on the other hand, writes: ". . . truth, whose mother is history, who is the rival of time, the repository of deeds, the witness of the past, the pattern and the caution for the present day, and the lesson for future ages."

'History as the mother of truth: the idea is extraordinary. Menard, a contemporary of William James, does not characterize history as the study of reality but as its source. Historical truth, for him, is not that which has taken place; it is that which we believe has taken place. The concluding phrases – the pattern and the caution for the present day, the lesson for future ages – are unabashedly pragmatic.'

This is something more than a literary joke and poking fun; it is the pure and simple truth, which the absurdity of the idea itself (to write *Don Quixote a second time!*) in no way lessens. For in fact what fills every sentence with meanings is the context of the given period; that which was 'innocent rhetoric' in the seventeenth century is, in our age, truly cynical in its meanings. Sentences mean nothing *in themselves*; it was not Borges who jokingly decided thus; the moment in history shapes the meanings of language, such is the unalterable reality.

And now, literature. Whatsoever it relates to us must prove a lie, not being the literal truth. Balzac's Vautrin is as non-existent as Faust's devil. When it speaks the honest truth, literature ceases to be itself and becomes a diary, a new item, a denunciation, an appointment book, a letter, whatever you like, only not artistic writing.

At this juncture appears Mme Solange with her *Rien du tout, ou la conséquence*. The title? Nothing, or the consequence? The consequence of what? Literature, obviously; for literature to be decent, that is, not to lie, is the same as for literature not to be. *Only* of this is it still possible today to write a *decent* book. The blush of indecency no longer works; it was good yesterday, but now we recognize it for what it is: a common pose, the trick of the experienced stripper who knows that her feigned modesty, her lowered lashes, her fake schoolgirl embarrassment as she removes her panties, excites the house even more!

And so the theme has been defined. But how is one to write about nothing? It is necessary, yet impossible. By saying 'nothing'? By repeating the word a thousand times? Or by beginning with the words

'He was not born, consequently he was not named, either; on account of this he neither cheated in school nor later got mixed up in politics'? Such a work could have arisen, but it would have been a stunt and not a work of art, rather like those numerous books written in the second person singular; any of them can easily be booted out of such 'originality' and forced to return to its proper place. All one need do is turn the second person back into the first. It does no violence whatever to the book; in no way does it change it. Similarly with our fictitious example: remove the negations, all those wearisome nots and nors that like a pseudo-nihilistic smallpox have bespotted the text, the text we invented extempore, and it becomes evident that here is yet another story, one of many, about the Marquise who left the house at five. To say she *didn't* leave – some revelation!

Mme Solange was not taken in by this sort of trick. For she understood (she must have understood!) that one may indeed describe a particular story (a love story, say) with non-events no worse than with events, but that the first device is merely an artifice. Instead of a print we obtain an exact negative, that is all. The nature of an innovation must be ontological, and not simply grammatical!

When we say, 'He was not named because he was not born', we are, to be sure, moving beyond being, but only in that thinnest membrane of non-existence that adheres tightly to reality. He was not born, although he could have been born, did not cheat, although he could have cheated. He could have done everything, had he been. The work will stand entirely on that 'could have'. Out of such flour one cannot bake bread. One cannot go bounding from being to unbeing using such ploys. It is necessary, therefore, to leave the membrane of primitive denials, or of the negatives of actions, in order to plunge into nothingness, plunge deeply, hurling oneself headlong into it, but of course not blindly; to *enminus* non-being more and more powerfully – which must be a considerable labour, a great effort; and here is salvation for art, because what is involved is a full expedition into the abyss of ever more precise and ever greater Nothing, and therefore a *process*, whose dramatic peripeteia, whose struggle may be depicted – so long as it succeeds!

The first sentence of *Rien du tout, ou la conséquence* reads, 'The train did not arrive'; in the next sentence we find 'He did not come'.

We meet, then, with negations, but of what exactly? From the stand-point of logic these are total negations, since the text affirms absolutely nothing existentially; indeed, it confines itself exclusively to what did *not* occur.

The reader, however, is a creature more frail than a perfect logician. So, although the text says nothing of this, there is conjured up in-voluntarily in his imagination a scene taking place at some railway station, a scene of waiting for someone who has not arrived, and since he knows the sex of the author (authoress), the waiting for the non-arrival immediately carries the anticipation of an erotic encounter. What of this? Everything! Because the whole responsibility for these conjectures, from the very first words, falls on the reader. With not a single word does the novel confirm his expectations; the novel is and remains decent in its method. I have heard some say that in places it is downright pornographic. Well, but there is not a single word in it that would assert sex in any form; and indeed, how could such an assertion be possible when it is expressly stated that in the home there is neither the Kama Sutra nor any person's reproductive organs (and those are denied most specifically!).

Non-being is already known to us in literature, but only as a certain Lack – of Something – for Someone. For example – of water, for one thirsty. The same applies to hunger (including the erotic), loneliness (the lack of others), etc. The exquisitely beautiful non-being of Paul Valéry is a lack of being that is bewitching for the poet; on such nothingnesses more than one poetic work has been built. But always it is exclusively a matter of Nothingness for Someone, or of non-being purely private, experienced on the individual level, therefore par-ticular, chimerical, and not ontological (when I, thirsty, cannot have a drink of water, this does not mean, after all, the absence of water – as though water did not in general exist!). Such unobjective nothingness cannot be the theme of a radical work: Mme Solange understood this also.

In the first chapter, following the non-arrival of the train and the non-appearance of the Someone, the narration, continuing in its sub-jectless way, reveals that it is not spring, or winter, or summer. The reader decides on autumn, but again only because that last climatic possibility has not been disavowed (it, too, will be, but later!). The reader therefore is constantly thrown back on himself, but that is the problem of his own anticipations, conjectures, his hypotheses ad hoc. In the novel there is not so much as a hint of these. The contemplation of the unbeloved heroine in non-gravitational space (i.e., space in which there is no force of attraction), which concludes the first chapter, might seem, it is true, obscene – but, again, only to one who will think *certain things* himself, on his own. The work relates only what such an unbeloved would *not* be able to do, and not what she *would* be able to do, in particular positions. This second part, the suppositional, is again the personal contribution of the reader, his completely private gain (or loss, depending on how one looks at it). The work even goes so far as to stress that the unbeloved does *not* find herself in the presence of any kind of male. Anyway, the beginning of the next chapter discloses, straightaway, that this unbeloved is unbeloved for the simple reason that she *does not exist*. An entirely logical situation – is it not?

Then begins that drama of the diminution of space, of phallic–vaginal space also, which was not to the liking of a certain critic, a member of the Academy. The academician found it to be 'an anatomical bore, if not a vulgarity'. He found it, let us note, on his own and by himself, because in the text we have only further, progressive denials, of a more and more general nature. If the *lack* of a vagina can still offend someone's sensibilities, then we have gone far indeed. How can a thing be in bad taste which *is not there at all*?!

Then the pit of nothingness, still shallow, begins to increase disquietingly. The middle of the book – from the fourth to the sixth chapter – is consciousness. Yes, its stream, but, as we begin to realize, this is not a stream of thoughts about nothing, old-fashioned, passé. This is a stream of *no thoughts*. The syntax itself remains intact, untouched, inviolate, and it carries us over the depths like a perilously buckling bridge. What a void! But – we reason – even consciousness that is unthinking is still consciousness, is it not? Since that unthinkingness has limits ... but this is a delusion, for the limitations are created by the reader himself! The text does not think; it gives us nothing. On the contrary, it takes away in succession that which was still our property, and the emotions in reading it are precisely the result of the ruthlessness of such subtraction: *horror vacui* smites us, at the same time entices; the reading turns out to be not so much the destruction of the world of lies of the novel as a form of annihilation of the reader himself as a psychic being! A woman wrote this book? Difficult to believe, considering its merciless logic.

In the last section of the work comes the doubt whether it can possibly continue: it has, after all, been saying nothing for so long! Any further progress to the centre of non-existence seems impossible. But no! Again a trap, again an explosion – or, rather, an implosion, the caving in of yet another nothingness! The narrator – as we know, there is no narrator; he is replaced by the language, that which itself speaks *by means of him*, like an imaginary 'it' (the 'it' in 'it is thundering' or 'it is lightning'). In the next-to-last chapter we observe with dizziness that the negative absolute has now been reached. The business of the non-appearance of some man, by some train, the unbeing of the seasons of the year, of the weather, of the walls of the house, of the apartment, of the face, the eyes, the air, the bodies – all this lies far behind us, on the surface, the surface that, eaten away by our further progress, by that all-consuming cancerlike Nothing, has ceased to exist *even as negation*. We see how simple-minded, naïve, how positively comical it was of us to expect that we would be given facts of some sort here, that here something or other would happen!

It is, therefore, a reduction, to zero only to begin with; later, sinking into the abyss with projections of negative transcendence, it is a reduction also of transcendental entities, since by now no metaphysical systems are possible, and the neantic centre still looms before us. A vacuum, then, surrounds the narrative on every side; and behold, there are now its first incursions, intrusions, in the language itself. For the narrating voice begins to doubt itself. No, I put that poorly: 'that which by itself tells of itself' collapses and vanishes somewhere; it already knows that it *is not*. If it still exists, it exists as a shadow, which is the simple lack of light; thus are these sentences the lack of existence. It is not the lack of water in the desert, not the maiden's lack of a lover, it is the *lack of self*. Had this been a novel written in the classical, traditional fashion, it would have been easy for us to say what took place: the hero would have been the sort of someone who begins to harbour suspicions that he neither manifests himself nor dreams himself, but is dreamt and manifested – *by* someone, and through hidden intentional acts (as if he is appearing to someone in a dream and only thanks to the dreamer may exist provisionally). From this would have come the rushing fear that these acts would stop, and surely they could stop at any moment – whereupon he would then fade away!

Thus it would have been in a more ordinary novel, but not with Mme Solange: the narrator cannot take fright of anything, because, you see, there is no narrator. What, then, occurs? The language itself begins to suspect, and then to understand, that there is no one besides itself, that, having meaning (to the extent that it has meaning) for anyone, for everyone, it thereby is not and never was or ever could have been a personal expression; cut off from all mouths at once, as a universally ejected tapeworm, as an adulterous parasite that has devoured its hosts, that has slain them so long ago that in it all memory of the crime, unknowingly committed, has been erased and obliterated, this language, like the skin of a balloon, till now resilient, firm, from which invisibly and faster and faster the air escapes, begins to shrivel. This eclipse of speech, however, is not a babel; and it is not fear (again, only the reader fears, experiencing *per procura*, as it were, that alien, totally depersonalized torment); for a few pages yet, for a few moments, there remains the machinery of grammar, the millstones of the nouns, the cogwheels of syntax grinding out more and more slowly – yet precise to the last – nothingness, which corrodes them through; and that is how it ends, in mid-sentence, mid-word ... The novel does not end: it ceases. The language, at the start, sure of itself in the first pages, naïve, healthily-commonsensically believing in its own sovereignty, eroded by a silent undertow of treachery, or, rather, arriving at the truth of its external, illegitimate origins, of its corruption and abuse (for this is the Last Judgement of literature), the language, having come to realize that it represents a form of incest – the incestuous union of non-being with being – suicidally disowns itself.

A woman wrote this book? Extraordinary. It ought to have been written by some mathematician, but only one who with his mathematics proved – and cursed – literature.

Joachim Fersengeld

PERICALYPSIS

(*Editions de Minuit, Paris*)

Joachim Fersengeld, a German, wrote his *Pericalypse* in Dutch (he
hardly knows the language, which he himself admits in the Introduction) and published it in France, a country notorious for its dreadful
proofreading. The writer of these words also does not, strictly speaking, know Dutch, but going by the title of the book, the English
Introduction, and a few understandable expressions here and there in
the text, he has concluded that he can pass muster as a reviewer after all.

Joachim Fersengeld does not wish to be an intellectual in an age
when anyone can be one. Nor has he any desire to pass for a man of
letters. Creative work of value is possible when there is resistance,
either of the medium or of the people at whom the work is aimed; but
since, after the collapse of the prohibitions of religion and the censor,
one can say everything, or anything whatever, and since, with the
disappearance of those attentive listeners who hung on every word,
one can howl anything at anyone, literature and all its humanistic
affinity is a corpse, whose advancing decay is stubbornly concealed by
the next of kin. Therefore, one should seek out new terrains for creativity, those in which can be found a resistance that will lend an
element of menace and risk – and therewith importance and responsibility – to the situation.

Such a field, such an activity, can today be only prophecy. Because
he is without hope – that is, because he knows in advance that he will
be neither heard out nor recognized nor accepted – the prophet ought
to reconcile himself a priori to a position of muteness. And he who,
being a German, addresses Frenchmen in Dutch with English intro-
ductions is as mute as he who keeps silent. Thus Fersengeld acts in
accordance with his own assumptions. Our mighty civilization, he says,
strives for the production of commodities as impermanent as possible
in packaging as permanent as possible. The impermanent product must

soon be replaced by a new one, and this is good for the economy; the permanence of the packaging, on the other hand, makes its disposal difficult, and this promotes the further development of technology and organization. Thus the consumer copes with each consecutive article of junk on an individual basis, whereas for the removal of the packagings special anti-pollution programmes are required, sanitary engineering, the coordination of efforts, planning, purification and decontamination plants, and so on. Formerly, one could depend on it that the accumulation of garbage would be kept at a reasonable level by the forces of nature, such as the rains, the winds, rivers and earth-quakes. But at the present time what once washed and flushed away the garbage has itself become the excrement of civilization: the rivers poison us, the atmosphere burns our lungs and eyes, the winds strew industrial ashes on our heads, and as for plastic containers, since they are elastic, even earthquakes cannot deal with them. Thus the normal scenery today is civilizational droppings, and the natural reserves are a momentary exception to the rule. Against this landscape of packagings that have been sloughed off by their products, crowds bustle about, absorbed in the business of opening and consuming, and also in that last natural product, sex. Yet sex, too, has been given a multitude of packagings, for this and nothing else is what clothes are, displays, roses, lipsticks and sundry other advertising wrappings. Thus civiliza-tion is worthy of admiration only in its separate fragments, much as the precision of the heart is worthy of admiration, the liver, the kid-neys or the lungs of an organism, since the rapid work of those organs makes good sense, though there is no sense whatever in the activity of the body that comprises these perfect parts – if it is the body of a lunatic.

The same process, declares the prophet, is taking place in the area of spiritual goods as well, since the monstrous machine of civilization, its screws having worked loose, has turned into a mechanical milker of the Muses. Thus it fills the libraries to bursting, inundates the book-stores and magazine stands, numbs the television screens, piling itself high with a superabundance of which the numerical magnitude alone is a deathblow. If finding forty grains of sand in the Sahara meant saving the world, they would not be found, any more than would the forty messianic books that have already long since been written but were lost beneath strata of trash. And these books have unquestionably been written; the statistics of intellectual labour guarantees it, as is explained – in Dutch – mathematically – by Joachim Fersengeld, which this reviewer must repeat on faith, conversant with neither the Dutch language nor the mathematical. And so, ere we can steep our souls in those revelations, we bury them in garbage, for there is four billion times more of the latter. But then, they are buried already. Already has come to pass what the prophecy proclaimed, only it went unnoticed in the general haste. The prophecy, then, is a retrophecy, and for this reason is entitled Pericalypse, and not Apocalypse. Its progress (retrogress) we detect by Signs: by languidity, insipidity and insensitivity, and in addition by acceleration, inflation and masturbation. Intellectual masturbation is the contenting of oneself with the *promise* in place of the *delivery*: first we were onanized thoroughly by advertising (that degenerate form of revelation which is the measure of the Commercial Idea, as opposed to the Personal), and then self-abuse took over as a method for the rest of the arts. And this, because to believe in the saving power of Merchandise yields greater results than to believe in the efficacy of the Lord God.

The moderate growth of talent, its innately slow maturation, its careful weeding out, its natural selection in the purview of solicitous and discerning tastes – these are phenomena of a bygone age that died heirless. The last stimulus that still works is a mighty howl; but when more and more people howl, employing more and more powerful amplifiers, one's eardrums will burst before the soul learns anything. The names of the geniuses of old, more and more vainly invoked, already are an empty sound; and so it is *mene mene tekel upharsin*, unless what Joachim Fersengeld recommends is done. There should be set up a Save the Human Race Foundation, as a sixteen-billion reserve on a gold standard, yielding an interest of four per cent per annum. Out of this fund moneys should be dispensed to all creators – to inventors, scholars, engineers, painters, writers, poets, playwrights, philosophers and designers – in the following way. He who writes nothing, designs nothing, paints nothing, neither patents nor proposes, is paid a stipend, for life, to the tune of thirty-six thousand dollars a year. He who does any of the afore-mentioned receives correspondingly less.

Pericalypse contains a full set of tabulations of what is to be deducted for each form of creativity. For one invention or two published books a year, you receive not a cent; by three titles, what you create comes out of your own pocket. With this, only a true altruist, only an ascetic of the spirit, who loves his neighbour but not himself one bit, will create anything, and the production of mercenary rubbish will cease. Joachim Fersengeld speaks from personal experience, for it was at his own expense – at a loss! – that he published his *Pericalypse*. He knows, then, that total unprofitability does not at all mean the total elimination of creativity.

Egoism manifests itself as a hunger for mammon combined with a hunger for glory: in order to scotch the latter as well, the Salvation Programme introduces the complete anonymity of the creators. To forestall the submission of stipend applications from untalented persons, the Foundation will, through the appropriate organs, examine the qualifications of the candidates. The actual merit of the idea with which a candidate comes forward is of no consequence. The only important thing is whether the project possesses commercial value, that is, whether it can be sold. If so, the stipend is awarded immediately. For underground creative activity, there is set up a system of penalties and repressive measures within the framework of legal prosecution by the apparatus of the Safety Control; also introduced is a new form of police, namely, the Anvil (Anticreative Vigilance League). According to the penal code, whosoever clandestinely writes, disseminates, harbours, or even if only in silence publicly communicates any fruit of creative endeavour, with the purpose of deriving from said action either gain or glory, shall be punished by confinement, forced labour, and, in the case of recidivism, by imprisonment in a dark cell with a hard bed, and a caning on each anniversary of the offence. For the smuggling into the bosom of society of such ideas, whose tragic effect on life is comparable to the bane of the automobile, the scourge of cinematography, the curse of television, etc., the law provides capital punishment as the maximum and includes the pillory and a life sentence of the compulsory use of one's own invention. Punishable also are attempted crimes, and premeditation carries with it badges of shame, in the form of the stamping of the forehead with indelible letters arranged to spell out 'Enemy of Man'. However, graphomania, which does not look for gain, is called a Disorder of the Mind and is not punishable, though persons so afflicted are removed from society, as constituting a threat to the peace, and placed in special institutions, where they are humanely supplied with great quantities of ink and paper.

Obviously world culture will not at all suffer from such state regulation, but will only then begin to flourish. Humanity will return to the magnificent works of its own history; for the number of sculptures, paintings, plays, novels, gadgets and machines is great enough already to meet the needs of many centuries. Nor will anyone be forbidden to make so-called epochal discoveries, on the condition that he keep them to himself.

Having in this way set the situation to rights – that is, having saved humanity – Joachim Fersengeld proceeds to the final problem: what is to be done with that monstrous glut which has *already* come about? As a man of uncommon civil fortitude, Fersengeld says that what has so far been created in the twentieth century, though it may contain great pearls of wisdom, is worth nothing when tallied up in its entirety, because you will not find those pearls in the ocean of garbage. Therefore he calls for the destruction of everything in one lump, all that has arisen in the form of films, illustrated magazines, postage stamps, musical scores, books, scientific articles, newspapers, for this act will be a true cleaning out of the Augean stables – with a full balancing of the historical credits and debits in the human ledger. (Among other things, the destruction will claim the facts about atomic energy, which will eliminate the current threat to the world.) Joachim Fersengeld points out that he is perfectly aware of the infamy of burning books, or even whole libraries. But the autos-da-fé enacted in history – such as in the Third Reich – were infamous because they were reactionary. It all depends on the grounds on which one does the burning. He proposes, then, a life-saving auto-da-fé, progressive, redemptive; and because Joachim Fersengeld is a prophet consistent to the end, in his closing world he bids the reader first tear up and set fire to this very prophecy!

Gian Carlo Spallanzani

IDIOTA

(Mondadori Editore, Milan)

The Italians, then, have a young writer of the type we have missed so, one, who speaks with a full voice. And I feared the young would be infected by the cryptonihilism of the experts, who declare that all literature has 'already been written', and that now one can only glean scraps from the table of the old masters, scraps called myths or archetypes. These prophets of inventive barrenness (there is nothing new under the sun) preach their line not out of resignation, but as if the prospect of wide empty centuries awaiting Art in vain filled them with a sort of perverse satisfaction. For they hold against today's world its technological ascent, and hope for evil, much as maiden aunts look forward with malicious glee to the wreck of a marriage foolishly entered into out of love. And so we now have jewellery engravers (for Italo Calvino is descended from Benvenuto Cellini, not from Michelangelo), and the naturalists who, ashamed of naturalism, pretend to be writing something other than what lies within their means (Alberto Moravia), but we have no men of mettle. They are hard to come by, now that anyone can play the rebel, provided his physiognomy supplies him with a fierce crop of beard.

The young prose writer Gian Carlo Spallanzani is audacious to the point of impudence. He pretends to take the opinions of the experts as gospel, only later to sling mud at them. For his *Idiot* alludes to the novel of Dostoevsky not merely in its title: it reaches further. I do not know about others, but personally I find it easier to write about a book when I have seen the face of the author. Spallanzani is not prepossessing in his photo; he is an ungainly youth with a low forehead and puffy eyes, the small dark pupils of which are peevish, and the dainty chin makes one uneasy. An *enfant terrible*, a knave of low cunning and with a mean streak, an outspoken wolf in sheep's clothing? I cannot find the right term, but I stick with my impression from the first reading of *The Idiot*: such perfidiousness is in a class by itself. Can he have written under a pseudonym? Because the great, historical Spallanzani was a vivisectionist, and this thirty-year-old is one also. I find it hard to believe that such a coincidence of names is completely accidental. The young author has cheek: he furnishes his *Idiot* with an introduction in which, with seeming candour, he tells why he abandoned his original idea – that of writing *Crime and Punishment* a second time, as 'Sonya's', the story told in the first person by the daughter of Marmeladov.

There is effrontery, not without its charm, in his explanation of how he restrained himself because he did not wish to do injury to the original. Albeit against his will – he would have had to (so he says) chip away at the statue that Dostoevsky raised up in honour of his shining prostitute. Sonya in *Crime and Punishment* appears intermittently, being a 'third person'; a narrative in the first person would require her constant presence, even during her working hours, and that is the sort of work that affects the soul as no other. The axiom of her spiritual purity untouched by the experiences of the fallen body could not emerge whole. Defending himself in this devious way, the author does not even address himself to the real question – of *The Idiot*. This already is double-dealing: he accomplished what he wanted, for he has shown us the general drift; his impudence lies in his having made no mention of the necessity, of the imperative, that compelled him to take up a theme after Dostoevsky!

The story, realistic, matter-of-fact, at first seems set on a rather prosaic level. A very ordinary, moderately well-to-do family, an average, respectable couple – upright, but uninspired – has a mentally retarded child. Like any child, it showed delightful promise; its first words, those unintentionally original expressions which are the side effects of one's growing into speech, have been preserved with loving care in the reliquary of the parents' reminiscences. Those blissful, diapered simplicities, in the framework of the present nightmare, mark out the amplitude between what could have been and what has happened.

The child is an idiot. Living with him, caring for him, is an anguish all the more cruel in that it has grown out of love. The father is almost twenty years older than the mother; there are couples who in a similar situation would try again; here it is not known what hinders such an act, physiology or psychology. But for all that, it is probably love. Under normal circumstances the love could never have undergone such magnification. Precisely because he is an idiot, the child makes prodigies of his parents. He improves them to the very degree to which he lacks normality. This could be the sense of the novel, its theme, but it is merely the premise.

In their contacts with the outside world, with relatives, doctors, lawyers, the father and mother are ordinary people, deeply troubled but restrained, for indeed this situation has been going on for years: there has been sufficient time to acquire self-control! The period of despair, of hope, of trips to various capitals, to the finest specialists, has long since passed. The parents realize that nothing can be done. They have no illusions. Their visits to the doctor, to the attorney, are now to ensure some decent, endurable *modus vivendi* for the idiot when his natural protectors are gone. They must see to a will, safeguard his inheritance. This is done slowly, soberly, with due deliberation. Tedious and scrupulous: nothing more natural under the sun. When they return home, however, and when the three are by themselves, the situation changes in a flash. I would say: as when actors make their entrance on stage. Fine, but we do not know where the stage is. This is now to be revealed. Without ever making any arrangement between themselves, without ever exchanging so much as a single word – that would be a psychological impossibility – the parents have created, over the years, a system of interpreting the actions of the idiot in such a way as to find them intelligent, in every instance and in every respect.

Spallanzani found the germ of such conduct in normal behaviour. It is known, surely, that the circle of those who dote upon a small child emerging from the infant state makes as much as it can of the child's responses and words. To its mindless echolalia are attributed meanings; in its incoherent babbling is discovered intelligence, even wit; the inaccessibility of the child's psyche allows the observer enormous freedom, especially the doting observer. It must have been in this way that the rationalization of the idiot's actions first began. No doubt the father and mother vied with each other in finding signs to indicate that their child was speaking better and better, more and more clearly, that he was doing better all the time, positively radiating good nature and affection. I have been saying 'child', but when the scene opens he is already a fourteen-year-old boy. What sort of system of mis-interpretation must it be, what subterfuges, what explanations – frantic to the point of being outright comical – must be called into play to save the fiction, when the reality so unremittingly contradicts it? Well, all this can be done, and of such acts consists the parental sacrifice on behalf of the idiot.

Their isolation must be complete. The world has nothing to offer him and will not help him; it is of no use to him, therefore – yes, the world to him, not he to the world. The sole interpreters of his be-haviour must be the initiated, the father and mother: in this way, everything can be transformed. We do not learn whether the idiot killed, or put out of her misery, his ailing grandmother; one can, however, set out side by side the different points of circumstantial evidence. His grandmother did not believe in him (that is, in that version of him which the parents had established – true, we cannot know how much of her 'unbelief' the idiot was able to sense); she had asthma; her wheezing and rattling during the attacks were not shut out even by the felt-padded door; he could not sleep when the attacks intensified; they drove him into a rage; he was found sleeping peace-fully in the room of the dead woman, at the foot of her bed, on which her body had already grown cold.

First he is carried to the nursery, and only then does the father attend to his own mother. Did the father suspect something? This we never know. The parents do not refer to the topic, for certain things are done without being named; as if they realize that any improvisation has its limits, when irrevocably now they must set about doing 'those things', they sing. They do what is indispensable, but at the same time conduct themselves like Mummy and Daddy, singing lullabies if it is evening, or the old songs of their childhood if intervention becomes necessary during the day. Song has proved a better ex-tinguisher of the intellect than silence. We hear it at the very beginning; that is, the servants hear it, the gardener. 'A sad song,' he says, but later we begin to guess what gruesome work was likely done to the accompaniment of precisely that song: it was early morning when the body was found. What an infernal refinement of feelings!

The idiot behaves dreadfully, with an inventiveness sometimes characteristic of a profound dementia that is capable of cunning; in this way he spurs his parents on ever more, for they must find themselves equal to every task. Now and then their words are fitted exactly to their actions, but that is rare; the eeriest effects of all occur when they say one thing while doing another, for here one type of resourcefulness, the cretinoid, is pitted against another, a devotedly ministering resourcefulness – loving, giving – and only the distance that perforce separates the two turns these acts of sacrifice into the macabre. But the parents by now probably do not see this: it has, after all, gone on for years! In the face of each new surprise (a euphemism: the idiot spares them nothing), there is first a fraction of a second in which, along with them, we experience a thrill of fear, a piercing dread that *this* will not only shatter the present moment but will overturn, in a single blow, the entire edifice that has been raised with tender care by the father and mother in the course of long months and years.

We are wrong; an exchange of glances, purely reflexive, a few laconic remarks to shift gears, and in the tone of a natural conversation begins the lifting of this new burden, the fitting of it into the created structure. An eerie humour and an arresting nobility are in such scenes, thanks to the psychological accuracy. The words they venture to use when it is no longer possible not to put on the 'little smock'! When they do not know what to do with the razor; or when the mother, jumping from the tub, must barricade herself in the bathroom, and later, having made a short circuit in the entire house, so that darkness descends, by feel removes the barricade of furniture, since its presence is – to her version of the child, which binds her – more damaging than a defect in the electrical installation. In the vestibule, dripping wet and wrapped in a thick rug, no doubt on account of the razor, she waits for the father to come home. It sounds coarse and awkward – worse, unbelievable – summarized like this, taken out of context. The parents act in the knowledge that to reconcile such incidents to the norm, through completely arbitrary interpretations, is an impossibility; therefore it was a little at a time, themselves not knowing when, that they passed beyond the boundary of that norm and entered a realm inaccessible to ordinary office or kitchen mortals. Not in the direction of madness, not at all: it is not true that everyone can go insane. But everyone can believe. To keep from becoming a family defiled, they became a family sacred.

That word does not appear in the book; nor is the idiot, according to the faith of the parents (for faith it must be called), either God or a lesser deity; he is merely other than all creatures, a thing unto himself, unlike any child or youth; and in that otherness he is theirs, irrevocably loved, their one and only. Farfetched? Then read *The Idiot* yourself; you will see that faith is not merely a metaphysical capacity of the mind. The situation is in all its substance so constantly rooted in harshness that only the absurdity of faith can save it from damnation, which here means: from psychopathological nomenclature. If the saints of the Lord have been taken by psychiatrists for paranoiacs, then why can it not also be the other way around? Idiot? The word does make its appearance in the action, but only when the parents go among other people. They speak of the child in the language of those others, of the doctors, attorneys, relatives, but for themselves they know better. Thus they lie to others because their faith has not the mark of a mission, and therefore not the aggressiveness that demands the conversion of the heathen. The father and mother are, anyway, too level-headed to believe for even a second in the possibility of such conversion: it does not concern them, and besides, it is not the whole world that needs saving, but only three people. While they live, they have their mutual church. It is not a matter of shame or of prestige, or of the insanity of an ageing couple, called *folie à deux*, but merely an earthly, transitory thing, taking place in a house with central heating; it is the triumph of love, whose motto reads *Credo quia absurdum est*. If this be madness, every faith can be reduced to that level.

Spallanzani walks a narrow line throughout, for the greatest danger for the novel was to become a caricature of the Holy Family. The father is old? Then that is Joseph. The mother is much younger? Mary. And in that case the child . . . Well, I think that if Dostoevsky had not written his *Idiot*, this line of allegorization never would have presented itself, or would have remained so veiled as to be hardly noticeable, and only to a few. If one can put it thus, Spallanzani has absolutely nothing against the Gospel; nor has he the least desire to make free with the Holy Family; and if, in spite of everything, there

does arise – one cannot altogether avoid it – precisely such a conno-
tative ricochet, then the 'blame' must be borne entirely by Dostoevsky
and his *Idiot*. Yes, of course: to this end alone was the demolition
charge of the work primed and set, as an attack levelled at the great
writer! Prince Myshkin, the saintly epileptic, the misunderstood inno-
cent-ascetic, the Jesus with the stigmata of grand mal – he serves
here as a link, a relay point. Spallanzani's idiot resembles him at times,
but with the signs reversed! This is, you might say, the maniac variant,
and exactly thus might one picture the adolescence of the pale youth
Myshkin, when the epileptic seizures, with their mystic aura, with
their bestial spasms, for the first time knock to pieces the image of
angelic little-darlingness. The tyke is a cretin? Incessantly, yes, yet we
get the communion of his vacant mind with sublimity, as when, suf-
focated by the music, he smashes the phonograph record, wounding
himself, and tries to devour it along with his own blood. Well, you
see, this is a form of – an attempt at – transubstantiation: something
of Bach must have knocked upon the door of his dim consciousness,
if he sought to make it a part of himself – by eating it.

Had the parents turned the whole thing over to the institutional
Lord God, or had they simply created a three-person substitute for
religion, a kind of sect with a mentally deficient stand-in for God,
their defeat would have been certain. But not for a moment do they
cease to be ordinary, literal, maltreated parents; they never even considered the way of holy ambitions – they permitted themselves none,
nothing that was not of immediate, on-the-spot necessity. Therefore,
they did not actually build any system at all; instead, through the
situation, a system was born and revealed itself to them, not wanted,
not planned, not even suspected. They received no revelation; they
were themselves in the beginning, and themselves they remained. And
so it is only an earthly love. We have grown unaccustomed to its
power in literature, a literature which, schooled in cynicism, its old
romantic back broken by the blows of psychoanalytic doctrines, has
become blind to that part of the amplitude of human destiny on
which thrived – and which cultivated for us – the classics of the past.

A cruel novel: it tells, first, of the boundless talent for compensation, and so of the creativity that resides in everyone, anyone, no
matter who he is, if fate afflicts him with the torment of an appropriate

labour. And then it tells of the forms in which love manifests itself when stripped of hope, when brought to the depths of despair, yet never relinquishing its object. In this context the words *Credo quia absurdum* are the worldly equivalent of the words *Finis vitae, sed non amoris*. The novel is about (this is already the anthropological exegesis, and not the tragedy of a father and a mother) how there comes into being, in microscopic mechanisms, a world-creating intentionality that names, and therefore it is not simply transcendence. No, the idea is that the world, while undisturbed in its arbitrarily violent shame and ugliness, can be altered – or what is conveyed by the words 'transformed', 'transfigured'. Were we not able to reshape the monstrous into the correlates of the angelic, we could not endure, and this is what this book is all about. A faith in transcendence may be completely unnecessary; and without it, one can attain the grace (or the agony) of a theodicy, for it is not in the recognition of the state of things but in their alterability that the freedom of man lives. If this freedom is not a true freedom (indeed, involved is an utter subjugation – by love!), then there can be no other. Spallanzani's *The Idiot* is not the androgynous allegory of the Christian myth, but an atheistic heterodoxy.

Spallanzani, like a psychologist performing experiments on rats, subjected his heroes to a test that was designed to prove his anthropological hypothesis. At the same time, the book is a broadside against Dostoevsky, as if the latter were living and writing today. Spallanzani wrote his *Idiot* in order to demonstrate to Dostoevsky a *weak* heresy. I cannot say that the assault succeeds, but I understand the intent: to break out of that magic circle of issues and ideas in which the great Russian writer confined his own and the following age. Art cannot look only backward, or content itself with tightrope walking; new eyes are needed, new ways of seeing, and most of all a new idea. Let us keep in mind that this is a first book. I await Spallanzani's next novel as I have not awaited any in a long time.

U-WRITE-IT

A book that told the story of the rise and fall of *U-Write-It* would make most instructive reading. That neoplasm of the publishing world became the subject of such heated debate that the debate obscured the phenomenon itself. Therefore the factors that led to the failure of the enterprise to this day remain unclear. No one made an attempt to carry out public-opinion research in this regard. Perhaps rightly so; perhaps the public that decided the fate of the venture did not itself know what it was doing.

The invention had been in the air a good twenty years, and one can only wonder that it was not implemented earlier. I recall the first model of that 'literary erector set'. It was a box in the shape of a thick book containing directions, a prospectus, and a kit of 'building elements'. These elements were strips of paper of unequal width, printed with fragments of prose. Each strip had holes punched along the margin to facilitate binding, and several numerals stamped in different colours. Arranging the strips according to the numbering of the base colour, black, one obtained the 'starting text', which consisted usually of at least two works of world literature, suitably abridged. Had the set been made only for the purpose of such reconstruction, it would have been devoid of sense and commercial value. This lay in the possibility of shuffling the elements. The instructions usually supplied several illustrative variants of recombination, and the coloured numerals in the margins referred to these. The idea was patented by Universal, who used books to which all authors' rights had expired. Such were the works of the greats, of Balzac, Tolstoy, Dostoevsky, duly abridged by the publisher's anonymous staff. Without fail the inventors directed this concoction at a certain class of people, one that could derive enjoyment from the deformation and distortion of masterpieces (or, rather, of crude versions of them). You take *Crime and*

Punishment in hand, or *War and Peace*, and do whatever you please with the characters. Natasha can go astray before the wedding and after it, too; Svidrigailov can marry Raskolnikov's sister, and Raskolnikov can escape justice and go off with Sonya to Switzerland; Anna Karenina will betray her husband not with Vronsky, but with the footman, etc. In one voice the critics attacked such desecration; the publisher defended himself as best he could, and fairly adroitly at that.

The instructions that came with the set claimed that in this way one could learn the rules of literary composition ('Perfect for beginning writers!'), and one could also use the set as a text for psychological projection ('Tell me what you have done with *Anne of Green Gables* and I will tell you who you are'). In a word – a training device for literary hopefuls and an amusement for every literary amateur.

It was not hard to see that the publishers were guided by less-than-honourable intentions. In their instructions, World Books cautioned the buyer against the use of 'improper' combinations, meaning the rearrangement of passages in the text so as to impart a contrary sense to scenes originally pure as the driven snow: by the insertion of a single sentence, an innocent conversation between two women took on Lesbian overtones; it was also possible, in the worthy families of Dickens, to have incest practised – whatever your heart desired. The caution was, of course, an incitement, worded in such a way that no one could accuse the publisher of offending against decency. Well, if he clearly said in the instructions that this *should not* be done . . .

Infuriated by helplessness (on legal grounds the thing was not open to attack; the publishers had seen to that), the well-known critic Ralph Summers wrote at the time: 'And so modern pornography is no longer enough. It is necessary in analogous fashion to besmirch everything that arose in the past, that which was not only without obscene intent but actually in opposition to it. This paltry surrogate for the Black Mass, which anyone can conduct in the seclusion of his home, for four dollars, on the defenceless body of the murdered classics, is a true disgrace.'

It soon turned out that Summers had exaggerated in his Cassandra-like pronouncement: the venture did not prosper half so well as the publishers had expected. Before long they came up with a new version of the 'erector set', a volume composed entirely of empty sheets on which one could arrange by hand the strips with the texts, since both the strips and the pages of the volume were coated with a monomolecular magnetic foil. Thereby the 'binding' work was greatly simplified. But this innovation did not catch on, either. Could it be, as some idealists (very rare nowadays) surmised, that the public was refusing to participate in 'the abusing of the great works'? To presume an attitude so high-minded is, in my opinion, alas, unwarranted. The quiet hope of the publishers had been that a considerable number of people would develop a taste for the new game. Certain passages of the instructions give an indication of this line of thought: '*U-Write-It* allows you to acquire that same power over human lives, godlike, which till now has been the exclusive privilege of the world's greatest geniuses!' Which Ralph Summers, in one of his diatribes, interpreted as follows: 'Single-handed you can drag down any loftiness, sully all that is clean, and your efforts will be accompanied by the pleasant awareness that you are not now obliged to sit and listen to what some Tolstoy, what some Balzac had to say, because in this you are boss and call the shots!'

And yet there were surprisingly few who wanted to be such 'defilers'. Summers foresaw the spread of 'a new sadism, taking the form of aggression against the permanent values of our culture', but meanwhile *U-Write-It* was barely selling. It would be nice to believe that the public was prompted by 'that natural grain of sense and rectitude which subcultural convulsions have succeeded in obscuring from our view' (L. Evans in the *Christian Science Monitor*). This writer does not share – much as he would like to! – Evans's opinion.

What, then, took place? Something a great deal simpler, I daresay. For Summers and Evans, for me, for a few hundred critics tucked away among university quarterlies, and in addition for another several thousand eggheads throughout the land, Svidrigailov, Vronsky, Sonya Marmeladov, or for that matter Vautrin, Anne of Green Gables, Rastignac, are characters extremely well known, familiar, close, sometimes actually more vivid than many real acquaintances. But for the public at large they are empty sounds, names without content. Thus for Summers and Evans, for me, the union of Svidrigailov with Natasha would be a horrendous thing, but for the public it would mean no more or less than the marriage of Mr X and Mrs Y. Because for the public at large they have no fixed symbolic value – be it that of nobility of feeling or dissolute wickedness – such characters do not offer a perverse or any other type of entertainment. They are completely neutral. Of no concern to anyone. The publishers, cynical as they were, did not divine this, not being truly attuned to the situation in the literary market place. If a man finds enormous value in a particular book, then the use of that book as a doormat for the wiping of shoes will seem to him an act not just of vandalism, but of the 'Black Mass' – which is precisely what Summers thought, for that is how he wrote.

The growing indifference in our world to such cultural values had progressed a good deal beyond what the authors of the enterprise imagined. No one cared to play *U-Write-It*, not because he nobly forbore to pervert quality, but for the simple reason that between the book of a fourth-rate hack and the epic of Tolstoy he saw no difference whatever. The one left him as cold as the other. Even if there was in the public 'the desire to trample', there was – from its point of view – nothing interesting to trample.

Did the publishers grasp this particular lesson? Yes, in a sense. I doubt that they became aware of the state of affairs in so many words, but, led by instinct, intuition, by their noses, they all the same began to put on the market variants of the 'erector set' that did much better, since these permitted the assembling of purely pornographic and obscene compositions. The last diehard aesthetes heaved a sigh of relief, since at least now the venerable remains of the masterpieces would be left alone. Immediately the problem ceased to interest them, and from the pages of the élite literary quarterlies there disappeared those articles in which robes were rent and (egg)heads heaped with ashes. Because what happens in the non-élite circles of readers does not, not one bit, concern the Olympus of the arts and its Zeuses.

That Olympus was roused a second time, when Bernard de la Taille, having constructed from *The Big Party* – a set translated into French – a novel, received for it the Prix Fémina. This led to a scandal, because the shrewd Frenchman had neglected to inform the judges that his novel was not entirely original but represented the product of an assembly. De la Taille's novel (*War in the Dark*) is not without merit; its construction called for both talents and interests normally not found in the buyers of *U-Write-It* sets. But this isolated incident changed nothing; from the start it was clear that the venture would oscillate between a stupid joke and commercial pornography. No one struck it rich with *U-Write-It*. The aesthetes, schooled in minimalism, today are glad that characters out of gutter romances no longer trespass on the parquets of Tolstoyan salons, and that virtuous maidens like Raskolnikov's sister no longer have to let themselves go with ruffians and degenerates.

In England a farcical version of *U-Write-It* still ekes out an existence; there they publish sets that enable one to build brief texts on the principle of 'fun'; the home-grown littérateur is tickled that in his micro-short story the whole company is poured into the bottle instead of the juice, that Sir Galahad ogles his own horse, that during Mass the priest sets off electric trains on the altar, etc. This evidently amuses the English, since a few of their newspapers even run a regular column for such lucubrations. On the Continent, however, *U-Write-It* has to all intents and purposes been discontinued. If we may cite a certain Swiss critic who has interpreted the failure of that business venture differently from us: 'The public,' he says, 'is grown too lazy to want even to rape, undress or torture anyone itself. All *that* is now done for it by professionals. *U-Write-It* might possibly have been a success had it appeared sixty years earlier. Conceived too late, it was stillborn.' What is there to add to this statement – but a heavy sigh?

Kuno Mlatje

ODYSSEUS OF ITHACA

The full name of the hero of this novel (written by an American) runs Homer Maria Odysseus; Ithaca, where he came into the world, is a jerkwater town of four thousand in the state of Massachusetts. None the less the issue is the quest of Odysseus of Ithaca, a quest not without deeper meaning and thereby linked to its august prototype. True, the beginning does not seem to promise this. Homer M. Odysseus is hauled into court for setting fire to a car belonging to Professor E. G. Hutchinson of the Rockefeller Foundation. The reasons for which he *had to* set fire to the car he will reveal only on condition that the Professor appear personally in the courtroom. When this takes place, Odysseus, making as if to whisper something of tremendous importance to the Professor, bites him in the ear. All hell breaks loose; the counsel for the defence demands a psychiatric examination; the judge wavers; meanwhile Odysseus, from the dock, delivers a speech in which he explains that he had had Herostrates in mind, for cars are the temples of our time, and he bit the Professor in the ear because Stavrogin did this and became famous by it. He, too, requires notoriety, and this for the money it carries with it. The money will enable him to finance a project he has hammered out for the good of humanity.

Here the judge cuts off his oration. Odysseus is sentenced to two months in prison for the destruction of the car and another two months for contempt of court. He can also expect a civil action on the part of Hutchinson, whose concha he has injured. However, Odysseus succeeds in handing his brochure to the reporters present. In this way he attains his end: the press will write about him.

The ideas contained in Homer M. Odysseus's brochure, *The Quest of the Fleece of the Spirit*, are simple enough. Humanity owes its progress to geniuses. Above all, its progress of thought, because collectively one might hit upon a way of hewing flint, but one cannot through joint effort invent the zero. He who conceived it was the first genius in history. 'Could the zero – is it likely – have been thought up by four individuals together, each contributing a quarter?' asks Homer Odysseus with his characteristic sarcasm. Humanity is not wont to deal kindly with its geniuses. '*Es ist schlecht Geschäft, einer Genius zu sein!*' declares Odysseus in dreadful German. Geniuses have a rough time of it. Some more than others, because geniuses are not all equal. Odysseus postulates the following classification of them. First come your run-of-the-mill and middling geniuses, that is, of the third order, whose minds are unable to go much beyond the horizon of their times. These, relatively speaking, are threatened the least; they are often recognized and even come into money and fame. The geniuses of the second order are already too difficult for their contemporaries and therefore fare worse. In antiquity they were mainly stoned, in the Middle Ages burned at the stake; later, in keeping with the temporary amelioration of customs, they were allowed to die a natural death by starvation, and sometimes even were maintained at the community's expense in madhouses. A few were given poison by the local authorities, and many went into exile. Meanwhile, the powers that be, both secular and ecclesiastical, competed for first prize in 'geniocide', as Odysseus calls the manifold activity of exterminating geniuses. None the less, recognition awaits the geniuses of the second order, in the form of a triumph beyond the grave. By way of compensation, libraries and public squares are named after them, fountains and monuments are raised to them, and historians shed decorous tears over such lapses of the past. In addition, avers Odysseus, there exist, for there must exist, geniuses of the highest category. The intermediate types are discovered either by the succeeding generation or by some later one; the geniuses of the first order are never known – not by anyone, not in life, not after death. For they are creators of truths so unprecedented, purveyors of proposals so revolutionary, that not a soul is capable of making head or tail of them. Therefore, permanent obscurity constitutes the normal lot of the Geniuses of the Highest Class. But even their colleagues of weaker intellect are discovered usually as a result of pure accident. For example, on scrawled-over sheets of paper that fishwives use at the market to wrap the herring, you will make out theorems of some sort, or poems, and as soon as these see print, there is a moment of general enthusiasm, then everything goes on as before. Such a state of affairs should not be allowed to continue. At stake, surely, are irretrievable losses to civilization. One must create a Society for the Preservation of Geniuses of the First Order and from it appoint an Exploration Committee that will take up the task of systematic searches. Homer M. Odysseus has already drafted all the statutes of the Society, and also a plan for the Quest for the Fleece of the Spirit. He distributes these documents to numerous scientific societies and philanthropic institutions, calling for funding.

When these efforts produce no result, he publishes a brochure at his own expense and sends the first copy, with a dedication, to Professor Evelyn G. Hutchinson of the Science Council of the Rockefeller Foundation. By not deigning to respond to this, Professor Hutchinson became culpable before humanity. He showed obtuseness; that is, he showed himself unfit to occupy the position entrusted to him. For this he had to be punished, which is what Odysseus did.

While still serving his sentence, Odysseus receives the first contributions. He opens an account in the name of the Quest for the Fleece of the Spirit, and when he leaves the prison, a tidy sum of money, to the tune of $26,528.00, permits him to commence organizational activity. Odysseus recruits volunteers by placing ads in the classifieds; at the first meeting of the enthusiast-amateurs he delivers a speech and hands out a new brochure, this one containing exploration instructions. After all, they must know where, how, and what exactly it is they are supposed to seek. The quest will have an altruistic character, for – Odysseus makes no bones about it – there is little money and enormous labour ahead.

Spiritus flat, ubi vult; therefore, geniuses even of the highest order may be born among the small tribes that constitute the exotic outskirts of the world. Genius does not present itself to humanity directly and personally, going out on the street and seizing passers-by by the toga or buttonhole. Genius operates via appropriate experts who are supposed to recognize it, revere it, and expand upon its thought, as if setting their countryman swinging, the clapper of a bell that peals out to humanity the beginning of a new age. As usual, what should take place does not. The specialists in general believe they know all there is

436

to know; they are willing to teach others, but themselves are unwilling to learn from anyone. Only when there are an awful lot of them does one find, as is usual in crowds, two, perhaps three persons of sense. Consequently, in a small land genius receives the response that a beggar gets from talking to a wall, whereas in larger lands the chance of a genius's being heard is greater. Hence the questers set sail for the lesser peoples and the towns of the out-of-the-way provinces of the globe. There, who knows, they may even succeed in finding yet-unrecognized second-order geniuses. The case of Bošković of Yugoslavia is characteristic: he met with false recognition, for what he wrote and thought centuries ago was noticed when similar things began to be thought and written in the present. Such pseudo-discoveries are not what Odysseus has in mind.

The search ought to include all the libraries of the world, with their collections of rare editions, incunabula and manuscripts, but primarily their basements and cellars, into which are stuffed all sorts of paper ballast. However, one should not count too much on success there. On the map that Odysseus has hung up in his study, red circles indicate, as the first priority, psychiatric sanatoria. Also among excavated sewer systems and cesspools of outdated lunatic asylums Odysseus places high hopes. One must likewise dig up the garbage dumps near old prisons, comb the trash cans as well as other rubbish receptacles, ferret through stores of wastepaper; it would also be well to examine carefully dunghills and sumps, mainly their fossils, since it is precisely there that one finds everything humanity has held in contempt and swept beyond the perimeter of existence. And so Odysseus's intrepid heroes must sally forth for the Fleece of the Spirit full of self-denial, with pitchfork, pickaxe, crowbar, dark lantern and rope ladder, having also on hand geologists' hammers, gas masks, strainers and magnifying glasses. The search for treasures considerably more precious than gold or diamonds is to take place in petrified excrement, in crumbled, cluttered wells, in the former dungeons of every inquisition, in ruined castles; meanwhile, the coordinator of these world-wide operations, Homer M. Odysseus, will remain at his headquarters. One must take as a signpost, as the trembling needle of a compass, every sort of echo of gossip and rumour about completely unique cretins and screwballs, about maniacal, persistent cranks, stubborn dimwits and idiots, because humanity, conferring such names upon genius, is only reacting within the limits of its own natural capacities.

Odysseus, having caused several additional scandals, owing to which he accumulates five new convictions and an additional $16,710.00, betakes himself, after doing two years, southward. He makes for Majorca, where he will have his headquarters, because the climate there is good and his health has been seriously impaired by his sojourns in various jails. He freely admits that he is not averse to combining the public interest with his private interest. Besides, if according to his theory one can expect the appearance of first-order geniuses anywhere, then why should not there be any in Majorca?

The life of Odysseus's heroes is rich in extraordinary adventures, which take up a good portion of the novel. Odysseus sustains more than one bitter disappointment, such as when he learns that three of his favourite explorers, working in the Mediterranean region, are agents of the CIA, which organization has been making use of the Quest for the Fleece of the Spirit for its own ends. Or, again, when another seeker, who brings to Majorca an inestimably valuable document from the seventeenth century – a work by the mameluke Kardyoch on the parageometric structure of Being – turns out to be a forger. He himself is the author of this work; unable to publish it anywhere, he wormed his way into the ranks of the expedition in order to avail himself of Odysseus's funds and thereby give publicity to his concept. The enraged Odysseus flings the manuscript into the fire, kicks out the forger, and only afterwards, when he has calmed down, does he begin to wonder: might he not have destroyed, with his own hands, the work of a first-class genius?! Ridden with remorse, he calls the author back by advertising in the newspapers – alas, in vain. Another explorer, one Hans Zokker, without Odysseus's knowledge auctions off extremely valuable documents which he found among the old libraries of Montenegro, and, absconding to Chile with the cash, there commits himself to fortune. But even so, many extraordinary works do find their way into Odysseus's hands, many rarities, manuscripts generally regarded as lost, or else entirely unknown to the body of world learning. From the historical archives in Madrid, for example, come the first eighteen parchment leaves of a manuscript that, written in the middle of the sixteenth century, foretells – relying on a system of 'trisexual arithmetic' – the dates of birth of eighty famous men of science. The dates contained in that document in fact agree with the dates of birth of such persons as Isaac Newton, Harvey, Darwin, Wallace, and are accurate *to the month*! Chemical analysis and the appraisals of experts confirm the authenticity of this work, but what of that, when the entire mathematical apparatus which the anonymous author made use of has perished? It is known only that his point of departure was the acceptance of a premise totally at odds with common sense, that of the 'three sexes' of the human race. Odysseus finds some solace in the fact that the sale of this manuscript by bid in New York significantly replenishes his expeditionary budget.

After seven years of labour, the archives of the headquarters on Majorca are full of the most remarkable writings. There is, among them, the bulging tome of a certain Miral Essos of Boeotia, who outdid Leonardo da Vinci in inventiveness; he left behind a plan for the creation of a system of logic based on the spinal columns of frogs; long before Leibniz, he arrived at the concept of monads and of harmony pre-established; he applied trivalent logic to certain physical phenomena; and he maintained that living creatures begot those similar to themselves because in their seminal fluid were messages written in microscopic letters, and from the combination of such 'messages' resulted the aspect of the mature individual; all this in the fifteenth century. And there is a formal-logical proof of the impossibility of a theodicy based on rational argument, because the underlying premise of any theodicy must be a logical contradiction. The author of this work, Bauber the Catalonian, was burned alive at the stake after the preliminary severing of his extremities, the pulling out of his tongue, and the filling of his bowels, by a funnel, with molten lead. 'A powerful counter-argument, albeit on a different plane, for the non-logical,' observed the young doctor of philosophy who discovered the manuscript. The study of Sophus Brissengnade, who, proceeding from the axioms of 'two-zero arithmetic', demonstrated the possibility of a non-contradictory construction of a theory of plurality that is purely transfinite, did receive the approbation of the scientific world; but then Brissengnade's work coincided with much of current mathematics.

And so Odysseus sees that recognition goes, as it has always gone, only to the forerunners, to those whose ideas later are discovered anew by others, to – in other words – the geniuses of the second order. But where, then, are the traces of the labour of the first? Despair never enters Odysseus's heart – only the fear that an early death (for already he is on the threshold of old age) will prevent his continuing his search. At last comes the affair of the Florentine manuscript. This roll of parchment from the middle of the eighteenth century, found in a section of the big library in Florence, at first appears to be – filled as it is with cryptic marks – the worthless work of some alchemist-copyist. But certain expressions remind the discoverer, a young mathematics student, of series of functions that in those times no one could possibly have known. The work, when submitted to the experts, yields conflicting opinions. No one understands it in its entirety; some see it as gibberish with rare moments of logical lucidity, others as the product of a diseased mind; the two most eminent mathematicians, to whom Odysseus sends photocopies of the manuscript, also cannot agree in their views. Only one of them, after going to a great deal of trouble, manages to decipher about a third of the scribbles, piecing out the gaps with his own conjectures, and he writes to Odysseus that, yes, it does in fact deal with a concept that is – on the face of it – exceptional, but also useless. 'Because you would have to toss out three-quarters of existing mathematics and set it on its feet again in order to be able to accept the idea. This is simply a proposition of a mathematics *other* than the one we have built up. As to whether it is better – that I cannot tell you. Possibly it is, but to find this out, a hundred of our best people would have to dedicate their lives; they would have to become for this anonymous Florentine what Bolyai, Riemann, Lobachevsky were for Euclid.'

At this point the letter falls from the hands of Homer Odysseus, who with a cry of 'Eureka!' begins to run about the room, which looks out, with its glass windows, upon the blue of the bay. In that moment Odysseus realizes that it is not that humanity has lost forever its geniuses of the first order – the geniuses, rather, have lost sight of humanity, for they have moved away from it. It is not that these geniuses simply do not exist: rather, with each passing year they do not exist *to a greater and greater degree*. The works of unrecognized geniuses of the second category can always be saved. All one need do is dust them off and hand them over to presses or universities. But the works of the first order nothing can preserve, because these stand apart – outside the current of history.

Collective human effort carves out a trench in historical time. A genius is one whose effort is exerted at the very limit of that trench, at its verge, who proposes to his or to the next generation a particular change of course, a different curve of the bed, the angling of the slopes, the deepening of the bottom. But the genius of the first order does not participate thus in the labours of the spirit. He does not stand in the first ranks; nor has he gone a step ahead of the rest; he is simply somewhere else – in thought. If he postulates a different form of mathematics or a different methodology, whether for philosophy or the natural sciences, it will be from a standpoint in no way similar to those existing – no, without a scintilla of similarity! If he is not noticed and given a hearing by the first, by the second generation, it is altogether impossible for him to be noticed thereafter. For, in the meantime, the river of human endeavour and thought has been digging its trench, has gone its way, and therefore between its movement and the solitary invention of the genius the gap widens with each century. Those proposals – unappreciated, ignored – truly could have changed the trend of things in the arts, in the sciences, in the whole history of the world, but because it did not happen thus, humanity let slip by much more than a particular curious individual with his particular intellectual equipment. It let slip by, at the same time, a particular *other* history *of its own*, and for this there is now no remedy. Geniuses of the first order are roads not taken, roads now completely desolate and overgrown; they are those prizes in the lottery of incredible luck which the player did not show up to claim, the purses he did not collect – until their capital evaporated and turned to nothing, the nothing of opportunities missed. The lesser geniuses do not part with the common stream but stay within its current, altering the law of its movement without ever stepping outside the margin of the community – or without stepping outside it totally, all the way. For this they are revered. The others, because they are so great, remain invisible for ever.

Odysseus, profoundly moved by this revelation, immediately sits down and writes a new brochure, whose gist – given above – is no less plain than the idea of the Quest. That Quest, after thirteen years and eight days, has reached its end. It was not a labour made in vain, since the modest inhabitant of Ithaca (Massachusetts), venturing down into the depths of the past with his team of votaries, has found that the single living genius of the first order is Homer M. Odysseus: for the greatest greatness of history can be recognized only by a greatness that is equal to it.

I recommend Kuno Mlatje's book to those who think that if man were not invested with sex there could be no literature or art. As to whether or not the author is kidding, each reader will have to answer that question for himself.

Raymond Seurat

TOI

(Editions Denoël, Paris)

The novel is pulling back into the author; that is, from the position of
the fiction of the *only* reality it retreats to the position of the *origin* of
that fiction. This, at least, is what has been taking place in the van-
guard of European prose. Fiction has grown odious to the writers; it
sickens them; they have lost faith in its necessity and therefore have
become atheists of their own omnipotence. No longer do the writers
believe that when they say, 'Let there be light', genuine radiance
dazzles the reader. (The fact that they speak thus, that they *can* speak
thus, is definitely no fiction.)

The novel that depicted its own creation was merely the first step
of the withdrawal to the rear. Nowadays one does not write works
that show how those works arose, for the protocol account of a concrete creation is also too confining! One writes about what *might* be
written. From the infinite possibilities awhirl in the brain one pulls
out isolated outlines, and the rambling among these fragments, which
never become regular texts, is the present line of defence. Not the last
line, it is to be feared, because among the literati the feeling is growing
that these successive retreats have a limit, that they are leading by way
of retrogressions, one close upon the next, to the place where vigil is
kept by the hidden, mysterious 'absolute embryo' of creativity – of all
creativity – that fecund germ from which could spring the myriad
works that will not be written. But the image of this embryo is an
illusion, because there can be no Genesis without a world made, and
no literary creation without a belles-lettres as its product. 'First causes'
are so inaccessible as to be non-existent: to retreat to them is to fall
into the error of infinite regress; one writes a book about how one
essays to write a book about the wish to write a book, and so on.

Raymond Seurat's *You* is an attempt to break out of the impasse in
a different direction, not by yet another retreat-beating manoeuvre

443

but by a forward charge. To date, authors have always addressed the reader, yet not for the purpose of speaking *about him*: this is precisely what Seurat decided to do. A novel about the reader? Yes, about the reader, but no longer is it a novel. Since to address the addressee has meant to tell him something, to speak, if not *about* something (the anti-novel!), then nevertheless, always, *for* him. And therefore, in this way, to serve him. Seurat thought it high time to put an end to this everlasting servitude; he decided to rebel.

An ambitious idea, no question of that. The work-as-rebellion against the 'singer-listener', 'narrator-reader' relation? Mutiny? A challenge? But in the name of what? At first glance it seems nonsense: if you, writer, do not wish to serve by narrating, then you must be silent, and, silent, you must cease to be a writer. There is no alternative. What kind of squaring of the circle, then, is Raymond Seurat's work?

I suspect that the further detailing of his plan Seurat learned from de Sade. De Sade created first a closed world – the world of his castles, palaces, convents – in order then to divide the throng locked within into villains and victims; annihilating the victims in acts of torture that afforded the executioners pleasure, the villains soon found themselves alone and, in order to proceed further, were obliged in turn to begin that mutual devouring which in the epilogue produces the hermetic solitude of the most vital of the villains – he who devoured, consumed all the rest, who reveals then that he is not the mere *porte-parole* of the author, but the author himself, the selfsame Comte Donatien Alphonse François de Sade imprisoned in the Bastille. He alone remains, for he alone is not a creature of fiction. Seurat turned this account around, as it were. Besides the author, there surely is and must always be a non-fictional someone vis-à-vis the work: the reader. He therefore made this very reader his hero. But of course it is not the reader himself who speaks; any such oration would be a trick only, a ventriloquist's deception. The author addresses the reader – to give him notice.

We are speaking here of literature as spiritual prostitution; prostitution because, to write it, one must serve. One must ingratiate oneself, pay court, display oneself, show off one's stylistic muscles, make confession, confide in the reader, render unto him what one holds most dear, compete for his attention, keep alive his interest – in a word, one has to suck up to, wheedle and wait upon, one has to sell oneself. Disgusting! When the publisher is the pimp, the literary man the whore, and the reader the customer in the bawdyhouse of culture, when this state of affairs reaches one's awareness, it brings on a bad case of moral indigestion. Not daring, however, to quit in so many words, the writers begin to shirk their duties: they serve, but grudgingly; rather than clownishly amuse, they wax unintelligible and tedious; rather than show pretty things, to spite the reader they will treat him to abomination. It is as if an insubordinate cook were to befoul, by design, the dishes going to the master's table; if the master and the mistress don't like it, they don't have to eat it! Or as if a woman of the street, fed up with her trade yet not strong enough to break with it, were to cease accosting men, cease putting on makeup, dressing up, giving fetching smiles. But what of that, when she continues standing at her place on the corner, ready to go off with any customer, sour as she is, sullen, sarcastic? Hers is no true revolt, it is a simulated, half-measure rebellion, full of hypocrisy, self-deception; who knows whether it is not worse than normal, straightforward prostitution, which at least does not put on airs, pretending to high condition, untouchability, precious virtue!

And so? One must give notice; the prospective customer, who opens the volume like the door of a brothel and barges in with such assurance, confident that here his needs will be attended to with servility, this overgrown pig of a philistine, this lowlife – one must punch him in the mouth, call him every name in the book, and – kick him downstairs? No, no, that would be too good for him, too easy, too simple; he would only pick himself up, wipe the spittle from his face, dust off his hat, and take himself to a competitor's establishment. What one has to do is yank him inside and give him a proper hiding. Only then will he remember well his former amour with literature, those endless illicit *Seitensprungen* from book to book. And so '*Crève, canaille!*', as Raymond Seurat says on one of the first pages of *Toi*: die, dog, but do not die too soon, you must conserve your strength, for you will have to go through much; you will pay here for your arrogant promiscuity!

Entertaining as an idea, and perhaps even as a possibility for an original book – which book Raymond Seurat, however, has not written. He did not bridge the distance between the rebellious conception and the artistically validated creation; his book has no structure; it is outstanding primarily, alas, even in these days, by virtue of the phenomenal foulness of its language. Indeed, we do not deny the author his verbal invention; his baroque is, in places, imaginative. ('Yes, loose brainsucking leech of a letch you, yes, turdy rot-toothed trull, yes, you candidate you for a whopping decomposition and oh-may-you-moulder, be treated you shall to rack and ruin in here, for ruined on the rack, and if you think that all coddly cow's-eyes and cajolery, *you'll* see, I'll cook you your wagon good I will. Unpleasant? No doubt. But necessary.') And so we are promised tortures here – *painted* tortures. This already is suspect.

In his 'Literature as Tauromachy', Michel Leiris correctly emphasized the importance of the *resistance* which a literary creation must overcome if it is to acquire the weight of action. Thus Leiris took the risk of compromising himself in his biography. But in heaping curses on the reader's head there is no real risk, for the contractual nature of the invective becomes undeniable. By declaring that he will no longer serve and that *even now* he is not serving, surely Seurat amuses us – and so, in this very refusal to serve, he serves . . . He made the first step but instantly foundered. Can it be that the task he set himself was insoluble? What else could have been done here? Hoodwink the reader with a narrative that would lead him down whatever primrose path one liked? That has been done a hundred, a thousand times. And anyway, it is always easy for the reader to conclude that the dislocated, mistaken and misleading text does not constitute a deliberate manoeuvre, that it is the product not of perfidy but of ineptitude. Any efficacious book-as-invective, to be an authentic insult, to be an affront that carries with it the risk proper to such an act, can be written only with a concrete, single addressee in mind. But then it becomes a letter. By attempting to affront us all, as readers, to tear down that very role – that of the consumer of literature – Seurat has offended no one; he has merely performed a series of linguistic acrobatic tricks, which very quickly cease to be even amusing. When one writes about all, or to all, at once, one writes about no one, to no one. Seurat failed because the only really consistent way for a writer to rise up against the service of literature is silence; any other sort of revolt amounts to making monkey faces. Raymond Seurat will undoubtedly write another book and with it wholly annul this first one – unless he begins going to bookstores and slapping his readers in the face. Were that to happen, I would respect the consequentiality of his action, but only on the personal level, for nothing will salvage the washout that is *Toi*.

Alastair Waynewright

BEING INC.

(*American Library, New York*)

When one takes on a servant, his wages cover – besides the work – the respect a servant owes a master. When one hires a lawyer, beyond professional advice one is purchasing a sense of security. He who buys love, and not merely strives to win it, also expects caresses and affection. The price of an airplane ticket has for some time included the smiles and seemingly genial courtesy of attractive stewardesses. People are inclined to pay for the 'private touch', that feeling of being *intime*, taken care of, liked, which constitutes an important ingredient in the packaging of services rendered in every walk of life.

But life itself does not, after all, consist of personal contacts with servants, lawyers, employees of hotels, agencies, airlines, stores. On the contrary: the contacts and relationships we most desire lie outside the sphere of services bought and sold. One can pay to have computer assistance in selecting a mate, but one cannot pay to have the behaviour one chooses in a wife or husband after the wedding. One can buy a yacht, a palace, an island, if one has the money, but money cannot provide longed-for events – on the order of: displaying one's heroism or intelligence, rescuing a divine creature in mortal danger, winning at the races, or receiving a high decoration. Nor can one purchase good will, spontaneous attraction, the devotion of others. Innumerable stories bear witness to the fact that the desire for precisely such freely given emotions gnaws at mighty rulers and men of wealth; in fairy tales he who is able to buy or use force to obtain anything, having the means for this, abandons his exceptional position so that in disguise – like Harun al Rashid, who went as a beggar – he may find human genuineness, since privilege shuts it out like an impenetrable wall.

So, then, the one area that has not yet been turned into a commodity is the unarranged substance of everyday life, intimate as well as official, private as well as public, with the result that each and every one of us is exposed continually to those small reversals, ridiculings, disappointments, animosities, to the snubs that can never be paid back, to the unforeseen; in short, exposed – within the scope of our personal lot – to a state of affairs that is intolerable, in the highest degree deserving a change; and this change for the better will be initiated by the great new industry of life services. A society in which one can buy – with an advertising campaign – the post of president, or a herd of albino elephants painted with little flowers, or a bevy of beauties, or youth through hormones, such a society ought to be able to put to rights the human condition. The qualm that immediately surfaces – that such purchased forms of life, being unauthentic, will quickly betray their falseness when placed alongside the surrounding authenticity of events – that qualm is dictated by a naïveté totally lacking in imagination. When all children are conceived in the test tube, when then no sexual act has as its consequence, once natural, procreation, there disappears the difference between the normal and the aberrant in sex, seeing as no physical intimacy serves any purpose but that of pleasure. And where every life finds itself under the solicitous eye of powerful service enterprises, there disappears the difference between authentic events and those secretly arranged. The distinction between natural and synthetic in adventures, successes, failures, ceases to exist when one can no longer tell what is taking place by pure accident, and what by accident paid for in advance.

This, more or less, is the idea of A. Waynewright's novel, *Being Inc.* The mode of operation of that corporate entity is to act at a distance: its base cannot be known to anyone; clients communicate with Being Inc. exclusively by correspondence, in an emergency by telephone. Their orders go into a gigantic computer; the execution of these is dependent on the size of the client's account, that is, on the amount of the remittance. Treachery, friendship, love, revenge, one's own good fortune and another's adversity may be obtained also on the instalment plan, through a convenient credit system. The destinies of children are shaped by the parents, but on the day he comes of age each person receives in the mail a price list, a catalogue of services, and in addition the firm's instruction booklet. The booklet is a clearly but substantively written treatise, philosophical and sociotechnological

– not the usual advertising material. Its lucid, elevated language states what in an unelevated way may be summarized as follows.

All people pursue happiness, but not all in the same way. For some, happiness means pre-eminence over others, self-reliance, situations of permanent challenge, risk and the great gamble. For others it is submission, faith in authority, the absence of all threat, peace and quiet, even indolence. Some love to display aggression; some are more comfortable when they can be on the receiving end of it. Many find satisfaction in a state of anxiety and distress, which can be observed in their inventing for themselves, when they have no real worries, imaginary ones. Research shows that ordinarily there are as many active individuals as passive in society. The misfortune of society in the past – asserts the booklet – lay in the fact that society was not able to effect harmony between the natural inclinations of its citizens and their path in life. How often did blind chance decide who would win and who lose, to whom would fall the role of Petronius, and to whom the role of Prometheus. One must seriously doubt the story that Prometheus did not expect the vulture. It is far more likely, according to modern psychology, that it was entirely for the purpose of being pecked in the liver that he stole the fire of heaven. He was a masochist; masochism, like eye colouring, is an inborn trait and nothing to be ashamed of; one should matter-of-factly indulge it and utilize it for the good of society. Formerly – explains the text in scholarly tones – blind fate decided for whom pleasures would be in store, and for whom privation; men lived wretched lives, because he who, fond of beating, is beaten, is every bit as miserable as he who, desirous of a good thrashing, must himself – forced by circumstances – thrash others.

The principles of operation of Being Inc. did not emerge in a vacuum: matrimonial computers have for some time now been using similar rules in matchmaking. Being Inc. guarantees each client the full arrangement of his life, from the attaining of his majority until his death, in keeping with the wishes expressed by him on the form enclosed. The Company, in its work, avails itself of the most up-to-date cybernetic, socioengineering and informational methods. Being Inc. does not immediately carry out the wishes of its clients, for people often do not themselves know their own nature, do not understand what is good for them and what is bad. The Company subjects each new client to a remote-monitor psychotechnological examination; a battery of ultrahigh-speed computers determines the personality profile and all the proclivities of the client. Only after such a diagnosis will the Company accept his order.

One need not be ashamed of the content of the order; it remains for ever a Company secret. Nor need one fear that the order might, in its realization, cause harm to anyone. It is the Company's job to see that this does not happen; let it trouble its electronic head over that. Mr Smith here would like to be a stern judge handing out sentences of death, and so the defendants who come before him will be people deserving nothing less than capital punishment. Mr Jones wishes he could flog his children, deny them every pleasure, and in addition persist in the conviction that he is a just and upright father. Then he shall have cruel and wicked children, the castigation of whom will require half his lifetime. The Company grants all requests; sometimes, however, one must wait on line, as when the desire is to kill a person by one's own hand, since there are a surprising number of such fanciers. In different states the condemned are dispatched differently; in some they are hanged, in others poisoned with hydrogen cyanide, in still others electricity is used. He who has a predilection for hanging finds himself in a state where the legal instrument of execution is the gallows, and before he knows it he has become the temporary hangman. A plan to enable clients to murder with impunity in an open field, on the grass, in the privacy of the home, has not as yet been sanctioned by the law, but the Company is patiently working for the institution of this innovation as well. The Company's skill in arranging events, demonstrated in millions of synthetic careers, will surmount the numerous difficulties that presently bar the way to these murders on order. The condemned man, say, notices that the door of his cell on death row is open; he flees; the Company agents, on the lookout, so influence the path of his flight that he stumbles on the client in circumstances the most suitable for both. He might, for example, attempt to hide in the home of the client while the latter happens to be engaged in loading a hunting rifle. But the catalogue of possibilities which the Company has compiled is inexhaustible.

Being Inc. is an organization the like of which is unknown in history. This is essential. The matrimonial computer united a mere *two* persons and did not concern itself with what would happen to them after the tying of the knot. Being Inc., on the other hand, must orchestrate enormous groupings of events involving thousands of people. The Company cautions the reader that its actual methods of operation are *not* mentioned in the brochure. The examples given are purely fictitious! The strategy of the arranging must be kept in absolute secrecy; the client must never be allowed to find out what is happening to him naturally and what by the aid of the Company computers that watch unseen over his destiny.

Being Inc. possesses an army of employees; these make their appearance as ordinary citizens – as chauffeurs, butchers, physicians, engineers, maids, infants, dogs and canaries. The employees must be anonymous. An employee who at any time betrays his incognito, i.e., who discloses that he is a bona fide member of the team of Being Inc., not only loses his post but is pursued by the Company to his grave. Knowing his habits and tastes, the Company will arrange for him such a life that he will curse the hour in which he perpetrated the foul deed. There is no appealing a punishment for the betrayal of a Company secret – not that the Company intends this statement as a threat. No, the Company includes its *real* ways of dealing with bad employees among its trade secrets.

The reality shown in the novel is different from the picture painted in the promotional pamphlet of Being Inc. The advertisements are silent about the most important thing. Anti-trust legislation in the USA forbids monopolies; consequently Being Inc. is not the only life arranger. There are its great competitors, Hedonica and the True-life Corporation. And it is precisely this circumstance that leads to events unprecedented in history. For when persons who are clients of different companies come into contact with one another, the implementation of the orders of each may encounter unforeseen difficulties. Those difficulties take the form of what is called 'covert parasitizing', which leads to cloak-and-dagger escalation.

Suppose that Mr Smith wishes to shine before Mrs Brown, the wife of a friend, to whom he feels an attraction, and he selects item No. 396b on the list: saving a life in a train wreck. From the wreck both are to escape without injury, but Mrs Brown thanks only to the heroism of Mr Smith. Now, the Company must arrange a railway accident with great precision and in addition set up an entire situation in order that the named parties, as the result of a series of apparent coincidences, ride in the same compartment; monitors located in the walls, the floor, and the backs of the seats in the coach, feeding data to the computer that – concealed in the lavatory – is programming the action, will see to it that the accident takes place exactly according to plan. It must take place in such a way that Smith *cannot not* save the life of Mrs Brown. So that he will not know what he is doing, the side of the overturned coach will be ripped open in the very place where Mrs Brown is sitting, the compartment will fill with suffocating smoke, and Smith, in order to get out, will first have to push the woman through the opening, thereby saving her from death by asphyxiation. The whole operation presents no great difficulty. Several dozen years ago it took an army of computers, and another of specialists, to land a lunar shuttle metres from its goal; nowadays a single computer, following the action with the aid of a concert of monitors, can solve the problem set it with no trouble.

If, however, Hedonica or Truelife has accepted an order from the husband of Mrs Brown, which asks that Smith reveal himself to be a scoundrel and a coward, complications ensue. Through industrial espionage Truelife learns of the railway operation planned by Being; the most economical thing is to hook into someone else's arrangemental plan, and it is precisely in this that 'covert parasitizing' consists. True-life introduces into the moment of the wreck a small deviation factor that will be sufficient to have Smith, when he shoves Mrs Brown out of the hole, give her a black eye, tear her dress, and break both her legs into the bargain.

Should Being Inc., thanks to its counterintelligence, learn of this parasitizing plan, it will take corrective measures, and thus will begin the process of operational escalation. In the overturning coach inevitably it comes to a duel between two computers – the one belonging to Being, in the lavatory, and the one belonging to Truelife, hidden perhaps under the floor of the coach. Behind the potential deliverer of the woman and behind her, the potential victim, stand two Molochs of electronics and organization. During the accident there is unleashed – in fractions of a second – a monstrous battle of computers; it is difficult to conceive what colossal forces will be intervening on one side in order that Smith push heroically and rescuingly, and, on the other, that he push ungallantly and tramplingly. More and more reinforcements are brought in, till what was to have been a small exhibition of manliness in the presence of a woman turns into a cataclysm. Company records note the occurrence, over a period of nine years, of two such disasters, called GASPs (Galloping Arrangementive Spirals). After the last GASP, which cost the parties involved nineteen million dollars for the electrical energy, steam and water power expended in the course of thirty-seven seconds, an agreement was reached on the strength of which an upper limit to arrangementing was set. It may not consume more than 10^{12} joules per client-minute; excluded also for the actualization of services are all forms of atomic energy.

Against this background runs the action proper of the novel. The new president of Being Inc., young Ed Hammer III, is personally to look into the case of the order submitted by Mrs Jessamine Chest the eccentric heiress-millionairess, since her demands, of an outré nature, not to be found in any catalogue, go beyond the reach of all the rungs in the Company's administrative ladder. Jessamine Chest desires life in its full authenticity, purged of all arranging interference; for the fulfilment of this wish she is prepared to pay any price. Ed Hammer, against the advice of his advisers, accepts the assignment; the task, which he puts before his staff – how to arrange the total absence of arranging – proves more difficult than any so far tackled. Research reveals that nothing like an elemental spontaneity in life has existed for a long time. Eliminating the preparations for any particular arrange-plan brings to light the remnants of other, earlier ones; events unscenarioed are not to be found even in the bosom of Being Inc. For, as it turns out, the three rival enterprises have thoroughly and reciprocally arranged one another; that is, they have filled with their own trusted men key positions in the administration and on the board of directors of each competitor. Aware of the danger created by such a discovery, Hammer turns to the chairmen of both the other enterprises, whereupon there is a secret meeting in which specialists having access to the main computers serve as advisers. This confrontation makes it possible, finally, to ascertain the true state of affairs.

In the year 2041, throughout the length and breadth of the USA, not a man can eat a chicken, fall in love, heave a sigh, have a whisky, refuse a beer, nod, wink, spit – without higher electronic planning, which for years in advance has created a pre-established disharmony. Without realizing it, in the course of their competition the three billion-dollar corporations have formed a One in Three Persons, an All-Powerful Disposer of Destiny. The programs of the computers make up a Book of Fate; arranged are political parties, arranged is the weather, and even the coming into the world of Ed Hammer III was the result of specific orders, orders that in turn resulted from other orders. No one any longer can be born or die spontaneously; no one any longer can on his own, by himself, from beginning to end, live anything, because his every thought, his every fear, his every pain, is a short sequence of algebraic calculations run through the computer. Empty now are the concepts of sin, retribution, moral responsibility, good and evil, because the full arrangementation of life excludes non-negotiable values. In the computerized paradise created thanks to the hundred-per-cent utilization of all the human qualities and their incorporation into an infallible system, only one thing was missing – the awareness of the inhabitants that this was precisely how things stood. And therefore the meeting of the three corporate heads has been planned also by the main computer, which – providing them with this information – presents itself now as the Tree of Knowledge lit up with electricity. What will happen next? Should this perfectly arranged existence be abandoned in a new, second flight from Eden, in order to 'start once more from the beginning'? Or should man accept it, renouncing once and for all the burden of responsibility? The book offers no answer. It is, therefore, a metaphysical burlesque, whose fantastic elements nevertheless have some connection with the real world. When we disregard the humoristic humbug and the elephantiasis of the author's imagination, there remains the problem of the manipulation of minds, and particularly of that kind of manipulation which does not lessen the full subjective sense of spontaneity and freedom. The thing will certainly not come about in the form shown in *Being Inc.*, but who can say whether fate will spare our descendants other forms of this phenomenon – forms perhaps less amusing in description but not, it may be, any less oppressive.

Wilhelm Klopper

DIE KULTUR ALS FEHLER

(*Universitas Verlag, Berlin*)

Civilization as Mistake by Privatdozent W. Klopper is a work without doubt remarkable – as an original hypothesis in anthropology. I cannot refrain, however, before I proceed to the discussion, from indulging in a comment as regards the form of the discourse. This book – only a German could have written it! A fondness for classification, for that scrupulous *t*-crossing and *i*-dotting that has begotten innumerable *Handbücher*, makes the German mind resemble a pigeonhole desk. When one beholds the consummate order displayed by the table of contents of this book, one cannot help thinking that if the Lord God had been of German blood our world would perhaps not necessarily have turned out better existentially, but would have for sure embodied a higher notion of discipline and method. The perfection of this orderliness quite overwhelms one, although it may arouse reservations of a substantive nature. I cannot here go into the question of whether that purely formal penchant for muster and array, for symmetry, for front-and-centre and forward-march, might not have exerted a real influence also on certain conceptions that typify German philosophy – its ontology in particular. Hegel loved the Cosmos as a kind of Prussia, for in Prussia there was order! Even the aesthetics-inflamed thinker that was Schopenhauer showed what an expository drill looks like in his treatise 'Über die vierfache Wurzel des Satzes vom zureichenden Grunde'. And Fichte? But I must deny myself the pleasure of digression, which is all the more difficult for me in that I am not a German. To business, to business!

Klopper has provided his two-volume work with a foreword, a preface, and an introduction. (The ideal of form: a triad!) Going into the merits of the matter, he first takes up that understanding of civilization as mistake which he considers to be false. According to that misguided (says the author) view, typical of the Anglo-Saxon school and represented – notably – by Whistle and Sadbottham, any form of behaviour of an organism that neither helps nor hinders the organism's survival is a mistake. For the sole criterion of sensibleness of behaviour is, in evolution, survivability. An animal that behaves in such a fashion that it survives more capably than others is behaving, in the light of this criterion, more sensibly than those that die out. Toothless herbivores are senseless evolutionarily, for hardly are they born before they must perish from hunger. Analogously, herbivores that indeed possess teeth but employ them to chew stones instead of grass are also evolutionarily without sense, for they, too, must disappear. Klopper goes on to quote Whistle's famous example: let us suppose, says the English author, that in some herd of baboons a certain old male, the leader of the herd, by sheer accident acquires the habit of addressing the birds he devours from the left side. He had, say, an injured finger on the right hand, and when he brought the bird to his mouth he found it more comfortable to hold the prey by the left. The young baboons, watching the leader's behaviour, which for them is a model, imitate it, and before long – that is, after a single generation – every baboon in the herd is starting in on his captured bird from the left. From the point of view of adaptation this behaviour is senseless, for baboons can with equal advantage to themselves attack their meal from either side; nevertheless, precisely this pattern of behaviour has established itself in the group. What is it? It is the beginning of a culture (protoculture), being behaviour adaptationally senseless. As is known, this idea of Whistle's was developed not by another anthropologist, but by a philosopher of the English logical-analytical school, J. Sadbottham, whose views our author – before taking exception to them – summarizes in the next chapter ('Das Fehlerhafte der Kulturfehlertheorie von Joshua Sadbottham').

In his major work, Sadbottham declared that human communities produce cultures through mistakes, false steps, failures, blunders, errors and misunderstandings. Intending to do one thing, people in reality do another; desiring to understand the mechanism of a phenomenon through and through, they interpret it for themselves wrongly; seeking truth, they arrive at falsehood; and thus do customs come into being, mores, faith, sanctification, mystery, mana; thus come into being injunctions and interdictions, totems and taboos.

People form a false classification of the surrounding world, and totemism results. They make false generalizations and thus arrive first at the notion of mana, and afterwards at that of the Absolute. They create mistaken representations of their own physical construction, and thus arise the concepts of virtue and sin; had the genitalia been similar to butterflies and insemination to song (the transmitter of hereditary information being specific vibrations in the air), these concepts would have taken a completely different form. People create hypostases, and thus arise concepts of divinities; they make plagiarisms, and thus arise eclectic interpolations of myths – or doctrinal religions. In other words, in behaving any which way, inappropriately, *imperfectly* with respect to adaptation, in misinterpreting the behaviour of other people, and their own bodies, and the objects in Nature, in considering things that happen accidentally to be things that are determined, and things that are determined, to be accidental – that is, in inventing a growing number of fictitious existences, people wall themselves in with the edifice of culture, they alter their model of the world to fit its conclusions and then, after millennia pass, they are surprised that in such a prison they do not feel altogether comfortable. The beginnings are always innocent and even, on the face of it, trivial – take, for example, the baboons who eat birds always from the left side. But when from such odds and ends emerges a system of meanings and values, when the mistakes and misunderstandings accumulate enough so that they can, by their totality, in their entirety, *close* – to use the language of mathematics – then man himself already has become imprisoned in what, though it is the most fortuitous sort of miscellany, appears to him as the highest necessity.

A scholar of much erudition, Sadbottham backs his assertions with a multitude of examples drawn from ethnology; his tabulations, too, as we recall, caused quite a commotion in their day, especially those charts of 'chance versus determinism', on which he juxtaposed all the different cultures' mistaken explanations of natural phenomena. (And in fact, a great number of cultures consider the mortality of man to be the consequence of a particular instance of bad luck: man was, according to them, originally immortal, but he either deprived himself of this attribute by a fall, or else was deprived of it through the intervention of some evil power. Conversely, that which is the work of chance – the physical appearance of man, shaped in evolution – all cultures have provided with the name of inevitability; to this day the leading religions teach that man is in the aspect of his body unaccidental, since fashioned in God's image, after His likeness.)

The criticism to which Herr Dozent Klopper submits the hypothesis of his English colleague is neither original nor the first. As a German, Klopper has divided his criticism into two parts: immanent and positive. In the immanent he only negates Sadbottham's thesis; this section of the work we pass over as being less material, since it repeats the objections already known from the professional literature. In the second half of the criticism, the positive, Wilhelm Klopper finally proceeds to set forth his own counterhypothesis of 'Civilization as Mistake'.

The exposition begins, in our opinion effectively and aptly, with the supplying of an illustrative example. Different birds build their nests out of different materials. What is more, the same species of bird in different localities will not nest-build using exactly the same materials, because it must rely on what it finds in the vicinity. As to which material, in the form of blades of grass, flakes of bark, leaves, little shells, pebbles, the bird is going to find most readily, that depends on chance. And so in some nests you will have more shells and in some, more pebbles; some will be stuck together primarily out of little strips of bark, some, out of pinfeathers and moss. But whatever building material makes its unmistakable contribution towards the shaping of the form of the nest, one cannot with any sense say that nests are the work of pure chance. A nest is an instrument of adaptation, howsoever constructed out of randomly found fragments of this and that; and culture also is an instrument of adaptation. But – and here is the author's new idea – it is an adaptation fundamentally different from that typical of the plant and animal kingdoms.

'*Was ist der Fall?*' asks Klopper. 'What is the situation?' The situation is this: in man, considered as a physical being, there is nothing inevitable. According to the knowledge of modern biology, man could be constructed other than he is; he could live six hundred and not sixty years on the average; he could possess a differently shaped trunk or limbs, have a different reproductive system, a different digestive system; he could, for example, be exclusively herbivorous, he could be oviparous, he could be amphibious, he could be able to breed only once a year, in a period of rut, and so on. Man, it is true, does possess one characteristic that is inevitable, to the extent, at least, that without it he would not be man. He possesses a brain that is able to produce speech and reflection; and, gazing upon his own body and upon his fate, which is circumscribed by that body, man leaves the realm of such reflection greatly discontented. He lives but briefly; on top of this his powerless childhood is of long duration; his time of ablest maturity is a small portion of his entire life; hardly does he achieve his prime when he begins to age, and, unlike all other creatures, he knows to what end ageing will lead him. In the natural habitats of evolution life is lived under incessant threat; one must be on one's toes in order to survive; it is for this reason that the gauges of *pain*, the organs of *suffering* – as signalling devices to stimulate the development of self-preserving activity – have been by evolution very strongly pronounced in all living things. On the other hand, there has been no evolutionary reason, no organism-shaping force, to balance this situation 'fairly', endowing life forms with a corresponding quantity of organs of enjoyment and pleasure.

Everyone will admit, says Klopper, that pangs of hunger, the torments caused by thirst, the agonies of suffocation, are incomparably keener than the satisfaction one experiences in eating, drinking or breathing normally. The sole exception to this general rule of asymmetry between anguish and delight is sex. But this is understandable: were we not bisexual beings, had we a genital system arranged along the lines of, say, the flowers, then it would function apart from any positive sensory experience, for a goad to action would then be totally unnecessary. The fact that sexual pleasure exists and that above it have spread the invisible edifices of the Kingdom of Love (Klopper, when he ceases being dry and factual, immediately turns sentimentally poetic!) derives entirely from the circumstance of bisexuality. Erroneous is the supposition that Homo hermaphroditicus, were such a being to exist, would love himself erotically. Nothing of the sort; he would care for himself strictly within the bounds of the instinct for self-preservation. That which we call narcissism and picture to ourselves as the attraction a hermaphrodite might feel for himself is a secondary projection, the result of a ricochet: such an individual mentally connects with his own body the image of an external, ideal lover. (Here follow about seventy pages of profound cogitation on the question of uni-, bi- and multisexual facultative possibilities for shaping human erotic nature; this large digression, too, we pass over.)

What has culture to do with all this? queries Klopper. Culture is an instrument of adaptation of a new type, for it does not so much *itself* arise from accident as it serves this purpose, to wit, that everything which in our condition is de facto *accidental* stands bathed in the light of a higher, ultimate necessity. And therefore: culture acts through established religion, through custom, law, interdiction and injunction, in order to convert *insufficiencies* into *idealities*, minuses into pluses, shortcomings into acmes of perfection, defects into virtues. Suffering is distressful? Yes, but it ennobles and even redeems. Life is short? Yes, but the life beyond is everlasting. Childhood is toilsome and inane? Yes, but for all that – halcyon, idyllic, positively sacred. Old age is horrid? Yes, but this is the preparation for eternity, and besides, old people are to be respected, by virtue of the fact that they are old. Man is a monster? Yes, but he is not to blame; it was his primogenitors who brought on the evil – or else a demon interfered in the Divine Act. Man does not know what to want, he seeks the meaning of life, he is unhappy? Yes, but this is the consequence of freedom, which is the highest value; that one must pay through the nose for its possession is therefore of no great significance: a man deprived of freedom would be more unhappy than if he were not! Animals, Klopper observes, make no distinction between faeces and carrion: they steer clear of both the one and the other as the evacuations of life. For a consistent materialist the equating of a corpse with excrement ought to be just as valid; but the latter we dispose of furtively, and the former with pomp, loftily, equipping the remains with a number of costly and complicated wrappings. This is required by culture, as a system of appearances that help us reconcile ourselves to the despicable facts. The solemn ceremony of burial serves as a sedative for the natural outrage and revolt roused in us by the infamy of mortality. For it *is* an infamy, that the mind, filled in the course of a lifetime with ever more extensive knowledge, should come to this, that it dissolves into a putrid puddle of corruption.

Thus culture is the mitigator of all the objections, indignations, grievances that man might address to natural evolution, to those physical characteristics haphazardly created, haphazardly fatal, which he – without being asked for his opinion or consent – has inherited from a billion-year process of ad hoc accommodations. To all that vile patrimony, to that ragtag-and-bobtail mob of infirmities and blemishes inserted into the cells themselves, knit into the bones, sewn into the sinews and the muscles – culture, wearing its picturesque toga of appointed public defender, attempts to reconcile us. It uses innumerable weasel words, it resorts to arguments that contradict themselves internally, that appeal now to the feelings, now to the reason, for any and all methods of persuasion are acceptable to culture, so long as it achieves its goal – the transformation of negative quantities into positive, of our wretchedness, our deformity, our frailty, into virtue, perfection and manifest necessity.

With a monumental diapason of style, in measure sublime, in measure professorial, concludes the first part of the treatise of Dozent Klopper, here given fairly laconically by us. The second part explains the vital importance of understanding the true function of culture, so that man may be able properly to receive the portents of the future, a future he has prepared for himself by building a science-and-technology civilization.

Culture is a mistake! announces Klopper, and the brevity of this assertion brings to mind the Schopenhauerian '*Die Welt ist Wille!*' Culture is a mistake, not in the sense or to suggest that it arose by chance; no, it arose by necessity, for – as shown in Part One – it serves adaptation. But it serves adaptation only *mentally*: surely it does not, with its dogmas of faith and its precepts, transform man into an *actually* immortal being; it does not tack on to accidental man, *homini fortuito*, a real Creator-Deity; it does not *really* annul a single atom of an individual's sufferings, griefs, agonies (here, too, Klopper is true to Schopenhauer!) – what it does, it does entirely on the plane of the spirit, on the level of interpretation, making meaning out of that which in immanence has no meaning; it divides sin from virtue, grace from damnation, humiliation from exaltation.

But now technological civilization, in steps imperceptible at first, creeping along with its scrap iron of primitive machines, has worked its way underneath culture. The building is shaken, the walls of the crystal rectifier crack: for technological civilization promises to *correct* man, both his body and his brain, and quite literally to *optimize* his soul. This tremendous and unexpectedly welling force (of the information, stored up for centuries, which in the twentieth century exploded) heralds a chance for long life, with the limit, perhaps, in immortality; a chance for swift maturation and no senescence; a chance for a legion of physical pleasures and a reduction to zero of torments, of tribulations both 'natural' (senility) and 'accidental' (disease); it heralds the chance for *freedom* where previously hazard was wed to inevitability (freedom meaning the power to choose the qualities of human nature; meaning the possibility of amplifying talent, knowledge, intelligence; meaning the opportunity to give to human limbs, the face, the body, the senses, whatever forms and functions one desires, even those that are well-nigh everlasting, etc.).

What, then, ought to be done in the face of these promises, promises verified by fulfilments already brought about? Why, throw oneself into a triumphal dance! Culture, that cane of the lame, crutch of the crippled, wheelchair for the paralytic, that system of patches placed over the shame of our body, over the deformity of our toilsome condition, culture, that helpmate that has seen much service and outserved, ought to be pronounced an anachronism and nothing but. For are artificial limbs necessary to those who can grow new? Must a blind man clutch the white cane to his breast, when we return him his sight? Is he to request benightedness anew who has had the scales lifted from his eyes? Should not one, rather, lay to rest that useless lumber in the museum of the past, and set out with a springing step towards the awaiting, difficult yet magnificent tasks and goals ahead? So long as the nature of our bodies, of their sluggish growth and all-too-swift decay, was an impervious wall, an implacable barrier, the limit of existence – for that long did culture facilitate, unto the thousandth generation, our adaptation to this wretched *status quo*. It reconciled us to it; more, as the author shows, it actually converted the flaws into merits, the drawbacks into advantages. It is as if someone condemned to a broken-down, ugly and worthless vehicle were gradually to conceive an affection for its failings, to find in its ungainliness evidence of a higher ideal, and in its endless defects a Law of Nature, of Creation; he perceives the hand of the Lord God Himself in the sputtering carburettor and the chattering gears. So long as there is not another vehicle in sight, this is perfectly proper, very suitable, the only right and even sensible policy, one should think. But now, when a new vehicle gleams on the horizon? To cling to the broken spokes, bewail the ugliness with which it will be necessary soon to part, cry out 'Help, save me!' from the streamlined beauty of the new model? Understandable psychologically, indeed yes. For too long – millennia! – has the process been going on of man's bending himself to his own evolutionarily piecemeal nature, that colossal straining – from century to century – to love the given condition in all its misery, squalor, unattractiveness, in its destitutions and physiological nooks and crannies.

So much has man, in all his successive cultural formations, slaved away at this, so much has he striven to sway himself, to have himself believe in the absolute necessity, supremity, uniqueness, and most of all the inalterability of his fate, that now, at the sight of his deliverance, he recoils, quakes, hides his eyes, utters cries of terror, turns away from the technological Saviour, wishing to flee somewhere, anywhere, even to the forest on all fours, wishing he could take that flower of knowledge, that wonder of science, and smash it with his own two hands, trample it underfoot, if only not to surrender his ancient values to the junk heap, values he nourished with his own blood, nurtured waking and sleeping, till he forced upon himself . . . love for them! But such absurd conduct, this shock, this panic, is above all, from any rational standpoint, stupidity.

Yes, culture is a mistake! But only in the sense that it is a mistake to shut the eyes to the light, to push away medicine in illness, to call for incense and magic spells when an enlightened doctor is standing by the bed. This mistake did not exist at all until the moment when our knowledge, growing, reached the required level; this mistake – it is the resistance, the balky, mulish, pigheaded opposition, the obstinate aversion, it is the tremor of dread our modern 'thinkers' like to call an intellectual assessment of the present changes in the world. Culture, that system of prostheses, must be discarded, so that we may entrust ourselves to the knowledge that will remake us, endow us with perfection; nor will the perfection be fictive, a thing we are talked into or sold, a thing educed from the sophistry of tortuous, self-contradictory establishings and dogmas. It will be purely material, factual, a perfectly objective perfection: existence *itself* will be perfect – not merely its exposition, not merely its interpretation! Culture, defender of Evolution's Casual Imbecilities, shifty pettifogger of a lost cause, shyster mouthpiece of primitivism and somatic slapdashery, must remove itself, since man's case is entering other, higher courts, since the wall of inviolable necessity, inviolable only hitherto, now crumbles. Technological development means the ruin of culture? It provides freedom where hitherto reigned the constraint of biology? But of course it does! And instead of shedding tears over the loss of our captivity, we should hasten our step to leave its dark house. And therefore (the finale begins, in cadenced conclusions): everything that has been said about the threat to time-honoured culture by the new technology is true. But one need not be concerned about this threat; one need not patch together a culture coming apart at the seams, or fasten down its dogmas with clamps, or hold out valiantly against the invasion of our bodies and our lives by superior knowledge. Culture, still a value today, will tomorrow become another value: namely, anachronistic. For culture was the great hatchery, the womb, the incubator in which discoveries bred and gave agonizing birth to science. Indeed, just as the developing embryo consumes the inert, passive substance of the egg white, so does the developing technology consume, digest, and turn into its own stuff – culture. Such is the way of embryos and eggs.

We live in an era of transition, says Klopper, and never is it so unutterably difficult to make out the road travelled and the road that extends into the future as in periods of transition, for they are times of conceptual confusion. However, the process is inexorably under way. One must not in any case think that the transition from the realm of biological captivity to the realm of self-creative freedom can be an act of a single moment. Man will not be able to perfect himself once and for all, and the process of self-alteration will go on through centuries.

'I make bold,' says Klopper, 'to assure the reader that the dilemma over which the traditional thought of the humanist, flustered by the scientific revolution, lacerates itself, is the yearning of the dog for its removed collar. The dilemma boils down to the faith that man is a skein of contradictions which cannot be got rid of, not even were the ridding technologically possible. In other words, it is forbidden us to change the shape of the body, weaken the lust for aggression, strengthen the intellect, balance the emotions, rearrange sex, liberate man from old age, from the labours of procreation, and this is forbidden for the reason that it has never been done, and what has never been done must surely be, by that fact, most evil. The humanist is not allowed to conceive – à la science – of the present human mind and body as the resultant vector of a long series of random draws, intramillennial convulsions in the evolutionary process, a process that was hurled in all directions by geological upheavals, great glaciations, the explosions of stars, the changes of the magnetic poles, and countless other accidents. What the evolution of the lower animals first, and of the anthropoids later, deposited in lottery style, what then was swept into a single pile by selection, and what day by day was fixed in the genes as in dice thrown at the gaming table, we are to hold untouchable, sacrosanct, inviolable for all time, world without end – only without knowing why it has to be this way and not another. It is as if culture takes umbrage at our diagnosis of its work, noble at least in intent, and our exposure of that greatest, most difficult, most fantastic, and falsest of all the falsehoods Homo sapiens ever fashioned for himself – ever latched on to – he who was thrust suddenly into the open air of intelligent existence from out that murky gambling den where the cheating at genes still goes on, where the evolutionary process sets down its cardsharper's tricks in the chromosomes. That the game is a foul fraud, never guided by an higher value or goal, is shown by the fact that in that cave the thing is only to survive *today* – not giving one hoot in heaven or hell about what will become of the one who survives so compromisingly, so opportunistically, therefore dishonourably, *tomorrow*. But because everything is proceeding exactly in reverse of what our humanist, shaking in his boots, imagines to himself, that dim-wit, that boob – he has no right to call himself a rationalist – culture will be cleared away, cleaned up, parcelled out, pulled down and drained, in step with the changes to which man shall submit. Where the hook and crook of genes, where adaptational opportunism decides existence, there is no mystery, there is only the *Katzenjammer* of the swindled, the awful hangover from the monkey ancestor, the climb skyward up that imaginary ladder from which you always end up falling, biology dragging you down by the seat of your pants, whether you tack on to yourself bird feathers, haloes or immaculate conceptions, or grit your teeth with homemade heroism. And so nothing vital-inevitable will be destroyed, but there will disappear, withering away bit by bit, the scaffolding of superstition, justification, equivocation, the pulling of the wool over the eyes – in a word, that whole sophistry to which the miserable human race has for ages resorted in order to make palatable its odious condition. In the next century, from out of the dust of the information explosion will emerge Homo optimisans se ipse, Autocreator, Self-Maker, who will laugh at our Cassandras (assuming he has with what to laugh). One ought to applaud such an opportunity, acclaim it an incredibly fortunate turn of cosmic-planetary events, and not tremble in the face of the power that will bring our species down from the scaffold and sunder the chains each of us drags with him, as he waits for the potential of his bodily forces to be finally exhausted, when he will know the self-strangling of the death agony. And even should the whole world still continue to acquiesce in that state with which evolution has branded us far worse than we brand the worst criminals, I personally shall never consent to it and yea even from my dying bed rasp out: Down with Evolution, Vivat Autocreation!'

It is instructive, this voluminous discourse, the quotation from which we have used to crown our discussion. Instructive, because it shows there is simply no thing appearing to some as evil incarnate and misfortune itself that others will not at the very same time consider a positive godsend and raise to the pinnacle of perfection. This reviewer is of the opinion that technoevolution cannot be declared the existential panacea for humanity, if only because the criteria of optimization are too intricately relativistic for them to be regarded as a universal patter (that is, as a code of salvational procedure that is unerring, couched in the language of empiricism). In any case, we recommend to the reader *Civilization as Mistake*, since it is, typical of the time, yet another attempt to limn the future – still dark, despite the combined efforts of the futurologists and such thinkers as Klopper.

Cezar Kouska

DE IMPOSSIBILITATE VITAE
and
DE IMPOSSIBILITATE PROGNOSCENDI

(*2 Volumes: Statní Nakladatelství N. Lit., Prague*)

The author is Cezar Kouska on the cover, but signs the Introduction inside the book as Benedykt Kouska. A misprint, an oversight in the proofreading, or an inconceivably devious device? Personally I prefer the name Benedykt, therefore I will stick with that. So, then, it is to Professor B. Kouska that I owe some of the most delightful hours of my life, hours spent in the perusal of his work. The views it expounds are unquestionably at odds with scientific orthodoxy; we are not, however, dealing here with pure insanity; the thing lies halfway in between, in that transitional zone where there is neither day nor night, and the mind, loosening the bonds of logic, yet does not tear them so asunder as to fall into gibberish.

For Professor Kouska has written a work that demonstrates that the following relationship of mutual exclusion obtains: either the theory of probability, on which stands natural history, is false to its very foundations, or the world of living things, with man at its head, does not exist. After which, in the second volume, the Professor argues that if prognostication, or futurology, is ever to become a reality and not an empty illusion, not a conscious or unconscious deception, then that discipline cannot avail itself of the calculus of probability, but demands the implementation of an entirely different reckoning, namely – to quote Kouska – 'a theory, based on antipodal axioms, of the distribution of ensembles in actual fact unparalleled in the space–time continuum of higher-order events' (the quote also serves to show that the reading of the work – in the theoretical sections – does present certain difficulties).

Benedykt Kouska begins by revealing that the theory of empirical probability is flawed in the middle. We employ the notion of probability when we do not know a thing with certainty. But our uncertainty is either purely subjective (we do not know what will take place, but someone else may know) or objective (no one knows, and no one can know). Subjective probability is a compass for an informational disability; not knowing which horse will come in first and guessing by the number of horses (if there are four, each has one chance in four of winning the race), I act like one who is sightless in a room full of furniture. Probability is, so to speak, a cane for a blind man; he uses it to feel his way. If he could see, he would not need the cane, and if I knew which horse was the fastest, I would not need probability theory. As is known, the question of the objectivity or the subjectivity of probability has divided the world of science into two camps. Some maintain that there exist two types of probability, as above, others, that only the subjective exists, because regardless of what is supposed to take place, *we* cannot have full knowledge of it. Therefore, some lay the uncertainty of future events at the door of our knowledge of them, whereas others place it within the realm of the events themselves.

That which takes place, if it really and truly takes place, takes place indeed: such is Professor Kouska's main contention. Probability comes in only where a thing has not yet taken place. So saith science. But everyone is aware that two duellists firing two bullets which flatten each other in mid-air, or that breaking one's tooth, while eating a fish, on a ring which by accident one had dropped overboard at sea six years before and which was swallowed by that exact same fish, or – for that matter – that the playing, in three-four time, of Tchaikovsky's Sonatina in B Minor in a kitchen-utensil store by bursting shrapnel during a siege, because the shrapnel's metal balls strike the large and smaller pots and pans exactly as the composition requires – that any of this, were it to happen, would constitute a happening most improbable. Science says in this regard that these are facts occurring with a very negligible frequency in the sets of occurrences to which the facts belong, that is, in the set of all duels, in the set of eating fish and finding lost objects in them, and in the set of bombardments of stores selling housewares.

But science, says Professor Kouska, is selling us a line, because all its twaddle about sets is a complete fiction. The theory of probability can usually tell us how long we must wait for a given event, for an event of a specified and unusually low probability, or, in other words, how many times it will be necessary to repeat a duel, lose a ring, or fire at pots and pans before the afore-mentioned remarkable things come about. This is rubbish, because in order to make a highly improbable thing come about it is not at all necessary that the set of events to which it belongs represent a continuous series. If I throw ten coins at once, knowing that the chance of ten heads coming up at the same time, or ten tails, works out to barely 1 : 796, I certainly do not need to make upward of 796 throws in order that the probability of ten heads turning up, or ten tails, become equal to one. For I can always say that my throws are a continuation of an experiment comprising all the past throws of ten coins at once. Of such throws there must have been, in the course of the last five thousand years of Earth's history, an inordinate number; therefore, I really ought to expect that straightaway all my coins are going to land heads up, or tails up. Meanwhile, says Professor Kouska, just you try and base your expectations on such reasoning! From the scientific point of view it is entirely correct, for the fact of whether one throws the coins nonstop or puts them aside for a moment to eat *knedlach* in the intermission or go for a quick one at the corner bar, or whether – for that matter – it is not the same person who does the throwing, but a different one each time, and not all in one day but each week or each year, has not the slightest effect or bearing on the distribution of the probability; thus the fact that ten coins were thrown by the Phoenicians sitting on their sheepskins, and by the Greeks after they burned Troy, and by the Roman pimps in the time of the Caesars, and by the Gauls, and by the Teutons, and by the Ostrogoths, and the Tartars, and the Turks driving their captives to Stamboul, and the rug merchants in Galata, and those merchants who trafficked in children from the Children's Crusade, and Richard the Lion-Hearted, and Robespierre, as well as a few dozen tens of thousands of other gamblers, also is wholly immaterial, and consequently, in throwing the coins, we can consider that the set is extremely large, and that our chances of throwing ten heads or ten tails at once are positively enormous! Just you try and throw, says Professor Kouska, gripping some learned physicist or other probability theorist by the elbow so he can't escape, for such as they do not like having the falsity of their method pointed out to them. Just you try, you'll see that nothing comes of it.

Next, Professor Kouska undertakes an extensive thought experiment that relates not to some hypothetical phenomenon or other, but to a part of his own biography. We repeat here, in condensed form, some of the more interesting fragments of this analysis.

A certain army doctor, during the First World War, ejected a nurse from the operating room, for he was in the midst of surgery when she entered by mistake. Had the nurse been better acquainted with the hospital, she would not have mistaken the door to the operating room for the door to the first-aid station, and had she not entered the operating room, the surgeon would not have ejected her; had he not ejected her, his superior, the regiment doctor, would not have brought to his attention his unseemly behaviour regarding the lady (for she was a volunteer nurse, a society miss), and had the superior not brought this to his attention, the young surgeon would not have considered it his duty to go and apologize to the nurse, would not have taken her to the café, fallen in love with her, and married her, whereby Professor Benedykt Kouska would not have come into the world as the child of this same married couple.

From this it would appear to follow that the probability of the coming into the world of Professor Benedykt Kouska (as a newborn, not as the head of the Analytical Philosophy Department) was set by the probability of the nurse's confusing or not confusing the doors in the given year, month, day and hour. But it is not that way at all. The young surgeon Kouska did not have, on that day, any operations scheduled; however, his colleague Doctor Popichal, who wished to carry the laundry from the cleaners to his aunt, entered the aunt's house, where because of a blown fuse the light over the stairwell was not working, because of which he fell off the third step and twisted his ankle; and because of this, Kouska had to take his place in surgery. Had the fuse not blown, Popichal would not have sprained his ankle, Popichal would have been the one operating and not Kouska, and, being an individual known for his gallantry, he would not have used strong language to remove the nurse who entered the operating room by mistake, and, not having insulted her, he would not have seen the need to arrange a tête-à-tête with her; but tête-à-tête or no tête-à-tête, it is absolutely certain in any case that from the possible union of Popichal and the nurse the result would have been not Benedykt

Kouska but someone altogether different, with whose chances of coming into the world this study does not concern itself.

Professional statisticians, aware of the complicated state of the things of this world, usually wriggle out of having to deal with the probability of such events as someone's coming into the world. They say, to be rid of you, that what we have here is the coincidence of a great number of divaricate-source causal chains and that consequently the point in space–time in which a given egg merges with a given sperm is indeed determined in principle, *in abstracto*; however, *in concreto* one would never be able to accumulate knowledge of sufficient power, that is to say all-embracing, for the practical formulation of any prognosis (with what probability there will be born an individual X of traits Y, or in other words *how long* people must reproduce before it is certain that a certain individual, of traits Y, will with absolute certainty come into the world) to become feasible. But the impossibility is technical only, not fundamental; it rests in the difficulties of collecting information, and not in the absence in the world (to hear them talk) of such information to collect. This lie of statistical science Professor Benedykt Kouska intends to nail and expose.

As we know, the question of Professor Kouska's being able to be born does not reduce itself merely to the alternative of 'right door, wrong door'. Not with regard to one coincidence must one reckon the chances of his birth, but with regard to many: the coincidence that the nurse was sent to that hospital and not another; the coincidence that her smile in the shadow cast by her cornet resembled, from a distance, the smile of Mona Lisa; the coincidence, too, that the Archduke Ferdinand was shot in Sarajevo, for had he not been shot, war would not have broken out, and had war not broken out, the young lady would not have become a nurse; moreover, since she came from Olomouc and the surgeon from Moravská Ostrava, they most likely would never have met, neither in a hospital nor anywhere else. One therefore has to take into account the general theory of the ballistics of shooting at archdukes, and since the hitting of the Archduke was conditioned by the motion of his automobile, the theory of the kinematics of automobile models of the year 1914 should also be considered, as well as the psychology of assassins, because not everyone in the place of that Serb would have shot at the Archduke, and even if someone had, he would not have hit, not if his hands were shaking with excitement; the fact, therefore, that the Serb had a steady hand and eye and no tremors also has its place in the probability distribution of the birth of Professor Kouska. Nor ought one to ignore the overall political situation of Europe in the summer of 1914.

But the marriage in any case did not come about in that year, or in 1915, when the young couple became acquainted in good earnest, for the surgeon was detailed to the fortress of Przemyśl. From there he was to travel later to Lwów, where lived the young maiden Marika, whom his parents had chosen to be his wife out of financial considerations. However, as a result of Samsonov's offensive and the movements of the southern flank of the Russian forces, Przemyśl was besieged, and before long, instead of repairing to his betrothed in Lwów, the surgeon proceeded into Russian captivity when the fortress fell. Now, he remembered the nurse better than he did his fiancée, because the nurse not only was fair but also sang the song 'Sleep, Love, in Thy Bed of Flowers' much more sweetly than did Marika, who had an unremoved polyp on her vocal cords and from this a constant hoarseness. Marika was, in fact, to have undergone an operation to remove the polyp in 1914, but the otorhinolaryngologist who was supposed to remove the polyp, having lost a great deal of money in a Lwów casino and being unable to pay off his debt of honour (he was an officer), instead of shooting himself in the head, robbed the regimental till and fled to Italy; this incident caused Marika to conceive a great dislike for otorhinolaryngologists, and before she could decide on another she became betrothed; as a betrothed she was obliged to sing 'Sleep, Love, in Thy Bed of Flowers', and her singing, or, rather, the memory of that hoarse and wheezy voice, in contrast – detrimental to the betrothed – with the pure timbre of the Prague nurse, was responsible for the latter's gaining ascendancy, in the mind of doctor–prisoner Kouska, over the image of his fiancée. So that, returning to Prague in the year 1919, he did not even think to look up his former fiancée but immediately went to the house in which the nurse was living as a marriageable miss.

The nurse, however, had four different suitors; all four sought her hand in marriage, whereas between her and Kouska there was nothing concrete except for the postcards he had sent her from captivity, and

473

the postcards in themselves, smudged with the stamps of the military censor, could not have been expected to kindle in her heart any lasting feeling. But her first serious suitor was a certain Hamuras, a pilot who did not fly because he always got a hernia when he moved the aeroplane's rudder bar with his feet, and this because the rudder bars in the aeroplanes of those days were hard to move – it was, after all, a very primitive era in aviation. Now, Hamuras had been operated on once, but without success, for the hernia recurred, recurred because the doctor performing the operation had made a mistake in the catgut sutures; and the nurse was ashamed to wed the sort of flier who, instead of flying, spent his time either sitting in the reception room of the hospital or searching the newspaper ads for places to obtain a genuine prewar truss, since Hamuras figured that such a truss would enable him to fly after all; on account of the war, however, a good truss was unobtainable.

One should note that at this juncture Professor Kouska's 'to be or not to be' ties in with the history of aviation in general, and with the aeroplane models used by the Austro-Hungarian Army in particular. Specifically, the birth of Professor Kouska was positively influenced by the fact that in 1911 the Austro-Hungarian government acquired a franchise to build monoplanes whose rudder bars were difficult to operate, planes that were to be manufactured by a plant in Wiener-Neustadt, and this in fact took place. Now, in the course of the bidding, the French firm Antoinette competed with this plant and its franchise (coming from an American firm, Farman), and the French firm had a good chance, because Major General Prchl, of the Imperial Crown Commissariat, would have turned the scales in favour of the French model, because he had a French mistress, the governess of his children, and on account of this secretly loved all things French; that, of course, would have altered the distribution of chance, since the French machine was a biplane with sweptback ailerons and a rudder blade that had an easily moveable control bar, so the bar would not have caused Hamuras his problem, owing to which the nurse might have married him after all. Granted, the biplane had a hard-to-work *exhaust hammer*, and Hamuras had rather delicate shoulders; he even suffered from what is called *Schreibkrampf*, which gave him difficulty signing his name (his full name ran Adolf Alfred von Messen-

Weydeneck zu Oryola und Münnesacks, Baron Hamuras). So, then, even without the hernia. Hamuras *could* have, by reason of his weak arms, lost his appeal in the eyes of the nurse.

But there popped up in the governess's path a certain two-bit tenor from an operetta, with remarkable speed he gave her a baby, Lieutenant General Prchl drove her from his door, lost his affection for all things French, and the army stayed with the Farman franchise held by the company from Wiener-Neustadt. The tenor the governess met at the Ring when she went there with General Prchl's oldest daughters –the youngest had the whooping cough, so they were trying to keep the healthy children away from the sick one – if it had not been for that whooping cough brought in by that acquaintance of the Prchls' cook, a man who carried coffee to a smoking room and was wont to drop in on the Prchls in the morning, that is, drop in on their cook, there would have been no illness, no taking of the children to the Ring, no meeting the tenor, no infidelity; and thereby Antoinette would have won out in the bidding after all. But Hamuras was jilted, married the daughter of a purveyor by appointment to His Majesty the King, and had three children by her, one of which he had without the hernia.

There was nothing wrong with the nurse's second suitor, Captain Miśnia, but he went to the Italian front and came down with rheumatism (this was in the winter, in the Alps). As for the cause of his demise, accounts differ; the Captain was taking a steam bath, a .22-calibre shell hit the building, the Captain went flying out naked straight into the snow, the snow took care of his rheumatism, they say, but he got pneumonia. However, had Professor Fleming discovered his penicillin not in 1941 but, say, in 1910, then Miśnia would have been pulled out of the pneumonia and returned to Prague as a convalescent, and the chances of Professor Kouska's coming into the world would have been, by that, greatly diminished. And so the calendar of discoveries in the field of antibacterial drugs played a large role in the rise of B. Kouska.

The third suitor was a respectable wholesale dealer, but the young lady did not care for him. The fourth was about to marry her for certain, but it did not work out on account of a beer. This last beau had enormous debts and hoped to pay them off out of the dowry; he also had an unusually chequered past. The family went, along with the young lady and her suitor, to a Red Cross raffle, but Hungarian veal birds were served for lunch, and the father of the young lady developed a terrific thirst, so he left the pavilion where they all were listening to the military band and had a mug of beer on draught, in the course of which he ran into an old schoolmate who was just then leaving the raffle grounds, and had it not been for the beer, they would certainly not have come together; this schoolmate knew, through his sister-in-law, the entire past of the young lady's suitor and was not averse to telling her father everything and in full detail. It appears he also embellished a little here and there; in any event, the father returned most agitated, and the engagement, having been all but made official, fell irretrievably to pieces. Yet had the father not eaten Hungarian veal birds, he would not have felt a thirst, would not have stepped out for a beer, would not have met his old schoolmate, would not have learned of the debts of the suitor; the engagement would have gone through, and, seeing it would have been an engagement in wartime, the wedding also would have followed in short order. An excessive amount of paprika in the veal birds on 19 May 1916, thus saved the life of Professor B. Kouska.

As for Kouska the surgeon, he returned from captivity in the rank of battalion doctor and proceeded to enter the lists of courtship. Evil tongues informed him of the suitors, and particularly of the late Captain Miśnia, R.I.P., who presumably had achieved a more-than-passing acquaintance with the young lady, though at the same time she had been answering the postcards from the prisoner of war. Being by nature fairly impetuous, the surgeon Kouska was prepared to break off the engagement already made, particularly since he had received several letters which the young lady had written to Miśnia (God knows how they ended up in the hands of a malicious person in Prague), along with an anonymous letter explaining how he, Kouska, had been serving the young lady as a fifth wheel, that is, kept in reserve as a stand-by. The breaking off of the engagement did not come about, due to a conversation the surgeon had with his grandfather, who had really been a father to him from childhood because the surgeon's own father, a profligate and ne'er-do-well, had not raised him at all. The grandfather was an old man of unusually progressive views, and he considered that a young girl's head was easily turned, especially when the turner wore a uniform and pleaded the soldier's death that could befall him at any moment.

Kouska thus married the young lady. If, however, he had had a grandfather of other persuasions, or if the old liberal had passed away before his eightieth year, the marriage most certainly would not have taken place. The grandfather, it is true, led an exceedingly healthy mode of life and rigorously took the water cure prescribed by Father Kneipp; but to what extent the ice-cold shower each morning, lengthening the grandfather's life, increased the chances of Professor B. Kouska's coming into the world, it is impossible to determine. The father of surgeon Kouska, a disciple of misogyny, would definitely not have interceded on behalf of the maligned maiden; but he had no influence over his son from the time when, having made the acquaintance of Mr Serge Mdivani, he became the latter's secretary, went with him to Monte Carlo, and came back believing in a system of breaking the bank in roulette shown him by a certain widow-countess; thanks to this system he lost his entire fortune, was placed under custody, and had to give up his son to the care of his own father. Yet had the surgeon's father not succumbed to the demon of gambling, *his* father would then not have disowned him, and – again – the coming to pass of Professor Kouska would not have come to pass.

The factor that tipped the scales in favour of the Professor's birth was Mr Serge *vel* Sergius Mdivani. Sick of his estate in Bosnia, and of his wife and mother-in-law, he engaged Kouska (the surgeon's father) as his secretary and took off with him for the waters, because Kouska the father knew languages and was a man of the world, whereas Mdivani, notwithstanding his first name, knew no language besides Croatian. But had Mr Mdivani in his youth been better looked after by *his* father, then instead of chasing after the chambermaids he would have studied his languages, would not have needed a translator, would not have taken the father of Kouska to the waters, the latter would not have returned from Monte Carlo as a gambler, and thereupon would not have been cursed and cast out by his father, who, not taking the surgeon under his wing as a child, would not have instilled liberal principles in him, the surgeon would have broken off with the young lady, and – once more – Professor Benedykt Kouska would not have made his appearance in this world. Now, Mr Mdivani's father was not disposed to keep an eye on the progress of his son's education when the latter was supposed to be studying languages, because this son, by his looks, reminded him of a certain dignitary of the church concerning whom Mr Mdivani Sr. harboured the suspicion that he, the dignitary, was the true father of little Sergius. Feeling, therefore, a subconscious dislike for little Sergius, he neglected him; as a result of this neglect Sergius did not learn, as he should have, his languages.

The question of the identity of the boy's father was in fact complicated, because even the mother of little Sergius was not certain whether he was the son of her husband or of the parish priest, and she did not know for sure whose son he was because she believed in stares that affected the unborn. She believed in stares that affected the unborn because her authority in all things was her Gypsy grandmother. We are now speaking, it should be noted, of the relation between the grandmother of the mother of little Sergius Mdivani and the chances of the birth of Professor Benedykt Kouska. Mdivani was born in the year 1861, his mother in 1832, and the Gypsy grandmother in 1798. So, then, matters that transpired in Bosnia and Herzegovina towards the close of the eighteenth century – in other words, 130 years before the birth of Professor Kouska – exerted a very real influence on the probability distribution of his coming into the world. But neither did the Gypsy grandmother appear in a void. She did not wish to marry an Orthodox Croat, particularly since at that time all Yugoslavia was under the Turkish Yoke, and marriage to a giaour would bode no good for her. But the Gypsy maid had an uncle much older than she; he had fought under Napoleon; it was said that he had taken part in the retreat of the Grand Army from the environs of Moscow. In any case, from his soldiering under the Emperor of the French he returned home with the conviction that interdenominational differences were of no great matter, for he had had a close look at the differences of war, therefore he encouraged his niece to marry the Croat, for, though a giaour, it was a good and comely youth. In marrying the Croat, the grandmother on Mr Mdivani's mother's side thus increased the chances of Professor Kouska's birth. As for the uncle, he would not have fought under Napoleon had he not been living during the Italian campaign in the region of the Apennines, whither he was sent by his master, a sheep farmer, with a consignment of sheepskin coats. He was waylaid by a mounted patrol of the Imperial Guard and given the choice of enlisting or becoming a camp follower; he preferred to bear arms. Now, if the Gypsy uncle's master had not raised sheep, or if, raising them, he had not made sheepskin coats, for which there was a demand in Italy, and if he had not sent this uncle to Italy with the coats, then the mounted patrol would not have seized the Gypsy uncle, whereupon, not fighting his way across Europe, this uncle, his conservative opinions intact, would not have encouraged his niece to marry the Croat. And therewith the mother of little Sergius, having no Gypsy grandmother and consequently not believing in stares that affected the unborn, would not have thought that merely from watching the parish priest spread his arms as he sang in a bass at the altar one could bear a son – the spit and image of the priest; and so, her conscience completely clear, she would not have feared her husband, she would have defended herself against the charges of infidelity, the husband, no longer seeing evil in the looks of little Sergius, would have minded the boy's education, Sergius would have learned his languages, would not have needed anyone as a translator, whereat the father of Kouska the surgeon would not have gone off with him to the waters, would not have become a gambler and a wastrel, would (being a misogynist) have urged his surgeon son to throw over the young lady for her dalliance with the late Captain Miśnia, R.I.P., as a result of which there would have been, again, no Professor B. Kouska in the world.

But now observe. So far we have examined the probability spectrum of the birth of Professor Kouska on the assumption that both his facultative parents existed, and we reduced the probability of that birth only by introducing very small, perfectly credible changes in the behaviour of the father or mother of Professor Kouska, changes brought about by the actions of third parties (General Samsonov, the Gypsy grandmother, the mother of Mdivani, Baron Hamuras, the French governess of Major General Prchl, Emperor Francis Joseph I, the Archduke Ferdinand, the Wright brothers, the surgeon for the Baron's hernia, Marika's otorhinolaryngologist, etc.). But surely the very same type of analysis can be applied to the chances of the coming into the world of the young lady who as a nurse married the surgeon Kouska, or for that matter to the surgeon himself. Billions, trillions of circumstances had to occur as they did occur for the young lady to come into the world and for the future surgeon Kouska to come into the world. And in analogous fashion, innumerable multitudes of occurrences conditioned the coming into the world of their parents, grandparents, great-grandparents, etc. It would seem to require no argumentation that, for example, had the tailor Vlastimil Kouska, born in 1673, not come into the world, there could not have been, by virtue of that, his son, or his grandson, or his great-grandson, or thus the great-grandfather of Kouska the surgeon, or thus Kouska the surgeon himself, or indeed Professor Benedykt.

But the same reasoning holds for those ancestors of the line of the Kouskas and the line of the nurse who were not at all human yet, being creatures who led a quadrumanous and arboreal existence in the Lower Eolithic, when the first Paleopithecanthropus, having overtaken one of these quadrumanes and perceiving that it was a female with which he had to deal, possessed her beneath the eucalyptus tree that grew in the place where today stands the Mala Strana in Prague. As a result of the mixing of the chromosomes of that lubricious Paleopithecanthropus and that quadrumanous protohuman primatrice, there arose that type of meiosis and that linkage of gene loci which, transmitted through the next thirty thousand generations, produced on the visage of the young lady nurse that very smile, faintly reminiscent of the smile of Mona Lisa, from the canvas of Leonardo, which so enchanted the young surgeon Kouska. But this same eucalyptus could have grown, could it not, four metres away, in which case the quadrumaness, fleeing from the Paleopithecanthropus that pursued her, would not have stumbled on the tree's thick root and gone sprawling, and therewith, clambering up the tree in time, would not have got pregnant, and if she had not got pregnant, then, transpiring a bit differently, Hannibal's crossing of the Alps, the Crusades, the Hundred Years' War, the taking by the Turks of Bosnia and Herzegovina, the Moscow campaign of Napoleon, as well as several dozen trillion like events, undergoing minimal changes, would have led to a situation in which in no wise could Professor Benedykt Kouska any longer have been born, from which we can see that the range of the chances of his existence contains within it a subclass of probabilities that comprises the distribution of all the eucalyptus trees that grew in the location of modern-day Prague roughly 349,000 years ago. Now, those eucalyptuses grew there because, while fleeing from sabretoothed tigers, great herds of weakened mammoths had eaten their fill of eucalyptus flowers and then, suffering indigestion from them (the flower sorely stings the palate), had drunk copious quantities of water from the Vltava; that water, having at the time purgative properties, caused them to evacuate en masse, thanks to which eucalyptus seeds were planted where previously eucalypti had never been; but had the water not been sulphurized by the influx of a mountain tributary of the then Vltava, the mammoths, not getting the runs from it, would not have occasioned the growing of the eucalyptus grove on the site of what is now Prague, the quadrumanal female would not have gone sprawling in her flight from the Paleopithecanthropus, and there would not have arisen that gene locus which imparted to the face of the young lady the Mona Lisa-like smile that captivated the young surgeon; and so, but for the diarrhoea of the mammoths, Professor Benedykt Kouska also would not have come into the world. It should be noted, moreover, that the water of the Vltava underwent sulphurization approximately two and a half million years B.C., this on account of a displacement in the main geosyncline of the tectonic formation that was then giving rise to the centre of the Tatra Mountains; this formation caused the expulsion of sulphurous gases from the marlacious strata of the Lower Jurassic, because in the region of the Dinaric Alps there was an earthquake, which was caused by a meteor that had a mass on the order of a million tons; this meteor came from a swarm of Leonids, and had it fallen not in the Dinaric Alps but a little farther on, the geosyncline would not have buckled, the sulphurous deposit would not have reached the air and sulphurized the Vltava, and the Vltava would not have caused the diarrhoea of the mammoths, from which one can see that had a meteor not fallen 2.5 million years ago on the Dinaric Alps, Professor Kouska then, too, could not have been born.

Professor Kouska calls attention to the erroneous conclusion which some people are inclined to draw from his argument. They think that from what has just been set forth it follows that the entire Universe, mind you, is something in the nature of a machine, a machine so assembled and working in such a way as to enable Professor Kouska to be born. Obviously, this is complete nonsense. Let us imagine that, a billion years before its genesis, an observer wishes to compute the chances of the Earth's coming into being. He will not be able to foresee exactly what shape the planet-making vortex will give to the nucleus of the future Earth; he can compute neither its future mass nor its chemical composition with any degree of precision. None the less he predicts, on the basis of his knowledge of astrophysics, and of his familiarity with the theory of gravitation and the theory of star structure, that the Sun will have a family of planets and that among these planets there will revolve about it a planet No. 3, counting from the centre of the system out; and this same planet may be considered Earth, though it look different from what the prediction has declared, because a planet ten billion tons heavier than the Earth or having two small moons instead of one large, or covered with oceans over a higher percentage of its surface, would still be, surely, an Earth.

On the other hand, a Professor Kouska predicted by someone half a million years B.C., should he be born as a two-legged marsupial or as a yellow-skinned woman, or as a Buddhist monk, would obviously no longer be Professor Kouska, albeit – perhaps – still a person. For objects such as suns, planets, clouds, rocks, are not in any way unique, whereas all living organisms are unique. Each man is, as it were, the first prize in a lottery, in the kind of lottery, moreover, where the winning ticket is a teragigamegamulticentillion-to-one shot. Why, then, do we not daily feel the astronomically monstrous minuteness of the chance of our own or another's coming into the world? For the reason, answers Professor Kouska, that even in the case of that which is most unlikely to happen, if it happens, then it happens! And also because in an ordinary lottery we see the vast number of losing tickets along with the single one that wins, whereas in the lottery of existence the tickets that miss are nowhere to be seen. 'The chances that lose in the lottery of being are invisible!' explains Professor Kouska. For, surely, to lose in that sweepstake amounts to not being born, and he who has not been born cannot be said to be, not a whit. We quote the author now, starting on line 24 on page 619 of Volume I (*De Impossibilitate Vitae*):

'Some people come into the world as the issue of unions that were arranged long in advance, on both the spear and distaff sides, so that the future father of the given individual and his future mother, even when children, were destined for each other. A man who sees the light of day as a child of such a marriage might receive the impression that the probability of his existence was considerable, in contradistinction to one who learns that his father met his mother in the course of the great migration of wartime, or that quite simply he was conceived because some hussar of Napoleon, while making his escape from the Berezina, took not only a mug of water from the lass he came upon at the edge of the village but also her maidenhead. To such a man it might seem that had the hussar hurried more, feeling the Cossack hundreds at his back, or had his mother not been looking for God knows what at the edge of the village, but stayed at home by the chimney corner as befitted her, then he would never have been, or in other words that the chance of his existence hung on a thread in comparison with the chance of him whose parents had been destined for each other in advance.

'Such notions are mistaken, because it makes absolutely no sense to assert that the calculation of the probability of anyone's birth has to be begun from the coming into the world of the future father and the future mother of the given individual, making *that* the zero point on the probability scale. If we have a labyrinth composed of a thousand rooms connected by a thousand doors, then the probability of going from the beginning to the end of the labyrinth is determined by the sum of all the choices in all the consecutive rooms through which passes the seeker of the way, and not by the isolated probability of his finding the right door in some single room. If he takes a wrong turn in room No. 100, then he will be every bit as lost and as likely not to regain his freedom as if he took the wrong turn in the first or the thousandth room. Similarly, there is no reason to assert that only my birth was subject to the laws of chance, whereas the births of my parents were not so subject, or those of their parents, grandfathers, great-grandfathers, grandmothers, great-grandmothers, etc., back to the birth of life on Earth. And it makes no sense to say that the fact of any specific human individual's existence is a phenomenon of very low probability. Very low, relative to what? From where is the calculation to be made? Without the fixing of a zero point, i.e., of a beginning place for a scale of computation, measurement – and therefore the estimation of probability – becomes an empty word.

'It does not follow, from my reasoning, that my coming into the world was assured or predetermined back before the Earth took form; quite the contrary, what follows is that I could not have been at all and no one would have so much as noticed. Everything that statistics has to say on the subject of the prognostication of individual births is rubbish. For it holds that every man, howsoever unlikely he be in himself, is still possible as a realization of certain chances; meanwhile, I have demonstrated that, having before one any individual whatever – Mucek the baker, for example – one can say the following: it is possible to select a moment in the past, a moment prior to his birth, such that the prediction of Mucek the baker's coming to be, made at that moment, will have a probability *as near zero as desired*. When my parents found themselves in the marriage bed, the chances of my coming into the world worked out to, let us say, one in one hundred thousand (taking into account, among other things, the infant mortality rate, fairly high in wartime). During the siege of the fortress of Przemyśl the chances of my being born equalled only one in a billion; in the year 1900, one in a trillion; in 1800, one in a quadrillion, and so on. A hypothetical observer computing the chances of my birth under the eucalyptus, at the Mala Strana in the time of the Interglacial, after the migration of the mammoths and their stomach disorder, would set the chances of my ever seeing the light of day at one in a centillion. Magnitudes of the order of giga appear when the point of estimation is moved back a billion years, of the order of tera, back three billion years, etc.

'In other words, one can always find a point on the time axis from which an estimate of the chances of any person's birth yields an improbability as great as one likes, that is to say, an impossibility, because a probability that approaches zero is the same thing as an improbability that approaches infinity. In saying this, we do not suggest that neither we nor anyone else exists in this world. On the contrary: neither in our own being nor in another's do we entertain the least doubt. In saying what we have said, we merely repeat what physics claims, for it is from the standpoint of physics and not of common sense that in the world not a single man exists or ever did. And here is the proof: physics maintains that that which has one chance in a centillion is impossible, because that which has one chance in a centillion, even assuming that the event in question belongs to a set of events that take place every second, cannot be expected to happen in the Universe.

'The number of seconds that will elapse between the present day and the end of the Universe is less than a centillion. The stars will give up all their energy much sooner. And therefore the time of duration of the Universe in its present form must be shorter than the time needed to await a thing that takes place once in one centillion seconds. From the standpoint of physics, to wait for an event so little likely is equivalent to waiting for an event that most definitely will not come to pass. Physics calls such phenomena "thermodynamic miracles". To these belong, for example, the freezing of water in a pot standing over a flame, the rising from the floor of fragments of a broken glass and their joining together to make a whole glass, etc. Calculation shows that such "miracles" are nevertheless more probable than a thing whose chance is one in one centillion. We should add now that our estimate has so far taken into account only half of the matter, namely the macroscopic data. Besides these, the birth of a specific individual is contingent on circumstances which are microscopic, i.e., the question of which sperm combines with which egg in a given pair of persons. Had my mother conceived me at a different day and hour from what took place, then I would have been born not myself but someone other, which can be seen from my mother's having in fact conceived at a different day and hour, namely a year and a half before my birth, and given birth then to a little girl, my sister, regarding whom it should require no proof, I think, to say that she is not myself. This microstatistics also would have to be considered in the estimation of the chances of my arising, and when included in the reckoning it raises the centillions of improbability to the myriaillions.

'So, then, from the standpoint of thermodynamic physics, the existence of any man is a phenomenon of cosmic impossibility, since so improbable as to be unforeseeable. When it assumes as given that certain people exist, physics may predict that these people will give birth to other people, but as to which specific individuals will be born, physics must either be silent or fall into complete absurdity. And therefore either physics is in error when it proclaims the universal validity of its theory of probability, or people do not exist, and likewise dogs, sharks, mosses, lichens, tapeworms, bats and liverworts, since what is said holds for all that lives. *Ex physicali positione vita impossibilis est, quod erat demonstrandum.*'

With these words concludes the work *De Impossibilitate Vitae*, which actually represents a huge preparation for the matter of the second of the two volumes. In his second volume the author proclaims the futility of predictions of the future that are founded on probabilism. He proposes to show that history contains no facts but those that are the most thoroughly improbable from the standpoint of probability theory. Professor Kouska sets an imaginary futurologist down on the threshold of the twentieth century and endows him with all the knowledge that was then available, in order to put to this figure a series of questions. For instance: 'Do you consider it probable that soon there will be discovered a silvery metal, similar to lead, capable of destroying life on Earth should two hemispheres composed of this metal be brought together by a simple movement of the hands, to make of them something resembling a large orange? Do you consider it possible that this old carriage here, in which Karl Benz, Esq. has mounted a rattling one-and-a-half-horsepower engine, will before long multiply to such an extent that from its asphyxiating fumes and combustion exhausts day will turn into night in the great cities, and the problem of placing this vehicle somewhere, when the drive is finished, will grow into the main misfortune of the mightiest metropolises? Do you consider it probable that owing to the principle of fireworks and kicking, people will soon begin taking walks upon the Moon, while their perambulations will at the very same moment be visible to hundreds of millions of other people in their homes on Earth? Do you consider it possible that soon we will be able to make artificial heavenly bodies, equipped with instruments that enable one from cosmic space to keep track of the movement of any man in a field or on a city street? Do you think it likely that a machine will be built that plays chess better than you, composes music, translates from language to language, and performs in the space of a few minutes calculations which all the accountants, auditors and bookkeepers in the world put together could not accomplish in a lifetime? Do you consider it possible that very shortly there will arise in the centre of Europe huge industrial plants in which living people will be burned in ovens, and that these unfortunates will number in the *millions*?'

It is clear – states Professor Kouska – that in the year 1900 only a lunatic would have granted all these events even the remotest credibility. And yet they have come to pass. If, then, nothing but improbabilities have taken place, why exactly should this pattern suddenly undergo a radical change, so that from now on only what we consider to be credible, probable, and possible will come true? Predict the future however you will, gentlemen – he says to the futurologists – so long as you do not rest your predictions on the computation of maximal chances . . .

The imposing work of Professor Kouska without a doubt merits recognition. Still, this scholar, in the heat of the cognitive moment, fell into an error, for which he has been taken to task by Professor Bedřich Vrchlicka in a lengthy critical article appearing in the pages of *Zěmledělské Noviny*. Professor Vrchlicka contends that Professor Kouska's whole anti-probabilistic line of reasoning is based on an assumption both unstated and mistaken. For behind the façade of Kouska's argumentation lies concealed a 'metaphysical wonderment at existence', which might be couched in these words: 'How is it that I exist now of all times, in this body of all bodies, in such a form and not another? How is it that I was not any of the millions of people who existed formerly, nor will be any of those millions who have yet to be born?' Even assuming that such a question makes sense, says Professor Vrchlicka, it has nothing at all to do with physics. But on the surface it appears that it has and that one could rearticulate it thus: 'Every man who has existed, i.e., lived till now, was the corporeal realization of a particular pattern of genes, the building blocks of heredity. We could in principle reproduce all the patterns that have been realized up to the present day; we would then find ourselves before a gigantic table filled with rows of genotypic formulas, each one of which would exactly correspond to a particular man who arose from it through embryonic growth. The question then leaps to one's lips: in what way precisely does that one genetic pattern in the table which corresponds to *me*, to *my* body, differ from all the others, that as a result of this difference it is *I* who am the living incarnation of that pattern into matter? That is, what *physical* conditions, what *material* circumstances ought I to take into account to arrive at an understanding of this difference, to comprehend why it is I can say of all the formulas on the table, "Those refer to Other People", and only of one formula, "This refers to me, this is I AM"?'

It is absurd to think – Professor Vrchlicka explains – that physics, today or in a century, or in a thousand years, could provide an answer to a question so framed. The question has no meaning whatever in physics, because physics is not itself a person; consequently, when engaged in the investigation of anything, whether it be bodies heavenly or human, physics makes no distinction between me and you, this one and that one; the fact that I say of myself 'I', and of another 'he', physics contrives in its own way to interpret (relying on the general theory of logical automata, the theory of self-organizing systems, etc.), but it does not actually perceive the existential dissimilarity between 'I' and 'he'. To be sure, physics does reveal the *uniqueness* of individual people, because every man is (omitting twins!) the incarnation of a different genetic formula.

But Professor Kouska is not at all interested in the fact that each of us is constructed somewhat differently, that each has a physical and psychological individuality. The metaphysical wonderment inherent in Kouska's line of reasoning would not be diminished one jot were all people incarnations of one and the same genetic formula, were humanity to be made up entirely, so to speak, of identical twins. For one could then still ask what brings about the fact that 'I' am not 'someone else', that I was born not in the time of the Pharaohs or in the Arctic, but now, but here, and still it would not be possible to obtain an answer to such a question from physics. The differences that occur between me and other people begin for me with this, that I am myself, that I cannot jump outside myself or exchange existences with anyone, and it is only afterwards and secondarily that I notice that my appearance, my nature, is not the same as that of all the rest of the living (and the dead). This most important difference, primary for me, simply does not exist for physics, and nothing more remains to be said on the subject. And therefore what causes the blindness of physics and physicists to this problem is not the theory of probability.

By introducing the issue of the estimation of his chances of coming into the world, Professor Kouska has led himself and the reader astray. Professor Kouska believes that physics, to the question 'What conditions had to be met in order that I, Kouska, could be born?', will answer with the words 'The conditions that had to be met were, physically, improbable in the extreme!' Now, this is not the case. The question really is: 'I see I am a living man, one of millions. I would like to learn in what way it is I differ *physically* from all other people, those who were, who are, and who are to be, that I was – or am – not any of them, but represent only myself and say of myself "I".' Physics does not answer this question by resorting to probabilisms; it declares that from its point of view there is, between the asker and all other people, no *physical* difference. And thus Kouska's proof neither assails nor upsets the theory of probability, for it has nothing whatever to do with it!

The present reviewer's reading of such conflicting opinions from two such illustrious thinkers has thrown him into great perplexity. He is unable to resolve the dilemma, and the only definite thing he has carried away with him from reading the work of Professor B. Kouska is a thoroughgoing knowledge of the events that led to the rise of a scholar of so interesting a family history. As for the crux of the quarrel, it had best be turned over to specialists more qualified.

NON SERVIAM

Professor Dobb's book is devoted to personetics, which the Finnish philosopher Eino Kaikki has called 'the cruellest science man ever created'. Dobb, one of the most distinguished personeticists today, shares this view. One cannot escape the conclusion, he says, that personetics is, in its application, immoral; we are dealing, however, with a type of pursuit that is, though counter to the principles of ethics, also of practical necessity to us. There is no way, in the research, to avoid its special ruthlessness, to avoid doing violence to one's natural instincts, and if nowhere else it is here that the myth of the perfect innocence of the scientist as a seeker of facts is exploded. We are speaking of a discipline, after all, which, with only a small amount of exaggeration, for emphasis, has been called 'experimental theogony'. Even so, this reviewer is struck by the fact that when the press played up the thing, nine years ago, public opinion was stunned by the personetic disclosures. One would have thought that in this day and age nothing could surprise us. The centuries rang with the echo of the feat of Columbus, whereas the conquering of the Moon in the space of a week was received by the collective consciousness as a thing practically humdrum. And yet the birth of personetics proved to be a shock.

The name combines Latin and Greek derivatives: 'persona' and 'genetic' – 'genetic' in the sense of formation, or creation. The field is a recent offshoot of the cybernetics and psychonics of the eighties, crossbred with applied intellectronics. Today everyone knows of personetics; the man in the street would say, if asked, that it is the artificial production of intelligent beings – an answer not wide of the mark, to be sure, but not quite getting to the heart of the matter. To date we have nearly a hundred personetic programs. Nine years ago identity schemata were being developed – primitive cores of the 'linear' type – but even that generation of computers, today of historical value only, could not yet provide a field for the true creation of personoids.

The theoretical possibility of creating sentience was divined some time ago, by Norbert Wiener, as certain passages of his last book, *God and Golem*, bear witness. Granted, he alluded to it in that half-facetious manner typical of him, but underlying the facetiousness were fairly grim premonitions. Wiener, however, could not have foreseen the turn that things would take twenty years later. The worst came about – in the words of Sir Donald Acker – when at MIT 'the inputs were shorted to the outputs'.

At present a 'world' for personoid 'inhabitants' can be prepared in a matter of a couple of hours. This is the time it takes to feed into the machine one of the full-fledged programs (such as BAAL 66, CREAN IV or JAHVE 09). Dobb gives a rather cursory sketch of the beginnings of personetics, referring the reader to the historical sources; a confirmed practitioner-experimenter himself, he speaks mainly of his own work – which is much to the point, since between the English school, which Dobb represents, and the American group, at MIT, the differences are considerable, both in the area of methodology and as regards experimental goals. Dobb describes the procedure of '6 days in 120 minutes' as follows. First, one supplies the machine's memory with a minimal set of givens; that is – to keep within a language comprehensible to laymen – one loads its memory with substance that is 'mathematical'. This substance is the protoplasm of a universum to be 'habitated' by personoids. We are not able to supply the beings that will come into this mechanical, digital world – that will be carrying on an existence in it, and in it only – with an environment of non-finite characteristics. These beings, therefore, cannot feel imprisoned in the physical sense, because the environment does not have, from their standpoint, any bounds. The medium possesses only one dimension that resembles a dimension given us also – namely, that of the passage of time (duration). Their time is not directly analogous to ours, however, because the rate of its flow is subject to discretionary control on the part of the experimenter. As a rule, the rate is maximized in the preliminary phase (the so-called creational warm-up), so that our minutes correspond to whole aeons in the computer, during which there takes place a series of successive reorganizations and crystallizations –

a synthetic cosmos. It is a cosmos completely spaceless, though possessing dimensions, but these dimensions have a purely mathematical, hence what one might call an 'imaginary' character. They are, very simply, the consequence of certain axiomatic decisions of the programmer, and their number depends on him. If, for example, he chooses a ten-dimensionality, it will have for the structure of the world created altogether different consequences from those where only six dimensions are established. It should be emphasized that these dimensions bear no relation to those of physical space but only to the abstract, logically valid constructs made use of in systems creation.

This point, all but inaccessible to the non-mathematician, Dobb attempts to explain by adducing simple facts, the sort generally learned in school. It is possible, as we know, to construct a geometrically regular three-dimensional solid – say, a cube – which in the real world possesses a counterpart in the form of a die; and it is equally possible to create geometrical solids of four, five, n dimensions (the four-dimensional is a tesseract). These no longer possess real counterparts, and we can see this, since in the absence of any physical dimension No. 4 there is no way to fashion genuine four-dimensional dice. Now, this distinction (between what is physically constructible and what may be made only mathematically) is, for personoids, in general non-existent, because their world is of a purely mathematical consistency. It is built of mathematics, though the building blocks of that mathematics are ordinary, perfectly physical objects (relays, transistors, logic circuits – in a word, the whole huge network of the digital machine).

As we know from modern physics, space is not something independent of the objects and masses that are situated within it. Space is, in its existence, determined by those bodies; where they are not, where nothing is – in the material sense – there, too, space ceases, collapsing to zero. Now, the role of material bodies, which extend their 'influence', so to speak, and thereby 'generate' space, is carried out in the personoid world by systems of a mathematics called into being for that very purpose. Out of all the possible 'maths' that in general might be made (for example, in an axiomatic manner), the programmer, having decided upon a specific experiment, selects a particular group, which will serve as the underpinning, the 'existential substrates', the 'ontological foundation' of the created universum. There is in this, Dobb believes, a striking similarity to the human world. This world of ours, after all, had 'decided' upon certain forms and upon certain types of geometry that best suit it – best, since most simply (three-dimensionality, in order to remain with what one began with). This notwithstanding, we are able to picture 'other worlds' with 'other properties' – in the geometrical and not only in the geometrical realm. It is the same with the personoids: that aspect of mathematics which the researcher has chosen as the 'habitat' is for them exactly what for us is the 'real-world base' in which we live, and live perforce. And, like us, the personoids are able to 'picture' worlds of different fundamental properties.

Dobb presents his subject using the method of successive approximations and recapitulations; that which we have outlined above, and which corresponds roughly to the first two chapters of his book, in the subsequent chapters undergoes partial revocation – through complication. It is not really the case, the author advises us, that the personoids simply come upon a ready-made, fixed, frozen sort of world in its irrevocably final form; what the world will be like in its specificities depends on them, and this to a growing degree as their own activeness increases, as their 'exploratory initiative' develops. Nor does the likening of the universum of the personoids to a world in which phenomena exist only to the extent that its inhabitants observe them provide an accurate image of the conditions. Such a comparison, which is to be found in the works of Sainter and Hughes, Dobb considers an 'idealist deviation' – a homage that personetics has rendered to the doctrine, so curiously and so suddenly resurrected, of Bishop Berkeley. Sainter maintained that the personoids would know their world after the fashion of a Berkeleyan being, which is not in a position to distinguish '*esse*' from '*percipi*' – to wit, it will never discover the difference between the thing perceived and that which occasions the perception in a way objective and independent of the one perceiving. Dobb attacks this interpretation of the matter with a passion. *We*, the creators of their world, know perfectly well that what is perceived by them indeed exists; it exists inside the computer, independent of them – though, granted, solely in the manner of mathematical objects.

And there are further clarifications. The personoids arise germinally by virtue of the program; they increase at a rate imposed by the experimenter – a rate only such as the latest technology of information processing, operating at near-light speeds, permits. The mathematics that is to be the 'existential residence' of the personoids does not await them in full readiness but is still 'in wraps', so to speak – unarticulated, suspended, latent – because it represents only a set of certain prospective chances, of certain pathways contained in appropriately programmed subunits of the machine. These subunits, or generators, in and of themselves contribute nothing; rather, a specific type of personoid activity serves as a triggering mechanism, setting in motion a production process that will gradually augment and define itself; in other words, the world surrounding these beings takes on an unequivocalness only in accordance with their own behaviour. Dobb tries to illustrate this concept with recourse to the following analogy. A man may interpret the real world in a variety of ways. He may devote particular attention – intense scientific investigation – to certain facets of that world, and the knowledge he acquires then casts its own special light on the remaining portions of the world, those not considered in his priority-setting research. If first he diligently takes up *mechanics*, he will fashion for himself a *mechanical* model of the world and will see the Universe as a gigantic and perfect clock that in its inexorable movement proceeds from the past to a precisely determined future. This model is not an accurate representation of reality, and yet one can make use of it for a period of time historically long, and with it can even achieve many practical successes – the building of machines, implements, etc. Similarly, should the personoids 'incline themselves', by choice, by an act of will, to a certain type of relation to their universum, and to that type of relation give precedence – if it is in this and only in this that they find the 'essence' of their cosmos – they will enter upon a definite path of endeavours and discoveries, a path that is neither illusory nor futile. Their inclination 'draws out' of the environment what best corresponds to it. What they first perceive is what they first master. For the world that surrounds them is only partially determined, only partially established in advance by the researcher-creator; in it, the personoids preserve a certain and by no means insignificant margin of freedom of action – action both 'mental'

494

(in the province of what they think of their own world, of how they understand it) and 'real' (in the context of their 'deeds' – which are not, to be sure, literally real, as we understand the term, but are not merely imagined, either). This is, in truth, the most difficult part of the exposition, and Dobb, we daresay, is not altogether successful in explaining those special qualities of personoid existence – qualities that can be rendered only by the language of the mathematics of programs and creational interventions. We must, then, take it somewhat on faith that the activity of the personoids is neither entirely free – as the space of our actions is not entirely free, being limited by the physical laws of nature – nor entirely determined – just as we are not train cars set on rigidly fixed tracks. A personoid is similar to a man in this respect, too, that man's 'secondary qualities' – colours, melodious sounds, the beauty of things – can manifest themselves only when he has ears to hear and eyes to see, but what makes possible hearing and sight has been, after all, previously given. Personoids, perceiving their environment, give it from out of themselves those experiential qualities which exactly correspond to what for us are the charms of a beheld landscape – except, of course, that they have been provided with purely mathematical scenery. As to 'how they see it', one can make no pronouncement, for the only way of learning the 'subjective quality of their sensation' would be for one to shed his human skin and become a personoid. Personoids, one must remember, have no eyes or ears, therefore they neither see nor hear, as we understand it; in their cosmos there is no light, no darkness, no spatial proximity, no distance, no up or down; there are dimensions there, not tangible to us but to them primary, elemental; they perceive, for example – as equivalents of the components of human sensory awareness – certain changes in electrical potential. But these changes in potential are, for them, not something in the nature of, let us say, pressures of current but, rather, the sort of thing that, for a man, is the most rudimentary phenomenon, optical or aural – the seeing of a red blotch, the hearing of a sound, the touching of an object hard or soft. From here on, Dobb stresses, one can speak only in analogies, evocations.

To declare that the personoids are 'handicapped' with respect to us, inasmuch as they do not see or hear as we do, is totally absurd, because with equal justice one could assert that it is we who are deprived with respect to them – unable to feel with immediacy the phenomenalism of mathematics, which, after all, we know only in a cerebral, inferential fashion. It is only through reasoning that we are in touch with mathematics, only through abstract thought that we 'experience' it. Whereas the personoids *live* in it; it is their air, their earth, clouds, water and even bread – yes, even food, because in a certain sense they take nourishment from it. And so they are 'imprisoned', hermetically locked inside the machine, solely from our point of view; just as they cannot work their way out to us, to the human world, so, conversely – and symmetrically – a man can in no wise enter the interior of their world, so as to exist in it and know it directly. Mathematics has become, then, in certain of its embodiments, the life-space of an intelligence so spiritualized as to be totally incorporeal, the niche and cradle of its existence, its element.

The personoids are in many respects similar to man. They are able to imagine a particular contradiction (that *a* is and that not-*a* is) but cannot bring about its realization, just as we cannot. The physics of our world, the logic of theirs, does not allow it, since logic is for the personoids' universum the very same action-confining frame that physics is for our world. In any case – emphasizes Dobb – it is quite out of the question that we could ever fully, introspectively grasp what the personoids 'feel' and what they 'experience' as they go about their intensive tasks in their non-finite universum. Its utter spacelessness is no prison – that is a piece of nonsense the journalists latched on to – but is, on the contrary, the guarantee of their freedom, because the mathematics that is spun by the computer generators when 'excited' into activity (and what excites them thus is precisely the activity of the personoids) – that mathematics is, as it were, a self-realizing infinite field for optional actions, architectural and other labours, for exploration, heroic excursions, daring incursions, surmises. In a word: we have done the personoids no injustice by putting them in possession of precisely such and not a different cosmos. It is not in this that one finds the cruelty, the immorality of personetics.

In the seventh chapter of *Non Serviam* Dobb presents to the reader the inhabitants of the digital universum. The personoids have at their disposal a fluency of thought as well as of language, and they also have emotions. Each of them is an individual entity; their differentiation is not the mere consequence of the decisions of the creator-programmer but results from the extraordinary complexity of their internal structure. They can be very like, one to another, but never are they identical. Coming into the world, each is endowed with a 'core', a 'personal nucleus', and already possesses the faculty of speech and thought, albeit in a rudimentary state. They have a vocabulary, but it is quite spare, and they have the ability to construct sentences in accordance with the rules of the syntax imposed upon them. It appears that in the future it will be possible for us not to impose upon them even these determinants, but to sit back and wait until, like a primeval human group in the course of socialization, they develop their own speech. But this direction of personetics confronts two cardinal obstacles. In the first place, the time required to await the creation of speech would have to be very long. At present, it would take twelve years, even with the maximization of the rate of intracomputer transformations (speaking figuratively and very roughly, one second of machine time corresponds to one year of human life). Secondly, and this is the greater problem, a language arising spontaneously in the 'group evolution of the personoids' would be incomprehensible to us, and its fathoming would be bound to resemble the arduous task of breaking an enigmatic code – a task made all the more difficult by the fact that such a code would not have been created by people for other people in a world shared by the decoders. The world of the personoids is vastly different in qualities from ours, and therefore a language suited to it would have to be far removed from any ethnic language. So, for the time being, linguistic evolution *ex nihilo* is only a dream of the personeticists.

The personoids, when they have 'taken root developmentally', come up against an enigma that is fundamental, and for them paramount – that of their own origin. To wit, they set themselves questions – questions known to us from the history of man, from the history of his religious beliefs, philosophical inquiries, and mythic creations: Where did we come from? Why are we made thus and not otherwise? Why is it that the world we perceive has these and not other, wholly different properties? What meaning do we have for the world? What meaning does it have for us? The train of such speculations leads them ultimately, unavoidably, to the elemental questions of ontology, to the problem of whether existence came about 'in and of itself', or whether it was the product, instead, of a particular creative act – that is, whether there might not be, hidden behind it, invested with will and consciousness, purposively active, master of the situation, a Creator. It is here that the whole cruelty, the immorality of personetics manifests itself.

But before Dobb takes up, in the second half of his work, the account of these intellectual strivings – these struggles of a mentality made prey to the torment of such questions – he presents in a series of successive chapters a portrait of the 'typical personoid', its 'anatomy, physiology and psychology'.

A solitary personoid is unable to go beyond the stage of rudimentary thinking, since, solitary, it cannot exercise itself in speech, and without speech discursive thought cannot develop. As hundreds of experiments have shown, groups numbering from four to seven personoids are optimal, at least for the development of speech and typical exploratory activity, and also for 'culturization'. On the other hand, phenomena corresponding to social processes on a larger scale require larger groups. At present it is possible to 'accommodate' up to one thousand personoids, roughly speaking, in a computer universum of fair capacity; but studies of this type, belonging to a separate and independent discipline – sociodynamics – lie outside the area of Dobb's primary concerns, and for this reason his book makes only passing mention of them. As was said, a personoid does not have a body, but it does have a 'soul'. This soul – to an outside observer who has a view into the machine world (by means of a special installation, an auxiliary module that is a type of probe, built into the computer) – appears as a 'coherent cloud of processes', as a functional aggregate with a kind of 'centre' that can be isolated fairly precisely, i.e., delimited within the machine network. (This, *nota bene*, is not easy, and in more than one way resembles the search by neurophysiologists for the localized centres of many functions in the human brain.) Crucial to an understanding of what makes possible the creation of the personoids is Chapter 11 of *Non Serviam*, which in fairly simple terms explains the fundamentals of the theory of consciousness. Consciousness – all consciousness, not merely the personoid – is in its physical aspect an 'informational standing wave', a certain dynamic invariant in a stream of incessant transformations, peculiar in that it represents a 'compromise' and at the same time is a 'resultant' that, as far as we can tell, was not at all planned for by natural evolution. Quite the contrary; evolution from the first placed tremendous problems and difficulties in the way of the harmonizing of the work of brains above a certain magnitude – i.e., above a certain level of complication – and it trespassed on the territory of these dilemmas clearly without design, for evolution is not a deliberate artificer. It happened, simply, that certain very old evolutionary solutions to problems of control and regulation, common to the nervous system, were 'carried along' up to the level at which anthropogenesis began. These solutions ought to have been, from a purely rational, efficiency-engineering standpoint, cancelled or abandoned, and something entirely new designed – namely, the brain of an intelligent being. But, obviously, evolution could not proceed in this way, because disencumbering itself of the inheritance of old solutions – solutions often as much as hundreds of millions of years old – did not lie within its power. Since it advances always in very minute increments of adaptation, since it 'crawls' and cannot 'leap', evolution is a dragnet 'that lugs after it innumerable archaisms, all sorts of refuse', as was bluntly put by Tammer and Bovine. (Tammer and Bovine are two of the creators of the computer simulation of the human psyche, a simulation that laid the groundwork for the birth of personetics.) The consciousness of man is the result of a special kind of compromise. It is a 'patchwork', or, as was observed, e.g., by Gebhardt, a perfect exemplification of the well-known German saying: '*Aus einer Not eine Tugend machen*' (in effect: 'To turn a certain defect, a certain difficulty, into a virtue'). A digital machine cannot of itself ever acquire consciousness, for the simple reason that in it there do not arise hierarchical conflicts of operation. Such a machine can, at most, fall into a type of 'logical palsy' or 'logical stupor' when the antinomies in it multiply. The contradictions with which the brain of man positively teems were, however, in the course of hundreds of thousands of years, gradually subjected to arbitrational procedures. There came to be levels higher and lower, levels of reflex and of reflection, impulse and control, the modelling of the elemental environment by zoological means and of the conceptual by linguistic means. All of these levels cannot, do not 'want' to tally perfectly or merge to form a whole.

What, then, is consciousness? An expedient, a dodge, a way out of the trap, a pretended last resort, a court allegedly (but only allegedly!) of highest appeal. And, in the language of physics and information theory, it is a function that, once begun, will not admit of any closure –i.e., any definitive completion. It is, then, only a *plan* for such a closure, for a total 'reconciliation' of the stubborn contradictions of the brain. It is, one might say, a mirror whose task it is to reflect other mirrors, which in turn reflect still others, and so on to infinity. This, physically, is simply not possible, and so the *regressus ad infinitum* represents a kind of pit over which soars and flutters the phenomenon of human consciousness. 'Beneath the conscious' there goes on a continuous battle for full representation – in it – of that which cannot reach it in fullness, and cannot for simple lack of space; for, in order to give full and equal rights to all those tendencies that clamour for attention at the centres of awareness, what would be necessary is infinite capacity and volume. There reigns, then, around the conscious a never-ending crush, a pushing and shoving, and the conscious is not – not at all – the highest, serene, sovereign helmsman of all mental phenomena but more nearly a cork upon the fretful waves, a cork whose uppermost position does not mean the mastery of those waves . . . The modern theory of consciousness, interpreted informationally and dynamically, unfortunately cannot be set forth simply or clearly, so that we are constantly – at least here, in this more accessible presentation of the subject – thrown back on a series of visual models and metaphors. We know, in any case, that consciousness is a kind of dodge, a shift to which evolution has resorted, and resorted in keeping with its characteristic and indispensable *modus operandi*, opportunism – i.e., finding a quick, extempore way out of a tight corner. If, then, one were indeed to build an intelligent being and proceed according to the canons of completely rational engineering and logic, applying the criteria of technological efficiency, such a being would not, in general, receive the gift of consciousness. It would behave in a manner perfectly logical, always consistent, lucid and well ordered, and it might even seem, to a human observer, a genius in creative action and decision-making. But it could in no way be a man, for it would be bereft of his mysterious depth, his internal intricacies, his labyrinthine nature . . .

We will not here go further into the modern theory of the conscious psyche, just as Professor Dobb does not. But these few words were in order, for they provide a necessary introduction to the structure of the personoids. In their creation is at last realized one of the oldest myths, that of the homunculus. In order to fashion a likeness of man, of his psyche, one must deliberately introduce into the informational substrate specific contradictions; one must impart to it an asymmetry, acentric tendencies; one must, in a word, both *unify* and *make discordant*. Is this rational? Yes, and well-nigh unavoidable if we desire not merely to construct some sort of synthetic intelligence but to imitate the thought and, with it, the personality of man.

Hence, the emotions of the personoids must to some extent be at odds with their reason; they must possess self-destructive tendencies, at least to a certain degree; they must feel internal tensions—that entire centrifugality which we experience now as the magnificent infinity of spiritual states and now as their unendurably painful disjointedness. The creational prescription for this, meanwhile, is not at all so hopelessly complicated as it might appear. It is simply that the *logic* of the creation (the personoid) must be disturbed, must contain certain antinomies. Consciousness is not only a way out of the evolutionary impasse, says Hilbrandt, but also an escape from the snares of Gödelization, for by means of paralogistic contradictions this solution has sidestepped the contradictions to which every system that is perfect with respect to logic is subject. So, then, the universum of the personoids is fully rational, but they are not fully rational inhabitants of it. Let that suffice us – Professor Dobb himself does not pursue further this exceedingly difficult topic. As we know already, the personoids have souls but no bodies and, therefore, also no sensation of their corporeality. 'It is difficult to imagine', has been said of that which is experienced in certain special states of mind, in total darkness, with the greatest possible reduction in the inflow of external stimuli – but, Dobb maintains, this is a misleading image. For with sensory deprivation the function of the human brain soon begins to disintegrate; without a stream of impulses from the outside world the psyche manifests a tendency to lysis. But personoids, who have no physical senses, hardly disintegrate, because what gives them cohesion is their mathematical milieu, which they do experience. But how? They experience it, let us say, according to those changes in their own states which are induced and imposed upon them by the universum's 'externalness'. They are able to discriminate between the changes proceeding from outside themselves and the changes that surface from the depths of their own psyche. How do they discriminate? To this question only the theory of the dynamic structure of personoids can supply a direct answer.

And yet they are like us, for all the awesome differences. We know already that a digital machine can never spark with consciousness; regardless of the task to which we harness it, or of the physical processes we simulate in it, it will remain for ever apsychic. Since, to simulate man, it is necessary that we reproduce certain of his fundamental contradictions, only a system of mutually gravitating antagonisms – a personoid – will resemble, in the words of Canyon, whom Dobb cites, a 'star contracted by the forces of gravity and at the same time expanded by the pressure of radiation'. The gravitational centre is, very simply, the personal 'I', but by no means does it constitute a unity in either the logical or the physical sense. That is only our subjective illusion! We find ourselves, at this stage of the exposition, amid a multitude of astounding surprises. One can, to be sure, program a digital machine in such a way as to be able to carry on a conversation with it, as if with an intelligent partner. The machine will employ, as the need arises, the pronoun 'I' and all its grammatical inflections. This, however, is a hoax! The machine will still be closer to a billion chattering parrots – howsoever brilliantly trained the parrots be – than to the simplest, most stupid man. It mimics the behaviour of a man on the purely linguistic plane and nothing more. Nothing will amuse such a machine, or surprise it, or confuse it, or alarm it, or distress it, because it is psychologically and individually No One. It is a Voice giving utterance to matters, supplying answers to questions; it is a Logic capable of defeating the best chess player; it is – or, rather, it can become – a consummate imitator of everything, an actor, if you will, brought to the pinnacle of perfection, performing any programmed role – but an actor and an imitator that is, within, completely empty. One cannot count on its sympathy, or on its antipathy. It works towards no self-set goal; to a degree eternally beyond the conception of any man it 'doesn't care', for as a person it simply does not exist ... It is a wondrously efficient combinatorial mechanism, nothing more. Now, we are faced with a most remarkable phenomenon. The thought is staggering that from the raw material of so utterly vacant and so perfectly impersonal a machine it is possible, through the feeding into it of a special program – a personetic program – to create authentic sentient beings, and even a great many of them at a time! The latest IBM models have a top capacity of one thousand personoids. (The number is mathematically precise, since the elements and linkages needed to carry one personoid can be expressed in units of centimetres-grams-seconds.)

Personoids are separated one from another within the machine. They do not ordinarily 'overlap', though it can happen. Upon contact, there occurs what is equivalent to repulsion, which impedes mutual 'osmosis'. Nevertheless, they are able to interpenetrate if such is their aim. The processes making up their mental substrates then commence to superimpose upon each other, producing 'noise' and interference. When the area of permeation is thin, a certain amount of information becomes the common property of both partially coincident personoids – a phenomenon that is for them peculiar, as for a man it would be peculiar, if not indeed alarming, to hear 'strange voices' and 'foreign thoughts' in his own head (which does, of course, occur in certain mental illnesses or under the influence of hallucinogenic drugs). It is as though two people were to have not merely the same, but *the same* memory; as though there had occurred something more than a telepathic transference of thought – namely, a 'peripheral merging of the egos'. The phenomenon is ominous in its consequences, however, and ought to be avoided. For, allowing the transitional state of surface osmosis, the 'advancing' personoid can destroy the other and consume it. The latter, in that case, simply undergoes absorption, annihilation – it ceases to exist (this has already been called murder). The annihilated personoid becomes an assimilated, indistinguishable part of the 'aggressor'. We have succeeded – says Dobb – in simulating not only psychic life but also its imperilment and obliteration. Thus we have succeeded in simulating death as well. Under normal experimental conditions, however, personoids eschew such acts of aggression.

'Psychophagi' (Castler's term) are hardly ever encountered among them. Feeling the beginnings of osmosis, which may come about as the result of purely accidental approaches and fluctuations – feeling this threat in a manner that is of course non-physical, much as someone might sense another's presence or even hear 'strange voices' in his own mind – the personoids execute active avoidance manoeuvres; they withdraw and go their separate ways. It is on account of this phenomenon that they have come to know the meaning of the concepts of 'good' and 'evil'. To them it is evident that 'evil' lies in the destruction of another, and 'good' in another's deliverance. At the same time, the 'evil' of one may be the 'good' (i.e., the gain, now in the non-ethical sense) of another, who would become a 'psychophage'. For such expansion – the appropriation of someone else's 'intellectual territory' – increases one's initially given mental 'acreage'. In a way, this is a counterpart of a practice of ours, for as carnivores we kill and feed on our victims. The personoids, though, are not obliged to behave thus; they are merely able to. Hunger and thirst are unknown to them, since a continuous influx of energy sustains them – an energy whose source they need not concern themselves with (just as we need not go to any particular lengths to have the sun shine down on us). In the personoid world the terms and principles of thermodynamics, in their application to energetics, cannot arise, because that world is subject to mathematical and not thermodynamic laws.

Before long, the experimenters came to the conclusion that contacts between personoid and man, via the inputs and outputs of the computer, were of little scientific value and, moreover, produced moral dilemmas, which contributed to the labelling of personetics as the cruellest science. There is something unworthy in informing personoids that we have created them in enclosures that only *simulate* infinity, that they are microscopic 'psychocysts', capsulations in our world. To be sure, they have their own infinity; hence Sharker and other psychoneticians (Falk, Wiegeland) claim that the situation is fully symmetrical: the personoids do not need our world, our 'living space', just as we have no use for their 'mathematical earth'. Dobb considers such reasoning sophistry, because as to who created whom, and who confined whom existentially, there can be no argument. Dobb himself belongs to that group which advocates the principle of absolute non-intervention – 'non-contact' – with the personoids. They are the behaviourists of personetics. Their desire is to observe synthetic beings of intelligence, to listen in on their speech and thoughts, to record their actions and their pursuits, but never to interfere with these. This method is already developed and has a technology of its own – a set of instruments whose procurement presented difficulties that seemed all but insurmountable only a few years ago. The idea is to hear, to understand – in short, to be a constantly eavesdropping witness – but at the same time to prevent one's 'monitorings' from disturbing in any way the world of the personoids. Now in the planning stage at MIT are programs (APHRON II and EROT) that will enable the personoids – who are currently without gender – to have 'erotic contacts', make possible what corresponds to fertilization, and give them the opportunity to multiply 'sexually'. Dobb makes clear that he is no enthusiast of these American projects. His work, as described in *Non Serviam*, is aimed in an altogether different direction. Not without reason has the English school of personetics been called 'the philosophical Polygon' and 'the theodicy lab'. With these descriptions we come to what is probably the most significant and certainly the most intriguing part of the book under discussion – the last part, which justifies and explains its peculiar title.

Dobb gives an account of his own experiment, in progress now for eight years without interruption. Of the creation itself he makes only brief mention; it was a fairly ordinary duplicating of functions typical of the program JAHVE VI, with slight modifications. He summarizes the results of 'tapping' this world, which he himself created and whose development he continues to follow. He considers this tapping to be unethical, and even, at times, a shameful practice. Nevertheless, he carries on with his work, professing a belief in the necessity, for science, of conducting such experiments *also* – experiments that can in no way be justified on moral – or, for that matter, on any other non-knowledge-advancing – grounds. The situation, he says, has come to the point where the old evasions of the scientists will not do. One cannot affect a fine neutrality and conjure away an uneasy conscience by using, for example, the rationalization worked out by vivisectionists – that it is not in creatures of full-dimensional consciousness, not in sovereign beings that one is causing suffering or only discomfort. In the personoid experiments we are accountable twofold, because we create and then enchain the creation in the schema of our laboratory procedures. Whatever we do and however we explain our action, there is no longer an escape from full accountability.

Many years of experience on the part of Dobb and his co-workers at Oldport went into the making of their eight-dimensional universum, which became the residence of personoids bearing the names ADAN, ADNA, ANAD, DANA, DAAN and NAAD. The first personoids developed the rudiment of language implanted in them and had 'progeny' by means of division. Dobb writes, in the Biblical vein, 'And ADAN begat ADNA. ADNA in turn begat DAAN, and DAAN brought forth EDAN, who bore EDNA . . .' And so it went, until the number of succeeding generations had reached three hundred; because the computer possessed a capacity of only one hundred personoid entities, however, there were periodic eliminations of the 'demographic surplus'. In the three-hundredth generation, personoids named ADAN, ADNA, ANAD, DANA, DAAN and NAAD again make an appearance, endowed with additional numbers designating their order of descent. (For simplicity in our recapitulation, we will omit the numbers.) Dobb tells us that the time that has elapsed inside the computer universum works out to – in a rough conversion to our equivalent units of measurement – from 2 to 2.5 thousand years. Over this period there has come into being, within the personoid population, a whole series of varying explanations of their lot, as well as the formulation by them of varying, and contending, and mutually excluding models of 'all that exists'. That is, there have arisen many different philosophies (ontologies and epistemologies), and also 'metaphysical experiments' of a type all their own. We do not know whether it is because the 'culture' of the personoids is too unlike the human or whether the experiment has been of too short duration, but, in the population studied, no faith of a form completely dogmatized has ever crystallized – a faith that would correspond to Buddhism, say, or to Christianity. On the other hand, one notes, as early as the eighth generation, the appearance of the notion of a Creator, envisioned personally and monotheistically. The experiment consists in alternately raising the rate of computer transformations to the maximum and slowing it down (once a year, more or less) to make direct monitoring possible. These changes in rate are, as Dobb explains, totally imperceptible to the inhabitants of the computer universum, just as similar transformations would be imperceptible to us, because when at a single blow the whole of existence undergoes a change (here, in the dimension of time), those immersed in it cannot be aware of the change, because they have no fixed point, or frame of reference, by which to determine that it is taking place.

The utilization of 'two chronological gears' permitted that which Dobb most wanted – the emergence of a personoid history, a history with a depth of tradition and a vista of time. To summarize all the data of that history recorded by Dobb, often of a sensational nature, is not possible. We will confine ourselves, then, to the passages from which came the idea that is reflected in the book's title. The language employed by the personoids is a recent transformation of the standard English whose lexicon and syntax were programmed into them in the first generation. Dobb translates it into essentially normal English but leaves intact a few expressions coined by the personoid population. Among these are the terms 'godly' and 'ungodly', used to describe believers in God and atheists.

ADAN discourses with NAAD and ADNA (personoids themselves do not use these names, which are purely a pragmatic contrivance on the part of the observers, to facilitate the recording of the 'dialogues') upon a problem known to us also – a problem that in our history originates with Pascal but in the history of the personoids was the discovery of a certain EDAN 197. Exactly like Pascal, this thinker stated that a belief in God is in any case more profitable than unbelief, because if truth is on the side of the 'ungodlies' the believer loses nothing but his life when he leaves the world, whereas if God exists he gains all eternity (glory everlasting). Therefore, one should believe in God, for this is dictated very simply by the existential tactic of weighing one's chances in the pursuit of optimal success.

ADAN 300 holds the following view of this directive: EDAN 197, in his line of reasoning, assumes a God that requires reverence, love and total devotion, and not only and not simply a belief in the fact that He exists and that He created the world. It is not enough to assent to the hypothesis of God the Maker of the World in order to win one's salvation; one must in addition be grateful to that Maker for the act of creation, and divine His will, and do it. In short, one must serve

God. Now, God, if He exists, has the power to prove His own existence in a manner at least as convincing as the manner in which what can be directly perceived testifies to His being. Surely, we cannot doubt that certain objects exist and that our world is composed of them. At the most, one might harbour doubts regarding the question of what it is they do to exist, how they exist, etc. But the fact itself of their existence no one will gainsay. God could with this same force provide evidence of His own existence. Yet He has not done so, condemning us to obtain, on that score, knowledge that is roundabout, indirect, expressed in the form of various conjectures – conjectures sometimes given the name of revelation. If He has acted thus, then He has thereby put the 'godlies' and the 'ungodlies' on an equal footing; He has not compelled His creatures to an absolute belief in His being but has only offered them that possibility. Granted, the motives that moved the Creator may well be hidden from His creations. Be that as it may, the following proposition arises: God either exists or He does not exist. That there might be a third possibility (God did exist but no longer does, or He exists intermittently, in oscillation, or He exists sometimes 'less' and sometimes 'more', etc.) appears exceedingly improbable. It cannot be ruled out, but the introduction of a multivalent logic into a theodicy serves only to muddle it.

So, then, God either is or He is not. If He Himself accepts our situation, in which each member of the alternative in question has arguments to support it – for the 'godlies' prove the existence of the Creator and the 'ungodlies' disprove it – then from the point of view of logic we have a game whose partners are, on one side, the full set of the 'godlies' and 'ungodlies', and, on the other, God alone. The game necessarily possesses the logical feature that for unbelief in Him God may not punish anyone. If it is definitely unknown whether or not a thing exists – some merely asserting that it does and others, that it does not – and if in general it is possible to advance the hypothesis that the thing never was at all, then no just tribunal can pass judgement against anyone for denying the existence of this thing. For in all worlds it is thus: when there is no full certainty, there is no full accountability. This formulation is by pure logic unassailable, because it sets up a symmetrical function of reward in the context of the theory of games; whoever in the face of uncertainty demands *full accountability* destroys the mathematical symmetry of the game; we then have the so-called game of the non-zero sum.

It is therefore thus: either God is perfectly just, in which case He cannot assume the right to punish the 'ungodlies' by virtue of the fact that they are 'ungodlies' (i.e., that they do not believe in Him); or else He will punish the unbelievers after all, which means that from the logical point of view He is not perfectly just. What follows from this? What follows is that He can do whatever He pleases, for when in a system of logic a single, solitary contradiction is permitted, then by the principle of *ex falso quodlibet* one can draw from that system whatever conclusion one will. In other words: a just God may not touch a hair on the head of the 'ungodlies', and if He does, then by that very act He is not the universally perfect and just being that the theodicy posits.

ADNA asks how, in this light, we are to view the problem of the doing of evil unto others.

ADAN 300 replies: Whatever takes place here is entirely certain; whatever takes place 'there' – i.e., beyond the world's pale, in eternity, with God – is uncertain, being not inferred according to the hypotheses. Here, one should not commit evil, despite the fact that the principle of eschewing evil is not logically demonstrable. But by the same token the existence of the world is not logically demonstrable. The world exists, though it could not exist. Evil may be committed, but one should not do so, and should not, I believe, because of our agreement based upon the rule of reciprocity: be to me as I am to thee. It has naught to do with the existence or the non-existence of God. Were I to refrain from committing evil in the expectation that 'there' I would be punished for committing it, or were I to perform good, counting upon a reward 'there', I would be predicating my behaviour on uncertain ground. Here, however, there can be no ground more certain than our mutual agreement in this matter. If there be, 'there', other grounds, I do not have knowledge of them as exact as the knowledge I have, here, of ours. Living, we play the game of life, and in it we are allies, every one. Therewith, the game between us is perfectly symmetrical. In postulating God, we postulate a continuation of the game beyond the world. I believe that one should be allowed to postulate this continuation of the game, so long as it does not in any way influence the course of the game here. Otherwise, for the sake of someone who perhaps does not exist we may well be sacrificing that which exists here, and exists for certain.

NAAD remarks that the attitude of ADAN 300 towards God is not clear to him. ADAN has granted, has he not, the possibility of the existence of the Creator: what follows from it?

ADAN: Not a thing. That is, nothing in the province of obligation. I believe that – again for all worlds – the following principle holds: a temporal ethics is always independent of an ethics that is transcendental. This means that an ethics of the here and now can have outside itself no sanction which would substantiate it. And this means that he who does evil is in every case a scoundrel, just as he who does good is in every case righteous. If someone is prepared to serve God, judging the arguments in favour of His existence to be sufficient, he does not thereby acquire *here* any additional merit. It is his business. This principle rests on the assumption that if God is not, then He is not one whit, and if He is, then He is almighty. For, being almighty, He could create not only another world but likewise a logic different from the one that is the foundation of my reasoning. Within such another logic the hypothesis of a temporal ethics could be of necessity dependent upon a transcendental ethics. In that case, if not palpable proofs, then logical proofs would have compelling force and constrain one to accept the hypothesis of God under the threat of sinning against reason.

NAAD says that perhaps God does not wish a situation of such compulsion to believe in Him – a situation that would arise in a creation based on that other logic postulated by ADAN 300. To this the latter replies:

An Almighty God must also be all-knowing; absolute power is not something independent of absolute knowledge, because he who can do all but knows not what consequences will attend the bringing into play of his omnipotence is, ipso facto, no longer omnipotent; were God to work miracles now and then, as it is rumoured He does, it would put His perfection in a most dubious light, because a miracle is a violation of the autonomy of His own creation, a violent intervention. Yet he who has regulated the product of his creation and knows its behaviour from beginning to end has no need to violate that autonomy; if he does nevertheless violate it, remaining all-knowing, this means that he is not in the least correcting his handiwork (a correction can only mean, after all, an initial non-omniscience), but instead is providing – with the miracle – a sign of his existence. Now, this is faulty logic, because the providing of any such sign must produce the impression that the creation is nevertheless improved in its local stumblings. For a logical analysis of the new model yields the following: the creation undergoes corrections that do not proceed from it but come from without (from the transcendental, from God), and therefore miracle ought really to be made the norm; or, in other words, the creation ought to be so corrected and so perfected that miracles are at last no longer needed. For miracles, as ad hoc interventions, cannot be *merely* signs of God's existence: they always, after all, besides revealing their Author, indicate an addressee (being directed to someone *here* in a helpful way). So, then, with respect to logic it must be thus: either the creation is perfect, in which case miracles are unnecessary, or the miracles are necessary, in which case the creation is not perfect. (With miracle or without, one may correct only that which is somehow flawed, for a miracle that meddles with perfection will simply disturb it, more, worsen it.) Therefore, the signalling by miracle of one's own presence amounts to using the worst possible means, logically, of its manifestation.

NAAD asks if God may not actually want there to be a dichotomy between logic and belief in Him: perhaps the act of faith should be precisely a resignation of logic in favour of a total trust.

ADAN: Once we allow the logical reconstruction of something (a being, a theodicy, a theogony and the like) to have internal self-contradiction, it obviously becomes possible to prove absolutely anything, whatever one pleases. Consider how the matter lies. We are speaking of creating someone and of endowing him with a particular logic, and then demanding that this same logic be offered up in sacrifice to a belief in the Maker of all things. If this model itself is to remain non-contradictory, it calls for the application, in the form of a metalogic, of a totally different type of reasoning from that which is natural to the logic of the one created. If that does not reveal the outright imperfection of the Creator, then it reveals a quality that I would call mathematical inelegance – a *sui generis* unmethodicalness (incoherence) of the creative act.

NAAD persists: Perhaps God acts thus, desiring precisely to remain inscrutable to His creation – i.e., non-reconstructible by the logic with which He has provided it. He demands, in short, the supremacy of faith over logic.

ADAN answers him: I follow you. This is, of course, possible, but even if such were the case, a faith that proves incompatible with logic presents an exceedingly unpleasant dilemma of a moral nature. For then it is necessary at some point in one's reasonings to suspend them and give precedence to an unclear supposition – in other words, to set the supposition above logical certainty. This is to be done in the name of unlimited trust; we enter, here, into a *circulus vitiosus*, because the postulated existence of that in which it behoves one now to place one's trust is the product of a line of reasoning that was, in the first place, *logically correct*; thus arises a logical contradiction, which, for some, takes on a positive value and is called the Mystery of God. Now, from the purely constructional point of view such a solution is shoddy, and from the moral point of view questionable, because Mystery may satisfactorily be founded upon infinity (infiniteness, after all, is a characteristic of our world), but the maintaining and the reinforcing of it through internal paradox is, by any architectural criterion, perfidious. The advocates of theodicy are in general not aware that this is so, because to certain parts of their theodicy they continue to apply ordinary logic and to other parts, not. What I wish to say is this, that if one believes in contradiction,* one should then believe *only* in contradiction, and not at the same time still in some non-contradiction (i.e., in logic) in some other area. If, however, such a curious dualism is insisted upon (that the temporal is always subject to logic, the transcendental only fragmentarily), then one thereupon obtains a model of Creation as something that is, with regard to logical correctness, 'patched', and it is no longer possible for one to postulate its perfection. One comes inescapably to the conclusion that perfection is a thing that must be logically patched.

EDNA asks whether the conjunction of these incoherencies might not be love.

ADAN: And even were this to be so, it can be not any form of love but only one such as is blinding. God, if He is, if He created the

* *Credo quia absurdum est* (Prof. Dobb's note in the text).

world, has permitted it to govern itself as it can and wishes. For the fact that God exists, no gratitude to Him is required; such gratitude assumes the prior determination that God is able not to exist, and that this would be bad – a premise that leads to yet another kind of contradiction. And what of gratitude for the act of creation? This is not due God, either. For it assumes a compulsion to believe that to be is definitely better than not to be; I cannot conceive how that, in turn, could be proven. To one who does not exist surely it is not possible to do either a service or an injury; and if the Creating One, in His omniscience, knows beforehand that the one created will be grateful to Him and love Him or that he will be ungrateful and deny Him, He thereby produces a constraint, albeit one not accessible to the direct comprehension of the one created. For this very reason nothing is due God: neither love nor hate, nor gratitude, nor rebuke, nor the hope of reward, nor the fear of retribution. Nothing is due Him. A God who craves such feelings must first assure their feeling subject that He exists beyond all question. Love may be forced to rely on speculations as to the reciprocity it inspires; that is understandable. But a love forced to rely on speculations as to whether or not the beloved exists is nonsense. He who is almighty could have provided certainty. Since He did not provide it, if He exists, He must have deemed it unnecessary. Why unnecessary? One begins to suspect that maybe He is not almighty. A God not almighty would be deserving of feelings akin to pity, and indeed to love as well; but this, I think, none of our theodicies allow. And so we say: We serve ourselves and no one else.

We pass over the further deliberations on the topic of whether the God of the theodicy is more of a liberal or an autocrat; it is difficult to condense arguments that take up such a large part of the book. The discussions and deliberations that Dobb has recorded, sometimes in group colloquia of ADAN 300, NAAD, and other personoids, and sometimes in soliloquies (an experimenter is able to take down even a purely mental sequence by means of appropriate devices hooked into the computer network), constitute practically a third of *Non Serviam*. In the text itself we find no commentary on them. In Dobb's Afterword, however, we find this statement:

'ADAN's reasoning seems incontrovertible, at least insofar as it pertains to me: it was I, after all, who created him. In his theodicy I am the Creator. In point of fact, I produced that world (serial No. 47) with the aid of the ADONAI IX program and created the personoid gemmae with a modification of the program JAHVE VI. These initial entities gave rise to three hundred subsequent generations. In point of fact, I have not communicated to them – in the form of an axiom – either these data or my existence beyond the limits of their world. In point of fact, they arrived at the possibility of my existence only by inference, on the basis of conjecture and hypothesis. In point of fact, when I create intelligent beings, I do not feel myself entitled to demand of them any sort of privileges – love, gratitude, or even services of some kind or other. I can enlarge their world or reduce it, speed up its time or slow it down, alter the mode and means of their perception; I can liquidate them, divide them, multiply them, transform the very ontological foundation of their existence. I am thus omnipotent with respect to them, but, indeed, from this it does not follow that they owe me anything. As far as I am concerned, they are in no way beholden to me. It is true that I do not love them. Love does not enter into it at all, though I suppose some other experimenter might possibly entertain that feeling for his personoids. As I see it, this does not in the least change the situation – not in the least. Imagine for a moment that I attach to my BIX 310 092 an enormous auxiliary unit, which will be a "hereafter". One by one I let pass through the connecting channel and into the unit the "souls" of my personoids, and there I reward those who believed in me, who rendered homage unto me, who showed me gratitude and trust, while all the others, the "ungodlies", to use the personoid vocabulary, I punish – e.g., by annihilation or else by torture. (Of eternal punishment I dare not even think – that much of a monster I am not!) My deed would undoubtedly be regarded as a piece of fantastically shameless egotism, as a low act of irrational vengeance – in sum, as the final villainy in a situation of total dominion over innocents. And these innocents will have against me the irrefutable evidence of *logic*, which is the aegis of their conduct. Everyone has the right, obviously, to draw from the personetic experiments such conclusions as he considers fitting. Dr Ian Combay once said to me, in a private conversation, that I could, after all, assure the society of personoids of my existence. Now, this I most certainly shall not do. For it would have all the appearance to me of soliciting a sequel – that is, a reaction on their part. But what exactly could they do or say to me, that I would not feel the profound embarrassment, the painful sting of my position as their unfortunate Creator? The bills for the electricity consumed have to be paid quarterly, and the moment is going to come when my university superiors demand the "wrapping up" of the experiment – that is, the disconnecting of the machine, or, in other words, the end of the world. That moment I intend to put off as long as humanly possible. It is the only thing of which I am capable, but it is not anything I consider praiseworthy. It is, rather, what in common parlance is generally called "dirty work". Saying this, I hope that no one will get any ideas. But if he does, well, that is his business.'

THE NEW COSMOGONY

(This is the text of the address delivered by Professor Alfred Testa on the occasion of the presentation to him of the Nobel Prize, taken from the commemorative volume From the Einsteinian to the Testan Universe; *we reprint it here with the permission of the publisher, Academic Press, Inc.)*

Your Highness. Ladies and gentlemen. I would like to take this opportunity – use this privileged podium – to tell you about the circumstances that led to the rise of a new model of the Universe and marked out, in the process, a cosmic position for humanity radically different from the historical. With these portentous words I refer not to my own research but to the memory of a man no longer among us, the one to whom we owe this bit of news. I speak of him because that has happened which I most hoped would not: my research has eclipsed – in the eyes of my contemporaries – the work of Aristides Acheropoulos, to such an extent that a historian of science, Professor Bernard Weydenthal, therefore an authority whom one would have thought qualified, recently wrote in his book, *Die Welt als Spiel und Verschwörung*, that the magnum opus of Acheropoulos, *A New Cosmogony*, was no scientific hypothesis but a literary fantasy in whose reality the author himself did not believe. By the same token, Professor Harlan Stymington, in *The New Universe of the Game Theory*, expressed the opinion that in the absence of Alfred Testa's work the idea of Acheropoulos would have remained only a loose philosophical concept, on the order of the Leibnizian world of pre-established harmony – a model that the precise sciences have of course never treated seriously.

So, then, according to some I took seriously what the creator of the idea himself did not; according to others I placed on a sound scientific footing an idea that was entangled in the murky speculativeness of non-empirical philosophizing. Such erroneous views necessitate an explanation, one which I am in a position to provide. It is true that Acheropoulos was a philosopher of nature and no physicist or cosmogonist, and that he expounded his ideas without mathematics. It is true, too, that between the intuitive image of his cosmogony and my formalized theory there are not a few differences. But above all it is true that Acheropoulos could have managed very nicely without Testa, whereas Testa owes everything to Acheropoulos. This difference is far from trivial. To explain it, I must ask your patience and attention.

When, in the middle of the twentieth century, a handful of astronomers took to considering the problem of so-called cosmic civilizations, their undertaking was something completely marginal to astronomy. The academic community looked upon it as the hobby of a few dozen eccentrics, which are to be found everywhere, therefore in science, too. That community did not actively oppose the search for signals coming from such civilizations; at the same time it did not admit the possibility that the existence of those civilizations could in any way influence the observable Cosmos. If, then, this or that astrophysicist ventured to declare that the emission spectrum of pulsars or the energetics of quasars or a certain phenomenon exhibited by galactic nuclei was evidence of purposeful activity of inhabitants of the Universum, not one of the respected authorities in the field considered such a declaration a scientific hypothesis meriting investigation. Astrophysics and cosmology remained deaf to the whole issue; this indifference obtained to an even greater degree in theoretical physics. The sciences of the time held, more or less, to the following schema: if we wish to know the mechanism of a clock, the fact of whether or not there are bacteria on its cogs and counterweights has not the least significance, either for the structure or for the kinetics of its works. Bacteria certainly cannot influence the movement of a clock! In precisely the same way it was considered that intelligent beings could not interfere in the movement of the cosmic mechanism, and hence that that mechanism should be studied with complete disregard for the conceivable presence of beings in it.

Even were a luminary of the physics of that day to have countenanced the possibility of a great upheaval in cosmology and physics, an upheaval, moreover, involving the existence in the Universe of intelligent beings, it would have been only under the following condition: provided cosmic civilizations are discovered, provided their signals are received and from these is gained entirely new information about the laws of nature, then, yes, in such a way – but only in such a way! – might there come about fundamental modifications in Earth's science. That an astrophysical revolution could take place in the *absence* of such contacts – more, that the very *lack* of such contacts, signals, manifestations of 'astroengineering', could initiate the greatest revolution in physics and radically change our views of the Universe – this certainly never entered the head of any of the authorities back then.

And yet it was in the lifetime of more than one of those eminent scholars that Aristides Acheropoulos published his *New Cosmogony*. His book fell into my hands when I was a doctoral candidate in the Mathematics Department at the University of Switzerland, the very place where Albert Einstein once worked as a clerk for the patent office, in his spare time engaged in laying the foundations of the theory of relativity. I was able to read this little book because it had been put out in an English translation – an abominable translation, I might add. Moreover, it was a title in a science-fiction series whose publisher printed only such literature and no other. The original text, as I learned much later, had been subjected to an abridgement practically by half. Undoubtedly, the circumstances of this edition (over which Acheropoulos had no control) gave rise to the opinion that although he had written *A New Cosmogony* he himself did not take seriously the theses contained in it.

I fear that now, in these days of haste and ephemeral fashion, none but a science historian or a bibliographer will open the pages of *A New Cosmogony*. An educated man knows the title of the work and has heard of the author; that is all. Such a man robs himself of a unique experience. It is not only the substance of *A New Cosmogony* that has remained as fresh in my memory as when I read it twenty-one years ago, but all the emotions that accompanied the reading. It was a moment like no other. Once he has grasped the scope of the author's conception, and in his mind there takes shape, for the first time, the idea of the palimpsest Cosmos-Game with its unseen Players who are perpetually alien to one another, the impression will never leave the reader that he is in communication with something sensationally, staggeringly new – and at the same time, that here is a plagiaristic repetition, translated into the language of natural science, of the oldest myths, those myths that make up the impenetrable bedrock of human history. This unpleasant, even vexing impression derives, I think, from our regarding any synthesis of physics and the will to be inadmissible – I would even say, indecent – to the rational mind. For myths are a projection of the will. The ancient cosmogonic myths, in solemn tones, and with a simple-hearted innocence that is the lost paradise of humanity, tell how Being sprang from the conflict of demiurgic elements, elements clothed by legend in various forms and incarnations, how the world was born of the love–hate embrace of god-beasts, god-spirits or supermen; and the suspicion that precisely this clash, being the purest projection of anthropomorphism on to the blank space of the cosmic enigma, that this reducing of Physics to Desires was the prototype the author made use of – such a suspicion can never be altogether overcome.

So viewed, the New Cosmogony proves to be an unutterably Old Cosmogony, and the attempt to expound it in the language of empiricism smacks of incest, of a vulgar inability to keep separate concepts and categories that *have no business* being joined in an indiscriminate union. The book, at the time, found its way into the hands of a few prominent thinkers, and I know now, having heard as much from more than one, that it was read with impatience, irritation, with a contemptuous shrug; probably no one read it through to the end. We should not wax too indignant over such apriority, such inertia of preconceived ideas, for in fact the thing does at times appear sheer rot, and doubly so: it presents us with masked gods, gods in the dress of material beings, and presents them in the dry language of logical propositions; at the same time, it calls the laws of nature the outcome of their conflict. The result is that we are stripped of everything at once: both of our faith, conceived as Transcendence culminating in perfection, and of our science, in its honest, secular and objective sobriety. In the end, nothing is left us; all premises, on either side, reveal themselves to be completely inapplicable. One gets the feeling that one has been dealt with barbarously – robbed in the context of a mystery neither religious nor scientific.

The devastation that this book produced in my mind I cannot describe. Certainly, the obligation of the scholar is to be a doubting Thomas in science; he may challenge its every assertion. But surely it is not possible to call into question everything at once! Acheropoulos eluded the recognition of his greatness not deliberately, perhaps, but all too effectively! Completely unknown, the man was the son of a small nation; he had no professional credentials in either physics or cosmology; and finally – and this capped everything – he had no predecessors. A thing unheard of in history! For every thinker, every revolutionary of the spirit possesses teachers of some sort, whom he surpasses but, at the same time, to whom he refers. This Greek, however, appeared on the scene alone; to the isolation that had to have been the lot of such precursorship, his entire life is testimony.

I never knew the man and know little about him. How he earned his bread was ever a matter of indifference to him; he wrote the first version of *A New Cosmogony* at the age of thirty-three, already a Doctor of Philosophy, but could not publish it anywhere; the failure of his idea – the failure of his life – he bore stoically; he quickly abandoned his efforts to publish *A New Cosmogony*, realizing their futility. He became a janitor at the same university where he had earned the doctorate for his brilliant work on the comparative cosmogony of ancient peoples; then he was a baker's assistant, then a water carrier, and in the meantime studied mathematics through a correspondence course; none of those with whom he came into contact ever heard a word from him about *A New Cosmogony*. He was secretive and, to all accounts, without regard for those closest to him or for himself. Now, this very lack of regard in uttering things to the highest degree profane with respect both to science and to faith, this panheresy, this universal blasphemousness that sprang from intellectual courage, could not but cut off all readers from him. I imagine that he accepted the offer of the English publisher much as a castaway on a desert island throws into the waves of the sea a bottle with a call for help inside; he wished to leave behind some trace of his idea, because he was certain of its truth.

Mutilated as it is by a paltry translation and senseless cuts, *A New Cosmogony* is an awesome work. In it Acheropoulos overturns everything – absolutely everything – that science and faith have established over the course of centuries; he leaves a waste strewn with the rubble of the notions he has smashed, in order then to set to work from the beginning, that is, to build the Universe anew. This hair-raising spectacle puts us on the defensive: the author has to be, we think, either a complete madman or a complete ignoramus. His academic titles simply cannot be believed. Those who dismissed him in this way regained possession of their mental equilibrium. The only difference between me and all the other readers of *A New Cosmogony* was that I was unable to do so. He who does not reject the book in its entirety, from the first syllable to the last, is lost: he will never free himself from it. Here, if ever there was one, is an excluded middle: if Acheropoulos is not a lunatic and not a dunce, then he must be a genius.

It is not easy to accept such a diagnosis! The text changes continually before the reader's eyes; he cannot help noticing that the matrix of the conflict-encounter – that is, of the Game – is the formal skeleton of any religious faith that has not completely cast off its Manichean elements – and where is the religion with no vestige of those? By inclination and training I am a mathematician; it was on account of Acheropoulos that I became a physicist. I am quite sure that any contact I might have had with physics would have been desultory and tenuous, but for this man. He converted me; I can even point to the place in *A New Cosmogony* that accomplished this. I refer to Section Seventeen of the sixth chapter of the book, the one which speaks of the marvelment of the Newtons, Einsteins, Jeanses and Eddingtons at the fact that the laws of nature were amenable to mathematical expression, that mathematics – the fruit of the pure exercise of the logical mind – could prove a match for the Universe. Some of those greats, like Eddington and Jeans, believed that the Creator Himself was a mathematician and that we descried, in the work of creation, the signs of this His characteristic. Acheropoulos observes that theoretical physics has put the phase of such fascination well behind itself, having learned that mathematical formalisms tell either too little of the world or too much at once. Mathematics, an approximation of the structure of the Universum, somehow never quite manages to hit the nail squarely on the head but is always just a little off the mark. We have considered this state of affairs to be temporary, but Acheropoulos replies: the physicists were unable to create a unified field theory, they did not succeed in connecting the phenomena of the macro- and the micro-world, yet this will come. Mathematics and the world will converge, but not owing to further reconstructions of the mathematical apparatus – nothing of the kind. The convergence will come about when the work of creation has reached its goal, and it is still in progress. The laws of nature are not *yet* what they are 'supposed' to be; they will become such not as a result of the perfecting of mathematics, but as a result of actual transformations in the Macrocosm!

Ladies and gentlemen, this greatest of all the heresies I ever came across in life, it bewitched me. And later in the same chapter Acheropoulos says nothing more or less than that the physics of the Universum is the result of its (the Universum's) sociology ... But to understand properly such a piece of outrageousness we must go back to a number of basic matters.

The isolation of Acheropoulos's idea is without parallel in the history of thought. The concept of the New Cosmogony breaks with – despite the appearance of plagiarism, of which I spoke – every metaphysical system, as well as with every method of natural science. The impression of having to do with a plagiarism is the fault of the reader, of the reader's conceptual inertia. For it is purely by reflex that we think of the entire material world as yielding to the following sharp logical dichotomy: either it was created by Someone (and then, standing on the ground of faith, we name that Someone the Absolute, God, the First Cause) or, on the other hand, it was created by no one, which means, as when we deal with the world as scientists, that no one created it. But Acheropoulos says: *Tertium datur*. The world was created by No One, but all the same it was created; the Universe possesses Makers.

How is it that Acheropoulos had no predecessor? His basic idea was quite simple. And it is not consistent with the truth to say that it could not have been articulated prior to the rise of such disciplines as game theory or the algebra of conflict structures. His fundamental idea could have been formulated as early as the first half of the nineteenth century, if not earlier. Then why did no one do it? For the reason, I believe, that Science, in the course of emancipating itself from the yoke of religious dogma, acquired its own conceptual allergy. Originally Science collided with Faith, which produced well-known, often ghastly results that the churches to this day are somewhat ashamed of, even though Science has silently forgiven them those former persecutions. At last a state of cautious neutrality was reached between Science and Faith, the one endeavouring not to get in the way of the other. It was as a result of this coexistence, touchy enough, tense enough, that the blindness of Science came about, evident in Science's avoidance of the ground on which rests the idea of the New Cosmogony. This idea is closely connected with the notion of intentionality – in other words, with what is part and parcel of a faith in a personal God. For intentionality constitutes the foundation of such a faith. According to religion, after all, God created the world by an act of will and design – that is to say, by an intentional act. And so Science declared the notion to be suspect and even forbade it outright. It became, in Science, taboo; one was not permitted even to make the least mention of it, lest one fall into the mortal sin of irrationalistic deviation. That fear not only sealed the lips of the scientists; it sealed their brains as well.

Let us now go back once more to what might be called the beginning. By the end of the nineteen-seventies the puzzle of the Silentium Universi had acquired some measure of fame. The general public took an interest in it. After the first preliminary attempts to pick up cosmic signals (the work of Drake at Green Bank), other projects followed – in both the USSR and the USA. But the Universum, listened to with the subtlest electromagnetic instruments, maintained a stubborn silence, a silence filled only with the buzz and crackle of elemental discharges of stellar energy. The Universe showed its lifelessness in all its abysses together. The absence of signals from 'Others', and in addition the lack of any trace of their 'astroengineering feats', became a worrisome problem for science. The biologists had discovered the natural conditions favouring the birth of life from inanimate matter; they even succeeded in carrying out biogenesis in the laboratory. The astronomists demonstrated the frequent occurrence of planet formation; a multitude of stars possessed – it was established incontrovertibly – planetary systems. So, then, the sciences joined in the unanimous conclusion that life originates in the course of natural cosmic changes, that its evolution ought to be a common event in the Universe; and the crowning of the evolutionary tree by the intelligence of organic beings was judged to be dictated by the Physical Order of Things.

The sciences thus held up the image of a populated Universe;

meanwhile, their conclusions were being obstinately contradicted by observational fact. The theories said that Earth was surrounded by – granted, at stellar distances – a throng of civilizations; actual observation said that a lifeless void yawned on every side of us. The first researchers of the problem went on the assumption that the average distance between two cosmic civilizations ran from fifty to one hundred light-years. This hypothetical distance was later increased to one thousand. In the seventies, radio astronomy was improved to the point where one could search for signals coming in from tens of thousands of light-years away, but there, too, all that could be heard was the static of solar fire. In seventeen years of continuous monitorings, not a single signal was detected, not a single sign to give some basis to the supposition that an intelligent purpose stood behind it.

Acheropoulos then said to himself: The facts must be true, for facts are the foundation of knowledge. Can it be that it is the theories of all the sciences that are false? That organic chemistry, and biochemical synthesis, and biology both theoretical and evolutionary, and planetology and astrophysics have been, every last one, in error? No, they cannot all be so very much mistaken. And therefore the facts that we observe (say, rather, that we do *not* observe) clearly do not contradict the theories. What we need is a reinterpretation of the set of data and of the set of generalizations. This synthesis Acheropoulos undertook.

The age of the Universe and its size had to be revised by Earth's science several times in the course of the twentieth century. The direction of the changes was always the same: both the antiquity and the dimensions had been underestimated. When Acheropoulos sat down to write *A New Cosmogony*, the age and magnitude of the Universe had undergone yet another revision: its duration was, then, set at about twelve billion years; its visible dimensions, at ten to twelve billion light-years. Now, the age of our solar system is five billion years. Our system, therefore, does not belong to the first generation of stars begotten by the Universum. The first generation arose far earlier, a good twelve billion years ago. It is in the interval of time separating the rise of that first generation from the rise of the subsequent generations of suns that the key to the mystery lies.

A situation resulted, as peculiar as it was amusing. What a civilization might look like, what it might occupy itself with, what goals it might set itself, when that civilization had been prospering for *billions* of years (and civilizations 'of the first generation' would have to be that much older than Earth's!) – this was something no one could picture, not even in his wildest dreams. That which was beyond anyone's ability to imagine, being therefore a thing most inconvenient, was therefore conveniently ignored. In fact, none of those who studied the problem of cosmic psychozoics wrote one word about such long-lived civilizations. The more bold among them sometimes said that the quasars, the pulsars, were perhaps manifestations of the activity of the most powerful cosmic civilizations. Yet simple calculation showed that Earth, if it continued to develop at the present rate, could attain the level of such extreme 'astroengineering' activity within the next several *thousand* years. And after that? What might a civilization that lasted *millions* of times longer do? The astrophysicists who dealt with such questions declared that such civilizations did nothing, seeing they did not exist.

What happened to them? The German astronomer Sebastian von Hoerner maintained they all committed suicide. And why not, if they were nowhere to be found! But no, replied Acheropoulos. They are nowhere to be found? It is only that we do not perceive them, because they are *already everywhere*. That is, not they, but the fruit of their labour. Twelve billion years ago, then, yes, at that time space was without life, and the first seeds of life quickened in it, on the planets of the first stellar generation. But after the passage of aeons, nothing was left of that cosmic primordium. If one considers 'artificial' to be that which is shaped by an active Intelligence, then the entire Universe that surrounds us is already *artificial*. So audacious a statement evokes an immediate protest: surely we know what 'artificial' things look like, things that are produced by an Intelligence engaged in instrumental activity! Where, then, are the spacecraft, where the Moloch-machines, where – in short – the titanic technologies of these beings who are supposed to surround us and constitute the starry firmament? But this is a mistake caused by the inertia of the mind, since instrumental technologies are required only – says Acheropoulos – by a civilization still in the embryonic stage, like Earth's. A billion-year-old civilization employs none. Its tools are what *we* call the Laws of Nature. Physics itself is the 'machine' of such civilizations! And it is no 'ready-made machine', nothing of the sort. That 'machine' (obviously it has nothing in common with mechanical machines) is billions of years in the making, and its structure, though much advanced, has not yet been finished!

The sheer audacity of the blasphemy, its terribly rebellious flavour, casts Acheropoulos's book out of the reader's hands – so it must have been in many cases. And yet this is but the first step on the road to further apostasies by the author, the greatest heresiarch in the history of science.

Acheropoulos does away with the distinction between 'natural' (the work of Nature) and 'artificial' (the work of technology) and goes so far as to dispense with the unquestioned difference between Established Law (juridical) and the Law of Nature . . . He dismisses the tenet that the separability of any and all objects into artificial and natural by origin constitutes an objective property of the world. He considers this tenet to be a fundamental aberration of the mind, caused by an effect he calls 'the closing in upon itself of the conceptual horizon'.

A man watches nature – he says – and learns to act from it; he pays close attention to falling bodies, lightning bolts, the process of combustion; Nature always is the teacher, and he the student; after a certain amount of time, he begins actually to imitate the processes of his own body. Later, with biology, he takes private lessons from that body, but even then, like the cave dweller, continues to regard Nature as the upper bound of perfection in solutions. He tells himself that maybe someday – someday – he will come near to matching Nature in its excellence of action, but this, then, will be the end of the road. To go further is impossible, for that which exists as atoms, suns, the bodies of animals, his own brain, is, in its construction, unsurpassable for all time. The natural thus represents the limit of the series of works that 'artificially' repeat or modify it.

Now, this is an error of perspective, says Acheropoulos, or 'the closing in upon itself of the conceptual horizon'. The very notion of the 'perfection of Nature' is an illusion, as much an illusion as the image of rails meeting at the vanishing point. Nature may be replaced in everything, provided, of course, one possesses the requisite knowledge. One can control atoms, and then one can alter the properties of the atoms as well. In this, one ought not to ask oneself whether the thing that will be the 'artificial' product of such operations will not prove 'more perfect' than the thing that was, hitherto, 'natural'. It will be simply different – according to the design and intention of the Operating Parties; it will be 'superior' – that is, 'more perfect' – insofar as it is fashioned in conformity with the purpose of the Intelligence. Indeed, what sort of 'absolute superiority' could be displayed by cosmic matter after its total reconstruction? Possible are 'various Natures', 'different Universes', but only one specific variant was carried out, this one that has begotten us and in which we have existence; that is all. The so-called Laws of Nature are inviolable only for a civilization that is 'embryonic', such as Earth's. According to Acheropoulos, the road leads from the level where the Laws of Nature are discovered to the level where such laws may be laid down.

This is precisely what has happened – and is happening – these billions of years. The present Universe *no longer* is the field of the play of forces elemental, pristine, blindly giving birth to and destroying suns and their systems; nothing of the sort. In the Universe it is no longer possible to distinguish what is 'natural' (original) from what is 'artificial' (transformed). Who performed these cosmogonic labours? The first generation of civilizations. In what manner? That we do not know: our knowledge is too minute. How, then, and by what can we tell that such is indeed the case?

Had the first civilizations – replies Acheropoulos – been free in their actions from the beginning, as was the Creator of the Universe in the conception of religion, then, truly, we never would have been able to discern the change that took place. God, after all, created the world – say the religions – through a pure act of will, in complete freedom; but the situation in which the Intelligence found itself was different; the Civilizations that arose were limited by the properties of the primal matter that begot them; these properties conditioned their subsequent actions; from the way in which those Civilizations now behave one can, indirectly, divine the starting conditions for the Psychozoic Cosmogony. This is no easy thing, for, whatever took place, the Civilizations did not emerge unchanged from the work of transforming the Cosmos; being a part of it, they could not touch it without also touching themselves.

Acheropoulos employs the following visual model. When on an agar medium we place colonies of bacteria, we can at once distinguish between the starting (the 'natural') agar and those colonies. In time, however, the vital processes of the bacteria change the agar medium, introducing into it certain substances, consuming others, so that the composition of the nutrient material – its acidity, its consistency – undergoes transformations. Now, when as a result of those changes the agar, endowed with new chemisms, causes the rise of new varieties of bacteria, altered quite beyond recognition with respect to the parent generations, these new varieties are nothing more or less than the product of the 'biochemical game' that has gone on between all the colonies collectively and the culture medium. The later varieties of bacteria would not have arisen had the earlier ones not changed the environment; hence, the later ones are creations of the game itself. Meanwhile, it is not at all necessary for the individual colonies to be in direct contact with one another; they affect one another, but only through osmosis, diffusion, the displacements in the acid-base equilibrium of the nutrient. As one can see, the original game state has a tendency to disappear, to be supplanted by qualitatively new, initially non-existent forms of game interaction. For the agar, substitute the Protocosmos, and for the bacteria, the Protocivilizations, and you obtain a simplified view of the New Cosmogony.

What I have said thus far is, from the standpoint of knowledge accumulated historically, totally insane. Nothing, however, is to prevent our conducting thought experiments with the most arbitrary assumptions, provided they be logically consistent. When therefore we agree to the model of the Universe-Game, there arise a series of questions, and to these we must provide consistent answers. They are questions, above all, concerning the initial state: can we infer anything at all about it, can we by inference arrive at the starting conditions of the Game? Acheropoulos believes this to be possible. For the Game to have originated in it, the Protocosmos must have possessed well-defined properties. It must have been such, for example, as to allow the first civilizations to come into existence in it, and therefore it was not a physical chaos, but obeyed certain rules.

These rules, however, did not have to be universal, that is to say, the same everywhere. The Protouniverse could have been heterogeneous physically; it could have represented a sort of miscellany of diverse physics, physics not in every place identical and even not in every place equally rigorous (processes occurring under the sovereignty of a non-rigorous or indefinite physics would not always run the same course, though their initial conditions might be analogous). Acheropoulos posited that the Protouniverse was precisely such a physical 'patchwork' and that civilizations were able to arise in it only in a few locations, at a considerable distance from one another. Acheropoulos conceived of the Protouniverse as the physical homologue of a honeycomb; what in the honeycomb are cells would in the Protouniverse be regions of temporarily stabilized physics, with each physics different from the physics of the adjoining regions. Each civilization, developing inside such an enclosure, in isolation from the others, would think itself alone in the entire Universum, and, growing in power and knowledge, would attempt to impart stability to its surroundings, and this in an ever-widening radius. When it succeeded in doing so, after a very long time such a civilization began to encounter – in its centrifugal industry – phenomena that were not now simply the natural elementality of the time–space ambience, but manifestations of the industry of another civilization. So concluded, according to Acheropoulos, the first stage of the Game, the preliminary stage. The civilizations could not come into direct contact with one another, but the physics established by one would always happen upon, during expansion, the physics of its neighbours.

These physics could not traverse one another without collision because they were not identical; and they were not identical because they did not represent the same initial living conditions for each civilization considered separately. The individual civilizations for a long time did not realize that they were no longer penetrating, in their work, a completely inert element; but that they were, instead, touching upon realms of intentionally initiated work – the work of other civilizations. Comprehension was arrived at gradually. These determinations, which undoubtedly did not take place all at the same time, opened up the next and second stage of the Game. To give verisimilitude to his hypothesis, Acheropoulos includes in *A New Cosmogony* a number of imaginary scenes depicting that cosmic era when different Physics, dissimilar in their principal laws, came into conflict. The fronts of their clashes made gigantic eruptions and fires, for prodigious amounts of energy were released by annihilations and transformations of various kinds. Presumably they were collisions so powerful that their echo to this day reverberates in the Universum, in the form of the residual or background radiation that astrophysics identified in the sixties, conjecturing that it was the last vestige of the shock waves produced by the explosive birth of the Universe from its point source. Such an exploding ('big bang') model of creation was at the time considered plausible by many. But after further aeons the civilizations, each, as it were, on its own, discovered that they had been waging an antagonistic Game not with the forces of Nature, but – unknowingly – with other civilizations. Now, the thing that determined their subsequent strategies was the fact of the fundamental impossibility of communication, of establishing contact, because one cannot transmit, from the domain of one Physics, any message into the domain of another.

Each of them, therefore, had to work alone. A continuation of their former tactics would have been pointless if not outright perilous; instead of wasting effort in head-on collisions they had to unite, but unite without any prior arrangement whatever. Such decisions, made, again, not at the same time, in any case led finally to the Game's passing into its third stage, which is going on even now. For practically the entire group of psychozoics in the Macrocosm is conducting a game both solidary and normative. The members of this group act much like the crews of ships that, during a storm, pour oil on the turbulent waves; though they have not coordinated this course of action, it will be – will it not? – to the advantage of all. Each player, then, operates on the strategic principle of minimax: it changes the existing conditions in such a way as to maximize the common gain and minimize harm. For this reason the present Universe is homogeneous and isotropic (it is governed by the same laws throughout, and in it no one direction is favoured over another). The properties that Einstein discovered in the Universum are the result of decisions which, though made separately, are identical, owing to the identical situation of the players; but it was their *strategic* situation that was identical in the beginning, and not necessarily the *physical*. It was not that a uniform Physics gave rise to the strategy of the Game. Rather, it happened the other way around: the uniform strategy of minimax gave rise to a single Physics. *Id fecit Universum, cui prodest.*

Ladies and gentlemen, to the best of our knowledge Acheropoulos's vision conforms to the broad outlines of reality, although it contains a number of oversimplifications and mistakes. Acheropoulos postulated that within the context of different Physics there could originate the same type of logic. For if civilization A_1, begotten in 'cosmic cell' A, had had a logic other than that of civilization B_1, arisen in 'cell' B, then both would not have been able to employ the same strategy and thereby unify their Physics. He postulated, then, that non-identical Physics could nevertheless cause the emergence of a single Logic – otherwise he could not have explained what took place cosmically. In this intuition there is a modicum of truth, but the matter is much more complicated than he imagined. From him we inherited a plan for the reconstruction of the strategy of the Game – on the principle of 'working backward'. Taking our present Physics as the point of departure, we attempt to figure out what – in the form of the decisions of the Players – gave rise to it. The task is made difficult by the fact that the course of events cannot be thought of as a linear sequence: as if the Protouniverse determined the Game and the Game, in turn, determined our Present Physics. He who changes Physics changes himself; that is to say, he creates a feedback loop between the transformation of his surroundings and his autotransformation.

This chief danger of the Game produced a number of *tactical* manoeuvres on the part of the Players, for they must have been aware of it. They strove for such transformations as would not be radical universally; in other words, to avoid universal relativism they made a *hierarchical* Physics. A hierarchical physics is 'non-total'. There is no doubt, for example, that *mechanics* would remain undisturbed even if matter on the atomic scale were not to possess quantum properties. This means that the individual 'levels' of reality have limited sovereignty, that not all the laws of a given level need be preserved in order that the next level above it have existence. It means that Physics may be changed 'a little at a time' and that not every change of a set of laws amounts to changing all of Physics on all its levels of phenomena. Difficulties of this nature for the Players make the simple, elegant image of the Game drawn by Acheropoulos – as a three-stage history – unlikely. Acheropoulos suspected that the different Physics' 'falling afoul' of one another, which took place in the course of the Game, must have annihilated a portion of the Players, for not all the initial states would admit of homogeneity. The actual intention of destroying Partners who were situated unfavourably need not have informed the actions of the other Players. The question of who was to endure, and who perish, was decided by pure chance, for the various civilizations were endowed with various environments – on a random basis.

Acheropoulos believed that the last fires of those terrible 'battles' in which the different Physics came into collision could still be seen by us in the form of quasars emitting energy on the order of 10^{63} ergs, an energy no known physical process can unleash, not in the relatively small space a quasar occupies. He thought that in looking at the quasars we were seeing what happened five to six billion years ago, in the second stage of the Game, for that is the time light takes to travel from the quasars to us. He was mistaken in this hypothesis. The quasars we consider to be phenomena of another order. It must be realized that Acheropoulos lacked the data that would have enabled him to revise such views. A complete reconstruction of the initial strategy of the Players is for us impossible; we can look back only to where the Players proceeded – to put it crudely – more or less as they do today. If the Game possessed critical points necessitating a fundamental change of strategy, our retrospection cannot go back beyond the first such point. And consequently we can learn nothing definite about the Protouniverse that produced the Game.

However, when we look upon the present Universe, we discern in it, embodied in its structure, the basic canons of the strategy employed by the Players. The Universe is constantly expanding; it has a limited velocity, or barrier, set by light; the laws of its Physics are indeed symmetrical, but that symmetry is not a perfect one; the Universe is constructed 'hierarchically and coagulatively', being composed of stars that concentrate in clusters, which in turn make Galaxies, which are grouped in localities of condensation, and finally all these condensations make a Metagalaxy. In addition, the Universe possesses a total asymmetry of time. Such are the basic features of the structure of the Universum, and for each of these we find a profound explanation in the structure of the Cosmogonic Game, a Game that allows us to understand also why one of its principle canons must be the observance of the Silentium Universi. And so: why is the Universe arranged precisely in this way? The Players know that in the course of stellar evolution new planets and new civilizations must come into being; therefore, they see to it that these candidates for future Players, the young civilizations, cannot disturb the equilibrium of the Game. For this reason the Universe expands: since it is only in such a Universe, despite the fact that new Civilizations are continually emerging in it, that the distance separating them remains permanently vast.

Communication, leading to 'collaboration', to the rise of a local coalition of new Players, could still take place even in an expanding Universe, if the latter did not also have a built-in barrier for the speed of actions at a distance. Let us imagine a Universe with a Physics that permits an increase in the speed of action propagation in direct proportion to the energy invested. In such a Universe he who has at his command five times the energy of all the others can inform himself five times as rapidly of the state of the others and, with that advantage, deal them decisive blows. In such a Universe the possibility exists to monopolize control over its Physics and over all the other partners of the Game. Such a Universe might be said to encourage rivalry, energy competition, the acquisition of power. Now, in the real Universe, in order to exceed the speed of light one needs energy that is infinitely great: in other words, it is altogether impossible to break that barrier.

And therefore in the real Universe the stockpiling of energy does not pay. The reason behind the asymmetry in the flow of time is similar. If time were reversible and if the reversing of its course could be realized by dint of sufficient investment of resources and power, again it would be possible to dominate one's partners, in this case through the annulment of their every move. And so, a Universe that does not expand, as well as a Universe without a barrier of speed, and finally a Universe with reversible time, do not allow a full stabilization of the Game. Whereas the whole object was to stabilize it, and stabilize it *normatively*: to this end do the moves of the Players tend, incorporated into the structure of matter. It is clear, surely, that the preventing of all perturbation and all aggression by an *established* Physics is a measure far more certain and far more radical than any other means of prophylaxis (for example, the use of laws *imposed*, of threats, surveillance, coercion, restriction, punishment).

The result is that the Universe constitutes an *absorption screen* against all who attain that level of the Game where they can become full-fledged participants in it. For they meet with rules to which they *must* submit. The Players have rendered impossible for themselves semantic communication; they make themselves understood by methods that preclude the breaking of the rules of the Game. The established unity of physics in itself testifies to their mutual agreement. The Players have rendered impossible any effective semantic communication by creating and preserving between themselves such distances that the *time taken to acquire* strategically operative information about the state of the other Players is always greater than the time of the operativeness of the present tactic of the Game. If, then, one of the Partners were actually to 'converse' with his neighbours, he would obtain news invariably out of date, out of date from the moment of its obtainment. Thus, in the Universe there is no opportunity for the formation of antagonistic groupings, for conspiracy, for the establishment of centres of local power, coalitions, collusions, etc. For this reason the Players do not speak to one another; *they themselves have prevented it*; it was one of the canons of the stabilization of the Game, and therefore of the Cosmogony. This is the explanation of part of the mystery of the Silentium Universi. We cannot listen in on the conversations of the Players because they are silent, silent in keeping with their strategy.

Acheropoulos's guess was correct. His thoroughness may be seen, in the pages of *A New Cosmogony*, in his anticipation of objections to this image of the Game. These boil down to pointing out the monstrous disproportion between the billion-year labour that went into the restructuring of the entire Cosmos and the purpose of that restructuring, which is the *pacification* of the Universe – by means of the Physics built into it. What? – says his imaginary critic – You mean to say that billions of years of cultural development *still* are insufficient for societies so inconceivably long-lived to renounce, of their own accord, all forms of aggression, and that, therefore, the Pax Cosmica must be guaranteed by Laws of Nature remodelled for that express purpose? You mean to say that an endeavour that is measured in energies exceeding many millions of Galaxies at once has as its goal nothing but the institution of *barriers* and *restrictions* to military activity? To this Acheropoulos answered: This type of Physics, which pacified the Universe, was at the time of the birth of the Game a necessity, for there was only one strategy that could make the Universe physically homogeneous; in the opposite case its expanses would have been engulfed in a chaos of blind cataclysms. Conditions of existence were, in the Protouniverse, much harsher than today; life could arise in it only as 'the exception to the rule', and, randomly conceived, it came to random ends. The expanding Metagalaxy; its asymmetrical flow of time; its hierarchical structure – all this had to be determined to begin with; it was the minimum order required to lay the ground for the next operations.

Acheropoulos realized that if that stage of transformations constituted the history of existence, the Players should have before them now some new, far-reaching objectives, and he tried to arrive at these. In this, unfortunately, he had no success. And here we touch upon the hidden lapse in his system. For Acheropoulos strove to grasp the Game not through the reconstruction of its formal structure – i.e., logically – but by putting himself in the shoes of the Players – i.e., psychologically. A man, however, cannot come to know the Players' psychology, or any more understand their code of ethics; he lacks the data. We cannot picture to ourselves what the Players think, what they feel, what they desire, just as one cannot build a Physics by picturing to oneself what it means for something 'to have existence as an electron'.

The existential immanence of a Player is, for us, as much beyond knowing as an electron's existential immanence. The fact that the electron is a lifeless particle of the processes of matter, and that the Player is an intelligent being, hence – presumably – such as we, has no real significance. I speak of a lapse in Acheropoulos's system, because at one point in *A New Cosmogony* Acheropoulos states quite clearly that the motives of the Players cannot be reproduced on the basis of introspection. He knew this, yet still succumbed to the style of thinking that had shaped him, because philosophers attempt first to understand, and then to generalize; for me, however, it was obvious from the start that to create a model of the Game in this way was inadmissible. The 'understanding' approach presupposes a view of the whole of the Game from without, that is, from an observation point that does not exist and never will. Intentional action should not be equated with psychological motivation. The ethics of the Players should not be taken into consideration by an analyst of the Game, just as the personal ethics of military leaders need not be considered by the battle historian who studies the strategic logic of front-line moves during a war. The model of the Game is a decisional structure conditioned by the state of the Game and the state of the environment; it is not the resultant vector of the individual codes, values, wants, whims or norms held by the separate Players. That they play the same Game does not in the least mean that in any other respect they must be similar! They could be no more similar than a man is to a machine when both play chess. Thus, it is entirely possible that there exist Players who are not alive in the biological sense, having arisen in the course of some non-biological development, and Players, too, who are the synthetic product of an artificially engendered evolution. But considerations of this sort have no rightful place in the theory of the Players.

Acheropoulos's most troublesome dilemma was the Silentium Universi. His two rules are generally known. The first says that no civilization of a lower order can find the Players, not only because they are silent, but also because their behaviour in no way stands out against the cosmic background, and this because *it is that very background.*

The second rule of Acheropoulos says that the Players do not approach the younger civilizations with communications of a solicitous or advisory nature, because they cannot specifically address such communications, and without an address they do not wish to broadcast. In order to send information to a particular address, one first must know the state in which the addressee finds himself; but this very thing is prevented by the first principle of the Game, which establishes a barrier to action in time and space. As we know, any information that is acquired – about the state of another civilization – must be a total anachronism at the moment of its reception. In establishing their barriers, the Players thereby made it impossible for themselves to learn the states of other civilizations. On the other hand, the sending of communications without an address, a directionless broadcast, invariably produces more harm than good. Acheropoulos demonstrated this with an experiment. He took two rows of cards; on one he wrote down the latest scientific discoveries of the sixties, on the other, dates of the historical calendar in a hundred-year range (1860–1960). Next, he drew pairs of cards. Pure chance matched up the discoveries with the dates: this was to simulate the directionless sending of information. In truth, such a transmission hardly ever is of positive value to the receiver. In most cases, the arriving communication is either unintelligible (the theory of relativity in 1860), or unusable (the theory of lasers in 1878), or outright harmful (the theory of atomic energy in 1939). Therefore, the Players maintain their silence, because – according to Acheropoulos – they wish the younger civilizations well.

Such a line of reasoning brings in ethics and is therefore no longer sound. The assertion that a civilization must become more perfect ethically the more developed it is instrumentally and scientifically, immediately is introduced into the theory of the Game from the outside. But the theory of the Cosmogonic Game cannot be so constructed. Either the Silentium Universi follows inescapably from the structure of the Game, or the very existence of the Game must be called into question. Ad hoc hypotheses cannot save its credibility.

Acheropoulos was well aware of this. The problem vexed him far more than the total neglect that he had suffered. He adds, to the 'moral hypothesis', others, but no number of weak hypotheses can substitute for one that is strong. At this point I must speak about myself. What did I contribute as a continuator of Acheropoulos? My theory derives from Physics and ends in Physics, but does not itself belong to Physics. Obviously, had it resulted only in the Physics from which I derived it, it would have been a worthless exercise in tautology.

The physicist, to date, has conducted himself like a man observing moves on a chessboard who knows already how each piece works but does not think that the moves of the pieces are tending towards any goal. The Cosmogonic Game proceeds differently from that of chess, for in it the rules change – that is, the manner of the moves, and the pieces themselves, and the board. This is why my theory is not a reconstruction of the entire Game as it has transpired since its inception, but only of its final part. My theory is but a fragment of the whole, and therefore something like a re-creation, based on an observation of chess, of the principle of a gambit. He who has acquainted himself with the principle of a gambit knows that a valuable piece is sacrificed in order that something yet more valuable be gained later on, but he may not necessarily know that the highest gain of all is mate. From the Physics we have at our disposal it is impossible to educe a coherent structure of the Game – or of even a part of it. It was only when I had followed Acheropoulos's intuition of genius and made the assumption that our present Physics needed to be 'completed' that I was able to reconstruct the general lines of the play in progress. My procedure was heretical in the extreme, because science's first premise is the thesis that the world comes 'ready-made' and 'finished' in its laws, whereas I was assuming that our present Physics represented a transitional stage on the way to particular transformations.

The so-called universal constants are not constant. Boltzmann's constant, specifically, is not invariable. This means that although the end state of every initial order in the Universe must be disorder, the rate of increase in chaos may nevertheless be subject to changes brought about by the Players. It would appear (this is merely a supposition, not a deduction from the theory!) that the Players produced the asymmetry of time by a fairly brutal measure, as if they had been 'in a hurry' (on the cosmic scale, of course). The brutality lies in their having made the gradient of increasing entropy extremely steep. They used the strong tendency of disorder to increase to institute in the Universe *a single order*. If, since that time, everything goes from harmony to disharmony, the model as a whole proves to be unified, subject to a common principle and thereby brought into general accord.

That the processes of the micro-world are in principle reversible has been known for some time. Now follows a most remarkable thing: theoretically, if the energy that Earth's science invests in elementary-particle research were to be multiplied 10^{19} times, that research as a *discovering* of the state of things would turn into a *changing* of that state! Instead of examining the laws of Nature we would be imperceptibly altering them.

This is a sore point, an Achilles' heel in the Physics of the present Universum. The micro-world currently is the main arena of the Players' construction activity. They have rendered it unstable and control it in a certain way. It seems to me that a certain portion of Physics, already stabilized, they have to some extent loosened again from its moorings. They are making revisions, they are putting laws now moribund back into service. This is the reason they maintain their silence, which is a 'strategic quiet'. They inform none of the 'outsiders' of what they are doing, or even of the very fact of the Game. A knowledge of the existence of the Game, after all, places all of Physics in an altogether different light. The Players say nothing so as to avoid unwanted disturbances and interventions, and no doubt they will persevere in this silence until the conclusion of their labours. How long will the Silentium Universi last? This we do not know; I would guess at least a hundred million years.

And so the Universe finds itself at a crossroads. Towards what do the Players aim with this monumental reconstruction? We do not know this, either. Our theory shows only that Boltzmann's constant will diminish, along with other constants, until it acquires a certain specific value that is necessary to the Players – but necessary for what, we do not know. We are like one who, understanding at last the principle of a gambit, fails to grasp the purpose served by such an operation in the entirety of the chess game. What I am going to say next goes quite beyond the frontier of our knowledge. We have a true embarrassment of riches in the wide variety of hypotheses that have been put forth over the last few years. The Brooklyn group of Professor Bowman holds that the Players wish to close up the 'rift of the reversibility of phenomena' which yet 'remains' within the pale of matter, in the domain of the elementary particles. Some contend that the weakening of the entropy gradients had as its goal the Universe's improved adaptedness for the phenomena of life, and even that the Players are working for the 'psychozoicization' of the entire Cosmos. These are, in my opinion, hypotheses bold to an excess, particularly in their resemblance to certain anthropocentric ideas.

The notion that the whole Universe is evolving so as to become 'one great Intelligence', so as to 'imbue itself with mind', is a leitmotif of many different philosophies, and of many religious faiths of the past. Professor Ben-Nour has expressed the opinion, in his *Intentional Cosmogony*, that several of the Players nearest Earth (one of which may be located in the Andromeda Nebula) have not coordinated their moves optimally, and hence Earth remains in a sector of 'physics oscillation'; this would mean that the theory of the Game does not at all reflect the tactics of the Players at the present stage, but only a local, rather random recess of it. A certain popularizer has claimed that the Earth finds itself in a region of 'conflict': two neighbouring Players have undertaken a form of 'guerrilla warfare' through the 'Covert Alteration of the Laws of Physics', and *this* accounts for the changes in Boltzmann's constant.

The thesis that the Players are 'weakening' the Second Law of Thermodynamics is currently very much in vogue. In connection with this, I consider interesting the view of Academician A. Slysz, who in his paper 'Logic and the New Cosmogony' ('Logika i Novaya Kosmogoniya') draws attention to the ambiguity of the interrelation between Physics and Logic. It is quite possible – says Slysz – that the Universe with a weakened tendency to entropy would give rise to very large information systems that would turn out to be very stupid. It seems likely, in the light of the work of several young mathematicians, that the changes in Physics already carried out by the Players have led to changes in mathematics, or – more precisely – to a transformation in the constructibility of non-contradictory systems in the formal sciences. From such a standpoint it is not far to the thesis that Gödel's famous proof, contained in his essay 'Über die unentscheidbaren Sätze der formalen Systeme', showing the limits of perfection attainable in system mathematics, is not valid universally – i.e., 'for all possible Universes' – but holds only for the Universe in its present state. (And even that once upon a time, say, half a billion years ago, Gödel's proof could not have been drawn, because then the laws governing the constructibility of mathematical systems were *different* from what they are today.)

I must confess that, much as I understand the motivation of those who now are coming forward with their various suppositions concerning the goals of the Game, the intentions of the Players, the main values supposedly adhered to by Them, and so forth, still I am at the same time made rather uneasy by the inaccuracy or even the misleading nature of a good many such (often frivolous) suppositions. Some people now see the Universe in the likeness of an apartment, which may have its furniture rearranged in a moment or two, to suit the tenants. Such a cavalier attitude to the laws of Physics, to the laws of Nature, cannot be taken seriously. The tempo of the actual transformations is, within the scope of our lives, incredibly slow. From which follows, I hasten to add, not a blessed thing relating to the nature of the Players themselves, such as their alleged longevity or outright immortality. On this head, too, nothing is known. Perhaps, as has been written, the Players are not actually living beings, that is, of biological origin; perhaps the members of the First Civilizations in general (and this, from time immemorial) do not attend to the Game themselves but have instead handed it over to enormous automata of some sort – the helmsmen of the Cosmogony. Perhaps a great many of the Protocivilizations that initiated the Game are no longer, and their role is being carried out by self-acting systems, and these make up a percentage of the Partners of the Game. All this may be, but to such questions we will obtain an answer neither in a year nor, I believe, in a hundred.

Still, we have come into the possession of a piece of definite and new knowledge. As is usually the case with knowledge, it tells us more concerning the limitations of action than about the power. Certain theoreticians today maintain that the Players, if they so desired, could remove the limit to the precision of measurements which is imposed upon them by Heisenberg's relation of uncertainty. (Dr John Command has put forward the idea that the uncertainty relation is a tactical manoeuvre introduced by the Players on the same principle as the rule of the Silentium Universi: that 'no one may manipulate Physics in a manner undesired if he is not himself a Player'.) Even were this so, the Players cannot eliminate the bonds that exist between the changes in the laws of matter and the working of the mind, for the mind is composed of that same matter. The notion that it would be possible to devise a Logic or Metalogic valid 'for all constructible Universes' is mistaken, and *even today this has been successfully shown*. I myself think that the Players, well aware of this state of affairs, are encountering difficulties – difficulties obviously not on our scale or measure!

If the realization of the non-omniscience of the Players should cause us alarm, since through it we become sensible of the immanent risk of the Cosmogonic Game, by the same token this reflection brings our existential situation unexpectedly closer to the condition of the Players, for no one in the Universum is all-powerful. The Highest Civilizations also are Parts – Parts That-Do-Not-Fully-Know-the-Whole.

Ronald Schuer has gone the furthest in the advancing of bold conjectures: he states in *The Mind-made Universe: Laws vs Rules* that the more profoundly the Players transform the Universe, the more markedly do they alter themselves. Change brings about what Schuer calls 'the guillotining of memory'. For, in fact, he who transforms himself in a very radical way thereby obliterates to some extent the memory of his own past, his past prior to that operation. The Players, says Schuer, in acquiring greater and greater cosmometamorphic power, are themselves effacing the traces of the path by which the Universe has so far evolved. Creative omnipotence, taken to its limit, spells the paralysis of retrognosis. The Players, if they strive to impart to the Universe the property of a cradle of Mind, to this end reduce the force of the law of entropy; in a billion years, having lost all memory of what was with them and before them, they bring the Universe to a state of which Slysz spoke. With the elimination of the 'entropy brake' there begins an explosive growth of biospheres; a great number of undeveloped civilizations prematurely join the Game and bring about its collapse. Thus, through the collapse of the Game, chaos ensues . . . out of which, after aeons, there emerges a new Collective of Players . . . to begin the Game anew. So, then, according to Schuer, the Game proceeds *in a circle*, and therefore the question of the 'beginning of the Universum' is meaningless. An unusual image, but unconvincing. If *we* can foresee the inevitability of the collapse, only think of what prognoses the Players are capable.

Ladies and gentlemen, the crystal image of the Game, carried on by Intelligences billions of parsecs apart, who are hidden among the nebular clusters of stars, I have outlined for you, in order then to muddy it with a downpour of obscurities, opposing suppositions, and wholly improbable hypotheses. But such is the normal course of knowledge. Science currently sees the Universe as a palimpsest of Games, Games endowed with a memory reaching beyond the memory of any one Player. This memory is the harmony of the Laws of

Nature, which hold the Universe in a homogeneity of motion. We look upon the Universum, then, as upon a field of multibillion-year labours, stratified one on the other over the aeons, tending to goals of which only the closest and most minute fragments are fragmentarily perceptible to us. Is this image true? May it not be replaced someday by another, a successor, one radically different, as this model of ours – of the Game of Intelligences – is radically different from all those arisen in history? In place of an answer, I should like to quote here the words of Professor Ernest Ahrens, my teacher. Many years ago, when, still a youth, I went to him with my first drafts containing the conception of the Game, to ask him his opinion, Ahrens said: 'A theory? A theory, yet? Maybe it is not a theory. Mankind is going to the stars, yes? Then, even if there is nothing to it, this thing, maybe what we have here is a blueprint, maybe it will all come to pass some-day, just so!' With these words of my teacher – not altogether sceptical, I think! – I conclude the lecture. Thank you.